JAMES WELDON JOHNSON

JAMES WELDON JOHNSON

WRITINGS

The Autobiography of an Ex-Colored Man
Along This Way
New York Age Editorials
Selected Essays
Black Manhattan
Selected Poems

THE LIBRARY OF AMERICA

Some of the material in this volume is reprinted with
permission of the holders of copyright and publication rights.
Acknowledgments are in the Note on the Texts, pages 892–96.

The paper used in this publication meets the
minimum requirements of the American National Standard for
Information Sciences—Permanence of Paper for Printed
Library Materials, ANSI Z39.48—1984.

Distributed to the trade
in the United States by Penguin Putnam Inc.
and in Canada by Penguin Books Canada Ltd.

Library of Congress Catalog Number: 2003044227
For cataloging information, see end of Notes.
ISBN 1–931082–52–9

———

First Printing
The Library of America—145

Manufactured in the United States of America

Contents

THE AUTOBIOGRAPHY
OF AN EX-COLORED MAN

PREFACE

THIS vivid and startlingly new picture of conditions brought about by the race question in the United States makes no special plea for the Negro, but shows in a dispassionate, though sympathetic, manner conditions as they usually exist between the whites and blacks to-day. Special pleas have already been made for and against the Negro in hundreds of books, but in these books either his virtues or his vices have been exaggerated. This is because writers, in nearly every instance, have treated the colored American as a *whole*; each has taken some one group of the race to prove his case. Not before has a composite and proportionate presentation of the entire race, embracing all of its various groups and elements, showing their relations with each other and to the whites, been made.

It is very likely that the Negroes of the United States have a fairly correct idea of what the white people of the country think of them, for that opinion has for a long time been and is still being constantly stated; but they are themselves more or less a sphinx to the whites. It is curiously interesting and even vitally important to know what are the thoughts of ten millions of them concerning the people among whom they live. In these pages it is as though a veil has been drawn aside: the reader is given a view of the inner life of the Negro in America, is initiated into the "free masonry," as it were, of the race.

These pages also reveal the unsuspected fact that prejudice against the Negro is exerting a pressure, which, in New York and other large cities where the opportunity is open, is actually and constantly forcing an unascertainable number of fair-complexioned colored people over into the white race.

In this book the reader is given a glimpse behind the scenes of this race-drama which is being here enacted,—he is taken upon an elevation where he can catch a bird's-eye view of the conflict which is being waged.

THE PUBLISHERS.

Chapter I

I KNOW that in writing the following pages I am divulging the great secret of my life, the secret which for some years I have guarded far more carefully than any of my earthly possessions; and it is a curious study to me to analyze the motives which prompt me to do it. I feel that I am led by the same impulse which forces the unfound-out criminal to take somebody into his confidence, although he knows that the act is liable, even almost certain, to lead to his undoing. I know that I am playing with fire, and I feel the thrill which accompanies that most fascinating pastime; and, back of it all, I think I find a sort of savage and diabolical desire to gather up all the little tragedies of my life, and turn them into a practical joke on society.

And, too, I suffer a vague feeling of unsatisfaction, of regret, of almost remorse from which I am seeking relief, and of which I shall speak in the last paragraph of this account.

I was born in a little town of Georgia a few years after the close of the Civil War. I shall not mention the name of the town, because there are people still living there who could be connected with this narrative. I have only a faint recollection of the place of my birth. At times I can close my eyes, and call up in a dream-like way things that seem to have happened ages ago in some other world. I can see in this half vision a little house,— I am quite sure it was not a large one;— I can remember that flowers grew in the front yard, and that around each bed of flowers was a hedge of vari-colored glass bottles stuck in the ground neck down. I remember that once, while playing around in the sand, I became curious to know whether or not the bottles grew as the flowers did, and I proceeded to dig them up to find out; the investigation brought me a terrific spanking which indelibly fixed the incident in my mind. I can remember, too, that behind the house was a shed under which stood two or three wooden tubs. These wash-tubs were the earliest aversion of my life, for regularly on certain evenings I was plunged into one of them, and scrubbed until my skin ached. I can remember to this day the pain caused by the strong, rank soap getting into my eyes.

Back from the house a vegetable garden ran, perhaps seventy-five or one hundred feet; but to my childish fancy it was an endless territory. I can still recall the thrill of joy, excitement, and wonder it gave me to go on an exploring expedition through it, to find the blackberries, both ripe and green, that grew along the edge of the fence.

I remember with what pleasure I used to arrive at, and stand before, a little enclosure in which stood a patient cow chewing her cud, how I would occasionally offer her through the bars a piece of my bread and molasses, and how I would jerk back my hand in half fright if she made any motion to accept my offer.

I have a dim recollection of several people who moved in and about this little house, but I have a distinct mental image of only two: one, my mother, and the other, a tall man with a small, dark mustache. I remember that his shoes or boots were always shiny, and that he wore a gold chain and a great gold watch with which he was always willing to let me play. My admiration was almost equally divided between the watch and chain and the shoes. He used to come to the house evenings, perhaps two or three times a week; and it became my appointed duty whenever he came to bring him a pair of slippers, and to put the shiny shoes in a particular corner; he often gave me in return for this service a bright coin which my mother taught me to promptly drop in a little tin bank. I remember distinctly the last time this tall man came to the little house in Georgia; that evening before I went to bed he took me up in his arms, and squeezed me very tightly; my mother stood behind his chair wiping tears from her eyes. I remember how I sat upon his knee, and watched him laboriously drill a hole through a ten-dollar gold piece, and then tie the coin around my neck with a string. I have worn that gold piece around my neck the greater part of my life, and still possess it, but more than once I have wished that some other way had been found of attaching it to me besides putting a hole through it.

On the day after the coin was put around my neck my mother and I started on what seemed to me an endless journey. I knelt on the seat and watched through the train window the corn and cotton fields pass swiftly by until I fell asleep. When I fully awoke we were being driven through the streets of a large city—Savannah. I sat up and blinked at the bright lights. At Savannah we boarded a steamer which finally landed us in New York. From New York we went to a town in Connecticut, which became the home of my boyhood.

My mother and I lived together in a little cottage which seemed to me to be fitted up almost luxuriously; there were horse-hair covered chairs in the parlor, and a little square piano; there was a stairway with red carpet on it leading to a half second story; there were pictures on the walls, and a few books in a glass-doored case. My mother dressed me very neatly, and I developed that pride which well-dressed boys generally have. She was careful about my associates, and I myself was quite particular. As I look back now I can see that I was a perfect little aristocrat. My mother rarely went to anyone's house, but she did sewing, and there were a great many ladies coming to our cottage. If I were around they would generally call me, and ask me my name and age and tell my mother what a pretty boy I was. Some of them would pat me on the head and kiss me.

My mother was kept very busy with her sewing; sometimes she would have another woman helping her. I think she must have derived a fair income from her work. I know, too, that at least once each a month she received a letter; I used to watch for the postman, get the letter, and run to her with it; whether she was busy or not, she would take it and instantly thrust it into her bosom. I never saw her read one of these letters. I knew later that they contained money and, what was to her, more than money. As busy as she generally was she, however, found time to teach me my letters and figures and how to spell a number of easy words. Always on Sunday evenings she opened the little square piano and picked out hymns. I can recall now that whenever she played hymns from the book her tempos were always decidedly largo. Sometimes on other evenings when she was not sewing she would play simple accompaniments to some old southern songs which she sang. In these songs she was freer, because she played them by ear. Those evenings on which she opened the little piano were the happiest hours of my childhood. Whenever she started toward the

instrument I used to follow her with all the interest and irrepressible joy that a pampered pet dog shows when a package is
opened in which he knows there is a sweet bit for him. I used
to stand by her side, and often interrupt and annoy her by
chiming in with strange harmonies which I found either on
the high keys of the treble or the low keys of the bass. I remember that I had a particular fondness for the black keys. Always on such evenings, when the music was over, my mother
would sit with me in her arms, often for a very long time. She
would hold me close, softly crooning some old melody without words, all the while gently stroking her face against my
head; many and many a night I thus fell asleep. I can see her
now, her great dark eyes looking into the fire, to where? No
one knew but she. The memory of that picture has more than
once kept me from straying too far from the place of purity
and safety in which her arms held me.

At a very early age I began to thump on the piano alone,
and it was not long before I was able to pick out a few tunes.
When I was seven years old I could play by ear all of the hymns
and songs that my mother knew. I had also learned the names
of the notes in both clefs, but I preferred not to be hampered
by notes. About this time several ladies for whom my mother
sewed heard me play, and they persuaded her that I should at
once be put under a teacher; so arrangements were made for
me to study the piano with a lady who was a fairly good musician; at the same time arrangements were made for me to
study my books with this lady's daughter. My music teacher
had no small difficulty at first in pinning me down to the
notes. If she played my lesson over for me I invariably attempted to reproduce the required sounds without the slightest recourse to the written characters. Her daughter, my other
teacher, also had her worries. She found that, in reading,
whenever I came to words that were difficult or unfamiliar I
was prone to bring my imagination to the rescue and read
from the picture. She has laughingly told me, since then, that I
would sometimes substitute whole sentences and even paragraphs from what meaning I thought the illustration conveyed. She said she sometimes was not only amused at the
fresh treatment I would give an author's subject, but that
when I gave some new and sudden turn to the plot of the

story she often grew interested and even excited in listening to hear what kind of denouement I would bring about. But I am sure this was not due to dullness, for I made rapid progress in both my music and my books.

And so, for a couple of years my life was divided between my music and my school books. Music took up the greater part of my time. I had no playmates, but amused myself with games—some of them my own invention—which could be played alone. I knew a few boys whom I had met at the church which I attended with my mother, but I had formed no close friendships with any of them. Then, when I was nine years old, my mother decided to enter me in the public school, so all at once I found myself thrown among a crowd of boys of all sizes and kinds; some of them seemed to me like savages. I shall never forget the bewilderment, the pain, the heart-sickness of that first day at school. I seemed to be the only stranger in the place; every other boy seemed to know every other boy. I was fortunate enough, however, to be assigned to a teacher who knew me; my mother made her dresses. She was one of the ladies who used to pat me on the head and kiss me. She had the tact to address a few words directly to me; this gave me a certain sort of standing in the class, and put me somewhat at ease.

Within a few days I had made one staunch friend, and was on fairly good terms with most of the boys. I was shy of the girls, and remained so; even now, a word or look from a pretty woman sets me all a-tremble. This friend I bound to me with hooks of steel in a very simple way. He was a big awkward boy with a face full of freckles and a head full of very red hair. He was perhaps fourteen years of age; that is, four or five years older than any other boy in the class. This seniority was due to the fact that he had spent twice the required amount of time in several preceding classes. I had not been at school many hours before I felt that "Red Head"—as I involuntarily called him—and I were to be friends. I do not doubt that this feeling was strengthened by the fact that I had been quick enough to see that a big, strong boy was a friend to be desired at a public school; and, perhaps, in spite of his dullness, "Red Head" had been able to discern that I could be of service to him. At any rate there was a simultaneous mutual attraction.

The teacher had strung the class promiscuously round the walls of the room for a sort of trial heat for places of rank; when the line straightened out I found that by skillful maneuvering I had placed myself third, and had piloted "Red Head" to the place next to me. The teacher began by giving us to spell the words corresponding to our order in the line. "Spell first." "Spell second." "Spell third." I rattled off, "t-h-i-r-d, third," in a way which said, "Why don't you give us something hard?" As the words went down the line I could see how lucky I had been to get a good place together with an easy word. As young as I was I felt impressed with the unfairness of the whole proceeding when I saw the tailenders going down before "twelfth" and "twentieth," and I felt sorry for those who had to spell such words in order to hold a low position. "Spell fourth." "Red Head," with his hands clutched tightly behind his back, began bravely, "f-o-r-t-h." Like a flash a score of hands went up, and the teacher began saying, "No snapping of fingers, no snapping of fingers." This was the first word missed, and it seemed to me that some of the scholars were about to lose their senses; some were dancing up and down on one foot with a hand above their heads, the fingers working furiously, and joy beaming all over their faces; others stood still, their hands raised not so high, their fingers working less rapidly, and their faces expressing not quite so much happiness; there were still others who did not move nor raise their hands, but stood with great wrinkles on their foreheads, looking very thoughtful.

The whole thing was new to me, and I did not raise my hand, but slyly whispered the letter "u" to "Red Head" several times. "Second chance," said the teacher. The hands went down and the class became quiet. "Red Head," his face now red, after looking beseechingly at the ceiling, then pitiably at the floor, began very haltingly, "f-u-." Immediately an impulse to raise hands went through the class, but the teacher checked it, and poor "Red Head," though he knew that each letter he added only took him farther out of the way, went doggedly on and finished, "r-t-h." The hand raising was now repeated with more hubbub and excitement than at first. Those who before had not moved a finger were now waving their hands above their heads. "Red Head" felt that he was lost. He looked very big and foolish, and some of the scholars began to snicker. His helpless condition went straight to my heart, and gripped my sympathies. I felt that if he failed it would in some way be my failure. I raised my hand, and under cover of the excitement and the teacher's attempts to regain order, I hurriedly shot up into his ear twice, quite distinctly, "f-o-u-r-t-h," "f-o-u-r-t-h." The teacher tapped on her desk and said, "Third and last chance." The hands came down, the silence became oppressive. "Red Head" began: "f"— Since that day I have waited anxiously for many a turn of the wheel of fortune, but never under greater tension than I watched for the order in which those letters would fall from "Red's" lips—"o-u-r-t-h." A sigh of relief and disappointment went up from the class. Afterwards, through all our school days, "Red Head" shared my wit and quickness and I benefited by his strength and dogged faithfulness.

There were some black and brown boys and girls in the school, and several of them were in my class. One of the boys strongly attracted my attention from the first day I saw him. His face was as black as night, but shone as though it was polished; he had sparkling eyes, and when he opened his mouth he displayed glistening white teeth. It struck me at once as appropriate to call him "Shiny face," or "Shiny eyes," or "Shiny teeth," and I spoke of him often by one of these names to the other boys. These terms were finally merged into "Shiny," and to that name he answered good naturedly during the balance of his public school days.

"Shiny" was considered without question to be the best speller, the best reader, the best penman, in a word, the best scholar, in the class. He was very quick to catch anything; but, nevertheless, studied hard; thus he possessed two powers very rarely combined in one boy. I saw him year after year, on up into the high school, win the majority of the prizes for punctuality, deportment, essay writing and declamation. Yet it did not take me long to discover that, in spite of his standing as a scholar, he was in some way looked down upon.

The other black boys and girls were still more looked down upon. Some of the boys often spoke of them as "niggers."

Sometimes on the way home from school a crowd would walk behind them repeating:

> "Nigger, nigger, never die,
> Black face and shiny eye."

On one such afternoon one of the black boys turned suddenly on his tormentors, and hurled a slate; it struck one of the white boys in the mouth, cutting a slight gash in his lip. At sight of the blood the boy who had thrown the slate ran, and his companions quickly followed. We ran after them pelting them with stones until they separated in several directions. I was very much wrought up over the affair, and went home and told my mother how one of the "niggers" had struck a boy with a slate. I shall never forget how she turned on me. "Don't you ever use that word again," she said, "and don't you ever bother the colored children at school. You ought to be ashamed of yourself." I did hang my head in shame, but not because she had convinced me that I had done wrong, but because I was hurt by the first sharp word she had ever given me.

My school days ran along very pleasantly. I stood well in my studies, not always so well with regard to my behavior. I was never guilty of any serious misconduct, but my love of fun sometimes got me into trouble. I remember, however, that my sense of humor was so sly that most of the trouble usually fell on the head of the other fellow. My ability to play on the piano at school exercises was looked upon as little short of marvelous in a boy of my age. I was not chummy with many of my mates, but, on the whole, was about as popular as it is good for a boy to be.

One day near the end of my second term at school the principal came into our room, and after talking to the teacher, for some reason said, "I wish all of the white scholars to stand for a moment." I rose with the others. The teacher looked at me, and calling my name said, "You sit down for the present, and rise with the others." I did not quite understand her, and questioned, "Ma'am?" She repeated with a softer tone in her voice, "You sit down now, and rise with the others." I sat down dazed. I saw and heard nothing. When the others were asked to rise I did not know it. When school was dismissed I went out in a kind of stupor. A few of the white boys jeered me, saying, "Oh, you're a nigger too." I heard some black children say, "We knew he was colored." "Shiny" said to them, "Come along, don't tease him," and thereby won my undying gratitude.

I hurried on as fast as I could, and had gone some distance before I perceived that "Red Head" was walking by my side. After a while he said to me, "Le' me carry your books." I gave him my strap without being able to answer. When we got to my gate he said as he handed me my books, "Say, you know my big red agate? I can't shoot with it any more. I'm going to bring it to school for you to-morrow." I took my books and ran into the house. As I passed through the hallway I saw that my mother was busy with one of her customers; I rushed up into my own little room, shut the door, and went quickly to where my looking-glass hung on the wall. For an instant I was afraid to look, but when I did I looked long and earnestly. I have often heard people say to my mother, "What a pretty boy you have." I was accustomed to hear remarks about my beauty; but, now, for the first time, I became conscious of it, and recognized it. I noticed the ivory whiteness of my skin, the beauty of my mouth, the size and liquid darkness of my eyes, and how the long black lashes that fringed and shaded them produced an effect that was strangely fascinating even to me. I noticed the softness and glossiness of my dark hair that fell in waves over my temples, making my forehead appear whiter than it really was. How long I stood there gazing at my image I do not know. When I came out and reached the head of the stairs, I heard the lady who had been with my mother going out. I ran downstairs, and rushed to where my mother was sitting with a piece of work in her hands. I buried my head in her lap and blurted out, "Mother, mother, tell me, am I a nigger?" I could not see her face, but I knew the piece of work dropped to the floor, and I felt her hands on my head. I looked up into her face and repeated, "Tell me, mother, am I a nigger?" There were tears in her eyes, and I could see that she was suffering for me. And then it was that I looked at her critically for the first time. I had thought of her in a childish way only as the most beautiful woman in the world; now I looked at her searching for defects. I could see that her skin was almost brown, that her hair was not so soft as mine, and that she did differ in some way from the other ladies who came to the house; yet, even so, I could see that she was very beautiful, more beautiful than any of them. She must have felt that I was examining her, for she hid her face in her hair, and said with difficulty, "No, my darling, you are not a nigger." She went on, "You are as good as anybody; if anyone calls you a nigger don't notice them." But the more she talked the less was I re-assured, and I stopped her by asking, "Well, mother, am I white? Are you white?" She answered tremblingly, "No, I am not white, but you—your father is one of the greatest men in the country—the best blood of the South is in you—" This suddenly opened up in my heart a fresh chasm of misgiving and fear, and I almost fiercely demanded, "Who is my father? Where is he?" She stroked my hair and said, "I'll tell you about him some day." I sobbed, "I want to know now." She answered, "No, not now."

Perhaps it had to be done, but I have never forgiven the woman who did it so cruelly. It may be that she never knew that she gave me a sword-thrust that day in school which was years in healing.

Chapter II

SINCE I have grown older I have often gone back and tried to analyze the change that came into my life after that fateful day in school. There did come a radical change, and, young as I was, I felt fully conscious of it, though I did not fully comprehend it. Like my first spanking, it is one of the few incidents in my life that I can remember clearly. In the life of every one there is a limited number of unhappy experiences which are not written upon the memory, but stamped there with a die; and in long years after they can be called up in detail, and every emotion that was stirred by them can be lived through anew; these are the tragedies of life. We may grow to include some of them among the trivial incidents of childhood—a broken toy, a promise made to us which was not kept, a harsh, heart-piercing word—but these, too, as well as the bitter experiences and disappointments of mature years, are the tragedies of life.

And so I have often lived through that hour, that day, that week in which was wrought the miracle of my transition from one world into another; for I did indeed pass into another world. From that time I looked out through other eyes, my thoughts were colored, my words dictated, my actions limited by one dominating, all-pervading idea which constantly increased in force and weight until I finally realized in it a great, tangible fact.

And this is the dwarfing, warping, distorting influence which operates upon each colored man in the United States. He is forced to take his outlook on all things, not from the view point of a citizen, or a man, or even a human being, but from the viewpoint of a *colored* man. It is wonderful to me that the race has progressed so broadly as it has, since most of its thought and all of its activity must run through the narrow neck of one funnel.

And it is this, too, which makes the colored people of this country, in reality, a mystery to the whites. It is a difficult thing for a white man to learn what a colored man really thinks; because, generally, with the latter an additional and different light must be brought to bear on what he thinks; and his thoughts are often influenced by considerations so delicate and subtle that it would be impossible for him to confess or explain them to one of the opposite race. This gives to every colored man, in proportion to his intellectuality, a sort of dual personality; there is one phase of him which is disclosed only in the freemasony of his own race. I have often watched with interest and sometimes with amazement even ignorant colored men under cover of broad grins and minstrel antics maintain this dualism in the presence of white men.

I believe it to be a fact that the colored people of this country know and understand the white people better than the white people know and understand them.

I now think that this change which came into my life was at first more subjective than objective. I do not think my friends at school changed so much toward me as I did toward them. I grew reserved, I might say suspicious. I grew constantly more and more afraid of laying myself open to some injury to my feelings or my pride. I frequently saw or fancied some slight where, I am sure, none was intended. On the other hand, my friends and teachers were, if anything different, more considerate of me; but I can remember that it was against this very attitude in particular that my sensitiveness revolted. "Red" was the only one who did not so wound me; up to this day O recall with a swelling heart his clumsy efforts to make me understand that nothing could change his love for me.

I am sure that at this time the majority of my white schoolmates did not understand or appreciate any differences between me and themselves; but there were a few who had evidently received instructions at home on the matter, and more than once they displayed their knowledge in word and action. As the years passed I noticed that the most innocent and ignorant among the others grew in wisdom.

I, myself, would not have so clearly understood this difference had it not been for the presence of the other colored children at school; I had learned what their status was, and now I learned that theirs was mine. I had had no particular like or dislike for these black and brown boys and girls; in fact, with the exception of "Shiny," they had occupied very little of my thought, but I do know that when the blow fell I had a very strong aversion to being classed with them. So I became something of a solitary. "Red" and I remained inseparable, and there was between "Shiny" and me a sort of sympathetic bond, but my intercourse with the others was never entirely free from a feeling of constraint. But I must add that this feeling was confined almost entirely to my intercourse with boys and girls of about my own age; I did not experience it with my seniors. And when I grew to manhood, I found myself freer with elderly white people than with those near my own age.

I was now about eleven years old, but these emotions and impressions which I have just described could not have been stronger or more distinct at an older age. There were two immediate results of my forced loneliness: I began to find company in books, and greater pleasure in music. I made the former discovery through a big, gilt-bound, illustrated copy of the Bible, which used to lie in splendid neglect on the center table in our little parlor. On top of the Bible lay a photograph album. I had often looked at the pictures in the album, and one day after taking the larger book down and opening it on the floor, I was overjoyed to find that it contained what seemed to be an inexhaustible supply of pictures. I looked at these pictures many times; in fact, so often that I knew the story of each one without having to read the subject, and then, somehow, I picked up the thread of history on which are strung the trials and tribulations of the Hebrew children; this I followed with feverish interest and excitement. For a long time King David, with Samson a close second, stood at the head of my list of heroes; he was not displaced until I came to know Robert the Bruce. I read a good portion of the Old Testament, all that part treating of wars and rumors of wars, and then started in on the New. I became interested in the life of Christ, but became impatient and disappointed when I found that, notwithstanding the great power he possessed, he did not make use of it when, in my judgment, he most needed to do so. And so my first general impression of the Bible was what my later impression has been of a number of modern books, that the authors put their best work in the first part, and grew either exhausted or careless toward the end.

After reading the Bible, or those parts which held my attention, I began to explore the glass-doored book-case which I have already mentioned. I found there "Pilgrim's Progress," "Peter Parley's History of the United States," Grimm's "Household Stories," "Tales of a Grandfather," a bound volume of an old English publication, I think it was called "The Mirror," a little volume called "Familiar Science," and somebody's "Natural Theology," which latter, of course, I could not read, but which, nevertheless, I tackled, with the result of gaining a permanent dislike for all kinds of theology. There were several other books of no particular name or merit, such as agents sell to people who know nothing of buying books. How my mother came by this little library which, considering all things, was so well suited to me, I never sought to know. But she was far from being an ignorant woman, and had herself, very likely, read the majority of these books, though I do not remember ever having seen her with a book in her hand, with the exception of the Episcopal Prayer-book. At any rate she encouraged in me the habit of reading, and when I had about exhausted those books in the little library which interested me, she began to buy books for me. She also regularly gave me money to buy a weekly paper which was then very popular for boys.

At this time I went in for music with an earnestness worthy of maturer years; a change of teachers was largely responsible for this. I began now to take lessons of the organist of the church which I attended with my mother; he was a good teacher and quite a thorough musician. He was so skillful in his instruction, and filled me with such enthusiasm that my progress—these are his words—was marvelous. I remember that when I was barely twelve years old I appeared on a program with a number of adults at an entertainment given for some charitable purpose, and carried off the honors. I did more, I brought upon myself through the local newspapers the handicapping title of "Infant prodigy."

I can believe that I did astonish my audience, for I never played the piano like a child, that is, in the "one-two-three" style with accelerated motion. Neither did I depend upon mere brilliancy of technic, a trick by which children often surprise their listeners, but I always tried to interpret a piece of music; I always played with feeling. Very early I acquired that knack of using the pedals which makes the piano a sympathetic, singing instrument; quite a different thing from the source of hard or blurred sounds it so generally is. I think this was due not entirely to natural artistic temperament, but largely to the fact that I did not begin to learn the piano by counting out exercises, but by trying to reproduce the quaint songs which my mother used to sing, with all their pathetic turns and cadences.

Even at a tender age, in playing, I helped to express what I felt by some of the mannerisms which I afterwards observed in great performers: I had not copied them. I have often heard people speak of the mannerisms of musicians as affectations adopted for mere effect; in some cases they may be so; but a true artist can no more play upon the piano or violin without putting his whole body in accord with the emotions he is striving to express than a swallow can fly without being graceful. Often when playing I could not keep the tears which formed in my eyes from rolling down my cheeks. Sometimes at the end or even in the midst of a composition, as big a boy as I was, I would jump from the piano, and throw myself sobbing into my mother's arms. She, by her caresses and often her tears, only encouraged these fits of sentimental hysteria. Of course, to counteract this tendency to temperamental excesses I should have been out playing ball or in swimming with other boys of my age; but my mother didn't know that. There was only once when she was really firm with me, making me do what she considered was best; I did not want to return to school after the unpleasant episode which I have related, and she was inflexible.

I began my third term, and the days ran along as I have already indicated. I had been promoted twice, and had managed each time to pull "Red" along with me. I think the teachers came to consider me the only hope of his ever getting through school, and I believe they secretly conspired with me to bring about the desired end. At any rate, I know it became easier in each succeeding examination for me not only to assist "Red," but absolutely to do his work. It is strange how in some things honest people can be dishonest without the slightest compunction. I knew boys at school who were too honorable to tell a fib even when one would have been just the right thing, but could not resist the temptation to assist or receive assistance in an examination. I have long considered it the highest proof of honesty in a man to hand his street-car fare to the conductor who had overlooked it.

One afternoon after school, during my third term, I rushed home in a great hurry to get my dinner, and go to my music teacher's. I was never reluctant about going there, but on this particular afternoon I was impetuous. The reason of this was, I had been asked to play the accompaniment for a young lady who was to play a violin solo at a concert given by the young people of the church, and on this afternoon we were to have our first rehearsal. At that time playing accompaniments was the only thing in music I did not enjoy; later this feeling grew into positive dislike. I have never been a really good accompanist because my ideas of interpretation were always too strongly individual. I constantly forced my accelerandos and rubatos upon the soloist, often throwing the duet entirely out of gear.

Perhaps the reader has already guessed why I was so willing and anxious to play the accompaniment to this violin solo; if not,—the violinist was a girl of seventeen or eighteen whom I had first heard play a short time before on a Sunday afternoon at a special service of some kind, and who had moved me to a degree which now I can hardly think of as possible. At present I do not think it was due to her wonderful playing, though I judge she must have been a very fair performer, but there was just the proper setting to produce the effect upon a boy such as I was; the half dim church, the air of devotion on the part of the listeners, the heaving tremor of the organ under the clear wail of the violin, and she, her eyes almost closing, the escaping strands of her dark hair wildly framing her pale face, and her slender body swaying to the tones she called forth, all combined to fire my imagination and my heart with a passion though boyish, yet strong and, somehow, lasting. I have tried to describe the scene; if I have succeeded it is only half success, for words can only partially express what I wish to convey. Always in recalling that Sunday afternoon I am subconscious of a faint but distinct fragrance which, like some old memory-awakening perfume, rises and suffuses my whole imagination, inducing a state of reverie so airy as to just evade the powers of expression.

She was my first love, and I loved her as only a boy loves. I dreamed of her, I built air castles for her, she was the incarnation of each beautiful heroine I knew; when I played the piano it was to her, not even did music furnish an adequate outlet for my passion; I bought a new note-book, and, to sing her praises, made my first and last attempts at poetry. I remember one day at school, after having given in our note-books to have some exercises corrected, the teacher called me to her desk and said, "I couldn't correct your exercises because I found nothing in your book but a rhapsody on somebody's brown eyes." I had passed in the wrong note-book. I don't think I have felt greater embarrassment in my whole life that I did at that moment. I was not only ashamed that my teacher should see this nakedness of my heart, but that she should find out I had any knowledge of such affairs. It did not then occur to me to be ashamed of the kind of poetry I had written.

Of course, the reader must know that all of this adoration was in secret; next to my great love for this young lady was the dread that in some way she would find it out. I did not know what some men never find out, that the woman who cannot discern when she is loved has never lived. It makes me laugh to think how successful I was in concealing it all; within a short time after our duet all of the friends of my dear one were referring to me as her "little sweetheart," of her "little beau," and she laughingly encouraged it. This did not entirely satisfy me; I wanted to be taken seriously. I had definitely made up my mind that I should never love another woman, and that if she deceived me I should do something desperate—the great difficulty was to think of something sufficiently desperate—and the heartless jade, how she led me on!

So I hurried home that afternoon, humming snatches of the violin part of the duet, my heart beating with pleasurable excitement over the fact that I was going to be near her, to have her attention placed directly upon me; that I was going to be of service to her, and in a way in which I could show myself to advantage—this last consideration has much to do with cheerful service.—The anticipation produced in me a sensation somewhat between bliss and fear. I rushed through the gate, took the three steps to the house at one bound, threw open the door, and was about to hang my cap on its accustomed peg of the hall rack when I noticed that that particular peg was occupied by a black derby hat. I stopped suddenly, and gazed at this hat as though I had never seen an object of its description. I was still looking at it in open-eyed wonder when my mother, coming out of the parlor into the hallway, called me, and said there was someone inside who wanted to see me. Feeling that I was being made a party to some kind of mystery I went in with her, and there I saw a man standing leaning with one elbow on the mantel, his back partly turned toward the door. As I entered he turned, and I saw a tall, handsome, well dressed gentleman of perhaps thirty-five; he advanced a step toward me with a smile on his face. I stopped and looked at him with the same feelings with which I had looked at the derby hat, except that they were greatly magnified. I looked at him from head to foot, but he was an absolute blank to me until my eyes rested on his slender, elegant, polished shoes; then it seemed that indistinct and partly obliterated films of memory began at first slowly then rapidly to unroll, forming a vague panorama of my childhood days in Georgia.

My mother broke the spell by calling me by name, and saying, "This is your father."

"Father, Father," that was the word which had been to me a source of doubt and perplexity ever since the interview with my mother on the subject. How often I had wondered about my father, who he was, what he was like, whether alive or dead, and above all, why she would not tell me about him. More than once I had been on the point of recalling to her the promise she had made me, but I instinctively felt that she was happier for not telling me and that I was happier for not being told; yet I had not the slightest idea what the real truth was. And here he stood before me, just the kind of looking father I had wishfully pictured him to be; but I made no advance toward him; I stood there feeling embarrassed and foolish, not knowing what to say or do. I am not sure but that he felt pretty much the same. My mother stood at my side with one hand on my shoulder almost pushing me forward, but I did not move. I can well remember the look of disappointment, even pain, on her face; and I can now understand that she

could expect nothing else but that at the name "father" I
should throw myself into his arms. But I could not rise to this
dramatic or, better, melodramatic climax. Somehow I could
not arouse any considerable feeling of need for a father. He
broke the awkward tableau by saying, "Well, boy, aren't you
glad to see me?" He evidently meant the words kindly enough,
but I don't know what he could have said that would have had
a worse effect; however, my good breeding came to my rescue,
and I answered, "Yes, sir," and went to him and offered him
my hand. He took my hand into one of his, and, with the
other, stroked my head saying that I had grown into a fine
youngster. He asked me how old I was; which, of course, he
must have done merely to say something more, or perhaps he
did so as a test of my intelligence. I replied, "Twelve, sir." He
then made the trite observation about the flight of time, and
we lapsed into another awkward pause.

My mother was all in smiles; I believe that was one of the
happiest moments of her life. Either to put me more at ease
or to show me off, she asked me to play something for my father. There is only one thing in the world that can make music, at all times and under all circumstances, up to its general
standard, that is a hand-organ, or one of its variations. I went
to the piano and played something in a listless, half-hearted
way. I simply was not in the mood. I was wondering, while
playing, when my mother would dismiss me and let me go;
but my father was so enthusiastic in his praise that he touched
my vanity—which was great—and more than that; he displayed that sincere appreciation which always aroused an artist
to his best effort, and, too, in an unexplainable manner,
makes him feel like shedding tears. I showed my gratitude by
playing for him a Chopin waltz with all the feeling that was in
me. When I had finished my mother's eyes were glistening
with tears; my father stepped across the room, seized me in
his arms, and squeezed me to his breast. I am certain that for
that moment he was proud to be my father. He sat and held
me standing between his knees while he talked to my mother.
I, in the meantime, examined him with more curiosity, perhaps, than politeness. I interrupted the conversation by asking, "Mother, is he going to stay with us now?" I found it impossible to frame the word "father"; it was too new to me; so

I asked the question through my mother. Without waiting for her to speak, my father answered, "I've got to go back to New York this afternoon, but I'm coming to see you again." I turned abruptly and went over to my mother, and almost in a whisper reminded her that I had an appointment which I should not miss; to my pleasant surprise she said that she would give me something to eat at once so that I might go. She went out of the room, and I began to gather from off the piano the music I needed. When I had finished, my father, who had been watching me, asked, "Are you going?" I replied, "Yes, sir, I've got to go to practice for a concert." He spoke some words of advice to me about being a good boy and taking care of my mother when I grew up, and added that he was going to send me something nice from New York. My mother called, and I said good-by to him, and went out. I saw him only once after that.

I quickly swallowed down what my mother had put on the table for me, seized my cap and music, and hurried off to my teacher's house. On the way I could think of nothing but this new father, where he came from, where he had been, why he was here, and why he would not stay. In my mind I ran over the whole list of fathers I become acquainted with in my reading, but I could not classify him. The thought did not cross my mind that he was different from me, and even if it had the mystery would not thereby have been explained; for notwithstanding my changed relations with most of my schoolmates, I had only a faint knowledge of prejudice and no idea at all how it ramified and affected the entire social organism. I felt, however, that there was something about the whole affair which had to be hid.

When I arrived, I found that she of the brown eyes had been rehearsing with my teacher, and was on the point of leaving. My teacher with some expressions of surprise asked why I was late, and I stammered out the first deliberate lie of which I have any recollection. I told him that when I reached home from school I found my mother quite sick, and that I had stayed with her a while before coming. Then unnecessarily and gratuitously, to give my words force of conviction, I suppose, I added, "I don't think she'll be with us very long." In speaking these words I must have been comical; for I noticed that my teacher, instead of showing signs of anxiety or sorrow, half hid a smile. But how little did I know that in that lie I was speaking prophecy.

She of the brown eyes unpacked her violin, and we went through the duet several times. I was soon lost to all other thoughts in the delights of music and love. I say delights of love without reservation; for at no time of life is love so pure, so delicious, so poetic, so romantic, as it is in boyhood. A great deal has been said about the heart of a girl when she stands "where the brook and river meet," but what she feels is negative; more interesting is the heart of a boy when just at the budding dawn of manhood he stands looking wide-eyed into the long vistas opening before him; when he first becomes conscious of the awakening and quickening of strange desires and unknown powers; when what he sees and feels is still shadowy and mystical enough to be intangible, and, so, more beautiful; when his imagination is unsullied, and his faith new and whole—then it is that love wears a halo—the man who has not loved before he was fourteen has missed a fore-taste of Elysium.

When I reached home it was quite dark, and I found my mother without a light, sitting rocking in a chair as she so often used to do in my childhood days, looking into the fire and singing softly to herself. I nestled close to her, and with her arms around me she haltingly told me who my father was,—a great man, a fine gentleman,—he loved me and loved her very much; he was going to make a great man of me. All she said was so limited by reserve and so colored by her feelings that it was but half truth; and so, I did not yet fully understand.

Chapter III

PERHAPS I ought not pass on this narrative without mentioning that the duet was a great success; so great that we were obliged to respond with two encores. It seemed to me that life could hold no greater joy than it contained when I took her hand and we stepped down to the front of the stage bowing to our enthusiastic audience. When we reached the little dressing-room, where the other performers were applauding as wildly as the audience, she impulsively threw both her arms around me, and kissed me, while I struggled to get away.

One day a couple of weeks after my father had been to see us, a wagon drove up to our cottage loaded with a big box. I was about to tell the men on the wagon that they had made a mistake, when my mother, acting darkly wise, told them to bring their load in; she had them unpack the box, and quickly there was evolved from the boards, paper and other packing material, a beautiful, brand new, upright piano. Then she informed me that it was a present to me from my father. I at once sat down and ran my fingers over the keys; the full, mellow tone of the instrument was ravishing. I thought, almost remorsefully, of how I had left my father; but, even so, there momentarily crossed my mind a feeling of disappointment that the piano was not a grand. The new instrument greatly increased the pleasure of my hours of study and practice at home.

Shortly after this I was made a member of the boys' choir, it being found that I possessed a clear, strong soprano voice. I enjoyed the singing very much. About a year later I began the study of the pipe organ and the theory of music; and before I had finished the grammar school I had written out several simple preludes for organ which won the admiration of my teacher, and which he did me the honor to play at services.

The older I grew the more thought I gave to the question of my and my mother's position, and what was our exact relation to the world in general. My idea of the whole matter was rather hazy. My study of United States history had been confined to those periods which were designated in my book as

"Discovery," "Colonial," "Revolutionary," and "Constitutional." I now began to study about the Civil War, but the story was told in such a condensed and skipping style that I gained from it very little real information. It is a marvel how children ever learn any history out of books of that sort. And, too, I began now to read the newspapers; I often saw articles which aroused my curiosity, but did not enlighten me. But, one day, I drew from the circulating library a book that cleared the whole mystery, a book that I read with the same feverish intensity with which I had read the old Bible stories, a book that gave me my first perspective of the life I was entering; that book was "Uncle Tom's Cabin."

This work of Harriet Beecher Stowe has been the object of much unfavorable criticism. It has been assailed, not only as fiction of the most imaginative sort, but as being a direct misrepresentation. Several successful attempts have lately been made to displace the book from northern school libraries. Its critics would brush it aside with the remark that there never was a Negro as good as Uncle Tom, nor a slave-holder as bad as Legree. For my part, I was never an admirer of Uncle Tom, nor of his type of goodness; but I believe that there were lots of old Negroes as foolishly good as he; the proof of which is that they knowingly stayed and worked the plantations that furnished sinews for the army which was fighting to keep them enslaved. But, in these later years, several cases have come to my personal knowledge in which old Negroes have died and left what was a considerable fortune to the descendants of their former masters. I do not think it takes any great stretch of the imagination to believe there was a fairly large class of slave holders typified in Legree. And we must also remember that the author depicted a number of worthless if not vicious Negroes, and a slave holder who was as much of a Christian and a gentleman as it was possible for one in his position to be; that she pictured the happy, singing, shuffling darkey as well as the mother wailing for her child sold "down river."

I do not think it is claiming too much to say that "Uncle Tom's Cabin" was a fair and truthful panorama of slavery; however that may be, it opened my eyes as to who and what I was and what my country considered me; in fact, it gave me my bearing. But there was no shock; I took the whole

revelation in a kind of stoical way. One of the greatest benefits I derived from reading the book was that I could afterwards talk frankly with my mother on all questions which had
been vaguely troubling my mind. As a result, she was entirely
freed from reserve, and often herself brought up the subject,
talking of things directly touching her life and mine and of
things which had come down to her through the "old folks."
What she told me interested and even fascinated me; and,
what may seem strange, kindled in me a strong desire to see
the South. She spoke to me quite frankly about herself, my
father and myself; she, the sewing girl of my father's mother;
he, an impetuous young man home from college; I, the child
of this unsanctioned love. She told me even the principal
reason for our coming North. My father was about to be
married to a young lady of another great Southern family. She
did not neglect to add that another reason for our being in
Connecticut was that he intended to give me an education,
and make a man of me. In none of her talks did she ever
utter one word of complaint against my father. She always
endeavored to impress upon me how good he had been and
still was, and that he was all to us that custom and the law
would allow. She loved him; more, she worshiped him, and
she died firmly believing that he loved her more than any
other woman in the world. Perhaps she was right. Who knows?

All of these newly awakened ideas and thoughts took the
form of a definite aspiration on the day I graduated from the
grammar school. And what a day that was! The girls in white
dresses with fresh ribbons in their hair; the boys in new suits
and creaky shoes; the great crowd of parents and friends, the
flowers, the prizes and congratulations, made the day seem to
me one of the greatest importance. I was on the programme,
and played a piano solo which was received by the audience
with that amount of applause which I had come to look upon
as being only the just due to my talent.

But the real enthusiasm was aroused by "Shiny." He was the
principal speaker of the day, and well did he measure up to the
honor. He make a striking picture, that thin little black boy
standing on the platform, dressed in clothes that did not fit
him any too well, his eyes burning with excitement, his shrill,
musical voice vibrating in tones of appealing defiance, and his

black face alight with such great intelligence and earnestness as to be positively handsome. What were his thoughts when he stepped forward and looked into that crowd of faces, all white with the exception of a score or so that were lost to view? I do not know, but I fancy he felt his loneliness. I think there must have rushed over him a feeling akin to that of a gladiator tossed into the arena and bade to fight for his life. I think that solitary little black figure standing there felt that for the particular time and place he bore the weight and responsibility of his race; that for him to fail meant general defeat; but he won, and nobly. His oration was Wendell Phillips' "Toussaint L'Ouverture," a speech which may now be classed as rhetorical, even, perhaps, bombastic; but as the words fell from "Shiny's" lips their effect was magical. How so young an orator could stir so great enthusiasm was to be wondered at. When in the famous peroration, his voice trembling with suppressed emotion rose higher and higher and then rested on the name Toussaint L'Ouverture, it was like touching an electric button which loosed the pent-up feelings of his listeners. They actually rose to him.

I have since known of colored men who have been chosen as class orators in our leading universities, of others who have played on the 'Varsity foot-ball and base-ball teams, of colored speakers who have addressed great white audiences. In each of these instances I believe the men were stirred by the same emotions which actuated "Shiny" on the day of his graduation; and, too, in each case where the efforts have reached any high standard of excellence they have been followed by the same phenomenon of enthusiasm. I think the explanation of the latter lies in what is a basic, though often dormant, principle of the Anglo-Saxon heart, love of fair play. "Shiny," it is true, was what is so common in his race, a natural orator; but I doubt that any white boy of equal talent could have wrought the same effect. The sight of that boy gallantly waging with puny, black arms, so unequal a battle, touched the deep springs in the hearts of his audience, and they were swept by a wave of sympathy and admiration.

But the effect upon me of "Shiny's" speech was double; I not only shared the enthusiasm of his audience, but he imparted to me some of his own enthusiasm. I felt leap within me pride that I was colored; and I began to form wild dreams of bringing glory and honor to the Negro race. For days I could talk of nothing else with my mother except my ambitions to be a great man, a great colored man, to reflect credit on the race and gain fame for myself. It was not until years after that I formulated a definite and feasible plan for realizing my dream.

I entered the high school with my class, and still continued my study of the piano, the pipe organ and the theory of music. I had to drop out of the boys' choir on account of a changing voice; this I regretted very much. As I grew older my love for reading grew stronger. I read with studious interest everything I could find relating to colored men who had gained prominence. My heroes had been King David, then Robert the Bruce; now Frederick Douglass was enshrined in the place of honor. When I learned that Alexander Dumas was a colored man, I re-read "Monte Cristo" and "The Three Guardsmen" with magnified pleasure. I lived between my music and my books, on the whole a rather unwholesome life for a boy to lead. I dwelt in a world of imagination, of dreams and air castles,—the kind of atmosphere that sometimes nourishes a genius, more often men unfitted for the practical struggles of life. I never played a game of ball, never went fishing or learned to swim; in fact, the only outdoor exercise in which I took any interest was skating. Nevertheless, though slender, I grew well-formed and in perfect health. After I entered the high school I began to notice the change in my mother's health, which I suppose had been going on for some years. She began to complain a little and to cough a great deal; she tried several remedies, and finally went to see a doctor; but though she was failing in health she kept her spirits up. She still did a great deal of sewing, and in the busy seasons hired two women to help her. The purpose she had formed of having me go through college without financial worries kept her at work when she was not fit for it. I was so fortunate as to be able to organize a class of eight or ten beginners on the piano, and so start a separate little fund of my own. As the time for my graduation from high school grew nearer, the plans for my college career became the chief subject of our talks. I sent for catalogues of all the prominent schools in the East, and eagerly gathered all the information I could concerning them from different sources. My mother told me that my father wanted me to go to Harvard or Yale; she herself had a half desire for me to go to Atlanta University, and even had me write for a catalogue of that school. There were two reasons, however, that inclined her to my father's choice: the first, that at Harvard or Yale I should be near her; the second, that my father had promised to pay a part of my college education.

Both "Shiny" and "Red" came to my house quite often of evenings, and we used to talk over our plans and prospects for the future. Sometimes I would play for them, and they seemed to enjoy the music very much. My mother often prepared sundry southern dishes for them, which I am not sure but that they enjoyed more. "Shiny" had an uncle in Amherst, Mass., and he expected to live with him and work his way through Amherst College. "Red" declared that he had enough of school and that after he got his high school diploma he would get a position in a bank. It was his ambition to become a banker, and he felt sure of getting the opportunity through certain members of his family.

My mother barely had strength to attend the closing exercises of the high school when I graduated; and after that day she was seldom out of bed. She could no longer direct her work, and under the expense of medicines, doctors, and someone to look after her, our college fund began to diminish rapidly. Many of her customers and some of the neighbors were very kind, and frequently brought her nourishment of one kind or another. My mother realized what I did not, that she was mortally ill, and she had me write a long letter to my father. For some time past she had heard from him only at irregular intervals; we never received an answer. In those last days I often sat at her bedside and read to her until she fell asleep. Sometimes I would leave the parlor door open and play the piano, just loud enough for the music to reach her. This she always enjoyed.

One night, near the end of July, after I had been watching beside her for some hours, I went into the parlor, and throwing myself into the big arm chair dozed off into a fitful sleep. I was suddenly aroused by one of the neighbors, who had come in to sit with her that night. She said, "Come to your mother at once." I hurried upstairs, and at the bedroom door met the woman who was acting as nurse. I noted with a dissolving heart the strange look of awe on her face. From my first glance at my mother, I discerned the light of death upon her countenance. I fell upon my knees beside the bed, and burying my face in the sheets sobbed convulsively. She died with the fingers of her left hand entwined in my hair.

I will not rake over this, one of the two sacred sorrows of my life; nor could I describe the feeling of unutterable loneliness that fell upon me. After the funeral I went to the house of my music teacher; he had kindly offered me the hospitality of his home for so long as I might need it. A few days later I moved my trunk, piano, my music and most of my books to his home; the rest of my books I divided between "Shiny" and "Red." Some of the household effects I gave to "Shiny's" mother and to two or three of the neighbors who had been kind to us during my mother's illness; the others I sold. After settling up my little estate I found that besides a good supply of clothes, a piano, some books and other trinkets, I had about two hundred dollars in cash.

The question of what I was to do now confronted me. My teacher suggested a concert tour; but both of us realized that I was too old to be exploited as an infant prodigy and too young and inexperienced to go before the public as a finished artist. He, however, insisted that the people of the town would generously patronize a benefit concert, so took up the matter, and made arrangements for such an entertainment. A more than sufficient number of people with musical and elocutionary talent volunteered their services to make a programme. Among these was my brown-eyed violinist. But our relations were not the same as they were when we had played our first duet together. A year or so after that time she had dealt me a crushing blow by getting married. I was partially avenged, however, by the fact that, though she was growing more beautiful, she was losing her ability to play the violin.

I was down on the programme for one number. My selection might have appeared at that particular time as a bit of affectation, but I considered it deeply appropriate; I played Beethoven's "Sonata Pathétique." When I sat down at the piano, and glanced into the faces of the several hundreds of people who were there solely on account of love or sympathy for me, emotions swelled in my heart which enabled me to play the "Pathétique" as I could never again play it. When the last tone died away the few who began to applaud were hushed by the silence of the others; and for once I played without receiving an encore.

The benefit yielded me a little more than two hundred dollars, thus raising my cash capital to about four hundred dollars. I still held to my determination of going to college; so it was now a question of trying to squeeze through a year at Harvard or going to Atlanta where the money I had would pay my actual expenses for at least two years. The peculiar fascination which the South held over my imagination and my limited capital decided me in favor of Atlanta University; so about the last of September I bade farewell to the friends and scenes of my boyhood, and boarded a train for the South.

Chapter IV

THE FARTHER I got below Washington the more disappointed I became in the appearance of the country. I peered through car windows, looking in vain for the luxuriant semi-tropical scenery which I had pictured in my mind. I did not find the grass so green, nor the woods so beautiful, nor the flowers so plentiful, as they were in Connecticut. Instead, the red earth partly covered by tough, scrawny grass, the muddy straggling roads, the cottages of unpainted pine boards, and the clay daubed huts imparted a "burnt up" impression. Occasionally we ran through a little white and green village that was like an oasis in a desert.

When I reached Atlanta my steadily increasing disappointment was not lessened. I found it a big, dull, red town. This dull red color of that part of the South I was then seeing had much, I think, to do with the extreme depression of my spirits—no public squares, no fountains, dingy street-cars and, with the exception of three or four principal thoroughfares, unpaved streets. It was raining when I arrived and some of these unpaved streets were absolutely impassable. Wheels sank to the hubs in red mire, and I actually stood for an hour and watched four or five men work to save a mule, which had stepped into a deep sink, from drowning, or, rather, suffocating in the mud. The Atlanta of to-day is a new city.

On the train I had talked with one of the Pullman car porters, a bright young fellow who was himself a student, and told him that I was going to Atlanta to attend school. I had also asked him to tell me where I might stop for a day or two until the University opened. He said I might go with him to the place where he stopped during his "layovers" in Atlanta. I gladly accepted his offer, and went with him along one of those muddy streets until we came to a rather rickety looking frame house, which we entered. The proprietor of the house was a big, fat, greasy looking brown-skinned man. When I asked him if he could give me accommodation he wanted to know how long I would stay. I told him perhaps two days, not more than three. In reply he said, "Oh, dat's all right den," at the same time leading the way up a pair of creaky stairs. I followed him and the porter to a room, the door of which the proprietor opened while continuing, it seemed, his remark, "Oh, dat's all right den," by adding, "You kin sleep in dat cot in de corner der. Fifty cents please." The porter interrupted by saying, "You needn't collect from him now, he's got a trunk." This seemed to satisfy the man, and he went down leaving me and my porter friend in the room. I glanced around the apartment and saw that it contained a double bed and two cots, two wash-stands, three chairs, and a time-worn bureau with a looking-glass that would have made Adonis appear hideous. I looked at the cot in which I was to sleep and suspected, not without good reasons, that I should not be the first to use the sheets and pillow-case since they had last come from the wash. When I thought of the clean, tidy, comfortable surroundings in which I had been reared, a wave of homesickness swept over me that made me feel faint. Had it not been for the presence of my companion, and that I knew this much of his history,—that he was not yet quite twenty, just three years older than myself, and that he had been fighting his own way in the world, earning his own living and providing for his own education since he was fourteen, I should not have been able to stop the tears that were welling up in my eyes.

I asked him why it was that the proprietor of the house seemed unwilling to accommodate me for more than a couple of days. He informed me that the man ran a lodging house especially for Pullman porters, and as their stays in town were not longer than one or two nights it would interfere with his arrangements to have anyone stay longer. He went on to say, "You see this room is fixed up to accommodate four men at a time. Well, by keeping a sort of table of trips, in and out, of the men, and working them like checkers, he can accommodate fifteen or sixteen in each week and generally avoid having an empty bed. You happen to catch a bed that would have been empty for a couple of nights." I asked him where he was going to sleep. He answered, "I sleep in that other cot to-night; to-morrow night I go out." He went on to tell me that the man who kept the house did not serve meals, and that if I was hungry we would go out and get something to eat.

We went into the street, and in passing the railroad station I
hired a wagon to take my trunk to my lodging place. We
passed along until, finally, we turned into a street that
stretched away, up and down hill, for a mile or two; and here I
caught my first sight of colored people in large numbers. I had
seen little squads around the railroad stations on my way
south; but here I saw a street crowded with them. They filled
the shops and thronged the sidewalks and lined the curb. I
asked my companion if all the colored people in Atlanta lived
in this street. He said they did not and assured me that the
ones I saw were of the lower class. I felt relieved, in spite of
the size of the lower class. The unkempt appearance, the
shambling, slouching gait and loud talk and laughter of these
people aroused in me a feeling of almost repulsion. Only one
thing about them awoke a feeling of interest; that was their dialect. I had read some Negro dialect and had heard snatches of
it on my journey down from Washington; but here I heard it
in all of its fullness and freedom. I was particularly struck by
the way in which it was punctuated by such exclamatory
phrases as "Lawd a mussy!" "G'wan man!" "Bless ma soul!"
"Look heah chile!" These people talked and laughed without
restraint. In fact, they talked straight from their lungs, and
laughed from the pits of their stomachs. And this hearty laughter was often justified by the droll humor of some remark. I
paused long enough to hear one man say to another, "W'at's
de mattah wid you an' yo' fr'en' Sam?" and the other came
back like a flash, "Ma fr'en'? He ma fr'en'? Man! I'd go to his
funeral jes' de same as I'd go to a minstrel show." I have since
learned that this ability to laugh heartily is, in part, the salvation of the American Negro; it does much to keep him from
going the way of the Indian.

The business places of the street along which we were passing consisted chiefly of low bars, cheap dry-goods and notion
stores, barber shops, and fish and bread restaurants. We, at
length, turned down a pair of stairs that led to a basement, and
I found myself in an eating-house somewhat better than those
I had seen in passing; but that did not mean much for its excellence. The place was smoky, the tables were covered with
oilcloth, the floor with sawdust, and from the kitchen came a
rancid odor of fish fried over several times, which almost nau-

seated me. I asked my companion if this were the place where we were to eat. He informed me that it was the best place in town where a colored man could get a meal. I then wanted to know why somebody didn't open a place where respectable colored people who had money could be accommodated. He answered, "It wouldn't pay; all the respectable colored people eat at home, and the few who travel generally have friends in the towns to which they go, who entertain them." He added, "Of course, you could go in any place in the city; they wouldn't know you from white."

I sat down with the porter at one of the tables, but was not hungry enough to eat with any relish what was put before me. The food was not badly cooked; but the iron knives and forks needed to be scrubbed, the plates and dishes and glasses needed to be washed and well dried. I minced over what I took on my plate while my companion ate. When we finished we paid the waiter twenty cents each and went out. We walked around until the lights of the city were lit. Then the porter said that he must get to bed and have some rest, as he had not had six hours' sleep since he left Jersey City. I went back to our lodging-house with him.

When I awoke the next morning there were, besides my new found friend, two other men in the room, asleep in the double bed. I got up and dressed myself very quietly, so as not to awake anyone. I then drew from under the pillow my precious roll of greenbacks, took out a ten dollar bill, and very softly unlocking my trunk, put the remainder, about three hundred dollars, in the inside pocket of a coat near the bottom; glad of the opportunity to put it unobserved in a place of safety. When I had carefully locked my trunk, I tiptoed toward the door with the intention of going out to look for a decent restaurant where I might get something fit to eat. As I was easing the door open, my porter friend said with a yawn, "Hello! You're going out?" I answered him, "Yes." "Oh!" he yawned again, "I guess I've had enough sleep; wait a minute, I'll go with you." For the instant his friendship bored me and embarrassed me. I had visions of another meal in the greasy restaurant of the day before. He must have divined my thoughts; for he went on to say, "I know a woman across town who takes a few boarders; I think we can go over there and get a good breakfast." With a feeling of mingled fears and doubts regarding what the break-fast might be, I waited until he had dressed himself.

When I saw the neat appearance of the cottage we entered my fears vanished, and when I saw the woman who kept it my doubts followed the same course. Scrupulously clean, in a spotless white apron and colored head handkerchief, her round face beaming with motherly kindness, she was picturesquely beautiful. She impressed me as one broad expanse of happiness and good nature. In a few minutes she was addressing me as "chile" and "honey." She made me feel as though I should like to lay my head on her capacious bosom and go to sleep.

And the breakfast, simple as it was, I could not have had at any restaurant in Atlanta at any price. There was fried chicken, as it is fried only in the South, hominy boiled to the consis-tency where it could be eaten with a fork, and biscuits so light and fluffy that a fellow with any appetite at all would have no difficulty in disposing of eight or ten. When I had finished I felt that I had experienced the realization of, at least, one of my dreams of Southern life.

During the meal we found out from our hostess, who had two boys in school, that Atlanta University opened on that very day. I had somehow mixed my dates. My friend the porter suggested that I go out to the University at once and offered to walk over and show me the way. We had to walk because, al-though the University was not more than twenty minutes dis-tance from the center of the city, there were no street-cars run-ning in that direction. My first sight of the school grounds made me feel that I was not far from home; here the red hills had been terraced and covered with green grass; clean gravel walks, well shaded, lead up to the buildings; indeed, it was a bit of New England transplanted. At the gate my companion said he would bid me good-by, because it was likely that he would not see me again before his car went out. He told me that he would make two more trips to Atlanta, and that he would come out and see me; that after his second trip he would leave the Pullman service for the winter and return to school in Nashville. We shook hands, I thanked him for all his kindness, and we said good-by.

I walked up to a group of students and made some inquiries. They directed me to the president's office in the main building.

The president gave me a cordial welcome; it was more than cordial; he talked to me, not as an official head of a college, but as though he were adopting me into what was his large family, to personally look after my general welfare as well as my education. He seemed especially pleased with the fact that I had come to them all the way from the North. He told me that I could have come to the school as soon as I had reached the city, and that I had better move my trunk out at once. I gladly promised him that I would do so. He then called a boy and directed him to take me to the matron, and to show me around afterwards. I found the matron even more motherly than the president was fatherly. She had me to register, which was in effect to sign a pledge to abstain from the use of intoxicating beverages, tobacco, and profane language, while I was a student in the school. This act caused me no sacrifice; as, up to that time, I was free from either habit. The boy who was with me then showed me about the grounds. I was especially interested in the industrial building.

The sounding of a bell, he told me, was the signal for the students to gather in the general assembly hall, and he asked me if I would go. Of course I would. There were between three and four hundred students and perhaps all of the teachers gathered in the room. I noticed that several of the latter were colored. The president gave a talk addressed principally to new comers; but I scarcely heard what he said, I was so much occupied in looking at those around me. They were of all types and colors, the more intelligent types predominating. The colors ranged from jet black to pure white, with light hair and eyes. Among the girls especially there were many so fair that it was difficult to believe that they had Negro blood in them. And, too, I could not help but notice that many of the girls, particularly those of the delicate brown shades, with black eyes and wavy dark hair, were decidedly pretty. Among the boys, many of the blackest were fine specimens of young manhood, tall, straight, and muscular, with magnificent heads; these were the kind of boys who developed into the patriarchal "uncles" of the old slave régime.

When I left the University it was with the determination to get my trunk, and move out to the school before night. I walked back across the city with a light step and a light heart. I felt perfectly satisfied with life for the first time since my mother's death. In passing the railroad station I hired a wagon and rode with the driver as far as my stopping place. I settled with my landlord and went upstairs to put away several articles I had left out. As soon as I opened my trunk a dart of suspicion shot through my heart; the arrangement of things did not look familiar. I began to dig down excitedly to the bottom till I reached the coat in which I had concealed my treasure. My money was gone! Every single bill of it. I knew it was useless to do so, but I searched through every other coat, every pair of trousers, every vest, and even each pair of socks. When I had finished my fruitless search I sat down dazed and heartsick. I called the landlord up, and informed him of my loss; he comforted me by saying that I ought to have better sense than to keep money in a trunk, and that he was not responsible for his lodgers' personal effects. His cooling words brought me enough to my senses to cause me to look and see if anything else was missing. Several small articles were gone, among them a black and gray necktie of odd design upon which my heart was set; almost as much as the loss of my money, I felt the loss of my tie.

After thinking for awhile as best I could, I wisely decided to go at once back to the University and lay my troubles before the president. I rushed breathlessly back to the school. As I neared the grounds the thought came across me, would not my story sound fishy? Would it not place me in the position of an impostor or beggar? What right had I to worry these busy people with the results of my carelessness? If the money could not be recovered, and I doubted that it could, what good would it do to tell them about it. The shame and embarrassment which the whole situation gave me caused me to stop at the gate. I paused, undecided, for a moment; then turned and slowly retraced my steps, and so changed the whole course of my life.

If the reader has never been in a strange city without money or friends, it is useless to try to describe what my feelings were; he could not understand. If he has been, it is equally useless, for he understands more than words could convey. When I reached my lodgings I found in the room one of the porters who had slept there the night before. When he heard what misfortune had befallen me he offered many words of sympathy and advice. He asked me how much money I had left. I told him that I had ten or twelve dollars in my pocket. He said, "That won't last you very long here, and you will hardly be able to find anything to do in Atlanta. I'll tell you what you do, go down to Jacksonville and you won't have any trouble to get a job in one of the big hotels there, or in St. Augustine." I thanked him, but intimated my doubts of being able to get to Jacksonville on the money I had. He reassured me by saying, "Oh, that's all right. You express your trunk on through, and I'll take you down in my closet." I thanked him again, not knowing then, what it was to travel in a Pullman porter's closet. He put me under a deeper debt of gratitude by lending me fifteen dollars, which he said I could pay back after I had secured work. His generosity brought tears to my eyes, and I concluded that, after all, there were some kind hearts in the world.

I now forgot my troubles in the hurry and excitement of getting my trunk off in time to catch the train, which went out at seven o'clock. I even forgot that I hadn't eaten anything since morning. We got a wagon—the porter went with me— and took my trunk to the express office. My new friend then told me to come to the station at about a quarter of seven, and walk straight to the car where I should see him standing, and not to lose my nerve. I found my role not so difficult to play as I thought it would be, because the train did not leave from the central station, but from a smaller one, where there were no gates and guards to pass. I followed directions, and the porter took me on his car, and locked me in his closet. In a few minutes the train pulled out for Jacksonville.

I may live to be a hundred years old, but I shall never forget the agonies I suffered that night. I spent twelve hours doubled up in the porter's basket for soiled linen, not being able to straighten up on account of the shelves for clean linen just over my head. The air was hot and suffocating and the smell of damp towels and used linen was sickening. At each lurch of the car over the none too smooth track, I was bumped and bruised against the narrow walls of my narrow compartment. I became acutely conscious of the fact that I had not eaten for hours. Then nausea took possession of me, and at one time I had grave doubts about reaching my destination alive. If I had the trip to make again, I should prefer to walk.

Chapter V

THE NEXT morning I got out of the car at Jacksonville with a stiff and aching body. I determined to ask no more porters, not even my benefactor, about stopping places; so I found myself on the street not knowing where to go. I walked along listlessly until I met a colored man who had the appearance of a preacher. I asked him if he could direct me to a respectable boarding-house for colored people. He said that if I walked along with him in the direction he was going he would show me such a place. I turned and walked at his side. He proved to be a minister, and asked me a great many direct questions about myself. I answered as many as I saw fit to answer; the others I evaded or ignored. At length we stopped in front of a frame house, and my guide informed me that it was the place. A woman was standing in the doorway, and he called to her saying that he had brought her a new boarder. I thanked him for his trouble, and after he had urged upon me to attend his church while I was in the city, he went on his way.

I went in and found the house neat and not uncomfortable. The parlor was furnished with cane-bottomed chairs, each of which was adorned with a white crocheted tidy. The mantel over the fireplace had a white crocheted cover; a marble-topped center table held a lamp, a photograph album and several trinkets, each of which was set upon a white crocheted mat. There was a cottage organ in a corner of the room, and I noted that the lamp-racks upon it were covered with white crocheted mats. There was a matting on the floor, but a white crocheted carpet would not have been out of keeping. I made arrangements with the landlady for my board and lodging; the amount was, I think, three dollars and a half a week. She was a rather fine looking, stout, brown-skinned woman of about forty years of age. Her husband was a light colored Cuban, a man about half one of her size, and one whose age could not be guessed from his appearance. He was small in size, but a handsome black mustache and typical Spanish eyes redeemed him from insignificance.

I was in time for breakfast, and at the table I had the opportunity to see my fellow-boarders. There were eight or ten of them. Two, as I afterwards learned, were colored Americans. All of them were cigar makers and worked in one of the large factories—cigar making is one trade in which the color-line is not drawn. The conversation was carried on entirely in Spanish, and my ignorance of the language subjected me more to alarm than embarrassment. I had never heard such uproarious conversation; everybody talked at once, loud exclamations, rolling "*carambas*," menacing gesticulations with knives, forks, and spoons. I looked every moment for the clash of blows. One man was emphasizing his remarks by flourishing a cup in his hand, seemingly forgetful of the fact that it was nearly full of hot coffee. He ended by emptying it over what was, relatively, the only quiet man at the table excepting myself, bringing from him a volley of language which made the others appear dumb by comparison. I soon learned that in all of this clatter of voices and table utensils they were discussing purely ordinary affairs and arguing about mere trifles, and that not the least ill-feeling was aroused. It was not long before I enjoyed the spirited chatter and badinage at the table as much as I did my meals,—and the meals were not bad.

I spent the afternoon in looking around the town. The streets were sandy, but were well shaded by fine oak trees, and far preferable to the clay roads of Atlanta. One or two public squares with green grass and trees gave the city a touch of freshness. That night after supper I spoke to my landlady and her husband about my intentions. They told me that the big winter hotels would not open within two months. It can easily be imagined what effect this news had on me. I spoke to them frankly about my financial condition and related the main fact of my misfortune in Atlanta. I modestly mentioned my ability to teach music and asked if there was any likelihood of my being able to get some scholars. My landlady suggested that I speak to the preacher who had shown me her house; she felt sure that through his influence I should be able to get up a class in piano. She added, however, that the colored people were poor, and that the general price for music lessons was only twenty-five cents. I noticed that the thought of my teaching white pupils did not even remotely enter her mind. None of this information made my prospects look much brighter.

The husband, who up to this time had allowed the woman to do most of the talking, gave me the first bit of tangible hope; he said that he could get me a job as a "stripper" in the factory where he worked, and that if I succeeded in getting music pupils I could teach a couple of them every night, and so make a living until something better turned up. He went on to say that it would not be a bad thing for me to stay at the factory and learn my trade as a cigar maker, and impressed on me that, for a young man knocking about the country, a trade was a handy thing to have. I determined to accept his offer and thanked him heartily. In fact, I became enthusiastic, not only because I saw a way out of my financial troubles, but also because I was eager and curious over the new experience I was about to enter. I wanted to know all about the cigar making business. This narrowed the conversation down to the husband and myself, so the wife went in and left us talking.

He was what is called a *regaliá* workman, and earned from thirty-five to forty dollars a week. He generally worked a sixty dollar job; that is, he made cigars for which he was paid at a rate of sixty dollars per thousand. It was impossible for him to make a thousand in a week because he had to work very carefully and slowly. Each cigar was made entirely by hand. Each piece of filler and each wrapper had to be selected with care. He was able to make a bundle of one hundred cigars in a day, not one of which could be told from the others by any difference in size or shape, or even by any appreciable difference in weight. This was the acme of artistic skill in cigar making. Workmen of this class were rare, never more than three or four of them in one factory, and it was never necessary for them to remain out of work. There were men who made two, three, and four hundred cigars of the cheaper grades in a day; they had to be very fast in order to make decent week's wages. Cigar making was a rather independent trade; the men went to work when they pleased and knocked off when they felt like doing so. As a class the workmen were careless and improvident; some very rapid makers would not work more than three or four days out of the week, and there were others who never showed up at the factory on Mondays. "Strippers" were the boys who pulled the long stems from the tobacco leaves. After they had served at that work for a certain time they were given tables as apprentices.

All of this was interesting to me; and we drifted along in conversation until my companion struck the subject nearest his heart, the independence of Cuba. He was in exile from the island, and a prominent member of the Jacksonville *Junta*. Every week sums of money were collected from *juntas* all over the country. This money went to buy arms and ammunition for the insurgents. As the man sat there nervously smoking his long, "green" cigar, and telling me of the Gomezes, both the white one and the black one, of Maceo and Bandera, he grew positively eloquent. He also showed that he was a man of considerable education and reading. He spoke English excellently, and frequently surprised me by using words one would hardly expect from a foreigner. The first one of this class of words he employed almost shocked me, and I never forgot it, 'twas "ramify." We sat on the piazza until ten o'clock. When we arose to go in to bed it was with the understanding that I should start in the factory on the next day.

I began work the next morning seated at a barrel with another boy, who showed me how to strip the stems from the leaves, to smooth out each half leaf, and to put the "rights" together in one pile, and the "lefts" together in another pile on the edge of the barrel. My fingers, strong and sensitive from their long training, were well adapted to this kind of work; and within two weeks I was accounted the fastest "stripper" in the factory. At first the heavy odor of the tobacco almost sickened me; but when I became accustomed to it I liked the smell. I was now earning four dollars a week, and was soon able to pick up a couple more by teaching a few scholars at night, whom I secured through the good offices of the preacher I had met on my first morning in Jacksonville.

At the end of about three months, through my skill as a "stripper" and the influence of my landlord, I was advanced to a table, and began to learn my trade; in fact, more than my trade; for I learned not only to make cigars, but also to smoke, to swear, and to speak Spanish. I discovered that I had a talent for languages as well as for music. The rapidity and ease with which I acquired Spanish astonished my associates. In a short time I was able not only to understand most of what was said at the table during meals, but to join in the conversation. I bought a method for learning the Spanish language, and with the aid of my landlord as a teacher, by constant practice with my fellow workmen, and by regularly reading the Cuban newspapers, and finally some books of standard Spanish literature which were at the house, I was able in less than a year to speak like a native. In fact, it was my pride that I spoke better Spanish than many of the Cuban workmen at the factory.

After I had been in the factory a little over a year, I was repaid for all the effort I had put forth to learn Spanish by being selected as "reader." The "reader" is quite an institution in all cigar factories which employ Spanish-speaking workmen. He sits in the center of the large room in which the cigar makers work and reads to them for a certain number of hours each day all the important news from the papers and whatever else he may consider would be interesting. He often selects an exciting novel, and reads it in daily installments. He must, of course, have a good voice, but he must also have a reputation among the men for intelligence, for being well posted and having in his head a stock of varied information. He is generally the final authority on all arguments which arise; and, in a cigar factory, these arguments are many and frequent, ranging from discussions on the respective and relative merits of rival baseball clubs to the duration of the sun's light and energy— cigar-making is a trade in which talk does not interfere with work. My position as "reader" not only released me from the rather monotonous work of rolling cigars, and gave me something more in accord with my tastes, but also added considerably to my income. I was now earning about twenty-five dollars a week, and was able to give up my peripatetic method of giving music lessons. I hired a piano and taught only those who could arrange to take their lessons where I lived. I finally gave up teaching entirely; as what I made scarcely paid for my time and trouble. I kept the piano, however, in order to keep up on my own studies, and occasionally I played at some church concert or other charitable entertainment.

Through my music teaching and my not absolutely irregular attendance at church I became acquainted with the best class of colored people in Jacksonville. This was really my entrance into the race. It was my initiation into what I have termed the freemasonry of the race. I had formulated a theory of what it was to be colored, now I was getting the practice. The novelty of my position caused me to observe and consider things which, I think, entirely escaped the young men I associated with; or, at least, were so commonplace to them as not to attract their attention. And of many of the impressions which came to me then I have realized the full import only within the past few years, since I have had a broader knowledge of men and history, and a fuller comprehension of the tremendous struggle which is going on between the races in the South.

It is a struggle; for though the black man fights passively he nevertheless fights; and his passive resistance is more effective at present than active resistance could possibly be. He bears the fury of the storm as does the willow tree.

It is a struggle; for though the white man of the South may be too proud to admit it, he is, nevertheless, using in the contest his best energies; he is devoting to it the greater part of his thought and much of his endeavor. The South to-day stands panting and almost breathless from its exertions.

And how the scene of the struggle has shifted! The battle was first waged over the right of the Negro to be classed as a human being with a soul; later, as to whether he had sufficient intellect to master even the rudiments of learning; and to-day it is being fought out over his social recognition.

I said somewhere in the early part of this narrative that because the colored man looked at everything through the prism of his relationship to society as a *colored* man, and because most of his mental efforts ran through the narrow channel bounded by his rights and his wrongs, it was to be wondered at that he has progressed so broadly as he has. The same thing may be said of the white man of the South; most of his mental efforts run through one narrow channel; his life as a man and a citizen, many of his financial activities and all of his political activities are impassably limited by the ever present "Negro question." I am sure it would be safe to wager that no group of Southern white men could get together and talk for sixty minutes without bringing up the "race question." If a Northern white man happened to be in the group the time could be safely cut to thirty minutes. In this respect I consider the conditions of the whites more to be deplored than that of the blacks. Here, a truly great people, a people that produced a majority of the great historic Americans from Washington to Lincoln now forced to use up its energies in a conflict as lamentable as it is violent.

I shall give the observations I made in Jacksonville as seen through the light of after years; and they apply generally to every Southern community. The colored people may be said to be roughly divided into three classes, not so much in respect to themselves as in respect to their relations with the whites. There are those constituting what might be called the desperate class,—the men who work in the lumber and turpentine camps, the ex-convicts, the bar-room loafers are all in this class. These men conform to the requirements of civilization much as a trained lion with low muttered growls goes through his stunts under the crack of the trainer's whip. They cherish a sullen hatred for all white men, and they value life as cheap. I have heard more than one of them say, "I'll go to hell for the first white man that bothers me." Many who have expressed that sentiment have kept their word; and it is that fact that gives such prominence to this class; for in numbers it is only a small proportion of the colored people, but it often dominates public opinion concerning the whole race. Happily, this class represents the black people of the South far below their normal physical and moral condition, but in its increase lies the possibility of grave dangers. I am sure there is no more urgent work before the white South, not only for its present happiness, but its future safety, than the decreasing of this class of blacks. And it is not at all a hopeless class; for these men are but the creatures of conditions, as much so as the slum and criminal elements of all the great cities of the world are creatures of conditions. Decreasing their number by shooting and burning them off will not be successful; for these men are truly desperate, and thoughts of death, however terrible, have little effect in deterring them from acts the result of hatred or degeneracy. This class of blacks hate everything covered by a white skin, and in return they are loathed by the whites. The whites regard them just about as a man would a vicious mule, a thing to be worked, driven, and beaten, and killed for kicking.

The second class, as regards the relation between blacks and whites, comprises the servants, the washer-women, the waiters, the cooks, the coachmen, and all who are connected with the whites by domestic service. These may be generally characterized as simple, kindhearted, and faithful; not over fine in their moral deductions, but intensely religious, and relatively,—such matters can be judged only relatively,—about as honest and wholesome in their lives as any other grade of society. Any white person is "good" who treats them kindly, and they love them for that kindness. In return, the white people with whom they have to do regard them with indulgent affection. They come into close daily contact with the whites, and may be called the connecting link between whites and blacks; in fact, it is through them that the whites know the rest of their colored neighbors. Between this class of the blacks and the whites there is little or no friction.

The third class is composed of the independent workmen and tradesmen, and of the well-to-do and educated colored people; and, strange to say, for a directly opposite reason they are as far removed from the whites as the members of the first class I mentioned. These people live in a little world of their own; in fact, I concluded that if a colored man wanted to separate himself from his white neighbors he had but to acquire some money, education and culture, and to live in accordance. For example, the proudest and fairest lady in the South could with propriety—and it is what she would most likely do—go to the cabin of Aunt Mary, her cook, if Aunt Mary was sick, and minister to her comfort with her own hands; but if Mary's daughter, Eliza, a girl who used to run around the lady's kitchen, but who has received an education and married a prosperous young colored man, were at death's door, my lady would no more think of crossing the threshold of Eliza's cottage than she would of going into a bar-room for a drink.

I was walking down the street one day with a young man who was born in Jacksonville, but had been away to prepare himself for a professional life. We passed a young white man, and my companion said to me, "You see that young man? We grew up together, we have played, hunted, and fished together, we have even eaten and slept together, and now since I have come back home he barely speaks to me." The fact that the whites of the South despise and ill-treat the desperate class of blacks is not only explainable according to the ancient laws of human nature, but it is not nearly so serious or important as the fact that as the progressive colored people advance they constantly widen the gulf between themselves and their white neighbors. I think that the white people somehow feel that colored people who have education and money, who wear good clothes and live in comfortable houses, are "putting on airs," that they do these things for the sole purpose of "spiting the white folks," or are, at best, going through a sort of monkey-like imitation. Of course, such feelings can only cause irritation or breed disgust. It seems that the whites have not yet been able to realize and understand that these people in striving to better their physical and social surroundings in accordance with their financial and intellectual progress are simply obeying an impulse which is common to human nature the world over. I am in grave doubt as to whether the greater part of the friction in the South is caused by the whites having a natural antipathy to Negroes as a race, or an acquired antipathy to Negroes in certain relations to themselves. However that may be, there is to my mind no more pathetic side of this many sided question than the isolated position into which are forced the very colored people who most need and who could best appreciate sympathetic coöperation; and their position grows tragic when the effort is made to couple them, whether or no, with the Negroes of the first class I mentioned.

This latter class of colored people are well-disposed towards the whites, and always willing to meet them more than half way. They, however, feel keenly any injustice or gross discrimination, and generally show their resentment. The effort is sometimes made to convey the impression that the better class of colored people fight against riding in "jim crow" cars because they want to ride with white people or object to being with humbler members of their own race. The truth is they object to the humiliation of being forced to ride in a *particular* car, aside from the fact that that car is distinctly inferior, and that they are required to pay full first-class fare. To say that the whites are forced to ride in the superior car is less than a joke. And, too, odd as it may sound, refined colored people get no more pleasure out of riding with offensive Negroes than anybody else would get.

I can realize more fully than I could years ago that the position of the advanced element of the colored race is often very trying. They are the ones among the blacks who carry the entire weight of the race question; it worries the others very little, and I believe the only thing which at times sustains them is that they know that they are in the right. On the other hand, this class of colored people get a good deal of pleasure out of life; their existence is far from being one long groan about their condition. Out of the chaos of ignorance and poverty they have evolved a social life of which they need not be ashamed. In cities where the professional and well-to-do class is large, they have formed society,—society as discriminating as the actual conditions will allow it to be; I should say, perhaps, society possessing discriminating tendencies which become rules as fast as actual conditions allow. This statement will, I know, sound preposterous, even ridiculous, to some persons; but as this class of colored people is the least known of the race it is not surprising. These social circles are connected throughout the country, and a person in good standing in one city is readily accepted in another. One who is on the outside will often find it a difficult matter to get in. I know of one case personally in which money to the extent of thirty or forty thousand dollars and a fine house, not backed up by a good reputation, after several years of repeated effort, failed to gain entry for the possessor. These people have their dances and dinners and card parties, their musicals and their literary societies. The women attend social affairs dressed in good taste, and the men in evening dress-suits which they own; and the reader will make a mistake to confound these entertainments with the "Bellman's Ball" and "Whitewashers' Picnics" and "Lime Kiln Clubs" with which the humorous press of the country illustrates "Cullud Sassiety."

Jacksonville, when I was there, was a small town, and the number of educated and well-to-do colored people was small; so this society phase of life did not equal what I have since seen in Boston, Washington, Richmond, and Nashville; and it is upon what I have more recently seen in these cities that I have made the observations just above. However, there were many comfortable and pleasant homes in Jacksonville to which I was often invited. I belonged to the literary society—at which we generally discussed the race question—and attended all of the church festivals and other charitable entertainments. In this way I passed three years which were not at all the least enjoyable of my life. In fact, my joy took such an exuberant turn that I fell in love with a young school teacher and began to have dreams of matrimonial bliss; but another turn in the course of my life brought these dreams to an end.

I do not wish to mislead my readers into thinking that I led a life in Jacksonville which would make copy as the hero of a Sunday School library book. I was a hail fellow well met with all of the workmen at the factory, most of whom knew little and cared less about social distinctions. From their example I learned to be careless about money; and for that reason I constantly postponed and finally abandoned returning to Atlanta University. It seemed impossible for me to save as much as two hundred dollars. Several of the men at the factory were my intimate friends, and I frequently joined them in their pleasures. During the summer months we went almost every Monday on an excursion to a seaside resort called Pablo Beach. These excursions were always crowded. There was a dancing pavilion, a great deal of drinking and generally a fight or two to add to the excitement. I also contracted the cigar-maker's habit of riding around in a hack on Sunday afternoons. I sometimes went with my cigar-maker friends to public balls that were given at a large hall on one of the main streets. I learned to take a drink occasionally and paid for quite a number that my friends took; but strong liquors never appealed to my appetite. I drank them only when the company I was in required it, and suffered for it afterwards. On the whole, though I was a bit wild, I can't remember that I ever did anything disgraceful, or, as the usual standard for young men goes, anything to forfeit my claim to respectability.

At one of the first public balls I attended I saw the Pullman car porter who had so kindly assisted me in getting to Jacksonville. I went immediately to one of my factory friends and borrowed fifteen dollars with which to repay the loan my benefactor had made me. After I had given him the money, and was thanking him, I noticed that he wore what was, at least, an exact duplicate of my lamented black and gray tie. It was somewhat worn, but distinct enough for me to trace the same odd design which had first attracted my eye. This was enough to arouse my strongest suspicions, but whether it was sufficient for the law to take cognizance of I did not consider. My astonishment and the ironical humor of the situation drove everything else out of my mind.

These balls were attended by a great variety of people. They were generally given by the waiters of some one of the big hotels, and were often patronized by a number of hotel guests who came to "see the sights." The crowd was always noisy, but good-natured; there was much quadrille dancing, and a strong-lunged man called figures in a voice which did not confine itself to the limits of the hall. It is not worth the while for me to describe in detail how these people acted; they conducted themselves in about the same manner as I have seen other people at similar balls conduct themselves. When one has seen something of the world and human nature he must conclude, after all, that between people in like stations of life there is very little difference the world over.

However, it was at one of these balls that I first saw the cake-walk. There was a contest for a gold watch, to be awarded to the hotel head-waiter receiving the greatest number of votes. There was some dancing while the votes were being counted. Then the floor was cleared for the cake-walk. A half-dozen guests from some of the hotels took seats on the stage to act as judges, and twelve or fourteen couples began to walk for a "sure enough" highly decorated cake, which was in plain evidence. The spectators crowded about the space reserved for the contestants and watched them with interest and excitement. The couples did not walk around in a circle, but in a square, with the men on the inside. The fine points to be considered were the bearing of the men, the precision with which they turned the corners, the grace of the women, and the ease with which they swung around the pivots. The men walked with stately and soldierly step, and the women with considerable grace. The judges arrived at their decision by a process of elimination. The music and the walk continued for some minutes; then both were stopped while the judges conferred, when the walk began again several couples were left out. In this way the contest was finally narrowed down to three or four couples. Then the excitement became intense; there was much partisan cheering as one couple or another would execute a turn in extra elegant style. When the cake was finally awarded the spectators were about evenly divided between those who cheered the winners and those who muttered about the unfairness of the judges. This was the cake-walk in its original form, and it is what the colored performers on the theatrical stage developed into the prancing movements now known all over the world, and which some Parisian critics pronounced the acme of poetic motion.

There are a great many colored people who are ashamed of the cake-walk, but I think they ought to be proud of it. It is my opinion that the colored people of this country have done four things which refute the oft advanced theory that they are an absolutely inferior race, which demonstrate that they have originality and artistic conception; and, what is more, the power of creating that which can influence and appeal universally. The first two of these are the Uncle Remus stories, collected by Joel Chandler Harris, and the Jubilee songs, to which the Fisk singers made the public and the skilled musicians of both America and Europe listen. The other two are ragtime music and the cake-walk. No one who has traveled can question the world-conquering influence of ragtime; and I do not think it would be an exaggeration to say that in Europe the United States is popularly known better by ragtime than by anything else it has produced in a generation. In Paris they call it American music. The newspapers have already told how the practice of intricate cake walk steps has taken up the time of European royalty and nobility. These are lower forms of art, but they give evidence of a power that will some day be applied to the higher forms. In this measure, at least, and aside from the number of prominent individuals the colored people of the United States have produced, the race has been a world influence; and all of the Indians between Alaska and Patagonia haven't done as much.

Just when I was beginning to look upon Jacksonville as my permanent home and was beginning to plan about marrying the young school teacher, raising a family, and working in a cigar factory the rest of my life, for some reason, which I do not now remember, the factory at which I worked was indefinitely shut down. Some of the men got work in other factories in town, some decided to go to Key West and Tampa, others made up their minds to go to New York for work. All at once a desire like a fever seized me to see the North again, and I cast my lot with those bound for New York.

Chapter VI

WE STEAMED up into New York harbor late one afternoon in spring. The last efforts of the sun were being put forth in turning the waters of the bay to glistening gold; the green islands on either side, in spite of their warlike mountings, looked calm and peaceful; the buildings of the town shone out in a reflected light which gave the city an air of enchantment; and, truly, it is an enchanted spot. New York City is the most fatally fascinating thing in America. She sits like a great witch at the gate of the country, showing her alluring white face, and hiding her crooked hands and feet under the folds of her wide garments,—constantly enticing thousands from far within, and tempting those who come from across the seas to go no farther. And all these become the victims of her caprice. Some she at once crushes beneath her cruel feet; others she condemns to a fate like that of galley slaves; a few she favors and fondles, riding them high on the bubbles of fortune; then with a sudden breath she blows the bubbles out and laughs mockingly as she watches them fall.

Twice I had passed through it, but this was really my first visit to New York; and as I walked about that evening I began to feel the dread power of the city; the crowds, the lights, the excitement, the gayety, and all its subtler stimulating influences began to take effect upon me. My blood ran quicker, and I felt that I was just beginning to live. To some natures this stimulant of life in a great city becomes a thing as binding and necessary as opium is to one addicted to the habit. It becomes their breath of life; they cannot exist outside of it; rather than be deprived of it they are content to suffer hunger, want, pain and misery; they would not exchange even a ragged and wretched condition among the great crowd for any degree of comfort away from it.

As soon as we landed, four of us went directly to a lodging-house in 27th Street, just west of Sixth Avenue. The house was run by a short, stout mulatto man, who was exceedingly talkative and inquisitive. In fifteen minutes he not only knew the history of the past life of each one of us, but had a clearer idea of what we intended to do in the future than we ourselves. He sought this information so much with an air of being very particular as to whom he admitted into his house that we tremblingly answered every question that he asked. When we had become located we went out and got supper; then walked around until about ten o'clock. At that hour we met a couple of young fellows who lived in New York and were known to one of the members of our party. It was suggested we go to a certain place which was known by the proprietor's name. We turned into one of the cross streets and mounted the stoop of a house in about the middle of a block between Sixth and Seventh Avenues. One of the young men whom we had met rang a bell, and a man on the inside cracked the door a couple of inches; then opened it and let us in. We found ourselves in the hallway of what had once been a residence. The front parlor had been converted into a bar, and a half dozen or so well dressed men were in the room. We went in, and after a general introduction had several rounds of beer. In the back parlor a crowd was sitting and standing around the walls of the room watching an exciting and noisy game of pool. I walked back and joined this crowd to watch the game, and principally to get away from the drinking party. The game was really interesting, the players being quite expert, and the excitement was heightened by the bets which were being made on the result. At times the antics and remarks of both players and spectators were amusing. When, at a critical point, a player missed a shot he was deluged by those financially interested in his making it with a flood of epithets synonymous to "chump"; while from the others he would be jeered by such remarks as "Nigger, dat cue ain't no hoe-handle." I noticed that among this class of colored men the word "nigger" was freely used in about the same sense as the word "fellow," and sometimes as a term of almost endearment; but I soon learned that its use was positively and absolutely prohibited to white men.

I stood watching this pool game until I was called by my friends, who were still in the bar-room, to go upstairs. On the second floor there were two large rooms. From the hall I looked into the one on the front. There was a large, round table in the center, at which five or six men were seated playing poker. The air and conduct here were greatly in contrast to what I had just seen in the pool-room; these men were evidently aristocrats of the place; they were well, perhaps a bit flashily, dressed and spoke in low modulated voices, frequently using the word "gentlemen"; in fact, they seemed to be practicing a sort of Chesterfieldian politeness towards each other. I was watching these men with a great deal of interest and some degree of admiration, when I was again called by the members of our party, and I followed them on to the back room. There was a door-keeper at this room, and we were admitted only after inspection. When we got inside, I saw a crowd of men of all ages and kinds grouped about an old billiard table, regarding some of whom, in supposing them to be white, I made no mistake. At first I did not know what these men were doing; they were using terms that were strange to me. I could hear only a confusion of voices exclaiming, "Shoot the two!" "Shoot the four!" "Fate me!" "Fate me!" "I've got you fated!" "Twenty-five cents he don't turn!" This was the ancient and terribly fascinating game of dice, popularly known as "craps." I, myself, had played pool in Jacksonville; it is a favorite game among cigar-makers, and I had seen others play cards; but here was something new. I edged my way in to the table and stood between one of my new-found New York friends and a tall, slender, black fellow, who was making side bets while the dice were at the other end of the table. My companion explained to me the principles of the game; and they are so simple that they hardly need to be explained twice. The dice came around the table until they reached the man on the other side of the tall, black fellow. He lost, and the latter said, "Gimme the bones." He threw a dollar on the table and said, "Shoot the dollar." His style of play was so strenuous that he had to be allowed plenty of room. He shook the dice high above his head, and each time he threw them on the table he emitted a grunt such as men give when they are putting forth physical exertion with a rhythmic regularity. He frequently whirled completely around on his heels, throwing the dice the entire length of the table, and talking to them as though they were trained animals. He appealed to them in short singsong phrases. "Come, dice," he would say. "Little Phoebe," "Little Joe," " 'Way down yonder in the cornfield." Whether these mystic incantations were efficacious or not I could not say, but, at any rate, his luck was great, and he had what gamblers term "nerve." "Shoot the dollar!" "Shoot the two!" "Shoot the four!" "Shoot the eight!" came from his lips as quickly as the dice turned to his advantage. My companion asked me if I had ever played. I told him no. He said that I ought to try my luck; that everybody won at first. The tall man at my side was waving his arms in the air exclaiming "Shoot the sixteen!" "Shoot the sixteen!" "Fate me!" Whether it was my companion's suggestion or some latent dare-devil strain in my blood which suddenly sprang into activity I do not know; but with a thrill of excitement which went through my whole body I threw a twenty dollar bill on the table and said in a trembling voice, "I fate you."

I could feel that I had gained the attention and respect of everybody in the room, every eye was fixed on me, and the widespread question, "Who is he?" went around. This was gratifying to a certain sense of vanity of which I have never been able to rid myself, and I felt that it was worth the money even if I lost. The tall man with a whirl on his heels and a double grunt threw the dice; four was the number which turned up. This is considered as a hard "point" to make. He redoubled his contortions and his grunts and his pleadings to the dice; but on his third or fourth throw the fateful seven turned up, and I had won. My companion and all my friends shouted to me to follow up my luck. The fever was on me. I seized the dice. My hands were so hot that the bits of bone felt like pieces of ice. I shouted as loudly as I could, "Shoot it all!" but the blood was tingling so about my ears that I could not hear my own voice. I was soon "fated." I threw the dice—seven—I had won. "Shoot it all!" I cried again. There was a pause; the stake was more than one man cared to or could cover. I was finally "fated" by several men taking "a part" of it. I then threw the dice again. Seven. I had won. "Shoot it all!" I shouted excitedly. After a short delay I was "fated." Again I rolled the dice. Eleven. Again I won. My friends now surrounded me and, much against my inclination, forced me to take down all of the money except five dollars. I tried my luck once more, and threw some small "point" which I failed to make, and the dice passed on to the next man.

In less than three minutes I had won more than two hundred dollars, a sum which afterwards cost me dearly. I was the hero of the moment, and was soon surrounded by a group of men who expressed admiration for my "nerve" and predicted for me a brilliant future as a gambler. Although at the time I had no thought of becoming a gambler I felt proud of my success. I felt a bit ashamed, too, that I had allowed my friends to persuade me to take down my money so soon. Another set of men also got around me, and begged me for twenty-five or fifty cents to put them back into the game. I gave each of them something. I saw that several of them had on linen dusters, and as I looked about I noticed that there were perhaps a dozen men in the room similarly clad. I asked the fellow who had been my prompter at the dice table why they dressed in such a manner. He told me that men who had lost all the money and jewelry they possessed, frequently, in an effort to recoup their losses, would gamble away all their outer clothing and even their shoes; and that the proprietor kept on hand a supply of linen dusters for all who were so unfortunate. My informant went on to say that sometimes a fellow would become almost completely dressed and then, by a turn of the dice, would be thrown back into a state of semi-nakedness. Some of them were virtually prisoners and unable to get into the streets for days at a time. They ate at the lunch counter, where their credit was good so long as they were fair gamblers and did not attempt to jump their debts, and they slept around in chairs. They importuned friends and winners to put them back in the game, and kept at it until fortune again smiled on them. I laughed heartily at this, not thinking the day was coming which would find me in the same ludicrous predicament.

On passing downstairs I was told that the third and top floor of the house was occupied by the proprietor. When we passed through the bar I treated everybody in the room,—and that was no small number, for eight or ten had followed us down. Then our party went out. It was now about half-past twelve, but my nerves were at such a tension that I could not endure the mere thought of going to bed. I asked if there was no other place to which we could go; our guides said yes, and suggested that we go to the "Club." We went to Sixth Avenue, walked two blocks, and turned to the west into another street. We stopped in front of a house with three stories and a basement. In the basement was a Chinese Chop-suey restaurant. There was a red lantern at the iron gate to the areaway, inside of which the Chinaman's name was printed. We went up the steps of the stoop, rang the bell, and were admitted without any delay. From the outside the house bore a rather gloomy aspect, the windows being absolutely dark, but within it was a veritable house of mirth. When we had passed through a small vestibule and reached the hallway we heard mingled sounds of music and laughter, the clink of glasses and the pop of bottles. We went into the main room and I was little prepared for what I saw. The brilliancy of the place, the display of diamond rings, scarf-pins, ear-rings and breast-pins, the big rolls of money that were brought into evidence when drinks were paid for, and the air of gayety that pervaded, all completely dazzled and dazed me. I felt positively giddy, and it was several minutes before I was able to make any clear and definite observations.

We at length secured places at a table in a corner of the room, and as soon as we could attract the attention of one of the busy waiters ordered a round of drinks. When I had somewhat collected my senses I realized that in a large back room into which the main room opened, there was a young fellow singing a song, accompanied on the piano by a short, thick-set, dark man. Between each verse he did some dance steps, which brought forth great applause and a shower of small coins at his feet. After the singer had responded to a rousing encore, the stout man at the piano began to run his fingers up and down the keyboard. This he did in a manner which indicated that he was master of a good deal of technic. Then he began to play; and such playing! I stopped talking to listen. It was music of a kind I had never heard before. It was music that demanded physical response, patting of the feet, drumming of the fingers, or nodding of the head in time with the beat. The barbaric harmonies, the audacious resolutions often consisting of an abrupt jump from one key to another, the intricate rhythms in which the accents fell in the most unexpected places, but in which the beat was never lost, produced a most curious effect. And, too, the player,—the dexterity of his left hand in making a rapid octave runs and jumps was little short of marvelous; and with his right hand, he frequently swept half the keyboard with clean cut chromatics which he fitted in so nicely as never to fail to arouse in his listeners a sort of pleasant surprise at the accomplishment of the feat.

This was ragtime music, then a novelty in New York, and just growing to be a rage which has not yet subsided. It was originated in the questionable resorts about Memphis and St. Louis by Negro piano players, who knew no more of the theory of music than they did of the theory of the universe, but were guided by natural musical instinct and talent. It made its way to Chicago, where it was popular some time before it reached New York. These players often improvised crude and, at times, vulgar words to fit the melodies. This was the beginning of the ragtime song. Several of these improvisations were taken down by white men, the words slightly altered, and published under the names of the arrangers. They sprang into immediate popularity and earned small fortunes, of which the Negro originators got only a few dollars. But I have learned that since that time a number of colored men, of not only musical talent, but training, are writing out their own melodies and words and reaping the reward of their work. I have learned also that they have a large number of white imitators and adulterators.

American musicians, instead of investigating ragtime, attempt to ignore it or dismiss it with a contemptuous word. But that has always been the course of scholasticism in every branch of art. Whatever new thing the *people* like is pooh-poohed; whatever is *popular* is spoken of as not worth the while. The fact is, nothing great or enduring, especially in music, has ever sprung full-fledged and unprecedented from the brain of any master; the best that he gives to the world he gathers from the hearts of the people, and runs it through the alembic of his genius. In spite of the bans which musicians and music teachers have placed upon it, the people still demand and enjoy ragtime. One thing cannot be denied; it is music which possesses at least one strong element of greatness; it appeals universally; not only the American, but the English, the French, and even the German people, find delight in. In fact, there is not a corner of the civilized world in which it is not known, and this proves its originality; for if it were an imitation, the people of Europe, anyhow, would not have found it a novelty. Anyone who doubts that there is a peculiar heel-tickling, smile-provoking, joy-awakening charm in ragtime needs only to hear a skillful performer play the genuine article to be convinced. I believe that it has its place as well as the music which draws from us sighs and tears.

I became so interested in both the music and the player that I left the table where I was sitting, and made my way through the hall into the back room, where I could see as well as hear. I talked to the piano player between the musical numbers, and found out that he was just a natural musician, never having taken a lesson in his life. Not only could he play almost anything he heard, but he could accompany singers in songs he had never heard. He had by ear alone, composed some pieces, several of which he played over for me; each of them was properly proportioned and balanced. I began to wonder what this man with such a lavish natural endowment would have done had he been trained. Perhaps he wouldn't have done anything at all; he might have become, at best, a mediocre imitator of the great masters in what they have already done to a finish, or one of the modern innovators who strive after originality by seeing how cleverly they can dodge about through the rules of harmony, and at the same time avoid melody. It is certain that he would not have been so delightful as he was in ragtime.

I sat by watching and listening to this man until I was dragged away by my friends. The place was now almost deserted; only a few stragglers hung on, and they were all the worse for drink. My friends were well up in this class. We passed into the street; the lamps were pale against the sky; day was just breaking. We went home and got into bed. I fell into a fitful sort of sleep with ragtime music ringing continually in my ears.

Chapter VII

I SHALL take advantage of this pause in my narrative to more closely describe the "Club" spoken of in the latter part of the preceding chapter,—to describe it, as I afterwards came to know it, as an habitue. I shall do this, not only because of the direct influence it had on my life, but also because it was at that time the most famous place of its kind in New York, and was well known to both white and colored people of certain classes.

I have already stated that in the basement of the house there was a Chinese restaurant. The Chinaman who kept it did an exceptionally good business; for chop-suey was a favorite dish among the frequenters of the place. It is a food that, somehow, has the power of absorbing alcoholic liquors that have been taken into the stomach. I have heard men claim that they could sober up on chop-suey. Perhaps that accounted, in some degree, for its popularity. On the main floor there were two large rooms, a parlor about thirty feet in length and a large square back room into which the parlor opened. The floor of the parlor was carpeted; small tables and chairs where arranged about the room; the windows were draped with lace curtains, and the walls were literally covered with photographs or lithographs of every colored man in America who had ever "done anything." There were pictures of Frederick Douglass and of Peter Jackson, of all the lesser lights of the prize-fighting ring, of all the famous jockeys and the stage celebrities, down to the newest song and dance team. The most of these photographs were autographed and, in a sense, made a really valuable collection. In the back room there was a piano; and tables were placed round the wall. The floor was bare and the center was left vacant for singers, dancers, and others who entertained the patrons. In a closet in this room which jutted out into the hall the proprietor kept his buffet. There was no open bar, because the place had no liquor license. In the back room the tables were sometimes pushed aside, and the floor given over to general dancing. The front room on the next floor was a sort of private party room; a back room on the same floor contained no furniture and was devoted to the use of new and ambitious performers. In this room song and dance teams practiced their steps, acrobatic teams practiced their tumbles, and many other kinds of "acts" rehearsed their "turns." The other rooms of the house were used as sleeping apartments.

No gambling was allowed, and the conduct of the place was surprisingly orderly. It was, in short, a center of colored bohemians and sports. Here the great prize fighters were wont to come, the famous jockeys, the noted minstrels, whose names and faces were familiar on every bill-board in the country; and these drew a multitude of those who love to dwell in the shadow of greatness. There were then no organizations giving performances of such order as are now given by several colored companies; that was because no manager could imagine that audiences would pay to see Negro performers in any other role than that of Mississippi River roustabouts; but there was lots of talent and ambition. I often heard the younger and brighter men discussing the time they would compel the public to recognize that they could do something more than grin and cut pigeon wings.

Sometimes one or two of the visiting stage professionals, after being sufficiently urged, would go into the back room and take the places of the regular amateur entertainers, but they were very sparing with these favors, and the patrons regarded them as special treats. There was one man, a minstrel, who, whenever he responded to a request to "do something," never essayed anything below a reading from Shakespeare. How well he read I do not know, but he greatly impressed me; and I can, at least, say that he had a voice which strangely stirred those who heard it. Here was a man who made people laugh at the size of his mouth, while he carried in his heart a burning ambition to be a tragedian; and so after all he did play a part in a tragedy.

These notables of the ring, the turf and the stage, drew to the place crowds of admirers, both white and colored. Whenever one of them came in there were awe-inspired whispers from those who knew him by sight, in which they enlightened those around them as to his identity, and hinted darkly at their great intimacy with the noted one. Those who were on terms of approach immediately showed their privilege over others less fortunate by gathering around their divinity. I was, at first, among those who dwelt in darkness. Most of these celebrities I had never heard of. This made me an object of pity among many of my new associates. I, however, soon learned to fake a knowledge for the benefit of those who were greener than I; and, finally, I became personally acquainted with the majority of the famous personages who came to the "Club."

A great deal of money was spent here; so many of the patrons were men who earned large sums. I remember one night a dapper little brown-skinned fellow was pointed out to me, and I was told that he was the most popular jockey of the day, and that he earned $12,000 a year. This latter statement I couldn't doubt, for with my own eyes I saw him spending at about that rate. For his friends and those who were introduced to him he bought nothing but wine;—in the sporting circle, "wine" means champagne—and paid for it at five dollars a quart. He sent a quart to every table in the place with his compliments; and on the table at which he and his party were seated there were more than a dozen bottles. It was the custom at the "Club" for the waiter not to remove the bottles when champagne was being drunk until the party had finished. There were reasons for this; it advertised the brand of wine, it advertised that the party was drinking wine, and advertised how much they had bought. This jockey had won a great race that day, and he was rewarding his admirers for the homage they paid him, all of which he accepted with a fine air of condescension.

Besides the people I have just been describing there was at the place almost every night one or two parties of white people, men and women, who were out sight-seeing, or slumming. They generally came in cabs; some of them would stay only for a few minutes, while others sometimes stayed until morning. There was also another set of white people who came frequently; it was made up of variety performers and others who delineated darky characters; they came to get their imitations first hand from the Negro entertainers they saw there.

There was still another set of white patrons, composed of women; these were not occasional visitors, but five or six of them were regular habitues. When I first saw them I was not sure that they were white. In the first place, among the many colored woman who came to the "Club" there were several just as fair; and, secondly, I always saw these woman in company with colored men. They were all good-looking and well dressed, and seemed to be women of some education. One of these in particular attracted my attention; she was an exceedingly beautiful woman of perhaps thirty-five; she had glistening copper-colored hair, very white skin and eyes very much like Du Maurier's conception of Trilby's "twin gray stars." When I came to know her I found that she was a woman of considerable culture; she traveled in Europe, spoke French, and played the piano well. She was always dressed elegantly, but in absolute good taste. She always came to the "Club" in a cab, and was soon joined by a well set up, very black young fellow. He was always faultlessly dressed; one of the most exclusive tailors in New York made his clothes, and he wore a number of diamonds in about as good taste as they could be worn by a man. I learned that she paid for his clothes and his diamonds. I learned, too, that he was not the only one of his kind. More that I learned would be better suited to a book on social phenomena than to a narrative of my life.

This woman was known at the "Club" as the rich widow. She went by a very aristocratic sounding name, which corresponded to her appearance. I shall never forget how hard it was for me to get over my feelings of surprise, perhaps more than surprise, at seeing her with her black companion; somehow I never exactly enjoyed the sight. I have devoted so much time to this pair, the "widow" and her companion, because it was through them that another decided turn was brought about in my life.

Chapter VIII

O N THE DAY following our night at the "Club" we slept until late in the afternoon; so late that beginning of search for work was entirely out of the question. This did not cause me much worry, for I had more than three hundred dollars, and New York had impressed me as a place where there was lots of money and not much difficulty in getting it. It is needless to inform my readers that I did not long hold this opinion. We got out of the house about dark, went round to a restaurant on Sixth Avenue and ate something, then walked around for a couple of hours. I finally suggested that we visit the same places we had been in the night before. Following my suggestion we started first to the gambling house. The man on the door let us in without question; I accredited this to my success of the night before. We went straight to the "crap" room, and I at once made my way to a table, where I was rather flattered by the murmur of recognition which went around. I played in up and down luck for three or four hours; then, worn with nervous excitement, quit, having lost about fifty dollars. But I was so strongly possessed with the thought that I would make up my losses the next time I played that I left the place with a light heart.

When we got into the street our party was divided against itself; two were for going home at once and getting to bed. They gave as a reason that we were to get up early and look for jobs. I think the real reason was that they had each lost several dollars in the game. I lived to learn that in the world of sport all men win alike but lose differently; and so gamblers are rated, not by the way in which they win, but by the way in which they lose. Some men lose with a careless smile, recognizing that losing is a part of the game; others curse their luck and rail at fortune; and others, still, lose sadly; after each such experience they are swept by a wave of reform; they resolve to stop gambling and be good. When in this frame of mind it would take very little persuasion to lead them into a prayer-meeting. Those in the first class are looked upon with admiration; those in the second class are merely commonplace; while those in the third are regarded with contempt. I believe these distinctions hold good in all the ventures of life. After some minutes one of my friends and I succeeded in convincing the other two that a while at the "Club" would put us all in better spirits; and they consented to go on the promise not to stay longer than an hour. We found the place crowded, and the same sort of thing going on which we had seen the night before. I took a seat at once by the side of the piano player, and was soon lost to everything except the novel charm of the music. I watched the performer with the idea of catching the trick; and during one of his intermissions, I took his place at the piano and made an attempt to imitate him, but even my quick ear and ready fingers were unequal to the task on first trial.

We did not stay at the "Club" very long, but went home to bed in order to be up early the next day. We had no difficulty in finding work, and my third morning in New York found me at a table rolling cigars. I worked steadily for some weeks, at the same time spending my earnings between the "crap" game and the "Club." Making cigars became more and more irksome to me; perhaps my more congenial work as "reader" had unfitted me for work at the table. And, too, the late hours I was keeping made such a sedentary occupation almost beyond the powers of will and endurance. I often found it hard to keep my eyes open and sometimes had to get up and move around to keep from falling asleep. I began to miss whole days from the factory, days on which I was compelled to stay at home and sleep.

My luck at the gambling table was varied; sometimes I was fifty to a hundred dollars ahead, and at other times I had to borrow money from my fellow workmen to settle my room rent and pay for my meals. Each night after leaving the dice game I went to the "Club" to hear the music and watch the gayety. If I had won, this was in accord with my mood; if I had lost, it made me forget. I at last realized that making cigars for a living and gambling for a living could not both be carried on at the same time, and I resolved to give up the cigar-making. This resolution led me into a life which held me bound more than a year. During that period my regular time for going to bed was somewhere between four and six o'clock in the mornings. I got up late in the afternoons, walked about a little, then went to the gambling house or the "Club." My New York was limited to ten blocks; the boundaries were Sixth Avenue from Twenty-third to Thirty-third Streets, with the cross streets one block to the west. Central Park was a distant forest, and the lower part of the city a foreign land. I look back upon the life I then led with a shudder when I think what would have been had I not escaped it. But had I not escaped it, I would have been no more unfortunate than are many young colored men who come to New York. During that dark period I became acquainted with a score of bright, intelligent young fellows who had come up to the great city with high hopes and ambitions, and who had fallen under the spell of this under life, a spell they could not throw off. There was one popularly known as "the doctor"; he had had two years in the Harvard Medical School; but here he was, living this gas-light life, his will and moral sense so enervated and deadened that it was impossible for him to break away. I do not doubt that the same thing is going on now, but I have rather sympathy than censure for these victims, for I know how easy it is to slip into a slough from which it takes a herculean effort to leap.

I regret that I cannot contrast my views of life among colored people of New York; but the truth is, during my entire stay in this city I did not become acquainted with a single respectable family. I knew that there were several colored men worth a hundred or so thousand dollars each, and some families who proudly dated their free ancestry back a half-dozen generations. I also learned that in Brooklyn there lived quite a large colony in comfortable homes, most of which they owned; but at no point did my life come in contact with theirs.

In my gambling experiences I passed through all the states and conditions that a gambler is heir to. Some days found me able to peel ten and twenty dollar bills from a roll, and others found me clad in a linen duster and carpet slippers. I finally caught up another method of earning money, and so did not have to depend entirely upon the caprices of fortune at the gaming table. Through continually listening to the music at the "Club," and through my own previous training, my natural talent and perseverance, I developed into a remarkable player of ragtime; indeed, I had the name at that time of being

the best ragtime player in New York. I brought all my knowledge of classic music to bear and, in so doing, achieved some
novelties which pleased and even astonished my listeners. It
was I who first made ragtime transcriptions of familiar classic
selections. I used to play Mendelssohn's "Wedding March" in
a manner that never failed to arouse enthusiasm among the patrons of the "Club." Very few nights passed during which I
was not asked to play it. It was no secret that the great increase
in slumming visitors was due to my playing. By mastering ragtime I gained several things; first of all, I gained the title of
professor. I was known as the "professor" as long as I remained in that world. Then, too, I gained the means of earning a rather fair livelihood. This work took up much of my
time and kept me almost entirely away from the gambling
table. Through it I also gained a friend who was the means by
which I escaped from this lower world. And, finally, I secured
a wedge which has opened to me more doors and made me a
welcome guest than my playing of Beethoven and Chopin
could ever have done.

The greater part of the money I now began to earn came
through the friend to whom I alluded in the foregoing paragraph. Among the other white "slummers" there came into
the "Club" one night a clean cut, slender, but athletic looking
man, who would have been taken for a youth had it not been
for the tinge of gray about his temples. He was clean shaven,
had regular features, and all of his movements bore the indefinable but unmistakable stamp of culture. He spoke to no
one, but sat languidly puffing cigarettes and sipping a glass of
beer. He was the center of a great deal of attention, all of the
old timers were wondering who he was. When I had finished
playing he called a waiter and by him sent me a five dollar bill.
For about a month after that he was at the "Club" one or two
nights each week, and each time after I had played he gave me
five dollars. One night he sent for me to come to his table; he
asked me several questions about myself; then told me that he
had an engagement which he wanted me to fill. He gave me a
card containing his address and asked me to be there on a certain night.

I was on hand promptly, and found that he was giving a dinner in his own apartments to a party of ladies and gentlemen,

and that I was expected to furnish the musical entertainment.
When the grave, dignified man at the door let me in, the place
struck me as being almost dark, my eyes had been so accustomed to the garish light of the "Club." He took my coat and
hat, bade me take a seat, and went to tell his master that I had
come. When my eyes were adjusted to the soft light I saw that
I was in the midst of elegance and luxury in a degree as I had
never seen; but not the elegance which makes one ill at ease.
As I sank into a great chair the subdued tone, the delicately
sensuous harmony of my surroundings drew from me a deep
sigh of relief and comfort. How long the man was gone I do
not know; but I was startled by a voice saying, "Come this
way, if you please, sir," and I saw him standing by my chair. I
had been asleep; and I awoke very much confused and a little
ashamed, because I did not know how many times he may
have called me. I followed him through into the dining-room,
where the butler was putting the finishing touches to a table
which already looked like a big jewel. The doorman turned me
over to the butler, and I passed with the butler on back to
where several waiters were busy polishing and assorting table
utensils. Without being asked whether I was hungry or not, I
was placed at a table and given something to eat. Before I had
finished eating I heard the laughter and talk of the guests who
were arriving. Soon afterwards I was called in to begin my work.

   I passed in to where the company was gathered, and went
directly to the piano. According to a suggestion from the host
I began with classic music. During the first number there was
absolute quiet and appreciative attention, and when I had finished I was given a round of generous applause. After that the
talk and the laughter began to grow until the music was only
an accompaniment to the chatter. This, however, did not dis-
concert me as it once would have done, for I had become accustomed to playing in the midst of uproarious noise. As the
guests began to pay less attention to me I was enabled to pay
more to them. There were about a dozen of them. The men
ranged in appearance from a girlish looking youth to a big
grizzled man whom everybody addressed as "Judge." None of
the women appeared to be under thirty, but each of them
struck me as being handsome. I was not long in finding out
that they were all decidedly blasé. Several of the women

smoked cigarettes, and with a careless grace which showed they were used to the habit. Occasionally a "damn it!" escaped from the lips of some one of them, but in such a charming way as to rob it of all vulgarity. The most notable thing which I observed was that the reserve of the host increased in direct proportion with the hilarity of the guests. I thought that there was something wrong which displeased him. I afterwards learned that it was his habitual manner on such occasions. He seemed to take a cynical delight in watching and studying others indulging in excess. His guests were evidently accustomed to his rather non-participating attitude, for it did not seem in any degree to dampen their spirits.

When dinner was served the piano was moved and the door left open, so that the company might hear the music while eating. At a word from the host I struck up one of my liveliest ragtime pieces. The effect was perhaps surprising, even to the host; the ragtime music came very near spoiling the party so far as eating the dinner was concerned. As soon as I began the conversation stopped suddenly. It was a pleasure to me to watch the expression of astonishment and delight that grew on the faces of everybody. These were people,—and they represented a large class,—who were ever expecting to find happiness in novelty, each day restlessly exploring and exhausting every resource of this great city that might possibly furnish a new sensation or awaken a fresh emotion, and who were always grateful to anyone who aided them in their quest. Several of the women left the table and gathered about the piano. They watched my fingers, asked what kind of music it was that I was playing, where I had learned it and a host of other questions. It was only by being repeatedly called back to the table that they were induced to finish their dinner. When the guests arose I struck up my ragtime transcription of Mendelssohn's "Wedding March," playing it with terrific chromatic octave runs in the base. This raised everybody's spirits to the highest point of gayety, and the whole company involuntarily and unconsciously did an impromptu cake-walk. From that time on until the time of leaving they kept me so busy that my arms ached. I obtained a little respite when the girlish looking youth and one or two of the ladies sang several songs, but after each of these it was, "back to the ragtime."

In leaving, the guests were enthusiastic in telling the host that he had furnished them the most unusual entertainment they had "ever" enjoyed. When they had gone, my millionaire friend,—for he was reported to be a millionaire,—said to me with a smile, "Well, I have given them something they've never had before." After I had put on my coat and was ready to leave he made me take a glass of wine; he then gave me a cigar and twenty dollars in bills. He told me that he would give me lots of work, his only stipulation being that I should not play any engagements such as I had just filled for him, except by his instructions. I readily accepted the proposition, for I was sure that I could not be a loser by such a contract.

I afterwards played for him at many dinners and parties of one kind or another. Occasionally he "loaned" me to some of his friends. And, too, I often played for him alone at his apartments. At such times he was quite a puzzle to me until I became accustomed to his manners. He would sometimes sit for three or four hours hearing me play, his eyes almost closed, making scarcely a motion except to light a fresh cigarette, and never commenting one way or another on the music. At first, I used sometimes to think that he had fallen asleep and would pause in playing. The stopping of the music always aroused him enough to tell me to play this or that; and I soon learned that my task was not to be considered finished until he got up from his chair and said, "That will do." The man's powers of endurance in listening often exceeded mine in performing— yet I am not sure that he was always listening. At times I became so oppressed with fatigue and sleepiness that it took almost superhuman effort to keep my fingers going; in fact, I believe I sometimes did so while dozing. During such moments, this man sitting there so mysteriously silent, almost hid in a cloud of heavy-scented smoke, filled me with a sort of unearthly terror. He seemed to be some grim, mute, but relentless tyrant, possessing over me a supernatural power which he used to drive me on mercilessly to exhaustion. But these feelings came very rarely; besides, he paid me so liberally I could forget much. There at length grew between us a familiar and warm relationship; and I am sure he had a decided personal liking for me. On my part, I looked upon him at that time as about all a man could wish to be.

The "Club" still remained my headquarters, and when I was not playing for my good patron I was generally to be found there. However, I no longer depended on playing at the "Club" to earn my living; I rather took rank with the visiting celebrities and, occasionally, after being sufficiently urged, would favor my old and new admirers with a number or two. I say, without any egotistic pride, that among my admirers were several of the best looking women who frequented the place, and who made no secret of the fact that they admired me as much as they did my playing. Among these was the "widow"; indeed, her attentions became so marked that one of my friends warned me to beware of her black companion, who was generally known as a "bad man." He said there was much more reason to be careful because the pair had lately quarreled, and had not been together at the "Club" for some nights. This warning greatly impressed me and I resolved to stop the affair before it should go any further; but the woman was so beautiful that my native gallantry and delicacy would not allow me to repulse her; my finer feelings entirely overcame my judgment. The warning also opened my eyes sufficiently to see that though my artistic temperament and skill made me interesting and attractive to the woman, she was, after all, using me only to excite the jealousy of her companion and revenge herself upon him. It was this surly black despot who held sway over her deepest emotions.

One night, shortly afterwards, I went into the "Club" and saw the "widow" sitting at a table in company with another woman. She at once beckoned for me to come to her. I went, knowing that I was committing worse than folly. She ordered a quart of champagne and insisted that I sit down and drink with her. I took a chair on the opposite side of the table and began to sip a glass of the wine. Suddenly I noticed by an expression on the "widow's" face that something had occurred. I instinctively glanced around and saw that her companion had just entered. His ugly look completely frightened me. My back was turned to him, but by watching the "widow's" eyes I judged that he was pacing back and forth across the room. My feelings were far from being comfortable; I expected every moment to feel a blow on my head. She, too, was very nervous; she was trying hard to appear unconcerned, but could not succeed in hiding her real feelings. I decided that it was best to get out of such a predicament even at the expense of appearing cowardly, and I made a motion to rise. Just as I partly turned in my chair, I saw the black fellow approaching; he walked directly to our table and leaned over. The "widow" evidently feared he was going to strike her, and she threw back her head. Instead of striking her he whipped out a revolver and fired; the first shot went straight into her throat. There were other shots fired, but how many I do not know; for the first knowledge I had of my surroundings and actions was that I was rushing through the chop-suey restaurant into the street. Just which streets I followed when I got outside I do not know, but I think I must have gone towards Eighth Avenue; then down towards Twenty-third Street and across towards Fifth Avenue. I traveled not by sight, but instinctively. I felt like one fleeing in a horrible nightmare.

How long and far I walked I cannot tell; but on Fifth Avenue, under a light, I passed a cab containing a solitary occupant, who called to me, and I recognized the voice and face of my millionaire friend. He stopped the cab and asked, "What on earth are you doing strolling in this part of the town?" For answer I got into the cab and related to him all that had happened. He reassured me by saying that no charge of any kind could be brought against me; then added, "But, of course, you don't want to be mixed up in such an affair." He directed the driver to turn around and go into the park, and then went on to say, "I decided last night that I'd go to Europe to-morrow. I think I'll take you along instead of Walter." Walter was his valet. It was settled that I should go to his apartments for the rest of the night and sail with him in the morning.

We drove around through the park, exchanging only an occasional word. The cool air somewhat calmed my nerves and I lay back and closed my eyes; but still I could see that beautiful white throat with the ugly wound. The jet of blood pulsing from it had placed an indelible red stain on my memory.

Chapter IX

I DID NOT feel at ease until the ship was well out of New York
harbor; and, notwithstanding the repeated reassurances of
my millionaire friend and my own knowledge of the facts in
the case, I somehow could not rid myself of the sentiment that
I was, in a great degree, responsible for the widow's tragic end.
We had brought most of the morning papers aboard with us,
but my great fear of seeing my name in connection with the
killing would not permit me to read the accounts, although, in
one of the papers, I did look at the picture of the victim, which
did not in the least resemble her. This morbid state of mind,
together with sea sickness, kept me miserable for three or four
days. At the end of that time my spirits began to revive, and I
took an interest in the ship, my fellow passengers, and the voyage in general. On the second or third day out we passed several spouting whales; but I could not arouse myself to make
the effort to go to the other side of the ship to see them. A
little later we ran in close proximity to a large iceberg. I was
curious enough to get up and look at it, and I was fully repaid
for my pains. The sun was shining full upon it, and it glistened
like a mammoth diamond, cut with a million facets. As we
passed it constantly changed its shape; at each different angle
of vision it assumed new and astonishing forms of beauty. I
watched it through a pair of glasses, seeking to verify my early
conception of an iceberg—in the geographies of my grammar-
school days the pictures of icebergs always included a stranded
polar bear, standing desolately upon one of the snowy crags. I
looked for the bear, but if he was there he refused to put himself on exhibition.

It was not, however, until the morning that we entered the
harbor of Havre that I was able to shake off my gloom. Then
the strange sights, the chatter in an unfamiliar tongue and the
excitement of landing and passing the customs officials caused
me to forget completely the events of a few days before. Indeed, I grew so light-hearted that when I caught my first sight
of the train which was to take us to Paris, I enjoyed a hearty
laugh. The toy-looking engine, the stuffy little compartment

cars with tiny, old-fashioned wheels, struck me as being extremely funny. But before we reached Paris my respect for our train rose considerably. I found that the "tiny" engine made remarkably fast time, and that the old-fashioned wheels ran very smoothly. I even began to appreciate the "stuffy" cars for their privacy. As I watched the passing scenery from the car window it seemed too beautiful to be real. The bright-colored houses against the green background impressed me as the work of some idealistic painter. Before we arrived in Paris, there was awakened in my heart a love for France which continued to grow stronger, a love which to-day makes that country for me the one above all others to be desired.

We rolled into the station Saint Lazare about four o'clock in the afternoon and drove immediately to the Hotel Continental. My benefactor, humoring my curiosity and enthusiasm, which seemed to please him very much, suggested that we take a short walk before dinner. We stepped out of the hotel and turned to the right into the Rue de Rivoli. When the vista of the Place de la Concorde and the Champs Elysées suddenly burst on me I could hardly credit my own eyes. I shall attempt no such supererogatory task as a description of Paris. I wish only to give briefly the impressions which that wonderful city made upon me. It impressed me as the perfect and perfectly beautiful city; and even after I had been there for some time, and seen not only its avenues and palaces, but its most squalid alleys and hovels, this impression was not weakened. Paris became for me a charmed spot, and whenever I have returned there I have fallen under the spell, a spell which compels admiration for all of its manners and customs and justification of even its follies and sins.

We walked a short distance up the Champs Elysées and sat for a while in chairs along the sidewalk, watching the passing crowds on foot and in carriages. It was with reluctance that I went back to the hotel for dinner. After dinner we went to one of the summer theaters, and after the performance my friend took me to a large café on one of the grand boulevards. Here it was that I had my first glimpse of the French life of popular literature, so different from real French life. There were several hundred people, men and women, in the place drinking, smoking, talking, and listening to the music. My millionaire

friend and I took seats at a table where we sat smoking and
watching the crowd. It was not long before we were joined by
two or three good-looking, well-dressed young women. My
friend talked to them in French and bought drinks for the
whole party. I tried to recall my high school French, but the
effort availed me little. I could stammer out a few phrases, but,
very naturally, could not understand a word that was said to
me. We stayed at the café a couple of hours, then went back to
the hotel. The next day we spent several hours in the shops
and at the tailor's. I had no clothes except what I had been
able to gather together at my benefactor's apartments the
night before we sailed. He bought me the same kind of clothes
which he himself wore, and that was the best; and he treated
me in every way as he dressed me, as an equal, not as a servant.
In fact, I don't think anyone could have guessed that such a
relation existed. My duties were light and few, and he was a
man full of life and vigor, who rather enjoyed doing things for
himself. He kept me supplied with money far beyond what ordinary wages would have amounted to. For the first two weeks
we were together almost constantly, seeing the sights, sights
old to him, but from which he seemed to get new pleasure in
showing them to me. During the day we took in the places of
interest, and at night the theaters and cafés. This sort of life appealed to me as ideal, and I asked him one day how long he intended to stay in Paris. He answered, "Oh, until I get tired of
it." I could not understand how that could ever happen. As it
was, including several short trips to the Mediterranean, to
Spain, to Brussels, and to Ostend, we did remain there fourteen or fifteen months. We stayed at the Hotel Continental
about two months of this time. Then my millionaire took
apartments, hired a piano, and lived almost the same life he
lived in New York. He entertained a great deal, some of the
parties being a good deal more blasé than the New York ones.
I played for the guests at all of them with an effect which to relate would be but a tiresome repetition to the reader. I played
not only for the guests, but continued, as I used to do in New
York, to play often for the host when he was alone. This man
of the world, who grew weary of everything, and was always
searching for something new, appeared never to grow tired of
my music; he seemed to take it as a drug. He fell into a habit

which caused me no little annoyance; sometimes he would come in during the early hours of the morning, and finding me in bed asleep, would wake me up and ask me to play something. This, so far as I can remember, was my only hardship during my whole stay with him in Europe.

After the first few weeks spent in sight-seeing, I had a great deal of time left to myself; my friend was often I did not know where. When not with him I spent the day nosing about all the curious nooks and corners of Paris; of this I never grew tired. At night I usually went to some theater, but always ended up at the big café on the Grand Boulevards. I wish the reader to know that it was not alone the gayety which drew me there; aside from that I had a laudable purpose. I had purchased an English-French conversational dictionary, and I went there every night to take a language lesson. I used to get three or four of the young women who frequented the place at a table and buy beer and cigarettes for them. In return I received my lesson. I got more than my money's worth; for they actually compelled me to speak the language. This, together with reading the papers every day, enabled me within a few months to express myself fairly well, and, before I left Paris, to have more than an ordinary command of French. Of course, every person who goes to Paris could not dare to learn French in this manner, but I can think of no easier or quicker way of doing it. The acquiring of another foreign language awoke me to the fact that with a little effort I could secure an added accomplishment as fine and valuable as music; so I determined to make myself as much of a linguist as possible. I bought a Spanish newspaper every day in order to freshen my memory on that language, and, for French, devised what was, so far as I knew, an original system of study. I compiled a list which I termed "Three hundred necessary words." These I thoroughly committed to memory, also the conjugation of the verbs which were included in the list. I studied these words over and over, much like children of a couple of generations ago studied the alphabet. I also practiced a set of phrases like the following: "How?" "What did you say?" "What does the word —— mean?" "I understand all you say except ——." "Please repeat." "What do you call ——?" "How do you say ——?" These I called my working sentences. In an astonishingly short

time I reached the point where the language taught itself,—
where I learned to speak merely by speaking. This point is the
place which students taught foreign languages in our schools
and colleges find great difficulty in reaching. I think the main
trouble is that they learn too much of a language at a time. A
French child with a vocabulary of two hundred words can express more spoken ideas than a student of French can with a
knowledge of two thousand. A small vocabulary, the smaller
the better, which embraces the common, everyday-used ideas,
thoroughly mastered, is the key to a language. When that
much is acquired the vocabulary can be increased simply by
talking. And it is easy. Who cannot commit three hundred
words to memory? Later I tried my method, if I may so term
it, with German, and found that it worked in the same way.

I spent a good many evenings at the Grand Opera. The
music there made me strangely reminiscent of my life in Connecticut, it was an atmosphere in which I caught a fresh breath
of my boyhood days and early youth. Generally, in the morning, after I had attended a performance, I would sit at the piano and for a couple of hours play the music which I used to
play in my mother's little parlor.

One night I went to hear "Faust." I got into my seat just as
the lights went down for the first act. At the end of the act I
noticed that my neighbor on the left was a young girl. I cannot
describe her either as to feature, color of her hair, or of her
eyes; she was so young, so fair, so ethereal, that I felt to stare at
her would be a violation; yet I was distinctly conscious of her
beauty. During the intermission she spoke English in a low
voice to a gentleman and a lady who sat in the seats to her left,
addressing them as father and mother. I held my programme
as though studying it, but listened to catch every sound of her
voice. Her observations on the performance and the audience
were so fresh and naïve as to be almost amusing. I gathered
that she was just out of school, and that this was her first trip
to Paris. I occasionally stole a glance at her, and each time I did
so my heart leaped into my throat. Once I glanced beyond to
the gentleman who sat next to her. My glance immediately
turned into a stare. Yes, there he was, unmistakably, my father!
looking hardly a day older than when I had seen him some ten
years before. What a strange coincidence! What should I say to

him? What would he say to me? Before I had recovered from my first surprise there came another shock in the realization that the beautiful, tender girl at my side was my sister. Then all the springs of affection in my heart, stopped since my mother's death, burst out in fresh and terrible torrents, and I could have fallen at her feet and worshiped her. They were singing the second act, but I did not hear the music. Slowly the desolate loneliness of my position became clear to me. I knew that I could not speak, but I would have given a part of my life to touch her hand with mine and call her sister. I sat through the opera until I could stand it no longer. I felt that I was suffocating. Valentine's love seemed like mockery, and I felt an almost uncontrollable impulse to rise up and scream to the audience, "Here, here in your very midst, is a tragedy, a real tragedy!" This impulse grew so strong that I became afraid of myself, and in the darkness of one of the scenes I stumbled out of the theater. I walked aimlessly about for an hour or so, my feelings divided between a desire to weep and a desire to curse. I finally took a cab and went from café to café, and for one of the very few times in my life drank myself into a stupor.

It was unwelcome news for me when my benefactor—I could not think of him as employer—informed me that he was at last tired of Paris. This news gave me, I think, a passing doubt as to his sanity. I had enjoyed life in Paris, and, taking all things into consideration, enjoyed it wholesomely. One thing which greatly contributed to my enjoyment was the fact that I was an American. Americans are immensely popular in Paris; and this is not due solely to the fact that they spend lots of money there, for they spend just as much or more in London, and in the latter city they are merely tolerated because they do spend. The Londoner seems to think that Americans are people whose only claim to be classed as civilized is that they have money, and the regrettable thing about that is that the money is not English. But the French are more logical and freer from prejudices than the British; so the difference of attitude is easily explained. Only once in Paris did I have cause to blush for my American citizenship. I had become quite friendly with a young man from Luxembourg whom I had met at the big café. He was a stolid, slow-witted fellow, but, as we say, with a heart of gold. He and I grew attached to each other and were together frequently. He was a great admirer of the United States and never grew tired of talking to me about the country and asking for information. It was his intention to try his fortune there some day. One night he asked me in a tone of voice which indicated that he expected an authoritative denial of an ugly rumor, "Did they really burn a man alive in the United States?" I never knew what I stammered out to him as an answer. I should have felt relieved if I could even have said to him, "Well, only one."

When we arrived in London my sadness at leaving Paris was turned into despair. After my long stay in the French capital, huge, ponderous, massive London seemed to me as ugly a thing as man could contrive to make. I thought of Paris as a beauty spot on the face of the earth, and of London as a big freckle. But soon London's massiveness, I might say its very ugliness, began to impress me. I began to experience that sense of grandeur which one feels when he looks at a great mountain or a mighty river. Beside London Paris becomes a toy, a pretty plaything. And I must own that before I left the world's metropolis I discovered much there that was beautiful. The beauty in and about London is entirely different from that in and about Paris; and I could not but admit that the beauty of the French city seemed hand-made, artificial, as though set up for the photographer's camera, everything nicely adjusted so as not to spoil the picture; while that of the English city was rugged, natural and fresh.

How these two cities typify the two peoples who built them! Even the sound of their names expresses a certain racial difference. Paris is the concrete expression of the gayety, regard for symmetry, love of art and, I might well add, of the morality of the French people. London stands for the conservatism, the solidarity, the utilitarianism and, I might well add, the hypocrisy of the Anglo-Saxon. It may sound odd to speak of the morality of the French, if not of the hypocrisy of the English; but this seeming paradox impresses me as a deep truth. I saw many things in Paris which were immoral according to English standards, but the absence of hypocrisy, the absence of the spirit to do the thing if it might only be done in secret, robbed these very immoralities of the damning influence of the same evils in London. I have walked along the terrace cafés of Paris and seen hundreds of men and women sipping their wine and beer, without observing a sign of drunkenness. As they drank, they chatted and laughed and watched the passing crowds; the drinking seemed to be a secondary thing. This I have witnessed, not only in the cafés along the Grand Boulevards, but in the out-of-the-way places patronized by the working classes. In London I have seen in the "Pubs" men and women crowded in stuffy little compartments, drinking seemingly only for the pleasure of swallowing as much as they could hold. I have seen there women from eighteen to eighty, some in tatters, and some clutching babes in their arms, drinking the heavy English ales and whiskies served to them by women. In the whole scene, not one ray of brightness, not one flash of gayety, only maudlin joviality or grim despair. And I have thought, if some men and women will drink—and it is certain that some will—is it not better that they do so under the sky, in the fresh air, than huddled together in some close, smoky room? There is a sort of frankness about the evils of Paris which robs them of much of the seductiveness of things forbidden, and with that frankness goes a certain cleanliness of thought belonging to things not hidden. London will do whatever Paris does, provided exterior morals are not shocked. As a result, Paris has the appearance only of being the more immoral city. The difference may be summed up in this: Paris practices its sins as lightly as it does its religion, while London practices both very seriously.

I should not neglect to mention what impressed me most forcibly during my stay in London. It was not St. Paul's nor the British Museum nor Westminster Abbey. It was nothing more or less than the simple phrase "Thank you," or sometimes more elaborated, "Thank you very kindly, sir." I was continually surprised by the varied uses to which it was put; and, strange to say, its use as an expression of politeness seemed more limited than any other. One night I was in a cheap music hall and accidentally bumped into a waiter who was carrying a tray-load of beer, almost bringing him to several shillings' worth of grief. To my amazement he righted himself and said, "Thank ye, sir," and left me wondering whether he meant that he thanked me for not completely spilling his beer, or that he would thank me for keeping out of his way.

I also found cause to wonder upon what ground the English accuse Americans of corrupting the language by introducing slang words. I think I heard more and more different kinds of slang during my few weeks' stay in London than in my whole "tenderloin" life in New York. But I suppose the English feel that the language is theirs, and that they may do with it as they please without at the same time allowing that privilege to others.

My "millionaire" was not so long in growing tired of London as of Paris. After a stay of six to eight weeks we went across into Holland. Amsterdam was a great surprise to me. I had always thought of Venice as the city of canals; but it had never entered my mind that I should find similar conditions in a Dutch town. I don't suppose the comparison goes far beyond the fact that there are canals in both cities—I have never seen Venice—but Amsterdam struck me as being extremely picturesque. From Holland we went to Germany, where we spent five to six months, most of the time in Berlin. I found Berlin more to my taste than London, and occasionally I had to admit that in some things it was superior to Paris.

In Berlin I especially enjoyed the orchestral concerts, and I attended a large number of them. I formed the acquaintance of a good many musicians, several of whom spoke of my playing in high terms. It was in Berlin that my inspiration was renewed. One night my "millionaire" entertained a party of men composed of artists, musicians, writers and, for aught I know, a count or two. They drank and smoked a great deal, talked art and music; and discussed, it seemed to me, everything that ever entered man's mind. I could only follow the general drift of what they were saying. When they discussed music it was more interesting to me; for then some fellow would run excitedly to the piano and give a demonstration of his opinions, and another would follow quickly doing the same thing. In this way, I learned that, regardless of what his specialty might be, every man in the party was a musician. I was at the same time impressed with the falsity of the general idea that Frenchmen are excitable and emotional, and that Germans are calm and phlegmatic. Frenchmen are merely gay and never overwhelmed by their emotions. When they talk loud and fast it is merely talk, while Germans get worked up and red in the face when sustaining an opinion; and in heated discussions are likely to allow their emotions to sweep them off their feet.

My "millionaire" planned, in the midst of the discussion on music, to have me play the "new American music" and astonish everybody present. The result was that I was more astonished than anyone else. I went to the piano and played the most intricate ragtime piece I knew. Before there was time for anybody to express an opinion on what I had done, a big bespectacled, bushy-headed man rushed over, and, shoving me out of the chair, exclaimed, "Get up! Get up!" He seated himself at the piano, and taking the theme of my ragtime, played it through first in straight chords; then varied and developed it through every known musical form. I sat amazed. I had been turning classic music ragtime, a comparatively easy task; and this man had taken ragtime and made it a classic. The thought came across me like a flash.—It can be done, why can't I do it? From that moment my mind was made up. I clearly saw the way of carrying out the ambition I had formed when a boy.

I now lost interest in our trip. I thought, here I am a man, no longer a boy, and what am I doing but wasting my time and abusing my talent. What use am I making of my gifts? What future have I before me following my present course? These thoughts made me feel remorseful, and put me in a fever to get to work, to begin to do something. Of course I know now that I was not wasting time; that there was nothing I could have done at that age which would have benefited me more than going to Europe as I did. The desire to begin work grew stronger each day. I could think of nothing else. I made up my mind to go back into the very heart of the South, to live among the people, and drink in my inspiration first-hand. I gloated over the immense amount of material I had to work with, not only modern ragtime, but also the old slave songs, —material which no one had yet touched.

The more decided and anxious I became to return to the United States, the more I dreaded the ordeal of breaking with my "millionaire." Between this peculiar man and me there had grown a very strong bond of affection, backed up by a debt which each owed to the other. He had taken me from a terrible life in New York and by giving me the opportunity of traveling and of coming in contact with the people with whom he associated, had made me a polished man of the world. On the other hand, I was his chief means of disposing of the thing which seemed to sum up all in life that he dreaded—Time. As I remember him now, I can see that time was what he was always endeavoring to escape, to bridge over, to blot out; and it is not strange that some years later he did escape it forever, by leaping into eternity.

For some weeks I waited for just the right moment in which to tell my patron of my decision. Those weeks were a trying time to me. I felt that I was playing the part of a traitor to my best friend. At length, one day, he said to me, "Well, get ready for a long trip; we are going to Egypt, and then to Japan." The temptation was for an instant almost overwhelming, but I summoned determination enough to say, "I don't think I want to go." "What!" he exclaimed, "you want to go back to your dear Paris? You still think that the only spot on earth? Wait until you see Cairo and Tokio, you may change your mind." "No," I stammered, "it is not because I want to go back to Paris. I want to go back to the United States." He wished to know my reason, and I told him, as best I could, my dreams, my ambition, and my decision. While I was talking he watched me with a curious, almost cynical, smile growing on his lips. When I had finished he put his hand on my shoulder.—This was the first physical expression of tender regard he had ever shown me—and looking at me in a big-brotherly way, said, "My boy, you are by blood, by appearance, by education and by tastes, a white man. Now why do you want to throw your life away amidst the poverty and ignorance, in the hopeless struggle of the black people of the United States? Then look at the terrible handicap you are placing on yourself by going home and working as a Negro composer; you can never be able to get the hearing for your work which it might deserve. I doubt that even a white musician of recognized ability could succeed there by working on the theory that American music should be based on Negro themes. Music is a universal art; anybody's music belongs to everybody; you can't limit it to race or country. Now, if you want to become a composer, why not stay right here in Europe? I will put you under the best teachers on the continent. Then if you want to write music on Negro themes, why, go ahead and do it."

We talked for some time on music and the race question. On the latter subject I had never before heard him express any opinion. Between him and me no suggestion of racial differences had ever come up. I found that he was a man entirely free from prejudice, but he recognized that prejudice was a big stubborn entity which had to be taken into account. He went on to say, "This idea you have of making a Negro out of yourself is nothing more than a sentiment; and you do not realize the fearful import of what you intend to do. What kind of a Negro would you make now, especially in the South? If you had remained there, or perhaps even in your club in New York, you might have succeeded very well; but now you would be miserable. I can imagine no more dissatisfied human being than an educated, cultured and refined colored man in the United States. I have given more study to the race question in the United States than you may suppose, and I sympathize with the Negroes there; but what's the use? I can't right the wrongs, and neither can you; they must do that themselves. They are unfortunate in having wrongs to right, and you would be foolish to unnecessarily take their wrongs on your shoulders. Perhaps some day, through study and observation, you will come to see that evil is a force and, like the physical and chemical forces, we cannot annihilate it; we may only change its form. We light upon one evil and hit it with all the might of our civilization, but only succeed in scattering it into a dozen of other forms. We hit slavery through a great civil war. Did we destroy it? No, we only changed it into hatred between sections of the country: in the South, into political corruption and chicanery, the degradation of the blacks through peonage, unjust laws, unfair and cruel treatment; and the degradation of the whites by their resorting to these practices; the paralyzation of the public conscience, and the ever overhanging dread of what the future may bring. Modern civilization hit ignorance of the masses through the means of popular education. What has it done but turn ignorance into anarchy, socialism, strikes, hatred between poor and rich, and universal discontent. In like manner, modern philanthropy hit at suffering and disease through asylums and hospitals; it prolongs the sufferers' lives, it is true, but is, at the same time, sending down strains of insanity and weakness into future generations.

My philosophy of life is this: make yourself as happy as possible, and try to make those happy whose lives come into touch with yours; but to attempt to right the wrongs and ease the sufferings of the world in general, is a waste of effort. You had just as well try to bale the Atlantic by pouring the water into the Pacific."

This tremendous flow of serious talk from a man I was accustomed to see either gay or taciturn so surprised and overwhelmed me that I could not frame a reply. He left me thinking over what he had said. Whatever was the soundness of his logic or the moral tone of his philosophy, his argument greatly impressed me. I could see, in spite of the absolute selfishness upon which it was based, that there was reason and common sense in it. I began to analyze my own motives, and found that they, too, were very largely mixed with selfishness. Was it more a desire to help those I considered my people or more a desire to distinguish myself, which was leading me back to the United States? That is a question I have never definitely answered.

For several weeks longer I was in a troubled state of mind. Added to the fact that I was loath to leave my good friend, was the weight of the question he had aroused in my mind, whether I was not making a fatal mistake. I suffered more than one sleepless night during that time. Finally, I settled the question on purely selfish grounds, in accordance with my "millionaire's" philosophy. I argued that music offered me a better future than anything else I had any knowledge of, and, in opposition to my friend's opinion, that I should have greater chances of attracting attention as a colored composer than as a white one. But I must own that I also felt stirred by an unselfish desire to voice all the joys and sorrows, the hopes and ambitions, of the American Negro, in classical music form.

When my mind was fully made up I told my friend. He asked me when I intended to start. I replied that I would do so at once. He then asked me how much money I had. I told him that I had saved several hundred dollars out of sums he had given me. He gave me a check for $500, told me to write to him care of his Paris bankers if I ever needed his help, wished me good luck, and bade me good-by. All this he did almost coldly; and I often wondered whether he was in a hurry to get rid of what he considered a fool, or whether he was striving to hide deeper feelings of sorrow.

And so I separated from the man who was, all in all, the best friend I ever had, except my mother, the man who exerted the greatest influence ever brought into my life, except that exerted by my mother. My affection for him was so strong, my recollections of him are so distinct; he was such a peculiar and striking character, that I could easily fill several chapters with reminiscences of him; but for fear of tiring the reader I shall go on with my narration.

I decided to go to Liverpool and take ship for Boston. I still had an uneasy feeling about returning to New York; and in a few days I found myself aboard ship headed for home.

Chapter X

AMONG the first of my fellow passengers of whom I took particular notice, was a tall, broad-shouldered, almost gigantic, colored man. His dark-brown face was clean shaven; he was well dressed and bore a decidedly distinguished air. In fact, if he was not handsome, he at least compelled admiration for his fine physical proportions. He attracted general attention as he strode the deck in a sort of majestic loneliness. I became curious to know who he was and determined to strike up an acquaintance with him at the first opportune moment. The chance came a day or two later. He was sitting in the smoking-room, with a cigar in his mouth which had gone out, reading a novel. I sat down beside him and, offering him a fresh cigar, said, "You don't mind my telling you something unpleasant, do you?" He looked at me with a smile, accepted the proffered cigar, and replied in a voice which comported perfectly with his size and appearance, "I think my curiosity overcomes any objections I might have." "Well," I said, "have you noticed that the man who sat at your right in the saloon during the first meal has not sat there since?" He frowned slightly without answering my question. "Well," I continued, "he asked the steward to remove him; and not only that, he attempted to persuade a number of the passengers to protest against your presence in the dining-saloon." The big man at my side took a long draw from his cigar, threw his head back and slowly blew a great cloud of smoke toward the ceiling. Then turning to me he said, "Do you know, I don't object to anyone having prejudices so long as those prejudices don't interfere with my personal liberty. Now, the man you are speaking of had a perfect right to change his seat if I in any way interfered with his appetite or his digestion. I would have no reason to complain if he removed to the farthest corner of the saloon, or even if he got off the ship; but when his prejudice attempts to move *me* one foot, one inch, out of the place where I am comfortably located, then I object." On the word "object" he brought his great fist down on the table in front of us with such a crash that everyone in the room turned to look. We both covered up the slightest embarrassment with a laugh, and strolled out on the deck.

We walked the deck for an hour or more, discussing different phases of the Negro question. I, in referring to the race, used the personal pronoun "we"; my companion made no comment about it, nor evinced any surprise, except to slightly raise his eyebrows the first time he caught the significance of the word. He was the broadest minded colored man I have ever talked with on the Negro question. He even went so far as to sympathize with and offer excuses for some white Southern points of view. I asked him what were his main reasons for being so hopeful. He replied, "In spite of all that is written, said and done, this great, big, incontrovertible fact stands out, —the Negro is progressing, and that disproves all the arguments in the world that he is incapable of progress. I was born in slavery, and at emancipation was set adrift a ragged, penniless bit of humanity. I have seen the Negro in every grade, and I know what I am talking about. Our detractors point to the increase of crime as evidence against us; certainly we have progressed in crime as in other things; what less could be expected? And yet, in this respect, we are far from the point which has been reached by the more highly civilized white race. As we continue to progress, crime among us will gradually lose much of its brutal, vulgar, I might say healthy, aspect, and become more delicate, refined, and subtile. Then it will be less shocking and noticeable, although more dangerous to society." Then dropping his tone of irony, he continued with some show of eloquence, "But, above all, when I am discouraged and disheartened, I have this to fall back on: if there is a principle of right in the world, which finally prevails, and I believe that there is; if there is a merciful but justice-loving God in heaven, and I believe that there is, we shall win; for we have right on our side; while those who oppose us can defend themselves by nothing in the moral law, nor even by anything in the enlightened thought of the present age."

For several days, together with other topics, we discussed the race problem, not only of the United States, but the race problem as it affected native Africans and Jews. Finally, before we reached Boston, our conversation had grown familiar and personal. I had told him something of my past and much about my intentions for the future. I learned that he was a physician, a graduate of Howard University, Washington, and had done post-graduate work in Philadelphia; and this was his second trip abroad to attend professional courses. He had practiced for some years in the city of Washington, and though he did not say so, I gathered that his practice was a lucrative one. Before we left the ship he had made me promise that I would stop two or three days in Washington before going on South.

We put up at a hotel in Boston for a couple of days and visited several of my friend's acquaintances; they were all people of education and culture and, apparently, of means. I could not help being struck by the great difference between them and the same class of colored people in the South. In speech and thought they were genuine Yankees. The difference was especially noticeable in their speech. There was none of that heavy-tongued enunciation which characterizes even the best educated colored people of the South. It is remarkable, after all, what an adaptable creature the Negro is. I have seen the black West India gentleman in London, and he is in speech and manners a perfect Englishman. I have seen natives of Haiti and Martinique in Paris, and they are more Frenchy than a Frenchman. I have no doubt that the Negro would make a good Chinaman, with exception of the pigtail.

My stay in Washington, instead of being two or three days, was two or three weeks. This was my first visit to the National Capital, and I was, of course, interested in seeing the public buildings and something of the working of the government; but most of my time I spent with the doctor among his friends and acquaintances. The social phase of life among colored people, which I spoke of in an earlier chapter, is more developed in Washington than in any other city in the country. This is on account of the large number of individuals earning good salaries and having a reasonable amount of leisure time to be drawn from. There are dozens of physicians and lawyers, scores of school teachers and hundreds of clerks in the departments. As to the colored department clerks, I think it fair to say that in educational equipment they average above the white clerks of the same grade; for, whereas a colored college graduate will seek such a job, the white university man goes into one of the many higher vocations which are open to him.

In a previous chapter I spoke of social life among colored people; so there is no need to take it up again here. But there is one thing I did not mention: among Negroes themselves there is the peculiar inconsistency of a color question. Its existence is rarely admitted and hardly ever mentioned; it may not be too strong a statement to say that the greater portion of the race is unconscious of its influence; yet this influence, though silent, is constant. It is evidenced most plainly in marriage selection; thus the black men generally marry women fairer than themselves; while, on the other hand, the dark women of stronger mental endowment are very often married to light-complexioned men; the effect is a tendency toward lighter complexions, especially among the more active elements in the race. Some might claim that this is a tacit admission of colored people among themselves of their own inferiority judged by the color line. I do not think so. What I have termed an inconsistency is, after all, most natural; it is, in fact, a tendency in accordance with what might be called an economic necessity. So far as racial differences go, the United States puts a greater premium on color, or better, lack of color, than upon anything else in the world. To paraphrase, "Have a white skin, and all things else may be added unto you." I have seen advertisements in newspapers for waiters, bell boys, or elevator men, which read, "Light colored man wanted." It is this tremendous pressure which the sentiment of the country exerts that is operating on the race. There is involved not only the question of higher opportunity, but often the question of earning a livelihood; and so I say it is not strange, but a natural tendency. Nor is it any more sacrifice of self respect that a black man should give to his children every advantage he can which complexion of the skin carries, than that the new or vulgar rich should purchase for their children the advantages which ancestry, aristocracy, and social position carry. I once heard a colored man sum it up in these words, "It's no disgrace to be black, but it's often very inconvenient."

Washington shows the Negro not only at his best, but also at his worst. As I drove around with the doctor, he commented rather harshly on those of the latter class which we saw. He remarked, "You see those lazy, loafing, good-for-nothing darkies, they're not worth digging graves for; yet they are the ones who create impressions of race for the casual observer. It's because they are always in evidence on the street corners, while the rest of us are hard at work, and you know a dozen loafing darkies make a bigger crowd and a worse impression in this country than fifty white men of the same class. But they ought not to represent the race. We are the race, and the race ought to be judged by us, not by them. Every race and every nation is judged by the best it has been able to produce, not by the worst."

The recollection of my stay in Washington is a pleasure to me now. In company with the doctor I visited Howard University, the public schools, the excellent colored hospital, with which he was in some way connected, if I remember correctly, and many comfortable and even elegant homes. It was with some reluctance that I continued my journey south. The doctor was very kind in giving me letters to people in Richmond and Nashville when I told him that I intended to stop in both of these cities. In Richmond a man who was then editing a very creditable colored newspaper, gave me a great deal of his time, and made my stay there of three or four days very pleasant. In Nashville I spent a whole day at Fisk University, the home of the "Jubilee Singers," and was more than repaid for my time. Among my letters of introduction was one to a very prosperous physician. He drove me about the city and introduced me to a number of people. From Nashville I went to Atlanta, where I stayed long enough to gratify an old desire to see Atlanta University again. I then continued my journey to Macon.

During the trip from Nashville to Atlanta I went into the smoking compartment of the car to smoke a cigar. I was traveling in a Pullman, not because of an abundance of funds, but because through my experience with my "millionaire," a certain amount of comfort and luxury had become a necessity to me whenever it was obtainable. When I entered the car I found only a couple of men there; but in a half hour there were half a dozen or more. From the general conversation I learned that a fat Jewish looking man was a cigar manufacturer, and was experimenting in growing Havana tobacco in Florida; that a slender be-spectacled young man was from Ohio and a professor in some State institution in Alabama;

that a white-mustached, well dressed man was an old Union soldier who had fought through the Civil War; and that a tall, raw-boned, red-faced man, who seemed bent on leaving nobody in ignorance of the fact that he was from Texas, was a cotton planter.

In the North men may ride together for hours in a "smoker" and unless they are acquainted with each other never exchange a word; in the South men thrown together in such manner are friends in fifteen minutes. There is always present a warm-hearted cordiality which will melt down the most frigid reserve. It may be because Southerners are very much like Frenchmen in that they must talk; and not only must they talk, but they must express their opinions.

The talk in the car was for a while miscellaneous,—on the weather, crops, business prospects—the old Union soldier had invested capital in Atlanta, and he predicted that that city would soon be one of the greatest in the country—finally the conversation drifted to politics; then, as a natural sequence, turned upon the Negro question.

In the discussion of the race question the diplomacy of the Jew was something to be admired; he had the faculty of agreeing with everybody without losing his allegiance to any side. He knew that to sanction Negro oppression would be to sanction Jewish oppression, and would expose him to a shot along that line from the old soldier, who stood firmly on the ground of equal rights and opportunity to all men; yet long traditions and business instincts told him, when in Rome to act as a Roman. Altogether his position was a delicate one, and I gave him credit for the skill he displayed in maintaining it. The young professor was apologetic. He had had the same views as the G.A.R. man; but a year in the South had opened his eyes, and he had to confess that the problem could hardly be handled any better than it was being handled by the Southern whites. To which the G.A.R. man responded somewhat rudely that he had spent ten times as many years in the South as his young friend, and that he could easily understand how holding a position in a State institution in Alabama would bring about a change of views. The professor turned very red and had very little more to say. The Texan was fierce, eloquent and profane in his argument and, in a lower sense, there was a direct logic in what he said, which was convincing; it was only by taking higher ground, by dealing in what Southerners call "theories" that he could be combatted. Occasionally some one of the several other men in the "smoker" would throw in a remark to reinforce what he said, but he really didn't need any help; he was sufficient in himself.

In the course of a short time the controversy narrowed itself down to an argument between the old soldier and the Texan. The latter maintained hotly that the Civil War was a criminal mistake on the part of the North, and that the humiliation which the South suffered during Reconstruction could never be forgotten. The Union man retorted just as hotly that the South was responsible for the war, and that the spirit of unforgetfulness on its part was the greatest cause of present friction; that it seemed to be the one great aim of the South to convince the North that the latter made a mistake in fighting to preserve the Union and liberate the slaves. "Can you imagine," he went on to say, "what would have been the condition of things eventually if there had been no war, and the South had been allowed to follow its course? Instead of one great, prosperous country with nothing before it but the conquests of peace, a score of petty republics, as in Central and South America, wasting their energies in war with each other or in revolutions."

"Well," replied the Texan, "anything—no country at all—is better than having niggers over you. But anyhow, the war was fought and the niggers freed; for it's no use beating around the bush, the niggers, and not the Union, was the cause of it; and now do you believe that all the niggers on earth are worth the good white blood that was spilt? You freed the nigger and you gave him the ballot, but you couldn't make a citizen out of him. He don't know what he's voting for, and we buy 'em like so many hogs. You're giving 'em education, but that only makes slick rascals out of 'em."

"Don't fancy for a moment," said the Northern man, "that you have any monopoly in buying ignorant votes. The same thing is done on a larger scale in New York and Boston, and in Chicago and San Francisco; and they are not black votes either. As to education making the Negro worse, you had just as well tell me that religion does the same thing. And, by the way, how many educated colored men do you know personally?"

The Texan admitted that he knew only one, and added that he was in the penitentiary. "But," he said, "do you mean to claim, ballot or no ballot, education or no education, that niggers are the equals of white men?"

"That's not the question," answered the other, "but if the Negro is so distinctly inferior, it is a strange thing to me that it takes such a tremendous effort on the part of the white man to make him realize it, and to keep him in the same place into which inferior men naturally fall. However, let us grant for sake of argument that the Negro is inferior in every respect to the white man; that fact only increases our moral responsibility in regard to our actions toward him. Inequalities of numbers, wealth and power, even of intelligence and morals, should make no difference in the essential rights of men."

"If he's inferior and weaker, and is shoved to the wall, that's his own look out," said the Texan. "That's the law of nature; and he's bound to go to the wall; for no race in the world has ever been able to stand competition with the Anglo-Saxon. The Anglo-Saxon race has always been and always will be the masters of the world, and the niggers in the South ain't going to change all the records of history."

"My friend," said the old soldier slowly, "if you have studied history, will you tell me, as confidentially between white men, what the Anglo-Saxon has ever done?"

The Texan was too much astonished by the question to venture any reply.

His opponent continued, "Can you name a single one of the great fundamental and original intellectual achievements which have raised man in the scale of civilization that may be credited to the Anglo-Saxon? The art of letters, of poetry, of music, of sculpture, of painting, of the drama, of architecture; the science of mathematics, of astronomy, of philosophy, of logic, of physics, of chemistry, the use of the metals and the principles of mechanics, were all invented or discovered by darker and what we now call inferior races and nations. We have carried many of these to their highest point of perfection, but the foundation was laid by others. Do you know the only original contribution to civilization we can claim is what we have done in steam and electricity and in making implements of war more deadly; and there we worked largely on principles which we did not discover. Why, we didn't even originate the religion we use. We are a great race, the greatest in the world to-day, but we ought to remember that we are standing on a pile of past races, and enjoy our position with a little less show of arrogance. We are simply having our turn at the game, and we were a long time getting to it. After all, racial supremacy is merely a matter of dates in history. The man here who belongs to what is, all in all, the greatest race the world ever produced, is almost ashamed to own it. If the Anglo-Saxon is the source of everything good and great in the human race from the beginning, why wasn't the German forest the birthplace of civilization?"

The Texan was somewhat disconcerted, for the argument had passed a little beyond his limits, but he swung it back to where he was sure of his ground by saying, "All that may be true, but it hasn't got much to do with us and the niggers here in the South. We've got 'em here, and we've got 'em to live with, and it's a question of white man and nigger, no middle ground. You want us to treat niggers as equals. Do you want to see 'em sitting around in our parlors? Do you want to see a mulatto South? To bring it right home to you, would you let your daughter marry a nigger?"

"No, I wouldn't consent to my daughter's marrying a nigger, but that doesn't prevent my treating a black man fairly. And I don't see what fair treatment has to do with niggers sitting around in your parlors; they can't come there unless they're invited. Out of all the white men I know, only a hundred or so have the privilege of sitting around in my parlor. As to the mulatto South, if you Southerners have one boast that is stronger than another, it is your women; you put them on a pinnacle of purity and virtue and bow down in a chivalric worship before them; yet you talk and act as though, should you treat the Negro fairly and take the anti-intermarriage laws off your statute books, these same women would rush into the arms of black lovers and husbands. It's a wonder to me that they don't rise up and resent the insult."

"Colonel," said the Texan, as he reached into his handbag and brought out a large flask of whiskey, "you might argue from now until hell freezes over, and you might convince me that you're right, but you'll never convince me that I'm wrong. All you say sounds very good, but it's got nothing to do with facts. You can say what men ought to be, but they ain't that; so there you are. Down here in the South we're up against facts, and we're meeting 'em like facts. We don't believe the nigger is or ever will be the equal of the white man, and we ain't going to treat him as an equal; I'll be damned if we will. Have a drink." Everybody, except the professor, partook of the generous Texan's flask, and the argument closed in a general laugh and good feeling.

I went back into the main part of the car with the conversation on my mind. Here I had before me the bald, raw, naked aspects of the race question in the South; and, in consideration of the step I was just taking, it was far from encouraging. The sentiments of the Texan—and he expressed the sentiments of the South—fell upon me like a chill. I was sick at heart. Yet, I must confess that underneath it all I felt a certain sort of admiration for the man who could not be swayed from what he held as his principles. Contrasted with him, the young Ohio professor was indeed a pitiable character. And all along, in spite of myself, I have been compelled to accord the same kind of admiration to the Southern white man for the manner in which he defends not only his virtues but his vices. He knows, that judged by a higher standard, he is narrow and prejudiced, that he is guilty of unfairness, oppression and cruelty, but this he defends as stoutly as he would his better qualities. This same spirit obtains in a great degree among the blacks; they, too, defend their faults and failings. This spirit carries them so far at times as to make them sympathizers with members of their own race who are perpetrators of crime. And, yet, among themselves they are their own merciless critics. I have never heard the race so terribly arraigned as I have by colored speakers to strictly colored audiences. It is the spirit of the South to defend everything belonging to it. The North is too cosmopolitan and tolerant for such a spirit. If you should say to an Easterner that Paris is a gayer city than New York he would likely to agree with you, or at least to let you have your own way; but to suggest to a South Carolinian that Boston is a

nicer city to live in than Charleston would be to stir his greatest depths of argument and eloquence.

But to-day, as I think over that smoking-car argument, I can
see it in a different light. The Texan's position does not render
things so hopeless, for it indicates that the main difficulty of
the race question does not lie so much in the actual condition
of the blacks as it does in the mental attitude of the whites; and
a mental attitude, especially one not based on truth, can be
changed more easily than actual conditions. That is to say, the
burden of the question is not that the whites are struggling to
save ten million despondent and moribund people from sinking into a hopeless slough of ignorance, poverty and barbarity
in their very midst, but that they are unwilling to open certain
doors of opportunity and to accord certain treatment to ten
million aspiring, education-and-property-acquiring people. In
a word, the difficulty of the problem is not so much due to the
facts presented, as to the hypothesis assumed for its solution.
In this it is similar to the problem of the Solar System. By a
complex, confusing and almost contradictory mathematical
process, by the use of zigzags instead of straight lines, the
earth can be proved to be the center of things celestial; but by
an operation so simple that it can be comprehended by a
schoolboy, its position can be verified among the other worlds
which revolve about the sun, and its movements harmonized
with the laws of the universe. So, when the white race assumes
as a hypothesis that it is the main object of creation, and that
all things else are merely subsidiary to its well being, sophism,
subterfuge, pervasion of conscience, arrogance, injustice, oppression, cruelty, sacrifice of human blood, all are required to
maintain the position, and its dealings with other races become indeed a problem, a problem which, if based on a hypothesis of common humanity, could be solved by the simple
rules of justice.

When I reached Macon, I decided to leave my trunk and all
my surplus belongings, to pack my bag, and strike out into the
interior. This I did; and by train, by mule and ox-cart, I traveled through many counties. This was my first real experience
among rural colored people, and all that I saw was interesting
to me; but there was a great deal which does not require de-

scription at my hands; for log cabins and plantations and dialect-speaking darkies are perhaps better known in American literature than any other single picture of our national life. Indeed, they form an ideal and exclusive literary concept of the American Negro to such an extent that it is almost impossible to get the reading public to recognize him in any other setting; but I shall endeavor to avoid giving the reader any already overworked and hackneyed descriptions. This generally accepted literary ideal of the American Negro constitutes what is really an obstacle in the way of the thoughtful and progressive element of the race. His character has been established as a happy-go-lucky, laughing, shuffling, banjo-picking being, and the reading public has not yet been prevailed upon to take him seriously. His efforts to elevate himself socially are looked upon as a sort of absurd caricature of "white civilization." A novel dealing with colored people who lived in respectable homes and amidst a fair degree of culture and who naturally acted "just like white folks" would be taken in a comic opera sense. In this respect the Negro is much in the position of a great comedian who gives up the lighter rôles to play tragedy. No matter how well he may portray the deeper passions, the public is loth to give him up in his old character; they even conspire to make him a failure in serious work, in order to force him back into comedy. In the same respect, the public is not too much to be blamed, for great comedians are far more scarce than mediocre tragedians; every amateur actor is a tragedian. However, this very fact constitutes the opportunity of the future Negro novelist and poet to give the country something new and unknown in depicting the life, the ambitions, the struggling, and the passions of those of their race who are striving to break the narrow limits of traditions. A beginning has already been made in that remarkable book by Dr. Du Bois, "The Souls of Black Folks."

Much, too, that I saw while on this trip, in spite of my enthusiasm, was disheartening. Often I thought of what my "millionaire" had said to me, and wished myself back in Europe. The houses in which I had to stay were generally uncomfortable, sometimes worse. I often had to sleep in a division or compartment with several other people. Once or twice I was not so fortunate as to find divisions; everybody slept on pallets on the floor. Frequently I was able to lie down and contemplate the stars which were in their zenith. The food was at times so distasteful and poorly cooked that I could not eat it. I remember that once I lived for a week or more on buttermilk, on account of not being able to stomach fat bacon, the rank turnip tops and the heavy damp mixture of meal, salt and water which was called corn bread. It was only my ambition to do the work which I had planned that kept me steadfast to my purpose. Occasionally I would meet with some signs of progress and uplift in even one of these backwoods settlements—houses built of boards, with windows, and divided into rooms, decent food and a fair standard of living. This condition was due to the fact that there was in the community some exceptionally capable Negro farmer whose thrift served as an example. As I went about among these dull, simple people, the great majority of them hard working; in their relations with the whites, submissive, faithful, and often affectionate, negatively content with their lot, and contrasted them with those of the race who had been quickened by the forces of thought, I could not but appreciate the logic of the position held by those Southern leaders who have been bold enough to proclaim against the education of the Negro. They are consistent in their public speech with Southern sentiment and desires. Those public men of the South who have not been daring and heedless enough to defy the ideals of twentieth century civilization and of modern humanitarianism and philanthropy, find themselves in the embarrassing situation of preaching one thing and praying for another. They are in the position of the fashionable woman who is compelled by the laws of polite society to say to her dearest enemy, "How happy I am to see you!"

And yet in this respect how perplexing is Southern character; for in opposition to the above, it may be said that the claim of the Southern whites that they love the Negro better than the Northern whites do, is in a manner true. Northern white people love the Negro in a sort of abstract way, as a race; through a sense of justice, charity and philanthropy, they will liberally assist in his elevation. A number of them have heroically spent their lives in this effort (and just here I wish to say that when the colored people reach the monument building stage, they should not forget the men and women who went South after the war and founded schools for them). Yet, generally speaking, they have no particular liking for individuals of the race. Southern white people despise the Negro as a race, and will do nothing to aid in his elevation as such; but for certain individuals they have a strong affection, and are helpful to them in many ways. With these individual members of the race they live on terms of the greatest intimacy; they intrust to them their children, their family treasures and their family secrets; in trouble they often go to them for comfort and counsel; in sickness they often rely upon their care. This affectionate relation between the Southern whites and those blacks who came into close touch with them has not been overdrawn even in fiction.

This perplexity of Southern character extends even to the mixture of the races. That is spoken of as though it were dreaded worse than smallpox, leprosy or the plague. Yet, when I was in Jacksonville, I knew several prominent families there with large colored branches, which went by the same name and were known and acknowledged as blood relatives. And what is more, there seemed to exist between these black brothers and sisters and uncles and aunts a decided friendly feeling.

I said above that Southern whites would do nothing for the Negro as a race. I know the South claims that it has spent millions for the education of the blacks, and that it has of its own free will shouldered this awful burden. It seems to be forgetful of the fact that these millions have been taken from the public tax funds for education, and that the law of political economy which recognizes the land owner as the one who really pays the taxes is not tenable. It would be just as reasonable for the relatively few land-owners of Manhattan to complain that they had to stand the financial burden of the education of the thousands and thousands of children whose parents pay rent for tenements and flats. Let the millions of producing and consuming Negroes be taken out of the South, and it would be quickly seen how much less of public funds there would be to appropriate for education or any other purpose.

In thus traveling about through the country, I was sometimes amused on arriving at some little railroad-station town to be taken for and treated as a white man, and six hours later, when it was learned that I was stopping at the house of the colored preacher or school teacher, to note the attitude of the whole town to change. At times this led even to embarrassment. Yet it cannot be so embarrassing for a colored man to be taken for white as for a white man to be taken for colored; and I have heard of several cases of the latter kind.

All this while I was gathering material for work, jotting down in my note-book themes and melodies, and trying to catch the spirit of the Negro in his relatively primitive state. I began to feel the necessity of hurrying so that I might get back to some city like Nashville to begin my compositions, and at the same time earn at least a living by teaching and performing before my funds gave out. At the last settlement in which I stopped I found a mine of material. This was due to the fact that "big meeting" was in progress. "Big meeting" is an institution something like camp-meeting; the difference being that it is held in a permanent church, and not in a temporary structure. All the churches of some one denomination—of course, either Methodist or Baptist—in a county or, perhaps, in several adjoining counties, are closed, and the congregations unite at some centrally located church for a series of meetings lasting a week. It is really a social as well as a religious function. The people come in great numbers, making the trip, according to their financial status, in buggies drawn by sleek, fleet-footed mules, in ox-teams, or on foot. It was amusing to see some of the latter class trudging down the hot and dusty road with their shoes, which were brand new, strung across their shoulders. When they got near the church they sat on the side of the road and, with many grimaces, tenderly packed their feet into those instruments of torture. This furnished, indeed, a trying test of their religion. The famous preachers come from near and far, and take turns in warning sinners of the day of wrath. Food, in the form of these two Southern luxuries, fried chicken and roast pork, is plentiful, and no one need go hungry. On the opening Sunday the women are immaculate in starched stiff white dresses adorned with ribbons either red or blue. Even a great many of the men wear streamers of vari-colored ribbons in the button-holes of their coats. A few of them carefully cultivate a fore lock of hair by wrapping it in twine, and on such festive occasions decorate it with a narrow ribbon streamer. Big meetings afford a fine opportunity to the younger people to meet each other dressed in their Sunday clothes, and much rustic courting, which is as enjoyable as any other kind, is indulged in.

This big meeting which I was lucky enough to catch was particularly well attended; the extra large attendance was due principally to two attractions, a man by the name of John Brown, who was renowned as the most powerful preacher for miles around; and a wonderful leader of singing, who was known as "Singing Johnson." These two men were a study and a revelation to me. They caused me to reflect upon how great an influence their types have been in the development of the Negro in America. Both these types are now looked upon generally with condescension or contempt by the progressive element among the colored people; but it should never be forgotten that it was they who led the race from paganism, and kept it steadfast to Christianity through all the long, dark years of slavery.

John Brown was a jet black man of medium size, with a strikingly intelligent head and face, and a voice like an organ peal. He preached each night after several lesser lights successively held the pulpit during an hour or so. As far as subject matter is concerned, all of the sermons were alike; each began with the fall of man, ran through various trials and tribulations of the Hebrew children, on to the redemption by Christ, and ended with a fervid picture of the judgment day and the fate of the damned. But John Brown possessed magnetism and an imagination so free and daring that he was able to carry through what the other preachers would not attempt. He knew all the arts and tricks of oratory, the modulation of the voice to almost a whisper, the pause for effect, the rise through light, rapid fire sentences to the terrific, thundering outburst of an electrifying climax. In addition, he had the intuition of a born theatrical manager. Night after night this man held me fascinated. He convinced me that, after all, eloquence consists more in the manner of saying than in what is said. It is largely a matter of tone pictures.

The most striking example of John Brown's magnetism and imagination was his "heavenly march"; I shall never forget how it impressed me when I heard it. He opened his sermon in the usual way; then proclaiming to his listeners that he was going to take them on the heavenly march, he seized the Bible

under his arm and began to pace up and down the pulpit platform. The congregation immediately began with their feet a
tramp, tramp, tramp, in time with the preacher's march in the
pulpit, all the while singing in an undertone a hymn about
marching to Zion. Suddenly he cried, "Halt!" Every foot
stopped with the precision of a company of well drilled soldiers, and the singing ceased. The morning star had been
reached. Here the preacher described the beauties of that celestial body. Then the march, the tramp, tramp, tramp, and the
singing was again taken up. Another "Halt!" They had
reached the evening star. And so on, past the sun and the
moon—the intensity of religious emotion all the time increasing—along the milky way, on up to the gates of heaven. Here
the halt was longer, and the preacher described at length the
gates and walls of the New Jerusalem. Then he took his hearers through the pearly gates, along the golden streets, pointing
out the glories of the City, pausing occasionally to greet some
patriarchal members of the church, well known to most of his
listeners in life, who had had "the tears wiped from their eyes,
were clad in robes of spotless white, with crowns of gold upon
their heads and harps within their hands," and ended his march
before the great white throne. To the reader this may sound
ridiculous, but listened to under the circumstances, it was
highly and effectively dramatic. I was a more or less sophisticated and non-religious man of the world, but the torrent of
the preacher's words, moving with the rhythm and glowing
with the eloquence of primitive poetry swept me along, and I,
too, felt like joining in the shouts of "Amen! Halleujah!"

John Brown's powers in describing the delights of heaven
were no greater than those in depicting the horrors of hell. I
saw great, strapping fellows, trembling and weeping like children at the "mourners' bench." His warnings to sinners were
truly terrible. I shall never forget one expression that he used,
which for originality and aptness could not be excelled. In my
opinion, it is more graphic and, for us, far more expressive
than St. Paul's "It is hard to kick against the pricks." He struck
the attitude of a pugilist and thundered out, "Young man yo'
arm's too short to box wid God!"

As interesting as was John Brown to me, the other man,
"Singing Johnson," was more so. He was a small, dark-brown,

one-eyed man, with a clear, strong, high-pitched voice, a leader of singing, a maker of songs, a man who could improvise at the moment lines to fit the occasion. Not so striking a figure as John Brown, but, at "big meetings," equally important. It is indispensable to the success of the singing, when the congregation is a large one made up of people from different communities, to have someone with a strong voice who knows just what hymn to sing and when to sing it, who can pitch it in the right key, and who has all the leading lines committed to memory. Sometimes it devolves upon the leader to "sing down" a long-winded or uninteresting speaker. Committing to memory the leading lines of all the Negro spiritual songs is no easy task, for they run up into the hundreds. But the accomplished leader must know them all, because the congregation sings only the refrains and repeats; every ear in the church is fixed upon him, and if he becomes mixed in his lines or forgets them, the responsibility falls directly on his shoulders.

For example, most of these hymns are constructed to be sung in the following manner:

Leader—   "Swing low, sweet chariot."
Congregation—   "Coming for to carry me home."
Leader—   "Swing low, sweet chariot."
Congregation—   "Coming for to carry me home."
Leader—   "I look over yonder, what do I see?"
Congregation — "Coming for to carry me home."
Leader—   "Two little angels coming after me."
Congregation—   "Coming for to carry me home."
     —   etc., etc., etc.

The solitary and plaintive voice of the leader is answered by a sound like the roll of the sea, producing a most curious effect.

In only a few of these songs do the leader and the congregation start off together. Such a song is the well known "Steal away to Jesus."

The leader and the congregation begin:

> "Steal away, steal away,
> Steal away to Jesus;
> Steal away, steal away home,
> I ain't got long to stay here."

Then the leader alone:

> "My Lord he calls me,
>   He calls me by the thunder,
>   The trumpet sounds within-a my soul."

Then all together:

> "I ain't got long to stay here."

The leader and the congregation again take up the opening refrain; then the leader sings three more leading lines alone, and so on almost ad infinitum. It will be seen that even here most of the work falls upon the leader, for the congregation sings the same lines over and over, while his memory and ingenuity are taxed to keep the songs going.

Generally the parts taken up by the congregation are sung in a three-part harmony, the women singing the soprano and a transposed tenor, the men with high voices singing the melody, and those with low voices, a thundering bass. In a few of these songs, however, the leading part is sung in unison by the whole congregation, down to the last line, which is harmonized. The effect of this is intensely thrilling. Such a hymn is "Go down Moses." It stirs the heart like a trumpet call.

"Singing Johnson" was an ideal leader; and his services were in great demand. He spent his time going about the country from one church to another. He received his support in much the same way as the preachers,—part of a collection, food and lodging. All of his leisure time he devoted to originating new words and melodies and new lines for old songs. He always sang with his eyes,—or to be more exact—his eye closed, indicating the tempo by swinging his head to and fro. He was a great judge of the proper hymn to sing at a particular moment; and I noticed several times, when the preacher reached a certain climax, or expressed a certain sentiment, that Johnson broke in with a line or two of some appropriate hymn. The speaker understood, and would pause until the singing ceased.

As I listened to the singing of these songs, the wonder of their production grew upon me more and more. How did the men who originated them manage to do it? The sentiments are easily accounted for; they are mostly taken from the Bible; but the melodies, where did they come from? Some of them so weirdly sweet, and others so wonderfully strong. Take, for instance, "Go down Moses." I doubt that there is a stronger theme in the whole musical literature of the world. And so many of these songs contain more than mere melody; there is sounded in them that elusive undertone, the note in music which is not heard with the ears. I sat often with the tears rolling down my cheeks and my heart melted within me. Any musical person who has never heard a Negro congregation under the spell of religious fervor sing these old songs, has missed one of the most thrilling emotions which the human heart may experience. Anyone who can listen to Negroes sing, "Nobody knows de trouble I see, Nobody knows but Jesus," without shedding tears, must indeed have a heart of stone.

As yet, the Negroes themselves do not fully appreciate these old slave songs. The educated classes are rather ashamed of them, and prefer to sing hymns from books. This feeling is natural; they are still too close to the conditions under which the songs were produced; but the day will come when this slave music will be the most treasured heritage of the American Negro.

At the close of the "big meeting" I left the settlement where it was being held, full of enthusiasm. I was in that frame of mind which, in the artistic temperament, amounts to inspiration. I was now ready and anxious to get to some place where I might settle down to work, and give expression the ideas which were teeming in my head; but I strayed into another deviation from my path of life as I had it marked out, which led me into an entirely different road. Instead of going to the nearest and most convenient railroad station, I accepted the invitation of a young man who had been present the closing Sunday at the meeting, to drive with him some miles farther to the town in which he taught school, and there take a train. My conversation with this young man as we drove along through the country was extremely interesting. He had been a student in one of the Negro colleges,—strange coincidence, in the very college, as I learned through him, in which "Shiny" was now a professor. I was, of course, curious to hear about my boyhood friend; and had it not been vacation time, and that I was not sure that I would find him, I should have gone out of my way to pay him a visit; but I determined to write to him as soon as the school opened. My companion talked to me about his work among the people, of his hopes and his discouragements. He was tremendously in earnest; I might say, too much so. In fact, it may be said that the majority of intelligent colored people are, in some degree, too much in earnest over the race question. They assume and carry so much that their progress is at times impeded, and they are unable to see things in their proper proportions. In many instances, a slight exercise of the sense of humor would save much anxiety of soul. Anyone who marks the general tone of editorials in colored newspapers is apt to be impressed with this idea. If the mass of Negroes took their present and future as seriously as do the most of their leaders, the race would be in no mental condition to sustain the terrible pressure which it undergoes; it would sink of its own weight. Yet, it must be acknowledged that in the making of a race over-seriousness is a far lesser failing than its reverse, and even the faults resulting from it lean toward the right.

We drove into the town just before dark. As we passed a large, unpainted church, my companion pointed it out as the place where he held his school. I promised that I would go there with him the next morning and stay a while. The town was of that kind which hardly requires or deserves description; a straggling line of brick and wooden stores on one side of the railroad track and some cottages of various sizes on the other side constituted about the whole of it. The young school teacher boarded at the best house in the place owned by a colored man. It was painted, had glass windows, contained "store bought" furniture, an organ, and lamps with chimneys. The owner held a job of some kind on the railroad. After supper it was not long before everybody was sleepy. I occupied the room with the school teacher. In a few minutes after we got into the room he was in bed and asleep; but I took advantage of the unusual luxury of a lamp which gave light, and sat looking over my notes and jotting down some ideas which were still fresh in my mind. Suddenly I became conscious of that sense of alarm which is always aroused by the sound of hurrying footsteps on the silence of the night. I stopped work, and looked at my watch. It was after eleven. I listened, straining every nerve to hear above the tumult of my quickening pulse.

I caught the murmur of voices, then the gallop of a horse, then of another and another. Now thoroughly alarmed, I woke my companion, and together we both listened. After a moment he put out the light, softly opened the window-blind, and we cautiously peeped out. We saw men moving in one direction, and from the mutterings we vaguely caught the rumor that some terrible crime had been committed, murder! rape! I put on my coat and hat. My friend did all in his power to dissuade me from venturing out; but it was impossible for me to remain in the house under such tense excitement. My nerves would not have stood it. Perhaps what bravery I exercised in going out was due to the fact that I felt sure my identity as a colored man had not yet become known in the town.

I went out and, following the drift, reached the railroad station. There was gathered there a crowd of men, all white, and others steadily arriving, seemingly from all the surrounding country. How did the news spread so quickly? I watched these men moving under the yellow glare of the kerosene lamps about the station, stern, comparatively silent, all of them armed, some of them in boots and spurs; fierce, determined men. I had come to know the type well, blond, tall and lean, with ragged mustache and beard, and glittering gray eyes. At the first suggestion of daylight they began to disperse in groups, going in several directions. There was no extra noise or excitement, no loud talking, only swift, sharp words of command given by those who seemed to be accepted as leaders by mutual understanding. In fact, the impression made upon me was that everything was being done in quite an orderly manner. In spite of so many leaving, the crowd around the station continued to grow; at sunrise there were a great many women and children. By the time I also noticed some colored people; a few seemed to be going about customary tasks, several were standing on the outskirts of the crowd; but the gathering of Negroes usually seen in such towns was missing.

Before noon they brought him in. Two horsemen rode abreast; between them, half dragged, the poor wretch made his way through the dust. His hands were tied behind him, and ropes around his body were fastened to the saddle horns of his double guard. The men who at midnight had been stern and silent were now emitting that terror instilling sound known as the "rebel yell." A space was quickly cleared in the crowd, and a rope placed about his neck; when from somewhere came the suggestion, "Burn him!" It ran like an electric current. Have you ever witnessed the transformation of human beings into savage beasts? Nothing can be more terrible. A railroad tie was sunk into the ground, the rope was removed and a chain brought and securely coiled around the victim and the stake. There he stood, a man only in form and stature, every sign of degeneracy stamped upon his countenance. His eyes were dull and vacant, indicating not a single ray of thought. Evidently the realization of his fearful fate had robbed him of whatever reasoning power he had ever possessed. He was too stunned and stupefied even to tremble. Fuel was brought from everywhere, oil, the torch; the flames crouched for an instant as though to gather strength, then leaped up as high as their victim's head. He squirmed, he writhed, strained at his chains, then gave out cries and groans that I shall always hear. The cries and groans were choked off by the fire and smoke; but his eyes bulging from their sockets, rolled from side to side, appealing in vain for help. Some of the crowd yelled and cheered, others seemed appalled at what they had done, and there were those who turned away sickened at the sight. I was fixed to the spot where I stood, powerless to take my eyes from what I did not want to see.

It was over before I realized that time had elapsed. Before I could make myself believe that what I saw was really happening, I was looking at a scorched post, a smoldering fire, blackened bones, charred fragments sifting down through coils of chain, and the smell of burnt flesh—human flesh—was in my nostrils.

I walked a short distance away, and sat down in order to clear my dazed mind. A great wave of humiliation and shame swept over me. Shame that I belonged to a race that could be so dealt with; and shame for my country, that it, the great example of democracy to the world, should be the only civilized, if not the only state on earth, where a human being would be burned alive. My heart turned bitter within me. I could understand why Negroes are led to sympathize with even their worst criminals, and to protect them when possible. By all the impulses of normal human nature they can and should do nothing less.

Whenever I hear protests from the South that it should be left alone to deal with the Negro question, my thoughts go back to that scene of brutality and savagery. I do not see how a people that can find in its conscience any excuse whatever for slowly burning to death a human being, or to tolerate such an act, can be entrusted with the salvation of a race. Of course, there are in the South men of liberal thought who do not approve lynching; but I wonder how long they will endure the limits which are placed upon free speech. They still cower and tremble before "Southern opinion." Even so late as the recent Atlanta riot those men who were brave enough to speak a word in behalf of justice and humanity felt called upon, by way of apology, to preface what they said with a glowing rhetorical tribute to the Anglo-Saxon's superiority, and to refer to the "great and impassable gulf" between the races "fixed by the Creator at the foundation of the world." The question of the relative qualities of the two races is still an open one. The reference to the "great gulf" loses force in face of the fact that there are in this country perhaps three or four million people with the blood of both races in their veins; but I fail to see the pertinency of either statement, subsequent to the beating and murdering of scores of innocent people in the streets of a civilized and Christian city.

The Southern whites are in many respects a great people. Looked at from a certain point of view, they are picturesque. If one will put oneself in a romantic frame of mind, he can admire their notions of chivalry and bravery and justice. In this same frame of mind an intelligent man can go to the theater and applaud the impossible hero, who with his single sword slays everybody in the play except the equally impossible heroine. So can an ordinary peace-loving citizen sit by a comfortable fire and read with enjoyment of the bloody deeds of pirates and the fierce brutality of Vikings. This is the way in which we gratify the old, underlying animal instincts and passions; but we should shudder with horror at the mere idea of such practices being realities in this day of enlightened and humanitarianized thought. The Southern whites are not yet living quite in the present age; many of their general ideas hark back to a former century, some of them to the Dark Ages. In the light of other days, they are sometimes magnificent. To-day they are often ludicrous and cruel.

How long I sat with bitter thoughts running through my mind, I do not know; perhaps an hour or more. When I decided to get up and go back to the house I found that I could hardly stand on my feet. I was as weak as a man who had lost blood. However, I dragged myself along, with the central idea of a general plan well fixed in my mind. I did not find my school teacher friend at home, so did not see him again. I swallowed a few mouthfuls of food, packed my bag, and caught the afternoon train.

When I reached Macon, I stopped only long enough to get the main part of my luggage, and to buy a ticket for New York. All along the journey I was occupied in debating with myself the step which I had decided to take. I argued that to forsake one's race to better one's condition was no less worthy an action than to forsake one's country for the same purpose. I finally made up my mind that I would neither disclaim the black race nor claim the white race; but that I would change my name, raise a mustache, and let the world take me for what it would; that it was not necessary for me to go about with a label of inferiority pasted across my forehead. All the while, I understood that it was not discouragement, or fear, or search for a larger field of action and opportunity that was driving me out of the Negro race. I knew that it was shame, unbearable shame. Shame at being identified with a people that could with impunity be treated worse than animals. For certainly the law would restrain and punish the malicious burning alive of animals.

So once again, I found myself gazing at the towers of New York, and wondering what future that city held in store for me.

Chapter XI

I HAVE now reached that part of my narrative where I must be brief, and touch only on important facts; therefore, the reader must make up his mind to pardon skips and jumps and meager details.

When I reached New York I was completely lost. I could not have felt more a stranger had I been suddenly dropped into Constantinople. I knew not where to turn or how to strike out. I was so oppressed by a feeling of loneliness that the temptation to visit my old home in Connecticut was well nigh irresistible. I reasoned, however, that unless I found my old music teacher, I should be, after so many years of absence, as much of a stranger there as in New York; and, furthermore, that in view of the step which I had decided to take, such a visit would be injudicious. I remembered, too, that I had some property there in the shape of a piano and a few books, but decided that it would not be worth what it might cost me to take possession.

By reason of the fact that my living expenses in the South had been very small, I still had nearly four hundred dollars of my capital left. In contemplation of this, my natural and acquired Bohemian tastes asserted themselves, and I decided to have a couple of weeks' good time before worrying seriously about my future. I went to Coney Island and the other resorts, took in the pre-season shows along Broadway, and ate at first class restaurants; but I shunned the old Sixth Avenue district as though it were pest infected. My few days of pleasure made appalling inroads upon what cash I had, and caused me to see that it required a good deal of money to live in New York as I wished to live, and that I should have to find, very soon, some more or less profitable employment. I was sure that unknown, without friends or prestige, it would be useless to try to establish myself as a teacher of music; so I gave that means of earning a livelihood scarcely any consideration. And even had I considered it possible to secure pupils, as I then felt, I should have hesitated about taking up a work in which the chances for any considerable financial success are necessarily so small. I had made up my mind that since I was not going to be a Negro, I would avail myself of every possible opportunity to make a white man's success; and that, if it can be summed up in any one word, means "money."

I watched the "want" columns in the newspapers and answered a number of advertisements; but in each case found the positions were such as I could not fill or did not want. I also spent several dollars for "ads" which brought me no replies. In this way I came to know the hopes and disappointments of a large and pitiable class of humanity in this great city, the people who look for work through the newspapers. After some days of this sort of experience, I concluded that the main difficulty with me was that I was not prepared for what I wanted to do. I then decided upon a course which, for an artist, showed an uncommon amount of practical sense and judgment. I made up my mind to enter a business college. I took a small room, ate at lunch counters, in order to economize, and pursued my studies with the zeal that I have always been able to put into any work upon which I set my heart. Yet, in spite of all my economy, when I had been at the school for several months, my funds gave out completely. I reached the point where I could not afford sufficient food for each day. In this plight I was glad to get, through one of the teachers, a job as an ordinary clerk in a downtown wholesale house. I did my work faithfully, and received a raise of salary before I expected it. I even managed to save a little money out of my modest earnings. In fact, I began then to contract the money fever, which later took strong possession of me. I kept my eyes open, watching for a chance to better my condition. It finally came in the form of a position with a house which was at the time establishing a South American department. My knowledge of Spanish was, of course, the principal cause of my good luck; and it did more for me; it placed me where the other clerks were practically put out of competition with me. I was not slow in taking advantage of the opportunity to make myself indispensable to the firm.

What an interesting and absorbing game is money making! After each deposit at my savings-bank, I used to sit and figure out, all over again, my principal and interest, and make calculations on what the increase would be in such and such a time.

Out of this I derived a great deal of pleasure. I denied myself as much as possible in order to swell my savings. Even so much as I enjoyed smoking, I limited myself to an occasional cigar, and that was generally of a variety which in my old days at the "Club" was known as a "Henry Mud." Drinking I cut out altogether, but that was no great sacrifice.

The day on which I was able to figure up $1,000.00 marked an epoch in my life. And this was not because I had never before had money. In my gambling days and while I was with my "millionaire" I handled sums running high up into the hundreds; but they had come to me like fairy god-mother's gifts, and at a time when my conception of money was that it was made only to spend. Here, on the other hand, was a thousand dollars which I had earned by days of honest and patient work, a thousand dollars which I had carefully watched grow from the first dollar; and I experienced, in owning them, a pride and satisfaction which to me was an entirely new sensation. As my capital went over the thousand dollar mark, I was puzzled to know what to do with it, how to put it to the most advantageous use. I turned down first one scheme and then another, as though they had been devised for the sole purpose of gobbling up my money. I finally listened to a friend who advised me to put all I had in New York real estate; and under his guidance I took equity in a piece of property on which stood a rickety tenement-house. I did not regret following this friend's advice, for in something like six months I disposed my equity for more than double my investment. From that time on I devoted myself to the study of New York real estate, and watched for opportunities to make similar investments. In spite of two or three speculations which did not turn out well, I have been remarkably successful. To-day I am the owner and part-owner of several flat-houses. I have changed my place of employment four times since returning to New York, and each change has been a decided advancement. Concerning the position which I now hold, I shall say nothing except that it pays extremely well.

As my outlook on the world grew brighter, I began to mingle in the social circles of the men with whom I came in contact; and gradually, by a process of elimination, I reached a grade of society of no small degree of culture. My appearance was always good and my ability to play on the piano, especially ragtime, which was then at the height of its vogue, made me a welcome guest. The anomaly of my social position often appealed strongly to my sense of humor. I frequently smiled inwardly at some remark not altogether complimentary to people of color; and more than once I felt like declaiming, "I am a colored man. Do I not disprove the theory that one drop of Negro blood renders a man unfit?" Many a night when I returned to my room after an enjoyable evening, I laughed heartily over what struck me as the capital joke I was playing.

Then I met her, and what I had regarded as a joke was gradually changed into the most serious question of my life. I first saw her at a musical which was given one evening at a house to which I was frequently invited. I did not notice her among the other guests before she came forward and sang two sad little songs. When she began I was out in the hall way where many of the men were gathered; but with the first few notes I crowded with others into the doorway to see who the singer was. When I saw the girl, the surprise which I had felt at the first sound of her voice was heightened; she was almost tall and quite slender, with lustrous yellow hair and eyes so blue as to appear almost black. She was as white as a lily, and she was dressed in white. Indeed, she seemed to me the most dazzlingly white thing I had ever seen. But it was not her delicate beauty which attracted me most; it was her voice, a voice which made one wonder how tones of such passionate color could come from so fragile a body.

I determined that when the program was over, I would seek an introduction to her; but at the moment, instead of being the easy man of the world, I became again the bashful boy of fourteen, and my courage failed me. I contented myself with hovering as near her as politeness would permit; near enough to hear her voice, which in conversation was low, yet thrilling, like the deeper middle tones of a flute. I watched the men gather around her talking and laughing in an easy manner, and wondered how it was possible for them to do it. But destiny, my special destiny, was at work. I was standing near, talking with affected gayety to several young ladies, who, however, must have remarked my preoccupation; for my second sense of hearing was alert to what was being said by the group of which the girl in white was the center, when I heard her say, "I think his playing of Chopin is exquisite." And one of my friends in the group replied, "You haven't met him? Allow me—" then turning to me, "Old man, when you have a moment I wish you to meet Miss——." I don't know what she said to me or what I said to her. I can remember that I tried to be clever, and experienced a growing conviction that I was making myself appear more and more idiotic. I am certain, too, that, in spite of my Italian-like complexion, I was as red as a beet.

Instead of taking the car I walked home. I needed the air and exercise as a sort of sedative. I am not sure whether my troubled condition of mind was due to the fact that I had been struck by love or to the feeling that I had made a bad impression upon her.

As the weeks went by, and when I had met her several more times, I came to know that I was seriously in love; and then began for me days of worry, for I had more than the usual doubts and fears of a young man in love to contend with.

Up to this time I had assumed and played my rôle as a white man with a certain degree of nonchalance, a carelessness as to the outcome, which made the whole thing more amusing to me than serious; but now I ceased to regard "being a white man" as a sort of practical joke. My acting had called for mere external effects. Now I began to doubt my ability to play the part. I watched her to see if she was scrutinizing me, to see if she was looking for anything in me which made me differ from the other men she knew. In place of an old inward feeling of superiority over many of my friends, I began to doubt myself. I began even to wonder if I really was like the men I associated with; if there was not, after all, an indefinable something which marked a difference.

But, in spite of my doubts and timidity, my affair progressed; and I finally felt sufficiently encouraged to decide to ask her to marry me. Then began the hardest struggle of my life, whether to ask her to marry me under false colors or to tell her the whole truth. My sense of what was exigent made me feel there was no necessity of saying anything; but my inborn sense of honor rebelled at even indirect deception in this case. But however much I moralized on the question, I found it more and more difficult to reach the point of confession. The dread that I might lose her took possession of me each time I sought to speak, and rendered it impossible for me to do so. That moral courage requires more than physical courage is no mere poetic fancy. I am sure I would have found it easier to take the place of a gladiator, no matter how fierce the Numidian lion, than to tell that slender girl that I had Negro blood in my veins. The fact which I had at times wished to cry out, I now wished to hide forever.

During this time we were drawn together a great deal by the mutual bond of music. She loved to hear me play Chopin, and was herself far from being a poor performer of his composition. I think I carried her every new song that was published which I thought suitable to her voice, and played the accompaniment for her. Over these songs we were like two innocent children with new toys. She had never been anything but innocent; but my innocence was a transformation wrought by my love for her, love which melted away my cynicism and whitened my sullied soul and gave me back the wholesome dreams of my boyhood. There is nothing better in all the world that a man can do for his moral welfare than to love a good woman.

My artistic temperament also underwent an awakening. I spent many hours at my piano, playing over old and new composers. I also wrote several little pieces in a more or less Chopinesque style, which I dedicated to her. And so the weeks and months went by. Often words of love trembles on my lips, but I dared not utter them, because I knew they would have to be followed by other words which I had not the courage to frame. There might have been some other woman in my set with whom I could have fallen in love and asked to marry me without a word of explanation; but the more I knew this girl, the less could I find it in my heart to deceive her. And yet, in spite of this specter that was constantly looming up before me, I could never have believed that life held such happiness as was contained in those dream days of love.

One Saturday afternoon, in early June, I was coming up Fifth Avenue, and at the corner of Twenty-third Street I met her. She had been shopping. We stopped to chat for a moment, and I suggested that we spend half an hour at the Eden Musée.

We were standing leaning on the rail in front of a group of figures, more interested in what we had to say to each other than
in the group, when my attention became fixed upon a man
who stood at my side studying his catalogue. It took me only
an instant to recognize in him my old friend "Shiny." My first
impulse was to change my position at once. As quick as a flash
I considered all the risks I might run in speaking with him, and
most especially the delicate question of introducing him to her.
I must confess that in my embarrassment and confusion I felt
small and mean. But before I could decide what to do he
looked around at me and after an instant, quietly asked, "Pardon me; but isn't this—?" the nobler part in me responded
to the sound of his voice, and I took his hand in a hearty clasp.
Whatever fears I had felt were quickly banished, for he seemed,
at a glance, to divine my situation, and let drop no word that
would have aroused suspicion as to the truth. With a slight
misgiving I presented him to her, and was again relieved of
fear. She received introduction in her usual gracious manner, and without the least hesitancy or embarrassment joined
in the conversation. An amusing part about the introduction
was that I was upon the point of introducing him as "Shiny,"
and stammered a second or two before I could recall his name.
We chatted for some fifteen minutes. He was spending his vacation North, with the intention of doing four or six weeks'
work in one of the summer schools; he was also going to take a
bride back with him in the fall. He asked me about myself, but
in so diplomatic a way that I found no difficulty in answering
him. The polish of his language and the unpedantic manner in
which he revealed his culture greatly impressed her; and after
we had left the Musée she showed it by questioning me about
him. I was surprised at the amount of interest a refined black
man could arouse. Even after changes in the conversation she
reverted several times to the subject of "Shiny." Whether it was
more than mere curiosity I could not tell; but I was convinced
that she herself knew very little about prejudice.

Just why it should have done so I do not know, but somehow the "Shiny" incident gave me encouragement and confidence to cast the die of my fate; but I reasoned that since I
wanted to marry her only, and since it concerned her alone, I
would divulge my secret to no one else, not even her parents.

One evening, a few days afterwards, at her home, we were going over some new songs and compositions when she asked me, as she often did, to play the "13th Nocturne." When I began she drew a chair near to my right and sat leaning with her elbow on the end of the piano, her chin resting on her hand, and her eyes reflecting the emotions which the music awoke in her. An impulse which I could not control rushed over me, a wave of exultation, the music under my fingers sank almost to a whisper, and calling her for the first time by her Christian name, but without daring to look at her, I said, "I love you, I love you, I love you." My fingers were trembling, so that I ceased playing. I felt her hand creep to mine, and when I looked at her her eyes were glistening with tears. I understood, and could scarcely resist the longing to take her in my arms; but I remembered, remembered that which has been the sacrificial altar of so much happiness—Duty; and bending over her hand in mine, I said, "Yes, I love you; but there is something more, too, that I must tell you." Then I told her, in what words I do no know, the truth. I felt her hand grow cold, and when I looked up she was gazing at me with a wild, fixed stare as though I was some object she had never see. Under the strange light in her eyes I felt that I was growing black and thick-featured and crimp-haired. She appeared to have comprehended what I said. Her lips trembled and she attempted to say something to me; but the words stuck in her throat. Then dropping her head on the piano she began to weep with great sobs that shook her frail body. I tried to console her, and blurted out incoherent words of love; but this seemed only to increase her distress, and when I left her she was still weeping.

When I got into the street I felt very much as I did the night after meeting my father and sister at the opera in Paris, even a similar desperate inclination to get drunk; but my self-control was stronger. This was the only time in my life that I ever felt absolute regret at being colored, that I cursed the drops of African blood in my veins, and wished that I were really white. When I reached my rooms I sat and smoked several cigars while I tried to think out the significance of what had occurred. I reviewed the whole history of our acquaintance, recalled each smile she had given me, each word she had said to me that nourished my hope. I went over the scene we had just gone through, trying to draw from it what was in my favor and what was against me. I was rewarded by feeling confident that she loved me, but I could not estimate what was the effect upon her of my confession. At last, nervous and unhappy, I wrote her a letter, which I dropped into the mail-box before going to bed, in which I said:

"I understand, understand even better than you, and so I suffer even more than you. But why should either of us suffer for what neither of us is to blame? If there is any blame, it belongs to me, and I can only make the old, yet strongest pleas that can be offered, I love you; and I know that my love, my great love, infinitely overbalances that blame, and blots it out. What is it that stands in the way of our happiness? It is not what you feel or what I feel; it is not what you are or what I am. It is what others feel and are. But, oh! Is that a fair price? In all the endeavors and struggles of life, in all our strivings and longings there is only one thing worth seeking, only one thing worth winning, and that is love. It is not always found; but when it is, there is nothing in all the world for which it can be profitably exchanged."

The second morning after, I received a note from her which stated briefly that she was going up in New Hampshire to spend the summer with relatives there. She made no reference to what had passed between us; nor did she say exactly when she would leave the city. The note contained no single word that gave me any clue to her feelings. I could gather hope only from the fact that she had written at all. On the same evening, with a degree of trepidation which rendered me almost frightened, I went to her house.

I met her mother, who told me that she had left for the country that very afternoon. Her mother treated me in her usual pleasant manner, which fact greatly reassured me; and I left the house with a vague sense of hope stirring in my breast, which sprang from the conviction that she had not yet divulged my secret. But that hope did not remain with me long. I waited one, two, three weeks, nervously examining my mail every day, looking for some word from her. All of the letters received by me seemed so insignificant, so worthless, because there was none from her. The slight buoyancy of spirit which I had felt gradually dissolved into gloomy heart sickness. I became preoccupied, I lost appetite, lost sleep, and lost ambition. Several of my friends intimated to me that perhaps I was working too hard.

She stayed away the whole summer. I did not go to the house, but saw her father at various times, and he was as friendly as ever. Even after I knew that she was back in town I did not go to see her. I determined to wait for some word or sign. I had finally taken refuge and comfort in my pride, pride which, I suppose, I came by naturally enough.

The first time I saw her after her return was one night at the theater. She and her mother sat in company with a young man whom I knew slightly, not many seats away from me. Never did she appear more beautiful; and yet, it may have been my fancy, she seemed a trifle paler and there was a suggestion of haggardness in her countenance. But that only heightened her beauty; the very delicacy of her charm melted down the strength of my pride. My situation made me feel weak and powerless, like a man trying with his bare hands to break the iron bars of his prison cell. When the performance was over I hurried out and placed myself where, unobserved, I could see her as she passed out. The haughtiness of spirit in which I sought relief was all gone, and I was willing and ready to undergo any humiliation.

Shortly afterward we met at a progressive card party, and during the evening we were thrown together at one of the tables as partners. This was really our first meeting since the eventful night at her house. Strangely enough, in spite of our mutual nervousness, we won every trick of the game, and one of our opponents jokingly quoted the old saw, "Lucky at cards, unlucky in love." Our eyes met and I am sure that in the momentary glance my whole soul went out to her in one great pleas. She lowered her eyes and uttered a nervous little laugh. During the rest of the game I fully merited the unexpressed and expressed abuse of my various partners; for my eyes followed her wherever she was, and I played whatever card my fingers happened to touch.

Later in the evening she went to the piano and began to play very softly, as to herself, the opening bars of the 13th Nocturne. I felt that the psychic moment of my life had come, a moment which if lost could never be called back; and, in as careless a manner as I could assume, I sauntered over to the

piano and stood almost bending over her. She continued playing; but, in a voice that was almost a whisper, she called me by
my Christian name and said, "I love you, I love you, I love
you." I took her place at the piano and played the Nocturne in
a manner that silenced the chatter of the company both in and
out of the room; involuntarily closing it with the major triad.

We were married the following spring, and went to Europe
for several months. It was a double joy for me to be in France
again under such conditions.

First there came to us a little girl, with hair and eyes dark like
mine, but who is growing to have ways like her mother. Two
years later there came a boy, who has my temperament, but is
fair like his mother, a little golden-headed god, a face and head
that would have delighted the heart of an old Italian master.
And this boy, with his mother's eyes and features, occupies an
inner sanctuary of my heart; for it was for him that she gave all;
and that is the second sacred sorrow of my life.

The few years of our married life were supremely happy, and
perhaps she was even happier than I; for after our marriage, in
spite of all the wealth of her love which she lavished upon me,
there came a new dread to haunt me, a dread which I cannot
explain and which was unfounded, but one that never left me.
I was in constant fear that she would discover in me some
shortcoming which she would unconsciously attribute to my
blood rather than to a failing of human nature. But no cloud
ever came to mar our life together; her loss to me is irreparable. My children need a mother's care, but I shall never marry
again. It is to my children that I have devoted my life. I no
longer have the same fear for myself of my secret's being found
out; for since my wife's death I have gradually dropped out of
social life; but there is nothing I would not suffer to keep the
"brand" from being placed upon them.

It is difficult for me to analyze my feelings concerning my
present position in the world. Sometimes it seems to me that I
have never really been a Negro, that I have been only a privileged spectator of their inner life; at other times I feel that I
have been a coward, a deserter, and I am possessed by a
strange longing for my mother's people.

Several years ago I attended a great meeting in the interest
of Hampton Institute at Carnegie Hall. The Hampton stu-

dents sang old songs and awoke memories that left me sad. Among the speakers were R. C. Ogden, Ex-Ambassador Choate, and Mark Twain; but the greatest interest of the audience was centered in Booker T. Washington; and not because he so much surpassed the other in eloquence, but because of what he represented with so much earnestness and faith. And it is this that all of that small but gallant band of colored men who are publicly fighting the cause of their race have behind them. Even those who oppose them know that these men have the eternal principles of right on their side, and they will be victors even though they should go down in defeat. Beside them I feel small and selfish. I am an ordinarily successful white man who has made a little money. They are men who are making history and a race. I, too, might have taken part in a work so glorious.

My love for my children makes me glad that I am what I am, and keeps me from desiring to be otherwise; and yet, when I sometimes open a little box in which I still keep my fast yellowing manuscripts, the only tangible remnants of a vanished dream, a dead ambition, a sacrificed talent, I cannot repress the thought, that, after all, I have chosen the lesser part, that I have sold my birthright for a mess of pottage.

ALONG THIS WAY

To my wife,

GRACE NAIL JOHNSON,

in love and comradeship.

CONTENTS

James Weldon Johnson   PHOTOGRAPH BY CARL VAN VECHTEN

ILLUSTRATIONS

PART ONE

I

IN 1802 Étienne Dillet, a French army officer in Haiti, placed Hester Argo, a native Haitian woman, together with her three children, aboard a schooner bound for Cuba. This was eleven years after the first insurrection of the slaves in Haiti, and during the war that resulted in the extermination of the French forces on the island and the establishment of Haitian independence. Hester Argo and her children were being sent to a place of refuge. One of these children was a boy, then about six years old, the son of the Frenchman by Hester. The boy's name became Stephen Dillet.

But the schooner never reached her destination; she was captured by a British privateer and taken into Nassau, the capital of the Bahama Islands. Some of the Haitian refugees fared very badly; but Hester Argo and her children, fortunately, were befriended by a well-to-do Spaniard (he may have been a Frenchman) named Lamotte. They had, however, been robbed of everything; and when young Stephen landed in Nassau his entire clothing consisted of the long shirt in which he was clad; and his sole possession, one to which he had somehow clung, was a sliver spoon.

A silver spoon . . . Young Stephen was apprenticed to a tailor. He became the tailor of the English garrison stationed at Nassau, and later the leading tailor of the town. England had abolished the slave trade by 1808; and in 1811 she made it a felony. On August 7, 1833, slavery was abolished in her colonies; but in 1830 she had already given the vote to free Negroes in the Bahamas. By 1835 bars that prevented Negroes from holding political office were removed. While still a young man, Stephen Dillet left trade for politics. He stood for election to the Bahaman House of Assembly as a member for the city of Nassau and was elected. The House, however, rather than seat him, effected a dissolution. But in the new House he was seated and remained a member for some thirty consecutive years. Early in the forties he was appointed Chief Inspector of Police and, soon after, Postmaster of the city of Nassau. He held these two offices conjointly about twenty years; that is, until they were separated by the legislature, when he was allowed to choose which of them he would retain. He choose to retain the post-mastership, and held that position until late in the seventies. It was also in the forties that he was made deputy Adjutant General of Militia and, so, a member of the Governor's staff. He was a vestryman of Christ Church Cathedral and a trustee of the Public Bank. He died at the age of eighty-four.

Hester Argo, the Haitian woman, was one of my maternal great-grandmothers, and this Stephen Dillet was my grandfather.

Ten or twelve years after the little schooner sailed with the refugees from Haiti, a slaver with a cargo bound for Brazil was captured by a British man-of-war and taken into Nassau. The Africans aboard were parceled out among the white inhabitants. To Captain Symonett, a former seafaring man, fell a slim, rather sharp-featured girl, who was later called Sarah. Just who Captain Symonett was, even just what his nationality was, I cannot tell. I know that he spoke English, and I know, too, that his vocabulary included all the sonorous and racy swear words of several languages. Had he been captain of a merchant vessel or had he been a buccaneer? The latter is quite possible. He did not live in the city of Nassau but across on one of the neighboring islands. There, as a sort of patriarchal head of a clan, he ruled; one of his rules being that at the sounding of a horn at daybreak all had to get up and assemble to receive the allowance of coffee and rum which he himself issued to each one: men, women, and children. I wish I knew more about this picturesque old sinner, but before I realized how much I would value the information its sources were cut off.

It was to his island domain that Captain Symonett took the slim African girl. Shortly afterwards his white wife died and he took Sarah to wife and by her reared a large family of sons and daughters, nine of them. Sarah, the African woman, was my other maternal great-grandmother, and one of her daughters, Mary Symonett, born November 16, 1823, was my grandmother

In the later forties of the last century James Johnson, my father, was working at the old Stevens House in Bowling Green,

New York City. He was born a freeman in Richmond, Virginia, August 26, 1830, and as a boy went to New York to work. And here I am again confronted with my lack of foresight; I know nothing of my father's early life and of his background, aside from the meager facts just stated. I never heard him speak of his childhood and what lay back of and beyond it; and I never questioned him. I have a hazy notion that he belonged to a fairly large family, but I never saw one of his relatives. There is among our family relics an old daguerreotype of his mother, a stern-looking woman, seated in a chair and wearing a silk skirt that ballooned about her. My only definite impression of her was one I gained as a child, derived from the fact that on my birth she wrote my father a letter telling him not to "spare the rod and spoil the child." It may be that this first impression had some bearings on my neglect in learning about my father's people. I do know, however, that this grandmother died in Richmond in 1887.

My maternal grandmother, following her eldest sister, Sarah, went to New York in the middle forties, taking with her her only child, Helen Louise Dillet, my mother, born in Nassau, August 4, 1842. My mother grew up in New York. She attended one of the public schools for colored children and secured a good English education. Special attention must have been paid to penmanship, for my mother, even in her old age, wrote a hand that was copperplate. At school she also had opportunity to cultivate her considerable talent for music. When she was between eighteen and nineteen she sang at a concert, and James Johnson, who was in the audience, fell in love with the singer. But the course of true love . . . Within a few months after the concert the Civil War was raging, and my grandmother, listening to the rumors that the colored people in the North would be put in slavery if the South won, became panic-stricken and, taking her daughter with her, boarded a ship and returned to Nassau.

Not long afterwards James Johnson sailed from New York to Nassau. He went to become headwaiter at the Royal Victoria Hotel and to continue his courtship of Helen Louise. They were married at Christ Church Cathedral on April 22, 1864. Nassau was the chief harbor for blockade runners during the War, and gold, English and American, was plentiful. James

Johnson was thrifty and enterprising, and he prospered. His job at the Royal Victoria was lucrative, and he added to his income by purchasing two small schooners and engaging in sponge-fishing, then a most flourishing business in the Bahamas. He also bought a team of horses, which he used for draying. He built a nice home and became a part of the local life. Helen Louise's voice gained her a place in the choir of Christ Church. A daughter, Marie Louise, was born to them on July 10, 1868. It looked as though James Johnson would become a British citizen and make his permanent home in Nassau.

But prosperity in Nassau had collapsed with the close of the Civil War; and the great hurricane of 1866 had blown away its remnants. James Johnson stayed on until the spring of 1869, but he had been thinking for some time of returning to New York. In the meantime some American guests at the Royal Victoria had talked to him about Florida and its possibilities, especially its possibilities as a winter hotel resort; so he resolved to look the field over. He left his family in Nassau and went to Jacksonville.

Jacksonville at that time was little more than a village. Bay Street, then the main street, turned its back as it still does, on the St. Johns River, and from the rear of a row of five or six blocks of low wooden and brick buildings several rickety wharves jutted out into the magnificent stream. (Of course, water-fronts had not yet entered the list of civic responsibilities.) From the river the town extended back eight or ten blocks and straggled out on the three sides. North and west of the town was a forest of tall pines, and to the east, where the river makes a bend northward before taking its course to the Atlantic, thus giving the present-day city a water-front on two sides, the east as well as the south, there was a thick grove of oaks. Most of the houses were cheaply constructed wooden buildings, but there were a few fine homes. The streets, straight and laid out at right angles, were of deep, grayish sand and were flanked along the sides by narrow boardwalks. In front of the better business places and richer homes the sidewalks were of brick. The streets in the main part of the town were lined with splendid, moss-draped oaks, and so were redeemed from barren ugliness. In almost every yard there were flowers and orange trees. On a spring night there actually was perfumed air. One street, Pine, was paved, paved with crushed oyster shells. It led out to the Shell Road, a road that extended four or five miles into the country and was used as a drive.

This was the Jacksonville James Johnson saw when he arrived: small, insignificant, and, for the most part, crude and primitive. So unlike the Richmond of his boyhood or the New York of his youth; even so unlike Nassau, where there was a high standard of English life. Perhaps he exercised foresight. Perhaps he relied on the tip that Northern people and capital were already interested in Jacksonville and Florida. At any rate, he decided to stay. In the western part of the town, in a suburb known as La Villa—a very misleading name—he bought a lot one hundred and five feet square, on the corner of which stood a four- or five-room dwelling, old, rough, and unpainted, a typical "poor white" house. For this property he paid three hundred dollars cash. This was to be home. He then sent for his family.

With all their transportable goods stored aboard a small sailing vessel, his wife and child arrived safely in Jacksonville in the winter of 1869; the only loss being several missing boxes of books. There also came his wife's mother, now Mary Barton, who, probably, was as apprehensive as she had been at the outbreak of the Civil War. Her husband, John Barton, a very good carpenter, came with her; they, too, came seeking a better field. Strictly attached to Helen Louise was one, Mary Bethel, who served her as nurse for the child and as cook, and who remained a sort of faithful retainer in the household more than thirty years. She took care of me and my brother in our babyhood and childhood. We knew her as "Bar," and in talking to us our elders always referred to her as "your Bar." We learned that "Bar" had been the result of Marie Louise's efforts to say "Bethel." Mary Bethel, in turn, and in true Cockney style, absolutely ignored the "H" in "Helen" and always said "Ellen," a name that Helen Louise detested.

When Helen Louise was ushered into her new home, she broke down and wept. The contrast with the cleanliness and comfort of the home she had just left was sufficient justification for tears. The comparatively cold weather greatly increased the discomfort. The frosty winds blew through the cracks in the walls and up through the cracks in the floor.

Within it was gloomy because the batten shutters to the sash-less, paneless windows had to be kept closed. The family sought comfort by huddling with scorching faces and chilly backs close around the smoky fireplace in the main room. The outlook from the house was equally disheartening; instead of the clean, dazzling white streets of Nassau, here were streets or rather roads of that grayish sand six inches deep, and no place to walk except through it. The surrounding houses were poorer and more dilapidated than the Johnson house. The neighbors—we still absurdly apply "neighbor" to people merely because they live near—spoke in terms and words often utterly foreign to Helen Louise. The nearest person who could possibly be a neighbor for her was a white woman who lived a block away on a corner diagonally across the main street or road. She was Mrs. McCleary. Her husband was the foreman at Clark's sawmill in the eastern end of the town, a large plant that employed a big force of Negroes and turned an immense quantity of Florida pine into lumber for local use, shipment North, and for export. Mrs. McCleary belonged to a family then rather prominent in Jacksonville, the Hollands. Her brother was at one time sheriff of the county.

And this was to be home! The heartsickness of Helen Louise can be understood. But it did become home. She and her husband lived together on that plot of ground forty-three years.

During this first winter little Marie Louise was taken sick, and died in June 1870.

II

I WAS born June 17, 1871, in the old house on the corner; but I have no recollection of having lived in it. Before I could be aware of such a thing my father had built a new house near the middle of his lot. In this new house was formed my first consciousness of home. My childish idea of it was that it was a great mansion. I saw nothing in the neighborhood that surpassed it in splendor. Of course, it was only a neat cottage. The house had three bedrooms, a parlor, and a kitchen. The four main rooms were situated, two on each side of a hall that ran through the center of the house. The kitchen, used also as a room in which the family ate, was at the rear of the house and opened on a porch that was an extension of the hall. On the front a broad piazza ran the width of the house. Under the roof was an attic to which a narrow set of steps in one of the back rooms gave access.

But the house was painted, and there were glass windows and green blinds. Before long there were some flowers and trees. One of the first things my father did was to plant two maple trees at the front gate and a dozen or more orange trees in the yard. The maples managed to live; the orange trees, naturally, flourished. The hallway of the house was covered with a strip of oilcloth and the floors of the rooms with matting. There were curtains at the windows and some pictures on the walls. In the parlor there were two or three dozen books and a cottage organ. When I was seven or eight years old, the organ gave way to a square piano. It was a tinkling old instrument, but a source of rapturous pleasure. It is one of the indelible impressions on my mind. I can still remember just how the name "Bacon" looked, stamped in gold letters above the keyboard. There was a center marble-top table on which rested a big, illustrated Bible and a couple of photograph albums. In a corner stood a what-not filled with bric-a-brac and knick-knacks. On a small stand was a glass-domed receptacle in which was a stuffed canary perched on a diminutive tree; on this stand there was also kept a stereoscope and an assortment of views photographed in various parts of the world. For my brother and me, in our childhood (my brother, John Rosamond, was born in the new house August 11, 1873), this room was an Aladdin's cave. We used to stand before the what-not and stake out our claims to the objects on its shelves with a "that's mine" and a "that's mine." We never tired of looking at the stereoscopic scenes, examining the photographs in the album, or putting the big Bible and other books on the floor and exploring for pictures. Two large conch shells decorated the ends of the hearth. We greatly admired their pink, polished inner surface; and loved to put them to our ears to hear the "roar of the sea" from their cavernous depths. But the undiminishing thrill was derived from our experiments on the piano.

When I was born, my mother was very ill, too ill to nurse me. Then she found a friend and neighbor in an unexpected quarter. Mrs. McCleary, her white neighbor who lived a block away, had a short while before given birth to a girl baby. When this baby was christened she was named Angel. The mother of Angel, hearing of my mother's plight, took me and nursed me at her breast until my mother had recovered sufficiently to give me her own milk. So it appears that in the land of black mammies I had a white one. Between her and me there existed an affectionate relation through all my childhood; and even in after years when I had grown up and moved away I never, up to the time of her death, went back to my old home without paying her a visit and taking her some small gift.

I do not intend to boast about a white mammy, for I have perceived bad taste in those Southern white people who are continually boasting about their black mammies. I know the temptation for them to do so is very strong, because the honor point on the escutcheon of Southern aristocracy, the *sine qua non* of a background of family, of good breeding and social prestige, in the South is the Black Mammy. Of course, many of the white people who boast of having had black mammies are romancing. Naturally, Negroes had black mammies, but black mammies for white people were expensive luxuries, and comparatively few white people had them.

When I was about a year old, my father made a trip to New York, taking my mother and me with him. It was during this visit that I developed from a creeping infant into a walking child. Without doubt, my mother welcomed this trip. She was, naturally, glad to see again the city and friends of her girlhood; and it is probable that she brought some pressure on my father to make another move—back to New York. If she did, it was without effect. I say she probably made some such effort because I know what a long time it took her to become reconciled to life in the South; in fact, she never did entirely. The New York of her childhood and youth was all the United States she knew. Latterly she had lived in a British colony under conditions that rendered the weight of race comparatively light. During the earlier days of her life in Jacksonville she had no adequate conception of her "place."

And so it was that one Sunday morning she went to worship at St. John's Episcopal Church. As one who had been a member of the choir of Christ Church Cathedral she went quite innocently. She went, in fact, not knowing any better. In the chanting of the service her soprano voice rang out clear and beautiful, and necks were craned to discover the singer. On leaving the church she was politely but definitely informed that the St. John's congregation would prefer to have her worship the Lord elsewhere. Certainly she never went back to St. John's nor to any other Episcopal church; she followed her mother and joined Ebenezer, the colored Methodist Episcopal Church in Jacksonville, and became the choir leader.

Racially she continued to be a nonconformist and a rebel. A decade or so after the St. John's Church incident Lemuel W. Livingston, a student at Cookman Institute, the Negro school in Jacksonville founded and maintained by the Methodist Church (North), was appointed as a cadet to West Point. Livingston passed his written examinations, and the colored people were exultant. The members of Ebenezer Church gave a benefit that netted for him a purse of several hundred dollars. There was good reason for a show of pride; Livingston was a handsome, bronze-colored boy with a high reputation as a student, and appeared to be ideal material for a soldier and officer. But at the Academy he was turned down. The examining officials there stated that his eyesight was in some manner defective. The news that Livingston had been denied admission to West Point was given out at a Sunday service at Ebenezer Church. When at the same service the minister announced "America" as a hymn, my mother refused to sing it.

My mother was artistic and more or less impractical and in my father's opinion had absolutely no sense about money. She was a splendid singer and she had a talent for drawing. One day when I was about fifteen years old, she revealed to me that she had written verse, and showed me a thin sheaf of poems copied out in her almost perfect handwriting. She was intelligent and possessed a quick though limited sense of humor. But the limitation of her sense of humor was quite the normal one: she had no relish for a joke whose butt was herself or her children; my father had the rarer capacity for laughing even at himself. She belonged to the type of mothers whose love completely surrounds their children and is all-pervading; mothers for whom sacrifice for the child means only an extension of love. Love of this kind often haunts the child in later years. He

runs back again and again through all his memories, searching
for a lapse or a lack or a falling short in that love so that he
might in some degree balance his own innumerable thought-
lessnesses, his petty and great selfishnesses, his failures to begin
to understand or value the thing that was once his like the air
he breathed; and the search is vain.

The childhood memories that cluster round my mother are
still intensely vivid to me; many of them are poignantly tender.
I am between five and six years old. . . . In the early evening
the lamp in the little parlor is lit. . . . If the weather is chilly,
pine logs are sputtering and blazing in the fireplace. . . . I
and my brother, who is a tot, are seated on the floor. . . . My
mother takes a book and reads. . . . The book is *David Cop-
perfield.* . . . Night after night I follow the story, always hungry for the next installment. . . . Then the book is *Tales of a
Grandfather.* . . . Then it is a story by Samuel Lover. I laugh
till the tears roll down my cheeks at the mishaps of Handy
Andy. And my brother laughs too, doubtless because he sees
me laughing. . . . My mother's voice is beautiful; I especially
enjoy it when she mimics the Irish brogue and Cockney accents. . . . My brother grows sleepy. . . . My mother closes
the book and puts us both to bed—me feverish concerning
the outcome of David's affairs or thrilling over the exploits of
Wallace or Robert the Bruce, or still laughing at Andy. She
tucks us in and kisses us good-night. What a debt for a child
to take on!

She was my first teacher and began my lessons in reading before ever I went to school. She was, in fact, the first colored
woman public school teacher in Florida; and, when my school
days began at Stanton, the central school in Jacksonville for
colored children, she was one of the teachers there. And that,
perhaps, is why I have no sharp recollection of just when I
started school. I have a blurred and hazy picture in my memory of being in a large room with fifty, maybe sixty boys and
girls, most of whom were several years older than I. The picture of the teacher is fainter, and would probably be fainter still
had I not afterwards come to know that she was Diana Grant,
the wife of the man who was for a number years the pastor of
Ebenezer Church. But I recall more clearly my sense of dis-

comfort. The room was too crowded; some of the children I was packed in with were not clean; I rebelled at the situation.

At this point there must have been some sort of a hiatus; I remember nothing further about that class and classroom, but I do remember distinctly being in a larger, less crowded room with nicer children and with a young lady named Carrie Sampson as my teacher. At once I fell in love with Miss Sampson; and small wonder, she was so lovely. When the time came for me to leave her class, the honor of promotion seemed to be no recompense for my desolation. I wanted to continue without end my education at her feet. It took persuasion and some sterner measures to induce a change of mind, if not of heart. The episode forms a pleasant memory of childhood; and the knowing that this my earliest judgment upon living beauty disclosed such exacting standards has always been a matter of certain pride to me. I saw my teacher many times when I was no longer a child, and I know she was one of the most beautiful women I have ever seen.

The development of the ability to read opened up for me a world of wonders that I never grew tired of exploring. My father gave me my first own books, a "library" consisting of seven volumes packed in a cardboard case four and a half inches high, three inches wide, and two inches deep. I still have the books; they are intact, but show the passage of the years. Each book contains a story about good little girls and good and bad little boys. I need not add that each story pointed a wholesome lesson. I list them: *Peter and His Pony*, *The Tent in the Garden*, *Harry the Shrimper*, *The White Kitten*, *Willie Wilson the Newsboy*, and *The Water Melon*.

Peter and His Pony opens thus:

"Dear papa," said Peter one morning to his father, "you said when I was nine years old, you would give me a pony to ride on. Don't you know that I shall be nine years old in three months' time? and will you keep your promise?"

Mr. Howard smiled at Peter's eagerness, and said, "I promised to give you a present of a pony when you should be nine years of age, provided you were sufficiently careful to be trusted with the charge of it; for, though I can afford to buy you a pony, I cannot afford to keep a man to clean and look after it."

"Oh, father," cried Peter, "I will do all that. I will brush his coat every day, and feed him regularly. I shall be fond of him, and he will be fond of me. If you will be so kind as to let me have a pony, I shall be very happy."

"I do not doubt that you will be very happy if I give you a pony," replied Mr. Howard; "but before I promise to give you one, I wish to be quite sure that the pony will be happy also; and if he is not well cleaned and regularly fed, and his shoes looked carefully after, he will not be happy."

"Dear papa," said Peter, "I do assure you that I will always attend to my pony before I eat my breakfast—you may be sure he shall want for nothing."

"Very well," said Mr. Howard, "I will think upon what you have said, and will let you know at the proper time what I intend to do."

Peter got the pony on his ninth birthday, and was very faithful in attending him. But for just once Peter neglected his duties, and when he rode that day the pony lost a shoe, cut his foot, and went lame. Peter's negligence brought upon him the retribution of being deprived for a month of the pleasure of riding.

The chief effect of the story on me was a long season of importuning my father to buy me a pony—the which I never got.

I finished these little books in short order, and looked for stronger meat. In fact, my father had underestimated my stage of development; my mother's readings had already carried me far beyond books of this grade. I read for myself *Pickwick Papers*, some of the *Waverly Novels*, *Pilgrim's Progress*, the fairy tales of the Brothers Grimm, and took my first dip into poetry through Sir Walter Scott. I think that of these books the stories by the Brothers Grimm made the deepest effect. These stories left me haunted by the elusiveness of beauty—elusiveness, its very quintessence. Years after, when I read Keat's *Ode to a Nightingale* the thought flashed through my mind that for one whose spirit had not been thus pervaded in childhood it would be impossible even to catch at the tenuous beauty in:

> The same that oft-times hath
> Charm'd magic casements, opening on the foam
> Of perilous seas, in faery lands forlorn.

I exhausted the little supply in our parlor and began laying hands on any book that came within my reach. I remember one day when I was absorbed in a novel I had got hold of with the title, as I remember it, *Vashti—Or Until Death Do Us Part*, my mother said to me, "You had better leave that book till you are older." How good were her grounds for censorship I cannot tell but I remember that I finished the book without, I think, doing myself any appreciable harm. Several years later I began buying regularly two magazines published for boys, *Golden Days* and *Golden Argosy*.

My mother was also my first music teacher. She had less than ordinary proficiency on the organ and piano, but she knew enough to give me and my brother a start. Before we began to learn our notes and the keys of the instrument, we used to stand, whenever we were allowed, close by on either side while she picked out hymns or other simple pieces. It was our great delight, my brother at one end of the keyboard and I at the other, to chime in with what were then wholly futuristic harmonies.

Pardonable sentiment does not make me completely forget that my mother's love was not manifested in unchanging gentleness. There were times when her love or her sense of responsibility for the kind of men her two boys would grow up to be prompted sterner treatment. Then the mental or moral lesson would be impressed upon us otherwise than through our intellectual processes or our higher emotions. Whenever I was spanked my brother always received vicariously whatever benefits there might be. When I cried he cried even more piteously or more lustily than I. These spankings were literally dark moments in my life. It was not the stinging sensation of the sole of the slipper or the back of the hairbrush that I dreaded, for the force applied was never excessive; it was the moment of darkness that terrified me. My mother's method was to put my head face down between her knees. This made the operation convenient for her, but it had on me somewhat the effect of a total eclipse of the sun on primitive peoples; the world was blotted out and, in addition, I underwent the horrors of the sensation of being smothered.

One instance stands out almost singly in my mind. Often a spanking comes to a child like a thunderclap out of a clear sky, and he doesn't fully realize why he is being punished. He suffers it like the brave man, who dies but once. But one evening after dark I and my brother, being in possession of a few pennies, conspired to run around the corner to Mrs. Handy's grocery store and buy two "prize" boxes of candy. We went without giving notice or asking permission. On starting back I became immediately aware of the gravity of the situation. With each step homeward my forebodings increased. I recognized the inevitable and had a thousand foretastes of it. When I entered the house it was with as heavy a sense of sin as any infant conscience could carry. However, summoning all the gayety we could, we exhibited the baubles we had won—these trinkets, not the candy, were the chief objects of our desires— but that did not stay the hand of fate.

Before my spanking days were entirely over, I took the matter up frankly with my mother and made a plea for open-air spanking. I conceded her right to punish me when I did wrong, but protested against having my eyes and nose and mouth buried in the dark depths of her skirts. She didn't fall back on parental prerogatives, but yielded me the point.

My Richmond grandmother's advice to my father about not sparing the rod and spoiling the child had no effect on him; not once in his life did he lay a finger in punishment on me or my brother. Nevertheless, by firmness and sometimes by sternness, he did exercise a strong control over us. But I am fogy enough to believe that the spankings my mother gave did me good.

I cannot remember when I did not know my mother, but I can easily recall the at first hazy and then gradually more distinct notions about my father. My impressions of him began to take shape from finding under my pillow in the mornings an orange, some nuts, and raisins, and learning that he had put them there after I had gone to sleep. Shortly after my father got to Jacksonville the St. James Hotel was built and opened. When it was opened he was the headwaiter, a job he held for twelve or thirteen years. Doubtless the hotel had been planned, and may even have been under construction, before he arrived; probably this was the definite prospect before him when he set out for Jacksonville. The St. James was for many years the most famous and the most fashionable of all the Florida resort hotels. A number of summers my father was the headwaiter at some mountain or seaside hotel in the North. So in my babyhood and first days of childhood I didn't see very much of him. His work at the St. James took him from home early in the mornings to see breakfast served, and he remained at the hotel until dinner was finished, by which time I had been put away in the little bed in which I slept. It was from the hotel that he brought the fruit and sweets that he put under my pillow. I remember, too, that our Sunday dinner always came from the hotel. It was brought in a hamper by one of the waiters, and the meat was usually fricasseed chicken.

I got acquainted with my father by being taken to the hotel to see him. As soon as Rosamond was big enough, he was taken too. My mother never went; one of the waiters fetched us until we were old enough to go alone. These visiting days were great days for us: the wide steps, the crowded verandas, the music, the soft, deep carpets of the lobby; this was a world of enchantment. My first definite thought about the hotel was that it belonged to my father. True, there was always around in the office a Mr. Campbell, a rather stooped man with a short reddish beard, who habitually gave me a friendly pat on the shoulder, and who evidently had something to do with the place. But just to the right, at the entrance to the big dining-room stands my father, peerless and imposing in full-dress clothes; he opens the door and takes me in; countless waiters, it seems, are standing around in groups; my father strikes a gong and the waiters spring to their stations and stand like soldiers at attention; I am struck with wonder at the endless rows of tables now revealed, the glitter of silver, china, and glass, and the array of napkins folded so that they look like many miniature white pyramids. Another gong, and the waiters relax; but one of them tucks a napkin under my chin and serves me as though I were a princeling. Then, with desires of heart and stomach satisfied and a quantity of reserves tied in a napkin, I am tucked away in a corner. Again the gong, the doors are thrown open, the guests stream in. My father snaps his fingers, waiters jump to carry out his orders, and guests smile him their thanks. He lords it over everything that falls within my ken. He is, quite obviously, the most important man in the St. James Hotel.

This childish portrait needs, of course, some rectification. No boy can make a fair estimate of his father. I was thirty years old before I was able to do it. The average boy all along thinks highly of his mother. In manhood he is likely even to sentimentalize her faults into tender virtues. With his male parent it is not so; his opinion goes through a range of changes and tends to be critical rather than sentimental. Up to ten a boy thinks his father knows everything; at twenty he indulgently looks upon the "old man" as a back number or, maybe, something less complimentary; at thirty, if the boy himself has any sense, he recognizes all of his father's qualities pretty fairly.

My father was a quiet, unpretentious man. He was naturally conservative and cautious, and generally displayed common sense in what he said and did. He never went to school; such education as he had was self-acquired. Later in life, I appreciated the fact that his self-development was little less than remarkable. He had a knowledge of general affairs and was familiar with many of the chief events and characters in the history of the world. I have the old sheepskin bound volume of *Plutarch's Lives* which he owned before I was born. He had gained by study a working knowledge of the Spanish language; this he had done to increase his value as a hotel employee. When he was a young man in New York, he attended the theater a good deal, and, before I was aware of where the lines came from or of what they meant, I used to go around the house parroting after him certain snatches from the Shakespearean plays. I particularly recall: "To be or not to be; that is the question" and "A horse! a horse! my kingdom for a horse!"

The quality in my father that impressed me most was his high and rigid sense of honesty. I simply could not conceive of him as a party to any monetary transaction that was questionable in the least. I think he got his greatest satisfaction in life out of the reputation he had built up as a man of probity, and took his greatest pride in the consequent credit standing that he enjoyed. This element in his character was a source of gratification to my pride and also, more than once, to my needs. One instance of double gratification was when I was at home in Jacksonville in 1910, just a few weeks before I was to be married. My father and mother discussed an appropriate gift to me and, finally, to my undisguised joy, decided upon a check for a thousand dollars. My father, excusably, did not have a thousand dollars in cash; but he said to me, "My boy, we'll go down town tomorrow and see if we can get the money." We went the next morning to one of the principal banks and my father spoke with John C. L'Engle, the president. The transaction was put through without any delay; he got the money on his note, without collateral security, without even an endorser. I was as proud to see him able to do such a thing as I was glad to have the money.

In the narrow sense, he was an unsociable man. My mother liked company; and when I was a boy we frequently had company at the house; occasionally there was a party. I, too, liked the company and the extra nice things to eat that were always a concomitant—especially ice cream of which in my whole life I have never had too much. My father took practically no part in these affairs. In his opinion the entertaining of company as "company" was a waste of time and money.

Yet he was not devoid of graces. He played the guitar well as a solo instrument, a use seldom made of it now. He possessed a vein of eloquence and had a good ear for the well-turned phrase. He liked to get off pithy aphorisms. He keenly enjoyed witticisms, particularly his own. Some of the latter, through repetition, became fixed in my mind. On a hot afternoon he would say to me, "Bubs, draw a fresh bucket of water from the well, and be sure to get it from the north side." Or on a still hotter afternoon, "Son, suppose while you're resting you take the ax and chop a little wood," Not infrequently he would achieve a penetrating truth. It was not until he was in his middle forties that he became a church member; when he was past fifty he became a preacher; one day, after he had been a preacher for some years, he said to me, "My boy, do you know I was never *compelled* to associate with bad people until I joined the church?"

He was a jolly companion for a boy, and I loved to be with him and go about with him. He made my first kites. He was adept at folding paper, and he made me windmills and fashioned little boats to be sailed in a tub. He made shadow-figures on the wall at night. He took me and my brother to places along the river where we could paddle about and learn to swim. After we were big enough to trot around with him, he played with us a good deal in this way during the times between hotel seasons. Before I was able to hold the instrument on my knees he began to teach me the guitar. I had to stand up to it in the same manner in which a player stands up to a bass viol. By the time I was ten years old I was, for a child, a remarkable performer—I judge; for I remember people, sometimes guests from the hotel, coming to our house to hear me play.

My father was a man of medium size, but constitutionally strong. One of the traditions of the home was that he was never sick. His color was light bronze, and so, a number of shades darker than that of my mother. She at fifty bore more than a slight resemblance to the later portraits of Queen Victoria; so much so that the family doctor christened her "Queen," a name to which she afterwards answered among her intimate friends.

The years as they pass keep revealing how the impressions made upon me as a child by my parents are constantly strengthening controls over my forms of habit, behavior, and conduct as a man. It appeared to me, starting into manhood, that I was to grow into something different from them; into something on a so much larger plan, a so much grander scale. As life tapers off I can see that in the deep and fundamental qualities I am each day more and more like them.

III

THERE was another force that I came under in those most plastic years. My grandmother Barton was a woman of strong will and determination. These traits were manifest in her physical appearance, her manner, and her speech. She had a spare, energetic body; and, in contradistinction to the tastes of her daughter, disdained the desire for ease and luxury. She was an expert laundress, and got high prices from the hotel guests in Jacksonville for her work. In this way she must have earned considerable money, because at that time the Florida season opened at Thanksgiving and lasted about five months,

A Childhood Portrait

and there was no competition from steam laundries. She also ran a little bake shop, and her bread and cake enjoyed a high reputation for excellency. In addition, she was an indefatigable church worker.

She was a comely woman with well-chiseled features. Her eyes were rather piercing, and she had a nose of which she was very proud, even boastful; a nose which, she said, she got from her own mother. As a child I used to feel that my grandmother's references to her aristocratic nose were frequently made as an implied comparison with the decidedly snub nose of my mother. But my mother could retort effectively by making any sort of a gesture with her lovely hands or breaking into the enhancing smile that disclosed her perfectly formed teeth. My grandmother was more than plain in her speech. She often said things that brought an "Oh, mother!" from my mother and a roar of laughter from my father. (I don't know how it happened that my brother and I were not taught to address our mother as "mother," as she did hers. For a long while we used "mamma," which as a word is little beyond the "bar-bar" of infancy. When we were big boys, we changed to the somewhat slangy "mumsey." I actually regret that I never had the direct use of this word of the greatest combined beauty, nobility and tenderness in the English language.) Her speech was sharp as well as plain, and she was well able to hold her own in a battle of tongues. She was a rigid disciplinarian and also, I judge, as firm a believer in the efficacy of the rod as my Richmond grandmother. But I was very fond of her and she was, perhaps, more fond of me. For reasons that were satisfactory for her I was her favorite grandchild. At times the display of her favoritism was so flagrant that it pained my mother and embarrassed me. My brother often manifested his recognition of it by loud wails.

John Barton was very indulgent toward me. I remember him quite distinctly, though I was but seven years old when he died. He was a tall, very dark brown man with a Lincoln-like face, even to the short beard. But he was dapper; I might say elegant. He was a grand sight, I thought, in his long-tailed, black broadcloth coat on Sundays. My grandmother used to say that she fell in love with him because of the graceful way in which he would handle himself in friendly boxing bouts. I liked John Barton very much. I called him "Pa John" and never knew until I had stopped using the term that it consisted of two words instead of one. He bought me a goat one day, a pretty white and black young billy goat. When Billy was presented to me, he was tied to a tree in the yard. He was a nice, tame goat; he let me pet him, and nibbled from my hand the grass or any other kind of food that I could forage. Pa John set to work to make a wagon and harness. Never did the anticipation of driving my own automobile equal in thrills the anticipation of driving my goat cart. But Billy got loose and out into the street; and the dogs chased and killed him. Such a thing could not seem less than a tragedy to a grown-up; what it meant to a child cannot be measured. I never got another goat, and the wagon and harness were never finished. Pa John died before he could attend to either.

I was in the room when he died, standing at the foot of the bed. How I got there I do not know. But there I stand, perhaps unnoticed because I am barely able to peep over the footpiece. I am bewildered. I cannot understand what is taking place. I see my grandmother almost hysterical, and my mother weeping. I see my father bend over the dying man and take his hand; I hear him call his name several times without any answer. Then my grandmother's wild scream; then the strange silence. I am snatched away, and I know nothing more about what has happened until the day of the funeral. I have never been to a funeral; but I understand that I shall not see Pa John any more. The thought saddens me; but how quickly I forget! There are five or six big carriages, each drawn by two horses. The carriages are all crowded, and I am boosted and perched on the high seat of one of them beside the driver. I ask him to let me drive, and he gives me the reins and puts his two big hands over my two tiny ones. I forget everything except the pull of the reins against the palms of my hands, the motion of the two great animals under me, and the aroma that rises from their sweating flanks. Of course, I do not want anybody else whom I know to die; but I would enjoy going to funerals, if I might sit on the high seat beside the driver and help hold the reins over the horses.

I loved to go down to my grandmother's house. The going of those two blocks alone was for a long time charged with a

sense of adventure, to which was often added the weight of responsibility as guardian for my brother. I would come out of
our front gate, turn to the right, and go some seventy-five or
eighty feet to the corner, where stood the old house that was
once home. I had to get on the other side of the street I had
reached, but I never crossed at this point because on the corner directly opposite lived Mr. Cole, a white man, and I was
dreadfully afraid of him. I was not afraid of him because he
was white—his or anybody else's being white had no special
significance for me at that time—I was afraid of him because
everybody said he was crazy. Perhaps he was—he was poor and
did no work of any kind—and perhaps he wasn't crazy. His
wife, a very good sort of a woman, took in sewing and did all
the rest of the necessary work. Mr. Cole, a tall, gaunt, black-
haired man, spent most of his time on his piazza seated in a
chair and grinding out wheezy tunes from an old music box.
He would periodically interrupt his artistic endeavors by leaping to his feet, striding up and down his piazza, and consign-
ing the whole neighborhood to hell with the most violent profanity. Usually some children, all colored, would be gathered
around to listen to the music or, probably, to tease Mr. Cole;
and when the outburst came they would scream and scamper
in all directions. I never dared the passage on the side of the
Cole house.

I always turned to the left and crossed over to the corner
where Aunt Elsie Andrews lived. Aunt Elsie lived in a little
house that was almost covered with honeysuckle vines. In her
yard was a marvelous fig tree. She was a very old and benign
woman with a noble, black face that took on a positive beauty
under the red bandanna she always wore over the white cotton
of her head. Whenever figs were in season and Aunt Elsie saw
me and my brother passing she would stop us and give us a
handful of the syrupy fruit. In the same yard, but in a separate
little house back of Aunt Elsie's, lived Aunt Venie. She was a
small, light-brown woman, much younger than Aunt Elsie
but, following the manner of according respect to a woman
who had reached a certain age, we addressed her also as
"Aunt." We were a little bit afraid of Aunt Venie, too; for she
was said to have fits. (In a former age she would have been
classed among those "possessed with devils.") Aunt Venie's fits

were probably the results of religious excesses. At St. Paul's Church, the colored church on the corner above to the west, she was the champion of all "ring shouters." When there was a "ring shout" the weird music and the sound of thudding feet set the silences of the night vibrating and throbbing with a vague terror. Many a time I woke suddenly and lay a long while strangely troubled by these sounds, the like of which my great-grandmother Sarah had heard as a child. The shouters, formed in a ring, men and women alternating, their bodies close together, moved round and round on shuffling feet that never left the floor. With the heel of the right foot they pounded out the fundamental beat of the dance and with their hands clapped out the varying rhythmical accents of the chant; for the music was, in fact, an African chant and the shout an African dance, the whole pagan rite transplanted and adapted to Christian worship. Round and round the ring would go: one, two, three, four, five hours, the very monotony of sound and motion inducing an ecstatic frenzy. Aunt Venie, it seems, never, even after the hardest day of washing and ironing, missed a "ring shout."

From Aunt Elsie's corner I usually crossed, passing under two very largely prickly pear trees, to where the Morrisons, a noisy colored family with five children, lived. Then I would go east down the length of the block, past three other colored families and around to the right at the next corner to my grandmother's. But when I was leading my brother I often kept on Aunt Elsie's side of the street, past the next house, where a big, ferocious dog always ran the length of the fence, giving every indication that he would chew us to bits if he could get at us. Rosamond would hold my hand more tightly; and it took all my prestige as an elder to assure him that there was no real danger. Once, discounting my assurances and my ability to protect him, he did break away and run back home. The sight of his skirts (all boys of his age then wore kilts) flying in the breeze and his feet digging up the sand was very funny to me. It was an incident that I related at home with a feeling of superiority.

At the end of the fence of the barking dog I would cut diagonally across the street to the corner around which my grandmother lived. I took this cut because I was always cautioned about passing Henry Arpen's. Henry Arpen was a Dutchman, short but not fat, who with his wife, a very tall and angular woman, ran a general store. The store included a bar, and it seemed that there were never less than a dozen drunks, black and white, hanging around. There were generally lots of profane and obscene language, and not infrequently a play of pistols and knives; so I always heeded the caution. But Arpen's store was a place that pricked my curiosity, and I was always glad of the chance to be taken there when something was to be bought. It was exciting; it was a glimpse into the big world; and, besides, Mr. Arpen and his wife were always nice to me. In their broken English they inquired about my health and as to whether I was a good boy or not while one of them fished out from a tall glass jar a ball of red and white candy for me. These hard candy balls were warranted to wear any ordinary child a full day and, in addition, to give him a gumboil on the roof of his mouth.

This little journey had, in mid-summer, one other element of adventure. The streets I have been talking about were actually very wide roads of loose, deep sand dotted here and there with little oases of grass. There were neither pavements nor sidewalks, except the veranda round Arpen's store. When the sands of these streets were heated, the sands of Sahara couldn't be hotter. And at that season the thing above all others that I and my brother implored of our mother was to let us leave off our shoes and stockings. Whenever she did, and often she didn't because of the prevalence of ground itch, we felt so light-footed; we could run so much faster; and the feel of the earth and water on naked feet made us such happy little animals. We sincerely envied the children around who had no shoes and stockings. And so sometimes the expedition to our grandmother's house gave us, in proportion, all the thrills that a traveler gets in exploring the world's perilous places. Our method was to run from one patch of grass to another, waiting at each until our feet cooled off before daring to set out for the next. But even these islands of refuge were not free from hazard; the grass was filled with sand-spurs that pierced the feet like hot needles. Under these conditions the journey was one that called for agility, endurance, and courage.

But the goal was always worth the dangers run; there were

sure to be small cakes and jumbles and benne candy, and at times a cool glass of limeade. But I must be fair to myself and say that it was more than a matter of the palate; to go into the little shop and catch the good, clean smell of fresh-baked bread and cake satisfied a sense related to, yet apart from hunger, and I liked the lively scene of coming and going customers. It was exciting to ramble round the comparatively strange yard; to play with a black dog named Bull, a much better playmate than our own dog, Stump, who had reached the philosophical age; to explore the recesses of the garden, help chase the chickens out, and search for blackberries that might be ripe along the edge of the fence. My grandmother's little parlor also had attractions, consisting of the few household treasures she had brought from Nassau. In the center was a table holding the photograph album, a stereoscope with views, and some trinkets. This table was of solid West Indian mahogany, with four straight, slender legs, two hinged leaves and a drawer. I use it now as a writing table in my study. On the wall hung a long, two-sectioned, gilt-framed mirror in which I could see myself from any part of the room. This mirror was flanked by two large portrait reproductions in color, one of Queen Victoria and the other of the Prince Consort in their royal robes. There was also a smaller portrait of the Prince of Wales dressed in the height of fashion. My grandmother remained a royalist. She never relinquished or forfeited her British citizenship. She took great pride in telling me about the Queen and about the Prince of Wales and his visit to New York. I admired these pictures very much, for they were larger and brighter than any we had at our house.

But the objects in this little room that held the greatest charm for me were two tall candlesticks, ornamented with lusters, that stood on the mantelpiece. My grandmother would take one down and let me look through the prismatic, cutglass pendants; instantly all that I saw was embroidered with crimson and purple and green and gold. How I longed to possess one of those magical glasses. If one would only drop off accidentally, and I might have it to carry round in my pocket so that I could turn it on any object I chose and make it more beautiful than it actually was; in fine, that I might always have an ever-ready rainbow.

After John Barton died I spent a good deal of time at my grandmother's house to keep her company. I made myself handy, especially in the shop, where I served a part of each day as clerk. I often slept at her house. On those evenings, after the shop was closed, she usually read to me for an hour or so. She read from the Bible and from a thick, illustrated book bound in green cloth called *Home Life in the Bible*. She also read me stories from books that she drew from the library of Ebenezer Church Sunday School. These stories were better written and slightly less juvenile than those in the "library" my father had given me, but they were of the same genre. My grandmother had had very little schooling, and could not read as my mother did; that, however, did not daunt her, she read a great deal, and more and more as she grew older. When she read Bible stories aloud to me she came across many names difficult to pronounce, especially in the stories from the Old Testament, but I never knew her to be stumped by a single one; she'd call it something and pass right on. In this way she coined, I am sure, a number of wonderful words.

It was during this period that she disclosed her consuming ambition, her ambition for me to become a preacher. She lived until I was thirty years old, and I believe she never felt that I had done other than choose the lesser part. She took me to Sunday school each week and to some of the church services. I was practically living at my grandmother's when there came a revivalist to Ebenezer. She attended the meetings every night, taking me along with her, always walking the distance of about a mile each way. Sometimes that homeward mile for my short legs seemed without end. In these revival meetings the decorum of the regular Sunday services gave way to something primitive. It was hard to realize that this was the same congregation which on Sunday mornings sat quietly listening to the preacher's exegesis of his text and joining in singing conventional hymns and anthems led by a choir. Now the scene is changed. The revivalist rants and roars, he exhorts and implores, he warns and threatens. The air is charged. Overlaid emotions come to surface. A woman gives a piercing scream and begins to "shout"; then another, and another. The more hysterical ones must be held to be kept from "shouting" out of their clothes. Sinners crowd to the mourners' bench.

Prayers and songs go up for the redemption of their souls. Strapping men break down in agonizing sobs, and emotionally strained women fall out in a rigid trance. A mourner "comes through" and his testimony of conversion brings a tumult of rejoicing.

I was only about nine years old but younger souls had been consecrated to God; and I was led to the mourners' bench. I knelt down at the altar. I was so wedged in that I could hardly breathe. I tried to pray. I tried to feel a conviction of sin. I, finally, fell asleep. . . . The meeting was about to close; somebody shook me by the shoulder. . . . I woke up but did not open my eyes or stir. . . . Whence sprang the whim, as cunning as could have occurred to one of the devil's own imps? The shaking continued, but I neither opened my eyes nor stirred. They gathered round me. I heard, "Glory to God, the child's gone off!" But I did not open my eyes or stir. My grandmother got a big, strong fellow who took me on his back and toted me that long mile home. Several people going our way accompanied us, and the conversation reverted to me, with some rather far-fetched allusions to the conversion of Saul of Tarsus. The situation stirred my sense of humor, and a chuckle ran round and round inside of me, because I did not dare to let it get out. The sensation was a delicious one, but it was suddenly chilled by the appalling thought that I could not postpone my awakening indefinitely. Each step homeward, I knew, brought the moment of reckoning nearer. I needed to think and think fast; and I did. I evolved a plan that I thought was good; when I reached home and "awoke" I recounted a vision. The vision was based on a remembered illustration in *Home Life in the Bible* that purported to be the artist's conception of a scene in heaven. To that conception I added some original embellishments. Apparently my plan worked out to the satisfaction of everybody concerned. Indeed, for me, it worked out almost too satisfactorily for I was called upon to repeat the vision many times thereafter—to my inward shame.

But I had put my hand to the plow, and there was no turning back. I was taken into the church for the probationary period, after which I would be made a full member if I proved worthy. My grandmother went with me to my home to tell my father and mother about it. The conference took place in our yard. My mother was hesitant, but acquiescent—she never reached the place where she could pit her will against her mother's. My father expressed his disapproval strongly, and it looked as though the matter would lead to a break between him and my grandmother. He said to my mother, "B" (his familiar name for her), "we ought not let the child join the church at his age; he doesn't understand what he's doing; he ought to be able to know what joining the church means before we allow him to take such a step." And to my grandmother, "Mrs. Barton" (he always addressed her in this formal manner), "you're doing the boy more harm than good; you're forcing him into something that he ought to be left to go into of his own free will. He'll make a better church member and a better Christian if he makes up his own mind about it." But the moral club was in my grandmother's hand and she wielded it vigorously. "If being a church member," she countered, "is a good thing, how can a child start too young? . . . Train up a child in the way he should go, because when he is old he may not choose that way." And she capped her arguments with the sanction of the words of Jesus, "Suffer little children to come unto me and forbid them not."

This controversy left me uneasy. Joining the church had seemed to me a matter of course, somewhat like entering school. Now I was impressed with its gravity and, in addition to the weight that a consideration of sin and salvation imposed upon me, I was disquieted by the family rift. After the family conference I talked church and religion a great deal with my grandmother. It was then she told me about my father's conversion. He was standing in the dining room of the St. James Hotel, looking out of a window, waiting for the doors to be thrown open, when suddenly he cried out aloud. His waiters ran to him, thinking he was ill. He told them that he had recognized himself as a sinner and had found God. He was then in his middle forties.

I was taken into the church as a full member on a Sunday morning. The church was crowded in pews and aisles. The space around the pulpit was filled with the church officers. As I stood at the altar rail in the long line of those being received as communicants my childish thoughts regarding religion vanished. The minister extended his hand to each probationer and welcomed him into the bond of Christian fellowship. When he reached me he paid special tribute to my tender years. I was lifted up, transported. The vision I had recounted came back a reality. I felt myself, like young Samuel, the son of Hannah, dedicated to the service of God.

Naturally, I could not hold such an emotional height. My normal boyish instincts, alone, would have caused some reaction. As it happened, the inevitable ebb of that first fervor was aided by contributing factors. My grandmother, with the highest motives and in furtherance of her great ambition for me, carried me along to church with her on every possible occasion. On Sundays I went to Sunday school, stayed for the preaching service, returned to an afternoon service, and occasionally went to the night meeting. I did not have to be forced to attend these meetings. I liked to mingle with the boys and girls at Sunday school. It was gayer than day school because the work and discipline were not so hard, and being dressed in our best clothes injected a holiday spirit. And the lessons attracted me, too; illustrated, as they generally were, by highly colored charts. And such attraction as the lessons lacked was made up for in a wholly mysterious and incomprehensible way by the presence of little Mamie Gibbs in my class. Nor was attendance at the other Sunday meetings a hardship; for I did fairly realize that I was a member of the church and in a manner set apart from most of the boys and girls that I knew, and I did to the extent of my powers try to fulfill my religious obligations.

It was attendance at weekday meetings that began to surfeit me. On Tuesday nights I was taken to class meetings. Class meeting is, in a measure, the Methodist substitute for the Catholic confession. Each member of a class rises in turn and tells his class leader what his spiritual experiences have been during the week past; whether there has been a falling from or a growth in grace. The leader then gives words of comfort and counsel to each as his case may require—a very self-satisfying function. However, through the many, many weeks that I attended class meetings I heard very few who did not testify to a constant growth in grace. The chief difficulty of the leader, it seemed, was to find terms devout and at the same time suffi-

ciently laudatory in which to make a fitting response at each of
these progressive stages toward sainthood. My grandmother
was my class leader, and I found this relationship exceedingly
embarrassing. She knew me as intimately as did my mother; so
any special emphasis on my growth in grace, probably, would
not carry much conviction; on the other hand, I recoiled from
exposing my little sins and failings before a group of virtual
strangers. Other weekday meetings that I attended were the
Friday afternoon prayer meetings for young people, the experience meetings, and the love feasts. The afternoon prayer
meetings caused me some regret when I saw boys I knew playing ball or marbles or tops or shinny—at all of which I was
adept—while I was on my way to church. But a greater infliction than the loss of an afternoon's play went with the prayer
meetings, and the same infliction, still heavier, went with the
experience meetings. In prayer meetings I was expected to lead
aloud in prayer, and in experience meetings to rise before the
whole congregation and give my testimony. In neither case
was there any escape. At prayer meetings the leader would say,
"We'll now be led in prayer by Brother James Johnson." And
at experience meetings the minister, who was the leader,
would say, "We haven't heard from Brother James Johnson
yet. Rise, Brother, and be a witness for the Lord." In both
cases I was confronted by the impossible; and not because I
objected to praying or being a witness for the Lord, but simply
because I was utterly incapable of making anything analogous
to a public utterance.

Once Rosamond and I were both down for recitations at
one of the Sunday school exhibitions—or concerts, as they
were called. He got off his "Little Tommy Tucker" in fine
style. I knew my recitation perfectly, but when the superintendent announced my name and I stood before the audience, I was as one struck dumb. I had no command over my
vocal organs. The promptings of my mother from behind the
curtained-off wings helped me not one whit. I remember
that I had on a pair of short, linen pants and that I caught
hold of the right leg at the knee and twisted it until I had
formed a regular corkscrew. The terrible tension broke in a
whimper, then tears; and I was led off in ignominy. My mother
was disappointed; but my stupid showing so humiliated my

grandmother that she then and there handed me a couple of resounding thwacks. My only successful appearance on the Sunday school stage was in a silent part; I recall that I made a hit as Joshua in a tableau, "Joshua Commanding the Sun to Stand Still." On my left arm I wore a cardboard shield covered with silver paper and in my right hand I carried a wooden spear, which I pointed after the manner of the illustration in our big Bible; but the words of Joshua I did not repeat. If anyone had predicted to me at that period that a good part of my life was to be spent on the platform as a public speaker, the future would have been filled with terror.

My distaste—that is the precise word—for the love feasts was a physical reaction. In this survival of a practice of the early Christians, long, narrow slices of bread with the crust cut away were distributed; then to the singing of hymns the members circulated among each other, shaking hands and exchanging pinches of bread that were to be eaten. This ceremony constituted a symbol of brotherly love. The pinch of bread came from some sweaty fingers a clammy lump of none-too-white dough, and I found that whatever impulse toward brotherly love that rose in my heart was routed by the revolt in my stomach against actual participation in the feast. I had also to overcome a reaction that was similar, though less in degree, at the communion service, that most barbarously insanitary practice—though at that time I did not know the term "insanitary" or its meaning. The sacrament raised many persons to a high emotional pitch and there was much weeping and slobbering into the cup from which all had to drink. But the taste of the wine—not grape juice in those days—afforded a recompense that the lumps of damp dough did not. I got a satisfaction from learning later that on these last two points my mother wasn't a very good Methodist either.

These combined factors at length produced reluctance, doubt, rebellion. I began to ask myself questions that frightened me. I groped within the narrow boundaries of my own knowledge and experience and between the covers of the Bible for answers, because I did not know to whom I could turn. I might, it seems, have turned to my father but I did not; and it was just as well, for a later incident showed that he would not have given me any real help. I was alone with my questionings and doubts, questionings and doubts that went deeper than mere recalcitrance; and alone I had to fight my way out. At fourteen I was skeptical. By the time I reached my Freshman year at Atlanta University I had avowed myself an agnostic. It can be imagined what an unholy distinction this position brought me in a missionary-founded school, in which playing a game of cards and smoking a cigarette were grave offenses. I now recall with some amusement how my agnostic reasoning left most of my fellow students aghast—there was only one other student in Atlanta University at that time who confessed similar views. Sometimes one or two of the more zealous ones would combat me; but I was well grounded in the arguments of Paine and Ingersoll, and was not an easy opponent. Efforts at reconverting me were futile. . . . I had been through all that. Certainly, the best retort the proselytizers might have made, but did not, was that I had never been converted. These debates usually ended with resolves to pray for God to save my soul from hell.

I examine my mind and heart to find out what has come to me from this early religious experience, this swing from almost the one extreme to almost the other. In that swing through the arc, rapidly forth and gradually back, I came to that conception of religion and that philosophy of life that are now my guide-posts, and I feel that if my experience had been otherwise I might not have come to an adjustment as nearly in emotional and intellectual balance as that which I have reached. And, too, because of that experience I became familiar with the Bible. I read it constantly; first to answer my doubts, then to confirm them, and, finally, with an increasing realization that, all in all, the King James Version is the greatest book in the world.

IV

MY religious experience preceded any experiences of race. Neither my father nor mother had taught me directly anything about race. Naturally, I gained some impressions and picked up some information. Many things I would have learned much sooner had I not been restricted in play. My vague, early impressions constituted what might be called an unconscious race-superiority complex. All the most interesting things that came under my observation were being done by colored men. They drove the horse and mule teams, they built the houses, they laid the bricks, they painted the buildings and fences, they loaded and unloaded the ships. When I was a child, I did not know that there existed such a thing as a white carpenter or bricklayer or painter or plasterer or tinner. The thought that white men might be able to load and unload the heavy drays or the big ships was too far removed from every-day life to enter my mind. There were yet some years for me to live before I would feel the brutal impact of race and learn how race prejudice permeated the whole American social organism.

At first, my brother was my only playmate. We had many ways of amusing ourselves, some of them our own inventions. We, of course, dug in the sand; and, according to the hygienic theories of the time, that did us lots of good. One of the first things Northern tourists were supposed to do was to strip the children and put them out in the sand. We used to sit on the floor with our legs outspread and roll a ball between us the length of the hallway of the house. On days when torrential semi-tropical showers came down, we liked to crawl under the chairs on the front piazza in which our mother or grandmother or "Bar" sat, and pull their skirts around as far as they would go—in those days they went pretty far. We sat in our "tents" very quiet, listening to the falling rain and feeling content and secure. On days when wind-pushed clouds rolled in ever-changing forms across the sky, we had exciting times watching for pictures. Like all normal children, we were not afraid to handle insects and bugs; we caught doodle-bugs; June bugs we kept captive on pieces of thread in order to have them go humming round and round our heads; of big grasshoppers we sought to make "horses," trying to train them to pull little loads. As we grew older we learned to play tops and marbles.

The first outside playmates I can recollect were two white boys, brothers, both of them older than I. I can't recall their names or where they lived, but I know they did for a while come from somewhere over to our yard to play. One day they were playing with me on our front steps; it must have been a few days after Christmas, for I had a new drum, my first. The bigger brother persuaded me to let him cut open the head of the drum so as to see where the sound came from. After his successful operation the only sounds made came from me. My mother rushed out and drove both boys away with a strong request to stay away. Those two playmates vanished from my life completely, but the incident remained in my mind. It was a low, mean trick; however, I am glad I remembered it.

As often as I got the chance I played in the street with the children of the neighborhood. They were the Morrisons, who lived diagonally across and whose father was a carpenter and often got pretty drunk; Beck and Carrie Wright, who lived next door to Mr. Cole; and Camilla Sherman, a pretty, saucy-looking little brown girl, who lived just above the Wrights. The games we played oftenest were hide-and-seek and prisoner's base. In the house on the lot adjoining us on the north lived the two little Ross girls, who looked white but were not. They went by the lovely pet names of "Sing" and "Babe." Sometimes my brother and I went over to their yard to play and sometimes they came over to ours. But the playmates that had our mother's unqualified approval lived at a considerable distance. We used to go across town to play with Alvin and Mamie Gibbs, whose father was steward on one of the steamboats that then plied the St. Johns River; with Sam and Charlie Grant, sons of the pastor of Ebenezer Church; and with Carrie, Fred, and "Trixie" (a boy) Onley, whose father was a contractor and builder. The houses of these playmates were very much like our own; that of the Onleys was, perhaps, a bit more pretentious. Our visits were regularly returned. The visit that for a long time interested me most was the one to the Gibbses. Mrs. Gibbs often invited us to dinner, and she generally gave us gumbo. Do not for an instant think it was the watery, tasteless concoction that goes by the same name in Northern hotels and restaurants. Mrs. Gibbs was a native of Charleston, South Carolina, and knew how to cook Charlestonian gumbo. Into the big pot went not only okra and water and salt and pepper, but at the proper intervals bits of chicken; ham first fried then cut into small squares; whole shrimps; crab meat, some of it left in pieces of the shell; onions and tomatoes; thyme and other savory herbs; the whole allowed to simmer until it reached an almost viscous consistency; then served in a deep plate over rice cooked as white and dry as it is cooked by the Chinese. This gumbo, a dish for—reference to the epicure and the *vrai gourmet* are not in place—this more than a savory dish—the dish irresistible—the most soul-satisfying of all the dishes that Negro cookery has given the South. Moreover, there was the subtle attraction of Mamie, and Alvin's ownership of a velocipede. After dinner we used to take the velocipede down to the St. James, where there was the best continuous sidewalk in town, and ride round and round the block. There were other houses that we visited, but not quite so regularly. But it was at school, when I was about eight years old, that I formed my closest boyhood friendship. D—— and I were unlike each other in more ways than one, yet we instantly became chums and mutual confidants—a relationship that was to run through boyhood, youth, and early manhood, and strangely to influence, cross, and interact upon both our lives.

Among this latter set of children, made up from a dozen or so families, birthday parties and parties in celebration of nothing in particular were frequently given. They were held in the afternoons, and we always had lemonade and cake and candies, sometimes ice cream; and we always played kissing games. I liked these kissing games, and didn't like them. There were always one or two girls that I knew I would prefer to kiss, but when I got into the ring I stood shamefaced; I did not find it easy to fly to the east and the west and to the very one that I loved best. I simply could not expose my delicate desires to the crowd; so, usually, I diffidently kissed some other girl in order to get out of the ring as quickly as possible. I frequently got out of the game altogether, watching with envy and admiration those who played with assurance, I might say effrontery. My prowess as a ring player was on a par with my ability as a public speaker; as a result, I went away from many a party filled with haunting regrets.

But it was not all play; I had certain tasks to do, and when my brother grew large enough he shared them with me. I raked the yard, cleaned the steel table knives by working them up and down in the sand and giving them a very bright polish. I cleaned, filled, and trimmed the lamps. Later Rosamond and I were assigned the job of washing and drying the dishes, a job we never stopped hating. Many of the children in the neighborhood performed a task that never fell to us because a supply of matches was always kept at our house. . . . Every morning they could be seen carrying a coal of fire between two sticks, blowing on it to keep it alive as they ran home. They had been sent to "borrow a piece of fire."

At school I learned the real boys' games, and played them with some pretty rough boys. I judge that Stanton, with respect to rough boys, held its own with any school in the country. I am glad, however, that the situation was such that my mother could not with good grace take me out and send me to a softer school. I learned in those school days democracy as it is practiced in the world of boys, and there it is practiced without hypocrisy and cant. In the world of boys it is always the frank and sometimes the brutal thing that democracy needs must be. This experience I count one of the most vital in the course of my education. Stanton School, so named after Lincoln's Secretary of War, was built shortly after Emancipation by the Freedmen's Bureau, I think, and later turned over to the county as a public school. The original structure (the one now standing is the fourth) was a large, two-story, frame building, extremely well built, that occupied, with the grounds, an entire city block, and was surrounded by a high fence. A little more than half of the grounds was on the "boys' side," but a strip of the boys' playground was taken up by a garden cultivated by the janitor, and woe to those who for a lost ball invaded the demesne of this old ogre. The first principal and most of the teachers were white. When I began as a pupil there were still several white women among the teachers, but the staff, including the principal, was practically all colored. The principal was James C. Waters, a well-educated man and an eloquent speaker. He was a brown-skinned man; he wore a cropped mustache and had what I thought of as fierce eyes. He was, I judge, a youngish man, but among themselves the boys called him "Old J.C.," and "Old J.C." was a terror to the toughest boys at Stanton. At recess, like a stalking Nemesis, he walked about on the boys' side with a long cane that he brought into action with lightning rapidity. I regarded him with awe, and could not have imagined a worse stroke of fate than to be called up before him. I never presumed on any immunity because my mother was one of the teachers; in fact, I had a feeling that with J.C. this would have aggravated the seriousness of my case.

School began with chapel exercises. All the pupils marched by classes in single file into the chapel, where devotions were held for twenty or thirty minutes. The chapel was an airy room that seated five or six hundred pupils. Running entirely across the farther end was a platform on which were a desk, a row of chairs, and a fine square piano, the latter a gift from a piano manufacturer who had visited the school. I have an uncertain recollection that on the walls there were framed pictures of Lincoln and several other important figures on the Union side in the Civil War. When chapel exercises began, the gates were locked, and the tardy scholars were kept in the street until they were over. J.C. would then go down to the lower hall with a strap or ruler in his hand and greet the late comers as they passed him one by one giving excuses that were seldom accepted. At recess we scurried out to play, and when it was over we marched back in strict order. There was a row of young oaks planted in a straight line; when the bell rang each class formed at its tree. Always there was a rush to be the first at the tree, and so head the line. The ambition to gain and hold this honor caused a good deal of pushing and scuffling and even fisticuffs that often brought J.C.'s long cane into action. It was, of course, infinitely far from my knowledge that J.C. was making a set of impressions on my mind against the time when I should stand in his place as the head of Stanton; impressions that would come back fresh and constrain me either to follow or avoid his example.

I never had any serious business with him; I was a small boy, and, before I was big enough to get into any scrapes that would bring down on me the sort of punishment then commonly meted out in public schools, there was another and milder principal at Stanton. I really look back with complacency—though that is a quality I positively dislike—upon my behavior as a boy in public school. I know I was slyly mischievous, but I stayed out of ugly, dishonorable things. I had the minimum number of fights that a boy in public school must have if he is to retain the respect of his fellows and his self-respect; but there is nothing ugly or dishonorable about that. I regret only that none of these fights can I now recollect as

James Johnson   *Helen Louise Johnson*

Teachers at Stanton

HELEN LOUISE JOHNSON—SECOND FROM THE LEFT, BOTTOM ROW
AGNES MARION EDWARDS—FIRST FROM LEFT, CENTER ROW

material for this record. I can see that I should have had at
least one gallant, memorable battle, with Victory flitting from
one side to the other before she finally perched upon my
shoulder.

The games I learned to play at school were: marbles, tops,
shinny, and baseball. Baseball was my game; the one in which I
developed more than ordinary expertness. I was well adapted
to the game physically, being slight of figure but muscular.
And I not only practiced steadily but studied assiduously. I
worked to master what is now known as "inside" baseball. I
read regularly a weekly publication called *Sporting Life*, which
was devoted chiefly to baseball, so I was familiar with the
names and records of all the noted professional players. My
favorite club was the old Detroits, and my particular heroes of
the diamond were Fred Dunlap and Dan Brouthers, its famous
second baseman and first baseman. Before I left Stanton to go
to Atlanta University, one of the pitchers on the "Cuban
Giants," the crack Negro professional team of New York, imparted to me the secrets of the art of curve pitching. (The
Cuban Giants were originally organized from among the waiters at the Ponce de Leon Hotel in St. Augustine. They played
professional ball in the North in the summer but for a number
of seasons they worked in winter in the St. Augustine hotels
and played ball, principally for the entertainment of the
guests.) Under my instructor, who had taken a liking to me
because he thought I showed the makings of a real player, I
gained control of a wide out-curve, a sharp in-shoot, a slow
and tantalizing "drop" and a deceptive "rise." I was at the
time the only local colored boy who could do the trick. I practiced by the hour with my friend Sam Grant as catcher. We
were the battery of our nine, "The Domestics" (why we chose
this name I cannot tell), a club made up of boys ranging from
fourteen to sixteen years of age. Our fame as a battery began
to spread.

My first taste of athletic glory came when Sam and I were
called on to serve as the battery for "The Roman Cities" (I
am more puzzled by the significance of this name than by
that of the club to which I belonged), the leading colored
club of Jacksonville and, thereby, the best club in the whole
city, in a big game with a formidable team from Savannah.

The Roman Cities was a first-rate club. The chief strength of the team was Bill Broad, so nicknamed because of the abnormal breadth of his face. Bill Broad was a wonderful outfielder and, I think, the best natural batter I have ever seen. In either capacity his most strenuous exertions always appeared to be effortless. There were other good players on The Roman Cities, but the team was a little apprehensive over the impending game, and decided to take a chance on strengthening their offensive with my style of pitching, which they had watched. They tried to fit Sam and me out in the blue and red uniforms of the club, but those were all too large; so we played in the white flannel suits, white caps and black stockings of our own club.

The crowd was big and vociferous. It was made up of both whites and blacks. (A good Negro team was then as great a drawing card for whites in the South as one is now for whites in the North.) The white people of Jacksonville were ardent boosters for The Roman Cities, especially when the club played against a team from a Georgia town. For this game a good many shops were closed, and street cars and hacks went out to the grounds loaded beyond capacity. When the visiting nine took the field, I glued my eyes on the opposing pitcher. He was a tall, slender fellow and a fine exponent of the classic style of pitching. He stood holding the ball in front of him in both hands while he intently studied the batter. Then shifting his entire weight to the right foot, he slowly twirled his body round to the right until he almost faced second base, his left foot rising from the ground as his body turned; then back again he twirled with accelerating speed. At the same time his right arm swung back, under, upward, forward and under, describing an almost complete figure 8. He turned swiftly. His left foot came down and dug into the earth, holding the momentum of his body in check, while the right rose into the air, and the ball shot out, projected by every ounce of his weight and energy. The motion began in a gentle sweeping curve and culminated in a pose, held for an instant, of tense power. It was an exhibition of the perfection of masculine grace. Beautiful pitching like that is among the lost arts.

This pitcher's strategy lay in a ball of blinding speed, change of pace, and the ability to trim the corners of the plate. I guessed at once that Sam and I would make a poor showing at the bat; and I guessed right. But we counterbalanced all that. When I ran out to go into the box for the home team, there was every reason for me to feel nervous, but I didn't. No medicine man ever appeared before the tribe with more confidence in his magic than I had in mine when I faced the crowd. As I stooped and picked up a handful of dirt to rub into the cover of the ball to roughen it somewhat, and glanced at the hulking young giant who came to bat, if I had the presumption to draw an analogy between myself and little David choosing his five smooth stones from the brook, I ought, perhaps, to be pardoned. But the analogy was not so far-fetched, at that; David used long-range artillery against a short sword, and I had up my sleeve what was practically a magic power, the power to make the ball suddenly change its course and dart out of the path of the on-coming bat. The advantage, over those to whom it was new, was so great as to amount to unfairness. Yet it was not apparent enough to prevent my being greeted by a chorus of groans and yells as well as applause and cheers.

My delivery was, necessarily, quite different from that of my opponent. It was overhand, rapid, even jerky, and ended with the quick snap of the wrist required to produce the curve. I started with the use of a wide out-curve aimed at the plate, and the break timed so as to tempt the batter to fan the air; varying it by aiming straight at the batter so that the break was over the plate, my purpose being to cause the batter to duck and have a strike called. The coaches finally solved this, and cautioned the batters, "When you see it coming for the plate, don't hit at it. Wait till you see it coming at you." Of course, I immediately began working in a straight ball, an in-shoot, and the drop; and the mystery deepened. As the game went on it assumed a humorous aspect. As many spectators as could do so crowded behind the catcher to watch the vagaries of the ball, and yells of derision greeted bewildered batters, especially when they lunged at the elusive, wide-breaking out-curves. The Roman Cities won the game by a one-sided score. I struck out sixteen men and held the others down to ineffectiveness. My reward was a pretty full cup of the sensation of being a popular hero.

One of the most interested spectators at the game was a man named Haines Spearing. He was a colored sport and said to be the best-dressed man in Jacksonville. He loudly declared that the whole thing was a hoax, a physical impossibility, merely an optical illusion—or words to that effect—and offered to bet that it could not be demonstrated. I couldn't cover his bet, but offered to give him a demonstration free of any risk on his part. I did what I had often done in practice and what I was confident I could do ninety-five times out of a hundred. A group followed us to where two trees stood ten or twelve feet apart. I took my stand in line with the trees and about fifty feet away. I stepped a couple of feet to the left and threw the ball so that it passed to the right of the first tree, between the two, and out to the left of the second tree. Q.E.D.

V

BEFORE the happenings just related—to be more precise, when I was about five years old—I made a memorable trip—"the trip to Nassau." I say "memorable" not because it was memorable for me but because it became memorable as a family tradition. Indeed, I remember very little about it. The trip over was made in a little two-masted schooner named the *Ida Smith*. I have a dim recollection of being on the water in a boat, and very uncomfortable. Less faintly comes back a sense of being suffocated in the place where I slept and a resurgence of the sickening odor of bilge water. The stay in Nassau was only a few months, but the trip back is a good deal clearer. The ship was bigger and I was happier. The captain, a colored man, was a very nice man and devoted some attention to me. I have a pretty clear recollection, too, of strange-looking women in Nassau coming by the house where we lived with trays or baskets on their heads loaded with mangoes, guavas, pineapples, pomegranates, sapodillas, sour-sops, tamarinds, and other tropical fruits, crying out their wares in words I couldn't understand beyond knowing that they meant things very good to eat. I retain a faint picture of streets dazzlingly white under the sun and ghostly pale under the moon. Other memory films are blurred and faded. Only one incident stands out: It was a bright morning. I was all dressed up. I was cautioned dozens of times not to soil my clothes by eating sticky, staining fruit. A very high wagon pulled up at the door. I could not imagine a higher one. It had four wheels and was drawn by two horses. My mother and grandmother and, seemingly, a lot of other people got into the wagon. They had to get in by stepping up on a chair. Baskets of food were also loaded in. We were going to visit the African Village, where a remnant of former slaves lived in primitive fashion under their own chief. The ride was for me a great adventure. When we got to the village, I went around with my elders looking at curious people, peeping into their huts, seeing them dance under a large, hut-like pavilion in the center of the village to the beating of drums—drums of many sizes and sounds, drums, drums, drums.

While I was in Nassau I must have many times seen Stephen Dillet, son of my grandfather, and himself a man of prominence, but I brought away no clear image of him. When we were leaving, he made me a present of a cricket bat, but I cannot recall his presenting me with it. When I got back home I found it among my possessions, and was told that it had been given to me by my Uncle Stephen. And it was in this way that I learned most of what I know about the trip to Nassau—by being told. In later years my wife and my brother's wife heard those incidents of the trip that concerned their respective husbands so often that they reached the point where they held up both hands whenever the subject was even indirectly introduced.

My cricket bat was the only tangible and substantial evidence I had of ever having been to Nassau. It was my convincing proof to all the boys who heard my second-hand versions of the adventures of the voyage; for not in all Jacksonville was there another bat like it. True, it was also proof that my uncle knew absolutely nothing about American athletic games; so the bat never rose to the punctilious use for which it was designed. Finally, it suffered the indignity of being worn out by Big Bill Broad in batting flies in our street for a crowd of youngsters.

It was during the visit to Nassau that I became vaguely aware of having a sister. My sister, Marie Louise, died before I was born. When my brother was about to be born, my mother was hoping for a girl, and picked out for her name, Rosamond.

When it turned out not to be that kind of child, she made the best of the situation by using the name, anyhow, and coupling it with a sex-indicating "John." But Rosamond is the name by which my brother was always called, and it caused him a good deal of embarrassment before he got it established, and even after.

My mother, however, was not to be outdone, so she adopted a daughter, not a baby, but a girl in her teens. Her name was Agnes Marion Edwards. This adopted daughter was one of the party that made the trip to Nassau, and she became one of the chief repositories of the lore relating to that epochal event. She was very gentle and capable of unselfish devotion to others that I have seen equaled in no one else. As I grew up I knew her and loved her as a sister.

When I was, perhaps, ten years old a strange being came to Jacksonville, the first colored doctor. He practiced there a number of years and made a success; but he had a hard, up-hill fight. Few were the colored people at that time who had the faith to believe that one of their own number knew how to make those cabalistic marks on a piece of paper that would bring from the drugstore something to stand between them and death. Dr. Darnes made himself a big chum to Rosamond and me, and we liked him tremendously. He constantly brought us some of the odds and ends so much prized by boys. He once gave us fifty cents apiece for learning the deaf and dumb alphabet within a given time. I suppose in doing that he merely wanted us to feel that we had done something to earn the money; for I couldn't see even then what practical benefit this knowledge would be to us. We did, however, for a while get some amusement out of trying to communicate with each other in this sign language. But, best of all, Dr. Darnes was an enthusiastic fisherman, and he opened up a new world of fun and sport by teaching us how to fish.

During my first decade two events from the big outside world made an impression on me; and that outside world was still a shadowy land. The most momentous decade in the history of the nation was the one preceding my birth, but, as yet, it had no real significance for me. I had heard talk about the Civil War from men who had seen it. I remember well a remnant in Jacksonville of a Negro regiment of the Union Army, which during Reconstruction had formed a part of the Florida militia. Some of these were friends of my father, and it was from them that I heard the talk. All the boys of my age knew something about "The War," and there was still plenty of evidence around Jacksonville that there had been a war. Any boy, by searching round a little, could make a collection of rusty bayonets, old belts, brass buttons, and the like; and nearly every boy had such a collection. The bayonets and buttons, polished bright, were highly prized. But I doubt that any of us had an idea of the meaning of the War. As for myself, my interest centered in tales about the fighting, and did not extend to what the fighting was about. But there were two names connected with the war that we knew well: Abraham Lincoln and General Grant. At that time Grant was for me the greater hero. He was President when I was born, so his name was sounded in my young ears a good many times. One of the clearest-cut of my early memories is of a very big colored man on a night of some excitement passing our house and yelling lustily, madly, truculently (he may have been drunk): "Hurrah for General Grant! Hurrah for General Grant!" In addition, through the tales of ex-soldiers I had caught some of the glamour of Grant's great military fame. And the news flashed and spread through the town that General Grant was coming to Jacksonville.

I was with my parents in the crowd that met him at the station. This visit must have taken place early in the year 1877. The crowd at the station was dense and mixed, white and black. There was no reason why the General should have been popular with the native whites; probably they were just curious to see the man. We waited, it seemed to me, for hours. Finally, the sound of the approaching train was heard; then the wood-burning locomotive, pouring a thick stream of black smoke from its wide-mouthed funnel and with a loud-clanging bell, hove into sight and drew alongside the dingy, shedless station. With hurrahs and yells the crowd swayed and bulged over the line that the police and militia were trying to maintain. Excitement and panicky fear struggled in me for the mastery; and I clutched my mother's hand more tightly.

The General with his party alighted and was standing in the open space receiving introductions of those in charge of his reception, when through the line burst an old harridan, well known to everybody in the town. She lived out our way, and there was not a child in that section who did not fear her violent tongue. Her real name was, I guess, Tucker; and I guess, too, that she was not so very old, but everybody called her "Old Dan Tucker." She was a woman brown in color, not at all bad-looking, and very active. On this day she was dressed in new clothes, but wore them in her usual manner: her long, wide calico skirt was tucked up about her waist so that it reached only a little below the knees; and a brand-new, bright red bandanna was wound round her head. In her hands she carried a big bunch of flowers. Before anyone could anticipate her intention, she darted across the open space straight for General Grant, threw her arms around his neck, gave him a resounding kiss on the cheek, then kneeling down presented him with her bunch of flowers. The crowd was too much astonished for expression. Some people, especially some of the colored people, were scandalized by "Old Dan's" action. What General Grant thought about it, no one ever found out.

Old Dan Tucker's *coup de théâtre* strengthened me in a much less daring project which I had been revolving in my own mind for several days. All the colored school and Sunday school children had been organized to pass in review before the General, and there were hundreds in line, with teachers, principals, and superintendents. He took his stand on the hotel veranda, and we were marched up the steps at one end, along and down and off at the other end. Along the veranda the crowd moved slowly. As we approached the reviewing group it took all that I could do to make my courage stick. When I reached the point where the General stood I timidly put out my hand; he took it in his for an instant, and I passed on. But it was a proud instant; I had carried out my project; I had shaken hands with General Grant.

The second of these two outside world events was the assassination of President Garfield. I was now four years older, old enough to take an interest in newspapers, and I kept up with the President's condition until he died. I thought it was a terrible thing to have shot down the President of the

United States. I think this sentiment was intensified by talk that I heard among the colored people, talk consisting of dark hints about a deep plot on the part of the ex-Confederates to capture the government. On the day that Garfield was buried, funeral exercises were held in Jacksonville. Those who took part in the program and other prominent citizens were seated on the veranda of the hotel. The crowd packed the street in front and extended back into St. James Park. I think the greater part of the crowd was made up of Negroes. The eloquence of the several orations that were pronounced left little impression on me, but the prayer that opened the exercises, because of its length, I remembered for years. This prayer was delivered by Reverend D. W. Culp. Mr. Culp was a slender young man of medium height, and was pure black. He was well educated, a graduate of Biddle University in North Carolina and of the theological seminary of Princeton. He had recently come to Jacksonville and was the pastor of the local colored Presbyterian Church, and had just been appointed as the new principal of Stanton School. The exercises were, naturally, in the hands of Federal officeholders, and Mr. Culp was chosen, representing the Negroes, to make the opening prayer, the which he did within the course of some thirty-five or forty minutes. He stammered terribly, but the length of this particular prayer could not be charged to the impediment in his speech. It was due rather, I suspect, to his realization that he had an opportunity to impress himself upon certain leading citizens of Jacksonville as well as upon the Lord. I have heard some queer prayers but never any one prayer in which so wide a range of topics was introduced. Many times I have been forced to conclude that the most absurd utterances that pass human lips are some of the prayers that are, ostensibly, addressed to God. Those officious, pompous prayers that summarize affairs on this terrestrial globe and offer Him specific directions for working out the difficulties and carrying on. If such prayers do reach God, and He can listen to them, He possesses an attribute no one ever thinks of ascribing to Him— an infinite sense of humor.

The Negro citizens of Jacksonville took great pride in the part they played in both of the ceremonies I have referred to. They were especially pleased with the brave showing they made before General Grant. I suppose, if the truth were known, the taciturn Grant was greatly bored by the performances of both whites and blacks. It occurs to me that the Negro citizens of Jacksonville would not at the present time be accorded an equivalent degree of recognition and participation in ceremonies or celebrations of this kind. And that comment would apply, I think, to Southern communities generally. Mr. Will Alexander of Atlanta holds that this shift in attitude is principally due to the rise to power of the poor whites, between whom and the Negro there is an old antagonism based on the differences in their actual economic status under the slave system, an antagonism that then bore more heavily upon the poor whites than upon the blacks. Of course, the settling down from the temporary heights of Reconstruction must be taken into account, but I feel that Mr. Alexander is, in the main, right. Long after the close of the Reconstruction period Jacksonville was known far and wide as a good town for Negroes. When I was growing up, most of the city policemen were Negroes; several members of the city council were Negroes; one or two justices of the peace were Negroes. When a paid fire department was established, one station was manned by Negroes. I was in my teens when the city government was reorganized and Joseph E. Lee, a Negro and a very able man and astute politician, was made Judge of the Municipal Court. Many of the best stalls in the city market were owned and operated by Negroes; Davis and Robinson, a firm of Negro commission merchants, were land stewards for the Clyde Steamship Company; and there was no such thing as a white-owned barber shop. I know that there was a direct relation between that state of affairs and the fact that Jacksonville was controlled by certain aristocratic families, families like the L'Engles, Hartridges, and Daniels's, who were sensitive to the code, *noblesse oblige*. The aristocratic families have lost control and the old conditions have been changed. Jacksonville is today a one hundred per cent Cracker town, and each time I have been back there I have marked greater and greater changes.

In this is epitomized one of the paradoxes of American democracy that the Negro has to wrestle with. We are told and we tell ourselves that as a race we belong to the proletariat and that our economic and political salvation lies in joining hands with our white fellow workers. Notwithstanding, it is true that the black worker finds getting into most of the white labor unions no easier than getting an invitation to a white bourgeois dinner party.

There is another fact that bears interestingly on Mr. Alexander's theory, perhaps to confirm it further, a fact that must strike every observant person who goes through the deep rural South: Among the white people of those regions, people who have not yet tasted social or political power nor yet possessed the rewards of industrialism or come within its brutal field of competition, active antagonism against the Negro is lowest; so low indeed, it would probably die out if it were not continuously and furiously stirred by the working classes and the politicians (the social factor is powerful and intransigent, but at this level is in abeyance); by the working classes, determined to hold certain grades of work for white men only, and by the politicians, bent on preserving their rotten oligarchy by keeping alive the sole political issue upon which the "Solid South" rests. An important part is played also by those intellectuals who write to uphold the present status, many of whom are, I know, conscious that the system is unjust and uncivilized but are too timid to oppose or even question it. Their timidity often sinks to pusillanimity.

VI

IN 1884, when I was between twelve and thirteen years old, my grandmother went to New York and took me with her. We made the trip by sea. She went to visit her sister, Sarah, who lived on what was then South Second Street in Williamsburg, Brooklyn. My grandaunt Sarah was older than my grandmother. She was quite stout and moved round with difficulty. She was also much lighter in complexion than my grandmother, but her features were slightly heavier. Still, when she smiled she showed that she had once been very pretty. Dimples came into her cheek and her mouth became winsome. My mother looked a great deal more like her aunt than she did like her own mother. The difference between the two sisters in temperament and disposition was even greater than it was in physical appearance. Aunt Sarah was jolly and

easy-going. She was nominally a member of the Episcopal
Church, but I am sure she did not contemplate the everlasting
fate of her soul with any particular anxiety. She loved her mug
of beer and was always willing to give me a generous taste. My
grandmother, who was one of the leaders of the Band of
Hope, a temperance crusading society to which I belonged,
objected to this strenuously; and her objections led one day to
a pretty hot row between the sisters.

Aunt Sarah's husband was named William C. H. Curtis. He
was a small, rather wizened, light brown man. He had a grave
face that was curiously lighted by his gray eyes. His head was
absolutely bald on the whole top, but the hair grew thick and
bushy low on the sides and in the back. He wore a beard of
medium length but scanty. He moved about the house almost
stealthily in slippers, and talked so little that everyone listened
whenever he did speak. Uncle William was a journeyman jew-
eler, but he had long given up his trade to become a manufacturer of regalia for secret societies. He carried on his business
at home, and a good part of each day he spent at a big table
cutting out badges and aprons and banners from bright-colored silks. My aunt and two hired women sat and stitched on
the gold and silver braid and fringe and tassels and the various
emblems and insignia. It must have been a profitable business,
for Aframerica did then and does now constitute a good market for these commodities. At any rate, he had been able to
purchase the house in which he lived, a two-story and basement brick building with a brownstone stoop. This house
seemed to me palatial, and I regarded my uncle as a very rich
man. I think he was in a way fond of me, but he never deviated
from the even tenor of his manner to demonstrate whatever affection he may have had. However, he did give me a gold ring
which he himself had made.

Moreover, he showed that he liked to take me with him
when he went over to New York to shop for materials for his
business; and that trip was always a great treat for me. We
would go to Broadway in Williamsburg and take the ferry to
Grand Street in New York. I loved the ferryboats—the rushing
crowds, the stamping teams and yelling teamsters, the tooting
whistles, the rattling windlasses and clanging chains when we
left and entered the slip. I loved to stand on the forward end

to watch the busy-body tugs; they amused me tremendously and made me think of what, in Jacksonville, we called "biggity" boys. But above all, I enjoyed the sensation of approaching the great city.

It would not have taken a psychologist to understand that I was born to be a New Yorker. In fact, I was partly a New Yorker already. Even then I had a dual sense of home. From the time that I could distinguish the meaning of words I had been hearing about New York. My parents talked about the city much in the manner that exiles or emigrants talk about the homeland; and I had long thought of New York, as well as Jacksonville, as my home. But being born for a New Yorker means being born, no matter where, with a love for cosmopolitanism; and one either is or is not. If, among other requirements for happiness, one needs neighbors; that is, feels that he must be on friendly terms with the people who live next door, and, in addition know all about them; if one must be able to talk across from front porches and chat over back fences; if one is possessed by a zeal to regulate the conduct of people who are neither neighbors nor friends—he is not born for a New Yorker.

When my uncle and I got off in New York we would take a horse car and go as far as Lord and Taylor's, then located in Grand Street. I had a lively time going through the big store while he bought his goods, some at one counter and some at another. When he had finished, we would go down to the Grand Street ferry and take the boat back to Williamsburg. I went to lots of other places in New York City, but my uncle never spent the time to take me. Yet, among the memories of all my goings about those of the excursions to Lord and Taylor's with him remain sharpest. I still love an old ferryboat because it is evocative of those days. I never board one and catch the smell from the deck planks redolent of horses that I do not recapture some of the sensations I experienced as a boy in crossing the East River and making the trip back and forth to Lord and Taylor's.

During my stay I learned to play all the New York sidewalk games; but, in comparison with the field games we played in Jacksonville, they seemed to me very childish. My playmates were for the greater part the white boys and girls who lived

near on our side of the street and those across. The only colored playmates I had were a girl named Edith Matthews, who
lived just around the corner, and two brothers by the name of
Jackson, who lived on the same street four or five blocks away.
When I went to the Jacksons, I frequently saw T. Thomas Fortune; he lived in the same house. I knew him well; he was a
native of Florida and before he moved to New York was a frequent visitor at our house. My two playmates and I were
sometimes in a room where he sat at a desk writing, covering
sheet after sheet that he dropped on the floor, and all the
while running his fingers through his long hair. He was writing his first book, *Black and White: Land, Labor, and Politics
in the South*, an economic study of the race problem. We were
usually playing parchesi on the floor, and when we annoyed
him too much he made us scamper. But we stood in no awe of
him; we had no conception of how great a man he was,
though not yet thirty, and of course no thought of how much
greater a man he was to become.

I did have another colored playmate, my aunt. She never felt
that the day was properly ended unless she and I had our
round of dominoes. She played a good game, and, at the same
time, was not above doing a little cheating. She always
crooned softly to herself when the game was going well for
her. It distressed her so much to lose that I didn't very much
enjoy winning. I got more fun out of her exuberant pleasure in
beating me, even when she had cheated a bit. After the
domino game there was one more thing to be done in which I
had to join her. Every night she took one of Carter's Little
Liver Pills—a product which gigantic advertising, then at its
beginning in the United States, had literally injected into hundreds of thousands of American households—and every night
during my stay in New York I took one too, whether I needed
it or not.

My grandmother took me about with her a good deal visiting old friends she had known twenty or thirty or more years
before. Most of the houses she visited were on Bleecker Street
or Sullivan Street or Thompson Street or in the vicinity, then
the principal Negro section of New York. None of her old
friends or acquaintances interested me; and hardly ever did I
meet anyone near my own age. I was bored terribly by long

conversations about old times and people who had died or, perhaps, done something worse; and I disliked the generally stuffy rooms in which I had to sit while the talk went on. But I loved to go on these trips because we rode endless miles, it seemed, on the horse cars and I was constantly seeing new sights. I especially enjoyed riding on the Broadway stage coaches. Only one of these old friends of my grandmother stuck in my memory. She was a gray-haired woman and quite stout, and sat all the while in a large armchair; she may have been lame. Suddenly she produced a pair of scissors and called me over to clip her finger nails. I found this job exceedingly distasteful; and, furthermore, she was very particular about how the work should be done. If I had been a modern-reared child I should have told the old lady to her face that I didn't want to and wouldn't clip her hard old nails; but to a product of the system under which I was brought up such action was unthinkable. When I had finished, she gave me a nickel, which I considered pretty poor pay. On one trip we went to Central Park, and I had the belated joy of riding in a goat wagon. And I mixed pleasure with duty by going round with a notebook industriously taking down a long list of the monuments to great men—names, dates, and deeds. I cannot imagine that this was a self-imposed duty, for I innately rebel at cataloguing statistical details. I must have been following the admonishment of one of my teachers. Nor do I remember that the collected data were ever of any use to me. I think the time could have been better spent in the monkey house. With my grandmother I made the trip across and back over Brooklyn Bridge. The great suspension bridges of New York are now commonplace; so the thrill of crossing Brooklyn Bridge when it was new cannot now be duplicated. But when I crossed, the echoes of the panic of the opening day, when the swaying of the great span under the tread of the crowd gave rise to the cry that the bridge was falling, had not quite died down; and I was far from feeling confident that it would not fall. Once we made a trip far up toward Harlem, a region then inhabited largely by squatters and goats.

But a good many of my happiest hours were passed in the house. In addition to watching gorgeous paraphernalia for Masons, Odd Fellows, Good Samaritans, and various Sons and

Daughters of this and that take form, partaking of surreptitious sips of beer with my aunt, and keeping up our domino playing and pill taking, I spent a lot of time reading. At home I had discovered a small bound volume of an old English periodical called *The Mirror*, which contained many things that interested me. But in my aunt's parlor I found perhaps a dozen volumes of a magazine (it may have been *The Waverly Magazine*) so large that the only way I could handle them was to lay them on the floor. These volumes were filled with illustrated serial stories, many of them Indian stories. Here was a mine of interest and excitement, and I worked it in long shifts; especially on rainy days. What a combination for contentment—a rainy day and a thirteen-year-old boy who loved to read stretched out on the floor with an inexhaustible supply of Indian stories! Sometimes I played the piano; at that age I played fairly well. One of the conditions on which I was given the trip was that I should keep up my piano lessons; so I studied once a week with a very good teacher with a French name that I cannot recall. During this stay in New York I formed a lasting affection for my grandaunt. While yet a boy I visited her twice again.

The following summer my mother visited Aunt Sarah and took my brother and my sister with her. I stayed at home with my grandmother, who had given up her cottage and moved to our house. She and I were practically alone, because my father had by this time gone into the ministry, and he spent most of his time in Fernandina, thirty miles away, where he was pastor of a large Baptist church. For a half-dozen years I had been able to boast to my brother that I had shaken hands with General Grant. When he got back home from New York, he could boast to me that he had seen General Grant's funeral. He related how they had gone up to Riverside Drive (then only one of the rocky frontiers of northern Manhattan) early in the morning with their lunch and camped there till the procession passed. He told me about the bands and the soldiers and the twenty-four colored men, each leading one of the black, black-plumed horses that drew the funeral car. I was compelled to admit that, between him and me, he had seen the best of General Grant.

But that was not the limit of our friendly rivalry. For several years I had been making a struggle, that grew more hopeless each day, to keep up with my brother in music. I played the guitar better than he; probably because he never exerted himself to learn that instrument. We considered the piano the greatest instrument, and my ambition was to maintain, at least, parity with him in piano playing. I finally gave over in the struggle and took up an instrument that did not attract him very much—the violin. But during the summer he was in New York my ambition was burning high. While he was away, I found a book entitled *Music and Some Highly Musical People*, a compilation of biographical sketches of a number of Negro musicians, including Blind Tom, The Black Swan, and others not so well known. In the back were various musical compositions by Negro composers. Among these compositions I found a piece, "Welcome to the Era," a stirring march, which I mastered after many hours of practice. At the first good opportunity I went to the piano and knocked the piece off for my brother. He at once wanted to know where I had got it; and I would not tell him. He searched through all the sheets of music and music books we had; naturally, not thinking to look in a book that appeared to be filled only with reading matter. I got keen joy out of the satisfaction that I had, at least, one piece that he couldn't beat me playing. However, my satisfaction lasted only until Rosamond let go the repertory of six or eight new pieces he had learned in New York, his star piece being *See-Saw*, a waltz song and the overwhelmingly popular hit of the year Eighteen Hundred and Eighty-Five. I may say that *See-Saw* snuffed out any future as a pianist that I might have had.

But I had in store another surprise for my brother; one that he didn't get over so easily; nor, for that matter, did my mother and father and sister. The pastor of Ebenezer Church at the time was the Reverend Peter Swearingen. I was a regular attendant at church, more regular during this period than ever before—or since; and so I heard Mr. Swearingen preach every Sunday. I thought that he was a very good preacher; but as much as his preaching I admired a pair of black broadcloth, "spring-bottom" trousers he wore. "Spring-bottom" trousers were extremely popular at the time. They were an adaptation of the style so long standard for sailors. As I think of it now, the style was not entirely in keeping with ministerial garb.

Notwithstanding, these "spring-bottoms" appealed to me as the acme of elegance; so much so that I set my heart on having a pair. I was wearing short pants, but my grandmother approved the idea; pleased, no doubt, that I was at any rate following clerical example. That much settled, it became a question of money, for I had already gone to Trumpeller, the leading merchant tailor, and inquired about the cost and had been dazed to learn that to make the trousers, finished in the best style, would cost fourteen dollars. I could not think of suggesting such an amount to my grandmother for a pair of boy's pants. I had been earning fifty cents on Saturdays. My father had torn down the old house on the corner and built a shop, which he rented to a white man named Mott. This man ran a grocery store, and gave me fifty cents for helping around on his busiest day. It was a very easy problem in arithmetic for me to figure out that at this rate I should have to work more than half a year before I could earn enough to pay for the pants; so I decided to look for another job.

One very hot morning I stopped under one of the great oaks on Laura Street and watched the work on the foundation for a new house. The building was being put up by Hart and DeLyons, a firm of Negro contractors. Here was a chance for a job. Why not? I walked up to Mr. Hart, whom I knew, and asked him to give me a job. He smiled and asked, "Well, what can you do?" I answered seriously, "I'll do anything." He took it as a joke, and said to me, "All right, get a board and bring bricks to the masons." I went to work at that task. When noon came, one of the men gave me a bite to eat, and I finished up the afternoon. It was hard labor, but whenever the heat seemed about to force me to weaken, I had only to think of my "spring-bottoms" to summon renewed energy. When we knocked off, Mr. Hart said to me, "Come back tomorrow, if you want to."

When I got home I found my grandmother anxious over my long absence; I told her what I had done, and she agreed that getting a job and earning some money would be the best way in which I could spend the summer. We planned for my making time the next morning. I said I should have to carry lunch, and she offered to fix me a nice basket. I told her a basket would not do; that I had seen no workman with a basket;

that they all carried pails. So the next morning I started to work with my tin pail. Mr. Hart was surprised to see me show up; of course, he knew nothing of the goad of desire that was driving me on. I carried bricks to the bricklayers until they began to work on scaffolds; then I was promoted with a raise of wages and made the driver of a horse and cart—another belated realization. As a brick carrier I was paid $2 a week, and as a driver of the cart I received $3. This seemed to me much more than a promotion; it was like being paid money for having a good time. Except for the fact that I wanted pants, I should have been glad to drive the cart for nothing. I worked the whole summer and earned about $40.

Of course, I got my black broadcloth "spring-bottom" trousers. The fact that the only coats I had were little bobtail jackets didn't embarrass me. I had worn my pants several times before my mother returned; my grandmother said I looked nice in them. When my mother saw me, she said seriously that I looked funny; my sister smiled and said that I looked funny; my brother laughed and said that I looked funny; and my father roared. Well, four people out of one family couldn't be absolutely wrong.

My father occasionally took me and my brother over to Fernandina to stay with him for a few days at a time. Fernandina was then and still is a small town. At the time of which I am writing it had a population of a couple of thousand; and at the present time it has only about a thousand more. As a Floridian, I often wondered why Fernandina failed to become the metropolis of the State. It is one of the oldest settlements in Florida, going back to the days of the Spanish. It is situated on the Atlantic Ocean, thirty miles north and east of Jacksonville, and has a deep, commodious, natural harbor. Jacksonville, on the other hand, is eighteen or twenty miles from the mouth of the St. Johns River, and was for a long time shut off from deep-draft vessels by a shallow bar. Perhaps the railroads made Jacksonville. We liked going over to Fernandina. There was the trip on the train; and in the town the streets, nice and grassy with a hard, white center of crushed oyster shells, were fine to play in; and beyond the town, the wide, firm beach. In Fernandina we got our first salt-water fishing experience. When we talked to the Fernandina boys, we displayed that superiority that metropolitans always assume over rustics. We overwhelmed them with stories of the grandeur of Jacksonville. The business section of Fernandina comprised a scanty block; and when we told them that Bay Street in Jacksonville had eight solid blocks of stores on both sides of the street, they could hardly believe their ears. But everything in life is relative; we did the same thing to boys in Jacksonville with stories of New York.

After my mother returned from New York, my grandmother continued to make our house her home; so, with my father's absence, our number was the same. She immediately took charge of the kitchen. She was a good cook; so was my father; my mother was a good schoolteacher. My father once gave my mother some lessons in cooking, and she essayed a pie for Sunday dinner. Our anticipations ran high. The interior of the pie was not bad, but getting to it was another matter. I thought I had played a clever practical joke when I went out and brought the ax in to the table. Anyhow, it was the only joke on herself, so far as I can remember, that my mother ever enjoyed. As long as she lived, I could make her laugh about it. My grandmother was especially skillful in the preparation of West Indian dishes: piquant fish dishes, chicken pilau, shrimp pilau, crab stew, crab and okra gumbo, poppin' John, and Johnny cake. She also knew how to cook the Southern delicacies. We talk a great deal about impressions made upon us in childhood that influence us through life, but we seldom recognize the importance of the tastes formed for the things we loved to eat. Whether I am eating in a humble home or an expensive restaurant, it is difficult for me to understand why there is not hominy for breakfast and rice for dinner—not the mushy, gruel-like messes some people make of these two staple foods, but hominy cooked stiff and rice cooked dry. Dry rice and a well-seasoned gravy make a satisfying dinner for me at any time.

The sensation of earning my first money was so pleasant that I was glad of the opportunity which came the next winter to get another job. *The Times-Union*, the morning newspaper, sent to the principal of Stanton and asked him to recommend three or four boys to deliver papers to local subscribers. The wages were $2.50 a week. I had to leave home by four o'clock in the morning, because the papers came from the press flat, and each carrier had to fold his own before starting out on his route. I took Rosamond along with me for company and gave him the odd fifty cents. The majority of the carriers, a half-dozen or so, were white schoolboys. I formed a fast friendship with two of them, the Lund boys, that lasted a good many years. George was freckled and red-haired, and Gilbert was very handsome with his pale face and jet-black hair. Gilbert and I had a binding common interest in baseball. Their mother was one of the best musicians in Jacksonville. Later, Rosamond and I came to know her quite well. There was another one of the white boys I can't forget. His name was Bob Bailey. Bob was a cracker boy with a whimsical, pinched face. He chewed tobacco and swore like a sailor. I gradually perceived that his orbit was in many respects farther from that of the Lund boys than was mine. He was older than the rest of us and a sort of super-carrier; he taught me my route and had done the same for all the other boys. I admired Bob; he was so capable and seemed to be so wise. He was the unquestioned authority among us on newspaper work from the carrier's end of it. He could fold papers at lightning speed, and was always willing to help out the slower boys.

This work was new and enjoyable. The camaraderie at the office was different from the companionship at school. It involved a common purpose and a definite object; school could be closed a day or a week for a holiday or four months for vacation, but what sort of a morning would it be in Jacksonville if the *Times-Union* failed to appear! All of us caught a share of the spirit of being a part of "the greatest newspaper in Florida." The work did me good physically; the breakfasts I ate were sufficient for a longshoreman. On my route I used to meet a certain milkman regularly and give him a paper for a pint of milk that I drank from his measure. I used to make another "exchange," one with a hobo-looking individual that drove a street car on the newly built line which passed within a half-block of our house, whom I dubbed "Old Grizzly." The Jacksonville street cars of that period were tiny one-man affairs with a coin box at the front end; they ran on a narrow-gauge track, each car pulled by a pair of small mules. As I write these lines I grow curious about this man I had half forgotten. It is strange that I have never before thought of him as a person. I try to recall him—a tall, broad-shouldered man with unkempt, reddish hair and beard, but a large, well-shaped head and a grave, intelligent face. When it was cold he wore a big, shabby, fuzzy overcoat; whence my nickname for him. His manner was taciturn, but he generally exchanged a pleasant word or two with me. He was always eager to get his copy of the paper, and whenever I missed him he was keenly disappointed. I rode with him many, many times; and only now it occurs to me to wonder who he had been and how he came to be what he was. To me he was only "Old Grizzly." Probably, to everybody else in Jacksonville he was a good deal less.

I worked at the *Times-Union* until I went away to school. I worked in several capacities. For a while I was office boy to the editor, Charles H. Jones, whom we all called "C.H." Later, Mr. Jones became editor of *The (New York) World*. Occasionally I held copy for proofreaders in the job office. When I left I was assistant in the mailing room, where the paper was wrapped and addressed to out-of-town subscribers and dealers. The world of the newspaper fascinated me, and I formed a new ambition.

My grandmother cherished the ambition for me to become a preacher. My father and mother never expressed a fixed ambition for me. The question of the child's future is a serious dilemma for Negro parents. Awaiting each colored boy and girl are cramping limitations and buttressed obstacles, in addition to those that must be met by youth in general; and this dilemma approaches suffering in proportion to the parents' knowledge of and the child's innocence of those conditions. Some parents up to the last moment strive to spare the child the bitter knowledge; the child of less sensitive parents is likely to have this knowledge driven in upon him from infancy. And no Negro parent can definitely say which is the wiser course, for either of them may lead to spiritual disaster for the child.

As I look back it appears that my parents must have followed a medium course. It seems to me that I acquired quite gradually the knowledge of the peculiar difficulties I should have to face; and it seems to me, too, that while I was acquiring that knowledge I never received from my parents a dash of cold water on any of my dreams. Once, I remember, a visiting preacher, Presiding Elder Robinson, put his hand on my head and pompously inquired, "Well, my boy, what are you going to be when you grow up?" And I replied in much the same tone, "I am going to be Governor of Florida." I was talking by the copybook. I was using the language of the high-minded young hero of the Sunday school romance, in whom it is set forth that the practice of the common virtues may lead to the Presidency of the United States; and, though I was not yet ten years old, I knew exactly that that was what I was doing. It is possible that my father and mother saw through me, but my pretentious proclamation met with no squelching.

Recollections of our fast-changing childhood ambitions ought to furnish amusement though they reveal nothing significant. The very earliest ambition that I can recall having was wanting to be the driver of a dray or any kind of a vehicle drawn by a horse or a mule. Holding the reins over these big beasts possessed a fascination for me that many of my later ambitions lacked. My next ambition was to be a drummer in a band. When I was quite small, the crack brass band of Jacksonville was the Union Cornet Band, a Negro band; in fact every good brass band in Florida at that time was a Negro band. I remember going to the state fair at Jacksonville and seeing a review of the state militia, all white. Every contingent in the review marched behind a black band, for the reason that there were no good white ones. The companies even from far-away Pensacola brought their own colored band. The Union Cornet Band had a wonderful drummer. He was Martin Dixon, a slim, good-looking black dandy, who had been a drummer boy in the Civil War. The boys in Jacksonville, black and white, boasted that when the band played for a funeral Martin could beat a continuous and unbroken roll on his muffled drum all the way from the church to the cemetery. I did not see how life could offer anything happier than marching behind the blaring brass beating a drum as Martin Dixon did and enjoying the admiration and envy of all the boys in town. I lost my ambition to be a drummer, but drums have never lost their tumultuous effect on me. Ambition then took me by the hand and pointed to the path that led to glory. I determined to be a soldier. But not a soldier like the men I knew who had been in the Civil War; I set my heart on going to

West Point, and I talked the matter over seriously with my father. I was familiar with the case of Lemuel Livingston, who had been turned down when he reported at the Academy, and understood that there would be special difficulties in my way, but I did not know the magnitude of those difficulties and was not discouraged. I also knew about Henry O. Flipper, the first of the three Negro graduates from West Point. But I was directly influenced by the case of Thomas Van Rensselaer Gibbs. He was a slender, indeed delicate-looking, light brown young man, who was a frequent visitor at our house. His father was a well-educated Northern Negro, who, during Reconstruction, had been State Superintendent of Public Instruction of Florida and was, in fact, the man who organized and established the Florida public school system. Tom Gibbs had spent a year at West Point. He used to talk about his cadet days, and assigned his physical condition rather than race prejudice as the reason for having to leave the Academy. This young man, despite his quiet, reserved, soft-spoken manner, always carried himself like a soldier. He impressed me as an exemplar more than anyone else that I used to see at our house; and I saw many men prominent at that time in the Negro world. Some of these I have mentioned; among the others, I have a very clear recollection of J. H. Menard, looking a good deal like the pictures of Alexandre Dumas; he was the first Negro elected to Congress, and, when I knew him, was running a weekly newspaper in Jacksonville; of Bishop Daniel A. Payne, a small shriveled figure, deep-lined face and sunken cheeks, the intellectual leader of the African Methodist Church; and of Joseph C. Price, broad-shouldered, vigorous, radiating vitality, jet-black and handsome, renowned as an orator and educator and who, had he not died young, might have rivaled Booker T. Washington for the leadership of the Negro race. Before I left my job at the *Times-Union* all dreams about leading my company or my regiment to fight for my country's glory—and my own—had vanished. I gradually became possessed with the idea that I should like to run a newspaper—to edit it—to write. From this idea I have swerved, but back to it again and again I have come.

In the year following my mother's visit to New York we found ourselves really a big family. My father had become pas-

tor of a little church in Jacksonville, and so was at home again.
Then one day Señor Echemendia, who was one of the heads of
El Modelo cigar factory, came to our house and brought with
him a very distinguished and aristocratic-looking gentleman,
Señor Ricardo Ponce of Havana. The elegance and courtliness
—such as I had never seen before—of this gentleman was emphasized by Señor Echemendia's dumpiness and untidy appearance. Señor Ponce had come to Jacksonville to find a family with which a Cuban boy in whom he was much interested
might live and learn English. Señor Echemendia knew us—he
lived in the same neighborhood—and brought the stranger in
the hope that we might take the boy. He acted as spokesman
because Señor Ponce spoke no English. My parents talked the
matter over with Señor Echemendia, my father exchanging a
few words in Spanish with Señor Ponce, and it was settled
that the boy would come. The boy was Ricardo Rodriquez—
later he added the name Ponce. He was about my age, very
good-looking, with the light bronze complexion that so many
colored Cubans have, and also with the proverbial Latin temperament. When he came, he knew but one English expression, "All right." He picked up English from Rosamond and
me quite rapidly, but not more rapidly than we picked up
Spanish from him. I think the early advantage lay with us. One
of the things our father had made a great effort to do was to
teach us the Spanish language. We used to sit for an hour at a
time while he drilled us in exercises from *Olendorf's Method*.
We committed to memory a great many useless sentences, like,
"Have you seen the tame antelope of the blacksmith's niece?"
but at the same time learned a large number of Spanish words.
He also gave us a pretty thorough drill in the principal Spanish
verbs. It was a natural then that Ricardo, when he found himself alone amidst strangers speaking an alien tongue, followed
the line of least resistance and took refuge in the fragmentary
Spanish that we knew. It was, of course, also natural that in the
end his knowledge and use of English exceeded ours of Spanish. When he came, my father was adding a second story to
our house. We made a dining room out of the room back of
the parlor, for the size to which the family had increased
would have made eating in the kitchen, as we formerly did, a
question of double shifts. And now with three boys at the

table carrying on a bi-lingual conversation, meals were little less than exciting.

In addition to learning to speak Spanish, I learned to smoke. Ricardo, though only fourteen, smoked incessantly. He smoked cigarettes made of Havana clippings wrapped in a dark brown, sweetish paper. He had dozens of packages, and periodically he received from home a box in which was packed a fresh supply. There also came in those boxes packages of Cuban sweets and preserves, and fresh supplies of fine linen handkerchiefs, hand-made shirts, initialed underwear, French neckties, French lisle socks, high-heeled Cuban shoes. Rosamond and I had always thought of ourselves as well-dressed boys—our mother spent a good part of her salary on clothes for us—but such finery as this, for a boy, we had not even imagined. Opening Ricardo's box was always an event. I smoked surreptitiously; at least, I thought I was doing so, but the aroma of Havana tobacco does not lend itself to deception. When I was found out, my father had hardly anything to say about it; he was a smoker himself and, perhaps, remembering when and how he learned, did not indulge in any cant. My mother was taken aback. The first time she saw me smoking she snatched the cigarette out of my mouth. I think she and my father must have talked the matter over and decided that it was best not to use any coercive measures. But my grandmother disapproved openly and vigorously. I think this was due in part to the fact that, like a true Britisher, she never fully approved of the foreigner in our midst. It was not until I was about twenty that I smoked freely in the presence of my parents.

Of course, in a city like Jacksonville smoking by boys was not the cardinal sin that it was in most communities and sections. Jacksonville was a cigar manufacturing center. It had a Cuban population of several thousand. Many boys learned the cigarmaker's trade; that was the trade my brother and my friend D—— learned. Every workman in a factory is allowed to make up for his own use a certain number of "smokers" each day. When I began to smoke cigars I started with the strong, "green smokers" given me by my many cigarmaker friends. After these "green smokers" the seasoned cigars bought from the dealer are pretty flat.

During this period there came to Jacksonville another distinguished man whose visit greatly stirred me. The Sub-Tropical Exposition was being held in the city, and Frederick Douglass was brought down to make a speech. I knew his story, for I had not only heard a great deal of talk about him, but a book I had won as a prize at Stanton was *The Life and Times of Frederick Douglass*, an autobiography, and I had read it with the same sort of feverish intensity with which I had read about my earlier heroes, Samson, and David, and Robert the Bruce. I looked forward to his coming with more than the glamorous curiosity with which I had looked forward to the coming of General Grant. I was now mature enough to experience an intellectual interest. I wanted to see him but, more, I wanted to hear him speak and catch his words. No one could ever forget a first sight of Frederick Douglass. A tall, straight, magnificent man with a lion-like head covered with a glistening white mane, who instantly called forth in one form or another Napoleon's exclamation when he first saw Goethe, "Behold a man!" As I watched and listened to him, agitator, editor, organizer, counselor, eloquent advocate, co-worker with the great abolitionists, friend and adviser of Lincoln, for a half century the unafraid champion of freedom and equality for his race, I was filled with a feeling of worshipful awe. Douglass spoke, and moved a large audience of white and colored people by his supreme eloquence. The scene, though on a less important scale, was similar to the one in which Booker T. Washington appeared nine years later at the Atlanta Exposition. Douglass was speaking in the far South, but he spoke without fear or reservation. One statement in particular that he made, I now wonder if any Negro speaker today, under the same circumstances, would dare to make, and, if he did, what the public reaction would be; Douglass, in reply to the current criticisms regarding his second marriage, said, "In my first marriage I paid my compliments to my mother's race; in my second marriage I paid my compliments to the race of my father."

Both my mother and my father had been worrying about my progress in school; contrary, however, to traditions, it was not the boy's fault. I started at Stanton advanced beyond my

years, and should have finished before I was thirteen; I was almost sixteen when I did finish. Mr. Culp, who succeeded Mr.
Waters as principal, was a well-educated man and may have
been a good preacher, but he was a poor teacher. As an administrator he had no success. The school got to be a sort of
go-as-you-please institution, and many parents took their
children out and sent them elsewhere. D——, to our mutual
sadness, was taken out by his father and sent to Cookman Institute, a school in Jacksonville founded and operated by the
Northern Methodist Church. My father was all for doing the
same, but my mother was now assistant principal of Stanton,
and she felt it was hardly proper for her to take her own child
out of the school. I and other pupils dawdled away our time in
Mr. Culp's class; he seemed to have no definite plans about
graduating us. Things came to such a pass that parents demanded that a change be made, and the school board acted
on their demand. The new principal was William Artrell. Mr.
Artrell had not had a college education, but he was thoroughly grounded in all the English branches. He was a native
of Nassau, and had been trained under the English public
school system; so, despite the fact that his education was not
extensive, he actually knew what he was supposed to know
and teach. He was an administrator, a good teacher, and a
strict disciplinarian. Like all educated West Indians, his handwriting was beautiful. Under him Stanton became a better
school than it had ever been. Pleasantly for my mother, she
found herself associated with a friend of her young womanhood. I finished at Stanton toward the end of May 1887. In the
same month D—— was graduated from Cookman Institute,
where he had covered the general high school subjects.

VII

Now I entered a period which, for excitement, surpassed
anything in my experience. For months my father and
mother had been forming plans for sending me off to school,
and the time for carrying out those plans was drawing nearer
day by day. My parents had reviewed information about several
schools: Howard University, Fisk University, Atlanta University, Biddle (now Johnson C. Smith) University, and Hampton

Institute. My father at first favored Hampton. He had practical ideas about life, one of them being that every boy should learn a trade. I think, too, he had a sentimental leaning toward Hampton because of the fact that he was by birth a Virginian. We, for I was taken into conference, finally decided on Atlanta University. Just what was the determining factor in this choice I do not remember. Perhaps my mother and I merely outvoted my father. Most likely it was the fact that Atlanta was nearest.

I was on the eve of an adventure, and its lure was powerful, but I had my moments of misgivings. I was leaving the familiar sights and objects and associations that had so far made up life for me. I was stepping off a well-known path upon a strange road. I watched my mother preparing me for the journey, but I could not know the anxious love she put into the task. Yet I am sure now that she knew she was packing my kit for me to take a road that would ultimately lead very far from the place where she stood.

Ricardo had been urging his people to let him go to Atlanta University with me. He argued that it would help him to achieve more quickly the object for which he had been sent to the United States; namely, to learn English and study dentistry. He was sincere, but I think he had also caught some of my enthusiasm and wanted to try the new experience. I think, too, he was loath to have me go and leave him in Jacksonville. There had grown between us a strong bond of companionship; and what was, perhaps, more binding, the bond of language. Up to that time my proficiency in Spanish was much greater than his in English; so he never exerted himself to speak to me except in his own language. Anyone who has undergone the agony of having to express himself inadequately in a foreign language knows what a sweet relief it is to find somebody who understands his mother tongue. Ricardo found that relief in me. There were things he could say to me which, if expressed in English, would have made him feel embarrassed. Among these were the confidences regarding his love affairs. These affairs were numerous but always intense. I had gone through phases of love common to a boy's lot; I had felt the pull and tug of that mysterious force; indeed, involved in my misgivings about leaving Jacksonville was Jennie, a golden-hued, fifteen-year-old bit of femininity, and my heart's desire;

but the idea that love could be the frenzied, frantic thing it was with Ricardo was not yet within my comprehension. One night after we had gone to bed he actually frightened me. He complained emphatically of violent pains in and round his heart; the indications were that that organ was about to break or explode. I called my mother and she came in and gave him a dose of tincture of lavender. My sympathy cooled when he divulged to me that the attack was caused by a sudden passion he had conceived for Jennie, my own heart's desire.

The letter and the money came from Havana. Ricardo was to go with me to Atlanta University. I was glad that I would have a friend and companion from the start. D—— and I had long expected that we should go off to school together, but early in the summer he confided to me that he was going to run away from home. His mother, whom he had loved very dearly, had died when he was small. His father married a second wife, who died shortly afterwards. He then took a third wife. D——'s second stepmother was very kind to him, but his father, always harsh, grew harsher. I tried to dissuade my friend from his plan to leave home. I begged him to stick it out until he got off to school. However, he did run away and go to New York. And so I was doubly glad that Ricardo was going with me. On the night my mother was putting the final touches on my packing there was a rumbling sound; the house trembled and swayed; we rushed downstairs and out, and became aware that there was an earthquake. This was a part of the tremor that came to be known as the Charleston Earthquake, and bore no relation whatever to the fact that I was leaving Jacksonville.

Ricardo and I boarded the train that left Jacksonville at night and arrived in Atlanta the next morning. We had first-class tickets, and my father put us in the first-class car. (This was the year in which Florida passed its law separating the races in railroad cars, and it was just being put into operation; a matter that I, at least, was then ignorant of.) We had a good send-off; many of our friends, boys and girls, came to bid us good-by. My heart's desire, looking very pretty, was there, and kept quite close to my mother. I wonder if keeping close to my mother was one of those feminine traits that a girl of fifteen knows intuitively. At any rate, the effect on me was full, and I clearly remember how strangely I was stirred by this simple, perhaps incidental, matter of juxtaposition. We got aboard midst a lot of noisy chatter that enabled me to cover up my choked condition when I kissed my mother good-by.

The train pulled out and we settled down comfortably in one seat after having arranged our packages, among which was a box of lunch. In those days no one would think of boarding a train without a lunch, not even for a trip of two or three hours; and no lunch was a real lunch that did not consist of fried chicken, slices of buttered bread, hard-boiled eggs, a little paper of salt and pepper, and orange or two, and a piece of cake. We had a real lunch and were waiting only for the train to get fully under way before opening it. A number of colored people had got on the train but we were the only ones in the first-class car. Before we could open our lunch the conductor came round. I gave him the tickets, and he looked at them and looked at us. Then he said gruffly, "You had better get out of this car and into the one ahead." "But," I answered, "we have first-class tickets; and this is the first-class car, isn't it?" It is probable that the new law was very new to him, and he said not unkindly, "You'll be likely to have trouble if you try to stay in this car." Ricardo knew there was something wrong but didn't fully understand the conversation or the situation, and asked me, *"¿Que dice?"* (What is he saying?) I explained to him what the conductor was trying to make us do; we decided to stay where we were. But we did not have to enforce the decision. As soon as the conductor heard us speaking a foreign language, his attitude changed; he punched our tickets and gave them back, and treated us just as he did the other passengers in the car. We ate our lunch, lay back in our seats, and went to sleep. We didn't wake up until it was broad daylight and the engine was puffing its way up through the gullies of the red clay hills on which Atlanta sits.

This was my first impact against race prejudice as a concrete fact. Fifteen years later, an incident similar to the experience with this conductor drove home to me the conclusion that in such situations any kind of a Negro will do; provided he is not one who is an American citizen.

Atlanta disappointed me. It was a larger city than Jacksonville, but did not seem to me to be nearly so attractive.

Many of the thoroughfares were still red clay roads. It was a long time before I grew accustomed to the bloody aspect of Atlanta's highways. Trees were rare and there was no city park or square within walking distance. The city was neither pictur-esque nor smart; it was merely drab. Atlanta University was a pleasant relief. The Confederate ramparts on the hill where the school was built had been leveled, the ground terraced, and grass and avenues of trees planted. The three main buildings were ivy-covered. Here was a spot fresh and beautiful, a rest for the eyes from what surrounded it, a green island in a dull, red sea. The University, as I was soon to learn, was a little world in itself, with ideas of social conduct and of the ap-proach to life distinct from those of the city within which it was situated. When students or teachers stepped off the cam-pus into West Mitchell Street, they underwent as great a tran-sition as would have resulted from being instantaneously shot from a Boston drawing room into the wilds of Borneo. They had to make an immediate readjustment of many of their fun-damental notions about life. When I was at the University, there were twenty-odd teachers, of whom all, except four, were white. These white teachers by eating at table with the students rendered themselves "unclean," not fit to sit at table with any Atlanta white family. The president was Horace Bum-stead, a cultured gentleman, educated at Yale and in Germany, yet there was only one white door in all Atlanta thrown open to him socially, the door of a German family. No observance of caste in India was more cruelly rigid. The year before I en-tered, the state of Georgia had cut off its annual appropriation of $8000 because the school stood by its principles and refused to exclude the children of the white teachers from the regular classes.

I was at the University only a short time before I began to get an insight into the ramifications of race prejudice and an understanding of the American race problem. Indeed, it was in this early period that I received my initiation into the arcana of "race." I perceived that education for me meant, funda-mentally: preparation to meet the tasks and exigencies of life as a Negro, a realization of the peculiar responsibilities due to my own racial group, and a comprehension of the application of American democracy to Negro citizens. Of course, I had

not been entirely ignorant of these conditions and requirements, but now they rose before me in such sudden magnitude as to seem absolutely new knowledge. This knowledge
was no part of classroom instruction—the college course at
Atlanta University was practically the old academic course at
Yale; the founder of the school was Edmund Asa Ware, a Yale
man, and the two following presidents were graduates of
Yale—it was simply in the spirit of the institution; the atmosphere of the place was charged with it. Students talked "race."
It was the subject of essays, orations, and debates. Nearly all
that was acquired, mental and moral, was destined to be fitted
into a particular system of which "race" was the center.

On the day of my arrival, the opening day, I took an examination and was assigned to the Junior Preparatory class. Ricardo was not examined. He was something of a puzzle. He
had a good elementary education in Spanish, but no equivalent of it in English; so he was made a special student in one of
the grammar school classes—the University then had such a
department. For weeks he stuck to me as closely as he could;
for he felt his status as a stranger more keenly than ever. His
embarrassment seemed greatest in the dining hall, where he
had to sit facing a whole row of girls. The dining hall was a
large, bright room that took up the main part of the basement
of North Hall, the girl's dormitory building. It was filled with
long tables, at each of which ten or twelve girls sat on one side
and about an equal number of boys on the other. Two teachers at a table acted as hosts; but there were not enough male
teachers to go round, so at a number of tables an advanced
student did the carving. And the position of carver was no
sinecure. The various dishes of food were placed between the
hosts. The carver asked each student, "What will you have?"
The girls were served first. They were generally dainty and
made certain choices. But from the boys' side there rolled out
a monotonous repetition of "Some of each." Three-fourths of
the boys would send back for a second helping with the request for "Some of each."

Ricardo and I talked Spanish at the table and this gave us
pleasant notoriety; we could not have excited more curiosity
and admiration had we been talking Attic Greek. Following
strictly in the Yale tradition, the students at Atlanta University

thought of a foreign language as something to be studied, not spoken. We were, naturally, assigned to the same room. It was a good-sized, clean, and comfortable room with a closet. In it were a table with a lamp, two chairs, a washstand with pitcher and basin, and a wooden slop-bucket. The floor was uncovered, except for a strip of carpet in front of the bed and an oil-cloth mat in front of the washstand. The walls were white and absolutely bare. There was not the slightest hint of decoration. The mattress on the bed was filled with fresh, sweet-smelling straw, and was fully two feet high before we started sleeping on it. When I first dived into it I felt as though I was plunging into the surf at Pablo Beach. We saw very little of each other during the day, except at meals; for on school days there were only about two hours, in the afternoons, that were not filled with duties of one kind or another. This proved to be the very thing that Ricardo needed, and he began mastering English with astonishing rapidity.

At some time during the day each student was required to put in one hour, at least, at work. It was the job of a group of a half-dozen boys to fill the wood bin in the kitchen each afternoon. We carried the wood in our arms, and I ruined a couple of good jackets keeping the kitchen fires burning. There was, however, an intangible recompense connected with this task that made us forget some of its irksomeness: the wood pile was located in the angle of the two wings of the girls' dormitory, and each boy could make a show of how much wood he could carry, while the unapproachable creatures looked down on him from their windows. I say "unapproachable," I ought to italicize the word; for there was no offense in the Atlanta University calendar that more perturbed the authorities than approaching a girl. A boy could see a girl upon a written application with the girl's name filled in, signed by himself and, if granted, countersigned by the president or dean. The caller was limited to twenty minutes in the parlor of North Hall; and he would find out that the matron was as particular about overtime as a long-distance telephone operator. He was also likely to overhear sundry remarks—in this day known as wise-cracks—made by various girls as they passed to and fro in the halls and up and down the main staircase. For the "caller" could be spotted as soon as he struck the bridge on his way to

North Hall, and word would be flashed from window to window and from room to room. If he was one of the constant sort, his visit did not arouse much interest, but, if he was of the other sort, it caused great speculation. Had the girls known how to gamble, they might have had exciting times betting on who the particular girl would be.

I found this whole procedure humiliating, and I made it a point of honor not to make out an application to call on a girl—a resolution I broke only twice during my six years, and for reasons that appeared to be sufficiently exigent. It might seem that these repressive regulations would have incited "sexy" talk among the boys, but they did not. The boys did talk a great deal about the girls across the bridge, but the talk was always on an expurgated, I might say, emasculated level. This was not prudery; it was idealism, and there was in it, too, something of an innate racial trait. There was an amazing absence of realistic discussion of sex; and no boy would have dared to bring the girls of North Hall into such a discussion. North Hall girls, love, and sex formed one of the spiritual mysteries. I remember that one day I was corrected by an older student in a group when I spoke of one of the teachers as "Miss." "We call her 'Miss' but she is really Mrs.," he said. This teacher was badly deformed, and, when I expressed mild surprise that she had found a husband, the whole group came down on my head. They pointed out to me that *true love* and physical passion were entirely distinct and unrelated—a doctrine that I found fully and forcibly set forth in the textbook on moral philosophy that I took up later in my course. This Sir Galahad attitude of the Atlanta University boys of that time appears to me in the present age in the light of a phenomenon.

The longest stretch of free time we had on school days was the two-hour period between the work hour and supper. The time on Sundays was pretty well filled; preaching in the morning, Sunday school in the afternoon, and prayer meeting at night. The couple of hours before the morning service we often whiled away walking about the campus, a sixty-five acre tract, part of it wooded. Saturday was our big day. We had to work two hours in the morning, but dinner was served at 1 o'clock and we had the whole afternoon up to supper time at 6. On Saturday afternoons during the fall there was usually a baseball game on. The baseball season closed with a big game on Thanksgiving Day. (We knew nothing about football until four or five years later, when it was encouraged by Professor Adams, who had been a player at Dartmouth.) These games were attended by the girls as well as the boys, and by crowds of townspeople. During the winter months Saturday afternoons were devoted to calling on friends in the city by those fortunate enough to know any Atlanta families. The girls also had the privilege, by permission, of visiting friends in town on this half-holiday. We would put on our best clothes—for Saturday not Sunday was the day we dressed up—and sally forth immediately after dinner. These afternoons formed one of the pleasantest parts of our student life; we met nice people, we would likely be offered something good to eat, and we ran a chance of meeting by accident, perhaps not wholly by accident, certain of the North Hall girls who might be visiting mutual friends.

I had been at the University a couple of weeks when, without notice, D—— appeared with his father. He had returned home from his runaway trip, and his father had agreed to let him come to Atlanta. I was glad and he was glad, for it meant that the thing we had dreamed about had come to pass. I took him to the matron, where we arranged to have a cot for him put in the room occupied by Ricardo and me. Three in a room made it a bit crowded, but the slight inconvenience didn't bother us because he was so anxious to tell me about his adventure in running away, and I wanted to talk to him about things at the University, most of them things that Ricardo would not be interested in or even understand. A good many nights, after lights were out and Ricardo had fallen asleep, D—— and I talked in subdued tones. In these talks we began to lay plans for the future: we would finish at Atlanta University, then we would study law and form a partnership.

D—— was assigned to the Freshman class; and I thought with vexation of the time I had lost with Mr. Culp as my teacher. He had some conditions to make up because Cookman Institute standards were not on a par with those of the preparatory school at the University, but this was no serious handicap for his quick mind, in fact, so quick that it often sped lightly over what should have been laboriously explored.

A few days after D——'s arrival I saw in the papers that the St. Louis Browns and another big league team were to play an exhibition game in Atlanta. I became feverish with desire to see them play. I especially wanted to see Arlie Latham, the famous third baseman of the Browns. Neither D—— nor Ricardo was much of a player, but they were both fans and caught my enthusiasm to see this game; in addition, it meant a half-day out of school for the three of us. I wrote out the application to be excused and took it to the proper authority. That authority, for the time, was Professor Francis. He read the application, looked up at me with sharp, dark eyes, then read the application again, presumably, to be sure he had read it aright the first time. Meanwhile, there ran through my mind some of the things I had already picked up about him from the older boys. He was disliked by the majority because he was regarded as a snooper. It was said that he walked about the halls of the boys' dormitory at night with rubbers on; that he was not above listening at keyholes; that nothing delighted him more than to "find out something," and that he had tracked down numberless plots and acts against the established order of the institution. It was felt that he had no understanding of or sympathy with boyhood, and known that he made no allowances for the deeds done by those still in that semi-savage state. He was the university pastor and was not far from fanaticism in his religious zeal. The unpopularity of Professor Francis was offset by the popularity of Professor Chase, our teacher of Greek. Mr. Chase was a stocky man with a head like the pictured one of the poet Aristophanes. His ruddy face held two merry eyes and was fringed by a cropped, reddish beard. On cold days he wore a shawl in the manner of Abraham Lincoln. He spoke haltingly, but was always eloquent in his defense of the boys. It may have been more than a coincidence that the two most understanding men—from a boy's point of view—at Atlanta during my time were both from Dartmouth, Professor Chase and Professor Adams. It was the latter who gave us our first lessons in the finer points of football. Mr. Francis was from Yale, and was the embodiment of all the stern virtues then traditional of that great school.

This was my first personal contact with Mr. Francis, and the contact made it hard to believe him to be as bad as he was

painted. While he pondered my application, I shyly studied
him. I was a little awe-struck. He, like Mr. Chase, was stocky
and had a Greek philosopher's head, but his complexion was
pallid, his eyes piercing, and his short beard—all the men
teachers, except two, wore beards of varying hues—was dark
and tinged with gray. He was gentle and soft-spoken; in fact, he
almost purred when he spoke. I noted a furtiveness in his
glance and manner that I afterwards recognized as a marked
characteristic. While I waited he squirmed round in his swivel
chair, frowned, plucked at his beard, and, picking up a ruler
from his desk, gave his skull several resounding whacks. Then
he turned and informed me in a kindly way that he had been
connected with the University from its founding and that never
before in its history had such a request been made—a request
to be absent from classes to attend a ball game. Also he gave me
to understand that had I been longer steeped in the spirit of the
institution I would not have dreamed of making it. Perhaps my
innocence or my ignorance appealed to him or it may have
been that he was, after all, a humorist in disguise; at any rate, he
turned suddenly to his desk and countersigned the application.
I left his office hurriedly with the precious scrap of paper
tucked away in my pocket. Among the three of us there was
sufficient worldly wisdom to make us keep our holiday a secret.

There was a large crowd at the ball grounds, but we were
there early and got good seats. On the way Ricardo bought a
package of cigarettes and, as soon as we were seated, he and
D—— lit up and began smoking. They, of course, offered me
a smoke, but I declined. Furthermore, I tried to dissuade
them, and once or twice snatched the lighted cigarettes from
their mouths and threw them away. This last resort roused
considerable anger in Ricardo, and he rolled at me a string of
sonorous and untranslatable Spanish oaths. Now, I was not being actuated by any goody-goody motive. It was true that each
of us on entering the University had signed the compulsory
pledge to abstain from alcoholic drinks, tobacco, and profanity; and I did have some regard for my pledge; but of, at least,
equal weight was my knowledge that smoking was considered
an offense meriting suspension or even expulsion, and, as my
knowledge on this point was, I knew, fuller than theirs, I was
trying my best to give my two friends the benefit of it.

We were delighted with the game. Arlie Latham fulfilled all our expectations of him, both as a baseball player and comedian. We returned to the University happy and after supper got great satisfaction out of relating to our envious fellow students the story of the game.

The next day I was called to the president's office. I stood waiting while Mr. Francis fumbled over the papers on his desk as though he was searching anxiously for an important misplaced document. While still fumbling and not looking up he said to me very quietly, "Johnson, what about the smoking at the ball grounds yesterday?" I was astounded. If I had been given an instant in which to collect myself I should have responded with a straightforward, honest lie, in full keeping with the code of honor of normal boys, but he continued talking and rehearsed the whole scene as it had taken place, and even the conversation, almost word for word. I was stupefied. The three of us had looked around quite carefully when the smoking began, and had seen no one that we knew. I felt that I was witnessing a feat of black magic. Mr. Francis dismissed me without further questioning, and I went out wondering if he was going to press the matter or was merely giving me a confirming demonstration of his reputed powers as a detective. I am sure now that he did get a great kick out of the interview; and I suspect that all of his similar exploits were a source of great pleasure. When I left him I also knew that I had, undeservedly, gone up to the top notch in his estimation.

As soon as I could get to D—— and Ricardo I told them that the cat was out of the bag and jumping; and I gave them the best tip I could as to the direction she was taking. Their mystification was as great as mine. That night we talked of nothing else. Ricardo was indifferent about the outcome; Atlanta University didn't mean more to him than the privilege of smoking meant. What stirred him most was curiosity as to how Mr. Francis knew. But D—— was much concerned; he had just patched things up with his father, who not unreluctantly had agreed to send him to college; and he knew that his future and our joint plans for the future were at stake. He and I hoped that the incident was closed. Our hope rested on the fact that neither he nor Ricardo had been sent for. However, we decided that there was no use in going up against the

indubitable powers possessed by Mr. Francis, and if they were
sent for the only thing to do would be to make a clean breast
of it. The summons came the following afternoon. Ricardo
went in the strength of his indifference and D—— in the
weakness of his concern. Mr. Francis rehearsed the scene and
conversation over for them; and, as with me, gave not the
slightest hint as to how the matter had become manifest to
him. D—— was repentant, but Ricardo stated as plainly as
possible that education or no education, he couldn't get
along without smoking. He clinched his statement by saying,
"Meester Francis, I wass born weet de cigarette in de mout."
They were both admonished and reprieved. I think it was Ricardo's indifference rather than D——'s penitence that saved
them. I am sure that Mr. Francis anticipated with pride that in
the next catalogue of Atlanta University would be listed, "Ricardo Rodriquez Ponce, Havana, Cuba." And there was no
way of punishing the compliant D—— while sparing the recalcitrant Ricardo.

I began my course in manual training in the carpenter
shop. I enjoyed going to the industrial building as much as
any of my classes, except my Latin class. I had no exceptional
difficulty with mathematics and I was interested in the subject, but I found that I had a love for language, and Latin
meant more for me than mere class work. It was the same
when it came to Greek, and French and German. Besides, I
had found Latin to be my "snap" course. The similarity to
Spanish, especially in the principal verbs, made it relatively
easy for me; and through Cæsar and Cicero and Vergil and
Horace and Tacitus and Livy I read at sight many lines that
cost my classmates much thumbing of dictionary and grammar. Work at the shops was fascinating. I liked the bright,
sharp tools, the peculiar fragrance that clings to a carpenter's
chest, the good smell of the wood as the saw cut into it or as
the shavings came curling up through the plane, and the experience of making things. I caught glimpses of boys working
at the forges, at the turning lathes and at the draughting tables. I was intensely interested in it all, and more than once
wished that my father, who believed in a trade for every boy,
could see me at work.

I had been going to the shops for quite a while before I saw the engineer; that is, the man who had charge of the engine room. He was a colored man, light yellow, with a mass of black hair, and a melancholy expression of the face that was deepened by a long, dark, drooping mustache. He looked like a reformed pirate, or as a pirate ought to look if he reformed. At first glance I wondered where I had seen the face before; I racked my brain, but, to my great irritation, could not tell. The rest of the day and somewhat through the night that face puzzled and haunted me. The next day at the shops I saw the man and looked at him long and hard. What happened? Did he for an instant give off a flicker that had already been caught on the film of my memory? I cannot say, but in a flash I knew him. He was the man who sat directly behind the three of us at the baseball game. In a following flash the workings of the occult powers of Mr. Francis were revealed in broad daylight, and they looked pretty mean.

On the ground floor of Stone Hall, the main building, was the general study room. It accommodated, perhaps, three hundred students, and was furnished with modern individual desks and chairs. In this room the boys and girls of the Preparatory and Normal departments sat and studied during school hours; from it they filed out on bells to the various classrooms for recitation. The daily devotional exercises were held there. The general study room was in charge of John Young, a graduate of the University and an instructor in Latin. Mr. Young was one of the handsomest men I have ever known—and he was one of the two men teachers who did not wear short beards. He had made a reputation as an excellent scholar and a fine athlete. All the boys were proud of him, and half the girls were in love with him. During my Middle Prep year he was preparing himself to go to Harvard for his Master's degree—the degree of doctor of Philosophy was not then the *sine qua non* of the teaching profession. He expected to return to Atlanta as a full professor of Latin. He did not enter Harvard, but died before he finished the year—of a broken heart, they said; but that is another story. Students in the College department studied in their rooms and went over to Stone Hall for recitations. The study room and recitation rooms of the Grammar department were located in South Hall, the boy's dormitory building.

The big room in Stone Hall was a pleasant place for study. The greatest distraction for a boy was the presence of so many pretty girls. Certainly, I had seen girls before, but their place in the scheme of things had been extrinsic, casual, subsidiary. Now, all at once, they assumed a vital position. They kept up a constant assault on the center of my thoughts. I could relegate them to their old place when I was on the baseball field or with a group of boys on the campus or at work in the shops, even when reciting with them in class; but sitting silently in the study room I fell, whether I would or not, under their pervasive and disquieting allure. Of course, there was the natural explanation; but more than biology was involved; there was also an element of æsthetics. The majority of these girls came from the best-to-do colored families of Georgia and the surrounding states. They really made up a selected group. Atlanta University was widely known as a school that attracted this type. As a result, the proportion of tastefully dressed, good-mannered, good-looking girls was very high. I had never seen their like in such numbers. To look at them evoked a satisfying pleasure. They ranged in color from ebony black to milk white. At one end of the scale eyes were dark and hair crisp, and at the other, eyes were blue or gray and the hair light and like fine spun silk. The bulk of them ran the full gamut of all the shades and nuances of brown, with wavy hair and the liquid velvet eyes so characteristic of women of Negro blood. There was a warmth of beauty in this variety and blend of color and shade that no group of white girls could kindle. I have been in far places and lived in strange lands since I sat in that study room in Stone Hall but the idea has grown stronger and stronger that, perhaps, the perfection of the human female is reached in the golden-hued and ivory-toned colored women of the United States, in whom there is a fusion of the fierceness in love of blond women with the responsiveness of black.

The thing of essential value that I got out of sitting through two years in this big room did not come from what I studied, but from the increasing power I gained to apply my mind to what I was studying, the power to shut out from it what I willed. This, of course, is the known power without which there can be but small achievement of intellectual or spiritual growth. And I have since found in it a boon; the ability to withdraw from the crowd while within its midst has never failed to yield me the subtlest and serenest of pleasures.

I was not long in finding my rank as a fellow student; and that is a rank not less important than the one in scholarship. It is, at any rate, a surer indicator of how the future man or woman is going to be met by the world. I found that I possessed a prestige entirely out of proportion to my age and class. Among the factors to which this could be attributed were: my prowess as a baseball pitcher, my ability to speak a foreign language, and the presumable superiority in worldly wisdom that having lived in New York gave me. I think, at the time, D—— and I were the only students who could boast of first-hand knowledge of the great city. I could boast of having traveled even to a foreign country. Another factor was my having a college student as my chum and roommate. D—— was only three months older than I, but he was more mature and far more sophisticated. Indeed, in his youth his face began to wear a jaded appearance; and, as a young man, he had a very low droop to the corners of his mouth. He had an unlimited self-assurance, while I was almost diffident; and he had inherited or acquired a good share of his father's roughness and coarseness. He had a racy style of speech, which I envied; but many of his choicest expressions I was unable to form in my own mouth. D—— was a *rara avis* at Atlanta University; nothing like him had ever before been seen in that cage. Yet he was popular with the boys and the girls, and, strange to say, even with the teachers. His very rakishness had a definite charm. And underneath his somewhat ribald manner he was tenderhearted and generous. Moreover, he was extremely goodlooking, having, in fact, a sort of Byronic beauty. He was short and inclined to stoutness. When he was a small boy, he was fat. His head, large out of proportion to his height, was covered with thick, dark brown hair that set off his pale face and fine hazel eyes. The only thing that marred his looks was the frequent raising of the drooping corners of his mouth in a cynical curl. But speaking of his face as pale does not convey the full truth; for neither in color, features, nor hair could one detect that he had a single drop of Negro blood.

D—— was entirely at ease with the older boys and the young men of the College department; and in his take-it-for-granted way he made an opening with them for me. So almost from the start my closest associates were not among the boys of the Prep school but among the students of the College classes. I became the acknowledged fifth member of a combination made up of two Juniors, a Sophomore, and D——, calling themselves the "Big Four." We grouped ourselves whenever and wherever possible. We exchanged stories, information, and confidences; and we borrowed each other's money, generally for the purpose of paying for a late supper. Why a boy in boarding school can never get enough to eat will, I suppose, always remain a question. The meals in the dining room were never stinted, but we were always ready for a late, clandestine supper. There was an old man named Watson, whose job it was to tend the fine herd of cows owned by the school. He and his wife lived in a little house on the campus. We called this house "Little Delmonico" because the good woman, who was also a good cook, furnished on short notice a supper of fried chicken, hot biscuits, and all the milk we could drink for fifteen cents. Whenever we had the money, we were ready to run the gantlet after lights were out for one of these suppers. Terms were cash, but we paid willingly; and without seeking to know whence came the milk—or the chickens either. We also passed many hours in the room of one or the other of us playing whist and seven-up, with shades drawn, hat over keyhole, crack under door chinked, and muffled voices; for playing cards was listed among the cardinal sins. But the greater part of our time together was spent seriously. We talked the eternal race question over and over, yet always found something else to say on the subject. We discussed our ambitions, and speculated upon our chances of success; each one reassuring the others that they could not fail. There was established a bond of comradeship—among men, a nobler and more enduring bond than friendship.

It is not difficult for me to blot out forty-five years and sit again with these comrades of my youth. There is A——, tall, fair, slender, and elegant . . . peering near-sightedly through his heavy, gold-rimmed spectacles, but with his agile mind always balancing the possibilities and discovering the vantage.

And H——, tall, too, but bronze-colored, broad-shouldered, heavy-jowled . . . in comparison with the ready, fluent A——, cumbrous of speech, using an almost Johnsonian vocabulary, and, when roused, vehemently eloquent. T——, brown, short, and jolly, with gray eyes looking out quizzically from his moon-round face . . . speaking in anecdotes as wiser men had spoken in parables . . . always fresh stories, stories of black and white in the South, stories which, although we roared at them, we knew to have their points buried deep in the heart of the race question. And D——, worldly-wise, dare-devilish, self-confident, and combative . . . invincible on his own ground, but in danger when he exposed a superficial knowledge of other things to the adroitness of A——, to the honest logic and common sense of H——, to the humor of T——, before which what any one of the rest of us posited might be blown away like dust before a strong puff of breath. We talked, we argued, we nursed ambitions and dreams; but none of us could foretell. There is no way of getting a peep behind that dark curtain, which simply recedes with each step we take toward it; leaving in front all that we ever know. In truth, if some mysterious being had appeared in our midst and announced to A—— that he would rise to the highest office in the church; to H—— that he was to become the most influential and powerful Negro of his time in our national politics; to T—— that he was to have his heart's desire granted in being widely recognized as a typically brilliant Georgia country lawyer; and to D—— that he was to be one of the most prosperous colored lawyers in the country, a member of the Jacksonville city council, and an important factor in Florida politics, we should all, probably, have been incredulous—but that is exactly what was behind the dark curtain. And it was also behind the dark curtain that before these lines would be written each of the four would have passed beyond the boundary of past, present, and future.

I now began to get my bearings with regard to the world and particularly with regard to my own country. I began to get the full understanding of my relationship to America, and to take on my share of the peculiar responsibilities and burdens additional to those of the common lot, which every Negro in the United States is compelled to carry. I began my mental and spiritual training to meet and cope not only with the hardships that are common, but with planned wrong, concerted injustice, and applied prejudice. Here was a deepening, but narrowing experience; an experience so narrowing that the inner problem of a Negro in America becomes that of not allowing it to choke and suffocate him. I am glad that this fuller impact of the situation came to me as late as it did, when my apprehension of it could be more or less objective. As an American Negro, I consider the most fortunate thing in my life to be the fact that through childhood I was reared free from undue fear or esteem for white people as a race; otherwise, the deeper implications of American race prejudice might have become a part of my subconscious as well as of my conscious self.

I began also in this period to find myself, to think of life not only as it touched me from without but also as it moved me from within. I went in for reading, and spent many of the winter afternoons that settle down so drearily on the bleak hills of North Georgia absorbed in a book. The university library was then the Graves Memorial Library. It contained ten thousand or so volumes, an array of books that seemed infinite to me. Many of the titles snared me, but I was often disappointed to find that the books were written from the point of view of divine revelation and Christian dogma or with a bald moral purpose. Among all the books in the Graves Library it was from books of fiction that I gained the greatest satisfaction. I read more Dickens; I read George Eliot; I read *Vanity Fair*, and that jewel among novels, *Lorna Doone*. It was during this period that I also read with burning interest Alphonse Daudet's *Sapho*, a book which was not in the library but was owned by one of the boys and circulated until it was all but worn out. The episode in which Sapho is carried up the flight of stairs left a disquieting impression on my mind that lingered long.

Before I left Stanton I had begun to scribble. I had written a story about my first plug (derby) hat. Mr. Artrell thought it was fine, and it made a hit when I read it before the school. Now an impulse set me at writing poetry, and I filled several notebooks with verses. I looked over these juvenilia recently and noted that the first of my poems opened with these three lines:

> Miserable, miserable, weary of life,
> Worn with its turmoil, its din and its strife,
> And with its burden of grief.

I did not follow this vein. Perhaps even then I sensed that there was already an over-supply of poetry by people who mistake a torpid liver for a broken heart, and frustrated sex desires for yearning of the soul. I wrote a lot of verses lampooning certain students and teachers and conditions on the campus. However, the greater part of my output consisted of rather ardent love poems. A number of these latter circulated with success in North Hall, and brought me considerable prestige as a gallant. It has struck me that the potency possessed by a few, fairly well written lines of passionate poetry is truly astounding, and altogether disproportionate to what really goes into the process of producing them. It is probable that the innate hostility of the average man toward the poet has its basis in this fact.

My chief shortcoming as an Atlanta University student I quickly recognized. It was my inaptitude as a public speaker. I was astonished to see boys no older than I rise and without fear or hesitation discourse upon weighty subjects; the weightier the subject, the more fluent the discourse. All the outstanding university orators were personages. They thrilled the large audiences that filled the chapel on special occasions; and the applause they received was without question a higher kind of approbation than the cheers given the players on the baseball field. The renown of several of the best speakers had spread beyond Atlanta. I determined to make as much of an orator out of myself as possible. I joined the Ware Lyceum, the debating society of the Preps, and looked forward to the time when I might shine in the Phi Kappa, the College society. I do not brag when I say that I achieved a measure of success. The first time I took part in a debate in the Ware Lyceum I was almost as terror-stricken as I was when I attempted my first Sunday school recitation. In my Sophomore year I won first prize in the principal oratorical contest; and in the following year I gained a tie with another speaker for that honor. Before I left Atlanta I had learned what every orator must know: that the deep secret of eloquence is rhythm—rhythm, set in motion by the speaker, that sets up a responsive rhythm in his audience. For the purpose of sheer persuasion, it is far more important than logic. There is now doubt as to whether or not oratory is an art—curiously, it is the only art in which the South as a section has gained and held pre-eminence—if it may still be classed among the arts, it is surely the least of them all. Oratory, it cannot be denied, has its uses; it has been of tremendous use to me. But the older I grow, the more I am inclined to get away from it. For rhetorical oratory I have absolute distrust. My faith in the soundness of judgment in a man addicted to opium could not be less than that in a man addicted to rhetorical oratory. Rhetorical oratory is the foundation upon which all the humbug in our political system rests.

These new activities crowded out music, and I hardly ever touched the piano during all my student days. I did, however, keep my guitar with me, and played it often. In my last two or three years I sang bass on the college quartet. I gave only the time required by the rules to religious observance. I attended all the Sunday services, because they were compulsory; but the Wednesday night prayer meetings, group prayer meetings in the reception room of the matron, and other voluntary activities I renounced. I did this at some cost. The school was founded in the missionary spirit and, although the original zeal had subsided, it was still quite high. Students who were religiously observant still enjoyed certain preferences. I am sure that I lowered Mr. Francis's first estimate of me very much; and he was, at the time, the administrative head of the institution. The preaching service on Sunday mornings was sometimes interesting. Not so much could I say for Sunday school in the afternoons. I already knew by heart the Bible stories and the lessons for the young to be drawn from them. The Sunday evening prayer meetings bored me terribly. They were conducted by Mr. Francis, and included the singing of hymns (in which he always joined loudly, and also always in a different key), a religious talk by him on student conduct, and brief admonitions by certain of the students to the others. Some students fulfilled their obligations by repeating Bible verses.

These quotations were most often apropos of no subject under consideration.

I doubt not that there were students who enjoyed these prayer meetings and were spiritually benefited, but I believe the main effect was to put a premium on hypocrisy or, almost as bad, to substitute for religion a lazy and stupid conformity. I remember that in my Middle Prep year, being, for reasons that I shall presently relate, without a roommate, the matron assigned to me a new student, a loutish young fellow, in order that he might come under my refining influence; that is, by example or otherwise, I was to be the inculcator of proper ideas about bathing, changing clothes, keeping teeth brushed and shoes shined, and about other niceties that would bring him up to Atlanta University standards. A good many new boys stood in need of this kind of tutorship. A few of the boys from the back country, who all their lives had been passing in and out of their houses over one or two steps at most, had to learn even how to go up and down stairs. I have seen such boys, generally free and easy in their movements, clinging desperately to the handrail while they painfully made their way up or down; and I realized that people who trip lightly up and down long flights of stairs are really performing a difficult acrobatic stunt, mastered by long years of practice. There was not much in common between me and my new roommate, but I did my best to be faithful to my trust. Each night during study hour he would sit gloomily pondering his books for a while, then would undress and kneel down to say his prayers. And each night after I had finished studying I would wake him up and make him get into bed. One night I didn't feel very well, and went to bed first leaving him to finish studying and say his prayers. When the rising bell woke me the next morning he was still on his knees. The time it took to get him awake and limbered up enough to dress himself made me late for breakfast.

One day late in the spring, not far from commencement time, I received another summons to see Mr. Francis in his office. I was curious but not worried. When I appeared before him, he was more direct and accusatory than he was on the former similar occasion. He at once put to me a series of questions that sounded like an echo of that famous list once propounded by Cicero to Catiline.

"Where were you yesterday afternoon?"

"Well, I was called to practice with the team, and I spent most of the afternoon on the ball field."

"Didn't you go out on West Hunter Street sometime during the afternoon?"

"No, sir."

"Didn't you go with some other boys to a place where you bought a bottle of wine and drank it, and smoked cigarettes?"

"No, sir."

The interview ended with Mr. Francis somewhat non-plussed. I was ignorant of what may have happened, but I saw D—— right away and told him about the inquisition I had been put through. His face blanched. He had not breathed a word to me; and now he did not need to. The "Big Four" got together at night, and I met with them. The facts were: the four had the afternoon before walked far out on West Hunter Street—this section of it only a clay road leading into the country—to a place where an old German (he may have been an Italian) cultivated a small vineyard and manufactured home-made wine; they had bought a bottle of his wine, drunk it, and smoked cigarettes. The meeting resolved itself into a board of strategy. We discussed the matter from every angle. I ventured the opinion that Mr. Francis, judging from the questions he had asked me, had firsthand knowledge of the whole affair. It was decided that one of the number be sent out to the old vintner to find out just what the situation was. T—— was selected to go. The night was stormy. We waited anxiously with lights out for him to return. It would have been better if any one of the others had gone and left T—— to keep our spirits up. He came back wet, spattered and stained with red clay. His report confirmed our worst fears. Mr. Francis had been out and seen the old man, and wheedled and wrung from him all that had taken place. The old man had given descriptions of persons, not names, because he didn't know the names. And that explained why I had been called; he had described one of the boys as having gray eyes, and my gray eyes being the most pronounced feature of my face had led Mr. Francis to send for me. How he overlooked the fact that T——'s eyes were gray we could not say. Probably, too, the old man repeated to Mr. Francis the first names, as well as he could remember them, that he heard the boys address each other by.

The evidence appeared to be overwhelming. How Mr. Francis got his first clue we never found out. Maybe he saw the four boys leave the campus together, and shadowed them. It is possible that some neighbor or some passerby saw the boys go into the old vintner's place, and reported the fact. Professor Chase pleaded for the boys in the faculty meeting that tried the case with tears streaming down his cheeks. But Mr. Francis with a majority could not be moved; and each of the four received a sentence of indefinite suspension. That night all of them showed wretchedness. T—— did attempt a story or two, but for the first time his efforts failed to provoke even a smile. D——, despite his superb self-confidence, was terribly broken up. He thought with dread of the effect of the news on his relations with his father. Through a part of the night he wept quietly, and I wept with him. The verdict cast a gloom over the whole school. Four such boys could not be sent away from a very small college without making a mighty hole in it. None of the four ever went back to Atlanta University.

I sometimes speculate on what might have happened had I not been called for baseball practice that spring afternoon. Would I have gone with the "Big Four"? If I had, would I have stood out? Would I have tried to dissuade them, and if so, could I have succeeded? Or would I have followed along and been sent away too? Of course, I cannot answer any one of these questions. But I do know that I have always been glad that I did not make myself liable for such punishment. For, in spite of petty regulations and a puritanical zeal, Atlanta University was an excellent school. In spite of the fact that its code of moral conduct was narrow as it was high, it was an excellent school. Its reputation for thorough work and scholarship was unsurpassed by any similar institution in the country; and the breadth of the social ideas that it carried out practically was, perhaps, unequaled. I have at times thought that, in some degree, its training might have cramped and inhibited me. But generally I have felt that for me there was probably no better school in the United States.

There is now and has been for some time a cry going up against the inadequacy of our school methods and their results. Without doubt, there is ground for complaint. But, at the same time, it is too easy to lose sight of the fact that not the school nor the teachers, but the student is the preponderant factor in education. The student who claims that he is handicapped or miscast for life through the mere inadequacy of the methods used for his instruction would not have profited discernibly more from the most superior methods in vogue or, as yet, only on paper. A good share of the complaint against the elementary schools rises out of the disappointment of fond and overambitious parents who look for a miracle. No kind of school can do the impossible; and any school that turns out the bulk of its students with a fair degree of developed mental and physical control may feel well satisfied with its work. In the higher institutions, teaching increases in importance as a factor; there must be both great teachers and capable students for the achievement of real education; but great teachers are almost as rare as great philosophers.

VIII

ON the morning after commencement I left Atlanta for Jacksonville. There were four in our party; besides Ricardo and me, there was a boy younger than either of us and a very pretty girl named Rosa DeVoe, whose father was collector of customs at the port of Savannah. The train carried a car for Negro passengers, but Georgia had not yet passed its "Jim Crow" law, and, as we had first-class tickets, we got into the first-class car. When the conductor took up our tickets, he suggested very strongly that we go into the car ahead. Our little party looked to me; and I, remembering how things had worked out on the trip from Jacksonville to Atlanta, told him that we were comfortable and preferred to stay where we were. The conductor said no more; but, when it was seen that we were not going to move, a murmur started in the car, and grew until it became a hubbub. The conductor was called upon to put us out; but doubtless his instructions were to stay on the safe side of the law in such cases and he took no action. The remarks in the car now became open and loud. Threats began to reach our ears. I affected nonchalance by scanning and turning the leaves of a book I held in my hand; I might just as well have held it upside-down. Soon a white man came to me and said in tones of one who had only a deep, friendly interest in us, "I advise you people to get into the next car; they have sent a telegram down to Baxley to have a mob come on and put you out when the train gets there." "Baxley, Baxley," when had I heard that name before? It came back. I remembered that one morning in the boys' reading room at the University I had seen in the *Atlanta Constitution* that a party of Negro preachers going to a convention somewhere in Georgia, and traveling in the first-class car, had been met by a mob at one of the stations along the line and forcibly ejected. Out on the station platform one of the mob, it was reported, said, "Niggers, dance us a jig." When the preachers protested that that would not be in keeping with their Christian practices and their dignity, this member of the mob started firing into the floor close to the preachers' feet, and they, naturally, began picking their feet up. The whole mob followed this lead, and kept the party of preachers doing some sort of Hopi Indian dance until some of them were exhausted. I remembered that the name of the station was Baxley; and we were now nearing Baxley and, to all appearances, nearing a mob with guns to put three boys and a girl out of a car in which they had a legal right to be. I was frightened, but I did not suggest to my companions that we move. Soon I saw the colored porter of the car forward beckoning to me. I went out on the platform to see what he wanted. He begged me to come out of the first-class car; he knew that a mob was going to meet the train at Baxley, and he was sure we should be hurt, perhaps killed. His warnings raised my fright to the point where it broke my determination to hold my ground; I went back to my friends and told them what the porter had said, and on my decision we gathered up our luggage and packages and went into the car ahead. This was my first experience with the "Jim Crow Car." While we were getting out of our car many of the passengers expressed their satisfaction. If their satisfaction rose from any idea that I was having a sense of my inferiority impressed upon me, they were sadly in error; indeed, my sensation was the direct opposite; I felt that I was being humiliated. When we passed through Baxley I saw a crowd but no indications of a mob; and I wondered if the colored porter had merely been made a tool of by the white passengers. The more I thought of this, the more I regretted that we had moved.

I have since been through a number of experiences with "Jim Crow." These experiences have always stirred bitter resentment and even darker passions in my heart. In two instances, however, the ridiculous aspect of the whole business was shown up so glaringly that, notwithstanding the underlying injustice, all sense of indignation was lost in the absurdity of the situation. In 1896 I was returning from New York to Jacksonville. I went by steamer to Charleston, and from there to Jacksonville by train. When I boarded the train at Charleston I got into the first-class car. (South Carolina had not yet enacted its separate car law; and all my life I have made it a principle never to "Jim Crow" myself voluntarily.) The car was almost full, but I found a seat to myself, arranged my luggage, and settled down comfortably. The conductor took my ticket quietly, and made no reference whatever to the fact that the train carried a special car for me. A while later, however, he came to me and said that I would have to go into the car forward. His manner was not objectionable; in fact, it was rather apologetic. I asked him why. He replied that we had just crossed the Georgia line, and that it was against the law in Georgia for white and colored people to ride in the same railroad car. I then asked him what he proposed to do if I did not move. We were discussing the question without heat, and he answered in a matter-of-fact manner that he would call the first available officer of the law and have me arrested. I realized that my opposition to the law and all the forces of the state of Georgia would have hardly any other effect in this instance than to land me in some small-town jail; but I said to the conductor that I would first take a look at the car designated for me.

I went forward and looked at the car. It was the usual "Jim Crow" arrangement: one-half of a baggage coach, unkempt, unclean, and ill smelling, with one toilet for both sexes. Two of the seats were taken up by the pile of books and magazines and the baskets of fruit and chewing gum of the "newsbutcher." There were a half-dozen or more Negroes in the car and two white men. White men in a "Jim Crow" car were not an unusual sight. It was—and in many parts still is—the custom for white men to go into that car whenever they felt like doing things that would not be allowed in the "white" car. They went there to smoke, to drink, and often to gamble. At times the object was to pick an acquaintance with some likely-looking Negro girl. After my inspection I went back and told the conductor that I couldn't ride in the forward car either. When he asked why, I gave as a reason the fact that there were white passengers in that car, too. He looked at me astonished, and hastily explained that the two men were a deputy sheriff and a dangerously insane man, who was being taken to the asylum. I listened to his explanation, but pointed out that it didn't change the race of either of the men. He pleaded, "But I can't bring that crazy man into the 'white' car." "Maybe you can't," I said, "but if I've got to break this law I prefer breaking it in the first-class car." The conductor was, after all, a reasonable fellow; and he decided to stand squarely by the law, and bring the two white men into the "white" car.

While this colloquy between the conductor and me was going on the passengers were fully aware of what it was about. There had been no open talk or threats regarding my being in the car. Probably they felt that the matter was in capable hands or it may be that there was no individual among them to take the initiative in stirring up protest or action. However, when I began to get my belongings together there were smiles and nudges and *sotto voce* comments all through the car. The sheriff and his insane charge were brought in, and I began to move out. The first thing the insane man did after sitting down was to thrust his manacled hands through the glass of the window, cutting himself horribly. Then he not only let out a stream of oaths and ordinary obscenity, but made use of all the unprintable (perhaps no longer so) four-letter words of Anglo-Saxon origin. As I left the car, there were protests from men and women against the change. The maniac continued his ravings; but both I and the conductor stood squarely by the law.

Several years later I was going from Jacksonville to New York. I had a Pullman ticket. Negroes who are interstate passengers on a Pullman car are not subject to the "Jim Crow" laws of the various states. Of course, they are not exempt from violence. There are still parts of the country where a Negro puts his life in jeopardy whenever he travels in a Pullman car. When I entered, the main body of the car was empty, except for two or three women passengers. The train left about seven-thirty in the evening, and as soon as it pulled out I asked the porter to make down my berth. When he began, I started for the men's room to smoke a cigar in the meantime. When I reached the door, from which the curtain had been drawn aside, a hurried glance showed me that there were five men in the compartment, sprawled out over practically all of the seating space. In an instant, as Negroes must often do, I was rapidly balancing the vital chances in a suddenly presented situation that involved "race." That instant took me past the open door to the extreme end of the car. There I came to a physical and a mental stop. I pulled myself together, and I said to me, "Jim Johnson, what's the matter with you?" I turned and walked quietly into the compartment. The three men on the long seat moved up. I sat down in the corner, and proceeded to light my cigar. Under the cover of that most handy of all masculine makeshifts I took in the scene. As I sat down, the conversation ceased, and I could feel myself being scrutinized more carefully than politely. My own quickened powers of observation were at work. A stout, ruddy, successful-looking man sat in the armchair, the dominating figure of the group, he had been talking animatedly when I entered. I learned later that he was an official of the railroad on which we were riding, with headquarters in Savannah. A clean-cut young man sat on the side seat, directly in front of me. He was regarding me in a not unfriendly way. I was to learn that he was the son of the stout man, had gone into the army as an officer during the Spanish-American War, and was just returning from Cuba. I was right in surmising that one of the men on the long seat was a preacher. He was pastor of a church in Tampa. The other two were nondescript. The silence was broken by the young man just back from Cuba, who said, "Dad, there's a genuine Panama hat." The elder man looked over intently at the hat I was wearing. Without saying anything, I took it off and passed it to him for closer inspection. Panama hats were then rare in the United States. The hat was passed round and examined with expressions of admiration; it was a very good one. When it reached the young man he noticed the

Havana-stamped lining and said to me, *"¿Habla Vd. español?"* *"Sí, señor,"* I answered. Thereupon he and I exchanged several commonplace phrases in Spanish; but in a short while his knowledge of that language was exhausted, and general conversation in English was resumed. I said little except in answer to some questions the preacher asked me about conditions in Cuba, where I had not yet been but concerning which I had a good deal of information. The preacher pressed an invitation on me to come and talk about Cuba at his church the next time I happened to be in Tampa. The run from Jacksonville to Savannah takes a little over three hours, but before we got out of Florida our train came to a standstill because of engine trouble, and we were a couple of hours late. The whole party spent the time in the smoking compartment, talking, joking, laughing. The railroad official went into his bag and brought out his private flask of whisky, from which each of us, including the preacher, took several samples, all drinking out of the same glass. Before we reached Savannah a bond of mellow friendship had been established. My newly made friends got off at Savannah, and I went to bed repeating to myself: In such situations any kind of a Negro will do; provided he is not one who is an American citizen.

IX

I WAS happy to get back home and see my parents, my brother and sister, and my heart's desire. Atlanta suddenly receded into something distant and unimportant. It was good to be again with the boys I had grown up with. I was burning to tell them my experiences and to show them how I had improved as a baseball player. In the single year I had grown much bigger and stronger, and practicing and playing almost daily during the season had developed my game remarkably. For a while I was kept busy noting changes. My parents and sister seemed the same, but my brother seemed almost like a different boy. I was surprised to see how much bigger and stronger he was. When I went away he was wearing short pants; now he was wearing long trousers and talking in a changed voice. When I saw my heart's desire I looked at her with some trepidation; I was anxious to see if she was going to stand the inevitable comparison with the girls of the University; and, too, I was anxious because I had rashly written a letter to one of the Jacksonville boys which contained a panegyric on the "Georgia peaches" and which he had with all possible speed shown to her. She stood the comparison easily. She was, indeed, pretty; so golden-hued, so soft-mannered, and yet so life-loving and gay. She played the piano better than any other colored girl in Jacksonville; and before jazz had become known, she knew the trick of transforming a piece of staid music into the most tantalizing rhythms.

It didn't take me long to discover that some connection that had existed between me and the boys I had known all my life had slipped its place. I found that the things that mutually interested them and me had abruptly shrunk. And I have noticed that this shrinkage has kept pace with the years. A good deal of sentiment is spilled over the subject of the friends of our childhood and youth, but except in the few cases where for mutually strong reasons the friendship is kept up and developed through the years, the idea is largely a myth. Rare is the situation that is more awkward than the one in which you are thrown for any length of time with the average friend of your childhood or youth. When "Do you remember this?" and "Do you remember that?" and "How is old Blank?" and "Where is old Blink?" are exhausted, the situation is likely to become painful, and the most absolute stranger would be a welcome relief.

Rosamond and I had much to say to each other. One of the first things he told me about was the new literary society. Two of the white teachers at Cookman Institute had organized a Browning Society among the young people. Rosamond took me to a meeting. It was held in the Presbyterian Church and was well attended. There were essays, orations, and a debate. There were also instrumental and vocal solos and music by the choir or chorus—of which Rosamond was, it appeared, a prominent member. I was astonished by the volume of his voice when he sang. Quite naturally, I was called on to "make a few remarks." My experience in the Ware Lyceum gave me a feeling of confidence, and I expressed great satisfaction in seeing such an organization as the Browning Society in my home city. It is more than probable that my "remarks" were a bit patronizing in tone. One of the members of the society in talking

with me after the meeting revealed that he had not the slightest idea why it was called the Browning Society. He had a hazy
notion that the name had some relation to colored people;
that the organization was in some special sense a society for
more or less brown-skinned people. This was during the great
vogue of Browning Societies, and I hazard the opinion that
there were throughout the country many, many members who
knew nothing or very little about Robert Browning; but I am
sure that the notion held by this particular member was absolutely unique.

D—— and I also had a great deal to talk over. I found that
his father had declared emphatically that he would not spend
another cent on his education. He had decided, instead, to put
his son to work. D——'s father was operating a small cigar factory in partnership with another colored man, who bore the
wholly non-Aframerican name of Eichelberger. When I went
to the factory I saw D—— working as a stripper, the first
step in learning the cigarmaker's trade. He stripped the stems
from the leaves of tobacco, smoothed out the "rights" and
"lefts" and put them in separate piles over the edge of a barrel
before which he was seated. He made no effort to disguise the
fact that the job was distasteful to him. He was a diminutive
Prometheus chained to a tobacco barrel.

The summer promised to bring happy days; there were picnics and rides on the river and excursions to Pablo Beach to
look forward to—but there were other things in store. One
day I found my mother lying across her bed groaning with
pain. The doctor was called. She went to bed and remained
there four months. When she got up she found herself crippled
by rheumatism, crippled for life. This was a great blow to
everyone in the house. Ever since she had been in Jacksonville
she had taken a leading part in the educational and cultural activities of the colored people; and to be thus handicapped in
the prime of her life, at the age of forty-six, was a great misfortune for her and not a small loss to the community. I was sent
to buy a pair of crutches for her, and Rosamond and I undertook to help her learn to use them. We both had a difficult
time choking back our emotions. She had been so active that
to see her struggling like an infant again was almost more than

we could stand. What made it all the more heart-breaking was her brave attempt to be cheerful; if she had complained and bemoaned her fate, we should not have been so keenly pierced.

In mid-summer, while my mother was lying ill, the great yellow fever epidemic broke out. Some people fled at the first notice; but a rigid quarantine quickly made prisoners of the rest, prisoners in a charnel. There were efforts at escape, most of them futile, some of them fatal. Business was paralyzed; the churches were closed, and all forms of assembly were restricted. Deaths reached a peak of more than a hundred a day. The county pest-house was enlarged by the addition of several temporary buildings, and patients were hurriedly taken there, unless they had behind them the advantage of strong influence. The people dreaded the pest-house as much as they did the disease; and every house upon which the yellow flag was nailed became, too, a pest-house. Many of the dead were buried in common graves; and that increased the terror. The cause of yellow fever had not yet been established; and I doubt that there were in Jacksonville in 1888 facilities for applying even the little that was then known about combating the plague. A few years later, the sure method of abolishing this disease was discovered.

But the possible was done. Money, supplies, and provisions were poured into Jacksonville from all over the country. The major part of the population was fed from commissariats. Some of the money contributed was expended in giving men work. I was given a job as time-keeper for a gang of men that was put at road building. For this I received two dollars a day. The fear, the suffering, the overhanging cloud of death, and my mother lying helpless, made this a memorable period of sadness for us. I watched my father grow more anxious and haggard as the days dragged slowly along. I went to bed for a couple of days with a temperature, and it looked as though the specter had entered our door. But we were among the fortunate; he passed us by. Expectations that medical skill and effort would stay the stalking pestilence were given up, and hearts finally clung to hope for an early frost.

The fall was ended before the fever had run its course and the quarantine was lifted. Reluctantly I resigned myself to the necessity of missing the year at school. I talked with my father and told him I wanted to keep it from being a lost year; that I wanted to go on with as many of my studies as possible—if I could find a tutor. He said that he knew a West Indian who was reputed to be a fine scholar. We went to see this man and found him in a small, dingy, cobbler's shop that he ran, pegging away at old shoes. He was a little man, very black, partially bald, with a scraggly beard, and but for bright, intelligent eyes an insignificant presence. At the sight of the surroundings my heart misgave me, and I was embarrassed both for my father and myself. I wondered if he misunderstood so much as to think that I wanted to be coached in spelling and arithmetic and geography. I was reassured when the little cobbler began to talk. He spoke English as no professor at the University could speak it. My father made arrangements, and I began to study with him every night. By a lamp that was often smoky and in an atmosphere filled with the odor of smelly old shoes I read Cæsar's *Gallic War* and Cicero's orations against Catiline. I also began the study of elementary geometry. My teacher did more than correct, when necessary, the way in which I translated or construed Latin sentences; he had a considerable store of collateral knowledge, and gave me the benefit of it. He talked to me about Julius Cæsar and Cicero, and about Roman power and Roman politics in their time. So I got more than a language out of what I read; this collateral information not only made it interesting, but gave it sense and connected it up with life. Perhaps, the most common fault among teachers is the lack of collateral knowledge or the failure to make use of it. I remember that when I came to read the Greek dramatists I was plunged directly into the texts. There was no enlightenment as to how and why the plays were written or how and where they were performed. In fact, for me they were not plays at all; they were exercises in Greek grammar.

I cannot recall the name of my West Indian teacher or which of the islands he came from. Nor can I say how he was able to use this method of instruction without, apparently, any books to which to refer. I have the impression that he was a Jamaican and was educated at one of the excellent colleges there. At any rate, in the whole course of my school work the only other teacher who made a subject as interesting to me as did this little cobbler was Brander Matthews at Columbia. I wonder just what it was that kept him down on a cobbler's bench?

One day early in the winter a young man stopped at our gate. I knew him; his name was Robert Goode; he had worked for my father at the St. James; he was now cook for the family of Dr. T. O. Summers. Dr. Summers was regarded as the outstanding surgeon in Florida. He had been, I think, a professor of surgery at Vanderbilt University. Robert Goode told my father that the doctor was in need of someone to take charge of his reception room for patients; that the place had been held by a young white woman; that he had spoken to the doctor about me, and that I could get the job. He also said that the work would allow me time for my studies.

I went to see Dr. Summers. His office consisted of a suite of three rooms in one of the business blocks. He was then the only physician in Jacksonville who did no have his office in his residence. I found a man of thirty-eight or forty, very handsome, and well dressed. His features were what we term "classic," his hair and his well-trained mustache were dark, and his eyes were brooding. When I entered he was seated in a large chair, holding in one hand a small tin containing something that he languidly sniffed, first up one nostril, then up the other. He asked me to have a seat, then said, "I suppose you can read and write." I gave him the answer and he asked, "What else have you studied?" I named the regular grammar school studies, then went on proudly with "Latin, algebra—" I got no further. He straightened up and questioned, "Can you read Latin?" I grew dismayed, and answered with sincerely felt modesty, "I can read a little." He rose quickly from his chair, went to a bookcase, took out a volume bound in black, limp leather, with gilt lettering and edges, and handing it to me said, "Read me something from that." A glance at the title showed me that the book was one unknown to me— the *Roman Missal*. I was not sure whether he wanted me to read or translate, but I proceeded as I had been taught; that is, to read the passage over first. I didn't think I should have made out so badly at translating, for the Latin did not strike me as difficult; but before I had finished reading the passage he said, "That will do," took the book from my hand and began telling me about my duties. These were the general duties of an attendant in a physician's reception room. But I had not been with him long before I took over entirely the matter of collecting his bills.

Since I have reached the point in life where the glance is more and more frequently backward, I look searching to discover the Key. I try to isolate and trace to their origins the forces that have determined the direction I have followed. This is a fascinating but inconclusive pursuit. The Key I do not find. I cannot separate the many forces that have been at work. I cannot unravel the myriad threads of influence that have drawn me here or there. The life, however simple, of every individual is far too complex for that sort of analysis. The number of forces, within and without, at work upon each one of us is infinite. Many of these forces are so subtle, so tangential that they are not even perceived. So when we set forth the manner in which we have definitely shaped the course of life, the precise steps by which certain ends have been reached, we are doing little more than rationalizing results. It is not possible to go back through the progression of causes. What more can any of us do than struggle to converge the forces at work toward some desired focus? We find some of them pliant and others stubborn. I have found many of them utterly unyielding. No intelligence or will power or industry that I possessed was able to bend or deflect them any fraction of a degree from their fixed and untoward direction. The forces at work on each individual are so manifold, so potent, so arbitrary, and often so veiled as to make fatalism a plausible philosophy.

Nevertheless, I know that in the moment in which Dr. Summers took his *Roman Missal* out of my hand and said, "That will do," I had made contact with one of those mysterious forces that play close around us or flash to us across the void from another orbit. Dr. Summers was an extraordinary man. Of course, he was educated; but I had by now known a number of educated people. What was unprecedented for me was that in him I came into close touch with a man of great culture. He was, moreover, a cosmopolite. He had traveled a good part of the world over, through Europe, to North Africa, to Greece and Turkey. He spoke French and German, the latter, because of his student days in Germany, as fluently as he did English. He had wide knowledge of literature, and was himself a poet. His local literary reputation was very high because of the poems he sometimes contributed to the *Times-Union*. He was an accomplished and brilliant talker. When alone, however, he was generally melancholy. He would sit for a long period inhaling from a small can of ether, seemingly lost in dreams. After I had learned something about ether, this habit caused me such anxiety that I spoke to him regarding it. He merely smiled sadly. I dared to speak to him about so personal a matter because from the beginning the relation between us was on a high level. It was not that of employer to employee. Less still was it that of white employer to Negro employee. Between the two of us, as individuals, "race" never showed its head. He neither condescended nor patronized; in fact, he treated me as an intellectual equal. We talked about things that only people in the same sphere may talk about. More than once, in conversation with others, he remarked that I had more sense than any of the Jacksonville doctors he knew anything about. This need not, however, be taken as extremely high praise; for his opinion with respect to the intellectuality of Jacksonville doctors in general was pretty low. In matters of money he was careless and, moreover, had the grand air. It was easy to believe what I vaguely gathered—that he had spent two fortunes, his own and his wife's. Mrs. Summers was pretty, petite, and rather demure. There were two beautiful children, "Bob" and Tom. "Bob," the elder, was about five years old, and a girl. She and I became great friends; and she never considered that I was at any time too busy to furnish her with information or entertainment.

My duties were light and gave me a good deal of the time to do things that appealed to me. I explored the books the doctor kept at his office. The number was not large but the range was wide; wider than that covered by the ten thousand books at the University library, many of those being, undoubtedly, donations from the libraries of defunct clergymen. A corner of the doctor's shelves was devoted to *erotica*; there I found the *Decameron* of Boccaccio and the *Droll Stories* of Balzac. It would be interesting, at least to me, if I could now determine what effect on me these forbidden books had. I can somewhat recall the glow that pervaded my body and my mind as I read some of these stories. Others of the stories struck me as very funny. I was stirred and entertained; was I damaged? The whole case for censorship is in that question. I cannot see that these books had the slightest deleterious effect. And I do not believe that any normal person is in any manner damaged by such reading. I grant that on persons of abnormal instincts or weaknesses there may not be this lack of bad effects, but those persons are anyhow bound to get at certain facts about life, and probably from sources far more contaminating than the wit and delicacy of Boccaccio and Balzac and the other masters of erotic literature. Did these books do me any good? That is a question the advocates of censorship might follow up with, but it raises a point not involved; a book may be 100 per cent "pure" and do nobody any good.

From the doctor's library I read some of Montaigne's essays, Thomas Paine's *Age of Reason*, and Robert Ingersoll's *Some Mistakes of Moses* and *The Gods and other Lectures*. I was so much impressed with *The Age of Reason* that I carried it along with me so that I could read and reread it. One day my father summarily commanded me to "take that book out of the house and never bring it here again." I don't believe he was familiar with the book. Whether this stern action was prompted by having scanned it at the time or by "Tom" Paine's popular reputation, I do not know. Indeed, I was too much astounded by the sudden show of intolerance on my father's part to question the reason for his order. I simply obeyed it. I spent some of the time at my desk copying the text from the Greek Testament that I discovered among the doctor's book. I found this fascinating, although I did not understand a single word that I copied. My pages of Greek text drew enthusiastic praise from Dr. Summers, and he declared that I should have lived when the copying of manuscripts by hand was a fine art.

In the course of collecting the doctor's bills I made several futile efforts to get some money long due him by a Mr. Short. One day, I left a memorandum on the doctor's table about the collections I had made; reporting on Mr. Short, I scribbled this bit of doggerel:

> Mr. Short—
> As I "thort"—
> Gave me not a single quarter;
> And every time
> I go to him
> He seems to turn up shorter.

He thought this rather clever. Certainly the verses could not be as funny to anyone else as they were to him. At any rate, they led to my showing Dr. Summers all the verses I had written, and to his giving to me the first worthwhile literary criticism and encouragement I had yet received.

Dr. Summers had worked very hard during the yellow fever epidemic and had recorded his observations on the disease. He had prepared a large number of slides for microscopic study. In the spring he was asked to come to Washington to confer with Army medical officials as to his findings. He said to me at once, "Jimmie, I'm going to Washington, would you like to go?" He decided to go to New York by sea, and from there down to Washington. We left Jacksonville aboard a sailing vessel with auxiliary steam power, belonging to Louis K. Bucky, a Jacksonville lumber-mill owner. The ship did not carry passengers, but the exception was made because of Mr. Bucky's friendship for the doctor. I have traveled many thousands of miles by sea, and I love ships; but I am a bad sailor. This trip is memorable because it was so pleasant. The vessel lazed along through tranquil seas and perfect weather. We did not have to be dressed up; we did not have to make acquaintances; there were no shuffleboard players to obstruct the decks; and there were no romping, shouting children to break the sense of peace and quiet. For once I had no sensation of seasickness. I went to meals with a ravenous appetite. I ate at table with the captain and Dr. Summers—just the three of us, ordinarily the captain ate alone. The food was excellent; this captain, as do most sea captains, lived aboard like a nabob. I remember he had brought for his table a barrel of oysters which we depleted in the seven or eight days of the trip. At meals the doctor was more talkative and gay than I had ever seen him. He matched the captain with stories of travels to far, strange places. He gave a thrilling recital of his experiences during the bombard- ment of Alexandria, seven years before. At other times he walked the small deck space alone, pausing frequently to look out broodingly on the sea, as though waiting for it to give him the answer to some question burning in his brain. Or he sat for long periods, a book in one hand, in the other his *vade mecum*, a tin of ether.

I am sure it was at Dr. Summer's suggestion, perhaps on his insistence, that I ate at the captain's table. He followed the same course at the hotels in New York and Washington. In each of these cities he engaged a double room in which both of us slept. We merely passed through New York, but our stay in Washington lasted a couple of weeks. I had practically noth- ing to do. The doctor sent me twice with communications to an official in the State, Army, and Navy Building; that is all I can remember having to do for him. He did not concern himself as to how I spent the time. I had much curiosity about Washington, which I went around satisfying. Naturally, the first sight was Pennsylvania Avenue. I was disappointed by its shabbiness, but amazed at its width. I went up and looked at the White House; I saw the Washington Monument; I visited various government buildings; but the major portion of my time I spent in the galleries of the Senate and the House of Representatives. The experience of looking at and for hours at a time listening to the leading figures on the floors of both houses did not tire me then. It was exciting, even when they discussed matters of which I had no comprehension. Of course I had no pre-knowledge that thirty-odd years later I should spend weeks and months between these same galleries, and in the offices of the leading figures on both floors, whom I should come to know well, in an effort to get them to do one particular thing.

When I returned to Atlanta University in the fall I was filled with regret at parting from Dr. Summers. The regret was mu- tual. He had formed a strong affection for me which he did not hide. I had made him my model of all that a man and a gentleman should be. The question rose in my mind whether I was not gaining more through contact with him than I would gain in going on in school. My father's estimate of this influence was not so high as mine. From my boastings at home he formed the opinion that the doctor was a very smart man, but visionary and impractical; in a word, without hard, common sense. My father was partially right. I myself could see that many of the things that Dr. Summers did and said were not governed by hard, common sense. But what my father did not appreciate, nor I, fully, was that that was the very point. I think he was glad that the time had come for me to return to Atlanta. The doctor did not intimate that I should do other than continue my schooling, but he urged upon me to choose medicine as a profession, and had a while before set me to the preliminary reading of a textbook on anatomy. Already, I had assisted him in several operations by administering the anæs-thetic. When I left him I had thrown over the idea of becoming a lawyer for that of becoming a physician and surgeon, with the emphasis on the surgeon. I left him also with an older ambition clarified, strengthened, and brought into some shape—the ambition to write. We exchanged letters, and I sent him regularly whatever new things I wrote. He moved to a western city, and we continued the correspondence for several years. Then one day I was shocked to learn that Dr. Summers had committed suicide. I was deeply grieved, for I had lost an understanding friend, one who was, in many ways, a kindred spirit.

X

AT the University I found myself in the Middle Prep class, a year behind the class I had started with. I at once asked for permission to do the two years' work in one. It was reluctantly granted after I gave evidence of the ground I had covered during the year that I was out. When I went home for the summer vacation, I looked for my cobbler, but he had disappeared; so I had to find another tutor. He was a former principal of the Duval High School, the white high school of Jacksonville. He had become partially paralyzed and, so, incapacitated for the position, and was living on the generosity of a friend. He was quite a pathetic figure; he had lost his health and his position; his wife had left him; and he was now glad to tutor a Negro boy for the small fee that was in it. He lived in

a little two-room cabin—it could hardly be called a cottage—
that sat far back in the yard to his patron's house. I went there
three times a week. I read Vergil's *Æneid* and continued the
study of algebra and geometry. My teacher was good enough,
as teachers go, and I got along; but he did not stir my curiosity and interest in what I studied as my little cobbler had. It
was a matter of hard study and routine recitation. Not that he
didn't talk to me; on the contrary, he talked a great deal, but
always about his misfortunes, his fair-weather friends, his in-
grate of a wife, and the general hard-heartedness of the world.
At the time, I knew the complete history of this bitter period
of his life. He roused my sympathies, for he was a broken and
forsaken man. So, I often lingered after lessons listening to
him only because I felt that it did him good to have someone
to talk to, someone to whom he could rail at fate.

I earned a little money during this vacation also. In my Middle Prep year I had taken wood-turning in the industrial shops.
I have said how much I liked the work in carpentry; I liked the
work in turning still more. Turning is considered a trade, but it
approaches very close to being an art. A rough block of wood,
dead-centered on the lathe; revolving slowly; gradually assuming cylindrical form under the tools in the hands of the turner;
then the lathe speeded up higher and higher; and the piece of
wood, under the deft touches of the workman, becoming
magically transformed into a thing of geometric beauty. There
is something in this akin to sculpture. Mr. Onley, a colored
contractor, ran a small mill. I presented myself as a wood-
turner, and got a job. I worked during the whole summer and
turned out quantities of banisters, corner blocks, and other
pieces used for ornamentation in a building. One day I was assigned the job of turning a newel post. The material given me
was a piece of eight by eight timber about five feet long. I had
never before handled such a big piece. With the help of a man
I got it dead-centered on the lathe, and began my work. But I
failed to estimate the amount of air resistance that a piece of
square timber of its weight and size would generate, and
started my lathe at too high a speed. In an instant there was a
commotion that shook the mill like an earthquake. The piece
of timber hummed like an airplane, but with a rapid crescendo.
In the next instant it had crashed up against and almost

through the ceiling. I was lucky not to be hurt; luckier not to be killed. The piece was put back on the lathe, and I kept it at the lowest speed until I had taken off all the rough corners and surfaces. Finally, the finished newel post was turned out. There was a deep satisfaction in seeing how sweetly that recalcitrant log spun at the higher speed after it began to take on beauty.

In the fall I returned to school. Rosamond had made up his mind that he preferred a musical to an academic education. He decided that he would go to Boston and study at the New England Conservatory; helping himself by working at his trade in the meantime. Ricardo decided that going through Atlanta University would be, for him, not a matter of time but eternity. He chose now to cast his lot with my brother. By this time he spoke English quite well. His plan was to go to Boston and work in the mechanical laboratory of some dentist, and continue his studies privately. He was still receiving his liberal allowance from Havana, and his plan looked like an easy one. It was easy; in fact, too easy. He found the opening in the mechanical laboratory, but Boston life took up all the time he thought he was going to devote to study. A month or so after I left, Rosamond and Ricardo sailed. D—— was left working in his father's cigar factory. When I reached the University I took the necessary examinations, skipped the Senior Prep class, and entered the Freshman year with my original class.

In this year the scarcity of the sense of humor in the faculty was reduced by the addition of a new member. Dean Hincks was a Yale graduate and had been the editor of a newspaper in Vermont. He was a man in his forties, tall, stoop-shouldered, with very blue eyes, that were shaded to a deeper color under his overhanging brow. He talked with a drawl, and his eyes twinkled when he was amused. He had a straightforward, rather blunt manner, but his heart was an understanding one. He was a good man for a boy in school to know. I was fortunate, and was brought into close contact with him. In my Freshman year I began work in the University printing office, and continued there through my Senior year, and Dean Hincks supervised the University publications. It was while I was one day working at a press that Dean Hincks brought a visitor into the printing office. The visitor was a brown-skinned man, forty-odd years of age, with shrewd gray eyes, and deep lines at the corner of his mouth. He was quite alert and asked many questions about what he was being shown. He came over to the press where I was working and watched me closely for a while. Dean Hincks introduced me to him. That was my first sight of Booker T. Washington, not at that time nationally known. As a writing man himself, the Dean took special interest in my literary efforts, and our personal relations became still closer.

I liked Dean Hincks. Perhaps, the thing I liked him for most was his freedom from cant. He would not indulge cant even if it was good form to do so. One afternoon there was a general assembly of the students to listen to an address by President Hickman, the new head of Clark University, a neighboring Negro college. President Hickman was a white Methodist preacher. After a year or two he gave up his work at Clark with the parting statement that he could not be expected to do for the Negro what God Almighty hadn't been able to do. On this particular afternoon the chapel was packed to the doors. That year the University had an enrollment of more than six hundred. The classes were overcrowded and rooming accommodations in some of the nearby homes had to be secured for many of the out-of-town students, the dormitories being taxed to capacity. President Hickman rose and made the kind of speech we had often heard before. He waxed sanctimoniously eloquent in commenting on the great number of students at Atlanta; and, turning to Dean Hincks on the platform, he exclaimed with fervor, "And we want more of them, don't we, brother?" And the Dean responded with equal fervor, "Hey, no; we've got enough." This response took the balance of the wind out of Brother Hickman's speech.

Dean Hincks had a section of the college students as his Sunday school class. We had one lesson on the "gift of tongues" as set down in the second chapter of *The Acts of the Apostles*, where it is recorded how the apostles, after the Pentecostal baptism of fire, addressed the multitude in all the known languages of the world, and how Peter met the charges of certain mockers that the apostles were drunk by declaring, "For these are not drunken, as ye suppose, seeing it is but the third hour of the day." In the course of the lesson I ventured the comment: that while I disagreed with the opinion of the

mockers, I felt that Peter's defense was not entirely sound; for
it seemed quite possible that a group of men could be drunk
by the third hour of the day, even on new wine, through the
simple expedient of sitting up drinking all night. Either at the
truth or the ignorance displayed in my comment, the Dean
laughed; the point of the incident being that he laughed.

Professor Chase, too, had a sense of humor, without fear of
letting others know that he had it. This quality made pretense
or pose impossible for him. When the University decided to
send out a quartet in the summers to interest people in the
school and raise funds, Mr. Chase was chosen to take charge of
the boys. I sang with the original quartet; the other members
were George Towns, my classmate—in our Senior year we were
roommates—and two younger students, Robert Gadsden and
Joseph Porter. In the course of time we sang, I should say, in
ninety-five per cent of all the inhabited spots in New England.
We sang in churches, hotel parlors, private drawing-rooms; in
fact, wherever there was a promising opening. Our program
consisted mainly of spirituals. George Towns and I made short
talks about the school, and Mr. Chase made the appeal for
funds. I filled two other spots on the program: I used to play a
couple of solo pieces on the guitar—the instrument was almost unknown in many of the smaller places—and recite a
story I had written about my experiences with a Georgia mule.
This latter feature proved to be a very popular one.

One other feature on the program, always a sure-fire hit,
was a popular song of the day entitled "He Never Came
Back." The first verse told the story of a soldier kissing his wife
good-by, going to the war, leaving "the one he did adore."
The chorus went on to relate that he never came back—and
"how happy she'll be, his sweet face to see, when they meet on
that beautiful shore." The second verse told the story of a man
going into a restaurant, calling the waiter, and ordering a
steak; of how the man waited and waited for the waiter; but—
in the chorus—he never came back, and "his face I will break,
if I don't get that steak, when we meet on that beautiful
shore." The remaining verses and choruses were equally incongruous with the first; however, we thought the song gave
our program a harmless touch of lightness. Mr. Chase chuck-
led over it night after night. One day he received a letter from

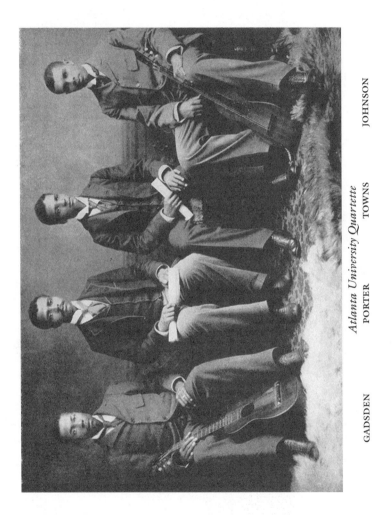

Atlanta University Quartette

GADSDEN   PORTER   TOWNS   JOHNSON

President Bumstead telling him to have the song cut from our program "at once." An elderly lady, who was a good friend of the University and the widow of a man who had lost his life in the Civil War, attended one of our concerts and wept over the singing of the first verse. She was shocked and pained by the second and remaining verses, and wrote to Dr. Bumstead about the song. Perhaps, the song didn't have a proper place in the serious business that was ours. I know it raised us many a laugh; I cannot say that it raised us any dollars. However, there was one instance in which it appealed to the most sober-minded in our audience. In a little town where we were to sing, George Towns went into the barber shop to get a shave, and was refused. A number of persons who heard of the incident expressed indignation. Just before the concert Towns and I got together and turned out an extra verse and chorus that were sung to tumultuous applause:

A certain little barber
In a certain little town,
Refused to shave another man
Because his face was brown.
That barber's face,
Although it's white—
His heart is very black;
And when he goes to regions warm
He never will come back.

He'll never come back, he'll never come back,
His face here we'll see never more;
O, but how he will crave for a brown face to shave,
When we meet on that beautiful shore.

I believe Professor Chase got as much fun out of these quartet tours as the boys did. He even got the amusing side of a concert we gave in one city for the entertainment of the inmates of the insane asylum—by the way, one of the most decorous and, apparently, one of the most thoughtful audiences I have ever appeared before.

These two grains of salt, Dean Hincks and Professor Chase, were wholesome ingredients in the Atlanta University faculty pot.

XI

I DID not spend the vacation after my Freshman year at home. Many of the students taught rural schools in the summer, and made enough money to cover their yearly expenses at the University. These expenses did not call for a large sum; at that time, the cost of room, board, and lodging was about one hundred dollars. The stories I had heard from these student-teachers made me want to try the summer in the backwoods of Georgia. This was going to be a new experience for me. True, I was born in a very small city, but it was one, nevertheless, that had quite a metropolitan air; and I knew nothing at all of rural life. So I looked forward to this venture. I wrote to my parents enthusiastically about it.

My roommate was Henry M. Porter, a Sophomore and a student with a shining record for scholarship. I had moved up from back rooms, and the training of young rustics, to a room looking over the front campus, and a congenial companion with whom to share it. Henry Porter and I roomed together three years. He was about a year older than I, and a youth with an earnest brown face, quite regular features, and very good dark eyes. He wore his hair in a tall pompadour; from which he was familiarly known as "Pompadour Porter." He had his hair cut in this style in order to add to his height, which was barely over five feet. He was an insatiable reader. He told me that during his first year he went off the campus but once, using all his spare time for reading, and so spent only five cents above his necessary expenses. He planned to be a lawyer, and cultivated the Websterian style of oratory. He was considered one of the best speakers at the University. He carried out his plan; he finished in law at the University of Michigan, and is now practicing his profession in Chicago. Porter and I bore the unpopular distinction of being the only self-acknowledged agnostics in the school. Perhaps, the distinction was not wholly unpopular; I am sure that by some of the students we were regarded with awe if not with admiration. His agnosticism went farther than mine and was based upon a more extensive reading. His renunciation of religious conformity went farther than mine. The aloofness of his attitude at the Sunday

night prayer meetings was one of the features of those gatherings. He always occupied a chair in the front row, directly in
front of the platform. He sat rigidly erect and as immovable as
a statue, his eyes fixed forward and his expression unchanging.
He held this position until he rose to leave. This sitter in the
seat of the scornful was, without doubt, a cause of great solicitude or of great irritation to Mr. Francis.

Porter knew all the steps to be taken in getting a country
school to teach. I kept thinking of the possibility of not getting
a place. He kept assuring me that there was no chance of such
an outcome. His positiveness left no room for doubt; and I
simply let him assume the entire responsibility. After commencement I went with him to a little town called Hampton,
about thirty miles south of Atlanta. Here Porter's school was
situated; it was the school he had taught the summer before.
His position was a very choice one, because his school was in a
town that had a railroad station. The station was the town's
nucleus. It was a small, dingy frame building; the most conspicuous thing about it being two bold signs, one lettered
"WHITE" and the other lettered "COLORED." The main portion of the station was divided into two rooms; over the door
to the larger room the "white" sign was placed, and the "colored" sign over the door to the smaller. The ticket office was
on the dividing line, so that one ticket seller could serve both
sides. However, it was not expected that he would turn to the
colored side as long as there was a white ticket purchaser in
sight. Back of the station and along the street on that side of
the railroad track was a short row of one-story brick and
wooden stores. This row was lengthened out on either side by
a line of residences, constantly dwindling in pretentiousness,
the Negro cabins at the extremities. Nowhere was there evidence of a sense of order, of beauty, or of community pride.
Hampton was not much of a town, but before the summer was
past it was for me a metropolitan center. Out from the town,
in all directions, lay the farms, the cotton plantations, and the
backwoods.

I went with Porter to his stopping place. It was the nicest
house in town occupied by a colored family. The owner of the
house was an intelligent, light-complexioned man, who had a
job with the railroad; the wife was a comely light-brown

woman; and there was a pretty little girl named Alma. I wondered how her parents came to choose that name, a word that
in Spanish means soul. I waited a day or two while Porter
made some preliminary arrangements about opening his
school, then the two of us started out in quest of a school for
me. He secured the use of a sleek, fast-trotting mule and a
buggy; and we radiated out from Hampton into the surrounding back country. We did not go to the school officials of the
county; we went directly to the patrons. The first two or three
of our excursions were fruitless; the people already had a
teacher or they didn't expect to have school that summer or
some other equally good reason made my services dispensable.
These disappointments did not spoil the fun of the trips. We
were having a good time and many a good laugh. I was
amazed and amused at hearing my friend dilate upon my qualifications as a teacher to the various local Negro school trustees
with whom we conferred. The way in which he impressed
them was wondrous, for his style of diction was elevated and
his tone of voice stentorian even in ordinary conversation, and
in putting forward my claims as a guide and teacher for youth
he surpassed himself. In addition, we generally got a supper of
fried chicken and biscuits. The swift drives back to Hampton
through the mild night, the silences broken only by the steady
tattoo of the mule's hoofs on the hard clay road, produced a
pleasurable sort of hypnosis.

   These disappointments brought back my doubts, but Porter
remained supremely confident. Before the end of a week he
got wind of a locality where they were looking for a teacher.
We hitched up our mule and drove out seven or eight miles to
the place; we were merely in the midst of a group of small and
large cotton farms. It was a locality without a center, without a
store, without even a name. We called on a man who, we had
been informed, was the head of the local board of trustees—a
farmer during the week and an "exhorter" on Sundays. He
summoned several other members of the board, and we talked
over the matter in hand. My advocate was more eloquent and
impressive than ever, and I was engaged as teacher. If my
memory is correct, I was to receive five cents a day for each day
of attendance of each pupil. Out of my wages I was to pay an
assistant, if one should be needed. These may not be the exact

figures, but this was the plan. And it was the plan, at that time, by which all the Negro children in the rural districts of the state of Georgia received their sixty to one hundred and twenty days a year of public school instruction, a plan with but one thing to recommend it—the economic incentive it gave the teacher to get and keep as many pupils as possible in school.

My stopping place was with a woman whose name I cannot recall. She was a dark, wiry woman of, perhaps, thirty-eight, who kept her house clean and cooked fairly well. She had been a widow for some time, but was now again a bride. Her husband was a hulking, dull, hard-working fellow, several years younger than she. A boy, Lem, about fourteen years old was her son by her former husband. With this family of three I made my home. The house was an old, unpainted, wooden structure consisting of two main rooms. The windows were without sash, and were closed by the use of wooden shutters. There was a shed addition on the back, in which there was space for cooking, eating, and washing up. There may also have been another small room under this shed roof. On the front of the house was a short shed-covered porch. The partition dividing the two main rooms was about six feet high. This partition, for the purpose of increasing the scant privacy, and, perhaps, to carry out ideas of decoration, was papered on both sides with sheets taken from illustrated publications. The walls of the rooms were in part covered in the same way. Each of the rooms contained a bed, a rough table, and a shelf or two. In the room that opened to the outside my landlady and her husband slept. At first it was proposed that Lem share the other room with me, and I was put in the awkward position of declining this arrangement with slightly more firmness than politeness. It was not that I objected to Lem personally, but to any further loss of the narrow margin of my privacy. Indeed, I liked Lem very much. He was a slim boy, tall for his age, with a lively, intelligent face. He had an inquiring mind, and I liked the unabashed way in which he would ask for information. I admired the long forelock that he carefully cultivated by wrapping it in twine, and on which he tied a gay ribbon for Sundays and all festive occasions. I enjoyed hearing his slow, musical laughter pitched in the middle tones of the flute. It was pleasant to watch him move; for already he walked with that easy swing from his hips, which is characteristic of Negro men and women. Lem was my daily companion to and fro on the two-mile walk between the house and the school. In fact, he was the most interesting companion I had. In our talks I learned a great deal from him about the country, about the trees and crops and animals and woodcraft in general; and I tried to satisfy his curiosity about books and the outside world.

And Lem liked me. He openly avowed that he had made me his pattern. One day he looked at me with his dancing eyes and his ingratiating smile, and asked,"Professor, that little bresh you use, is that what keeps your teeth so white?" Now, in truth, Lem's teeth were whiter than mine; kept so with a homemade toothbrush consisting of a piece of twig chewed at one end until it became a soft, fibrous miniature mop. But Lem had an inquiring mind; and I explained to him the hygienic and social reasons for the toothbrush. Several days later I surprised him working industriously on his teeth with my "little bresh." I promptly made him a present of it and he was delighted. But, for some days, I couldn't get rid of the question as to how long he had been using it before it became his own. I wonder what became of that boy. He deserved a better opportunity than his locality could ever give him.

Speaking comparatively, I was comfortable. The house was situated back from the road on a rise; there were some fine trees round it, and the yard, front and back, was kept scrupulously clean by daily sweeping. I was gratefully surprised by the fare my landlady set before me; the main course being fried chicken twice a day, for breakfast and supper. However, at the end of two or three weeks it appeared that I had eaten every chewable chicken on the place. At first, this was something of a relief, for I had made the astounding discovery that man cannot live by fried chicken alone. But the table steadily degenerated until my diet was chiefly fat pork and greens and an unpalatable variety of corn bread. For a while I lived almost exclusively on buttermilk, because I could no longer stomach this coarse fare. Then it was that I looked longingly at every chicken I passed, and would have given a week's wages for a beefsteak. I was incommoded mainly by the lack of conveniences for taking a bath, and the lack of a suitable light by which to read or study at night. For my bath, I had to have a washtub brought into my room and filled. There were a couple of lamps in the house but they were used like lanterns—carried wherever they might be needed. In fact, they were hardly more than torches, because neither one of them had more than a fragment of a chimney. So I was obliged to spend my evenings before going to bed talking with Lem and his mother and step-father, and sometimes with their neighbors who came in. I got used to the washtub—it is not difficult for any normal person in normal health to adapt himself to mere inconveniences. As for light: well, I was no worse off than the philosophers and poets of Greece in her age of highest culture. I was actually being forced to gather some valuable information not to be found in books.

School was held in a shanty of a church, a rough, unpainted, board structure that had, probably, been built by the volunteer labor of the farmers round about. It was a rectangular building with sashless windows and without any attempt at architectural effect, except for a small belfry that straddled the roof at the front end, and in which there was no bell. There was, however, one pleasant outside feature; the church stood in the midst of a fine grove. Within, it was as crude as without. A shed at the back formed a niche for the pulpit. In front of the pulpit was a table used principally when collections were taken, for it was the custom—general in Negro churches—to have the members of the congregation march up the aisle and put their offerings on the table. The seats were benches, originally of rough boards, but now worn smooth and shiny by long rubbing. There was no organ or place for a choir. Nor was there a choir; the singing was all congregational. The sole hymn book was used by the preacher, and from it he lined out the hymns two lines at a time, so that they could be carried in mind by the congregation. Listening to this hymn-book singing was not a cheerful experience. The hymns were sung in a long-drawn-out and doleful manner, and with so many turns and quavers that the original melody was hardly recognizable. A prime favorite was Isaac Watt's immortal but lugubrious:

> Hark! From the tomb a doleful sound,
> Mine ears attend the cry—
> Ye living men, come view the ground,
> Where ye must shortly lie.

The congregation was natural, spontaneous, and musical only when they sang spirituals.

The only equipment I had was a table, which I used as a desk. There was not a single desk for a pupil, nor was there a blackboard. Nevertheless, I went at my work with enthusiasm. On the opening day I had two dozen or so pupils, most of them bright and eager to learn, and all of them, I guess, curious about the new teacher. I immediately started grading and classifying them. As soon as I got my school organized, I began canvassing the district for more pupils. They were slow coming in because so many children were still busy "choppin' cotton"; but when the crop was "laid by" they piled in. By the middle of the summer the number was more than doubled, and I had to have an assistant. These half-hundred children, who had so much to do with my education, who taught me so many things, who revealed to me some of my powers and more of my weaknesses; these children who were individuals to me, each one registering himself upon my mind by his appearance, his speech, his abilities, are now only a sort of composite picture in my memory. I try to recall them, and I get only a scene of blurred faces and forms. Only five of them can I separate from this blurred group image: Lem, of course, my prize scholar. The three Laster children; and just why I am able to remember them I cannot tell. They were not particularly bright; perhaps, it was their names. The eldest was a boy, known as "Pig" Laster, the middle was a girl named "Tempe," and the youngest a boy called "Tunk." "Tunk" is more than a memory with me; he remains a personality. I became interested in him the first day of school, when I found out that although it was his third term he had failed to master the alphabet. I wondered how he had managed to perform such a feat and I determined to make him break the series. (I never learned whether I succeeded or not.) I devoted my best per-

sonal effort to "Tunk" throughout the whole term, and I
made the easy discovery that by the time he got slightly familiar with X, Y, Z, he had forgotten all about A, B, C. So it was
not surprising that in his nine months' vacation his mind grew
absolutely blank regarding everything from A to Z. "Tunk"
was not stupid; he had consciously or unconsciously made up
his mind that he wasn't going to study. Neither old-fashioned
nor modern methods made any impression on him. I used to
watch the little rascal, his book held up in front of his face, his
brow wrinkled as though he was grappling with some Einsteinian problem, peeping at intervals around the corner of the
book to see if I was watching. It was very amusing. "Tunk" so
impressed his personality on me that a few years later I did my
best to immortalize him in a poem that bears his unique name.
The other pupil that I remember was a little mulatto girl of
eight or nine whose surpassing beauty made me uneasy about
her lot in the coming years.

I arranged my program so that school opened at eight
o'clock in the morning and closed at three-thirty in the afternoon, with a forty-five-minute recess at eleven, and a fifteen-
minute intermission in the middle of the afternoon. I was
pretty well satisfied with my program and the way in which it
worked. The children were willing and teachable, and I was
proud of the progress they were making. I was also proud of
the order and discipline I had established. "Self-expression"
methods for primary schools had not yet, so far as I knew,
been discovered. Just when I thought everything was going
finely, I received a visit from my local board of trustees. They
filed in quite solemnly a little before the time for dismissal, so
I correctly surmised that they hadn't come to witness an exhibition of what the pupils and the teacher had accomplished.
Indeed, they had come for an opposite reason; they had come
to lodge a complaint against at least one of my ideas about
conducting a school. When the pupils were let out, my board
went into business session, and officially notified me that the
hours per day I was devoting to teaching were too few. They
informed me that all the teachers they had had prior to me had
taught from "sun to sun"—meaning, from the rising thereof
to the going down of the same. Euphemistically they expressed the opinion that since a farmhand had to work twelve

hours a day, there was no sound reason why a schoolteacher should work only six. I listened to them respectfully, but with difficulty because of the temptation to yield to the humor of the situation; the difficulty being greater because of their earnest solemnity. When they had finished, I proceeded to give them all the pedagogical and other kinds of arguments I could muster to convince them that the children would learn more through being kept in school six hours a day than they could through being kept double that time. I pointed to the hard, backless benches and asked if any of them could stand being made to sit on them all day long. They went away acquiescent, but, I fear, unconvinced. This scene remained in my mind and some ten years afterwards I utilized it in a skit. I now ask myself, why? Was it really laughable? It takes little analysis to find that one of the mainsprings of laughter is a situation which has a fundamental element of pathos, often of cruelty, in it.

A few days after the call from my board of trustees I had another visitor. The pupils were out at recess and I was sitting at my table reading a book. The book was a copy of *Don Quijote* in the original. I became conscious that someone was standing in front of me, and looking up I saw a very tall, white man, who I knew at once, did not belong in the locality. He introduced himself as the County Superintendent of Schools. He was making his official visit. I asked him to take my chair. As he sat down he glanced with curiosity at my book; being, perhaps, puzzled by the Spanish spelling, "Quijote." In answer to his question I told him that the book was a copy in Spanish of *Don Quixote*; and I noted the occurrence, in some degree, of the phenomenon to which I have referred in previous pages. I rang the "bell" by striking with one piece of iron on another piece suspended from a wire, and the children came scampering to the door with loud cries and laughter; but they formed their lines in good order and marched in quietly. The Superintendent heard me conduct a class, and asked a few questions, then addressed the scholars, speaking well of their behavior and progress, not omitting to say some complimentary things about their teacher. We had received a clean bill from the County Superintendent.

I enjoyed this rustic life. It was new, in some ways exciting, and I was interested in my school. I was getting a taste of the never-failing satisfaction in telling others important things they do not know. I had carried a baseball to the country and even tried to teach Lem how to pitch curves; but that was labor lost, for the boys thereabouts didn't play baseball. The only standard game they played was marbles. The easy expla- nation was they had no suitable grounds on which to play baseball.

But not many weeks had passed before I realized a great loss, the loss of letters, letters from home, letters from friends, letters from a University girl who had promised to write me, letters with news from the world I had left. To get mail I had to go to Hampton; and the most convenient and dependable way I found of getting there was by walking. I used to set out on Friday afternoons after I had closed school and walk the seven or eight miles to town, keeping up a steady medium gait. Sometimes I would be late in starting, and I would not reach Hampton before nightfall; then, after the lonely dark of the road how welcome a sight were the lights of the town. How good it was to see Porter and have him hand me the small but precious package of mail that had come addressed to me in his care. And the appetizing smell of a specially prepared supper gave a youngster who had just finished trudging miles of dusty roads a full measure of the zest of life.

I always tried to reach Hampton before night, because I knew enough to know that a strange Negro on a backcountry road in Georgia was not entirely secure, not even in daylight. But I was never in any way molested. One day I found myself passing over a section of road that was being repaired in accor- dance with the "road laws" of Georgia; that is, it was being "worked" by the abutting landowners—all white men. The af- ternoon was hot, and I passed along between the two rows of men, holding my umbrella over my head. The men stood stock-still, spades in hand, looking at me as I passed, in an amazement sprung from a sight of the incredible. I suppose that no such thing had ever happened before in the whole his- tory of Henry County. I turned my eyes neither right nor left, but I could feel their gaze, burning me more fiercely than the sun. I had nearly covered the ground before one of the crowd found voice enough to yell, "Hey, Nigger! don't you know better'n to walk over a road whar white men's workin'?—and with a umbrella up?" I kept on walking, with, I confess, a slight acceleration.

There is nothing more effective as a thirst producer than walking over a hot clay road; and several times I had to stop and ask for a drink of water at a white farmhouse. This, too, is an act not without hazard for a strange Negro in the backwoods of Georgia. My requests each time brought the water, and no unpleasant consequences. These people, despite my youth, perhaps on account of my clothes, addressed me as though I were a preacher. The usual greeting was, "Well, Elder, whar you preachin' this Sunday?" The most alarming happenings on these journeys were not caused by men but by dogs. One very dark night when I was passing a place where the house stood far back from the road, I heard two or three dogs rushing down toward me with loud barking and baying—dangerous dogs. I was in terror, and cried out at the top of my voice, "Call your dogs off! Call your dogs off!" A man at the house called to them in a command they obeyed; and he added a sort of apology to me. My friend, William Pickens, who is black and also sometime star student at Yale, laughingly tells that he frequently and involuntarily passes for white. He says that in the deepest South he often finds it is most convenient to transact certain small matters of business with white people over the telephone; and in no instance does he fail to receive a "Yes, sir. Yes, sir." I judge that it was my speech coming out of the darkness that brought me at least the apology.

I always stayed with Porter until Sunday afternoon. The time passed quickly; we had so much to talk about. I would tell him about my school and community, and get his advice on the things that bothered me. We always went to the railroad station on Saturdays to see the four trains come in and go out, two in the morning and two in the afternoon. I never saw anybody that I knew get off, but there was a faint excitement in watching the traffic. At any rate, I got an understanding of why country people love to meet passing trains. Occasionally we would take a Saturday to drive to some other community to attend a picnic or a fish-fry, confident that we should meet some other student-teachers. One Saturday we went to the county seat of an adjoining county. "Big Court" was in session, and court and Saturday combined had brought crowds

of people to town. The main street was lined with hundreds of
horse teams, mule teams, and ox teams packed in as automobiles are now parked on Main Street everywhere. We had an
exciting day. We met some old friends and made some new
ones. H—— and T—— of the old "Big Four" were there;
they were teaching in that county. We found them standing
near the courthouse. I had not seen either of them since they
left the University, so the day wasn't long enough for us to talk
ourselves out. They said that they had no intention of ever returning to Atlanta. In fact, they were going in the fall for their
last year in law at the University of Michigan. Porter was anxious to see the court in action, so he and I joined H—— and
T—— and listened to the trial of a black man charged with
stealing a hog. We did not have to listen very long; the defense
was perfunctory; the prosecutor made no pretense of extending himself in either effort or time; his speech in substance
was, "Gentlemen of the jury, I don't have to tell you this nigger is guilty; you know it as well as I do. All you've got to do is
to bring in a verdict of guilty." The verdict of "guilty" was
promptly brought in. What I was witnessing was not actually
the processes of a court of justice, but a circus, a Roman holiday; and the whites in the courtroom, at least those who had
trekked into town in search of excitement, enjoyed it as such.
They packed the hot, ill-smelling room, watching and laughing at the men, women, and children, too, caught and held
and strangled in the meshes of the law, much in the same spirit
as the Roman crowd howled its enjoyment at the sight of the
victims thrown to the lions.

I do not recall how Porter and I went to this town, but I
clearly remember how we got back. He rode a little horse, and
I drove in a buggy with a fellow named Wilkins. We started
late in the night, but the moon was radiant. As we drove
through the fields of corn and cotton on either side of the road
it seemed to me that I was experiencing something that I had
dreamed or read in a poem or a story. I had never seen cotton
growing until I went to Georgia; and driving through far-
spreading miles of it in full bloom under the moon evoked a
sense of enchantment. Porter was anything but a good horse-
man and he had continual and arduous ups and downs in trying to keep up with our fast-trotting mule. More than once we

had to stop and wait for him. When we were passing where the road ran through a large cornfield Wilkins remarked to me, "Do you know, this mule hasn't had anything to eat since morning." "Well," I asked, "where are you going to get anything for him at this time of night?" He halted the mule, paused for a moment while he looked at me, then stated with an interrogating tone in his voice, "Here's lots of corn handy; I don't see why we shouldn't get some of that." Porter rode up and disapproved very strongly of Wilkin's plan. The latter, however, insisted that he simply could not drive the mule all day, and put him up at night with nothing to eat. Porter would have no part in the business, and rode along. I got out with Wilkins and helped him gather some corn. Breaking off the ears made a startling noise in the stillness of the night. We got what we thought was sufficient and drove on and overtook Porter. I did not become actually frightened about this episode until later, when I learned that for such an act we might have been "justifiably" shot down or sent to the penitentiary for something like life.

About the middle of the summer I changed stopping places. In visiting round among the school patrons and the Negro families of the locality I became acquainted with a man named Woodward. He was a keen, intelligent, enterprising farmer, who had just finished building a new house for himself. The house was weatherboarded and had windowpanes. On the inside it was ceiled and partitioned. I inspected a room that I was told I could have; it contained a comfortable bed, some other necessary furniture, and, above all, a real lamp. There was another inducement to change; Mr. Woodward owned two mules, and he told me that I could use one of them whenever I needed to do so. This, it struck me, would make the trip to Hampton to get my mail and see Porter feasible even in the middle of the week. My new stopping place necessitated a longer walk to school, but this, I felt, was overbalanced by the advantages. Moreover, Mr. Woodward interested me and I liked to talk with him. He was an uneducated man, but one with a good share of native intelligence—a cottonfield philosopher. He frequently delighted me with his original phraseology. I remember asking one morning for his forecast of the weather. He looked up, and pointing to a mass of cirrocumulus clouds, said, "Fessar, see them rain eggs up there; hatch out 'fore noon." And they hatched out. Another day, in commenting to me on a piece of folly committed by one of his neighbors, he said in disgust, "I didn't believe the man knowed so much ignunce." In talking with him I learned that he was an elder brother of Sidney Woodward, the celebrated Boston Negro tenor, and that Sidney had been reared in the locality.

But with the good must be taken what is not so good; and, in my case, that was Mrs. Woodward. She was an unprepossessing woman of Amazonian proportions, addicted on weekdays to a snuff-stick, and on Sundays to cologne, a starched white dress, and vari-colored ribbons; of the latter she wore yards enough to fit out an ordinary Maypole. She was an atrocious cook, and her biscuits were marvels of size and weight. Her love of perfumery extended to her cooking. Once, she asked me if I had any cologne. I informed her that I didn't use it. She wanted it to flavor a cake. Mr. Woodward missed going to church whenever he had or could invent a fair excuse. One Sunday morning, when his wife had arrayed herself in an extra yard or two of ribbon, Mr. Woodward came up with an excuse, and asked me if I would not drive her to the meeting. I suspected that Mrs. Woodward was his real excuse. But I had no way out; I had already announced that I wanted to go and hear the man who was to preach; his fame was great throughout the region; so I responded with as much of a show of gallantry as I could put on, and served as the lady's escort. But my embarrassment rose till it reached the point of pain, and I determined that I should not again let this honor be thrust upon me.

In making the next trip to Hampton I became acquainted with Gypsy. Gypsy was the elder of Mr. Woodward's two mules. She was a venerable animal that, long before I met her, had earned the right to have nothing more to do than rest in green pastures. Her many years had added to her original endowment of mule sense; and mule sense, I think, involves a greater amount of intelligence than the so highly esteemed horse sense. An aristocratic horse, especially when caparisoned, will use up an incalculable amount of energy in merely capering round for show. The average horse, under the lash, will work himself to exhaustion. But no mule can be made, either through cajolery or by lambasting, to lose his dignified and balanced attitude toward life or labor. I at once found out that Gypsy had no intention of overtaxing her waning forces simply because of my impetuous desire to get to Hampton to read some letters or to talk to somebody. In riding this mule to town, the only advantage over going on foot was my safety from dogs. I must have made a comic figure astride this prehistoric-looking beast. Porter, at first sight of me, threw off his air of a Roman senator and gave vent to a burst of laughter that would not have sounded strange coming from the throat of a Mississippi roustabout.

I made one never-to-be-forgotten trip with Gypsy. My school had grown so large that I had to have an assistant. I wrote to the principal of one of the Atlanta public schools, and he sent me down a boy who had just finished the eighth grade. Before my assistant could begin work he had to pass an examination. Why I was not examined I cannot remember; probably, an examination was not required of accredited Atlanta University students. For reasons of appearances, as well as of speed and certainty, I wanted to use the other mule for the trip to the county seat, where the examination was to be held, but Mr. Woodward couldn't spare him; so Gypsy was hitched to the buggy. Outward bound, we had little or no trouble. While waiting for my assistant to pass his test, I talked a bit with the County Superintendent, then walked round for a look at the town. I had not visited the place before, but it was typical, and I saw nothing to excite special attention. Before leaving I bought a fine watermelon. On the way home Gypsy performed very well until we had covered about half the distance; then she stopped. I used all the terms for addressing mules that I had picked up, but Gypsy responded to none of them. I thought the mule might, perhaps, be sick, and I got down and examined her as carefully as I knew how. She didn't look sick; merely meditative. Then I thought she might be hungry; and I took the watermelon and burst it on the ground before her. She ate it with relish, but still didn't move. I then tried to coax her along by pulling on the bridle. When I did this she began to back; and the harder I pulled, the more she backed. This convinced me that, at least, the animal was not incapable of motion; so I got up in the buggy again and employed all known devices for urging a mule forward, including the application of a hickory, but to no effect. I rested a while then tried pulling on the bridle again, and Gypsy started backing again. We should have been home in time for supper; and it was now nearing midnight. I sat dejected on the side of the road.

I worked this incident into a short story, the ending to the story being that I was seized with the idea of hitching the mule in upside down or wrongside out or stern end fore; that I then got back into the buggy and pulled on the bridle while the mule backed all the way home. Now, the reader may accept or reject that sequel, as he chooses. Recalling all I went through with that mule, it makes very little difference.

In all of my experience there has been no period so brief that has meant so much in my education for life as the three months I spent in the backwoods of Georgia. I was thrown for the first time on my own resources and abilities. I had my first lesson in dealing with men and conditions in the outside world. I underwent my first tryout with social forces. Certainly, the field was limited, the men and conditions simple, and the results not particularly vital; nevertheless, taken together they constituted the complex world in microcosm. It was this period that marked the beginning of my psychological change from boyhood to manhood. It was this period which marked also the beginning of my knowledge of my own people as a "race." That statement may not be entirely clear; I mean: I had in the main known my own people as individuals or as groups; and now I began to perceive them clearly as a classified division, a defined section of American society. I had learned something about the Negro as a problem, but now I was where I could touch the crude bulk of the problem itself with my own hands, where the relations between Black and White in the gross were pressed upon me. Here there were no gradations, no nuances, no tentative approaches; what Black and White meant stood out starkly.

As I worked with my children in school and met with their parents in the homes, on the farms, and in church, I found myself studying them all with a sympathetic objectivity, as though they were something apart; but in an instant's reflection I could realize that they were me, and I was they; that a force stronger than blood made us one. In this study it was impossible to eliminate the element of hopelessness. I lived in this community three months without ever being on speaking terms with a single white person in it, yet knowing each one fairly well, knowing fairly well his family history, his habits, his reputation, his worth; and not being able among them all to find one, however ignorant or depraved, who was not superior to any and every Negro—superior in the eyes of the law, in opportunities, and in all the awards that the public decencies may assure to the individual. But the "race problem" is paradoxical; and, with all my inexperience, I could not fail to see that this superior status was not always real, but often imaginary and artificial, bolstered up by bigotry and buttressed by the forces of injustice. Nor could I fail to see that what is imaginary, artificial, and false cannot eternally withstand actuality and truth.

But had I been totally blind to any crack or weak spot in the thick wall standing on the line of race and color, I should not have come through this phase of my education a victim of utter hopelessness; intellectual curiosity would have saved me. I was anxious to learn to know the masses of my people, to know what they thought, what they felt, and the things of which they dreamed; and in trying to find out, I laid the first stones in the foundation of faith in them on which I have stood ever since. I gained a realization of their best qualities that has made any temptation for me to stand on a little, individual peak of snobbish pride seem absurd. I saw them hedged for centuries by prejudice, intolerance, and brutality; hobbled by their own ignorance, poverty, and helplessness; yet, notwithstanding, still brave and unvanquished. I discerned that the forces behind the slow but persistent movement forward of the race lie, ultimately, in them; that when the vanguard of that movement must fall back, it must fall back on them. The situation in which they were might have seemed hopeless, but they themselves were not without hope. The patent proof of this was their ability to sing and to laugh. I know something about the philosophy of song; I wish I knew as much about the philosophy of laughter. Their deep, genuine laughter often puzzled and irritated me. Why *did* they laugh so? How *could* they laugh so? Was this rolling, pealing laughter merely echoes from a mental vacuity or did it spring from an innate power to rise above the ironies of life? Or were they, in the language of a line from one of the blues, "Laughing to keep from crying"? Were they laughing because they were only thoughtless? Were they laughing at themselves? Were they laughing at the white man? I found no complete answer to these questions. Probably, some of all the elements suggested entered in. But I did discover that a part of this laughter, when among themselves, was laughter at the white man. It seems to me that for the grim white man in the backwoods of the South this deep laughter of the Negro should be the most ominous sound that reaches his ears.

We of the vanguard often look with despair at these very characteristics of the masses. We feel that these easy-going traits constitute our chief racial weaknesses and the chief hindrance to faster progress. This impatience on our part is understandable, but I believe it involves an underestimation. It takes no account of the technique for survival that the masses have evolved through the experience of generations. It does not give them credit for the fact that in their ignorance and defenselessness, with the weight of outnumbering millions on their shoulders, they persisted, they straightened up their bent backs by degrees, and from the travail of their agony buried in laughter brought us forth as tokens of their potentialities. They used the methods available; and those methods were not always aimlessness and dumb servility. For one thing, they learned the white man with whom they had to deal. They learned him through and through; and without ever completely revealing themselves. Their knowledge of that white man's weaknesses as well as his strength came to be almost intuitive. And when they felt it futile to depend upon their own strength, they took advantage of his weaknesses—the blind side of arrogance and the gullibility that always goes with overbearing pride. It is possible that these masses might have done much better—I am not unmindful of their numerous shortcomings—yet, it is certain that they might have done much worse.

The most vital factor in the future of a race is the power to survive; and the masses have an instinctive knowledge of their possession of that power. Firm confidence is theirs through having survived every degree of hardship and oppression to which any race may be subjected. I saw strong men, capable of sustained labor, hour for hour, day for day, year for year, alongside the men of any race. I saw handsome, deep-bosomed, fertile women. Here, without question, was the basic material for race building. I use the word "handsome" without reservations. To Negroes themselves, before whom "white" ideals have so long been held up, the recognition of the beauty of Negro women is often a remote idea. Being shut up in the backwoods of Georgia forced a comparison upon me, and a realization that there, at least, the Negro woman, with her rich coloring, her gayety, her laughter and song, her alluring, undulating movements—a heritage from the African jungle—was a more beautiful creature than her sallow, songless, lipless, hipless, tired-looking, tired-moving white sister.

I was graduated in 1894. The Atlanta University commencement program indicated no distinctions, but it was unwritten opinion that the first and last places on the program were the honor points; I was given last place. On this occasion I made the attempt to break through the narrow and narrowing limitations of "race," if only for the hour. I went as far beyond the boundaries as I could go, farther, certainly, than my capabilities warranted me in going, and made the subject of my oration, "The Destiny of the Human Race." At graduation I had two choices before me: through President Bumstead I had a chance for a scholarship in medicine at Harvard; in Jacksonville Mr. Artrell was retiring, and I had a call to take charge of Stanton School. I was weary of going to school; I wanted to get out and do something. I became principal of Stanton.

I frequently live again my days at Atlanta; and, now, the hardships that once appeared so huge have, naturally, dwindled to infinitesimal proportions. Indeed, I have to brush away a glamorous haze, in order to see things as they appeared to me then. Grown older, I occasionally meditate upon the kind of education Atlanta University gave me. The conception of education then held there and at other Negro colleges belonged to an age that, probably, is passing never to return. The central idea embraced a term that is now almost a butt for laughter—"service." We were never allowed to entertain any thought of being educated as "go-getters." Most of us knew

that we were being educated for life work as underpaid teachers. The ideal constantly held up to us was of education as a
means of living, not of making a living. It was impressed upon
us that taking a classical course would have an effect of making
us better and nobler, and of higher value to those we should
have to serve. An odd, old-fashioned, naïve conception?
Rather.

PART TWO

XII

THE time of the psychological passing over from boyhood to manhood is a movable feast. The legal date fixed on the twenty-first birthday has little or no connection with it. There are men in their teens, and there are boys in their forties. This passing over is really not across a line, but across a zone. There are some who are driven across early in life by the steady pressure of responsibility. A few, projected by some sudden stroke of fate, take the zone in a single leap. But most of us wander across somewhat as the Israelites wandered across the Arabian Desert; and a good many of us grow old without ever getting completely over.

This train of thought ran through my mind as I sat in front of the Stanton teachers, whom I had called together a day or two before the opening of school. I looked at them—some had been teachers when I was a pupil at Stanton, among these, my sister—and they looked at me. I talked to them a while; then we discussed school matters. But what I wanted most to know was their unexpressed thoughts about me; doubtless, they had a corresponding curiosity. I found myself talking almost mechanically about things not at the center of my thoughts. I am three months past any twenty-third birthday. . . . I have in my hands the administration of a public school with a thousand pupils and twenty-five teachers. . . . This is not a job for a boy; it's a man's job. . . . Can I actually do it? . . . Of course, I can; it's essentially the same job as my school in the backwoods of Georgia. . . . Yes, it's that, but it's more. It is so much more complex that it is practically a different job. Here, first of all, are twenty-five assistants, whose respect for my ability I've got to get. Some of these assistants will have to be convinced. They would laugh if I failed. . . . My position is an important one. Relatively, it is far more important than the principalship of the white grammar school. Its disproportionate importance makes me a mark. I shall be scrutinized. I shall meet with envy and antagonism on the outside; and, perhaps, with disloyalty on the inside. . . . What sort of a start am I making? . . . The first impression these teachers get of me will be far-reaching; of what sort is it?— Through all these thoughts run alternating currents of confidence and doubt.

I had an academic education, but had had no special training as a teacher. But I had already discovered for myself that three-fourths of the art of teaching consists in the ability to rouse the pupil's interest—at least, his curiosity—in the thing he is to learn; and that that ability is not imparted by a course in pedagogy. My work at Stanton, however, was not that of teaching, but of organization and administration; in fact, it was the business of conducting a large institution. Here was something concerning which I knew nothing; but it was on the technical side and could easily be learned; in the main it entailed a knowledge of methods of systematization; and I determined to learn as much about it as I could and as quickly as possible.

It seemed that the first practical step for me to take would be to see how they did things at the white central grammar school and make a comparison with the way we did things at Stanton. I talked with Mr. Glenn, the superintendent of schools, and my plan seemed to strike him favorably. He said to me, "You know McBeath; go up and see him, and tell him what you want." Mr. McBeath was the principal of the white school. I had met him a number of times in the superintendent's office, and we were on rather friendly terms. Early one morning I presented myself at his office in the Jacksonville Grammar School, and at once gave him the reason for my visit. He was pleased, perhaps flattered. He answered my questions and offered me information on methods of administration he had found to be effective. I thanked him; but there was one other thing I wanted to accomplish on my visit; I wanted to make a direct comparison between the classroom work of the teachers in his school and those in mine. I expressed my desire to go into the classes. He took me to the primary department and introduced me to one of the teachers. He saw that I had a chair, then left me, saying that I was free to visit any of the classes. I spent the entire forenoon going from class to class observing and making mental notes. As I entered each room I introduced myself to the teacher as the principal of Stanton School; at the same time stating that Mr. McBeath had extended me the privilege of visiting the classrooms. My self-introductions were met with varying degrees of graciousness, politeness, embarrassment, and stiffness. Most of the pupils exhibited undisguised curiosity. I went away feeling that I had gained a good deal.

Several days later I was astounded to learn that my visit to the white grammar school had raised a hullabaloo. It appeared that a number of parents, hearing of it through teachers and pupils, were outraged and alarmed over my unprecedented behavior. The affair was fomented to such an extent that the board of education felt it necessary to hold a meeting to inquire into the matter and fix the responsibility for my action. This explosion from what I had thought of as merely a natural and reasonable act was not only an overwhelming surprise to me, it was a manifestation of the limits of utter asininity to which race prejudice can go. This manifestation was so clear that, in talking the matter over with members of the board, I could not but feel the superiority of my position. I knew the majority of the men on the board quite well; they were men of intelligence; and I wanted to feel for their sakes that they were ashamed of the silly exhibition they had been called to take part in. Mr. Glenn stood his ground; so did Mr. McBeath, and the affair blew over. The incident was the beginning of a close acquaintance between Mr. McBeath and me.

I did not have to teach at Stanton, but I liked to go into a teacher's room and take her class for a while. I particularly liked to take a class in arithmetic. After I left Stanton I spent six years studying branches of higher mathematics. When I returned as principal, I found that I did not know arithmetic; so I started in to remedy that defect in my educational foundation. It was pleasant work; arithmetic is not only an interesting study, it is also a most fascinating pastime. With excusable vanity, I sometimes amazed a class by performing an arithmetical stunt for them. I mastered a formula for extracting the cube root of numbers at sight. I would set the pupils to work cubing numbers, and calling off the cube—which often ran up into the hundreds of thousands—to me while I stood at the blackboard and wrote it down; then, without pausing, I would write down the cube root. This stunt never failed to rouse the interest of a class in arithmetic. It had some analogy to the inspiring of faith by the working of a miracle. I tried to discover and prove the principles that underlay the "rules of arithmetic." I saw that the "rules of arithmetic" were accepted as axiomatic and so used. For example, the rule for the division of fractions used to read: Invert the terms of the divisor, and proceed as in multiplication. I found no pupils and few teachers who understood and could explain the reason for this process. Getting at simpler and more understandable methods of solution became an absorbing game. I made frequent use of a very simple problem to illustrate the rational method of reduction to unity. The problem was: One pumping engine can fill a boiler in a minute; another can fill it in a half-minute; how long will it take both of them pumping together to fill it? I have seen pupils and teacher stumped by this problem. I have seen college graduates resort to algebra to solve it. The direct solution, of course, is: The two engines can fill the boiler *three* times in *one* minute; therefore they can fill it once in one-third of a minute, or twenty seconds.

I was astonished and amused to find myself using mannerisms when I taught a class. I found myself walking up an down, gesticulating with a ruler, and occasionally giving myself a resounding thwack on the skull with it. These were the mannerisms of Mr. Francis. At recess I walked round the grounds on the boys' side; I tried to avoid giving the impression that I was watching and seeing things; I carried a slender rattan cane, which I sometimes used to flick the legs of unruly boys; I couldn't resist a chuckle over the boyhood memories of "Old J.C." that came back to me; I discovered with a very pleasurable satisfaction that the boys spoke of me as "Old Man Johnson"; I observed that play was not so rough as it was in my boyhood at Stanton; shinny had been abandoned, baseball was the predominant game; I enjoyed giving the boys pointers on play and explanations on the workings of "inside baseball."

The matter of patrol, rattan cane, and all that sounds rather old-fashioned. The question at the bottom of the matter caused me much anxiety at the time. The attitude of the teacher toward his pupils and the response to it that he draws from them constitute a delicate problem. Shall he act the

tyrant, and be feared as one? Or shall he be just one of the
fellows, and loved as one? It seemed to me that efforts from
either end of the scale would be about equally inefficient, so
far as the business of teaching was concerned; that no fixed
policy could be laid down; that it was a matter of adjustment
to varying conditions. I am glad that my principalship of Stanton was in a period before the time when a director of play—
or whatever is the exact title for the new profession—might
have been annexed to my teaching force. That sounds more
than old-fashioned, I know. It sounds archaic. We speak of carrying coals to Newcastle; the language is not capable of a
metaphor to convey the idea of superfluity in an adult teaching
children how to play. I know that large groups of children at
play require oversight, especially is this true in the case of boys,
in order that the smaller and weaker may not be molested or
imposed upon by the bigger and stronger fellows, and that the
spirit of rowdyism likely to crop out in any crowd of healthy
boys be held in check. Aside from that, they ought to be let
alone. When children play to themselves they are natural,
naïve, and spontaneous. Furthermore, they are inventive,
imaginative, ingenious, and resourceful; capable not only of
devising games but the things needed for playing them. One
of the greatest delights an adult can experience is to obliterate
himself and watch them. It is an experience through which he
may, perhaps, recapture some of the joy of being a happy child.
But as soon as an adult pokes his nose into the business, children become unnatural, self-conscious, imitative, embarrassed,
insincere, even priggish. Against this breaking into and spoiling the Child's World I should be willing to see a law passed.

At the close of my first year, twenty-six were ready to be
graduated from the eighth grade. This was all the education
the city of Jacksonville gave me, and it was all it was giving
them. I had been thinking about them for some time. . . .
They are entitled to as much as others. . . . Why shouldn't
they get it? . . . But how? . . . Well, that sounds like a feasible
plan. . . . Can I carry it through? . . . I think I can. . . . I'll
try it. . . . I'll do it. I did do it; I made Stanton a high school.

In these latter years, since I have witnessed and participated
in so many hard fights by Negroes, through petitions, legal
proceedings, and by political action, to secure high schools, I

look back with almost unbelief at the simplicity, the assurance
and ease with which I accomplished what I set out to do.
Scarcely did the school board, to say nothing of the white people in general of Jacksonville, know it was being done. This is
all there was to the plan in its beginning: I first got the members of the class interested in the project; then I persuaded
their parents to let them come back the following year. I laid
out a course for them that was practically the Junior Prep
course at Atlanta University. I myself taught the class. The next
year I followed the same procedure; told the superintendent
what I had done, and asked for an assistant. I discontinued the
use of the general assembly room for devotions and converted
it, by using curtains for partitions, into extra classrooms. The
next year I obtained another assistant. I introduced Spanish as
the modern language in the course, and taught it myself. That,
in short, is the plan by which Stanton Grade School was developed into Stanton High School. Of course, the plan could not
have succeeded if the superintendent had not supported me
after that first year, and if the board of education had not
accepted a *fait accompli*.

Seven years had wrought changes. I noted that Jacksonville
was for me, in many ways, a different place. There were
changes in the life at home—Rosamond was away; Ricardo
was away; my mother was permanently lame; my grandmother
was fast aging, and her terrific energies slowing down; and my
father, for the first time, struck me as an elderly man. A house
that had been lively, gay, and, because of the activities of three
growing boys, sometimes noisy, had become quiet and subdued. So my father and I were thrown together a good deal,
and in a new relationship: not only as father and son, but as
two men. It was at this point that I began to distinguish between my love for him as a good father and my admiration for
him as a good man. I gauged the respect he had won from the
community through the simple virtues of industry and integrity. I saw the evidences of it wherever I went with him.
And I saw the regard in which he was held for the work to
which he had given himself. He was the pastor of a very small
church made up of very poor people. He showed no ambition
to have charge of larger and richer congregation. He said to

me a number of times, "I am not a preacher by trade." By
which he meant that he was not influenced by the emoluments
of the office. His spirit of self-sacrifice might be somewhat
minimized by the fact that he had acquired a competence, but
not wholly discounted. In addition to the work in his little
church, he did a sort of general missionary work. He was the
only colored minister—I do not know if there was any white
one—who was willing or not afraid to go and pray for a dying
woman in the quarter for prostitutes in Jacksonville. The
women of the quarter called him "Father Johnson" and they
knew whenever they sent for him in such cases that he would
come. He was very simple and unostentatious in all this. He
did not even affect a noticeable clerical appearance. Indeed, he
was at that time one of the only two preachers I knew who did
not seem to believe that a long-tailed black coat was one of the
evidences of Christianity; Joseph Twitchell of Hartford was
the other. This adaptation by my father of Christianity to life in
good measure made a deeper impression on me than all the
formal religious training I had been given.

My mother, on account of her lameness, had stopped teaching, but she was still the choir leader of her church. She asked
me to join the choir, and I did. My voice had developed into a
fairly good baritone, and I enjoyed the singing. My mother
frequently assigned me a solo part in an anthem. My choir duties took me to church mornings and evenings each Sunday, so
I was a regular attendant. An effort was made to have me take
the superintendency of the Sunday school; but this, in spite of
the pleas of my grandmother and my mother, I absolutely refused to do.

My mother talked to me a good deal about a matter she had
mentioned in letters written to me while I was still at the University, but concerning which she could not be as free in writing as in talking. It was much in her mind; one of her best
friends, Alonzo Jones, was involved. He was one of a number
of colored men who, because of the steady change from the
old and rather favorable attitude towards Negroes in Jacksonville, resolved to prepare to meet the worst. They ordered a
rifle and a quantity of ammunition for each man in the group.
Alonzo Jones made the great error of having the whole shipment consigned to him. This action was indicative of the man.

He was impulsive and incautious. It is probable that some of
the men were timid, and he rashly assumed the entire responsibility. But he had real courage, and would never humbly or
quietly tolerate any infringement upon what he believed to be
his rights. At this time he was a man of about fifty, stoutish,
very dark, and rather morose in disposition His father had
been a bricklayer and a successful man, who had bought several pieces of property on a street that became one of the principal thoroughfares of the city. The son followed the father's
trade and worked industriously to improve the property that
had been left to him. When the incidents I am relating took
place he was worth, perhaps, fifty or sixty thousand dollars.
Events followed fast after the arrival of the rifles. A Negro
walking along the street eating a banana throws the peel on
the sidewalk. A white policeman orders him to pick it up. He
refuses. The policeman draws his club, and a struggle ensues.
The Negro is down and is being severely clubbed by the policeman. He somehow gets hold of the policeman's pistol and
shoots him through the heart. The Negro is rushed to the
Duval County jail. Excitement runs high and increases hourly.
"Crackers" from the surrounding country pour into town.
Lynching is in the air. The county jail is bounded on three
sides by the houses of Negroes, and several hundred colored
men with rifles, shotguns, and revolvers man the windows and
roofs of these houses. Women supply them with food and hot
coffee. Some of the more daring of the women parade cans of
kerosene, vowing that if the prisoner is lynched, they will lay
the town in ashes. Two or three local companies of militia are
called out and thrown round the jail. They make no attempt to
dislodge or disperse the armed Negroes on guard. Some of the
Negro leaders confer with the militia officers and declare that,
together with the troops or without them, they will defend the
prisoner against any mob. The prisoner is not lynched.

My mother is stopping at a boarding house at Pablo Beach.
Alonzo Jones has run down for a few days. The boarders are all
friends and acquaintances. In the night the sheriff and his
deputies come and demand entrance in the name of the law.
They arrest Alonzo Jones, charging him with conspiracy to in-
cite a riot. They take him away handcuffed, amidst the tears
and cries of the women, who believe he is being dragged to his

death. The whole affair, especially the arrest in the middle of the night, makes an impression of terror on my mother's mind that she cannot rid herself of. I am deeply moved by her recital of these happenings, and I feel an exultant pride in the men who manned the windows and housetops to safeguard the prisoner, and in the women who brought them food and coffee.

Alonzo Jones was not the only one involved; several others, all prominent Negroes, were arrested. But the chief onus was fixed on him because of the record in the office of the express company which proved it was to him that a large number of rifles had been consigned and delivered. Two or three influential white men used their good offices in behalf of the Negro leaders charged with conspiracy. Mr. Jones was released under heavy bond; another, Dan Tresvan, chef in one of the hotels, was paroled for a number of months as cook for a young millionaire; D——'s father and several others were saved from imprisonment. The affair blew over. The whites recovered from the jolt they had received, tranquilized, no doubt, by the feeling that the spirited figures among the blacks had been taught an unforgettable lesson. Alonzo Jones was financially ruined. He heeded what was probably the best advice, and jumped his bail. He went to Port Chester, New York, to live and work at his trade. His wife remained in Jacksonville to look after the property, but all of this was eventually swallowed up by the bond. He died in Port Chester, a broken man.

There were changes outside of home. D—— was away— working in a cigar factory in Tampa. Some of the boys and girls I had known best were scattered. Heart's Desire, even if she had not forgotten me, had married and gone to live in another town. More marked was the change in social life. During my boyhood the social affairs among colored people in Jacksonville were for the most part public or semi-public. There were church festivals and bazaars; there were picnics and excursions, up the river to Green Cove Springs or down to the sea at Pablo Beach; there were concerts and entertainments in National Hall, Jones' Hall, Redwood, and other halls. At secular affairs there was a band for dancers, but dancing was strictly under the ban for people who belonged to the church. Now, I found that there was a social life which had a degree of exclusiveness. There were many more homes that were comfortable and commodious; and entertainment among those who went in for society had become largely a private matter. The women who were leaders in affairs social were sharply divided into two groups: a Chautauqua group that took up culture and serious thinking, and gave mild entertainments; and a group which put more stress on the mere frivolities, gave whist parties and house dances, and served a punch of more than one-half of one per cent strength. Certainly, in my boyhood the well-to-do colored people gave entertainments of one sort or another in their homes, to which they invited those with whom they associated, but I don't think there was such a thing as "society." "Society" was one of the new things I found. I also found that the men had gone in for it. There had been organized a social club called *The Oceolas*, which gave two or three dances each winter. I was, quite naturally, invited to join this club, and I did join; thereby unwittingly starting some trouble for myself.

This social life was, in its proportionate degree, a replica of all the pettinesses of "society" in general. There were present the same snobbishness, the same envies and jealousies, the same strivings and heartburns, the same expenditure of time and energy upon futilities. And, as in "society" in general, it was the women who were the chief sticklers and arbiters; among the men there was a certain democracy. In the Oceola Club a man's occupation had little or nothing to do with his eligibility. Among the members were lawyers, doctors, teachers, bricklayers, carpenters, barbers, waiters, Pullman porters. This democracy, however, was not exactly laxness; I knew of one or two cases in which, for one reason or another, the possession of money failed to force entrance. On one point, this black "society" was precisely like Southern white "society"—anyone belonging to an "old family," regardless of his pecuniary condition or, in fact, his reputation, was eligible. Knowledge of this fact would have struck Southern white people as funny, probably, without their being able to tell just why. In Charleston, South Carolina, colored "society" was quite old, having its beginnings among the free Negroes of that city before the Civil War. And a member of the Charleston set was as proud of his social standing as any member of the *St. Cecilia*.

There were then similar social groupings in all the Southern cities, in fact, in all the cities of the country where there was a considerable Negro population; and there was an interchange of privileges like those accorded to a member of an order in good standing in going from one lodge to another. At the present time, just as with white people, this punctilious phase of "society" is fast becoming obsolete among Negroes in the larger cities.

One of the first things I did with the money I was earning as a teacher was to gratify a wish that had long been denied fulfillment. When I was a small boy I longed for two playthings, above all others: a real snare drum—not of the toy kind, but of the kind used in bands—and a velocipede. But, although around Christmas time, for a number of years, I used to lie stretched out in front of the hearth and write dozens of cajoling letters to Santa Claus, I never got either of the gifts. Once, the drum seemed to be within my grasp. Some white young men had organized a brass band, and my father had in some way stood good for the purchase of the instruments. The band failed and the instruments reverted to him. I pleaded with my father to give me the drum, but in vain. The whole outfit was displayed in the window of Campbell's music store and sold piecemeal to members of the various Negro bands. The velocipede I did not get, perhaps, because there was no place within a half mile of our house where it could be ridden. On one of my childhood journeys to the St. James Hotel I saw a boy riding a bicycle, one of the old-fashioned, high-wheeled affairs, round and round in the bandstand that stood in the center of St. James Park. I watched him as long as I could, entranced. The rider was Ralph D. Paine, whose father was then pastor of the white Methodist church that stood on the side of the park opposite the hotel. My wish was then transferred from a velocipede to a bicycle. The time had now come when I could gratify that wish. I bought a second-hand machine of the old safety type, a Victor that weighed sixty or seventy pounds, and was almost as difficult to mount as the old high-wheeled variety. Shortly afterwards, I discarded the Victor and bought a low, light model, quite like the machines used today. It was a good investment; it afforded me exercise, fresh air, and a lot of enjoyment. I rode to and from school. On many nights a crowd of bicycle owners would meet and we would ride the ten miles of shell road that ran out from Main Street and circled back along the river into the city. Also, I got lots of fun out of the then current gallantry of teaching the art of riding to young ladies, many of whom, at the first wobbling of the machine, would with nice little screams turn loose the handlebar and throw both arms around your neck.

I bought my bicycle from a man named Gilbert; and I stopped in at his shop whenever I needed repairs. He was a pleasant sort of man, and we grew rather friendly, so friendly that I formed the habit of stopping in occasionally when I didn't need repairs, merely for a chat. In those days the bicycle shop rivaled the barber shop as a place for the exchange of masculine talk and gossip. I used to talk freely about race and racial injustices with white men in town that I knew; perhaps more freely than cautious judgment would have warranted. I got away with it, probably, because most of the men I talked with knew my father well, and had known me since my boyhood. Once, however, I did get a mild warning. One afternoon I stopped in at Gilbert's and found a half-dozen or so white men gathered there, none of whom I knew particularly well. I joined in the talk, which, through me, I suppose, finally shifted to the race question. I was expressing some of my opinions when I was interrupted by a nondescript fellow, who remarked with a superb sneer, "What wouldn't you give to be a white man?" The remark hit me between the eyes. The sheer insolence of it rocked me. The crowd tittered. The hot retort surged up for utterance. With great effort I collected and held myself and replied in as measured and level a tone as I could command, "Let me see. I don't know just how much I would give. I'd have to think it over. But, at any rate, I am sure that I wouldn't give anything to be the kind of white man you are. No, I am sure I wouldn't; I'd lose too much by the change." He went livid, then purple. The titter died. For an instant it looked as though a physical clash would break from the dark cloud of silence. But the young fellow himself seemed to realize that to beat me up would not improve his position in the eyes of the witnesses to the incident. He was spiritually licked. I rode away satisfied. I, at least, felt free from that regret which comes from thinking later of something that might have been said. Yet, I was disturbed; and I thought: I must go over this question frankly with myself; I must go down to its roots; drag it up out of my subconsciousness, if possible, and give myself the absolutely true answer. I made a sincere effort to do this. I watched myself closely and tried to analyze motives, words, actions, and reactions. The conviction I always arrived at was that the answer I gave the young man in the bicycle shop was the true one; and true not only so far as it went, but farther.

That same remark, implied if not expressed, has many times since been thrown at me. I judge that every intelligent Negro in the United States has met it in one form or another. And it is most likely that all of us have at some time toyed with the Arabian Nights–like thought of the magical change of race. As for myself, I find that I do not wish to be anyone but myself. To conceive of myself as someone else is impossible, and the effort is repugnant. If the jinnee should suddenly appear before me and, by way of introduction, say, "Name the amount of wealth you would like to have, and it shall be given you," I, gauging my personal needs and a sum sufficient to enable me to do freely the things I like to do, should reply, "Give me three hundred thousand dollars in (if such there still be) sound securities." If I thought of the sum in terms of some other things I might do with money, I should test the limits of the jinnee's generosity and power. If he should say, "Name some boon you desire, and it shall be granted," I think I should reply, "Grant me equal opportunity with other men, and the assurance of corresponding rewards for my efforts and what I may accomplish." If, coming to the principal matter, he should say, "Name any person into whom you would like to be changed, and it shall be done," I should be absolutely at a loss. If, continuing, he should say, "Name any race of which you would like to be made a member, and it shall be done," I should likewise be at a loss. If the jinnee should say, "I have come to carry out an inexorable command to change you into a member of another race; make your choice!" I should answer, probably, "Make me a Jew."

Among my youthful ambitions, teaching had never had a place. Not until I was about to finish at Atlanta University had I given it any thought as a vocation. But I liked the work, and

I was intensely interested in my plan to develop Stanton into a high school. Toward the end of my first year of principalship, however, my thoughts began to rotate around one of my early ambitions; I thought again about publishing and editing a newspaper. I finally decided to undertake it. I took the few hundred dollars I had saved from my salary, borrowed from my father more than I had saved, and formed a partnership with a young man named M. J. Christopher. We planned to publish an afternoon paper to be called *The Daily American*, believing—and, so far as I can learn, we were right—that it would be the first Negro daily ever published. I was to be the editor and he the business manager; I estimated that my duties on the paper would not interfere with my school work. Two of my former classmates at Atlanta, George A. Towns and N. W. Collier, also put some money into the enterprise. We bought on time a flat-bed cylinder press that was run by a gas engine, and the necessary composing room equipment. We arranged with a concern in Atlanta to furnish us an electrotyped dispatch service. When *The Daily American* appeared, it met with the enthusiastic acclaim of the colored people.

Immediately after the closing of this first school year I went to Tampa to attend the annual meeting of the state association of colored teachers. There I saw D—— again. He was working in a cigar factory and was in a discouraged state of mind. Much had happened in his venturesome life since I had last seen him, several years before, sitting in front of a barrel stripping tobacco in his father's little factory. Between two and three thousand dollars had been realized from the sale of a piece of property that had been left to him by his mother. He had had a stiff row with his father over this money, but, by legal action, had got possession of the cash. For this, it seems, his father never forgave him. With the money in his possession he immediately left Jacksonville. This time, as Ricardo had done, he followed Rosamond's trail and went to Boston. He went with some undefined plans of continuing his education, and studying law at Harvard. Before getting down to work, he yielded to an impulse to take a little fling at life. He procured an expensive wardrobe—clothes by a fashionable tailor and haberdashery and shoes by custom makers. He ate only in the smartest places, and never took a street car if a cab was obtainable. He moved in the quiet exclusive social set of Negro Boston, doubtlessly dazing those staid, more or less dark New Englanders with his opulent display. In Negro sporting circles he was an even greater favorite, a "Little Napoleon."

Before he got round to his plans, the money was gone. His jewelry and the best of his clothes found their way to the pawnshop. He steadily settled to that low level which we politely call reduced circumstances. Finally, eating regularly became a problem involving the unknown. He then made his way back to Jacksonville, and from there to Tampa.

These experiences of D——, which I have condensed into three hundred words, filled the major part of his talk with me during the six days I was in Tampa. I sat late into the night listening to his adventures. He related incident after incident in his racy, half-cynical manner, giving a punch to the whole recital by his not meager command of profanity. He caused me to laugh heartily over some of his most dire situations. I knew that he had acted recklessly, but I admired, perhaps envied, the way in which he could challenge life. I asked him if he would come to Jacksonville and take a place on *The Daily American*. He was happy to do it. When we left Tampa it was together; and he started work as a reporter at fifteen dollars a week.

The meeting of the teachers' association was not an exceptionally brilliant affair. The majority of the papers were dull or immature. The discussions that followed were often more interesting and enlightening than the papers; occasionally they were exciting. The social features were more satisfying, and, perhaps, more important than the intellectual features. It was a great pleasure to meet and know teachers from all parts of the state; and, at any rate, I gained more valuable information about the work of educating Negro youth in Florida from conversations with individuals and groups than I did from the laboriously written papers. The large number of visitors added to the social success of the gathering. Of one of these visitors I carried away a haunting recollection. I remembered her only because of her extraordinary beauty; in fact, I spoke scarcely a score of words to her, but I could hardly take away my eyes from her face. The color of her face was that delicate brown, light enough to glow rosily, which is so commonly found among women of mixed black and white blood. But under her raven hair, parted simply in the middle, her low, lovely brow took on the tint of mellow ivory. The curve of her cheek and the line of her throat were faultless. The nose was slightly fleshy, but perfectly molded. Her eyes, dark, liquid, and deeply shaded, produced in me a sensation akin to the fascinating dread of looking into unknown depths. Her red, ripe, sensuous mouth was in disquieting contrast to the Madonna-like upper portion of the face and head. That provocative mouth, with its vivid splash of color, its hint of wantonness, quickened the whole countenance out of the cold placidity of saintly beauty. What a face, I kept thinking, for a painter!

The initial success of *The Daily American* astonished its founders. Subscriptions poured in. There were, perhaps because of curiosity to know what was going on among Negroes, quite a number of white subscribers. Congratulatory letters were written by patrons and encomiastic sermons delivered by preachers. Applications from persons wishing to be agents came in from many towns in Florida and south Georgia. The plant and offices became a Mecca for visitors. I was elated. I felt that the undertaking transcended any personal ambition; that an instrument had been created that would be a strong weapon in the Negro's defense against racial inequalities and injustices; that the colored people of the community had come into possession of an adequate medium through which they could express themselves, of a voice by which they could make themselves heard across the race boundaries.

I was over-sanguine. We kept the paper going for eight months, then were forced to suspend. As I watched the press turn for the last time I was a sadly discouraged young man. It was my first disappointment at the failure of the masses to respond to what I myself felt to be an important effort towards racial advancement. Had I known how many similar experiences were in store for me, I should have taken this one more philosophically. And yet, I had used myself up so fully between my school duties and the struggle to keep the paper afloat that the definite silence of the press brought me a sense of relief. The failure of *The Daily American* was my first taste of defeat in public life, and for quite a while was bitter in my mouth; so bitter, that at a meeting held shortly thereafter in which the need of Negro business enterprises was being discussed I made the statement that the only sound investment I could at the moment think of was a Negro cemetery, because Negroes had to die, had to be buried, and, with few exceptions, had to be buried in Negro graveyards.

My disappointment at failure was natural, but I have now for a long time known that I was by no means blameless. I had allowed enthusiasm to overshoot good judgment. I ought to have discovered by other than empiric methods that the colored people of Jacksonville, regardless of what their will might be, were not able to support the kind of newspaper I sought to provide for them. There were two contributing reasons for the failure. One was the mistake of tying up all our cash capital in a plant. The other was the competition of the "colored columns" carried in the two white afternoon papers, which reported religious, fraternal, and social activities among the colored people of the city. The reader is, of course, at liberty to add another reason: the possibility that the paper was not as well run as it might have been. All in all, I now look back on this experience with satisfaction. I even reason, perhaps consolingly, that defeat was better for me then than easy success. But my biggest satisfaction has come from looking over the files of this paper. I have reread my editorials and seen that I would not feel called upon to make any apology for them today.

The closing down of the paper left D—— high and dry; and for six months or so the going for him was pretty hard. His father grudgingly gave him food and shelter, but would do nothing beyond that. He evidently got a sweet satisfaction out of proclaiming that his prediction that the boy would never amount to anything had come true. In the summer of 1896 D—— got a break. The local Democrats had split. The younger element in the party had grown recalcitrant, and was making an effort to wrest control of the machine from the old wing. This younger element, known as the Straightouts, was led by John N. C. Stockton, a banker. Mr. Stockton, as I remember, was ambitious to go to Congress. The fight was fierce and close; and while it was being waged there happened the thing that is bound to happen whenever there is a split in

the Democratic Party in the South: both sides made bids for
the Negro vote. The fear that such a thing might happen
generally is the nightmare of the Southern political oligarchy.
The determination to keep it from happening is the single
foundation stone on which the political solidarity of the
South rests; it is also the chief reason why white men in the
South have very little if any more political independence than
black men.

   In some way D—— came to the attention of Mr. Stockton
and was engaged by him to campaign for the Straightout
ticket. He addressed colored meetings in various sections of
the town and throughout Duval County. He was well fitted for
this work; his rough and tumble style made him a very effective stump speaker. I wondered then and many times afterwards at the things he could say to Negroes about themselves.
They took from him with indulgent laughter statements for
which from me they would have demanded my head. D——
was again affluent, and life was once more a game to be played
gaily. But in the election in the fall the machine won—which,
except for a miracle, it always does. Within several months
D——'s prosperity had dwindled, and within several months
more he was back in his former condition. All that remained to
him from his political activity was Mr. Stockton's promise to
"do something for him"; a promise which probably meant
when it was made that D—— would get some sort of political
job, if the Straightouts won.

   While D—— was getting his first lessons in practical politics,
my thoughts were rotating around another of my earlier ambitions; I began planning to study law. Early in the fall I made
arrangements and started. I didn't go to law school, but studied by the then most approved method in the Old South; that
is, by reading law in a lawyer's office. The man who made it
possible for me to do this was Thomas A. Ledwith, a young
and, as the term is used, brilliant member of the Jacksonville
bar. Mr. Ledwith's father had been a prominent man in
Florida. He was a Republican of the Reconstruction era and
had held several high federal offices. He was also wealthy; he
had owned the building used as the city market, the Ledwith
block on the principal street, and other properties. But when

he died it was discovered that his wealth had shrunk to almost nothing; and young Ledwith, reared as a rich man's son, was faced with the struggle of making his own way and a living. In this struggle he did not follow the political path of his father, but, recognizing the changes, joined the Democratic Party. His office was in the Law Exchange Building, and there I spent a part of each day; when there was no school, I spent the whole day. After I had been studying about six months Mr. Ledwith turned over to me the duty of drawing most of the necessary papers. This lightened his work and was very advantageous for me. He had a good practice in divorce matters, and I gained proficiency in drawing bills in these cases. He gave me a good deal of his time in discussing knotty questions and in quizzing me in various legal subjects.

At the end of eighteen months my friend—we had become friends—said he thought I ought to try the examination for admission to the bar. I didn't feel so sure about it as he; however, my application was filed and the day for my examination set. The nearer the day approached, the more anxious I grew. I think Mr. Ledwith passed through a similar experience. This was the first time in Duval County and, for all I could learn, in the state of Florida, that a Negro had sought admission to the bar through open examination in a state court. There were two or three Negro lawyers in Jacksonville, but each of these, I believe, had been admitted in the Federal Courts during or shortly after the Reconstruction period, and were admitted to practice in the state courts through comity.

The day came. I went over to the courthouse in a state of high tension. I had spent the greater part of the night before in a last effort at preparation. There was one fact that was reassuring to me as I entered the building: I was to be examined before Judge R. M. Call, a very fair man. Negroes in the South have a simple and direct manner of estimating the moral worth of a white man. He is good or bad according to his attitude toward colored people. This test is not only a practical and logical one for Negroes to use, but the absolute truth of its results average pretty high. The results on the positive side are, I think, invariably correct; I myself have yet to know a Southern white man who is liberal in his attitude toward the Negro and on the race question and is not a man of moral worth. Judge

Call, in the estimation of the colored people of Jacksonville, was a "good man," and he was a good man. My bit of reassurance was quickly lost in the realization that my examination had taken on the aspect of a spectacle. The main courtroom was full. Probably half the lawyers in Jacksonville were present. More people were present than I had many times seen at a murder trial in the same room. I judged that some were there out of curiosity, some out of mild interest, and others to see the fun. I did not look at the crowd. I felt that there was only one face in it that would reflect sympathy; and my eyes did occasionally seek the face of my friend, Ledwith; there I could read at a glance the barometric rise and fall of my chances. But Ledwith was a highly nervous man and he freely exhibited his deep concern. He constantly fidgeted and ran his fingers through his very red hair. His undisguised anxiety was far from being a source of confidence for me. I determined to let nothing interfere with the working of my mind. I concluded that I would need to know all that I knew, and know it on the instant. So I kept my attention focused as steadily as could on my examining committee, before whom I was seated six or eight feet away.

The judge had appointed a committee of three. One was E. J. L'Engle, a son of one of Florida's ruling families, who had been admitted to the bar several months before. Another member was Major W. B. Young. I do not know whether his military rank was derived from membership in the militia or whether he had been a very young major in the Civil War or had merely been breveted because of the legal battles he had fought. He was a medium-sized, bantam-like man; a man who, in the Negro idiom, "strutted his stuff." He had reddish hair, fierce gray eyes, a beak of a nose, and wore a mustache and imperial after the pictured tradition of the Southern aristocrat. His presence on the committee disturbed me, because by the "Negro test" and in the general estimation of the colored people of Jacksonville he was a "bad" white man. The third member was Duncan U. Fletcher, one of the outstanding members of the Jacksonville bar. In my mind, his presence on the committee balanced that of Major Young; for I knew of his reputation as a fair and just man. Mr. Fletcher is now the senior United States Senator from Florida.

The examination started. The questions were fired at me rapidly; little time being allowed for consideration. Sometimes the same question would be camouflaged and fired a second time. As the examination proceeded I gained confidence. Before it was over Major Young took up a copy of *The Statutes of Florida* and began examining me therefrom. It was my impression that the unfairness of this unprecedented procedure was regarded with disapproval by the other members of the committee and by Judge Call. After two hours there was a lull in the questioning. A lawyer named W. T. Walker, sitting near the committee, leaned over and asked, "Well, what are you going to do about it?" Mr. Fletcher answered, "He's passed a good examination; we've got to admit him." Major Young commented—I quote him precisely; for his words blurted out in my face, made their sizzling imprint on my brain: "Well, I can't forget he's a nigger; and I'll be damned if I'll stay here to see him admitted." With that he stalked from the courtroom. Mr. Fletcher conferred for a moment with Judge Call. The judge then asked me a few questions in equity and international law. Mr. Fletcher conferred with him a moment more, then stood before the bench and made the motion for my admission. Judge Call bade me rise and swore me in as a counselor, attorney-at-law, and solicitor in the courts of the State of Florida. Mr. Fletcher and Mr. L'Engle both congratulated me. Two or three other lawyers offered me a good word. My friend, Ledwith, was nowhere in sight; he explained to me later that when the committee began to confer he could stand the strain no longer. I found him in the office. He had already heard the news, and was beaming with satisfaction. But his first words of congratulation were: "That was the damnedest examination I ever heard or heard of."

One day, almost a year before my admission to the bar, D—— came to me and said, "Mr. Stockman wants to carry out the promise he made to do something for me. He doesn't know what he can do, and I don't know just what to ask him to do." I suggested, "Why don't you ask him to send you to law school? Ask him to send you to Ann Arbor; it's one of the best in the country." D—— jumped at the suggestion. His enthusiasm, always either very high or very low, bubbled over.

He was jubilant at the prospect, and at once wanted to know, "If Mr. Stockton sends me to Ann Arbor, why can't you go too?" My answer was, "I'd certainly like to go, but I can't do it. There are two reasons: I haven't got the money; I went broke and in debt on *The Daily American*; and even if I had the money, I wouldn't want to break off my plans to develop Stanton into a high school." Mr. Stockton did carry out his pre-election promise, despite the fact that he had been defeated—which, perhaps, was evidence that he had no real aptitude for practical politics—and in the fall D—— left for the University of Michigan. At the end of his first year he returned to Jacksonville, just a few days after my admission to the bar.

While we were talking about my examination it is probable that D——'s quick mind was working something like this: If Jim can pass without having gone to any kind of a law school, why can't I after a year at the University of Michigan? At any rate, he revealed his intention of trying the examination. I knew what his reasoning had been, and I told him that I had had the advantage of a year of practical legal work and of familiarity with the rules and forms of practice in Florida; that, however, with some hard work I believed he could prepare himself to pass. We worked together the whole summer and late into the fall, using the quiz method and studying the forms used in the Florida courts. D—— took the examination and was admitted. His examination was not so well attended as mine; I judge the first novelty had worn off. Immediately he and I formed a partnership. We did what I doubt would now be possible—we secured rooms in one of the principal office buildings of the town. We planned a division of work: he was to give the main attention to the office and the work in court, while I was to give as much time at the office as my school duties would allow, and draw the papers. The new firm began to pick up business from the start. We got cases of many kinds. It took me a while to rid myself of the state of depression resulting from the fact that our client in our first murder case was hanged. I gained some relief, however, from the reflection that he, being a Negro, would have been hanged anyhow, had his lawyer been Duncan U. Fletcher or even the redoubtable Major Young.

In the following spring the state teachers' association met at Tallahassee. I was bound by duty to go, and D—— thought that it would be a good thing for both of us to be there and look for the opportunity to be admitted to the State Supreme Court. In quest of that opportunity, we climbed the central red hill of the town, up to the capitol. In one of the corridors we met a man who shouted, "Hey, what are you two fellows doing here?" The man was Frank T. Clark, a Jacksonville lawyer. We told him that our main reason for visiting the capitol was to find someone, if we could, who would help us in being admitted to the Supreme Court. Mr. Clark said at once, "Why, come long with me; I'll do it myself." We followed him into the Supreme Courtroom, and in less time than it takes to tell about it he had made the motion and we had been admitted. A short while afterwards Mr. Clark was elected to Congress. For a number of years he justified his presence there by introducing at each session a bill to provide for "Jim Crow" street cars in the District of Columbia.

Years later, while I was secretary of the National Association for the Advancement of Colored People, I appeared at a hearing before the Census Committee of the House of Representatives. The Association was laying before the Committee facts concerning the prevention of Negroes from voting in Southern states, especially Florida, at the preceding general elections, and demanding the reduction of the Congressional representation of Southern states in accordance with the Fourteenth Amendment. Mr. Clark rose and made a perfect demagogic speech, which undoubtedly was mailed to his whole constituency. After the hearing adjourned, he complimented me on my presentation of our case.

XIII

ROSAMOND came back home in the spring of 1897. He had been away seven years, six of which he had spent studying music and working in Boston, and one in traveling with a theatrical company. John W. Isham had been the advance agent for the *Creole Show*, the forerunner of all the modern Negro musical comedies. Later, Mr. Isham produced *The Octoroons*. In 1896 he planned a more ambitious production, and for it secured the best trained Negro singers and musicians then available. From Boston he secured Sidney Woodward, the tenor, and my brother. The show was called *Oriental America*. Rosamond came back eager about the theater. Also, he had had two popular instrumental pieces published and was full of ideas and plans about songs and plays and operas that he and I should write together. He was impatient at finding me immersed in the study of law. His enthusiasm roused my curiosity about this new world into which he had had a peep, and I became, as I had at times before and have many times since, keenly aware of the love of venture that runs in me, a deep, strong current. But I have from my father a something—which I have often thought limits me as an artist—that generally keeps that deep, strong current from bursting out and spreading over the surface. This something hinted to me: You had better finish the business you have in hand before you jump into another that you know absolutely nothing about. So I told my brother that I should have to get through with my studies and take my examination before I could begin work with him. I have often rebelled against these cautious admonitions; but, generally, I have followed them, saying to myself in justification: One need not be an irresponsible fool in order to be a good artist. Three times in my life, however, with a vital decision before me, I have thrown caution to the winds, and in each instance the results have somehow worked out better than I had dreamed.

While I went on with my study of law, Rosamond began establishing himself as a teacher of music. In starting he showed more than a mere knowledge of music; first, he took one of the front rooms of our house and converted it into a studio; then, following the formulas of exclusive teachers of music in big cities, formulas that are based on sound principles of psychology, he announced that "Mr. Johnson, etc., etc., etc., will accept a limited number of pupils in piano and voice on terms of twenty half-hour lessons for fifteen dollars or twenty forty-five minute lessons for twenty dollars." This was revolutionary. Most of the colored people in Jacksonville who had studied music had been taught by peripatetic teachers who were glad to collect twenty-five cents a lesson. The result of this bold stroke together with his ability as a teacher was the rapid accumulation of a waiting list of pupils. Several of the older local music teachers came to study under him. In addition, he became choirmaster and organist for one of the large Baptist churches, and taught music once a week at the Baptist Academy. After he had been teaching seven or eight months he "presented" his pupils in a recital. Public performance of music by children and young people was nothing new to the colored people of Jacksonville. They had long been hearing and applauding the extremely *adagio* playing of *Maiden's Prayers* and the dashing off of familiar *gavottes* with steady acceleration, but they were not prepared to hear little girls play worthwhile music with such a show of virtuosity. This recital set a new standard for musical entertainments in Jacksonville. And it did another new thing; it started local white music lovers coming to concerts given by colored people.

In the meantime, Rosamond had thumbed through my notebooks and found several lyrics which he liked and to which he composed music. One of these was a poem on Easter. He made an anthem of it, and had it sung by his choir. This anthem increased his local reputation more than was warranted, I think. Indeed, my personal feeling is that it would not be gross injustice to give the composers of most of the anthems written for church choirs a light jail sentence for each offense. Of course, if my brother ever writes a book, I shall not object to his saying that something of the sort ought to be done with the poets who write most of the poems on Easter.

The closing exercises of Stanton constituted an important social as well as educational event. They were held in the local theater because of the large crowd that had to be accommodated. They had been of the conventional kind—songs, solos, vocal and instrumental, original essays and declamations by the graduates, and the presentation of diplomas by the Superintendent of Schools. For the closing in the year after my brother's return, he and I decided to try an innovation. We planned the program in two parts; the first to be an operetta performed by the pupils, and the second to consist of the graduation exercises and the presentation of diplomas. We concocted a juvenile libretto with a plot adapted to music taken from *The Geisha* and *The Runaway Girl*. The operetta was a grand success. The audience was enthusiastic over it; but the joy of the children who took part in it was what pleased us most. I can remember with what verve, what sheer delight they sang "O, Listen to the Band" from *The Runaway Girl*. They had never sung such music before. But, for the finale we had arranged a simple dance movement that was performed by the whole company, and thereby was brought down on my head the wrath of several of the colored clergy; the special wrath and condemnation of the pastor of one of the large Baptist churches, who declared I was "leading the children to the ballroom." This same pastor ran a weekly newspaper which carried one of those "We Know" columns in which responsibility for slander was avoided by not using names. However, he came out openly in his paper and lambasted me on what he asserted was my reputation as one of the best dancers at the affairs given by the Oceola Club; he harshly criticized me for being the club's president and for being a smoker. These attacks caused some talk, but did not produce the effect that the reverend gentleman unquestionably expected. They nevertheless annoyed me more than I cared to confess. On the board of education they made no impression at all. The members took the matter as something to be smiled at, knowing that each year, following the custom in colleges, the white high school gave a "Junior Prom" at which students, teachers, parents, and friends danced together; and also that most of the men teachers in the white public schools smoked. The dancing finale to the operetta brought on my first skirmish with a group of colored preachers in Jacksonville over matters which I considered innocent, and which they professed to consider sinful.

My bar examination was over, school was closed, and, aside from coaching D——, I had nothing pressing to do; so I was ready to begin with Rosamond on one of his big ideas. The idea he picked for a start was big enough; it was that he and I should write a comic opera. Rosamond felt pretty confident about the music, but I felt rather shaky about a libretto. We cast around for a story; and, as unlikely as it might seem that two such amateurs could do it, we found a capital one. The United States had, the year before, annexed Hawaii, and was at the time engaged in the Spanish-American War. We decided to write a comic opera satirizing the new American imperialism. The setting was an island kingdom in the Pacific. The story was concerned with Tolsa, the beautiful princess; her prime minister, a crafty old politician; the entrance of an American man-of-war; the handsome, heroic American lieutenant; and finally annexation. Old stuff now, but not so then. In fact, nothing of the sort had yet been produced on the American stage. We worked earnestly, and at the end of about a year had the opera finished. While we were working on it Rosamond frequently played completed parts over for the leading musical people of the town: Mr. Kerrison, the director of the Jacksonville Conservatory of Music; Mr. Kahn, the manager of the principal music store; Mrs. Lund, a musician and a beautiful and aristocratic woman, and the mother of the Lund boys mentioned in an early chapter of this account; and one or two others. One night Mr. Benedict, a partner of the firm of Furchgott and Benedict, the largest dry goods store in Jacksonville, "threw a party" for us. Mr. Benedict was a business man who was at heart an artist. He had two boys still in their teens for whom, it seemed, his highest ambition was that they should become accomplished musicians. There were a dozen or so people present, and they spoke enthusiastically of our work when Rosamond played and sang parts of the opera. The host served a supper of sandwiches, potato salad, more kinds of cold meats than I knew that there were, and beer. This was the first interracial-artistic party in our experience.

The attention and praise we received from the people in Jacksonville who knew most about music, naturally, increased our confidence in our work. We decided to try our fate in New York, and early in the summer of 1899 we set out for the metropolis. We left Jacksonville with the good wishes of friends, white and colored. Mr. Kahn gave us a letter to Mr. Freund, editor of one of the New York music trade journals. Mr. Kerrison gave us a word of warning. He cautioned us that we had a valuable piece of work which was not copyrighted, and to be very careful, because New York was full of pirates just waiting for the chance to plunder. We set out sanguine of success.

This was one of the determinative incidents in my life. As I look back on it now I can see that it was almost quixotic; that in the undertaking there was none of my father's practical sense. Two young Negroes away down in Florida, unknown and inexperienced, starting for New York thirty-three years ago to try for a place in the world of light opera. I can now recognize all the absurdities and count up all the improbabilities in it.

As soon as we had settled in a couple of rooms in West 53rd Street we presented our letter of introduction to Mr. Freund. He, in turn, gave us a letter to Mr. Witmark and Sons, music publishers, who had published a number of light opera scores. We got an appointment and played the opera for Isadore Witmark. We were with him a couple of hours, and he appeared to be favorably impressed by the songs and choruses. Just as we finished, Harry B. Smith and Reginald DeKoven, then the two greatest American writers of light opera, entered. Mr. Witmak introduced us as two young men who had written an opera. "Well," said Mr. Smith, "let's hear it; we might be able to steal something from it." Mr. DeKoven and Mr. Witmark laughed. We didn't quite see the joke—if it was a joke—and, remembering Mr. Kerrison's warning, gathered up our precious manuscript and made a quick exit. Later we did laugh about it; and later we did collaborate with both Mr. Smith and Mr. DeKoven, realizing that had it not been for our caution and the extremely high value we placed on our work we might have collaborated with them immediately following that first introduction.

The opera, *Tolosa*, was never, as such, produced, but it served to introduce us to practically all of the important stars and producers of comic opera and musical plays in New York. The great Oscar Hammerstein climbed to our modest rooms in West 53rd Street to hear it played. It seemed to open doors by magic. Of course, the temerity of youth, our utter innocence with respect to their impassability of any doors—I hesitate to add, our invincible faith in ourselves—had something to do with this. We ultimately adapted most of the single numbers, and they were produced in one or another Broadway musical show. I have often looked over the score of our opera and seen that a practiced hand could have whipped it into shape for production. It is possible that the managers were a bit afraid of it; the Spanish-American War had just closed, and they may have thought that audiences would consider a burlesque of American imperialism as unpatriotic. Not long afterwards, however, George Ade, in *The Sultan of Zulu*, used the same theme successfully.

In the fall Rosamond and I went back to our teaching in Jacksonville and to do more writing. Before we left New York we met Bob Cole. Bob was one of the most talented and versatile Negroes ever connected with the stage. He could write a play, stage it, and play a part. Although he was not a trained musician, he was the originator of a long list of catchy songs. We also met Williams and Walker and Ernest Hogan, the comedians; Will Marion Cook, the Negro composer; Harry T. Burleigh, the musician and singer; and a number of others, doing pioneer work in Negro theatricals. I attended rehearsals of two Negro companies that were preparing for the coming season, and I took in something of night life in Negro Bohemia, then flourishing in the old Tenderloin District. Into one of the rehearsals I was attending walked Paul Laurence Dunbar, the Negro poet. The year before he had written in collaboration with Cook an operetta called, *Clorindy—The Origin of the Cakewalk*, which had been produced with an all-Negro cast and Ernest Hogan as star by George Lederer at the Casino Theater Roof Garden, and had run with great success the entire summer. Mr. Lederer was the principal and most skillful musical play producer of the period. His production, *The Belle of New York*, with Dan Daly and Edna May, was one of the greatest successes the American stage had seen. But he learned some new things from *Clorindy*. He judged correctly that the practice of the Negro chorus, to dance strenuously and sing at the same time, if adapted to the white stage would be a profitable novelty; so he departed considerably from the model of the easy, leisurely movements of the English light opera chorus. He also judged that some injection of Negro syncopated music would produce a like result. Mr. Lederer was, at least, the grandfather of the modern American musical play. Ironically, these adaptations from the Negro stage, first made years ago, give many present-day critics reason for condemning Negro musical comedy on the ground that it is too slavish an imitation of the white product. I had met Dunbar five years before, when he was almost unknown; now he was at the height of his fame. When he walked into the hall, those who knew him rushed to welcome him; among those who did not know him personally there were awed whispers. But it did not appear that celebrity had puffed him up; he did not meet the homage that was being shown him with anything but friendly and hearty response. There was no hint of vainglory in his bearing. He sat quiet and unassuming while the rehearsal proceeded. He was then twenty-seven years old, of medium height and slight of figure. His black, intelligent face was grave, almost sad, except when he smiled or laughed. But notwithstanding this lack of ostentation, there was on him the hallmark of distinction. He had an innate courtliness of manner, his speech was unaffectedly polished and brilliant, and he carried himself with that dignity of humility which never fails to produce a sense of the presence of greatness. Paul and I were together a great deal during those last few weeks. I was drawn to him and he to me; and a friendship was begun that grew closer and lasted until his death. A day or two before I left he took me into Dutton's on 23rd Street, where he bought a copy of his *Lyrics of Lowly Life* and inscribed it for me. It is one of my most treasured books.

These glimpses of life that I caught during our last two or three weeks in New York were not wholly unfamiliar to Rosamond, but they showed me a new world—an alluring world, a tempting world, a world of greatly lessened restraints, a world of fascinating perils; but, above all, a world of tremendous artistic potentialities. Up to this time, outside of polemical essays on the race questions, I had not written a single line that had any relation to the Negro. I now began to grope toward a realization of the importance of the American Negro's cultural background and his creative folk-art, and to speculate on the superstructure of conscious art that might be reared upon them. My first step in this general direction was taken in a song that Bob Cole, my brother, and I wrote in conjunction during the last days in New York. It was an attempt to bring a higher degree of artistry to Negro songs, especially with regard to the text. The Negro songs then the rage were known as "coon songs" and were concerned with jamborees of various sorts and the play of razors, with gastronomical delights of chicken, pork chops and watermelon, and with the experiences of red-hot "mammas" and their never too faithful "papas." These songs were for the most part crude, raucous, bawdy, often obscene. Such elements frequently are excellencies in folk-songs, but rarely so in conscious imitations. The song we did was a little love song called *Louisiana Lize* and was forerunner of a style that displaced the old "coon songs." We sold the singing rights to May Irwin for fifty dollars—our first money earned. With the check the three of us proceeded joyfully to the Garfield National Bank, then at Sixth Avenue and 23rd Street, where Bob was slightly known. The paying teller looked at the check and suggested we take it over on the next corner to the Fifth Avenue Bank, on which it was drawn and have it O.K.'d It is always disconcerting to have a bank teller shove a check back to you, whatever his reasons may be, so we went over to the other bank not without some misgivings. The teller there looked at it and said, "Tell them over at the Garfield Bank that the check would be good if it was for fifty thousand dollars." Bob delivered the message. Next, we took the manuscript to Jos. W. Stern and Co., who published the song.

When I got back to Jacksonville I found that my artistic ideas and plans were undergoing a revolution. Frankly, I was floundering badly: the things I had been trying to do seemed vapid and non-essential, and the thing I felt a yearning to do was so nebulous that I couldn't take hold of it or even quite make it out. In this state, satisfactory expression first came through writing a short dialect poem. One night, just after I had finished the poem, I was at Mr. McBeath's house talking about school matters; then about books and literature. He read me a long poem he had written on Lincoln—a Lincoln poem, the expression of a Southern white man. I thought it was good and told him so. I also thought but did not say that there was yet to be written a great poem on Lincoln, the expression of a Negro. Aloud, I repeated for him my dialect poem, *Sence You Went Away.* He thought it was good enough for me to try it on one of the important magazines. I sent it to *Century*, and it was promptly accepted and printed. Outside of what had appeared in Atlanta University periodicals and in the local newspapers, this was my first published poem. Some years later my brother set this little poem to music. It has proved to be one of the most worthwhile and lasting songs he has written. It was first sung by Amato, the Metropolitan Opera baritone; it was afterwards recorded for the phonograph by John McCormack, with a violin obbligato played by Kreisler; and was again recorded by Louis Graveure and still again by Paul Robeson. It continues to find a place on concert programs.

During the winter I wrote more dialect poems, some of them very trite, written with an eye on Broadway. Rosamond made some pretty songs out of these trivialities and put them aside for our next migration to New York. In the same winter Rosamond planned a concert such as had not before been given by or for colored people in Jacksonville. He brought Sidney Woodward down from Boston. The affair was successful, artistically and financially, beyond our expectations. The concert sent the level of musical entertainment among the colored people many degrees higher. Nor were its effects limited to the colored people; it was a treat for the hundred or so local white music lovers who were present, for, indeed, not all of them had before heard a tenor with Woodward's voice and technical finish.

A group of young men decided to hold on February 12 a celebration of Lincoln's birthday. I was put down for an address, which I began preparing; but I wanted to do something else also. My thoughts began buzzing round a central idea of writing a poem on Lincoln, but I couldn't net them. So I gave up the project as beyond me; at any rate, beyond me to carry out in so short a time; and my poem on Lincoln is still to be written. My central idea, however, took on another form. I talked over with my brother the thought I had in mind, and we planned to write a song to be sung as a part of the exercises. We planned, better still, to have it sung by schoolchildren—a chorus of five hundred voices.

I got my first line: —Lift ev'ry voice and sing. Not a startling line; but I worked along grinding out the next five. When, near the end of the first stanza, there came to me the lines:

Sing a song full of the faith that the dark past has taught us.
Sing a song full of the hope that the present has brought us.

the spirit of the poem had taken hold of me. I finished the stanza and turned it over to Rosamond.

In composing the two other stanzas I did not use pen and paper. While my brother worked at his musical setting I paced back and forth on the front porch, repeating the lines over and over to myself, going through all of the agony and ecstasy of creating. As I worked through the opening and middle lines of the last stanza:

God of our weary years,
God of our silent tears,
Thou who hast brought us thus far on our way,
Thou who hast by Thy might
Let us into the light,
Keep us forever in the path, we pray;
Lest our feet stray from the places, our God, where we met
    Thee,
Lest, our hearts drunk with the wine of the world, we forget
    Thee . . .

I could not keep back the tears, and made no effort to do so. I was experiencing the transports of the poet's ecstasy. Feverish ecstasy was followed by that contentment—that sense of serene joy—which makes artistic creation the most complete of all human experiences.

When I had put the last stanza down on paper I at once recognized the Kiplingesque touch in the two longer lines quoted above; but I knew that in the stanza the American Negro was, historically and spiritually, immanent; and I decided to let it stand as it was written.

As soon as Rosamond had finished his noble setting of the poem he sent a copy of the manuscript to our publishers in New York, requesting them to have a sufficient number of mimeographed copies made for the use of the chorus. The song was taught to the children and sung very effectively at the celebration; and my brother and I went on with other work. After we had permanently moved away from Jacksonville, both the song and the occasion passed out of our minds. But the schoolchildren of Jacksonville kept singing the song; some of them went off to other schools and kept singing it; some of them became schoolteachers and taught it to their pupils. Within twenty years the song was being sung

in schools and churches and on special occasions throughout
the South and in some other parts of the country. Within that
time the publishers had recopyrighted it and issued it in several arrangements. Later it was adopted by the National Association for the Advancement of Colored People, and is now
quite generally used throughout the country as the "Negro
National Hymn." The publishers consider it a valuable piece
of property; however, in traveling round I have commonly
found printed or typewritten copies of the words pasted in
the backs of hymnals and the songbooks used in Sunday
schools, Y.M.C.A.'s, and similar institutions; and I think that
is the method by which it gets its widest circulation. Recently
I spoke for the summer labor school at Bryn Mawr College
and was surprised to hear it fervently sung by the white students there and to see it in their mimeographed folio of
songs.

Nothing that I have done has paid me back so fully in satisfaction as being the part creator of this song. I am always
thrilled deeply when I hear it sung by Negro children. I am
lifted up on their voices, and I am also carried back and enabled to live through again the exquisite emotions I felt at the
birth of the song. My brother and I, in talking, have often
marveled at the results that have followed what we considered
an incidental effort, and effort made under stress and with no
intention other than to meet the needs of a particular moment. The only comment we can make is that we wrote better
than we knew.

XIV

SCHOOLS were again closed, and Rosamond and I left Jacksonville on our second trip to Broadway. We did not carry
much new work, for his teaching was taking up more and
more of his time, and I had given most of my spare hours to
my law practice. D—— was not exactly pleased when I announced that I was going to New York again, and I saw that
our partnership could not last much longer on such a basis. A
short while after we reached New York I went into another
partnership, a curious partnership. My brother, Bob Cole,
and I formed a partnership to produce songs and plays. I have

not known of just such another combination as was ours. The three of us sometimes worked as one man. At such times it was difficult to point out specifically the part done by any one of us. But, generally, we worked in a pair, with the odd man as a sort of critic and adviser. Without regard to who or how many did the work, each of us received a third of the earnings. There was an almost complete absence of pride of authorship; and that made the partnership still more curious. At first, we printed the three names at the top of the sheet, but three names on little songs looked top-heavy; so we began printing only two; sometimes we printed but one. Our first firm name for the title page was, "Johnson, Cole, and Johnson." After Bob and Rosamond became noted in vaudeville under the name of Cole and Johnson, we changed our title-page signature to "Cole and Johnson Brother." Furthermore, the agreement was actually a rather loose one; Rosamond collaborated with Harry B. Smith and other librettists, and I did some songs with other composers. I also worked with Will Marion Cook on a comic opera called *The Cannibal King*. The partnership lasted seven years, in which time we wrote some two hundred songs that were sung in various musical shows on Broadway and on "the road." We gained our start as a firm in the early part of the summer by writing several songs for May Irwin's new play.

On the night of August 15, 1900, we were at our rooms in West 53rd Street. Bob Cole's company had begun rehearsals for the coming season, but he had been sick for several days and unable to attend them. For that reason, Billy Johnson, his theatrical partner, had come up to 53rd Street to rehearse some of their numbers. Rosamond played the songs, but the rehearsal took longer that he expected and he had to break an engagement to go with a friend, Barry Carter, and two young women to an entertainment of some sort. He was very much disappointed over this. He worked until about ten-thirty, then he and I walked to the corner of Eighth Avenue with Billy, who would there take a street car to go down where he lived, somewhere around Thirtieth Street. We waited fifteen minutes, a half-hour, an hour; no car passed going in either direction. We thought it strange. Billy finally hailed a hansom. We had just gone off to sleep when our door bell rang. There was a young white man at the door, who asked if we knew Barry Carter. He went on to tell us that Carter had been beaten up and was in the Jefferson Market jail. When we expressed the determination of going down to see what we could do, the young man impressed on us that we shouldn't even try to go; that a mob was raging up and down Eighth Avenue and the adjacent side blocks from 27th to 42nd Streets attacking Negroes wherever they were found, and that it was not safe for any colored person to go through that section. We followed his advice. The next morning the newspapers told the story of a great race riot. We found Carter in a sad condition. He had kept the appointment, and was walking along one of the side streets with both the young women, ignorant of what was going on, when a crowd of young hoodlums ran up from behind and began beating him over the head with pieces of lead pipe. He struggled away and ran to a squad of policemen on the Avenue, but they met him with more clubbing. His scalp was cut open in several places, and his arms were terribly bruised and swollen to twice their natural size from the blows received in trying to protect his head. It was a beating from which he never fully recovered.

This was the fourth great clash in New York involving the Negro. The first the so-called "Negro Insurrection" in 1712; the second was the so-called "Conspiracy (of the Negro slaves) to burn New York and murder its inhabitants" in 1741; the third was the draft riots in 1863. The riot of 1900 grew out of an altercation between a white policeman in plain clothes and a Negro, in which the former was killed. The outbreak was, beyond doubt, fomented by New York police, but it had more than local significance; it was, in fact, only a single indication of the national spirit of the times toward the Negro. By 1900 the Negro's civil status had fallen until it was lower than it had been at any time since the Civil War; and, without noticeable protest from any part of the country, the race had been surrendered to Disfranchisement and Jim-Crowism, to outrage and violence, to the fury of the mob. In the decade ending in 1899, according to the records printed in the daily press, 1665 Negroes were lynched, numbers of them with a savagery that was satiated with nothing short of torture, mutilation, and burning alive at the stake.

◆

At the end of the summer my brother and I were fully satisfied with the advancement we had made in gaining recognition, but the financial returns had been small; so small that we
had to borrow money to get back to Jacksonville. The outlook, except from the point of view of art for art's sake, did not
appear very encouraging. At home again in Jacksonville, Rosamond found that his pupils and classes and recitals took more
of his time than ever before. And now that Stanton was a high
school, it allowed me very little time for anything else, even for
my law practice. Nevertheless, I continued writing poems,
most of them in dialect, and after the style of Dunbar.

But just at this time I came across Whitman's *Leaves of Grass*.
I was engulfed and submerged by the book, and set floundering again. I felt that nothing I had written, with exception of
the hymn for the Lincoln celebration, rose above puerility. I
got a sudden realization of the artificiality of conventionalized
Negro dialect poetry; of its exaggerated geniality, childish optimism, forced comicality, and mawkish sentiment; of its limitation as an instrument of expression to but two emotions, pathos
and humor, thereby making every poem either only sad or only
funny. I saw that not even Dunbar had been able to break the
mold in which dialect poetry had, long before him, been set by
representations made of the Negro on the minstrel stage. I saw
that he had cut away much of what was coarse and "niggerish,"
and added a deeper tenderness, a higher polish, a more delicate
finish; but also I saw that, nevertheless, practically all of his
work in dialect fitted into the traditional mold. Not even he
had been able to discard those stereotyped properties of min-
strel-stage dialect: the watermelon and the possum. He did,
however, disdain to use that other ancient "prop," the razor.

I could see that the poet writing in the conventionalized dialect, no matter how sincere he might be, was dominated by
his audience; that his audience was a section of the white
American reading public; that when he wrote he was expressing what often bore little relation, sometimes no relation at all,
to actual Negro life; that he was really expressing only certain
conceptions about Negro life that his audience was willing to
accept and ready to enjoy; that, in fact, he wrote mainly for the
delectation of an audience that was an outside group. And I

could discern that it was on this line that the psychological attitude of the poets writing in the dialect and that of the folk
artists faced in different directions: because the latter, although working in the dialect, sought only to express themselves for themselves, and to their *own group*. I have frequently
speculated upon what Dunbar might have done with Negro
dialect if it had come to him fresh and plastic.

In my muddled state of mind I tried to gain orientation
through a number of attempts in the formless forms of Whitman.

In the early part of the spring I had the opportunity of talking these questions through with Dunbar. Following the example of Rosamond's successful venture of the winter before
with Sidney Woodward, I arranged to have Paul come to Jacksonville for a public reading. This affair was equally as successful as the Woodward concert, and, likewise, it was attended by
a large number of local white people. Dunbar's success on the
platform, and it was great, was due not only to his fame as a
poet, but also to his skill as a reader. His voice was a perfect
musical instrument, and he knew how to use it with extreme
effect. I furthermore arranged with Mr. Campbell, the manager of the St. James, for a reading in the hotel parlors.

But Paul's visit to Jacksonville was more than professional;
in arranging for him to come down, my brother and I had
asked him to stay with us as long as he liked. He visited with
us about six weeks. In that time I grew to know him intimately. He was the Dunbar of the courtly manners, polished
speech, and modest behavior that I had marked; but, as lov-
able as he was with people he liked, I learned that under this
polite tongue there was a sac of bitter sarcasm that he spat out
on people he did not like, and often used in his own defense.
He formed a decided dislike for D——'s roughness, his aggressive and cock-sure manner. He could not tolerate what he
termed D——'s "vulgar streak." So the two never met but
that Paul kept his tongue moistened from that little sac and
read always to strike out at this instinctive foe. It was astonishing that D——, so glib of speech, was never able or never
wanted to get back at him.

Paul and I did not clash. I recognized his genius, and in a
measure regarded myself as his disciple. He was often as head-

strong, as impulsive, and as irresponsible as a boy of six, but none of his whims seemed unreasonable to me. I got pleasure out of humoring him. I remember how scrupulous I was in seeing that he was provided with the bedtime snack that he wanted every night, a raw onion with salt and a bottle of beer. He had great faith in this smelly combination as an antidote for tuberculosis—the disease that he knew would some day set at naught all antidotes. During his visit he wrote a half dozen or so poems. As quickly as he finished them he sent them off; two of them, I remember, to the *Saturday Evening Post*; and I was amazed at seeing how promptly he received checks in return. Whatever he wrote was in demand.

We talked again and again about poetry. I told him my doubts regarding the further possibilities of stereotyped dialect. He was hardly less dubious than I. He said, "You know, of course, that I didn't start as a dialect poet. I simply came to the conclusion that I could write it as well, if not better, than anybody else I knew of, and that by doing so I should gain a hearing. I gained the hearing, and now they don't want me to write anything but dialect." There was a tone of self-reproach in what he said; and five years later, in his fatal illness, he sounded that same tone more deeply when he said to me, "I've kept on doing the same things, and doing them no better. I have never gotten to the things I really wanted to do." In the evenings when we did not go visiting or have visitors at the house we sat and smoked and continued our discussions. Sometimes we would break the discussion and listen to Rosamond play. Paul never told me definitely what the things were that he really wanted to do. I surmised that it was not that he desired merely to write more poems in literary English, such as he had already done, but that it was his ambition to write one or two long, perhaps epical, poems in straight English that would relate to the Negro. I could not tell him what the things were that I wanted to do, because I myself didn't know. The thing that I was sure of and kept repeating to him was that he had carried traditional dialect poetry as far as and as high as it could go; that he had brought it to the fullest measure of charm, tenderness, and beauty it could hold. We agreed that the public still demanded dialect poetry, but that as a medium, especially for the Negro poet, it was narrow and limited.

Some years later these ideas were so thoroughly clarified in my mind and I was so certain of their truth, I made a precise statement of them. No Negro poets are today writing the poetry that twenty-five years ago was considered their natural medium of expression. They realize that the essential of traditional dialect poetry—the painting of humorous, contented, or forlorn "darkies" in standardized colors against a conventional Arcadian background of log cabins and cottonfields—is itself a smooth-worn stereotype.

In the course of our talks I showed Paul the things I had done under the sudden influence of Whitman. He read them through and, looking at me with a queer smile, said, "I don't like them, and I don't see what you are driving at." He may have been justified, but I was taken aback. I got out my copy of *Leaves of Grass* and read him some of the things I admired most. There was, at least, some personal consolation in the fact that his verdict was the same on Whitman himself.

While he was in Jacksonville Rosamond set two of his poems to music: *When the Colored Band Comes Marchin' down the Street* and *Li'l Gal.* The second of these is a classic in its field, and is still popular with concert singers who like to include a dialect song on their programs. But it was the first one that particularly delighted Paul. While Rosamond played the spirited music and sang the gay words, he liked to give a one-man impersonation of the marching band. This impersonation was, in the main, some pretty cleverly executed cakewalk steps.

Paul returned to his home in Washington early in the spring. He always spoke of his stay in Jacksonville in high terms. Before he left, the Negro Masons decided to organize a lodge of young men, and in honor of Paul, name it the Paul Laurence Dunbar Lodge. The lodge was organized, and Paul and twenty-five or thirty more of us were one night initiated and carried through the first three degrees of Masonry. The Negro Masons of that day in Jacksonville were a horny-handed set. The Odd Fellows lodges were made up of white collar workers, but the Masonic lodges were recruited largely from the stevedores, hod carriers, lumber mill and brickyard hands, and the like. The initiation was rough, and lasted all night. One of our young friends was lame for a number of weeks on account of a fall to the floor while being tossed in a blanket. I was made

Worthy Master of the lodge, but it did not take me long to see that being a good Mason demanded more time than I should be willing to devote to it. The first time that I had to "turn out" with the lodge, arrayed in regalia, settled the question definitely.

XV

WE were in the last days of May. Stanton was closed. Rosamond was conducting the final rehearsals for the closing exercises of the Baptist Academy, and asked me to go over and give him a hand. We mounted our bicycles one morning and rode the three or four miles through the city to the Academy, situated in the eastern part. At the beginning of the afternoon the rehearsal was over and we started home. We had been riding only a few minutes when we noticed a curling volume of smoke that appeared to be rising from a point in the western end of the town. The point seemed to us to be in a line not far away from our house. We pedaled faster and faster. The cloud of smoke spread wider and grew darker. Now, under and through its mass we could see the lurid glow, and now, the vivid, darting tongues of the flames. We rode harder, and now we could see that Stanton was on the line running to the center. When we reached the school, the fire was still two or three blocks to the west. We met many people fleeing. From them we gathered excitedly related snatches:—the fiber factory catches afire—the fire department comes—fanned by a light breeze, the fire is traveling directly east and spreading out to the north, over the district where the bulk of Negroes in the western end of the city live—the firemen spend all their efforts saving a long row of frame houses just across the street on the south side of the factory, belonging to a white man named Steve Melton—when complaints about this reach the chief he exclaims, "It will be a good thing for some of these damned niggers to get burnt out."—The breeze increases to a high wind—the fire is now beyond control—Jacksonville is doomed.

Rosamond and I realize at once that if Stanton escapes it can be made a temporary lodging place for the homeless. We think there is a chance. The school consists of three buildings, but

the main building is of brick and stands in the center of a
block, with wide playgrounds on either side. We rush into the
main building to see that the windows are all shut tight. Already people are seeking refuge. The grounds are being
quickly transformed into a refugee camp. People are rushing in
with household utensils hardly worth the effort to save. It is almost laughable to watch a woman running into the yard with
a mattress on her head, ignorant of the fact that sparks have lit
upon it and that it is already aflame. When we reach the second
story we look out to the west. There we see an immense, on-
rolling cloud of dense black smoke, and under it a roaring,
crouching and leaping pack of ravenous flames. We realize that
Stanton must go unless the firemen get to work on it at once.
Where are the firemen? We haven't yet seen a single stream of
water. We run down into the street, where we find a half-
dozen firemen pulling on a line of hose. We appeal to them—
if the school building is saved it can shelter hundreds of
people. They look at us listlessly and make no answer, but continue to drag the hose along, the flames almost on their heels.
We hear excited rumors:—all the fire apparatus has been
burned up—the fire chief has committed suicide. On top of it
all, these half-dozen dazed firemen, in automatic response to
some reflex, are struggling to save a few feet of hose.

I know that Stanton is to go. I rush, my brother with me,
into my office on the ground floor and take out the principal
records of the school. We jump on our bicycles and start for
home. But we must pass, on the corner above, the fine home
of S. H. Hart, the man who gave me my first job. We go in to
see if we can lend a hand. The house is open, but deserted; the
family has walked out and left it as it was. We ride to the south,
skirting around the burning sea, and reach home. My father is
silent; my mother and sister excited; my grandmother, who is
in bed with what was her last illness, is worried about
Ebenezer Church. But there stands our house. Due either to
the reported race prejudice of the fire chief or to the direction
of the wind, it is unharmed; at any rate, we are fortunate, for
the house is only three block from the fiber factory, but due
south. It isn't just our house for long. Before night, it is the
refuge of more than twenty of our friends who have no other
roof.

Without thought of food, Rosamond and I rush out again. We learn that all of the nearby towns in Florida and south Georgia have been telegraphed to for aid, and that special trains are rolling in from them with firemen and apparatus, even from so far away as Savannah. But all efforts are vain. The breeze has turned into a gale that hurtles a section of a burning roof through the air and sets it down on a building blocks away—a breath-taking pyrotechnical show. The speed and spread of the flames are constantly increased by the many hundreds of pitch pine houses. The fire travels east, all the while spreading to the north. Then it shifts to the south, burning to the river's edge and destroying the business section of the town. It follows the water to the eastern end of the city, and widens its zone on the north to Hogan's Creek. By nightfall more than one hundred and fifty blocks are smoldering ashes. But the row of frame houses belonging to Steve Melton, across the street from the fiber factory, is still standing.

A catastrophe! But, among the strangest paradoxes is the fact that people can take a catastrophe philosophically, good-naturedly, almost cheerfully. If a man's home burns down, he will curse his fate or lament his misfortune. But here were thousands who had lost their homes and all their household goods, and the general comment was, "Lucky it didn't happen at night."

Immediately, as in the yellow fever epidemic, relief began pouring in—money, provisions, and clothing from all parts of the country. Commissary depots were at once established. I was asked to take charge of one. For days I was kept busy issuing packages of assorted food to destitute families. Work to supply temporary housing started within a day or two, and unsightly board buildings with corrugated iron roofs sprang up as if by magic. Our "family" remained at about twenty-five for a couple of weeks; eating in camp style and sleeping on sofas, in chairs, and even on the floor. D—— had become one of the "family." In the meantime, civil law had been suspended and martial law established. Companies of state militia from central and western counties had been mustered to form a provost guard. These troops from the backwoods district of the state had many unnecessary clashes with the colored people of Jacksonville, Negroes of a kind they were not accustomed to dealing with. They interfered with me and made me move on when I tried to persuade a group of Negro men and boys not to pose for some photographers, who were taking fake pictures of "looting." I knew that the pictures were being taken for use in periodicals throughout the country.

There was a lady from New York who was an occasional contributor to various papers and magazines visiting in Jacksonville at the time of the fire. A very handsome woman she was, with eyes and hair so dark that they blanched the whiteness of her face. One afternoon she came to the commissary depot where I was engaged and told me that she had written an article on the fire, dealing especially with its effects on the Negro population, which she would like to have me read over before she sent it off. I readily consented to read the article, but told her I couldn't possibly do so until after four o'clock, when the depot closed. It was a sweltering afternoon, and I was hot and tired; so I suggested that after closing time we might take a street car and ride out to Riverside Park, where we could sit and go over the article leisurely and in comfort. She decided that instead of waiting around for me to close she would go out to the park and wait there.

At four o'clock I washed up and boarded a car. I had not yet been to this new Riverside Park; in fact, it was not yet quite a park. There was an old Riverside Park that I knew very well; but the city had recently acquired a large oak and pine covered tract on the bank of the river, a few miles farther out, which it was converting into a new park. I was, perhaps, more interested in seeing how this work had progressed than I was in reading the lady's article. When I reached the end of the car-line, I noticed a rustic waiting-pavilion near the edge of the river. I made my way to it, expecting to find the lady there. She was not there, and I looked about but saw no sign of her. I judged that she had grown tired of waiting and had returned to the city. I walked back to the car-line. The car I had come out on was still there. The conductor and motorman were standing on the ground near the rear end. I waited until they were about ready to start, then got aboard. The car was empty, except for me, and I took a seat near the center—there were then no "Jim Crow" street car laws in Jacksonville. As I settled

in my seat and glanced out of the window I saw a woman approaching across a little rustic bridge a hundred or so feet away
whom I at once recognized by her dress and the black and
white parasol she carried to be the lady I was to meet. I
jumped off the car and walked over to join her. We went back
across the bridge, then along some newly laid out paths until
we came to a little clearing on the other side of which was a
barbed wire fence. I helped her through the fence and followed. We then walked through the trees until we came to the
bank of the river, where we found a bench and sat down. She
read the article to me, and I offered one or two suggestions.

We sat talking. The sun was still bright, but was preparing
for his plunge under the horizon, which he makes more pre-
cipitantly in the far south than he does in the north. At the
point where we were sitting the St. Johns River is several miles
wide. Across the water the sun began cutting a brilliant swath
that constantly changed and deepened in color until it became
a flaming road between us and the dark line of trees on the opposite bank. The scene was one of perfect semi-tropical beauty.
Watching it, I became conscious of an uneasiness, an uneasiness that, no doubt, had been struggling the while to get up
and through my subconscious. I became aware of noises, of
growing, alarming noises; of men hallooing back and forth,
and of dogs responding with the bay of bloodhounds. One
thought, that they might be hunters, flashed through my
mind; but even so, there was danger of a stray shot. And yet,
what men would hunt with such noises, unless they were beating the bush to trap a wild, ferocious beast? I rose to go, and
my companion followed. We threaded our way back. The
noises grew more ominous. They seemed to be closing in. My
pulse beat faster and my senses became more alert. I glanced at
my companion; she showed no outward sign of alarm. Suddenly we reached the barbed wire fence. There we stopped.
On the other side of the fence death was standing. Death
turned and looked at me and I looked at death. In the instant
I knew that the lowering of an eyelash meant the end.

Just across the fence in the little clearing were eight or ten
militiamen in khaki with rifles and bayonets. The abrupt appearance of me and my companion seemed to have transfixed
them. They stood as under a spell. Quick as a flash of light the

series of occurrences that had taken place ran through my mind: The conductor and motorman saw me leave the street car and join the woman; they saw us go back into the park; they rushed to the city with a maddening tale of a Negro and a white woman meeting in the woods; there is no civil authority; the military have sent out a detachment of troops with guns and dogs to get me.

I lose self-control. But a deeper self springs up and takes command; I follow orders. I take my companion's parasol from her hand; I raise the loose strand of fence wire and gently pass her through; I follow and step into the group. The spell is instantly broken. They surge round me. They seize me. They tear my clothes and bruise my body; all the while calling to their comrades, "Come on, we've got 'im! Come on, we've got 'im!" And from all directions these comrades rush, shouting, "Kill the damned nigger! Kill the black son of a bitch!" I catch a glimpse of my companion; it seems that the blood, the life is gone out of her. There is the truth; but there is no chance to state it; nor would it be believed. As the rushing crowd comes yelling and cursing, I feel that death is bearing in upon me. Not death of the empty sockets, but death with the blazing eyes of a frenzied brute. And still, I am not terror-stricken, I am carrying out the chief command that has been given me, "Show no sign of fear; if you do you are lost." Among the men rushing to reach me is a slender young man clad in a white uniform. He breaks through the men who have hold of me. We look at each other; and I feel that a quivering message from intelligence to intelligence has been interchanged. He claps his hand on my shoulder and says, "You are my prisoner." I ask him, "What is the charge?" He answers, "Being out here with a white woman." I question once more, "Before whom do I answer this charge?" "Before Major B——, the provost marshal," he replies. At that, I answer nothing beyond "I am your prisoner."

The eternity between stepping through the barbed wire fence and the officer's words putting me under arrest passed, I judge, in less than sixty seconds. As soon as the lieutenant put his hand on me and declared me his prisoner, the howling mob of men became soldiers under discipline. Two lines were formed, with my companion and me between them, and marched to the street car. The soldiers filled the seats, jammed the aisle, and packed the platforms, and still some of them, with two men in civilian clothes holding the dogs in leash, were left over for the next car. As we began nearing the city my companion had the reactions natural to a sensitive woman. Both of us were now fairly confident that the danger of physical violence was passed, but it was easy to see that she was anxious; perhaps, about the probable notoriety; perhaps, about the opportunity for malicious tongues. I assured her as best I could that everything would come out all right. I said to her, "I know Major B——, the provost marshal, very well; he is a member of the Jacksonville bar." On the way in, the car stopped at the electric power house. It was met by a crowd of conductors, motormen, and other employees, who hailed our car with cries of, "Have you got 'em?" "Yes, we've got 'em," the soldiers cried back.

Before the car left the power house, the young lieutenant, whom I had hardly been able to see after we left the park, made his way to our seat. Again I felt the waves of mental affinity. In the midst of the brutishness that surrounded us I felt that between him and me there was somewhere a meeting place for reason. He leaned over and said, "I'm going to put these men off the car here and take you in myself." He ordered the men off. Of course, they obeyed, but they were openly a disappointed and disgruntled lot. The car moved across the aqueduct and into the heart of the city. I was thankful for the lieutenant's action; because, for reason or no reason, I did not want to be paraded through the streets of Jacksonville as a prisoner under guard of a company of soldiers. In my gratitude I was tempted to tell him what I did not have a chance to tell before I was put under arrest. But I was now comparatively light-hearted. I was already anticipating the burlesque finale to this melodrama—melodrama that might have been tragedy— and I disliked spoiling any of the effects. However, I did say to him, "The lady with me *is* white, but not legally so." He looked at her curiously, but made no comment; instead he said to me, "You know where the provost headquarters are, don't you?" I answered that I did. He continued, "When you get off the car you walk on ahead; I'll follow behind, and nobody will know you are under arrest." I thanked him again. We got off

and walked to the provost headquarters, passing numbers of
people, colored and white, who knew me. We went into the
provost marshal's tent, followed by the lieutenant, who turned
his prisoners over.

Major B—— showed astonishment and some embarrassment when he recognized me. I said to him, "Major, here I
am. What is the charge?" He repeated the charge the lieutenant had made. "Major," I went on, "I know there is no use
in discussing law or my rights on any such basis as, 'Suppose
the lady *is* white?' so I tell you at once that according to the
customs and, possibly, the laws of Florida, she *is not* white." In
spite of appearances, he, of course, knew that I spoke the
truth. He was apologetic and anxious to dismiss us and the
matter. He spoke of the report that had been brought in, of his
duty as commanding officer of the provost guard, of how he
never even dreamed what the actual facts were. In answering, I
told him that I appreciated how he felt about it personally but
that that did not balance the jeopardy in which my life had
been put. I added, "You know as well as I do, if I had turned
my back once on that crowd or taken a single step in retreat,
I'd now be a dead man." He agreed with me and said he was
as glad as I that nothing of the kind had happened. At this
point my companion began to speak. She spoke slowly and deliberately at first; then the words came in torrents. She laid on
the Major's head the sins of his fathers and his fathers' fathers.
She charged him that they were the ones responsible for what
had happened. As we left, the Major was flushed and flustered.
I felt relieved and satisfied, especially over the actually minor
outcome of the avoidance of any notoriety for my companion.
It was now dark, and I took her to her stopping place, The
Boyland Home, a school for colored girls supported by
Northern philanthropy.

I did not get the nervous reaction from my experience until
I reached home. The quick turn taken by fate had buoyed me
up. When I went into the provost marshal's tent my sense of
relief had mounted almost to gayety. Now, the weight of all
the circumstances in the event came down and carried me under. My brother was the only one of the family to whom I confided what had taken place. He was terrified over what might
have happened; I never mentioned it to my parents. For weeks

and months the episode with all of its implications preyed on my mind and disturbed me in my sleep. I would wake often in the night-time, after living through again those few frightful seconds, exhausted by the nightmare of a struggle with a band of murderous, bloodthirsty men in khaki, with loaded rifles and fixed bayonets. It was not until twenty years after, through work I was then engaged in, that I was able to liberate myself completely from this horror complex.

Through it all I discerned one clear and certain truth: in the core of the heart of the American race problem the sex factor is rooted; rooted so deeply that it is not always recognized when it shows at the surface. Other factors are obvious and are the ones we dare to deal with; but, regardless of how we deal with these, the race situation will continue to be acute as long as the sex factor persists. Taken alone, it furnishes a sufficient main-spring for the rationalization of all the complexes of white racial superiority. It may be innate; I do not know. But I do know that it is strong and bitter; and that its strength and bitterness are magnified and intensified by the white man's perception, more or less, of the Negro complex of sexual superiority.

XVI

SHORTLY after the happenings just related, Rosamond and I decided to get away from Jacksonville as quickly as possible and go to New York. I went to see the mayor, a man I had known nearly all my life, and told him we were going to New York and that we should try to arrange a benefit there for the relief of fire sufferers. We stopped in Washington to see Paul Dunbar, but he was away on a reading tour. His young and beautiful wife, Alice Ruth, informed us that he would be back in a couple of days, and pressed us to stay. But we had written to Bob Cole regarding the benefit, and he was enthusiastic about starting to put it on; so we did not wait over. We had no difficulty in getting Negro theatrical performers and other artists in New York to give their services. The benefit was well attended and netted nearly a thousand dollars. The amount was sent to the major of Jacksonville. After we left Jacksonville, D—— set up office temporarily in Rosamond's studio.

We found that some marked changes had taken place in West 53rd Street. Two hotels that had been opened by Negro proprietors the previous fall were now running in full blast. It is true they were hotels more in name than in fact—in each case the building was an adapted private house—but they fulfilled their main purpose, providing good food, quite adequately. The Marshall, located between Sixth and Seventh Avenues, occupied a brownstone, four story and basement house which in the years before had been a fashionable dwelling. Both hotels served very good meals. On Sunday nights there was a special dinner with music. The Sunday night dinners had become so popular that tables were booked days in advance. The music was good also. At the Marshall there was a four-piece orchestra that was excellent. The leader, a man named Wiggins, was, to me, a most remarkable man. After he had been earning his living for a number of years as a violinist, he suffered an injury to the fingers of his left hand that completely incapacitated him. What did he do? He set out at once to learn to play by bowing with his left hand and fingering with his right. There may be those who cannot appreciate the difficulty of this feat; but one who has any knowledge of the long and arduous drill in the co-ordination of brain and hands necessary to learn to play the violin can understand what it meant to make the change involved in stringing and playing the instrument backwards. It entailed the direct reversal of reflexes that had become second nature.

These hotels brought about a sudden social change. They introduced or made possible a fashionable sort of life that hitherto had not existed. Prior to their opening there was scarcely a decent restaurant in New York in which Negroes could eat; I knew of only one place with excellent food and a social air where they were welcome. The sight offered at these hotels, of crowds of well-dressed colored men and women lounging and chatting in parlors, loitering over their coffee and cigarettes while they talked or listened to the music, was unprecedented. The sight had an immediate effect on me and my brother; we decided to give up our lodgings with our old landlady at No. 260, and move to the Marshall. We took the large backroom on the second floor, put in a piano, and started to work. This move had consequences we did not dream of.

Bob Cole lived two doors from the Marshall, and that made it convenient for the trio to work together. We worked according to a schedule. We rose between nine and ten o'clock, breakfasted at about eleven, and began work not later than twelve. When we didn't go to the theater, our working period approximated ten hours a day. We spent the time in actual writing or in planning future work. In our room and without stopping work, we snatched a bite to eat at the fag-end of the afternoon. Always, we went downstairs for a midnight supper. And this was by no means a light supper; it was our main and most enjoyed meal. Sometimes it consisted of planked steak or broiled lobster. This supper generally cost us more than we were justified in spending; but, if we had done a good day's work, the money spent seemed a minor matter; if we hadn't made much progress, the gay air of the dining room, gayer around midnight than at any other hour, stimulated us. Looking back at those days, the elation and zest with which we usually worked seem prodigious. We laid down a strict rule against interruptions; but there were several intimates who were not included under the rule: Harry T. Burleigh who sometimes brought along the manuscript of an "art song" he had just finished and played it over; Will Marion Cook, despite his animosity against Bob Cole; Theodore Drury, who had begun his productions of grand opera at the Lexington Opera House; and Paul Dunbar, who, however, had lost interest in things theatrical. Another intimate whom we were always glad to see was young Jack Nail, then the most popular young colored man in New York, an exceedingly handsome boy. He belonged because of his real appreciation of the things the members of this group were trying to do. He came in frequently of evenings. If we were busy, he took a chair and sat quietly smoking his pipe while we, after a grunt of greeting, went on working. There was in him a quality that made his presence more helpful than distracting.

Our room, particularly of nights, was the scene of many discussions; the main question talked and wrangled over being always that of the manner and means of raising the status of the Negro as a writer, composer, and performer in the New York theater and world of music. The opinions advanced and maintained, often with more force than considerateness, were as

diversified as the personalities in the group. However, the only
really bitter clashes were those occurring between Cole and
Cook. Seldom did they meet and part without a clash. Cole
was the most versatile man in the group and a true artist. In
everything he did he strove for the fine artistic effect, regardless of whether it had any direct relation to the Negro or not.
Nevertheless, there was an element of pro-Negro propaganda
in all his efforts; and it showed, I think, most plainly when he
was engaged in matching the white artist on the latter's own
field. Cook was the most original genius among all the Negro
musicians—probably that statement is still true. He had received excellent training in music, both in this country and in
Berlin at the Hochschule; he studied the violin under Joachim.
But he had thrown all these standards over; he believed that
the Negro in music and on the stage ought to be a Negro, a
genuine Negro; he declared that the Negro should eschew
"white" patterns, and not employ his efforts in doing what
"the white artist could always do as well, generally better."
Both these men tended toward eccentricity, both were hot-
tempered, and the argument did not always oscillate between
their divergent points of view; it did not always keep itself
above personalities. Cook never hesitated to make belittling
comments on Cole's limitations in musical and general education; he would even sneer at him on a fault in pronunciation.
Cole was particularly sensitive on this side, and Cook's taunts
both humiliated and maddened him.

Burleigh's position was unique. He had been a student at
the National Conservatory while Dvorák was the director. He
had studied harmony with Rubin Goldmark and counterpoint
with Max Spicker. Not only had he studied with Dvorák but
he had spent considerable time with him at his home. It was he
who called the attention of the great Bohemian composer to
the Negro spirituals. He had been the baritone soloist at St.
George's Church for seven years—a position he still holds. His
reputation as a composer was already well in the making, based
on a number of "art songs" written in the best modern manner. Among us, however, it was as a master that he was held.
On all questions in the theory and science of music he was the
final authority. In this acceptance, both Cook and my brother,
with their own very good musical training, always joined.

Some years later Kurt Schindler said to me that on a question in the theory of music he would accept Mr. Burleigh's decision as quickly as that of any other musician in New York. Drury was the picturesque one. He was light bronze in color and quite good-looking, especially when he flashed his teeth in a smile. He cultivated a foreign air, in fact, a foreign appearance; he might easily have been taken for a member of one of the African nationalities of the Mediterranean border. He was a singer, and had forced his voice up to enable him to sing certain grand opera rôles; the result being the making of a straining tenor out of an excellent baritone. He was at the beginning of his enterprise which annually, for four or five years, gave Negro New York a one-night season of grand opera. Whatever may have been said of these productions artistically, they were, as popular social events, huge successes. They were for the first two or three seasons huge successes financially. Drury was naturally shy, and talked very little; but both these traits in him were more than offset by his personal representative and business manager, Theodore Pankey. Pankey was a small, very light-colored young man who at one time had been a jockey. He had rubbed against the world, and possessed aplomb to that degree which is irritating. Nothing short of a locked door could keep him out, if he took a notion to come in. Talk from him was always sufficient for two; and besides, no topics of conversation or discussion imposed silence upon him. Notwithstanding, all of us liked Pankey. All of us conceded that in one field we did not know his peer. No one else could have sold so many tickets and packed so many people in the Lexington Opera House for Drury's productions of Verdi, Wagner, Gounod, and Bizet. Moreover, he did qualify as an "artist" through a good tenor voice that he used very well. As for the operas, none of us, with the exception of Pankey, took them too seriously—that statement possibly includes Drury himself.

In all of our discussions and wrangles we were unanimous on one point; namely, that the managers, none of whom at that time could conceive of a Negro company playing anything but second and third-class theaters, had to be convinced. It is true that Cook's operetta, *Clorindy*, had been produced at the Casino Theater Roof Garden, and the following summer, his operetta, *Jes Lak White Folks*, had been produced at the New York Theater Roof Garden, also that many top-notch Negro performers had appeared in the best vaudeville houses; but as yet, no professional Negro company had played a regular engagement on the stage proper of any first-class, legitimate "Broadway" house.

About this time Cook persuaded me to use my good offices to have Dunbar collaborate with him on another piece, a full-length opera to be called *The Cannibal King*. *Clorindy*, for which Dunbar was the librettist, had been a big success. For *Jes Lak White Folks* Cook was his own librettist, and the piece did not go over so well as its predecessor; so Cook wanted Dunbar's touch and, still more, his name again. But the great success of the first piece was not due alone to Dunbar, nor was the partial failure of the second piece due alone to Cook. In *Clorindy*, New York had been given its first demonstration of the possibilities of Negro syncopated music, of what could be done with it in the hands of a competent and original composer. Cook's music, especially his choruses and finales, made Broadway catch its breath. In *Jes Lak White Folks*, the book and lyrics were not so good, nor was the cast; and, naturally, the music was not such a startling novelty. I did my best to persuade Paul to do the book and lyrics for *The Cannibal King*, but he was obdurate. He told me with emphasis, "No, I won't do it. I just can't work with Cook; he irritates me beyond endurance." Finally, I undertook the work of writing the lyrics and actually got Cook to agree to have Bob Cole do the book. We began work on neutral ground, four or five blocks over, at Harry Burleigh's apartment on Park Avenue. We celebrated the end of the first day's work with a beefsteak dinner, deliciously cooked by Harry's brother, Reginald. But despite the inaugural love feast, discord entered and prevailed, and *The Cannibal King* was never wholly completed. Enough was finished, however, to enable Cook to negotiate a sale to a producer for a flat cash price that gave us several hundred dollars apiece. This was my first work with Cook; later, through the years, we wrote a number of songs in collaboration.

The Marshall gradually became New York's center for Negro artists. For a generation that center had been in Negro Bohemia, down in the Tenderloin. There, in various clubs, Negro

theatrical and musical talent foregathered. The clubs of Negro
Bohemia were of diverse sorts. There were gambling clubs and
poker clubs—a fine distinction between the two being involved; there were clubs frequented particularly by the followers of the ring and turf, where one got a close-up of the noted
Negro prize fighters and jockeys; there were "professional"
clubs, that served as meeting places and exchanges for Negro
theatrical performers. Among the clubs of Negro Bohemia
were some that bore a social aspect corresponding to that of
the modern night club. These had their regular habitués, but
they also enjoyed a large patronage of white sightseers and
slummers and of white theatrical performers on the lookout
for "Negro stuff," and, moreover, a considerable clientele of
white women who had or sought to have colored lovers. The
most popular of the "professional" clubs was Ike Hine's. It
was principally a club for Negroes connected with the theater,
but it drew the best elements from the various circles of Bohemia—except the gamblers. No gambling was allowed, and
the conduct of the place was in every respect surprisingly orderly. This club occupied what formerly was a three-story and
basement dwelling. In the basement was a chop suey restaurant. The parlor, on the main floor, was carpeted and furnished
with chairs and tables. The walls of this room were entirely
covered with photographs and lithographs of Negro "celebrities." The back parlor contained a few chairs and tables, a
piano, and also a buffet. The floor of the room was bare and
provided space for the entertainers and for dancing. On the
floor above one or two of the rooms were given over to "acts"
for rehearsals. The top floor was used as living quarters by the
proprietor and his wife.

As the Marshall gained in popularity, the more noted theatrical stars and the better-paid vaudevillians deserted the
down-town clubs and made the hotel their professional and
social rendezvous. Up to 53rd Street came Bert Williams; tall
and broad-shouldered; on the whole, a rather handsome figure, and entirely unrecognizable as the shambling, shuffling
"darky" he impersonated on the stage; luxury-loving and indolent, but highly intelligent and with a certain reserve which
at times exhibited itself as downright snobbishness; talking
with a very slow drawl and getting more satisfaction, it

seemed, out of being considered a great raconteur than out of being a great comedian; extremely funny in his imitations in the West Indian dialect. (He was himself a West Indian; born in Nassau.) Bert was a good story teller, but not a better one, we thought, than his very pretty wife, Lottie. All of Lottie's stories centered around one character, and that character was Bert. She recited very comically—the comicality heightened by her prettiness—her trials and tribulations with Bert on the "road," the chief of them being the many devices to which she had to resort to get him out of bed in time to catch early trains, Bert the while listening meekly and grinning good-naturedly. Up, too, came George Walker, very black, very vigorous, and very dapper, being dressed always a point or two above the height of fashion. George, the hail-fellow-well-met, the mixer, the diplomat; frequently flashing that celebrated row of gleaming teeth in making his way to his objective; but serious withal and the driving force of the famous team; working tirelessly to convince New York managers that Negro companies should be booked in first-class houses, and, finally, succeeding. And Aida Overton, George Walker's wife; not as good-looking as Lottie Williams, but more than making up for what she lacked in looks by her remarkable talent; a wonderful dancer, and the possessor of a low-pitched voice with a natural sob to it, which she knew how to use with telling effect in "putting over" a song; beyond comparison, the brightest star among women on the Negro stage of the period, and hardly a lesser attraction of the Williams and Walker company than the two comedians. And up came Ernest Hogan, not an Irishman, but a natural-black-face comedian; ranked by some critics, erroneously, I think, as a greater comedian than Bert Williams; expansive, jolly, radiating infectious good humor; provoking laughter merely by the changing expressions of his mobile face—a face that never, even on the stage, required cork or paint to produce comical effects. Behind these well-known performers came others less noted, and also a crowd of those who love to follow the clouds of glory trailed by the great. In time, the Marshall came to be one of the sights of New York. But it is more than a "sight"; its importance as the radiant point of the forces that cleared the way for the Negro on the New York stage cannot be overestimated.

Soon after our trio got settled down to work, we went to see Miss Irwin; the result of our visit was a commission to do the feature songs for her new play, *The Belle of Bridgeport*. This stroke of good fortune filled us with enthusiasm and confidence such as to make the conquest of New York seem a very easy matter. We also did the music for Peter Dailey's play, *Champagne Charlie*, and collaborated in writing a two-act musical comedy, *The Supper Club*, produced by the Sire Brothers at the Winter Garden. There were forty-odd people in the cast of *The Supper Club*, and among them were some of the best-known stars of the day: Virginia Earle, Ada Lewis, Josie Sadler, Toby Claude, Thomas Q. Seabrooke, Alexander Clarke, Junie McCree, and—not known at all then, but later of *Merry Widow* fame—Donald Brine (as his name appeared on the program). Bob Cole helped to stage the show, and taught Donald Brian his dance steps.

One day Bob came in breathless with excitement. He had just met Ben Teal on Broadway. Teal was then stage director for the Klaw and Erlanger productions, and Klaw and Erlanger were already the most powerful factors in the whole theatrical business. Many a time we had passed their offices on Broadway and looked longingly at those awe-inspiring names in gold on the windows across the whole front of the building. Teal had asked Bob, "Do you know where I can find two brothers named Johnson, who wrote a song called *Run, Brudder Possum, Run* for the Rogers Brothers show last season?" And Bob had answered, "I know just where I can put my hands on them for you."

Klaw and Erlanger had arranged to bring over from London the Drury Lane Pantomimes, and produce them in an Americanized version in New York. They were at the time engaged in preparations for the first of these productions, *The Sleeping Beauty and the Beast*. Mr. Teal had been much impressed by the little song we had done for the Rogers Brothers, and wanted us to collaborate on *The Sleeping Beauty*. We wrote three specialty numbers for that piece: *Tell Me, Dusky Maiden*, *Come Out, Dinah, on the Green*, and *Nobody's Lookin' but the Owl and the Moon*, and suddenly found ourselves programmed with "top-notchers" among the writers of musical comedy. *The Sleeping Beauty and the Beast* was produced at the old Broadway Theater, the only stage in New York that was adequate in size and facilities. The success of the pantomime was instantaneous and overwhelming. New York had some years before seen *The Black Crook* but never had it seen anything to compare with *The Sleeping Beauty.* Never before had it seen such massing of performers, such lavishness of scenery and costumes, and such marvels in stage effects. New York gazed wide-eyed at the fairy parliament, the witch's cave, the palace of crystal, the prismatic fountains and, above all, the flying ballet. I myself, even after seeing at rehearsals and backstage the mechanics of the ballet, never outgrew the wonder of watching those lovely ladies rise and float through the air and alight always with such consummate ease and grace on the pointed toes of one foot. The critics and reviewers found it necessary to go to the circus advertisements (the pre-view advertisements of the movies were not yet born) and appropriate such adjectives as "stupendous," "dazzling," "gorgeous," "amazing." Among the principals in *The Sleeping Beauty and the Beast* were Joseph Cawthorne, Harry Bulger, Charles J. Ross, Ella Snyder, Viola Gillette, and the Hengler Sisters; but all the individual performers were dwarfed by the production itself. These adaptations of the Drury Lane Pantomimes continued to be the grandest spectacle on the American stage until the opening of the New York Hippodrome in 1905.

Just as the spectacular effects of *The Sleeping Beauty* dwarfed the individual performers, it dwarfed the individual musical numbers. Our songs were well applauded but their sales did not begin to reach what we thought they ought to be. But during this summer of 1901 we wrote a song that was to send our reputation to the top and make us some money. The song was *The Maiden with the Dreamy Eyes*; it was sung by Anna Held in her play, *The Little Duchess. The Maiden with the Dreamy Eyes* fitted Miss Held perfectly, and was one of her greatest song successes. The popularity which the song achieved was due principally to her, but not wholly; a good share of it was due to Elsie Janis. Miss Janis was then about twelve years old, extraordinarily clever and very pretty. I remember that her mother brought her to our studio several times, when Rosamond played the song over and over while she committed it to memory and perfected her imitation of Anna Held singing it.

We had a theory that great popularity in the case of any song was based upon a definite and sufficient reason; that it was not merely accidental. A song might be popular because it was silly; but silliness sufficient to give a song popularity would have to be the result of a certain cleverness. In those days a song was popular and profitable only when it reached the point where people bought it to play and sing at home. Today, a popular song is just another dance tune. In those days the royalties of a writer depended largely upon the young fellow who would buy a copy of the song and take it along with him when he went to call on his girl, so that she would play it while the two of them gave vocal vent to the sentiments. Alas, the piano in the parlor and the girl who played it are about passed. In writing *The Maiden with the Dreamy Eyes* we gave particular consideration to these fundamentals. It needed little analysis to see that a song written in exclusive praise of blue eyes was cut off at once from about three-fourths of the possible chances for universal success; that it could make but faint appeal to the heart or pocketbook of a young man going to call on a girl with brown eyes or black eyes or gray eyes. So we worked on the chorus of our song until, without making it a catalogue, it was inclusive enough to enable any girl who sang it or to whom it was sung to fancy herself the maiden with the dreamy eyes. It ran:

> There are eyes of blue,
> There are brown eyes too,
> There are eyes of every size
> And eyes of every hue;
> But I surmise
> That if you are wise
> You'll be careful of the maiden
> With the dreamy eyes.

Anna Held's singing of *The Maiden with the Dreamy Eyes* naturally introduced us to her husband and manager, Florenz Ziegfeld, and led to our doing further work for her. Indeed, the next year Mr. Ziegfeld invited us to come for a week up to Thousand Islands, where he and Miss Held were summering, and try over some songs that we thought would be suitable for

her. I recall how explosively voluble Miss Held was about a
song, whether in praise or condemnation of it, and how un-
demonstrative was her husband. But if he finally drawled out,
"It's a good song, I think," it was enough to make us know
that he intended to use the piece and give it every possible
chance.

Mr. Ziegfeld was then on the threshold of his career as the
greatest of all American producers of musical plays, but I
doubt that there were many who recognized the master in
him; he was so utterly different from the dictatorial, obstreper-
ous musical producers of the period. He was always quiet and
unobtrusive. He was at that time so thin and meek-looking
that he struck me as a sort of semi-invalid. However, some
years later than the time of which I am writing he astonished
me by the amount of force and anger he could display. Rosamond and I had an appointment with him at his apartment in
the Ansonia, which occupied an entire section of one of the
floors of the hotel. We stepped into a waiting elevator and told
the operator that we wished to go up to Mr. Ziegfeld's apartment; and he informed us that he couldn't take us up; that we
should have to take the service elevator. We went over to the
desk and said to the man in charge that we had a business appointment with Mr. Ziegfeld, and that the elevator boy refused to take us up. The man at the desk coldly informed us
that the elevator boy was carrying out the rules of the hotel.
We then called Mr. Ziegfeld on the telephone and told him we
were downstairs but would not be able to come up because we
were denied the use of the elevators, except one designated
"service." Mr. Ziegfeld asked us to wait. He came down at
once and for some minutes had the stormiest kind of scene at
the desk. He protested and threatened. In protesting he said,
"These gentlemen have business with me; they are my guests;
they are my friends." The man at the desk pleaded that the
rule was not of his making and that it was not in his power to
change it. Thereupon, Mr. Ziegfeld escorted us to the elevator, ushered us in, stepped in himself and ordered the boy to
take him up to his apartment. Up we went. At the end of a
couple of hours, when our visit was over, he came out with us,
rang for the elevator, went through a like procedure; and
down we came.

This incident was indicative of Mr. Ziegfeld's attitude on race. As a producer, he not only recognized that there was Negro talent, but he dared to give that talent an opportunity. He did a brave and unprecedented thing when back in 1910 he made Bert Williams one of the principals of *The Follies*. Mutterings about quitting were made by some of the white principals, but when they learned that it was Mr. Ziegfeld's intention that Mr. Williams was to stay, whether they did or not, they stayed. Without exaggeration it may be said that when Ziegfeld put on *Show Boat*, the greatest of all his shows, he also put on the greatest colored musical show ever staged.

All in all, the summer of 1901 promised much. In August we gathered together the manuscripts of fifteen songs and took them to Jos. W. Stern and Co., our publishers. We talked the list over with the two partners, Mr. Stern and Mr. Marks, and pointed out to them that most of the songs were slated to be used in productions of the 1901–2 season. The result of our conference was the signing of a three-year contract to write for publication exclusively by Jos. W. Stern and Co., with a cash guarantee to be paid to us monthly and to be deducted from our semi-annual royalty accounts. There were, of course, other Negro song writers in New York. One of them, Gusse L. Davis, was at the height of his popularity and more widely known than we. The whole country and a good part of the world were singing his famous ballads: *In A Lighthouse by The Sea*, *Down in Poverty Row*, *The Fatal Wedding*, *The Baggage Coach Ahead*. But we had achieved a certain uniqueness due to the entrée we had gained to the Broadway musical stage; and our contract with Jos. W. Stern and Co. increased our uniqueness, for it was, I believe, the first contract of its kind ever executed.

During these months that we were in New York the rebuilding of Jacksonville was going ahead feverishly. Stanton was being rebuilt, but I learned that the new building would not be ready in October; then that it would not be ready in November or even in December. Finally, I received word from the board of education that the first week in February was set for the opening. This postponement was no disappointment to me; I was too eager to see the shows in which we had music.

The Sleeping Beauty was to open in November and *The Supper Club* in December. The others opened on the road. I was also anxious, for reasons that are plain, to get my royalty statement, due in January, before going South.

We spent these early winter months pleasantly enough; our only handicap being a shortage of cash. Our main revenue was from our publishers. Bob Cole's circumstances were far more precarious than Rosamond's and mine, for he had a mother and four sisters to support. Furthermore, he had dissolved his theatrical partnership with Billy Johnson, and was not going out with a show for the first time in ten years or more. Rosamond had also cast the die. He had decided, win or lose, that he was going to try his fortune in New York. I hesitated. I argued that the decisions reached by Bob and Rosamond did not demand as much courage as the one confronting me; that they had put down work which they could freely take up again; while I should be giving up a definite position that I could not expect to get back. I decided to return to Jacksonville. I arranged with Rosamond that while I was drawing salary in Jacksonville he could draw and use my share of the monthly stipend from our publishers.

About the middle of January we went down to our publishers to get our royalty statement. We received the statement, but no royalties. We had not broken even; we found that we were in debt to the firm for nearly $1300. We went back to our studio in the Marshall a discouraged and disheartened trio. We discussed the situation until late at night—"The songs had not yet begun to sell." That was evident. "They were good songs, well placed, and would sell during the height of the season." That was problematic. We were worried. But there is nothing like youth. The gloom was lifted and we began to laugh when I suggested that, perhaps, Stern and Co. were more worried than we.

A few days before I left for Jacksonville, Bob and Rosamond received a call to entertain for a party at Sherry's, then at Fifth Avenue and 44th Street. They were to get one hundred dollars for the job. Of course, they were jubilant. They decided to sing and play only original compositions, and spent several hours rehearsing certain of our songs. While they were rehearsing, in walked Theodore Pankey. Pankey waxed so enthusiastic over what was going on that Bob and Rosamond concluded to take him along for good measure; and mighty good measure he proved to be. The three of them arrayed in evening clothes started for Sherry's, and I went to bed. About four o'clock in the morning the three of them roused me out of bed. They were excited and hilarious. Each one had with him a quart of champagne brought from the party. They roused Jimmie Marshall, our genial proprietor, and made him bring up sandwiches; then the five of us, while the "entertainers" talked about the party, sat and drank champagne till the bottles were empty.—It was a grand party—Lillian Russell was there in all her beauty—the vivacious Edna Wallace Hopper was there—a dozen other stars and a dozen influential producers and managers. But the high spot in the recital related to Pankey. He had sung *Li'l Gal* to a lady who was seated on a gentleman's knee. The lady begged him to sing it over and over. At the finish the gentleman peeled off a hundred-dollar bill and handed it to him—an action, without doubt, prompted more by interest in the lady than by interest in the song.

We were all elated and voted the party a momentous affair. For Bob and Rosamond it proved so to be.

XVII

I REACHED Jacksonville a few days before the date scheduled for the opening of Stanton. The first thing I did was to inspect the new building. I don't think I ever saw a more hideous structure. It was a huge, crude, three-story frame building that looked more like a mill or a granary than like a schoolhouse. I came in for some criticism from the colored citizens who felt that it would have been different had I been on the ground when it was being planned and built. I was forced to admit to myself that this criticism was well founded. I talked with members of the board of education and learned that their plans contemplated doing away with Stanton as a central school, and for that reason they had erected a purely temporary building. The Stanton plot was an entire block in one of the best sections of the city. The blocks to the north were occupied by the residences of some of the wealthiest white citizens in Jacksonville, who, undoubtedly, had for years

looked upon the school as a nuisance and considered it a factor that held back the more rapid increase in value of their
neighboring property. The necessity of rebuilding the city
gave an opportunity to have the school moved, and they
brought pressure on the board of education to have this done.
Similar situations have risen in, probably, every southern community. The town grows and a certain site becomes "too
good" or "too valuable" for the use of Negroes; then by one
means or another the Negroes are evicted and shoved farther
out and back. The school board planned to sell the Stanton
plot as soon as it could do so profitably or, failing in that, to
use it as the site for a white school and to build in each of the
Negro districts a schoolhouse that would be "more accessi-
ble." These plans meant the destruction of a tradition and important element in the life of Jacksonville Negro citizens and
the sweeping away of one of its main centers of pride and affection. Furthermore, they probably meant the end of a Negro
high school.

There was, however, a fact athwart the course that had been
laid out; a fact of which no member of the school board
seemed to be aware. I presented it as promptly as I could, and
it was no less important a fact than that the Stanton plot did
not belong to the board of education or the city or the county
or the state. It had been deeded to a board of trustees made up
of white and colored men as a site for a Negro school by Governor Hart, a Reconstruction governor of Florida. I had from
childhood been familiar with this beginning of Stanton's history. When I was a small boy, the old and deserted Hart mansion stood in the center of the adjoining block south of the
school. I remember that frequently we used to run the risk of
punishment by going over to the Hart place to hunt for berries
and chinquapins during recess. And I knew it was the man
who had lived in the old house who had given us the land for
our school. This deed, furthermore, stated that, if the property
ceased to be used for the purpose of a Negro school, it would
revert to the heirs of the Hart estate. In the years, the board of
education had changed so many times that sight had been lost
of the original conditions under which it held the Stanton
property. A search of the records verified these conditions. Indeed, the whole matter worked out for the best: the property

rights of the colored people in the property were clarified and settled once and for all; and even the temporariness of the building the board had erected proved a blessing in disguise, for it was not long before the structure was condemned as unsafe and the school board erected the modern and beautiful Stanton High School which stands in its stead, such a building as it would not have built at an earlier time.

I settled down to hard work with the school. I gave almost no time to the practice of law; I no longer had sufficient interest in it. Indeed, D—— and I had about reached the mutual understanding that he would go it alone. I wrote nothing, that is, for Broadway; perhaps, my brother's absence was responsible for my lack of incentive. I had the year before been elected president of the State Teacher's Association, and I did my best to make the meeting that was to be held in Fernandina the latter part of May a success. I was actually and rapidly resigning myself to the idea that teaching was to be my main vocation, and any other pursuit secondary. Those certain qualities inherited from my father were shaping my ideas and behavior. Moreover, the girl with the forehead of a Madonna and the mouth of a Thais, whom I had seen at the meeting of the teacher's association in Tampa several years before, had come to Jacksonville on a visit. In Tampa I had adored her rather at a distance; in Jacksonville I was with her almost daily. Her disturbing beauty shook my ambitions for a New York career, and more and more made the odds against winning seem longer and less worth taking. I wrote to the State Superintendent of Education and made arrangements to take an examination at Tallahassee in the coming summer for a life certificate, so that I might continue teaching, with exemption from all further examinations.

I had been back in Jacksonville a couple of months when I received a letter from Rosamond saying that one of the managers who had been present at the party at Sherry's had engaged him and Bob to appear in vaudeville, singing and playing their original compositions. This meant an end of their immediate money worries, for they started at a salary of three hundred dollars a week. But it seemed to me that this stroke of fortune for them so altered our partnership plans that my individual chances were greatly reduced; so, amidst suffusing thoughts of love in a cottage, I applied myself as doggedly as I could to preparation for my examination.

Stanton closed after a short term of four months, but I did not leave for New York. I spent the greater part of each day studying; and I have never set a tougher task for myself. Despite the state of my heart, my mind kept running off to Broadway and the group at the Marshall. I was disturbed by the thought that my caution amounted to cowardice. Why not play the game, win or lose? One very hot afternoon I was stretched in a hammock boning Vergil's *Æneid*, one of the subjects I was to be examined in, when the postman's whistle blew, and my sister, a moment later, brought me up two letters. They were both from my brother. I studied the postmarks to learn which one had been mailed at the earlier hour, and found that the two had been mailed at the same time. I fingered them a moment, and decided to open the lighter letter first. It contained a brief note and a money order for eighty-odd dollars royalty. I then opened the second. It contained a long communication and a money order for four hundred dollars, more of the same royalty money. The cost of an extra money order was Rosamond's method of perpetrating a practical joke; I don't know why he surmised that I should open the right envelope first and not spoil the joke. The letter was written in high spirits:—*The Maiden with the Dreamy Eyes* was selling—the other songs were beginning to move—in the January to June period we had earned enough to pay off all our indebtedness to our publishers and net nearly fifteen hundred dollars—the vaudeville act was a hit, and was now a headline attraction—why in the world was I hanging on down in Jacksonville?

"Why in the world was I hanging on in Jacksonville?" I threw Vergil the length of the porch, sprang out of the hammock, and rushed downstairs. I emptied several dollars in silver from my pockets into my mother's lap; then did a dance round her chair. The more curious my mother and sister became about the cause of my behavior, the wilder became my antics. I finally sobered down enough to ask them to help me pack for New York. I hurried down to the Post Office and cashed my two money orders. What sweet money it was! It was sweeter than money merely worked for. This was money gained for materializing the intangible. I had actually minted some rather inconsequential dreams, and the process seemed to possess an element of magic. This, for me, considerable sum gave me a larger measure of satisfaction than any money I had hitherto earned.

When I reached New York I met several surprises. I was, first of all, surprised at the opulence of Bob and Rosamond; at their clothes, modest in pattern and design but nevertheless expensive; at their dozen pairs of shoes each; at the abundance of their shirts and ties and socks. I felt like a country cousin. They were quick to assure me that this outlay was part of their stock in trade. I was also surprised to see that they had taken the front and middle rooms connecting with the back room in which Rosamond and I had lived, and that Bob himself had moved over to the Marshall. The whole floor provided ample sleeping quarters for the three of us, after reserving the back room exclusively as a workshop. My biggest surprise was Bob and Rosamond's act. They were at the time playing an engagement as headliners of the bill at Keith's 14th Street Theater, then one of the principal vaudeville houses of the country. Of course, I went at once to see them.

The act was unlike anything ever done by Negro performers; it was quiet, finished, and artistic to the minutest details. The two entered dressed in evening clothes—they did make a handsome appearance—and talking casually about the program they had best give in entertaining a party to which they were on their way. Rosamond seating himself at the piano, suggested that they open with an instrumental number, and proceeded to play Paderewski's *Minuet*, which went over well. Rosamond then suggested further that they ought to follow with a little classic song. Bob demurred slightly, but Rosamond went ahead and sang *Still wie die Nacht* in German. The singing of this song never failed to gain applause; perhaps, somewhat for the reason that Dr. Johnson assigned for admiration at seeing a dog walk on his hind legs. Bob then expressed the fear that classic music might be what the people at the party (in fact, the audience) would least like to hear, and suggested the singing of their own little song, *Mandy*. From this point on the program consisted of original songs, sung one after another, Rosamond playing the accompaniments.

And novel accompaniments they were, for he was among the first musicians in America to go beyond the one-two-three and one-two-three-four styles of arrangements and to adapt counterpoint to the accompaniments of popular songs. A comparison of the arrangements of *The Maiden with the Dreamy Eyes*, *Under the Bamboo Tree*, and *The Congo Love Song* with those of other songs of that period will substantiate this statement. The interludes were furnished by Bob's graceful soft shoe dancing to the choruses played almost pianissimo. Those who remember their performance, certainly, do not forget the pleasing manner in which Bob Cole handled a white silk handkerchief, both in singing and dancing. This was the framework of an act that these two men played for seven or eight years with tremendous success in the United States and Europe. No small part of the success of the act was due to the fact that its planned simplicity and studied naïveté gave it the spontaneous air of an impromptu. This was the act that started a vogue of acts consisting of two men in dress suits and a piano.

Bob and Rosamond were now regularly playing two shows a day; nevertheless, we began again at once on our work of composition. Much of the time I worked alone, but the three of us worked together, sometimes in the mornings and sometimes late at nights. We worked the harder because the team was booked to play the Orpheum Circuit in the winter, and that meant playing to the Pacific Coast and back. One of the first songs we wrote in this period was *Under the Bamboo Tree*. We saw George Lederer, and he introduced us to Marie Cahill, who was playing in his *Sally in Our Alley*. Miss Cahill was delighted with the song and began using it as soon as an orchestration could be made. Before *Sally in Our Alley* was closed, Miss Cahill had set the world singing *Under the Bamboo Tree*. This song led to more work for her, and a warm relationship that has continued up to the present time.

Before I realized it, the fall of the year was on me and I was confronted with the necessity of deciding whether or not I was going back to Jacksonville as the principal of Stanton. Making the decision was by no means a simple matter. I weighed the question up and down: the prospects looked bright; I was making headway along a line that seemed to lead straight to the center of the American light opera world; *The Maiden with the Dreamy Eyes* was selling; several other songs had begun to move; and *Under the Bamboo Tree* was very promising. But, as yet, our compositions had not brought in sufficient money to live on. True, Bob and Rosamond were earning a dependable wage, but I could not and would not put myself in a position where I might become their pensioner; perhaps it would be wisest to continue my school work and come to New York in the summers as I had been doing. This last consideration was strengthened by my realization of the fact that our combination was no longer a trio working as one man, but a majority and a minority. While I was debating these questions, I wrote a letter to my father telling him that I was thinking of giving up my position in Jacksonville and remaining in New York. I wrote a somewhat similar letter to D———. My father wrote a very fatherly letter in reply, advising me to be careful, to think well before I gave up my position; but he left it for me to use my own judgment. D——— advised strongly against the step; that if I wanted to give up schoolteaching— and he had small reverence for that occupation—I ought to devote myself entirely to law; that Jacksonville was one of the best fields in the country for a colored lawyer. I also received letters from several friends who had somehow become privy to the plans I was contemplating, giving me additional advice. One of these blankly asked, "What's the matter with you, thinking of giving up a life position to take a chance, and a Negro's chance, at writing music in New York? Have you gone crazy?"

No, I had not quite gone crazy, but my mind for a while was whirling in a void of indecision. But time put an end to that, and the day arrived when I had to act. I sat down and wrote out my resignation. I carried it in my pocket through the following day; then, at night while walking up Broadway with Bob and Rosamond I stopped suddenly at a mail box, dropped it in, and burned my bridges. As the letter dropped into the box, a load dropped from my shoulders. I at once became aware of an expanse of freedom I had not felt before. Immediately it seemed that the goal of my efforts was no longer marked by a limit just a little way in front of my eyes but reached out somewhere toward infinity. From the thought that the things I had already done, I had done, perhaps, fairly well, I got a solid satisfaction; but stepping off my beaten road on to a path that led I knew not just where gave me a thrill.

In January, a few days before Bob and Rosamond started their western tour, we went down to our publishers for an accounting. We went with high expectations. *The Maiden with the Dreamy Eyes* and *Under the Bamboo Tree* were popular hits, and some of our other songs appeared to be selling well. With my expectations were mingled fervent hopes; for, although Rosamond had now in turn allowed me to draw his share of the monthly royalty advance, I was finding it hard to make both ends meet. We were handed our statement with the sales of the songs itemized and advances deducted, and a check for the balance due. Bob took the check and statement, and the three of us glanced quickly at the one then studied the other. We were disappointed. We felt that the songs should have made a better showing, and so expressed ourselves. Bob spoke strongly. There were words, some of them hot. Bob threw the check on the table, and the three of us walked out. We walked the half-block to Broadway, turned in at the old Continental Hotel, went into the bar, and ordered a drink. We needed it, for by the time we got that far we realized that we had actually scorned a check for close to six thousand dollars. The drink made me philosophically detached, and I mused over the matter. I made a nimble computation which showed that I had contemptuously tossed aside a sum of money accruing in six months that it would have taken me two years and six months to earn as principal of Stanton—and I marveled that such a thing could really be.

We remained away from our publishers a couple of days, but the matter was patched up and Bob and Rosamond started for the Coast. But the rumor spread that Cole and Johnson Brothers had had a serious breach with their publishers, and offers came to us from several other houses. One of the leading publishing firms in the city sent an urgent request for me to come and see them. I went, and the head of the firm kept me in conference a long time. He emphasized to me the advantage of being on the staff of their older, larger, and richer concern. He spread in front of me a contract—a very liberal one—and offered me a pen, together with a certified check for ten thousand dollars against future royalties, drawn to my order. I could not resist studying the check curiously; and, without the aid of a drink, I was again forced to marvel that such things could really be. But I declined to take the pen. I parried with the remark that my partners were out of the city and that sole action on my part would not bind them. The publisher said he knew my partners were away, but that he would be satisfied to have me sign the contract and turn over the manuscripts of such new songs as were in my possession and to wait for their signatures. I called to his attention the fact that we were still under contract. He smilingly observed that grounds were sometimes found on which contracts could be broken. But the breaking of a contract did not appear to me to be so simple or advantageous a matter as it seemed to appear to him, and I came out leaving the unsigned document and the ten-thousand-dollar check. I wrote to Rob and Rosamond about the offer; they fully agreed with my view.

One of the first things I did after we cashed our royalty check was to send my father a thousand dollars with the request that he invest it in Jacksonville property for me. I was proud to do this, and I gloated over the effect it would have on the friend who had written to ask if I had gone crazy. This was a precedent, however, that I did not follow regularly enough.

We never regretted not making the attempt to break our contract. Our relations with our publishers became entirely cordial again. At the end of another six months they gave us a check for an amount more than double that of the previous check, and we were at a height of popularity and success equal, at least, to that of any other writers of popular songs in America. We had a clean business record and a list of hits that included: *The Maiden with the Dreamy Eyes*; *Mandy, Won't You Let Me Be Your Beau*; *Nobody's Lookin' but the Owl and the Moon*; *Tell Me, Dusky Maiden*; *The Old Flag Never Touched the Ground*; *My Castle on the Nile*; *Under the Bamboo Tree*; and *Oh, Didn't He Ramble*. We had written a new song for Miss Cahill, *The Congo Love Song*, that she was to sing and to make as famous as *Under the Bamboo Tree*; and there were others still to follow. In the fullness of our vogue there were times when songs of ours were being sung in three or four current musical productions on Broadway. We managed to break in even upon the rather exclusive Weber and Fields stage with a song for Lillian Russell. The reviewers built up for us a sort of reputation as physicians for ailing musical plays. We got used to seeing notices and paragraphs and articles about ourselves in the press of New York and other cities; but the appearance of a four-column-wide cartoon of the three of us in *The Evening World* did shake us up a bit. In truth, we became, in a measure, Broadway personalities. I remember D——'s utter amazement when one night during a visit of his to the city, as he and I were walking up the famous street, a little newsboy ran up to me shouting, "Mr. Johnson, you want the latest edition?" I didn't want it, but I bought it. All of this seems to me now to belong to a distant and distinct existence.

With Bob and Rosamond away so much of the time, even New York frequently seemed lonely. I wrote and jotted down ideas for new work; I read a great deal; I went to the theater as a part of my job; nearly every Saturday night, because it was popular price night, I went to the opera, and in that way heard the whole Metropolitan repertory, but, even so, I found time on my hands. It was then that I discovered an explanation as good as any of whatever success that has come my way: I discovered my abhorrence of "spare time." I thereupon cast about to find a means of using up all I had of it in some worthwhile manner. I lit upon doing some studying at Columbia University. I secured a catalogue, and determined to take up courses in English and the history and development of the drama. I decided to go up to the University and talk the matter over with Professor Brander Matthews, whom I knew by his writings. I was flattered to find that Professor Matthews knew of my work in musical comedy, a phase of the theater that he followed and studied closely. My reception was extremely cordial. As soon as the greetings were over and I had taken a seat, he produced his cigarette case and offered me a smoke. For the life of me, I could not prevent the inculcated inhibitions of my years at Atlanta University from rushing out in full force upon me. I accepted the cigarette and smoked it, but it was difficult for me not to feel that I was breaking school rules. Of course, I had smoked constantly since my graduation from Atlanta, but to be smoking with a professor in his office

on the university grounds struck me for the time as being not
only incongruous but slightly unholy.

This meeting was the beginning of a warm and lasting
friendship between Brander Matthews and me. He talked to
me a great deal about the musical comedy stage and the important people connected with it. In his lectures he frequently
set me in an enviable light before the class. When we reached
the classic drama of Spain, he often called on my knowledge of
the language in dealing with the plays in the original. When
we came to the contemporary American stage he cited me a
good many times as a journeyman in the theater. I was fascinated with my work under him. I was especially impressed
with his catholicity, his freedom from pedantry, and his common sense in talking about the theater. I believe that he
shocked most of us in his class when he declared that the best
plays of Weber and Fields were the same sort of thing as the
theater of Aristophanes; that, except for the fact that no Weber
and Fields playwright ever attempted to imitate the occasional
lofty lyrical flights of the Greek comedian, the two theaters
were comparable.

I continued my work at Columbia for three years, not allowing for an interruption of several months in the spring of 1905.
Before I left I talked with Professor Matthews about my more
serious work, and showed him the draft of the first two chapters of a book which, I said to him, I proposed to call *The Autobiography of an Ex-Colored Man*. He read the manuscript and
told me he liked the idea and the proposed title, and that I was
wise in writing about the thing I knew best. I also showed him
some of my poems. After he had looked them through, he
gave me a note to Professor Harry Thurston Peck, who was
then editing *The Bookman*. Professor Peck took two poems for
the magazine, and appeared to be much interested in the
things I was planning to do; and talked with me quite a while
in his precise, punctilious manner.

I saw Professor Peck only once after that interview, about
ten years later. I was on 43rd Street, just east of Fifth Avenue,
and about to enter the offices of G. Ricordi and Co., the music publishers, when I saw a man approaching, walking in a
dazed sort of way. As he came nearer I recognized him to be
Harry Thurston Peck. He was dressed, as was his custom, in a

frock coat and silk hat, but both were extremely shabby. He passed, looking neither right nor left; he seemed entirely oblivious to his surroundings. I felt a strong impulse to go after him and speak to him. I knew something of the difficulties he had had at Columbia, and which had led to his severance from the University, and it appeared as though he was in great need. The thought flashed through my mind that I might offer him some little help. But I hesitated, something held me back, and some intangible apprehensions intervened; it may have been the shadow of race; and he passed on. A day or two later I read that he had committed suicide in his room in a cheap lodging-house at Stamford, Connecticut. I never recall this incident without a pang of regret that I did not speak the words that were in my mind to say to him.

XVIII

SUCCESS is a heady beverage. It can be as deleterious as any alcoholic drink. It seems to me that a man drunk with success is more of a fool than the maudlin inebriate; and, certainly, he is more dangerous to himself and to others. Success is safe only when it comes slowly, and even then is not entirely so. We had been struggling for four years; yet, when success did come, it seemed sudden. It magically blotted out the memory of all our disappointments and defeats and carried us up into a region above doubts and fears, to that height where success of itself begets success. There is a line in the blues which runs:

I got de world in a bottle an' de stopper—in-a ma hand.

No single line of poetry that I know of contains a more graphic figure to suggest the reaction to success.

I regard it as pardonable that we were made tipsy; why we did not get drunk I do not know. As for Rosamond and myself, I might definitely attribute our salvation to that precept of Solomon, "Train up a child in the way he should go, and when he is old he will not depart from it," were it not for the fact that so many times its teachings appear to have failed. And, furthermore, Solomon gives not even an intimation of what may happen in the years between. Or I might claim that

I was safeguarded by a patent or latent strength of character; but I should be hard put to it to analyze satisfactorily for myself "strength of character." It is probable that one of the reasons why I did not fly off at a tangent was that I was not able to feel completely that our success was real. This trait has persisted in me through all the years of my manhood. When success with me has seemed brightest, there has never failed to lurk somewhere the shadow of doubt. Always, the sense of security is greater in the struggle to succeed. For many years I have been disturbed by a frequently recurring dream, the pattern of which is: I am taking a terribly difficult examination, on the passing of which my future and my means of existence depend; I awake before I know the result of the test, and sometimes seconds pass in an effort to shake off the dream and seize the reality. A psychoanalyst could, I suppose, tell the significance of this dream, but I never consulted one about it.

With prosperity, we added a degree or so of luxury to our mode of living. We bought furniture, books, and "objects of art," and had the set-up supervised by a professional decorator. Across one wall was stretched a seine, to which was attached with clips our collection of autographed photographs. This collection grew to include nearly all the important persons connected with the musical theater. Our studio now became a center for both Negro and white artists. Among the principals in Broadway musical plays who were singing our music, there were those who found it pleasant to come to the studio to rehearse their numbers. We also began to give parties. Our first big party was given for Miss May Irwin and friends she might wish to bring. She brought eight or ten persons; and we had invited about an equal number of colored guests. The party was a success. One evening we gave a party for G. P. Huntley and principals in the English company playing *Three Little Maids* at Daly's. Several times we entertained Charles Hawtrey, later by the grace of his good friend, King Edward VII, Sir Charles Hawtrey, when he was playing *The Man from Blankney's*. This entertaining entailed considerable expenditure, but we justified it to ourselves under the head of publicity. No doubt, it did bring us returns in publicity, and a certain éclat.

Be that as it may; in the artistic world, anything, from wearing strange-looking clothes to committing manslaughter, may be justified under the head of "publicity."

The fame of the Marshall spread. We lent Jimmie Marshall money to enable him to acquire and adapt the twin house adjoining, and, so, double the capacity of the hotel. Bert Williams and two or three other leading Negro performers and musicians moved in and made the Marshall their home. It was now one of the most interesting places in New York. During this period, Rosamond and I brought our mother and sister north several summers. We brought our father up one summer; he had not been to New York in more than twenty-five years; he had a great time going about with us and pointing out spots where old landmarks used to stand.

We continued to ride the crest of the wave. *The Ladies' Home Journal* then made it a custom to publish musical pieces as a part of the regular edition of the magazine; and Edward Bok, the editor, asked us to contribute. I went over to see Mr. Bok, and made arrangements, with the consent of our publishers, to have certain of our compositions appear in that way. We published, in all, seven or eight pieces in *The Ladies' Home Journal*. Some while after the first conference, I had another talk with Mr. Bok, and he showed me a letter which had given him, it appeared, one of the biggest laughs of his life. He had accepted a song that had been submitted to him by a young Negro composer in Georgia. Following the acceptance, he announced in the magazine that in a subsequent issue such a song would appear. Promptly he received a letter from a white woman in a little town also in Georgia protesting against it. She declared that no Negro had the musical skill or the artistic taste to interpret even his own race, much less the ability to do anything worthy of going into the pages of *The Ladies' Home Journal*. She ended her letter by imploring Mr. Bok to "give us some more of those little Negro classics by Cole and Johnson Brothers." The very serious-looking Mr. Bok read me the letter and laughed uproariously over it. I laughed too; but my laughter was tempered by the thought that there was anybody in the country, notwithstanding the locality being Georgia, who, knowing anything at all about them, did not know that Cole and Johnson Brothers were Negroes.

◆

We received another call from Klaw and Erlanger; the call
this time did not come through Ben Teal, who was no longer
with the concern, but directly from A. L. Erlanger himself, the
Grand Mogul of the theatrical business. We had a conference
with Mr. Erlanger, and he told us pointedly what he wanted,
and that was to have us write exclusively for the Klaw and Erlanger productions. There was some question in our minds as
to whether it would be more advantageous to do this or remain free lances. Our publishers felt strongly that we should
hold ourselves open to work for all producers. We finally did
sign a contract for three years, which stipulated the payment to
us of a definite sum monthly and, in addition, a flat sum for
each ensemble number; the royalty rights in all our numbers
being reserved to us.

This arrangement made us members of the Klaw and Erlanger producing staff and brought us into intimate contact
with Mr. Erlanger. When a new play was being planned, the
staff was called by Mr. Erlanger to meet with him in his offices
as often as was necessary—possibly more often than was necessary. We met with John J. McNally, Herbert Gresham, Ned
Wayburn, and Fred Solomon. Ernest D'Auban was present if
there was to be a ballet in the production. Mr. Erlanger completely dominated these meetings. His word was law, and he
brooked no opposition. Members of the staff would offer
counter-suggestions but none ever flatly disagreed with him.
He was a man of tremendous energy. Short of stature and
somewhat portly, he would walk with the pompous strut natural to men of his build and temperament, up and down the
room, carrying a lighted or unlighted cigar in his mouth at a
forty-five-degree angle, and lay down for us what he wanted
done. He impressed me as possessing certain Napoleonic qualities. At times he made himself a bit absurd—a failing common
to all Napoleonic figures—by pre-empting more of the creative field of the theater than he could hold, and attempting to
picture and outline a whole play in a few words. He would
pace up and down saying:—Now, over here I want this—And
over there I want that—Then we'll do such and such things—
And after that such and such other things. At these times an

Bob Cole, James and Rosamond Johnson

imperceptible smile ran round the members of the staff, and
we made little or no mental note of what he was saying; for
these fragmentary suggestions usually had no value.

When a play was nearing the time for production, Mr. Erlanger frequently attended rehearsals; and he carried his dictatorial manner there. He would stand at the back of the theater
watching, then suddenly come striding down the aisle to the
stage, storming at directors and performers and yelling out his
dissatisfaction at the way in which things were being done.
These outbursts never failed to upset everybody concerned
with the making of the play, but nobody dared to flare back.
Only once did I see such an incredible thing take place. We
were down to the final rehearsals of *Humpty Dumpty*, another
of the Drury Lane Pantomimes, and everybody was on edge.
There was a part in the piece that called for a better-trained
voice than was, in those days, easily found in the ranks of musical play performers, and a young lady who, as I remember,
was the soprano soloist in a prominent church choir had been
engaged to sing it. Rosamond had worked with her assiduously, and she knew the score well and sang it beautifully. But
in these rehearsals before a cold jury she became timid, nervous, and frightened. Her voice quivered and broke constantly.
Mr. Erlanger yelled his dissatisfaction with her several times.
Finally, he rushed down the aisle shouting, "Rossmore (the
name by which he always called my brother), we'll have to take
that woman out and get somebody who can sing the part."
Rosamond jumped up from the piano and shouted back,
"How in the world can you expect her to sing it when you
keep yelling at her?" A silence, I judge, the same in kind if not
in duration as that recorded in Rev. viii, 1, fell on the theater.
Mr. Erlanger was for an instant the most surprised man in New
York. He turned and walked slowly to the back of the theater
muttering under his breath something that sounded like
"Well, I'll be damned." The silence gave Rosamond opportu-
nity to realize the enormity of his act.

And yet, A. L. Erlanger had a considerate kindly side. We
had been with the K & E institution but a short while when
Mr. Erlanger called us for a conference in his offices at eight
o'clock in the morning. We got in about fifteen minutes late.
As we entered, he took out his watch saying, "Good morning,

boys. For what hour did I call this conference?" We somewhat
lamely offered as an excuse the fact that we had worked late
the night before, feeling that we were in for a sharp reproof.
Instead, Mr. Erlanger said to us rather gently, "No matter how
late I work, I am up at six, riding in the park at seven, and at
my desk by eight. When you are dealing with *busy* men, never
be late for an appointment. Try and remember that." I never
forgot it. We saw little of Mr. Klaw, the other half of the firm.
I saw him periodically at times when I went to collect money
due us. He was a quiet, unobtrusive man, who seemed to hide
himself behind the dark luxuriant whiskers he then wore. He
had the reputation among his associates of being scholarly. It
appeared that he paid no attention to the production of plays,
but devoted himself to the business end of the enterprise; and
that meant, principally, looking after the percentage tribute
that flowed into the coffers of Klaw and Erlanger from companies all over the United States and Canada that had been
booked through their offices.

Humpty Dumpty, for which we did the lyrics and music, was
the first play produced in Klaw and Erlanger's new New Amsterdam Theater, at the time the last word in New York theaters. We also did the lyrics and music for the show that
opened their Aerial Theater, atop the New Amsterdam. In this
show Fay Templeton scored a popular success with one of our
songs called *Fishing*. Another play for which we did the lyrics
and music opened another new Klaw and Erlanger theater; it
was *In Newport*, and was produced at the Liberty Theater. In
In Newport we got the first setback since gaining recognition.
The play had a good cast; in it were Peter Dailey, Joseph
Coyne, Lee Harrison, the beautiful Virginia Earle, and the
temperamental Fay Templeton; but the work had been hastily
and carelessly done. Our part of it was pretty far below the
standard we had been maintaining. On the opening night I
stood back of the orchestra rows and watched the performance; I thought the play was pretty poor. As it went along, I
stepped over to where Mr. Erlanger stood and asked him what
he thought of it. He answered tersely, "Rotten." For once, at
least, his critical judgment was sound. We were called the next
day into conference. The case of *In Newport* was discussed and
diagnosed, but there seemed to be nothing the doctors could

prescribe to save it. Mr. Erlanger decided to withdraw it at the end of the week. In the conference Mr. Erlanger remarked, "We've got some mighty good reports from a show Georgie Cohan has on the road. I think we'll cancel his road dates and bring him in to the Liberty." He did as he said, and George Cohan came to the Liberty Theater with *Little Johnny Jones.* George Cohan's eccentric manner of singing and dancing captured Broadway; and furthermore he had two such songs to sing as *Give My Regards to Broadway* and *I'm a Yankee-Doodle Dandy.* Within forty-eight hours after the closing of *In Newport*, George Cohan had started on his rapid rise in the American theater.

We got an idea for a genuine American pantomime, which we worked on for a while; then took to Mr. Erlanger an outline of the play with some of the musical numbers in a finished state. Our idea was to make a pantomime out of the *Uncle Remus* stories. Mr. Erlanger thought well of it; so well that he said that I should go to Atlanta to talk with Joel Chandler Harris and see if suitable arrangements for rights could be made. I have lost all recollection of what would explain my not going to Atlanta to see Mr. Harris or our failure to push the idea. I am puzzled, because we had the greatest resources in the country back of us, and, without doubt, *Uncle Remus*, made into an artistic music spectacle, would have been successful at that time. The idea still has possibilities.

While we were with Klaw and Erlanger, we observed that through an organized agency—the Southern Society, if I remember correctly—certain leaflets were being placed, before performances, in the seats of New York theaters. The purpose was to disseminate anti-Negro propaganda, and in particular to rouse and strengthen sentiment against Negroes being seated in any part of a theater, except the top gallery. We brought this to Mr. Erlanger's attention, and he at once issued orders that stopped it in all the theaters in New York under his control.

It was difficult to see why this agency should display such solicitude, for the conditions were already humiliating enough. In the "Broadway" houses it was the practice to sell Negroes first balcony seats, but, if their race was plainly discernible, to refuse to sell them seats in the orchestra. (The

Metropolitan Opera House, Carnegie Hall, and in general, the
East Side and West Side theaters were exceptions.) The same
practice was and still is common in most of the cities of the
North; it is not necessary to mention the practice in Southern
cities. In Washington, where race discrimination is hardly less
than in any city in the South, Negroes are not allowed to enter
the National Theater; nor was that rule broken when *The
Green Pastures* recently played a two weeks' engagement at
that house. In that case the colored people made strong
protest, and the management compromised by setting aside
one night "for Negroes only," stating that even this concession
would offend many of their regular patrons. Just how those
patrons could feel like that and at the same time be able to feel
in any degree the beauty and ecstasy conveyed through the
acting of Richard B. Harrison and the great Negro cast of the
play presents a mystery of the human soul which only God or
perhaps the devil can explain.

Some years ago one of my old Jacksonville friends, a physician, came to New York on a visit. My wife and I thought it
would give him a real treat to take him to see a show. We
bought orchestra seats several days in advance for an operetta
playing at one of the Shubert houses. When we reached the
theater, my wife passed through the gate first, I followed with
the tickets and my friend followed me. The ticket taker probably was not aware that we were a group of colored people until we had passed through. Inside, each usher we approached
was "very busy," and we had to find our own seats. After we
were seated, I signaled an usher, asking her to bring us programs. She never brought them. A gentleman seated next to
me courteously proffered the use of his program. As the lights
were being lowered for the first act, I felt some one tap me on
the shoulder from the row behind. I turned. A man from the
box office was bending over my chair.

"Have you coupons for these seats?" he asked.

"Yes," I replied.

"May I see them?"

"Certainly."

I held the coupons up to him, displaying the numbers, but
kept them tightly gripped between my thumb and forefinger.

"I'd like to look at them."

"You're looking at them."

"You don't think I want to steal them?"

"I don't intend to give you the chance."

He went away. Had I handed him the coupons he would have rushed off with them to the box office, then come back and told us that there had been a mistake made about the tickets and that we would have to give up our seats. I was determined not to undergo that injustice and humiliation, so held fast to my coupons. But I was so blind with anger and resentment that I did not actually see the first act. In relation to the whole scheme of life such an experience appears insignificant, but at the moment it is charged with elements of tragedy.

A marked change in these conditions has taken place in New York City. It began in 1921 with the popular Negro musical play *Shuffle Along* at the 63rd Street Theater, where Negroes in considerable numbers were seated on the ground floor, and increased with *Blackbirds, Porgy, The Green Pastures,* and other Negro plays. It was established more firmly by the big moving pictures theaters, which, whatever may have been the reason, never adopted a policy of segregation. At the present time the sight of colored people in the orchestras of "Broadway" theaters is not regarded a cause for immediate action or of utter astonishment.

XIX

IN Jacksonville for a while after my graduation from Atlanta University social life took up a good deal of my time, but as the years went along the additional work that I undertook constantly reduced the margin of time which I felt I could spare for social affairs. Before I left Jacksonville, I had withdrawn almost entirely from such activities.

When I came to New York to live, there was not such a thing as "society" among the colored people who lived in Manhattan. There were, of course, concerts, big dances, the Drury opera performances, and other public events, that anybody who paid the price of admission could attend. In summer there were "picnics" that began at ten o'clock at night. The most popular picnic place was Sultzer's Park out at the Harlem River end of Second Avenue. Many picnics were given there during a season, but there were two that were more select than any of the others: one given annually by the Sons of New York, a society made up of native-born New Yorkers, and another given by the Guild of St. Phillip's Episcopal Church, the richest Negro church in the world. These summer picnics were jolly and promiscuous, but usually quite orderly. But cultivated Negroes living in Manhattan had, for many years, necessarily been going to Brooklyn for the social intercourse that is confined more or less to the people one knows or knows about. Forty years before, there had been a general exodus of the better-off Negroes from Manhattan to Brooklyn. For some years still farther back, there had been the steady lure of the better opportunity to buy homes on that side of the East River; but the Draft Riots in 1863 precipitated a wholesale migration. A number of these older families in Brooklyn were positively rich; their money, made in the days when Negroes in New York were successful caterers, fashionable dressmakers, and the janitors of big buildings, having come down through two or three generations. I knew a family in which, after the death of the parents, four children were left around sixty thousand dollars each in cash and securities, besides valuable real estate.

Rosamond and I knew some of the old families of Brooklyn, and we devoted an occasional Sunday afternoon and evening to paying calls. Naturally, we made the acquaintance of others that we had not known. We got to know the younger people of the "Brooklyn set" and were invited to parties and dances. We went to these when we could make it convenient. I found these social gatherings much the same as those in Jacksonville; the chief difference being that in Brooklyn the number of well-off people was larger, and the houses we went into were more imposing. Today, I should think of those houses as stuffy, too filled with heavy furniture, heavy pictures, heavy curtains, and heavy carpets; then, I thought of them as being very sumptuous.

My social visits to Brooklyn were not regular or frequent, but much more so than Rosamond's, because his vaudeville work left him scarcely any time to use in that way. I went over one night to see an amateur theatrical performance. I have found that amateur theatricals anywhere are generally a bore; and this one was not an exception. After the performance there was an hour or so of dancing; and that closed the evening pleasantly. Without doubt, the whole affair would have faded completely from my memory had it not been for the fact that it marked the time when I first saw Grace Nail, Jack Nail's sister. She was there with her mother, and was taking, it appeared to me, an initiatory peep at life. Her sensitive response to what she saw was enchanting. She was in her middle teens, but carried herself then like a princess. Her delicate patrician beauty stirred something in me that had not been touched before, and I went away carrying a vivid picture of her in my mind.

I went down to Atlanta University on the tenth anniversary of my graduation to receive an honorary degree. There it was that I first met W. E. B. Du Bois, who was now one of the professors. The year before, he had issued *The Souls of Black Folk* (a work which, I think, has had a greater effect upon and within the Negro race in America than any other single book published in this country since *Uncle Tom's Cabin*) and was already a national figure. I had been deeply moved and influenced by the book, and was anxious to meet the author. I met a quite handsome and unpedantic young man—Dr. Du Bois was then thirty-six. Indeed, it was, at first, slightly difficult to reconcile the brooding but intransigent spirit of *The Souls of Black Folk* with this apparently so light-hearted man, this man so abundantly endowed with the gift of laughter. I noted then what, through many years of close association, I have since learned well, and what the world knows not at all: that Du Bois in battle is a stern, bitter, relentless fighter, who, when he has put aside his sword, is among his particular friends the most jovial and fun-loving of men. This quality has been a saving grace for him, but his lack of the ability to unbend in his relations with people outside the small circle has gained him the reputation of being cold, stiff, supercilious, and has been a cause of criticism amongst even his adherents. This disposition, due perhaps to an inhibition of spontaneous impulse, has limited his scope of leadership to less than what it might have been, in that it has hindered his attracting and binding to himself a body of zealous liegemen—one of the essentials to the headship of a popular or an unpopular cause. The great influence Du Bois has exercised has been due to the concentrated force of his ideas, with next to no reinforcement from that wide appeal of personal magnetism which is generally a valuable asset of leaders of men.

Just before spring in 1905, Bob and Rosamond started again over the Orpheum Circuit; I made the trip with them. Some other performers who were playing the same circuit and who left Denver for San Francisco on the same train with us had planned to stop off for a day in Salt Lake City to visit the Mormon Tabernacle and see the town. They persuaded us to do likewise. We had our tickets adjusted for a stop-over until the next day and got off the train at Salt Lake City. We took a carriage, and directed the driver, a jovial Irishman, to take us to a good hotel. He took us to the best. Porters carried our luggage into the lobby, and I went to the desk, turned the register round and registered for the three. The clerk was busy at the key-rack. He glanced at us furtively, but kept himself occupied. It grew obvious that he was protracting the time. Finally, he could delay no longer and came to the desk. As he came his expression revealed the lie he was to speak. He turned the register round, examined our names, and while his face flushed a bit said, "I'm sorry, but we haven't got a vacant room." This statement, which I knew almost absolutely to be false, set a number of emotions in action: humiliation, chagrin, indignation, resentment, anger; but in the midst of them all I could detect a sense of pity for the man who had to make it, for he was, to all appearances, an honest, decent person. It was then about eleven o'clock, and I sought the eyes of the clerk and asked if he expected any rooms to be vacated at noon. He stammered that he did not. I then said to him that we would check our bags and take the first room available by night. Pressure from me seemed to stiffen him, and he told us that we could not; that we had better try some other hotel. Our bags were taken out and a cab called, and we found ourselves in the same vehicle that had brought us to the hotel. Our driver voluntarily assumed a part of our mortification, and he attempted to console us by relating how ten or twelve years before he had taken Peter Jackson (the famous Negro pugilist) to that same hotel and how royally he had been entertained there. We tried two other hotels, where our experiences were similar but

briefer. We did not dismiss our cabman, for we were being fast
driven to the conclusion that he was probably the only com-
passionate soul we should meet in the whole city of the Latter-
Day Saints.

We had become very hungry; we felt that it was necessary
for us to eat in order to maintain both our morale and our endurance. Our cabman took us to a restaurant. When we entered it was rather crowded, but we managed to find a table
and sat down. There followed that hiatus, of which every Negro in the United States knows the meaning. At length, a man
in charge came over and told us without any pretense of palli-
ation that we could not be served. We were forced to come
out under the stare of a crowd that was conscious of what had
taken place. Our cabman was now actually touched by our
plight; and he gave vent to his feelings in explosive oaths. He
suggested another restaurant to try, where we might have
"better luck"; but we were no longer up to the possible facing
of another such experience. We asked the cabby if he knew of
a colored family in town who might furnish us with a meal; he
did not, but he had an idea; he drove along and stopped in
front of a saloon and chophouse; he darted inside, leaving us
in the carriage; after a few moments he emerged beaming
good news. We went in and were seated at a wholly inconspic-
uous table, but were served with food and drink that quickly
renewed our strength and revived our spirits.

However, we were almost immediately confronted with the
necessity of getting a place to sleep. Our cabby had another
idea; he drove us to a woman he knew who kept a lodging
house for laborers. It was a pretty shabby place; nevertheless,
the woman demurred for quite a while. Finally, she agreed to
let us stay, if we got out before her regular lodgers got up. In
the foul room to which she showed us, we hesitated until the
extreme moment of weariness before we could bring ourselves
to bear the touch of the soiled bedclothes. We smoked and
talked over the situation we were in, the situation of being
outcasts and pariahs in a city of our own and native land. Our
talk went beyond our individual situation and took in the common lot of Negroes in well-nigh every part of the country, a
lot which lays on high and low the constant struggle to re-
nerve their hearts and wills against the unremitting pressure of

unfairness, injustice, wrong, cruelty, contempt, and hate. If what we felt had been epitomized and expressed in but six words, they would have been: A hell of a "my country."

We welcomed daybreak. For numerous reasons we were glad to get out of the beds of our unwilling hostess. We boarded our train with feelings of unbounded relief; I with a vow never to set foot again in Salt Lake City. Twenty-three years later, I passed through Salt Lake City, as one of a large delegation on the way to a conference of the National Association for the Advancement of Colored People held in Los Angeles. Our train had a wait of a couple of hours, and the delegation went out to see the town, the Tabernacle, and the lake. I spent the time alone at the railroad station.

Concerning this particular lapse from democracy in America, I have heard many people declare that the remedy for the situation is for Negroes to have places of their own. Aside from any principle of common rights, the suggestion is absurd. At the time of which I have been speaking, Negroes in Salt Lake City constituted an infinitesimal element in the community, and Negroes who visited there, a still smaller element; therefore it is evident that no hotel nor even a modest boarding house for "Negroes only" could have been operated on a commercial basis. Such an institution would have demanded a subsidy. Negroes in many localities where their numbers are large have, from necessity, and as often from choice, provided certain places of public accommodation for themselves; but to say that they should duplicate the commercial and social machinery of the nation is to utter an inanity. It takes all New York and its hundreds of thousands of visitors to support one grand opera company. If I want to hear grand opera in New York I must go to the Metropolitan Opera House. To tell Negroes that they ought to get their own opera house in Harlem if they want to hear grand opera would not be less unreasonable than to tell them to get their own railroads if they want to ride in Pullman cars, and just about as reasonable as telling them to have hotels in all cities and towns in which a Negro traveler might, perchance, stop over.

I was delighted with San Francisco. Here was a civilized center, metropolitan and urbane. With respect to the Negro race,

I found it a freer city than New York. I encountered no bar against me in hotels, restaurants, theaters, or other places of public accommodation and entertainment. We hired a furnished apartment in the business area, and took our meals wherever it was most convenient. I moved about with a sense of confidence and security, and entirely from under that cloud of doubt and apprehension that constantly hangs over an intelligent Negro in every Southern city and in a great many cities of the North. Bob and Rosamond were booked for four weeks in San Francisco, but were held over for another two weeks; so I, with nothing in particular to do, had time in which to learn the town quite well. At every turn San Francisco roused my admiration; but on one occasion it also gave me proof that I was a good typical New Yorker. The grand opera season was on and an acquaintance invited me to go with him to witness a performance. It struck me as curious to go all the way to San Francisco to attend grand opera; I had heard all the grand operas; there were other things in the Pacific Coast metropolis that would interest me more. My friend insisted that I should hear one of the greatest coloratura sopranos in the world, if not the greatest. This struck me as ridiculous, and I said, "Now, now, if she's all you say she is, what is she doing singing in a small company out here? Why hasn't she been heard at the Metropolitan?" The singer was Tetrazzini; but I did not hear her until she sang in New York.

When I had been in San Francisco a few days I received a cardboard cylinder which contained an ornate signed and sealed commission certifying to my appointment as a "Colonel" in the Roosevelt inaugural parade; the honor being conferred in recognition of services I was adjudged to have rendered in the presidential campaign the year before. Under separate cover I received a letter from a division commander of the Civic Grand Division of the parade, in which he said, "A number of very prominent men have been invited to serve on my staff, and I have every reason to believe that the civic division of the parade will surpass any similar feature on any former occasion. I should like to have you serve on my staff, and, if you accept the appointment, you will be expected to serve rain or shine. Kindly let me hear from you by return mail. The only expense attached to the appointment will be for the hire of a

horse." I appreciated the honor and have preserved the commission, but the inducement of being one of a large number of
non-equestrian civilians seated for several uncomfortable
hours astride an unknown horse was not sufficient to cause me
to cut short my stay in San Francisco.

During my stay I made many acquaintances. I was invited to
speak in one of the colored churches on a Sunday afternoon,
and from that became acquainted with a number of people of
my race. The black population was relatively small, but the colored people that I met and visited lived in good homes and appeared to be prosperous. I talked with some of them about
race conditions; the consensus of their comment was that San
Francisco was the best city in the United States for a Negro.
This may, of course, have been in some degree a reflex of
prevalent Pacific Coast boosting.

I think the most interesting person I met was Jack Johnson,
who was to be, three years later, the champion prize fighter of
the world. I saw him first at the theater, where he had come to
see Bob and Rosamond. He came frequently to our apartment, and his visits were generally as long as our time permitted, for he was not training. These visits put the idea in my
head of improving myself in "the manly art of self-defense"—
the manner in which gentlemen used to speak about taking
boxing lessons. Jack often boxed with me playfully, like a
good-natured big dog warding off the earnest attacks of a
small one, but I could never get him to give me any serious instruction. Occasionally, he would bare his stomach to me as a
mark and urge me to hit him with all my might. I found it an
impossible thing to do; I always involuntarily pulled my
punch. It was easy to like Jack Johnson; he is so likable a man,
and I liked him particularly well. I was, of course, impressed by
his huge but perfect form, his terrible strength, and the
supreme ease and grace of his every muscular movement; however, watching his face, sad until he smiled, listening to his soft
Southern speech and laughter, and hearing him talk so wist-
fully about his big chance, yet to come, I found it difficult to
think of him as a prize fighter. I had not yet seen a prize fight,
but I conceived of the game as a brutal, bloody one, demanding of its exponents courage, stamina, and brute force as well
as skill and quick intelligence, and I could hardly figure gentle

Jack Johnson in the rôle. Frederick Douglass had a picture of
Peter Jackson in his study, and he used to point to it and say,
"Peter is doing a great deal with his fists to solve the Negro
question." I think that Jack, even after the reckoning of his big
and little failings has been made, may be said to have done his
share.

Back in New York, Bob and Rosamond found that they
were booked for six weeks at the Palace Theater in London.
We were all excitement; and at once decided to make of the
engagement a tour rather than just a trip. We planned to spend
three months. I went to Columbia for the few last lectures that
I could attend, and took an opportunity to consult Brander
Matthews about our trip abroad. He suggested that we go first
to Paris, and radiate out from there to the surrounding places
we wished to visit; then to go up through Belgium and Holland, and come back to Ostend for the trip across the Channel.
We followed his suggestions.

From the day I set foot in France, I became aware of the
working of a miracle within me. I became aware of a quick
readjustment to life and to environment. I recaptured for the
first time since childhood the sense of being just a human
being. I need not try to analyze this change for my colored
readers; they will understand in a flash what took place. For my
white readers . . . I am afraid that any analysis will be inadequate, perhaps futile . . . I was suddenly free; free from a sense
of impending discomfort, insecurity, danger; free from the
conflict within the Man-Negro dualism and the innumerable
maneuvers in thought and behavior that it compels; free from
the problem of the many obvious or subtle adjustments to a
multitude of bans and taboos; free from special scorn, special
tolerance, special condescension, special commiseration; free
to be merely a man.

On the boat we had made some pleasant acquaintances from
among our white compatriots. Of several of these I still have a
distinct recollection. One was a West Point cadet; another was
a young man going to Paris to study at the *Académie Julien*—
the two were relatives, I think, and were traveling with two
middle-aged ladies, who were aunts or something of that sort;
a third was the fashion plate of the ship, a young man who

seemingly had an inexhaustible supply of clothes, and changed four or five times a day. It was this young man who strongly recommended that we put up in Paris at the Hotel Continental. We knew nothing of Paris hotels, and he appeared to know so much; we followed his advice. When we had registered and been assigned to our rooms, we found ourselves in possession of a suite of two bedrooms, sitting room, and bath, opening on the beautiful court. We were appalled in thinking of what the cost would be. What had they taken us for, South American millionaires or what? Bob and Rosamond were inclined to blame me, the one who knew the most about French, with letting the clerk or manager or whoever he was put it over on us. We decided that we should stay at the Continental a day or two for the sake of appearances, then look for a good *pension*.

When we had finished laying out this plan of action, it was near dinner time. We dressed and started out. As we stepped from our rooms a uniformed attendant standing at the door— waiting, it seemed for our exit—bowed low and said, "Messieurs." We walked toward the elevator, and there stood another uniformed attendant, who bowed low and said, "Messieurs." As we entered the elevator, the operator bowed low and said, "Messieurs." As we passed through the office, there came from various functionaries a chorus of "Messieurs." As we went out of the great gate, an attendant uniformed like a major general saluted and said, "Messieurs." We laughed heartily over all this when we got back to our rooms, and declared that whatever it cost to stay at the Continental, it was worth it.

In coming through the office we had been joined by a young man we had met on the ship. He knew his Paris, and we were glad to be taken in tow. After dinner, we went to see the performance at the Marigny; and after the theater our friend piloted us to Olympia. I was amazed at the size of the place, the size of the orchestra seated in the center, and the great gayety of the whole scene. We found a table and were seated. The next number played by the orchestra was *Under the Bamboo Tree*. We attached no particular importance to that; but when it was followed by *The Congo Love Song*, we took notice and sent our compliments to the leader with the request that he and his men order whatever they wished. Soon four girls joined our party; only one of them, a German girl with lovely dark eyes, being able to speak any English, and she knew only a few words. Nevertheless, they all chatted with and at us gayly while they sipped their beer or black coffee drunk from tall, thin glasses. All the while we were in Paris we generally ended up each evening at Olympia; and, generally, this same group of girls joined us at our table. I stopped trying to make an interpreter out of the German girl, and took my first plunge into the practical use of French. My ability to talk the language increased in geometrical progression. I had studied French at school, and had taken the Cortina course in New York, but Olympia proved to be the best school for learning French I ever attended.

A few days after our arrival we were invited to a studio party. Our hostess was an American singer at the Paris Opera House; her husband being the secretary, if I remember correctly, of the American Chamber of Commerce in Paris. Among the guests were the West Point cadet and the art student with their aunts. It was through them that we had received the invitation to the party. There were a number of artists of one kind or another present, and each who could did a turn. This party was our sole opportunity for a peep at Paris on the inside, but, in the short time we had, we saw about all that could be seen on the outside. However, we didn't make a business of seeing Paris; we made a pleasure of it. We looked with something like pity on tourists groups working on a schedule, being hustled from point to point, pausing only while their guide repeated his trite and hasty lecture on this building or that painting or the other monument. I was glad that on my first visit I was able to see what I did see leisurely; not forced to gulp it down but able to take the time to note the taste of it. I kept congratulating myself that I had declined the chance to visit Europe the summer after I graduated from Atlanta as a member of a tourist party of colored Baptist preachers. I quickly discovered that "historical points" interested me less than almost anything else; that a good picture and the facts well told were, generally, as satisfying as the actual sight. What I wanted most, and what cannot be gotten vicariously, was impressions from the life eddying round me and streaming by. I wanted to see people, people at every level, from an élite audience at the Opera House to a group of swearing fish-mongers in the market.

I left Paris with few anticipations. It was true that Bob and Rosamond's engagement was still before us in London, but I feared that so far as seeing things was concerned our trip would follow the steps of an anticlimax. I was relieved to find Brussels *un vrai petit Paris.* The city was in gala attire. We learned that the seventy-fifth anniversary of the independence of Belgium was being celebrated. As soon as we were located, we went out to see the sights. We tried to get a street car; we hailed a dozen or more, only to hear the conductor shout back to us, *"Complet, complet."* Bob looked at me in his quizzical way and asked, "What are they doing, drawing the color line?" The *"complet"* of the conductors did not, so far as our knowledge went, give a clear explanation; for the cars, according to the American practice, were not full, there was lots of standing room. At last, we secured a cab and drove along through the crowded streets. The Belgian peasants, of whom there were great numbers in the city for the festival, made the most picturesque of all the sights. Our cab driver insisted that we go to see Manneken-Pis. I suppose that every Brussels cabby takes his fares who are strangers to see this famous little statue; we went without any idea of what we were going to see. When we arrived, there were two or three dozen country people looking at the figure. As soon as we stepped out of our cab, we, instead of the Manneken, became the center of their attention. We were at once almost surrounded by them, and they gazed at us respectfully but with undisguised curiosity. Judging that they had never before seen dark people, we stood long enough to enable them to satisfy their eyes; we felt it would be ungracious to rob them of something to tell the folks back home.

We spent our first night in Brussels at the *Palais d'Été.* Nothing on the program particularly interested us until a man in evening clothes stepped before the curtain and made an announcement in French regarding the closing act on the bill. We were confident that the man was colored, but we could not make up our minds whether he was East Indian, West Indian, African, or American. We decided to go to the stage door after the performance and see if we could find out something about him. We met him and found out that he was not only colored,

Paris

but an American Negro, born in South Carolina. His name was Woodson; he had started out as an acrobat; for eighteen years he lived in Europe, working as a circus performer the greater part of the time; for seven years he had been stage manager of the *Palais d'Été*. To me, his story was an amazing one. Had it been told to me, I should have taken the "stage manager" climax with a grain of salt. But I myself did see that he held that important and respected position. Mr. Woodson invited us to take breakfast with him at his home the next morning. I was glad to go, for it meant another of those peeps inside, that are rare for a stranger in a strange land. I was not disappointed in Mr. Woodson's home; it was pleasant and tasteful. We met his wife and daughter, a girl about twelve. Mrs. Woodson, like her husband, was brown. She was quite stout but had an extremely nice face. The daughter was brown like her parents, and very vivacious and pretty. I had an immediate foretaste of talking with this little Negro family about Paris and Brussels and Europe and America, too, from a common point of view. We quickly learned that Mrs. Woodson spoke only German. She was born in Germany of a German mother and a Negro father, and had never learned to speak English. We enjoyed the breakfast and the chance to talk with Mr. Woodson. He appeared to know Europe from one end to the other. His memory about his native land was rather faint, but he expressed no desire of reviving it. We left Brussels and hurried through visits to Antwerp and Amsterdam. The London engagement, now only seven or eight days away, was beginning to pull on the nerves of Bob and Rosamond, and they were anxious to get on the ground.

Great, rumbling London; stupendous, overwhelming London gave us, in a manner, a personal reception. Every bus, and there seemed to be thousands of them, carried along its whole length a placard announcing the appearance for the first time at the Palace Theater of "Cole and Johnson, the Great Coloured Comedians" or "Cole and Johnson, the Great American Musicians." Similar announcements were carried on other vehicles, plastered over numerous hoardings, and displayed in many shops. We were astonished, for we had never seen vaudeville performers advertised in such a way in any

American city. Bob and Rosamond got a tremendous thrill out
of it; they could not help but be thrilled at the thought that
probably a million people had noted that Cole and Johnson
were coming to London. London blotted out the rest of Europe, for London was a city not to be visited, but to be captured. This inspiriting thought carried, however, a penalty of
anxiety that heightened as the opening of the engagement approached. It is needless to say that I shared in the thrill and the
anxiety.

A day or two before the opening we met Marie Dressler on
the street. She talked with us about the opening night, and radiated buoyancy and confidence in a way that made them infectious. She promised to be present to give the boys a hand.
Miss Dressler kept her promise; and, more than that, she
rounded up every American performer in London she could
get hold of and brought them along to help in "giving a
hand." It was a big-hearted thing that she did. We had only
two guests that night, Samuel Coleridge-Taylor, the colored
English composer, and his wife; they sat with me. I was impressed by the Palace Theater, its splendor, the width and
comfort of the seats. I particularly noticed that each chair had
two arm-rests, which obviated the American custom of yielding the use of the single arm-rest in common to two chairs to
the person who pre-empts it. When the orchestra filed in, I
counted forty men, and made a quick contrast with the scant
nine-piece orchestra in the best American vaudeville theaters
and with the solitary piano player in a great many of them. I
was still more impressed by the audience; all the men and
women in the orchestra chairs and boxes were in strict evening
dress. The elegance of the whole atmosphere was somewhat
like a night at the Metropolitan Opera House.

Bob and Rosamond were the headliners of the bill; so they
did not appear until well down the program. I was distrait until they did appear; and, when they did, I was seized with a sort
of panic. I stiffened under the tension, and gripped the arms of
my chair like a person fortifying himself for the extraction of a
tooth. Rosamond's piano solo was courteously received; his
song in German more warmly; but I knew, and I knew that
they knew, that the audience was not yet theirs. When Rosamond struck the opening bars of *The Congo Love Song*, I knew

that the die was about to be cast; that it was now win or lose. They sang the song with flawless artistry, and finished so softly that it induced an intense silence. Then there was an outburst of spontaneous and prolonged applause. They had won; and I was able to let down and enjoy the act as though I had never seen it before.

These states of pain and pleasurable reaction under similar circumstances are more keenly experienced by Negroes, perhaps, than by any other people. For them, the central persons are not individuals, they become protagonists of the whole racial cause. Certainly, all people have similar experiences whenever there are high feelings of partisanship. For example, white Americans who witnessed the recent Olympic Games at Los Angeles experienced the peculiar thrill of the transition from anxiety to elation whenever an American was the victor; but I do not think it possible that any of them experienced in degree what was felt by the Negroes who saw Eddie Tolan, the diminutive black sprinter, win the hundred-meter race by breaking the world record with Ralph Metcalf, another Negro, second, and the two-hundred-meter race by setting a new Olympic record. They saw him gain not only two glorious victories for the United States but a victory of unique significance for them.

We lived in a quite nice furnished apartment, which we had had no difficulty in leasing; it was when we came to give it up that we ran into complications. We had, without anything like exhaustive examination, signed a voluminous document of, I should say, twenty or twenty-five pages written entirely in longhand, never imagining that it was an instrument empowering the landlord to enforce a limitless number of minute exactions, indeed, to make us practically buy the apartment, if he was disposed to press the matter that far.

We had two minor encounters with English business customs. Rosamond went into an exclusive shop to buy a new silk hat for the act. It was handed to him in a box that was constructed, I judge, out of English oak. When Rosamond made what he intended as a jocose remark about the weight of the box, the shopkeeper turned on him and said, "We've been packing our hats in those boxes a hundred and fifty yeahs, sir, a hundred and fifty yeahs," and in a tone that implied, "If you don't like the box, you needn't take the hat." As soon as I could get at it, I made some snapshots of the busses carrying the "Cole and Johnson" placards, and took them to a place to be developed and printed. I went back after four or five days to get the prints; they had not been touched. "But," I pressed, "I left them here four or five days ago." The shopkeeper snapped at me, "If you want them in a hurry, sir, take them to a hurry shop. Take them to an American shop."

I enjoyed my stay in London. I learned to love London. Its gravity in design and temper does not, it is true, allow much for that levity which debonair and sprightly Paris almost forces, but I felt that the spirit of London approached closer to the realities of life. Of course, this feeling may, after all, have been fundamentally a matter of language. In the English city I was able to speak not only the language of words but, more or less, the language of ideas of the people I came in contact with, whether on the streets, in the shops, or in a drawing room. I grew aware of the beauty in the ruggedness of London. I rode atop busses for hours, not knowing or caring where they went, and was grateful for the intrinsic quality in so teeming a city that enabled a man to be alone.

We met a good many people in London, a number of Americans, some of whom we had known in the United States. It is a wise general rule for American Negroes in Europe to steer clear of their white fellow-countrymen, but, although we did not stick to this rule, we ran into no unpleasant or awkward situations. During our stay, Charles Hawtrey made a return of our hospitality to him in New York by inviting us to lunch with him and to go afterwards on an automobile trip to Windsor Castle. That part of the invitation which concerned the trip to Windsor Castle excited us greatly; first, because trips by automobiles were still rare enough to constitute an event; secondly, because we knew of the close friendship between Charles Hawtrey and King Edward. We had no anticipations of supper with the King, but we did feel that we should see the Castle under auspices far beyond the reach of the average tourist. But, alas! those were the automobile days when one merely hoped to get to one's destination and hardly dared to expect to get back. The day was beautiful, and we left the hotel in grand style. We threaded our way out of London and skimmed rapidly over the roads, but not so rapidly that we could not take in the surpassing beauty of the English countryside. As we sped along, our spirits mounted higher and higher. Then suddenly, for reasons that were yet among the mysteries, the car stopped. We went to an inn for a sandwich and a bottle of ale, while the chauffeur would do whatever was necessary to get the car started. When we got back, the chauffeur was still working, but already there were signs of despair on his face. He explained to Mr. Hawtrey what he thought was the trouble; but such terms as "carburetor," "ignition," "sparking plug," "transmission," and "differential" meant less to me then than do the terms of Einsteinian astronomy now. The chauffeur worked doggedly, but nothing he did started the machine. Finally, we left him and the car and made our way to the nearest railroad station and back by train to London; Mr. Hawtrey and Bob and Rosamond reaching the city just in time to get on the stages of their respective theaters.

One night, walking home from the theater we passed a man standing at a window on the ground floor of a house not far from where we lived. The evening was warm, and he was, presumably, trying to catch a breath of air. We could not see his face very well, but his form was sharply outlined by the light in the room. As we passed, Bob remarked, "That man looks like Gus Kerker." Whereupon, the man at the window put his head out and said, "I am Gus Kerker. Who are you?" We retraced the step or two, and when he saw who we were he invited us in. We sat until long past midnight talking about the theater; or, more exactly, listening to him talk about *The Belle of New York*. He rehearsed the whole history of the show; how they had with trepidation brought it to London; its tumultuous English success; the personal triumphs of Edna May and Dan Daly—and his own, the triumph of being the composer of the first American musical play to be unreservedly acclaimed in England. There was no pose of the braggart in his attitude; his manner was rather that of one restating incontestable truths. This *magnum opus* of his had put his name well up in the list of composers of light opera and had earned him a fortune—a very happy combination; and I judge that from then until he died his breath of life was the fame of *The Belle of New York*.

We were short of money on leaving London. Indeed, I had days before cashed my last American Express Company check. During our last week we sold for thirty pounds the singing rights of a song to the producers of a play at the Drury Lane Theater; and that helped. Nevertheless, when we boarded the Cunarder at Liverpool, all the money the three of us could show could be counted in shillings. Getting on the boat with so little cash was easy, but getting off was another matter. As the ship approached New York, I began to reckon the smallest possible tips that I could offer to my waiter, the state-room steward, the bathroom steward, and the deck steward, but by no shifting of figures could all these items be covered. The situation began to loom up as something quite serious. I was actually depressed by the moral element involved. It was something like having a note fall due at the bank with no funds in sight to meet it. As we steamed through the Narrows I stood leaning on the rail, reduced to juggling various plausible subterfuges, when a young man whom I had met only in a casual manner on board came up and said, "You don't look very happy about getting back home." "Oh, I'm happy enough on that score," I assured him, "but the three of us have run short of cash, and I am wondering how we are going to get off the ship honorably." He laughed and offered to lend me whatever I needed. I got twenty-five dollars from him and his address, promising that I should return the money promptly after I got ashore; which, perhaps I should add, I did. I could not but wonder why this virtual stranger voluntarily lent me twenty-five dollars. It was a friendly act of the sort that lingers warmly in the memory.

XX

IN the middle of the summer of 1904 Charles W. Anderson had come to me with what struck me as a strange request. Mr. Anderson and I had been friends for a number of years; I considered him one of the ablest politicians in the country. I regarded him as being, beyond any doubt, the very ablest

Negro politician. The campaign to elect Theodore Roosevelt to succeed himself in the Presidency was just beginning to warm up. Mr. Anderson dropped in at the studio one evening and revealed to me his plans for establishing a "Colored Republican Club" in West 53rd Street. The plans were: to lease one of the three-story and basement houses across the street from the Marshall; to furnish it in good style, billiard and pool room in the basement, assembly room on the main floor, lounge and card rooms on the second floor, and committee rooms on the top. Mr. Anderson informed me that the money for these initial expenses had already been provided. He said, finally:

"Jim, I've got to have your help."

"But, Charlie, how can *I* help you?"

"You can help me in making the club a success; and that's going to be a big job. You can do it better than anybody I know."

"How?"

"I want somebody who'll know where every dollar comes from and where every dollar goes, and who'll keep the records straight. I want a man for chairman of the house committee, and you're the man."

I protested that my work kept me too busy to afford the necessary time; that, in addition, I was studying at Columbia University; that, furthermore, I knew nothing about politics or political organizations. Mr. Anderson summed up his request by saying, "Well, I want you to do it *for me*." The request put in that form I could not refuse. After I had begun, I became enthusiastic about my new job. The club started off with a grand opening. Visitors were surprised at the elegance and completeness of its appointments. The membership increased by leaps and bounds. Big guns of the campaign boomed in its assembly room. I was able to secure a sufficient number of volunteers from amongst the "talent" at the Marshall to have an "entertainment night" once a week; these nights were particularly popular with the New York newspaper men. The trio got busy and wrote a campaign song for "Teddy."

One verse of the song, the verse commenting on Alton B. Parker's famous telegram to the gold standard wing of the

Democrats in convention, went the rounds of the press. It ran:

> Oh, Mr. Parker thinks
> That he is like the Sphinx
> But we're inclined to think he is a clam.
> He's bound to get a tilt
> Upon a platform built
> Out of a Western Union Telegram.
> Chorus
> You're all right Teddy, etc., etc., etc.

Rosamond carefully made a manuscript copy, which was sent to Mr. Roosevelt. He wrote complimenting us on having written "a bully good song."

My new activities gave me a chance to learn something about the workings of practical politics; something about how men deal and are dealt with in this, the greatest American game. I got some understanding of what "political loyalty" is and of its strength as a force in our civic system. I learned that the loyalty of the active, practical politicians—that vast army of actual and prospective holders of political jobs, from street cleaner up—is primarily given not to the party candidate or standard bearer, but to the boss. I learned that the practical politicians who are active in politics three hundred and sixty-five days a year, are those who directly or indirectly gain a living or more than a living from politics. They control the political machinery and, so far as its manipulation is concerned, nobody else really counts. In fact, nobody else is really interested in politics. The contrary premise leads to a great many errors and futile efforts.

Mr. Anderson was the president of the Club. He was the recognized colored Republican leader of New York, an astute politician, keen in his study of men and the uses to be made of them. A versatile man; much more than an ordinary orator, in the style of the day; capable of intelligently discussing the English poets, the Irish patriots, or the contemporary leaders of the British Parliament. A cool, calculating player in the hard game of politics, but always playing the game rather on the grand scale for the higher stakes. On friendly terms with

Theodore Roosevelt, Elihu Root, Chauncey M. Depew, Tom
Platt, and other Republican leaders. Nor was there an important Tammany leader who did not know "Charlie" and greet
him cordially. He made New York take note of the Colored
Republican Club.

The campaign ended. Theodore Roosevelt was gloriously
elected, and made that so characteristic expression of thanks to
the American people, which was to come up to plague him
when later he decided to accept that "third cup of coffee."
Within a reasonable time he appointed Charles W. Anderson
to the position of Collector of Internal Revenue for that district which includes the Wall Street section of New York City.
Mr. Anderson held his office through the Taft administration,
and, though his district was changed, through the Wilson administrations; and is, at this writing, still Collector of Internal
Revenue—not a slight evidence of political sagacity. After his
appointment he decided to resign the presidency of the Club.
Again he requisitioned my services. He impressed upon me
that the Club was a power and an influence, socially as well as
politically, and that it must be kept alive. In accordance with
his desires and plans, I became president of the Club. I learned
many lessons from this job, some of them hard, all of them
valuable.

When I returned from Europe, I sometimes visited Mr. Anderson at his office in the Custom House to talk over Club
matters. These visits were generally in the afternoon, and he
would, at times, say, "You're not in a hurry, are you? I'll be
through in a little while, and we'll walk along and talk." These
walks that seemed like nothing to him taxed me terribly. His
antidote for fatigue was to stop in somewhere and get a pint of
champagne. I frequently had to rebel against walking another
step. I remember that on one afternoon we started from
Bowling Green and ended up at the Marie Antoinette Hotel
at Broadway and 66th Street. In one of our talks, Mr. Anderson suggested that it would be a nice thing for me to go into
the United States Consular Service; he felt sure that President
Roosevelt would be willing to appoint me. The idea was interesting. I asked some questions. Mr. Anderson supplied me
with information: the Service had recently been reorganized
by Elihu Root (then Secretary of State); the standard had

been raised; applicants were required to pass a real examination and had to possess a knowledge of at least one of the principal foreign languages; the Service had been classified into grades that ranged in salary from two thousand dollars to twelve thousand dollars a year; a new man entered the lowest grade, and would be promoted; the whole Service had been divorced from the spoils system, and consuls henceforth would be secure in their positions and sure of merited promotion. His recital set my imagination in action, but I dismissed the whole matter for the time by laughingly remarking, "But, Charlie, it would take about one-third of my salary just to keep my life insurance going."

During the winter the trio continued to write. Our songs were still selling, with *Lazy Moon* quite popular. Bob and Rosamond were still headliners on the "big time" in vaudeville, but a new idea was working in Bob's mind. He had first let it out in occasional hints, then broached it. The idea was that he and Rosamond drop vaudeville and go out at the head of a theatrical company. His argument was that they should capitalize their reputation; that there was the chance of clearing thirty or forty thousand dollars a year with a company of their own; that, whatever happened, they could always go back into vaudeville. Rosamond was influenced, but I opposed the idea as strongly as I could. I pointed out that their position was unique; that they were independent and free from the responsibilities and worries that a large company would entail; that they played only the best houses in the biggest cities; that this gave them time for composition; and that while they were on the road with a show their Broadway reputation would be fading. I agreed that there would be a chance of clearing thirty or forty thousand dollars a year if they played all New Yorks and Chicagos, but I reminded them that they would have to play a great many second-class houses in one-night stands. I had reasons in addition to those that primarily concerned Bob and Rosamond. I knew that it was in Bob's plans to have me go as business manager of the company, and I had no desire to go trouping around the country and undergoing the hardships that every colored company had to put up with; nor did I have any intentions of doing so, if there was any way to avoid it. The idea was allowed to sleep for a while.

The idea slept, but I knew it would be wakened. I applied myself with more diligence to my work at Columbia and I began planning some more literary work. I found that less and less was I able to go at the work for Broadway on sheer enthusiasm; I had to spur myself forward. Being light enough for Broadway was beginning to be, it seemed, a somewhat heavy task. Unconscious of what was taking place I was actually making a mental shift and adjustment.

The extension of their vaudeville engagements kept Bob and Rosamond out of New York more than ever before. I went to the theater quite regularly, and occasionally to some social affairs. I attended the St. Phillip's Guild picnic, and saw Grace Nail there. She was quite a young lady now. I asked her to dance with me; and I remember distinctly my slight confusion and timidity in asking. I took with me from the picnic an intense vivification of the memory of her that I had taken from the amateur theatrical performance in Brooklyn several years before.

In the spring, D—— came to New York. In the new Jacksonville that rose out of the fire, he had prospered. His law practice had grown; he had accumulated considerable property; he had been elected to the city council, and was counted an influence in politics. For several summers back he had been coming to New York on vacation, so between his trips north and my occasional trips to Jacksonville to visit my parents, we had seen a good deal of each other. But this trip was to be a final one. He had closed his office in Jacksonville, disposed of most of his property, and bought a half-interest in the practice of a colored lawyer in Brooklyn. As D—— had disapproved of my moving to New York, so I had disapproved of his. And I felt that my advice was more disinterested than was his. The personal element could hardly be absent from the advice he had given me: unwillingness to have our companionship and partnership broken, and dislike of my living in the great metropolis and his remaining in the small city. I was glad enough to have D—— in New York, but I felt that, in leaving Jacksonville, he was doing a foolish thing to himself.

Toward the latter part of this same winter, Bob and Rosamond learned that they were booked for a return engagement
at the Palace Theater in London. Bob then again brought up
the question of a theatrical company of their own. His plan
was to play the Palace engagement as a farewell to vaudeville,
and, on their return to the United States in the fall, to start out
with their own show. He and Rosamond decided on that plan.
Furthermore, Bob had already made an outline of the play. It
was to be in three scenes; time, the outbreak of the Spanish-
American War; the first and third scenes in a Negro industrial
school in the South, the second scene in the Philippine Islands.
The play was to be called *The Shoo-Fly Regiment*. We started
writing it at once, and before time for the trip to London, I
had done the lyrics and worked with Bob on the dialogue; and
Rosamond had set quite a bit of music. I experienced strange
emotions while doing my part creating *The Shoo-Fly Regiment*,
for I felt that it was the last piece of work the three of us
should do together.

While we were working on the play, Mr. Anderson spoke to
me again about going into the Consular Service. I asked him
to let me think it over a little while. When I saw him next I
said, "Charlie, if the President will appoint me, I'll go." Mr.
Anderson started immediately to take the steps to secure an
appointment for me. Arriving at this decision was not an easy
matter; not nearly so easy as the decision to leave Jacksonville.
New York had been a good godmother to me, almost a fairy
godmother, and it gave me a wrench to turn my back on her.
Over against all that life and work in New York meant, I balanced three things, and tipped the scales. I put into the scales
my desire to avoid the disagreeable business of traveling round
the country under the conditions that a Negro theatrical company had to endure; as I proposed to cite, among my qualifications for the Service, Spanish as my foreign language, I
expected to be appointed to a South American post, so there
was added the lure of the adventure of life on a strange continent; but heavier than either of these was the realization,
which came upon me suddenly, that time was slipping and I
had not yet made a real start on the work that I had long kept
reassuring myself I should sometime do, that the opportunity
for seizing that "sometime" had come, and that I ought not

let it pass. Then, the feeling came over me that, in leaving New York, I was not making a sacrifice, but an escape; that I was getting away, if only for a while, from the feverish flutter of life to seek a little stillness of the spirit.

I went to Washington and took my examination. My appointment was United States Consul at Puerto Cabello, Venezuela. And so, while D—— was setting himself up in New York, I was pulling up my stakes. Once again our see-saw of advice and counter-advice got into action. His expression of opinion, this time, was sharper than it was on my leaving school position and law practice to move to New York. He simply could not accept or understand any reason for leaving New York to go to "the jungle of South America." He dropped into his old racy style of speech and so disparaged the job I had taken and the surroundings in which I should find myself that strictures turned to humor, and the irritation and tension dissipated. Bob and Rosamond said little; nothing in direct opposition to my plans. I had put these plans before them fully, and they had accepted them. I believe they reasoned that I could always come back to New York; that my sojourn would be brief, and, probably, advantageous, for I should be likely to return with new ideas for Broadway and for Cole and Johnson shows.

Spring came to an end. Bob and Rosamond sailed to fill their return engagement in London; I sailed for my post in Venezuela; and the trio was dissolved.

PART THREE

XXI

I HAVE traveled thousands of miles in ships, but have always been an uncertain sailor. I have crossed a choppy English Channel without the slightest nausea, and been seasick unto death on a Sound steamer, going from New York to Fall River. I was between these two states, a condition worse than outright seasickness, during the entire trip to Venezuela. I went more or less regularly to the dining saloon, but had no relish for food. In the dining saloon I had been given the place of honor, the seat at the right of the Captain. There began at table a friendly relation between him and me that lasted throughout my stay in Venezuela. The ship stopped a day in San Juan, Porto Rico. A friend, Arthur A. Schomburg, who is a native of Porto Rico, had given me a letter to the mayor of the city. I presented the letter and received a cordial welcome. I spent the day ashore, but was seasick, it seemed, even on land. I dreaded going aboard again.

I got my first real relief when the ship entered the quiet waters of the harbor of Curaçao, or Willemstad, as the city itself is known. As a matter of fact, the excitement of approaching the harbor caused me to forget my stomach. The ship pointed her nose directly at what appeared to be an unbroken volcanic shore. It looked as though the Captain was intentionally running his ship aground. It was not until we were close enough to make out a bridge that had been drawn from across the mouth of a narrow channel that we saw any place where it was possible to enter. We steamed through this channel into a spacious landlocked harbor, which, I learned, was the crater of an extinct volcano that had been filled by the sea. It was plain to observe what a perfect pirates' stronghold this most important island of the Dutch West Indies had been in buccaneer days. Around the edges of the harbor and along the sides of several canals formed by inlets from this inner bay, sat the picturesque

town of Willemstad, a miniature Amsterdam, dazzlingly clean
and bright under a cloudless sky. It seldom, almost never rains
in Curaçao, and water is or was peddled from door to door,
like milk. Nevertheless, drawing the conclusion from my observations, there is not a cleaner place in the world. I was told
that Willemstad was the origin of Sapolio's popular advertising
slogan, "Spotless Town." In this, in particular, its standards
were much higher than what I found on the South American
continent only twelve hours away.

Dutch is the official language of Curaçao and is, of course,
spoken by the Dutch officials, garrison and civilians. But the
mass of the population, which is Negro, speaks *Papaimento*.
Indeed, everybody who lives in Curaçao knows and uses Papaimento. This is not a mere patois; it is a language, a composite language made up of Spanish, Portuguese, French, English,
and a little German and Dutch. It might well serve as a universal medium. It is grammatically constructed, is the language of
most of the textbooks used in the public schools, and the language in which the newspapers are published and into which a
number of books of literature are translated. It is, probably, for
this reason that every Curaçaoan is a linguist. For them, differences caused by language hardly exist. A boatman, an old black
man, paddling me across to my steamer, addressed me in four
languages in an effort to discover what was my mother
tongue. At the club I saw four or five men playing a game of
pool, and was astonished at the lightness with which the conversation was tossed from one language to another.

My first sight of South America was that eastern spur of the
Andes which rises up, a sheer wall from the Atlantic, where La
Guaira stretches along a narrow ledge of shore between
mountains and sea. It is a majestic sight—the mountains, not
the town. La Guaira, dingy and squalid and fetid, made me decide to stay aboard. But the ship was unbearable; a June sun
heated it to the temperature of an oven. We were tied to a
wharf with an iron roof, and that radiated heat like a furnace. I
couldn't find an endurable spot. My head began to feel
strange, and I confided to Captain Crockett my fear that I had
symptoms of sunstroke. He said, "The ship will be here two
days, loading and unloading; you had better take a train and

go up to Caracas and stay there until tomorrow afternoon. Go to the Grand Hotel Klint." The trip from La Guaira is, I should judge, the most wonderful twenty-five mile railroad ride in the world. For more than three thousand feet the train makes its way up over a cogwheel track, and drops into the cup of the mountain, where sits Caracas, the capital of Venezuela. The trip takes about two hours. When I had been riding an hour, I felt a change of climate and like a new man. When I reached Caracas, the temperature was like early June in the Berkshire Hills of western Massachusetts.

I found Caracas not a large city but quite a gay one. A season of Italian Grand Opera opened on the night of my arrival, and I attended. The performance was interesting, but much more interesting to me was a sight of General Juan Vicente Gómez, the Vice-President, and the view which the occasion afforded of Venezuelan rank and fashion on parade. In watching this pageant of Caracas society, I estimated that seven out of every ten women in it under, say, twenty-five years of age, were beautiful. The sight of General Gómez disclosed a calm, stern, morose-looking man. He seemed to bear very little relation to the brilliant military retinue that accompanied him. Between the acts, he came out of the presidential box and moved around or stood in a very sober, almost rustic manner. He was at every point, as I was to learn later, the opposite of the volatile, arrogant, cantankerous Castro. From this glimpse I sensed power in the man—the man who was a brief while later to seize the reins of government from Castro; keep his former chief out of the country for sixteen years, down to an exile's death; and hold Venezuela in his hands for, till now, twenty-five years.

Steaming into the harbor of Puerto Cabello I gained a favorable first impression of my "home." The hills and mountains lay back some distance from the coast and allowed the air to circulate and the town to spread itself out. I caught sight of a pleasant-looking plaza and park just beyond the wharf. The Consulate was an airy, clean, and fairly commodious house. Unlike most houses in Spanish-speaking countries, it was two stories high. Certainly, a big enough house for one man. I kept the Consulate there about a year, then moved it to a better-adapted house. For the first few months, I took my meals at

Consulate at Puerto Cabello, Venezuela

the best of the hotels, but grew tired of that and decided to set up my own establishment. I got echoes of slight censure because, in hiring domestic help, I raised the general wages of three dollars (American gold) a month to four dollars. I engaged and kept four persons, the equivalent, perhaps, of two efficient American servants. I hired a cook, a girl to wait on table and help in the kitchen, a girl to clean the house, and a boy to make himself handy.

I immediately found out that, in addition to being the American Consul, I was consul for Cuba, consul for Panama, and in charge of consular affairs for France, with which country Castro had broken off all relations. I received in fees from these extra duties an amount equal to my salary from the United States. I cleared all vessels bound for any one of the four countries I was representing, and transacted all consular business for their respective citizens. Within a short time Cuba appointed her own consul; and, just before I left Puerto Cabello, diplomatic relations were re-established between Venezuela and France, and the French consul resumed charge of French consular affairs. My duties were not arduous; and even at that, there was a vice consul to perform any or all of them. Most of the routine work and all of the clerical work was done between the vice consul and the clerk; I, however, assumed personal responsibility for writing all consular reports on commercial and political matters. As it was, I had considerable leisure time.

I fell easily into the tropical mode of life; even into the quite sensible habit of taking a siesta. In the better house to which I moved the Consulate, my manner of living was semi-luxurious. The house, evidently, had been built for some Venezuelan grandee. The front faced the plaza and the harbor, and a side overlooked one of the three parks of the town. This was also a two-story house, but the living quarters were confined to the second floor; the ground floor, except for the portion taken up by the bath, being given over to business. The bath was of vast proportions; in it were not only a shower and a large tin tub that I had imported, but also a pool built of concrete in which one could even swim a couple of strokes. The patio of the house was on the upper floor, and so formed a sort of roof garden. It was always cooler there at noon than any other spot in the house, and there I took my siesta. The *sala* was a room capable of accommodating a grand ball. On the park side of the house were three connecting rooms, which I used as office, private office, and bedroom.

I generally got up quite early, as is the custom in Latin America. When I started down to the bath, the housemaid announced to the cook that I was up, and then laid out my fresh clothes—I usually dressed in white from hat to shoes. By the time I put my clothes on, *desayuno*, consisting of coffee, a roll or toast, and an egg, was ready. From eleven o'clock to one, every business door in Puerto Cabello was closed; that was the hour for *almuerzo*, a four-course meal, and the siesta. Five o'clock was the closing hour, and seven o'clock the general hour for dinner. I bought a good horse—horses were comparatively cheap—and learned to ride; and spent many afternoons on horseback until dinnertime. Frequently on Sundays I joined a group of horsemen and rode out to neighboring haciendas.

A few days after my arrival in Puerto Cabello I received a thirty-day card of courtesy from the club and an invitation to join. The club was housed in a low, picturesque building that sat behind a high brick wall with an ornamental gate entrance. In front of the house was a garden, and from the back a wharf extended a little way out into the bay. The wharf was occasionally the landing place for pleasure boats, but it was constantly used as a sitting place on fair afternoons and evenings. But the blades of the club had a sitting place much more popular with them. They would take their chairs and line them along the outer side of the wall, and watch the passers-by, with particular attention to the ladies. That was when I learned of the custom of Venezuelan men of addressing remarks to any pretty woman passing in the streets. Every pretty woman who ran the gantlet of that line of chairs would hear successive explosions of "*Que bonita!*" "*Que linda!*" "*Que hermosa!*" "*Que graciosa!*" An expression I frequently heard was, "*Ah, si tuviera un millón!*" ("Ah, if I only had a million dollars!") I never witnessed an instance in which any lady appeared to take offense at these remarks.

I spent most of my evenings at the club, and used many of those evenings trying to learn to play billiards or chess. I spent enough time in the reading room to go through each monthly issue of the leading French and Spanish illustrated magazines. Often I joined in a discussion or merely listened to one. The common sentiment of the members, as of Venezuelans in general, was anti-American, but I do not remember that it was ever directed against me individually. I had a feeling that I was rather popular. After I had been a member about a year, I was elected to the executive committee. I was aware that the common verdict of the club was that I was *muy simpático*. I was made to feel that there was a special appreciation of the unique experience of having an American consul who spoke the language of the country. The social intercourse that the club afforded me helped very much to make life in Puerto Cabello pleasant. And I am certain that it was the source of the greater part of all I learned about Venezuela that was valuable to me officially or personally.

At the club I observed a confutation of the idea that only women gossip. I heard a great deal of gossip, some of it important, a lot of it idle. But no gossip is unimportant for a man in the foreign service of any country. What might appear to be trivial gossip may shed light on what is serious. Whenever the talk was about Venezuela or Venezuelans I *listened* only. Often gossip gave way to semi-confidential discussions of scandal. Most of these scandalous things that I heard I set down as inventions of the imagination or as malicious lies. I discounted such tales ninety-five per cent; but a friend in whom I had the highest confidence assured me that they were generally ninety-five per cent true, and explained the mystery of how the information was commonly obtained. A Venezuelan matron was forced to be too proud to go to market for herself; such an act was regarded as degrading, and would cause her a loss of caste; but she was not above extracting from a trusted servant every bit of gossip and morsel of scandal that could be gathered. (It should, however, in fairness to the women be said that the men of what we should term the white-collar class were equally careful to avoid in public any task that might be looked upon as menial. The clerk in my office was a young Curaçaoan; I sent him one day to buy something that made a small package weighing not more than a couple of pounds. Imagine my astonishment on looking up the street and seeing him marching proudly ahead of a small boy to whom he had given a penny to carry the package. He did not dare to let it be suspected that he was anything other than a *clerk* at the American Consulate. I tried to teach him a practical lesson by going out and bringing home a ten-pound ham, but it is probable that I merely surprised him as much as he had surprised me.) All the marketing was done by servants. They went out early in the morning, and each one returned with not only provisions for the day but with every piece of interesting news she had been able to gather from the servants of other households that she had met. Naturally, in getting these items she had to trade her own; and it was through this clearing-house process that every family in Puerto Cabello knew something about what was going on in every other family.

Through Captain Crockett I took up hunting. He wanted to go hunting both because he loved the sport and because he felt it was the best method he could find to keep himself physically fit. He wanted to get out and tramp through the woods. He brought me down a shotgun from New York; and it was understood that, whenever he was in port, he and I should have a morning of shooting, starting out as early as four o'clock. Later, he brought down a canoe so that we could paddle up into the little inlets from the bay and shoot ducks. Our first experience with the canoe came near having tragic results. We started one afternoon from the ship, he in one end of the canoe, I in the other, the guns laid in the bottom, both of us paddling. I considered a canoe a craft for shallow lakes and streams, and was frightened as I thought that it was only a thin, narrow shell that stood between us and the depth of fathoms of water. I felt less nervous when we got up into the inlets. We picked out what we thought was a good spot and beached the canoe; the Captain started round the water's edge in one direction and I in the other. I heard him bang away; then a few minutes later I heard him calling to me for help. There was that in his voice that struck me with terror. I ran back and saw him twenty-five or thirty yards from the shore up to his waist in mud. He had tried to retrieve a wounded duck by floundering in after it through what appeared to be just shallow water. He had failed to get the duck, and had found that he couldn't get back on shore. He was stuck in a bed of mud, where every effort he made to get out only hastened the process of being sucked down. He directed me to get the canoe. While I was trying in my unpracticed, clumsy way to get the boat into the water, I heard him calling to me frantically to hurry. When I reached him he had sunk to his armpits. He took hold of the front end of the canoe while I sat on the farthest extreme of the other end, in order to provide the greatest leverage possible. The Captain went at the work of extricating himself in a methodical manner, like a man accustomed to dealing with an exigency; had he been panicky, both of us should have been precipitated into the same plight. Gradually, inch by inch, he forced himself up and out and closer to the shore. Before he was completely out, that darkness which comes down so rapidly in the tropics, was beginning to fall and, powerful a man as he was, he was wholly exhausted. I related this incident at the club in the evening and heard in return some weird tales of quicksands abounding in the region, of men disappearing in them, and of their bodies never being recovered. Whether these tales were true or not, I already knew enough to make me vow that I should never let a duck or any other game decoy me to any spot where I could not be sure of my footing.

Yet, the prospects of shooting ducks did lead me into another experience somewhat similar. The Italian Consul and I sat in the club and planned that, as soon as the torrential rains that had been falling for weeks stopped, we would go out to a lagoon twelve or fifteen miles from town, where, it was said, the ducks were plentiful. We started before daylight and used for our transportation a horse and buggy owned by the Consul. We got out into the country and were feeling our way cautiously along the miry road with the aid of a lantern in the buggy, when suddenly and silently, as if by magic, the horse disappeared. We got out to look for him, and found that he had slipped forward into a mud hole and had sunk up to his neck. He was a brave-hearted animal and made heroic efforts to get himself out, but his efforts did nothing more than sap his strength. The Consul got down and helped the horse to keep his nose above the mud, while I ran for help. I came back with a half-dozen *mozos*. They stripped and went into the mud. After hard work the horse was rescued, but he lay panting on the side of the road for, perhaps, an hour before we could hitch him in and start back to town.

The Consul sent out by Cuba was Señor Zangroniz. He was a well-educated man, an engineer by profession. In appearance, he was far from being typically Cuban; his complexion was almost ruddy; his eyes were blue-gray; he cultivated a short but rather fierce mustache; was punctilious with regard to the finer points of Spanish etiquette; indeed, he might easily have passed for a Spaniard of one of the northern provinces. Señor Zangroniz was, I judged, ten years older than I, but our personal relationship somehow adjusted itself in correspondence with the political relationship between our two countries. We became very close friends, and spent lots of time together. We established the custom that regularly he would dine at my house on one night in each week and I at his on another. I do not doubt that one of the strong elements in his preference for my companionship was the fact that mine was the only ear into which he felt he could pour certain criticisms which, otherwise, he would have kept to himself—an element at the base of all close companionship. He never exhausted the subject of the comparison of the standards of civilization and social life in Cuba with those in Venezuela; with the judgment always in favor of Cuba. Particularly enthusiastic and magniloquent did he grow in contrasting the beauty and graces and virtues of Cuban women with those of the women of Venezuela. But this element of the confidential ear was not all on one side; there were some things that appeared to be shortcomings in the Venezuelans and Venezuela that I felt I could discuss only with Zangroniz, of all the foreign language men in Puerto Cabello. Even so, on my side, I sensed limitations; for I realized that, after all, in language, religion, and traditional background, Zangroniz and the Venezuelans were one.

Our friendship, however, went far beyond the considerations of mutual satisfaction in the freedom to discuss Venezuela. We genuinely liked each other. We talked about many things. Sometimes we took long walks—for the tropics —while we talked. It was on one of these walks that I saw a sight that afterwards gained for me among my best friends the reputation of being, if not a liar, the teller of a very fishy fish story. Zangroniz and I had walked along the edge of the bay until we came to the mouth of a narrow inlet; and there we saw a native fishing. Now fishing, it may be said, is the laziest of all the sports; and here was a fisherman without rod or line or hook, who sat puffing languidly on his cigarette while the fish jumped into his boat. His only effort in the meantime was to observe his catch occasionally to see if it was sufficient. Among my regrets in life, one of the keenest is that I didn't have my kodak with me; for in relating this incident, and I have related it scores of times, I have yet to meet the person who seemed to believe that I was telling the truth. Perhaps, now, since trick photography in the movies has become so commonplace, the proof of the camera would not be regarded as positive. At any rate, this is the inside story: The fisherman, just before the tide turned to run out, paddled his boat to the inlet and anchored it across the mouth, which was hardly wider than the length of his craft; then a yard or so on the up-stream side of his boat, he stretched a seine entirely across the inlet with about a foot of the net above the water. He then sat in his boat and smoked while he waited. At the turn of the tide, the fish that had been chasing their prey up the bay and into the inlet, started back toward the sea, and found their passage obstructed by the seine; at least a fair number of them simply backed up and took a flying leap over the barrier; some fell short of the boat and others shot over it, but enough of them fell in to reward the fisherman for his ingenuity and patience. We watched until the satisfied fisherman removed his seine, pulled in his anchors, and paddled away; and we agreed that laziness, not necessity, is the mother of invention.

Señor Zangroniz also liked to hunt, and he wanted very much to go along with Captain Crockett and me. On one of his stays in port I informed Captain Crockett that I had invited the Cuban Consul to join us. The Captain expressed great dissatisfaction at this, and declared emphatically that he did not want to be bothered with any "spiggoty." However, the three of us went. All the way out I found myself in the uncomfortable position of mediator and interpreter. The Captain's expressions of his dissatisfaction at the presence of Zangroniz increased in vehemence as we went along; and Zangroniz, noticing the Captain's hostile manner, was concerned about what he was saying. Captain Crockett, although he had been

sailing to South American ports many years, spoke only wharf
Spanish, and Señor Zangroniz spoke no English at all; so I
kept getting from the Captain, "What's that he said?" and
from the Consul, "¿Que dice?" I translated for each of them,
but I took great liberties with the Captain's speeches; for I
knew that a true translation might have resulted in a complete
break of relations. Of course, Zangroniz was too intelligent
not to see that my translations did not always accord with the
Captain's tone of voice. When we reached the hunting
grounds we set up our blinds at separate points and sat waiting. A flock of ducks alighted to feed and we began banging
away. In the midst of the banging I heard Zangroniz yelling to
me that the Captain had shot him, and saw him running to the
cover of the woods. When I reached him he had taken off his
leather puttees, which bore a great many marks of small bird-
shot, and was searching his legs for wounds. I helped him in
the search but we found no marks on his flesh. I was never able
to discover to my complete satisfaction whether the Captain
had merely shot wild at the rising birds or had in malicious
humor discharged a volley at a point close to the Consul's
blind. But I do know that Zangroniz expressed no further desire to join any hunting party of which Captain Crockett was a
member.

XXII

IN the tropics, "Do not do today what *can* be put off till to-
morrow," is a maxim that contains many grains of wisdom.
There have come to the tropics men from a foreign clime who
have attempted to put into practice the strenuous life. The effects on them have generally been disastrous. And yet not so
disastrous as the effects on those who have yielded too much
and become lotus eaters. I saw examples of both classes, and
the plight of those who had broken down physically was less
pitiable than the plight of those who had broken down spiritually. I strove while taking life easily not to take it too easily. The
social day in Venezuela did not begin until five o'clock in the
afternoon, and between early morning and that hour there was
scarcely ever anything that one could do except attend to one's
own business. When I had no official duties to perform, I

made it my business to use that period in getting ahead with my writing, to do which had been one of my chief reasons for entering the Consular Service. Before leaving New York, I had made myself known to Richard Watson Gilder, the editor of the *Century Magazine*, and to William Hayes Ward, the editor of *The Independent*. I began mailing manuscripts to them, and my poems began appearing in the two publications. Mr. Gilder and Dr. Ward both evinced personal interest in the work I was doing. Mr. Gilder wrote me enthusiastically about my poem, *O Black and Unknown Bards*.

It was while I was in Venezuela that I had my one and only experience in line with a tradition about poetic inspiration, the tradition of the poet seizing his pen and in "fine frenzy" taking dictation from a spirit hovering about his head. I had come home from the club, and with no conscious thought of poetry in my mind I undressed for bed. When I had finished undressing I turned out my light and threw open the shutters to my bedroom windows. The open windows admitted enough light from the electric light opposite in the park to enable me to see my way about the room. I got into bed and immediately went to sleep. Later in the night, I woke suddenly, completely. For some reason, the light in the park had gone out and the room was in impenetrable darkness. I felt startled; then the darkness and silence combined, brought down on me a feeling of uttermost peace. I lay thinking for a long while; then I got up and fumbled for the light, took pen and paper, and almost without hesitation wrote a sonnet which I called *Mother Night*. Hardly bothering to read it over, I got back into bed and at once went off to sleep. The next day I made one or two slight revisions in the poem, typed it, and sent it to *The Century*. Promptly I got a letter from Mr. Gilder in which he said, "We are overwhelmed with poetry but we must take *Mother Night*."

I began earnest work on *The Autobiography of an Ex-Colored Man*, of which I had already made a first draft of the opening. The story developed in my mind more rapidly than I had expected that it would; at times, outrunning my speed in getting it down. The use of prose as a creative medium was new to me; and its latitude, its flexibility, its comprehensiveness, the variety of approaches it afforded for surmounting technical difficulties gave me a feeling of exhilaration, exhilaration similar to that which goes with freedom of motion. I turned over in my mind again and again my original idea of making the book anonymous. I also debated with myself the aptness of *The Autobiography of an Ex-Colored Man* as a title. Brander Matthews had expressed a liking for the title, but my brother had thought it was clumsy and too long; he had suggested *The Chameleon.* In the end, I stuck to the original idea of issuing the book without the author's name, and kept the title that had appealed to me first. But I have never been able to settle definitely for myself whether I was sagacious or not in these two decisions. When I chose the title, it was without the slightest doubt that its meaning would be perfectly clear to anyone; there were people, however, to whom it proved confusing. When the book was published (1912) most of the reviewers, though there were some doubters, accepted it as a human document. This was a tribute to the writing, for I had done the book with the intention of its being so taken. But, perhaps, it would have been more farsighted had I originally affixed my name to it as a frank piece of fiction. But I did get a certain pleasure out of anonymity, that no acknowledged book could have given me. The authorship of the book excited the curiosity of literate colored people, and there was speculation among them as to who the writer might be—to every such group some colored man who had married white, and so coincided with the main point on which the story turned, is known. I had the experience of listening to some of these discussions. I had a rarer experience, that of being introduced to and talking with one man who tacitly admitted to those present that he was the author of the book. Only two or three people knew that I was the writer of the story—the publishers themselves never knew me personally; yet the fact gradually leaked out and spread. The first printed statement was made by George A. Towns, my classmate at Atlanta University, who wrote a piece in which he gave his reasons for thinking I was the man. When the book was republished,* I affixed my name to it, and Carl Van Vechten was good enough to write an Introduction, and in it to inform the reader that

*Alfred A. Knopf, New York, 1927.

Mother Night.

Eternities before the first-born day,
Or e'er the first sun fledged his wings of flame
Calm Night, the everlasting and the same,
A brooding mother, over chaos lay.

And whirling suns shall blaze and then decay,
Shall run their fiery courses and then claim
The haven of the darkness whence they came,
Back to the Nirvanic peace shall grope their way.

So when my feeble sun of life burns out,
And sounded is the hour for my long sleep,
Shall I, full weary of the feverish light,
Welcome the darkness without fear or doubt,
And, heavy-lidded, I shall softly creep
Into the quiet bosom of the Night.

⏑—|⏑ —|⏑ —|⏑ —|⏑ —

Pto Bello.
Dec. 1908.

Facsimile of "Mother Night" Manuscript

the story was not the story of my life. Nevertheless, I continue to receive letters from persons who have read the book inquiring about this or that phase of my life as told in it. That is, probably, one of the reasons why I am writing the present book.

At the end of the year I was granted the statutory sixty-day leave of absence. I spent about a week in Washington, during which I visited the State Department several times. I went to Jacksonville for a brief stay with my parents; then returned to New York. In Washington, I found myself a non-resident member of the "Black Cabinet." This was a group made up of colored men who held important federal positions in the capital. At the time, it included the Register of the Treasury, the Recorder of Deeds for the District, the Auditor of the Navy Department, an Assistant United States Attorney General, a Judge of the Municipal Court, and the Collector for the Port of Washington. Charles W. Anderson was a member of the group, and so was P. S. B. Pinchback, former Lieutenant Governor of Louisiana. Those of the group who lived in Washington customarily met at lunch and discussed the political state of the nation, with special reference to its Negro citizens. On such matters, Booker T. Washington was chief adviser to President Roosevelt, and became the same to President Taft; but the "Black Cabinet" was not without considerable influence and power. The "Cabinet" no longer exists, and for the reason that Presidents since Taft have adopted a policy of appointing fewer and fewer Negroes to important positions; the lowest mark, close to zero, being reached in President Hoover's administration.

In New York, I found Bob and Rosamond back from their tour with *The Shoo-Fly Regiment*. They had started out with a company of sixty people, with some fairly good bookings and promises of more; but the bulk of it all turned out to be in one-night stands in popular-price theaters. Not yet had the fight for colored companies to play first-class houses been won. A good part of their tour had been laid out to cover small towns in the South. With a large and expensive company, it was impossible for them to make money at the prices to which they were compelled to play. Indeed, they lost money; so much that the management under which they were booked failed them and left the show to shift for itself somewhere in the far South. Bob and Rosamond used their own money to keep the company intact and bring it back to New York. A short engagement at the Bijou Theater in New York had the result of bringing them under the more reliable management of Stair and Havlin for the coming season.

New York did not seem the same to me. Some of the shine seemed to have come off. I enjoyed going to the theater again, especially because most of the times I went with Grace Nail. She had been a theater-goer since childhood, and was well informed about plays, players, and playwrights. The performances that we saw together we talked over from the three angles. But my enthusiasm about being back in my old surroundings was not as high as I had expected it would be. Bob and Rosamond were in low spirits over the financial failure of the *Shoo-Fly Regiment*, and worried about the prospects and outcome of the approaching season. The wear and tear of "trouping" coupled with anxiety had worn on Rosamond physically and showed particularly in the almost complete loss of his singing voice. Bob, more used to the ups and downs of theatrical life, showed no marked ill effects, and, probably because the plans gone awry were chiefly of his making, maintained a defensive show of optimism. But neither of the two, though they were sincerely happy to see me back, were in the mood or condition to kill a fatted calf. The studio was changed, and I could not feel at home in it. During the months that Bob and Rosamond had been on the road, D—— had used it as living quarters; it was rearranged and cluttered up; it had lost its air. The Marshall itself seemed to have deteriorated. There was still a large clientele of patrons and sightseers, but I missed the Broadway stars, the important newspaper men, and other writers that had been frequent visitors. There seemed to me to have been an all-round cheapening process going on. Some of these reactions may have been due purely to subjective causes, but they were not for that reason any less real.

When Bob and Rosamond came back to town, D—— moved out of the studio, but took another room in the Mar-

shall, so I saw him every day. I found that he had dissolved his
partnership with the Brooklyn lawyer and had set up for himself, with offices downtown in Beekman Street. I visited him
there several times. He kept a suite of well-furnished rooms,
and appeared to be building up a good practice. He was surely
far from being discouraged and I was forced to admit that my
advice to him not to leave Jacksonville had apparently been no
sounder than his to me. From what I saw, his clientele was almost entirely white. In taking lunch or dinner downtown with
him, I found that he was on terms of breezy intimacy with a
number of professional and business men in his district. On
one occasion when I was in his office a strikingly beautiful
woman came in. She was young, about twenty-two, and her
face was symmetrically perfect. She was tall and slender, but
with that breadth of shoulders that presages an Amazonian air
in middle life. But middle life to her was a long way off, and I
recognized her beauty for what it was in the present. D——
took in the homage I silently paid her; I could see from the
way he smiled that he relished it. It did not require the slight
proprietary air that he assumed for my benefit to make me perceive that the young lady's visit was not that of a client to her
lawyer. When she had gone, D—— proceeded to enlighten me
fully on what I had already guessed to be the main point. The
young lady was a Jewess; she belonged to a very nice family;
she knew that he was colored but her family did not; he was
deeply in love with her; she was in love with him. He enlarged
on the last two points.

Throughout our lives, D—— in all his love affairs had
sooner or later made me a sort of confessor. He frequently did
something that I should rather have lost a finger than to do, he
would read me most ardent letters from his lady loves; I recall,
in particular, letters he received for several years from a girl he
met at the University of Michigan, letters too tender, too sincere, yes, too sacred to be seen by a third pair of eyes; yet he
read them to me. It may have been an injustice to him, but I
always suspected that the act was not purely confidential in its
nature, but was more or less mixed with vainglory. A confession about a great love from D—— had for some time since
ceased to strike me as a crisis in his life; so I took no extreme
heed of this latest one.

I would not say that I was pleased to get away from New York, when my leave was over; but when I got aboard ship it was with a feeling of relief that I was bound for my great house, where I commanded not only my time but my actions and my near surroundings, where I should not be so tightly wedged in by the will and presence of others.

I think I have indicated that the little city of Puerto Cabello constituted a man's world. The women of Puerto Cabello had very little part in that world, and where they did touch it they did so mainly through contact with men of their immediate families. Business, politics, community activities, were wholly and exclusively masculine provinces. Even social life was preponderantly the affair of men; directly the opposite of what it is in the United States, where "society" is run and ruled by women.

But in 1908 Puerto Cabello was the scene of two consecutive weeks of social activity in which the women played a full part. Late in August, *El Restaurador* steamed into port. *El Restaurador* was the flagship of the Venezuelan Navy; in fact, almost the whole Navy. Formerly a steam yacht belonging to one of the Goulds, she had been purchased by the government, converted into a war vessel, and named in honor of President Castro, who had assumed the title, *El Restaurador de Venezuela* (The Restorer of Venezuela). On board were General Cipriano Castro, President of the Republic; his wife, Doña Zoila de Castro; numerous military aides; a full military band, and an entourage of several dozen pretty young women. It was said that the General never traveled without a large number of maids-in-waiting, as it were.

General Castro was by no means universally popular among the Venezuelans, but he was universally feared; and for the good reason that his power and his ruthlessness were both unbounded. There was, in fact, great opposition to Castro; there was opposition to him among the men I knew in Puerto Cabello, but it was never expressed openly. No one would be foolhardy enough to oppose a dictator like Castro through the expression of opinion; opposition had to be kept covert until it was able to manifest itself in armed rebellion. And, even then, one must feel fairly certain of the chances for success, because no imaginable fate could be worse than being made a political prisoner. I used to talk with a man who had lain for months in a filthy dungeon, weighted down in *grillos* (irons). In his case, he and another man were bound together by heavy shackles that were riveted on their ankles and connected by a short chain; they were never able to be more than three feet apart. His story caused me nausea. So, in the welcome to Puerto Cabello given to General Cipriano Castro, *Restaurador de Venezuela*, there was no voice of audible dissent. Men who bitterly hated Castro, though they took no active part in entertaining him, hardly dared to decline to attend affairs to which they were bidden.

But no one, friend or enemy to the Dictator, could escape the intoxication engendered by the festivities. Various officials invited guests *a tomar una copa de champagne* in honor of the General. The presidential band, a good one, played every afternoon in the principal park, while the populace and society promenaded round and round. A special *Te Deum* was sung at the church. The high spot, however, came at the beginning: it was the grand ball given by the Collector of the Port. All of Porteña society was present. I was surprised that it could boast so many lovely women. The orchestra had been brought down from Valencia. I have not yet heard a finer orchestra for the kind of dances it played. It was composed entirely of strings and woodwinds, and played only waltzes and quadrilles. I danced most of the waltzes—they were played ravishingly—and omitted all of the quadrilles. The women were beautiful, the music enchanting, and the champagne, unusual for the tropics, was dry—a trinity that left little for a man's attention elsewhere. I could not help but note that one of Castro's generals present at the ball was a gigantic, full-blooded Negro; and I was mildly surprised, because there were, comparatively, only a few Negroes in Venezuela. But something else made a still stronger pull on my attention—General Castro.

This was the first good opportunity I had had to observe the man—this man who for seven years had been the absolute master of Venezuela; who had snapped his fingers at the power of England, of Germany, of Italy, of France, and of the United States; who compared himself with Napoleon, slightly to the latter's disadvantage; this man who had risen from the bottom level of his country's peasantry to be the overlord of all; who until he was thirty had never worn a pair of shoes and now lived the life of a sybarite; who was a superlative combination of vanity, arrogant ignorance, cruelty; and of courage, too; this despot who was able to decree the prosperity or the ruin of any Venezuelan citizen, under whose disfavor security crumbled away, in whose hands life and death actually lay. It was like seeing the sinister hero of some barbarous page in history brought to life.

During the early part of the evening, General Castro sat in a high-backed chair, where he received those who were presented to him. I was presented as the American Consul. He extended his hand to me with the palm turned down and fingers hanging limp. He took my hand with the ends of those limp fingers and expressed a perfunctory greeting, taking no pains to disguise the contempt he had for all foreigners. He was an exceptional figure in the throng of men about him. Short in stature—his height, within a fraction of an inch, was that of Napoleon's—he, nevertheless, did not look small in the great chair in which he sat; his haughty and disdainful manner filled it up. His complexion showed his Indian ancestry, but he had a sallow hue. His head was square rather than round. Looking at his face, it appeared that from the line of his eyes the length to the extremity of his forehead was much greater than it was to the point of his chin. This appearance was magnified by the top of his head being bare, except for a very thin and rat-like growth of hair. A jet-black, luxuriant beard and mustache did not entirely cover his sensual mouth. But the dominant feature was the eyes; black, hard, unresponsive, impassive, they darted a quick glance here or there, but immediately recovered their insensitivity. I had seen such eyes in some animal, somewhere.

There was a note on the invitation to the ball saying, full dress *es de rigor*; but General Castro did not comply with the requirement. He was attired neither in full dress nor, like his aides, in uniform. He wore a long, fawn-colored Prince Albert coat, with vest and trousers of the same material, patent leather shoes, and on his head a dark velvet skull-cap embroidered with a wreath pattern in gold. This cap was his only insignia of rank. He took it off frequently to mop his face and brow and the top of his head with his handkerchief. The manner in which he was arrayed seemed to me to be strangely at variance with his known vanity. At any rate, he was dressed more sensibly than any other man present; for one of the follies of man in tropical America is the slavish fashion of wearing black clothes at state and high official affairs, a folly that is an actual hardship. The man in equatorial America who will design a light and cool style of dress for such occasions will be a benefactor worthy of a monument.

Toward the middle of the evening, the announcement ran round in whispers that the President would dance. No one could stay in Venezuela thirty days and not learn that Castro was a remarkable dancer; but I was not prepared for the exhibition I witnessed. He took part in a quadrille, and for a while went through the figures in the customary manner. By degrees, the spirit of the dance seemed to get into his blood, to run through his nerves, to seize and control his muscles. He became more and more animated, and finally took the center of the floor to himself. He chasséd right and left, forward and backward. He pranced round and round, spreading out the skirts of his coat with his hands. No other dancer in the set was now making any move. He executed fantastic figures and steps, at one time squatting on his haunches and kicking out his feet alternately, somewhat after the manner of a familiar Russian folk dance movement. His dancing quickened the tempo of the music; he jumped, he leaped, he pirouetted, he spun himself round like a whirling dervish. He was, it was evident, bordering on a state of frenzy. When he stopped, wet with streaming perspiration, the set in which he had been dancing ended; but he danced again in the same manner many times before the ball was over, coming up, seemingly fresh, for each new dance. I was told that at a ball he always had on hand a supply of extra shirts, at least a dozen, and made changes whenever the moisture of a garment reached the point of saturation. Without doubt, it was these extraordinary antics that had led to his being dubbed *El Mono de los Andinos* (the Monkey of the Andes). It was difficult for me to reconcile these grotesqueries with the air and actions of the man I had an hour before been observing as he sat in his high-backed chair.

This series of festivities was brought to a close with a grand ball given by General Castro himself in honor of *la sociedad carabobeña*. The ball was given in Valencia, the chief city of

the State of Carabobo. A number of invited guests went up
from Puerto Cabello. I went for a double reason; I wanted to
attend the ball and I wanted to see Valencia, where I had not
yet been, although it was in my consular district. I found it a
beautiful city of about thirty thousand, twice the population
of Puerto Cabello, with some very nice shops and a great
many fine dwelling houses. It was more typically Spanish than
the Port, because foreign interests and influence were not so
strong there as they were in the city on the coast. I liked Valencia so much that I decided to be a frequent visitor; but I
never got back. The ball was similar to the one given in Puerto
Cabello; the difference being in degree rather than in kind. In
each particular it was on a grander scale because of the larger
number of persons of wealth and culture in Valencia. The
President danced with even wilder energy than he had displayed on the former occasion. I began to suspect that he was
dancing against death. Castro was then forty-eight, and at the
peak of his power, a comparatively young man, who had conquered the world about him; but, as some knew, he was also a
sick man. A close study of his face in repose, the deep lines,
the weary mouth, the cadaverous aspect lurking just behind
the countenance, revealed even to the unpracticed eye that the
dread hand was preparing to strike. Beyond a doubt, Castro
had forebodings of this; but it is improbable that he had a single inkling that it was the hand of political fate that was to
strike first.

Several months passed, and Puerto Cabello had entirely settled back to its leisurely pace. Then, suddenly, there was excitement at the club. Rumors and more rumors came down
from the capital regarding the President's health: that his
physical condition was approaching a critical point; that his
doctors had informed him that only a surgical operation, one
which they did not dare perform, could save his life; that he
had cabled to Germany for the services of a great specialist;
that the German specialist was willing to take the case, but declined to operate in Venezuela; that this disinclination developed into a blank refusal in the face of a proffered fee of fifty
thousand dollars. This last item in the succession of rumors

was hotly discussed at the club; some asserting that the German was unwilling to risk his reputation with the hospital facilities of Caracas; some that he feared he would never get out of Venezuela alive if the operation was not successful; and still others that he probably knew, if he came and performed even a successful operation, Castro would bilk him.

In the end, General Castro reluctantly yielded to the pressure of his advisers and decided to go to Germany for the operation. He took nearly all the space on a large French liner; for, with him went not only a full complement of aides and friends, but also, as the reports had it, more than a hundred of the most beautiful women of Venezuela. As the ship prepared to get under way, Castro sat dejectedly on a great strong-box, which contained, as other reports had it, an immense amount of money in gold currency. It is more than probable that many of the friends who accompanied Castro felt that they would be safer on the ocean with him than in Venezuela without him. Among these was one, Gumersindo Rivas, the editor of Castro's personal organ, *El Constitucional.* In the field of press agency, American journalism has never produced anything to compare with this man Rivas. His praise of Castro strained even the grandiloquence of the Spanish language. Venezuelans read daily about "The Restorer," "The Invincible Hero," "The Supreme Leader," "The Savior of His People." Frequently Rivas listed in an ascending scale the names and deeds of the world's great heroes, ages, and saints, including the name of Jesus, and rose to climax with the name and deeds of Cipriano Castro. When Castro was making the tour that took in Puerto Cabello and Valencia, the progress of his itinerary was published in a series of articles under the title, "The Apotheosis of the Hero." I used to read *El Constitucional* every day, not omitting to read Rivas's leading editorial. The man's ingenuity and his ability to ring in Castro's name, no matter upon what subject he was writing, was astonishing. If he wrote an article, say, on the solar system, he would end it by declaring that as the sun is the center of the solar system, so is Castro the center of Venezuela. I took up *El Constitucional* one Sunday morning and read an eloquent, perfervid article on Easter. And that article did end: "As Christ rose to save the world, so has Castro risen to save Venezuela." For Gumersindo Rivas, Castro was the breath of life and the staff of life, so it was natural that he could not exist separated from him.

The ship had hardly cleared the harbor of La Guaira before the university students of Caracas rose in revolt against the Castro administration. General Vincent Gómez, Vice President of the Republic, promptly put down the "revolution," and as promptly took over the Presidency. There is no doubt that Castro got the news on shipboard by wireless. What were his thoughts? Did he have full confidence in the lieutenancy of Gómez? Did he believe that the subordinate had merely taken strong measures to hold the power until the return of his chief? Or did he have misgivings and doubts? There must have occurred to Castro's mind the success of a most simple expedient which he had himself employed a few years before. At that time he had wanted very much to get rid of the French Minister to Venezuela. One day that official went down to La Guaira and made a visit aboard a French steamship. Now, there was a regulation in Venezuela that no one was allowed to go aboard a vessel without an authorization signed by the officer of the port. The French Minister, relying on the courtesy usually accorded to foreign representatives with regard to the ships of their own nations, simply walked aboard. When he started off, Castro's soldiers, under orders from Caracas, asked to see his permit and, when he was not able to show one, refused to let him go ashore. The Minister was obliged to sail without bag or baggage.

Castro's operation was successful. He came through in better health than he had had for years. When he sought to return to Venezuela, Gómez would not let him land; an eventuation that produced satisfaction, even if disguised, in our Department of State. Castro retired long enough to raise an expedition of several thousand men, and effected a landing on the north coast of the country. But Venezuelans did not flock to his standard, and in a single battle he was defeated. He spent the remainder of his life in efforts to regain his lost power. He had an idea that he might further his cause among Venezuelan expatriates in the United States, through a visit to New York; but our government detained him at Ellis Island and finally denied him admission. He hovered round Venezuela as closely as he could, and finally died, an exile, at San Juan, Porto Rico, in 1924.

XXIII

LIFE in Puerto Cabello ran along evenly. I enjoyed it, but I didn't want to slip so deep into the rut of it that I shouldn't be able to get out. The consulship at this indolent little port afforded ideal conditions for me to carry on my principal aim in entering the service; but I had grown ambitious as a consul, and I worked to make a record that would entitle me to promotion. I did my best to make my commercial reports more than perfunctory communications. I kept both eyes open as wide as possible for opportunities for American business. I sent in frequent suggestions gathered in the method pursued by the Germans, who did the greater part of all the foreign business done in Venezuela. Actuated by the fact that baseball was so popular and well played in Cuba, I promoted the idea of organizing two clubs in Puerto Cabello. There was, at least, the result of an order for complete outfits from a New York sporting goods house. I can't ever forget the first game they played; it was so much more vocal than athletic. When I left Puerto Cabello there were indications that our national game was gaining a foothold in that section of Venezuela. The gathering of commercial information and a supervision over American ships and seamen are prime duties of a consul. However, when the post lies within the sphere of American influence, the gathering of political information and the protection of American citizens also become prime duties.

I sent in frequent political reports, because our State Department had more than the conventional interest in the internal political situation of Venezuela. But, because there were practically no American citizens resident in Puerto Cabello and the only American visitors were passengers en route who came ashore while their ship was in port, I had little or nothing to do about the protection of American citizens. "Protecting American citizens" is the bane of a consul's life; and the point of the difficulty is not that of seeing that an American citizen's rights are not violated, but of seeing that his physical needs are taken care of. This is especially true in many of the Latin American countries, where there are so many destitute Americans. Among the beachcombers in these countries, applying to the consul for aid is a regular "racket." A consul is authorized to draw on the Treasury of the United States for any necessary amount to aid the destitute seaman, to provide them with food, shelter, clothes, medical treatment, and passage back to an American port, if the situation warrants; but he is not allowed a penny for the aid of mere citizens; any financial aid that he gives them comes out of his own pocket. Not in my entire experience, however, did I meet a fellow consul who could say that he had ever been able to convince an applicant of that fact. The applicant, when he failed to receive as much as he thought he was entitled to, usually expressed his doubts as to the consul's interest or sincerity or his honesty. Sometimes an outspoken individual would express his opinion about his country, declaring that he didn't consider it worth a damn.

Among the American visitors to Puerto Cabello came a shipload of Congressmen headed by "Uncle" Joe Cannon. As I remember, they were on their way to see how the digging of the Panama Canal was coming on. I knew that the party had been touring around the Caribbean several weeks, so I met the ship with my latest batch of *New York Heralds*, which I placed in Mr. Cannon's hands. He expressed great appreciation of this; and I felt sure there was nothing I might have done for him in Puerto Cabello that would have pleased him more. He came ashore and, running his arm through mine, walked along to pay a short visit at the Consulate. He asked me a number of pointed questions about Venezuela and about myself. Strangely, with him, I felt no reticence in answering the latter questions. I put him down as a fine, democratic gentleman. The only member of the junketing party that I recall was Congressman, later Senator, William B. McKinley.

The visitor at the Consulate who caused me the greatest excitement was an officer from aboard an American man-of-war that had just anchored in the harbor. He presented me the compliments of the Captain, and advised me that the launch would be at my service at the hour when I wished to pay my official visit aboard. I appointed the hour, then set myself to

reading over the regulations governing the conduct of a consul paying an official visit aboard an American war vessel. Both
the launch and the ship flew the consular flag; the ship was
manned as I went aboard; the Captain met me at the gangplank and escorted me to his cabin. When the visit was concluded, he escorted me back to the gangplank. When the
launch cleared the ship, I was given the consular salute of
seven guns, which I received standing with bared head. The
ceremony was, later, to become rather commonplace with me,
but this first experience was the thrill of a lifetime.

After I had served two years at Puerto Cabello, my thoughts
turned more and more to the matter of a promotion. It was
not that I was dissatisfied with Puerto Cabello; I was simply
anxious to go up in the Service, and I knew that a consul who
stayed too long a time at one post was likely to become regarded as a fixture there. Before my first year was up, President Roosevelt had expressed a willingness to name me as
consul at Nice, but Secretary Root had said that it simply
could not be done. Consideration of me for the post at Nice
was a by-product of the riot at Brownsville, Texas, August
1906, in which a battalion of the Twenty-fifth Regiment (Negro) United States Infantry was implicated. In November, the
President issued an order dismissing the entire battalion without honor and disqualifying its members from military or civil
service thereafter. This order aroused a wave of disapproval and
criticism. But from the colored people came a storm of protest
which burst over the President with a force that must have
shocked him, for he was genuinely proud of the fact that he
held a greater degree of the confidence and affection of the
Negro people than had been given to any president since
Abraham Lincoln. A Congressional investigation smoothed
the matter out somewhat by opening a way for members of
the battalion to re-enlist, and the President revoked the civil
disability order, but he was still disturbed by the resentment of
the colored people, and was ready and willing to do anything
he properly could to allay that feeling.

When the matter of a promotion was uppermost in my
mind, I awoke to find that I was trapped in Venezuela. An epidemic of bubonic plague broke out, and every American representative got out of the country, except me. Certainly, I did

not stay on because I wished to; but there I was, the only one left. I suffered no great fright; I felt that my habits of living secured me more than a fair degree of immunity. I, of course, kept clean and I took the further precaution of not going to any place where there was likelihood of contagion. But those were dreary weeks. Shipping fell off to a minimum. The few ships that did put in guarded against rats going aboard by placing midway up their hawsers metal disks a foot and a half or two feet in diameter. I spent much of my time reading about rats. I was surprised at the large amount of literature on the subject, and to find that it was so interesting. In the spring of 1909, a cable from the State Department came advising me that I had been appointed Consul at Corinto, Nicaragua, and that I should proceed to my post by way of Washington. My new post carried a promotion to the next grade above and an increase in salary of a thousand dollars a year. But when the moment came, I felt some keen regrets at leaving Puerto Cabello. I had established many kindly associations, and life had been very pleasant. I confess that the biggest emotional strain came in saying good-by to my ménage; two of the women had been in my employ for three years, and they wept as though I was going to my death. A group of men I knew best were at the ship to see me off; and bade me good luck and Godspeed in, as is the custom in Latin America, many a glass of champagne. When the ship touched at Curaçao I went ashore and to the shop of a filigree worker, where I purchased one of his masterpieces, a heart done in gold, to be worn as a pendant. I made it a gift to Grace Nail.

XXIV

WHEN I reached New York, I went directly to Washington to report at the State Department and receive instructions. My instructions were brief; they were that I should proceed to my post as promptly as possible, with the added instruction that my duties would be more diplomatic than consular. I took the time to run over to Baltimore for a night to see Bob and Rosamond; they had written a new show called *The Red Moon*, and were playing there. My two former partners were enthusiastic about the future under their new managers. I returned to New York and spent a feverish ten days or so in preparations to sail.

I felt less at home in the city than ever before. The studio was closed. Bob had bought a house in West 136th Street, in Harlem, and moved his family in. He was, I believe, the first colored person to buy a home in Harlem, west of Lenox Avenue. Rosamond had taken an apartment in West 99th Street, and I stayed there. I went down to The Marshall only once; it seemed like a place I had known and almost forgotten. West 53rd Street was already beginning to lose its place as the Negro center, and the trek to Harlem was taking on significant proportions. D—— had married; he had married the beautiful Jewess I had seen at his office on my former visit to New York. But his marriage made no change in his relations toward me; nor, in fact, any marked change in his relations with his other Negro friends. D—— was, so far as I can remember, the only man I have known to "pass"—and I have known numbers of them—without feeling it was necessary to "pass up" his colored friends. One of his first acts was to have me up to his apartment for dinner with him and his wife.

During the time I was in New York I saw Grace Nail as often as I could. We went many places together, to the theater a number of times. I remember, specifically, that we saw *Anna Karenina* at the old Herald Square Theater; but clearer than any memory of the play is my memory of the fact that, through my clumsiness, one of her hatpins was lost under the seats. I replaced the pin, and was superstitious enough to exact a penny from her in payment. She was at the steamer to see me sail; and, as the ship slipped out from the pier, the thought came down on me heavily that I was a lonely man; and I knew that I was really and deeply in love.

The voyage was uneventful, except that I got my initiation into the science and art of poker. A quartet of young men insisted on my taking the fifth hand at table, and we played every night in the smoking room. I liked the game, and also I was lucky enough to get my lessons at small cost. I had reasons, later, to be thankful for this primary instruction. Our vessel docked at Colon—which reminds me that there was a man on board who got lots of fun out of inveigling victims into making the losing bet that Colon, on the Atlantic, was east of Panama, on the Pacific. The Panama Canal was still in course of construction; so, transportation across the Isthmus had to be made by train. I had considerable baggage to be transferred, because I was taking with me a good many articles that I needed and which I doubted could be obtained in Nicaragua. But the manager of the Panama Railroad was good enough to extend to me the courtesies of the company, and all my baggage was carried across without trouble or expense on my part.

I was glad to get out of Colon; the town was utterly unattractive and unbearably hot. Panama was an agreeable change. I found this old city, originally built by the Spaniards in 1518, exceedingly interesting and charming. As soon as I was installed at my hotel, I drove the several miles to Ancon, the port, to verify the arrangements for my passage to Corinto. At the offices of the Pacific Mail Steamship Company, I learned that the ship on which I was to sail had sunk at the dock. True it was; I went down on the dock and looked at her, or rather, at what could be seen of her. I learned, further, that I should have to wait fully two weeks for the next ship. This was not a pleasing prospect; that length of time was more than I required for seeing Panama; moreover, in view of my instructions, I was anxious to get to my post. But there was no way out of the dilemma. While I was at the offices of the Pacific Mail Steamship Company talking with the agent, I became aware of the presence of a dozen or more Negroes in the large counting room back of the outer office. Now, Negroes were not a rare sight in Panama; they were almost as ubiquitous there as they are now in Harlem; the spade work on the Canal was being done mainly by Negroes. So these that I saw in the Pacific Mail office made no special demands on my attention until I gradually perceived that they were not working as janitors or laborers, but doing clerical work. I noted that they were making entries in the big ledgers and handling stacks of bills of lading and other shipping documents. I was particularly impressed by their nonchalant skill in the trick of making pen and pencil racks of their ears. I could not refrain from asking the agent about them. He informed me that the very best accountants and bookkeepers to be found in Panama were educated Jamaican Negroes.

I spent the time seeing Panama. In the afternoons I took a drive. In the evenings I listened to the band play in the park and watched the crowds or explored the places of amusement—some of them tough places. I did not omit seeing the world-famous Panama "red light" district. I had only two or three more days to wait. I went out on a morning to make some purchases: Panama hats, which, as ought to be known, are made in Ecuador, not Panama, and some trinkets from the Chinese shops. I had hitherto avoided going out in the heat of the day; and, when I got back to the hotel about noon, I was wet with perspiration and felt extremely fatigued. I took off my coat and threw myself on the bed under a window through which a delightful breeze was blowing. I intended to relax only a few minutes before going down to lunch, but I fell sound asleep. I got up in time for dinner, and after dinner went out to the band concert. In the night I woke with terrible pains in my chest and back, which were intensified each time I breathed. I managed to ring for a bell boy. When he came, he grew quite concerned about my condition. I asked him to call me a doctor at once. He left and came back with two porous plasters, one of which he applied to my chest and the other to my back, and told me that the doctor was out but would come as soon as he got the message. I asked him if he could not call some other doctor, but he seemed to go on the assumption that there was only one doctor in Panama—this probably was the one who had special arrangements with the hotel.

The doctor came the next morning. I had one additional symptom, I could not swallow. He took my temperature and examined me; it was four or five, I don't remember exactly how many, degrees above normal; I had a severe case of tonsillitis; and symptoms of pleurisy. The doctor urged me to go to the hospital immediately. I told him that it was impossible; my ship sailed within thirty-six hours, and I could not miss it; I'd stay, at least, through the day at the hotel and see how I felt. He shrugged his shoulders, prescribed for me, and said that he would come again in the evening. The next morning I felt no better and the rain was coming down as it can only in the tropics. On his visit the doctor again advised my going to the hospital. I declined to go. I lay in bed weighing the situation;

sick in Panama, no friends, not a single person interested in me, not sure even that I had a competent physician; I had better take my chances on board an American ship with the ship's doctor. I made the decision. With the aid of a bell boy I got dressed and packed. I then hired a wagon and drove through the rain to the Pacific Terminals of the Railroad, where I picked up my goods being held in storage for me there, then to the docks, and, soaking wet, caught my ship within fifteen minutes of her sailing time. I don't know what to attribute it to, but this rash action had none of the results to be expected. I felt better as soon as I got aboard, and I improved rapidly each day at sea. It was only the tonsillitis that hung on and made swallowing uncomfortable for six or seven days.

My first view of Corinto sent my heart down like a plummet. What I saw was not a city or a town, but a straggling, tropical village. H. H. Leonard, the Vice-Consul, came aboard and courteously took charge of my belongings. When I got ashore, I found that the close-up was less flattering than the view from the bay. The bay itself was beautiful; landlocked by several islands, with Cardon, a great rock, standing up in strong relief. Directly across the bay, three or four miles, was a large, finely wooded island, and along the left ran the shore of the mainland with its skyline of five volcanoes. Of the surroundings, only what man had done in making Corinto was vile. It was a shanty town, built entirely of wood. There were less than a half-dozen attractive houses in it. The streets were unpaved; there was no electricity. Except for a couple of primitive grocery stores, there was not a shop in the place. There was a rambling old building on the waterfront, the Hotel Papi, run by a fat Italian of that name. It was a wooden structure, built largely of mahogany, and in a more or less tumbledown condition; but its airy *cantina* and dining room made it the pleasantest place in Corinto. Adjoining the Hotel Papi were the comparatively splendid houses of the brothers Palacio, also Italians and the leading importers and exporters in Nicaragua. A block back was another hotel, a crude, new building, which lacked the picturesqueness that the old Hotel Papi possessed. It was run by a tall, gaunt but handsome old Irishman, whom the English-speaking people called Dan Finnegan. Dan wrote his last name "Finucane," pronouncing it as a three-syllable word with the accent on the "u." The natives made it a four-syllable word, with the accent on the "a." Dan, with his aristocratic face and soldierly bearing, running a crude hotel in Corinto, never, during the four years I knew him, ceased stirring my curiosity as to the whys and wherefores of his being there.

As soon as I had settled myself at the Hotel Papi, I went to the Consulate. It was located in a room that was part of a private dwelling adjoining Dan's hotel. I was the first consul appointed to Corinto; the office up to that time had been in charge of a vice-consul who was under the Consul at Managua, the capital. I saw at once that it would not be possible to organize the office properly in the limited quarters it occupied; so I signed a lease for the third-best house in town, which, fortunately for me, had just become vacant. The house consisted of three rooms built in a straight line facing the street. Two of the rooms were each twenty by twenty. There was an ell on the back that contained the kitchen and quarters for servants. There was an elevated porch on the front, that also served as a sidewalk for the public; and on the back was a wide veranda that looked out over a very lovely flower garden. At the far end of the garden was a shower bath, supplied with water from a tank which was filled by a force pump at the well. One of the large rooms I took as an office, the other for my personal use, and the third as a filing room. I requisitioned office furniture from Washington, bought a commodious, native-built cedar wardrobe, and some other pieces for myself; and in a short while the Consulate was presentable and I was comfortable.

When I arrived at Corinto, there was an American warship anchored in the harbor. I was prompt in paying my official visit aboard. She was in command of Captain William S. Benson (later, the American representative in drawing up the naval terms of the Armistice with Germany and the Central Powers, and naval adviser to the American Commission to Negotiate Peace). Captain Benson was glad to talk with someone who had recently come from Washington. He had been anchored in Corinto bay several months, and he was anxious to get some sign, however slight, as to why he was being held there and when he would be relieved. I could give him no sign that was hopeful; but a little while after, he was relieved, when another warship came in and took his place.

Within my first few days in Corinto, I paid another official visit. I learned that President Zelaya was living at his summer house on Cardon Island. I went over to pay my respects to him, and was cordially received. Here was another famous dictator, the man who had held autocratic power in Nicaragua for sixteen years. It was inevitable that I should compare him with Castro. He was like Castro, in that he was a ruthless tyrant and also "in bad" with the United States. In every other respect he was unlike the Venezuelan. Castro was boorish, and took refuge in his ignorance; Zelaya was urbane and well educated. He spoke three languages; his English was very good. Castro made a boast of his provincialism; whenever he might be asked why he never visited Paris, he would answer sarcastically that he had no need to go to Paris, Caracas was in every way as fine a city as Paris, only smaller. Zelaya was a cosmopolite who knew his Paris and the Riviera. The President of Nicaragua was light bronze in color, slightly bald, rather stout, and possessed of perfect poise and charming manners. He chatted with me without constraint for half an hour. I do not question that he had as great distrust of the United States and dislike for its citizens as Castro, but he was too suave to make any exhibition of it under the circumstances. I left carrying a pleasant impression of Zelaya although I already knew that, officially, my hand was to be against him.

I quickly found that Corinto was not to be at all so close to a sinecure as Puerto Cabello had been. There were more ships to be cleared, and the seamen on the American ships were different from those I had been dealing with; many of them were Mexicans, and they gave considerably more work and worry. Occasionally, there were fights among them, in which someone was seriously hurt. In one instance there was a killing. In such cases, the Consul has preliminary extraterritorial powers, which he is called on to exercise. The American warships, always present in the harbor, entailed another set of duties. Then there were duties involved in protecting American citizens, of whom there were, relatively, a great many in Nicaragua: American businessmen, American plantation owners,

American concession hunters, prospectors, adventurers, soldiers of fortune, beachcombers, and a steady stream of tourists. An American citizen, dead, in a foreign country and without adult next of kin, puts a heavier responsibility on the Consul than any live one could. The Consul at once becomes the custodian and administrator of all his possessions, whether they consist of gold and lands or only a valiseful of old clothes. There was a coffee planter living in Nicaragua with his wife and two grown sons. The wife and both sons, within a matter of months, died under tragic if not suspicious circumstances. The coffee planter decided to go back to the United States. He was making his way on muleback down from the far interior, but was taken sick and got no farther than the city of Leon, where he died. I had to take charge of all his affairs and property at once. (The Consular Regulations are extremely rigid on this point.) I held ten thousand dollars in my safe and looked after the income from a coffee plantation worth fifty thousand dollars or more, while search was being made for heirs of the dead man in the United States. Inquiries by the State Department brought no results; but, in going through the planter's papers, I found a letter written to him by a brother living in Philadelphia. It was a letter in which the writer stated that two of his daughters would be unable to attend school because he could not buy shoes for them, and begged for a small sum of money. I cabled the news of the planter's death to this brother, then wrote and told him about the estate, directing him to come to Nicaragua immediately with proof of his kinship so that I could turn the property over into his hands. He replied saying that could not come to Nicaragua; that I could send the ten thousand dollars to him (I suppose he meant by mail), and implying that he had no particular use for a coffee plantation; that if I sent him the cash I could keep the plantation. I do not know what perils this man thought lay in traveling from Philadelphia to the interior of Nicaragua. I promptly informed him that he would have to come in person or through a proper power of attorney. He gave his power of attorney to a lawyer—a Philadelphia lawyer— who came down at once, and to whom I turned over the property with feelings of great relief. In addition to these duties, there was the one of keeping both eyes and ears open for political developments, to interpret them correctly and keep the State Department informed.

I found, too, in Corinto—unlike in Puerto Cabello— that occasionally race prejudice bumped into me. I mean to indicate specifically that I did not bump into it. In other words, I was not concerned with its stupid outbursts or with how it bruised its own head. A man, from South Carolina, came into the Consulate on a matter of business. His gaze at once met a white man (the Vice Consul) seated at a long table just to the right of the entrance. And, up center of the room, a Negro (myself) seated at a desk, just back of which an American flag draped the wall. This set-up evidently did not accord with his sense of the fitness of things, for he stood perplexed for a moment. But conditioned reflexes forced him over to the Vice-Consul, to whom he made known his case. The Vice-Consul informed him that it was a matter which he had better take up with the Consul, and directed him to me. The man's perplexity gave way to confusion, perhaps to something worse; he appeared incapable of taking the three or four steps over to my desk. I went on with what I had been doing, allowing him all the time he needed to make up his mind whether he would ask for what he wanted or not; to adjust himself to meet the humiliation which confronted him or avoid it by walking out. He finally came over to me, and I dispatched the business he had come to have done. He went out—having slain a bugbear or sustaining a smarting wound to his Nordic pride?—I don't know which. There were several other cases of individuals, caught unawares and psychologically unprepared to meet the situation. I found it best always to let them work out their own recovery from the shock and embarrassment.

In October, news flashed across the country that a revolution to overthrow Zelaya had been started on the east coast at Bluefields, under the head of General Juan B. Estrada. I easily put together all the intimations I had gathered; and the import of the instructions given me at the Department of State became perfectly clear. I had not asked for further instructions from the Department, because I had been in the Service long enough to learn that in certain phases of diplomacy definite instructions are not given, and an officer is valuable only so far as his ability to divine the main objects of his government goes. I knew that our government would be glad to see Zelaya overthrown. He had been an energetic and capable administrator of Nicaraguan affairs, but his hostility to the United States had made him a thorn in the thumb of the Department of State. The American Minister had thrown up his hands and his commission, saying that he could not deal with such an uncivilized ruler as Zelaya. On the surface was his hostile and tricky attitude toward American concessionaires; and deep down at the center was his attitude regarding the Nicaraguan Canal route. And now I saw that our government had had foreknowledge that this revolutionary blow against him was to be struck, and that it stood definitely on the side of the revolutionists.

The revolutionists had a great advantage and a great disadvantage in starting their operations in Bluefields. They were relatively close to New Orleans and New York, their main bases of supplies and resources, and were free from any danger of their line of communications being cut or interrupted. On the other hand, they were some two hundred miles from the real Nicaragua; for the capital, the government, the overwhelming portion of the population and wealth of Nicaragua—as in each of the Central American republic—are on the Pacific rather than the Atlantic side. The comparatively wide stretch between the Caribbean and the two great lakes of Nicaragua was a wild region without a railroad or even adequate roads. To march and sustain an army through this jungle and over an intervening range of mountains called for tremendous courage and endurance. The revolutionists did make and fight their way toward the lakes, and almost within striking distance of Managua. But, for the reason that the American interests in control of the great Deitrick concession, which was a big part of the milk in the revolutionary coconut, were still not quite sure where Estrada stood on the question of concessions (the insurgent leader had declared himself opposed to all "monopolistic" concessions; later, upon inquiries from the United States, he had declared that he would protect "lawful American interests"), negotiations in New York for money to finance the revolution came to a standstill, and the revolutionists, who had advanced on promises of forthcoming support, found themselves in the interior without ammunition. General

Chamorro, the commander in the field, thus caught, was defeated by the government forces, and compelled to fall back on Bluefields.

The fighting in eastern Nicaragua was farther away from Corinto than the fighting in the World War was from San Francisco. Business and life at the port went on as usual. I made trips up to Leon, the largest city; to Managua, the capital; and to Granada, the third city in importance, in order to get in closer touch with what was taking place. Very little authentic news could be gained; there were rumors aplenty, but they had to be weighed, compared, and sifted. The safest method was to infer what was going on from the action of government and military officials. At any rate, from these trips, I got a view of the cultural life of Nicaragua. Leon was an old, sleepy, typical Spanish-American city, of about forty thousand inhabitants, very proud of its primacy in distinguished families and culture. On these two points, there was a fierce rivalry between the people of Leon and the people of Granada. In fact, this rivalry widened into a breach that constituted the political cleavage in Nicaragua. The struggle for the control of the government was a fight waged between *Los Liberales* (the Liberals) of Leon and *Los Conservadores* (the Conservatives) of Granada. The terms, it hardly needs to be said, had no more of intrinsic significance than the terms "Republicans" and "Democrats" in the United States. Indeed, it seemed to me that it would have been more fitting if these two cities had exchanged their political labels; for Leon was much less modern in its attitude toward politics and everything else than Granada. Thus it was that the political division of the country was also a geographical division, and it was, to say the least, politically uncomfortable for persons of one party to live in the geographical territory of the other.

In the political sense, Managua, lying between these two cities, was the territory to be captured. Managua was a smaller city than Leon, but was more of a metropolis. In the capital there was considerable movement and some approach to the gayeties of life. This aspect was heightened by the presence of the foreign representatives and a fairly large number of foreign residents. A good club and the Grand Hotel Luponi, the latter kept by an Italian, afforded meeting places of a fashionable air.

At the brewery there was an outdoor beer garden which was popular in the afternoons and evenings. The National Band gave concerts in the park. In Leon, as I remember, the most popular diversion was a walk on Sunday afternoons out to the cemetery. I used to visit Leon often, because it was near to Corinto. I was an accepted visitor at a number of houses there, and became acquainted with members of Leon's literary group. Among the boasts of Leon was its leadership in literature; and it was not an empty boast; Leon was the birthplace and home of Rubén Darío (1867–1916), the foremost and widest known figure in Latin American letters in his generation, and a world influence on modern literature in the Spanish language.

I could not help but note, as I had done in Venezuela, the strong position of the Germans in business. I saw that in both countries they did not limit their relationships and activities to business; they entered fully into the social life. The unmarried men connected with the German commercial houses were more than likely to marry into the native families. This unified social relationship gave them an inside advantage over the English and Americans, their chief business rivals. I think it was true of all Latin American countries that Englishmen and Americans were unable to enter the social life without reservations and reticences. A solitary individual might approach doing so, but whenever either nationality numbered as many as three, there was inevitably formed a group within a group; wherever the number was sufficient, a separate and distinct group was formed. This seemed to be especially true of the English. Marrying into a native family appeared to be no part of an Englishman's stock of ideas. He might keep a low caste native woman as a mistress, and raise a family by her, but, when it came to marriage, he chose an Englishwoman of any class in preference to the highest-class woman of the country in which he was only sojourning.

When I moved into the new Consulate, I did not hire a cook; I took my meals at Dan's, which was only two doors away. At Dan's there was one long table at which twelve to sixteen men sat (rarely was there a woman), and served themselves from large dishes that were passed around. Dan's table gave me some degree of the opportunity to keep an ear open to local reports and opinions that in Puerto Cabello had been afforded me by the club. There was no social life in Corinto, no places of amusement. This monotony was broken by invitations to dine with the Commander or at the officers' mess aboard our warships. I followed more or less regularly the custom for the Consul to dine with the captains of American merchant vessels in port. Occasionally the officers of one of the ships would give a dance aboard, and invite persons from as far away as Leon. There was but one important social event given in the town of Corinto during my whole stay there. An Italian cruiser put into harbor, and the Comandante of Corinto tendered the officers a banquet. The leading local men were invited, as were the officers of the American warship then in port. I was among those asked to speak. I spoke in Spanish because none of the Italians were familiar with English. I remember two ensigns from our ship endeavoring to hold a conversation across the table with one of the Italian officers, who sat beside me. One of these ensigns was using his Annapolis Spanish and the other his Annapolis French; meanwhile the Italian sat smiling suavely and nodding his head. A dispute, stimulated by the champagne, arose between the two Americans as to which of them the Italian understood better. The dispute developed into a wager, and I was called on to act as referee and stakeholder, two five-dollar pieces being posted in my hands. I rendered the decisions by returning the stakes, because it turned out that the Italian didn't understand either one.

Often for recreation I sat with the Vice-Consul late in the afternoons on the front porch of the Consulate and watched the people go by and the trains from Managua come in. The railroad terminus was the open street directly in front of the Consulate. Across the street from the Consulate was a long, low, frame building which contained the municipal headquarters and the school for boys. Frequently there was excitement at the headquarters caused by the *policia* bringing in arrested persons; and periodically from the school came outbursts of sing-song recitations in concert. I finally got so used to hearing these recitations that I did not hear them, but I never got accustomed to the sight of the teacher patrolling his schoolroom with a big stick in his hand and a long cigar in his mouth.

One afternoon as I sat on the porch, three ragged fellows came along and offered to sell me a pearl. I had not then been long in Corinto and asked Mr. Leonard where these fellows would get a pearl. I learned that pearls were found just off Cardon Island, and that the soldiers of the garrison there dove for them. The leader of the trio unwrapped a soiled bit of newspaper and showed me a pear-shaped pearl about three quarters of an inch in length. I asked him how much he wanted for it, and he named a price equal to about twenty dollars gold. Mr. Leonard, seeing my willingness to make the purchase, shook his head violently and said to me in English, "Don't appear so anxious. Offer him half; he may go off, but he'll be back in five minutes, and you'll save six or seven dollars, at least." I knew that the Vice-Consul had had years of experience in Nicaragua, but I yielded to his advice with great reluctance. The fellows did go off, but they did not come back in five, nor ten, nor fifteen minutes. I grew panicky and sent the office boy to find them and bring them back. He met them returning from a steamer lying at the wharf, where they had sold the pearl to one of the passengers. I was very much vexed, and Mr. Leonard very much mortified. The men passed the Consulate, and I told them, if they would give me first choice, I'd buy whatever catch they made. Carrying out this agreement, I bought nearly a tumblerful of baroque pearls; which, however, cost me only a few dollars. But one day the leader came in with a broad grin on his face and said: *"Ah, señor Consul, tengo una cosa muy bonita."* On my desk he slowly unwrapped his little package and out rolled two evenly matched, almost perfectly round pearls of beautiful luster. I could scarcely conceal my delight and anxiety. His price was twelve dollars gold, which I paid without hesitation. The pearls later became a pair of ear rings for Grace Nail.

From time to time, I ran across some persons among the people making the trip up and down the Pacific who interested me. On one ship was the daughter of Lillian Russell, Dorothy, whom I had known in New York, a young woman who had her mother's beauty and a great deal of talent. On another was Mrs. Luders, the wife of the composer of *The Prince of Pilsen*, and still on another day, the wife of George Primrose, the famous minstrel, who had sung many of our songs. On one ship

I found Peter Clark MacFarlane, at that time a well-known story writer. He was seated on deck in the coolest spot he could find, banging away on his typewriter. He asked me if he could pick up any worthwhile material in Nicaragua. I told him that he might if he took a trip up into the interior. He followed my suggestion. In his going up and back, I made him my guest for a couple of days; it was so good to have a writer to talk with. But he taught me an unforgotten lesson about talking too freely with anyone of that unscrupulous tribe— from which I do not exclude myself. I told MacFarlane my choicest South American story about the value and fluctuations of exchange. I told him I had stopped off at Baranquilla, Colombia, and that when I asked a porter at the wharf how much he would charge to take my bags up to the hotel, the fellow had looked at them and answered, *"Tres cientos pesos, señor."* (Three hundred dollars, sir.) I didn't know what the rate was in Colombia, but I took a chance and proffered the man an American dollar in payment; and he promptly returned to me in the paper currency of the country, seven hundred dollars in change. MacFarlane enjoyed the story immensely; but imagine my chagrin when later I saw in *Collier's Weekly* an article on Nicaragua by him, in which he related the story as having happened to him, and without even so much as intimating that he knew there was an American consul at Corinto.

XXV

IT appeared that the insurrection against Zelaya had collapsed. Some weeks dragged along, and I resolved to ask for a leave of absence to visit the United States. I had a decided reason for wanting to get back to New York. I cabled my request to the Department and it was granted by cable. I made immediate preparations to sail; among my preparations was arranging with the owner of the house in which the Consulate was located to have two rooms added to it and the whole house painted. Aboard the Pacific Mail Steamer, I made a change in my itinerary. In order to see a new country, I decided to cross to the Atlantic side by way of Costa Rica instead of Panama, so I debarked at the port of Punta Arenas. The change from Nicaragua to Costa Rica was comparable to a change from Costa Rica to France. The difference was immediately noticeable. Even in the small port there were cleanliness and order and, in every respect, a higher plane of civilization was obvious. One of the boasts of Costa Rica at that time was that she spent more money on her schools than on her army. The pleasurable anticipations of my trip across the country received a shock, however, when I learned that between Punta Arenas and San José, five thousand feet up in the mountains, there was a gap in the railroad—perhaps it was twenty miles—that had to be covered by horseback. I looked in dismay at my two very big trunks and three or four bags and packages; nevertheless, there was nothing for me to do but go ahead. My train left the next morning and made very good speed over the coastal plain, but soon began puffing laboriously up the grade of the mountain. In the early afternoon we came to a stop at a long steel bridge over a river; and the conductor came through advising the passengers that they should get off and precede the train across the bridge on foot; that those who remained aboard did so at their own risk. It was in the rainy season and the river, which in the dry season was a beautiful little mountain stream, was a swirling, foaming, rushing, roaring flood that every moment threatened the utter destruction of the bridge. Several men passengers were foolhardy enough to stay on the train; I was not of their number. Walking across the quivering bridge, I could not keep my eyes off the ominous torrent rolling below, and I had as little sense of security as I should have had in walking a tightrope over Niagara Falls. We anxiously watched the train come over like a snail, then again got aboard. We reached the terminus of the first section of the railroad and I went with some other passengers to an inn for the night. I learned that to catch the train at the other end of the gap, the start would have to be made before daylight. I hired a horse and engaged a man to transport my baggage. This man used two mules. Of course, they were not the big Missouri breed, common to the United States, but the Spanish breed, small but strong, willing, and sure-footed on mountain trails. My porter showed astonishing skill in strapping the baggage on the backs of the mules, but an old-fashioned, sky-scraper wardrobe trunk that I had seemed to be beyond his ingenuity. When daylight broke, a mountain scene of great beauty was revealed; I should have enjoyed the thrill of the rest of the ride had not my wardrobe trunk kept slipping and the continual delays to readjust it kept me in a state of apprehension about missing my train. The other travelers, with their lighter packs, forged ahead. We got in sight of the station just in time to see the train for San José pulling out; and I was forced to spend twenty-four hours in a little mountain village with nothing I could do but nurse my chagrin. I found the capital of Costa Rica the finest Spanish-American city that I had seen. I was sorry that my sailing schedule allowed me only one full day to see it; but promised myself to come again. I left to catch my steamer down to Limon, taking one of the most amazing railroad rides in the world.

After I reached New York, I went directly to Washington and made in person as full a report as I could on the political situation in Nicaragua. Then I returned to New York on what was to me a more important and delicate mission. I went back to New York to ask Grace Nail to be my wife. There was one consideration that disturbed me in an increasing measure, one that could not be removed or escaped; that consideration was Corinto itself. Before I left Nicaragua I questioned myself whether I had any sort of right to ask a girl who had lived all her life in New York to come and live in Corinto. I justified myself, saying: I had no idea of spending the rest of my days in Corinto; yet, I don't know how much longer I may be held there; and there is only one girl I want to marry; and she is more than three thousand miles away. I tried sincerely to paint Corinto for her in true colors, but, it is probable that, in spite of myself I threw some splashes of light upon its dull, drab background. We became engaged.

I took the opportunity to go out to Chicago and spend a few days with Bob and Rosamond, who were playing the *The Red Moon* there. I also made the trip to Jacksonville to see my parents. On my trip up from Jacksonville I stopped in Washington and visited the Department. Things had been happening in Nicaragua—the revolution was in full swing—Zelaya had committed an inexplicable blunder, for so astute a statesman, in sanctioning the execution of Groce and Cannon, two Americans charged with filibustering—the United States had severed diplomatic relations, dismissed the Zelaya representa-

tives in Washington, and declared it would hold those concerned in the killing of the two American citizens personally
responsible—Zelaya, recognizing the hopelessness of the situation, had "deposited the power" in Doctor José Madriz, and
fled; taking refuge with his friend Porfirio Diaz, President of
Mexico.

It was plain to those familiar with the situation that Zelaya's
move of self-elimination was made not only to save himself but
in the hope of robbing the revolution of its reason for being;
that it was made with the intention of reserving the power to
his régime, possibly, with the hope of reserving it for himself in
a happier day. It was a highly strategic move, but it did not
win; the revolution, backed by the resources and power of
the United States, continued; not against Zelaya but against
"Zelayaism." Doctor Madriz was a fine man, a scholarly man,
an honest man; at some other period he might have made a
good president for Nicaragua; but he did not possess the dominating strength to hold the reins that had just been held by
Zelaya's hands.

It was necessary for me to get back to my post as quickly as
was convenient. I induced the Department to furnish a reception room at the Consulate, and I purchased in New York furniture, rugs, and curtains to fit out the large room I had been
using as a bedroom. At the same time, I bought on my own
account bedroom furniture and household utensils. Grace Nail
and I were married, and with the good wishes of many friends
sailed to Corinto. The trip down was now an old experience
for me, but it became fresh and new, seen through Grace's
eyes. It was her first ocean voyage, but she proved a first-rate
sailor. We had some stormy weather, but she never tired of
standing where she could watch the big waves break over the
prow of the ship. Kingston, Jamaica, with its black custom
house officials, black soldiers, black policemen, black street car
conductors, black clerks in the big shops, black girls in the
telegraph office and at the news-stand of the fashionable Myrtle Bank Hotel, struck her as white civilization turned topsy-
turvy. She was fascinated with old Panama; and in the flying
fish and phosphorescent waters of the Pacific she took almost
childish delight. But I was anxious about her first view of Corinto, the place that was to be home. On the morning that our

steamer slipped into the harbor, I wondered that I had not before noticed how miserable an appearance Corinto could present. I plainly saw that Grace was dazed in disappointment; and that, as we made our way over the long, hot wharf, through unlovely streets to the Consulate, her disappointment increased. Mr. Leonard had the office spick and span. The floor had been scrubbed until the boards shone white; there were flowers on my desk and flowers in the bedroom; but the carpenters had not quite finished the addition they were building, and the new part of the house was still littered with tools and lumber and sawdust and shavings. I was smitten with an agonizing sympathy for my young wife. But she quickly recovered herself and immediately made a display of the courage that she showed under trying conditions for the next two years. Within a few days, the carpenters cleared out, and we excitedly unpacked and set up our new furniture. Into the living room went the cool, green, grass-woven furniture, and rugs of the same material; into the larger new room, opening off the living room, went the new bedroom furniture; and into the smaller went the bedroom furniture I had been using. Into the living room went also what proved to be the greatest pleasure-giving piece of all, a fine victrola with a large supply of records, a wedding present from Bob Cole. The curtains were hung and some water colors and prints placed on the walls. With the portières of the living room and front bedroom undrawn there was a vista straight through the four rooms that faced on the street. Set up in this manner, the Consulate gained the reputation of being the most charming house in Nicaragua.

Grace took great pride in her house, and with the help of two girls kept it immaculate—"immaculate" is a word with great religious but little domestic significance in Latin America. She started in earnest to learn Spanish, and in a month or so was able to give all the directions to her two maids. I was her teacher, but, as I frequently said to her, she made remarkable progress because she had to talk Spanish with her domestic help, and because with them she was not held back by the fear of making mistakes. Her absorption in acquiring the language went far toward making many of the discomforts of life in Corinto less apparent. She enjoyed the trips we made to Leon and Managua, and meeting people there; to be able to

Grace Nail

talk with them better on each succeeding visit became an interesting game. Her first big excitement came, however, one
night when we were sitting quietly in our living room reading
through a batch of New York newspapers that had just come
down. Suddenly, the lamp on the table began to shiver and
pictures on the walls to sway. I had learned the meaning of
these signals, and said to Grace as quietly as possible, "Get out
into the street. Get out into the street." We ran out of the
house and found the streets filled with people. The ground
was heaving under our feet and the birds and fowls, shaken out
of the trees, were flying around and making weird noises. In
cataloguing for Grace the things she might expect in
Nicaragua, I had failed to include the item of earthquakes; and
my statement that it was because of their very frequency that
they were not regarded with great concern did not, for the
time, wholly reassure her. In truth, the question, "Did you feel
the earthquake last night?" was asked with scarcely any greater
agitation than, "Did you hear the rain?"

But at Corinto itself there was an occasional social flurry.
Because of the impending crisis of the revolution, there were,
at times, two and even three United States naval vessels in
port, and my wife and I were frequently invited aboard for
luncheon or dinner. And there came down to spend a season at
the shore and take the baths, Mrs. Madriz, the wife of the
President, and a party of ladies from the capital. In total disregard of the political factors at work, a couple of dances were
given aboard ship in honor of the President's wife. Certainly
we could not be merely recipients of hospitality. The Consul
was a standing host for the officers of the warships; whenever
they called, they met a hospitable welcome. This was pleasant,
officially and socially, but financially it was quite a burden. It
was a case of one hundred to one; all the officers entertained
the Consul, and the consul entertained all the officers. Champagne and other French wines were comparatively cheap, but
the price of American whisky was exorbitant. Champagne was
an indispensable element in diplomatic and official intercourse
with the Latin Americans, but U.S. Americans preferred to
drink to each other's health in something less effervescent.

A good many of the navel officers seemed to enjoy the Consulate. Every once in a while, a group of them would say,

"Consul, wouldn't it be possible for us to have a little game of poker ashore tonight?" And the Consul would answer, "Why, certainly." I remember vividly the first of these parties. Five officers came ashore to play. I provided the sandwiches and the beverages. When we sat down one of them asked, "Well, what shall we make it?" And another answered, "Let's make it ten dollars a stack." I felt a cold moisture on my brow. I was no poker player; my highest flying had been a penny-ante game with a ten-cent limit; and here, with no way of escape, I faced the possibility of losing a half month's pay as well as the cost of the refreshments. This thought might not have been so appalling in former days, but now with a wife to take care of, it was a serious matter. I must have had extraordinary luck, or the officers were no better players than I, for I came out just about even, counting the refreshments. In self-defense, I showed the naval men after that how much more fun there was in playing for Nicaraguan instead of American money—enjoying the thrill of high bets without the danger of large losses, for often a pot ran up to several thousand "dollars."

For a long while back, American soldiers of fortune have played parts in Central American history. In the time of which I am writing, the two most famous were "General" Lee Christmas and "General" H. O. Jeffries. I never saw "General" Christmas, but one day in the latter part of March 1910, "General" Jeffries landed at Corinto and handed me a letter of introduction written by the American consul at Panama. I was curious about this man because he had been one of the chief factors in the revolution that separated Panama from Colombia and made the Panama Canal possible. He had also been the principal actor in a tragedy of private life that had shaken Panama City. In appearance he was disappointing. There might have been a time when, as an adventurer staking his life against long odds for big gains, he had looked the part of the gaunt, picturesque, rakish soldier of fortune; if so, ease and prosperity had changed all that. He was now inclined to portliness, was well fed and well dressed, almost sleek—the image of a successful American businessman. But under this commonplace surface was the "General" Jeffries of other days—venturesome and daredevilish, taking the hazards of life as a joke. During a whole evening he was the center of a small group that he kept hanging on the tales of his exploits. He told about his revolutionary activities, and he told how he had gone into the office of a Panama editor to avenge a woman's honor. One of the charms of his recital was that he took none of these episodes over-seriously. He related how once, at the head of a band of insurgents, he was surprised by a superior force, and gave commands for an orderly retreat back down the railroad track; how the speed of the retreat increased under the increasing pressure and fire of his pursuers, until, finally, "we were going down that railroad track so fast that the telegraph poles looked like teeth in a fine-toothed comb." "General" Jeffries told a great many things, but he did not tell just what his mission to Nicaragua was. I judged that it was not simply a matter of pleasure.

The revolution against "Zelayaism" continued. On December 18, 1909, the commander of the U.S.S. *Des Moines* had declared Bluefields a neutral zone and thereby, to the great advantage of the Conservatives, prevented Zelaya forces from attacking revolutionary forces in that territory. On December 23, the revolutionists had defeated Zelaya's troops at Rama; and on the next day Zelaya "deposited the power" in José Madriz and fled to Corinto, where he boarded a Mexican gunboat and took refuge in Mexico. Later, he went to Paris. But the United States refused to recognize Madriz, and the revolution continued. President Madriz, perplexed and harassed, did all he could to work out an adjustment and maintain the power of his party. He canceled the government's procedure initiated by Zelaya to void the Deitrick concession; but that action did not avail, and the United States continued to withhold recognition. In August of 1910 he fled to Corinto and with a large party of followers boarded a Pacific Mail steamer and sailed away. The flight of Zelaya and of Madriz constituted the only close-ups that Corinto got of the revolution.

General Juan B. Estrada, the political head of the revolutionary party, and provisional President, was later chosen President—his official term of office beginning December 31, 1910—and was recognized by the United States. Estrada proceeded to the capital over land from the east coast, but Adolfo Diaz, who was later chosen Vice-President, came by way of the

Panama Canal and Corinto. In the group that accompanied him was Thomas W. Moffat, the American Consul at Blue-fields. I had known Mr. Moffat in Venezuela; he was consul at La Guaira while I was at Puerto Cabello; we had both been transferred to Nicaragua at the same time and with the same instructions. I entertained Señor Diaz and Mr. Moffat at the Consulate until they left for Managua. Don Adolfo was a quiet-mannered man, rather small of stature and quite dapper. He spoke English very well, but had little to say. I was to know him better and to learn that, despite his slight figure and gentle demeanor, he was a man of iron nerve.

Estrada, formerly a Liberal, now a Conservative (he was in command of the Bluefield District, under Zelaya, when he turned revolutionist), a man of no exceptional force or qual-ifications, was President, but the chief factors in the future of Nicaragua were Don Adolfo Diaz, General Emiliano Chamorro, and General Luis Mena. Of this trio, Diaz was the intellectual, the student, the diplomat. General Chamorro, a Granada aristocrat, proud of his almost pure Spanish ancestry, was a man of courage and much military resourcefulness. The strong man of the trio was General Mena, a giant of a man, a man of great physical magnetism, showing a large proportion of Indian blood and, apparently, a tinge of Negro, rough, au-dacious, fearless, and the idol of his soldiers. Each of the three was ambitious; and, unfortunately for Nicaragua, the ambition of each had the presidency as its goal. Suspicion and mistrust developed into open hostility first between President Estrada and General Mena, Minister of War. Estrada tried the iron hand and threw Mena into prison. The latter's soldiers, hear-ing that the life of their hero was in danger, marched from all sides, several thousand strong on Managua. Estrada became panic-stricken. At three or four o'clock in the morning of May 12, I was wakened by the whistling and rumbling of a train. I did not understand it, for no regular trains ran at night in Nicaragua. A moment later, there was a loud knocking at my door. When I opened it, a lone, terror-haunted man stood there. He was President Estrada. He asked for asylum. On the first ship leaving Corinto, after only four months in office, he fled in fear of his life. Adolfo Diaz succeeded to the presidency amidst shouts of "Viva Diaz!"

In the midsummer I received sad news from New York. Bob
and Rosamond had closed the season in the spring with *The
Red Moon*. They had come to the conclusion that they could
neither make money nor break even playing the popular-price
theaters, the only ones in which they could get bookings, and
determined to go back into vaudeville. They went back at a
salary of $750.00 a week, and made their appearance on the
vaudeville stage at Keith's Fifth Avenue Theatre. On the last
night of their engagement there, Bob was stricken with a
mental breakdown. His condition continued to grow worse for
several weeks. Then his mother took him to a little resort in
the Catskills, where, it was hoped, the quiet and rest would do
him good. The first few days seemed to benefit him a great
deal. He enjoyed going for a swim in a nearby lake; he was an
excellent swimmer. He and his mother were sitting on the
porch of the house. A lady arrived, passed them by, and entered. In the hallway she remarked to someone, loudly enough
to be overheard, "Isn't that Bob Cole? Poor fellow. Too bad,
isn't it?" Bob got up and said to his mother that he was going
to take his swim. She did not see him again until his body was
dragged from the bottom of the lake.

I was shocked and disturbed beyond measure. I had lost one
of the closest friends of my lifetime, a friend whom I loved not
only for his unchanging fidelity, but whom I admired for his
unquestionable genius. I thought back over the twelve years of
our relations; I again lived through experiences that we had
suffered or enjoyed together; I tried to reckon the degree of
his influence on the course my life had taken; and I felt only
deep contentment in the fact that we had been friends and co-
workers. Bob Cole's death was a vital loss to the Negro stage.

The year was coming to a close. My wife and I had been
more than twenty months in Corinto. She had not been sick a
day, but I was anxious for her to have a change, for I knew that
no woman from a northern climate ought to stay longer than
two years at a time in the tropics. There was some political un-
rest; General Mena, through control of the Assembly, had in
October had himself elected President for four years, his term
of office to begin in 1913. Our government looked on this action with grave concern. Mena had been one of the strongest

forces in making the revolution successful, but formerly he had been a stanch supporter of Zelaya. Pressure was brought to have him renounce the election; our representative at Managua pointed out that the Assembly under the new Constitution had not the right to elect the President. Mena acquiesced but sulked in his tent. He remained, however, in control of the army.

In the lull, I requested a leave of absence. It was granted, and Grace and I sailed for a visit to the United States. Remembering my promise to myself to visit San José again, and wanting Grace to see Costa Rica, I arranged our passage that way. Certainly, I should not have done this had I not known that the Costa Rica railroad was now complete from Punta Arenas to San José. I did not dream that, even so, Grace would be in for trunk trouble. The harbor of Punta Arenas is an open roadstead, and passengers going ashore must be transferred into small boats. On the day that we arrived a very heavy swell was running in, and that made getting off the ship into a small boat an uncomfortable if not risky feat. All of the passengers got ashore without mishap, but when the trunks were being swung over the side, one slipped out of the sling and fell into the water. It proved to be one of Grace's, the one in which she had packed the light pretty things she expected to wear in San José and on the Atlantic trip during the warm days. The news reached us at the hotel, when we were getting ready for dinner. Grace was heartbroken. We got the trunk and opened it; everything in it was water-soaked. The hotel proprietor secured us first-aid in the shape of a Chinese laundryman, who promised to have everything "back fine" in time for us to catch our train in the morning. He got the things back in time, but Grace declared that their present was worse than their former state. She and the laundryman had a stiff row. The pidgin Spanish of the Chinese amused me, but the scope, color, warmth, and volubility of Grace's Spanish completely astounded me. Parts of her vocabulary did not come out of any textbook she had studied.

The elegance of the hotel in San José, its air of urbanity, its faultless menu and service, its well-dressed, well-mannered patrons, were our first taste of metropolitan life in nearly two years; and it affected Grace like wine. I had achieved the ability to make the best of almost any conditions, but I could not help catching some of her intoxication. When we went to our room to change, we heard the Band of the Republic, a band of nearly a hundred pieces, marching through the streets on its way to the park for the *retreta* that evening. I became as excited as Grace, and we hustled into our clothes like eager children. The band was an excellent one, but good bands may be heard in many places; on the other hand, in no place in the world, so far as I know, can such rapturously beautiful women be seen as in San José, Costa Rica. The park was crowded; all San José seemed to be out. The people did not sit down and listen to the music, but, in the Spanish-American custom, the men and youths promenaded round and round the park on the outer side of the walk, while on the inner side, the *señoritas*, accompanied by the older women of their families, or by their *dueñas*, promenaded in the opposite direction. The chatter made the music sound far away; very red lips constantly disclosed very white teeth, and very dark eyes constantly flashed all the signals of coquetry and love. Grace's comment was that the girls were too beautiful to seem real. She said that the scene was like a multiplied Ziegfeld chorus out of doors. And, although the prevailing type was brunette instead of blond, that was an apt comparison.

We spent a week in San José seeing the shops and places of interest. We went to the National Theater, which cost something like a million dollars and is probably one of the finest theater buildings on the western continent. One night while walking through a lesser street, we heard a strange but familiar sound. It was nothing other than the singing of a Methodist hymn, led by a lusty voice. We drew alongside the house whence the singing came and found that it was an improvised church. The preacher was just about to begin his sermon, and the preacher was a jet-black Negro. The congregation was composed of a few Negroes and overwhelmingly of Costa Ricans. That constituted the most curious sight we saw in Catholic San José.

We spent a while in New York, then went to Jacksonville; Rosamond joined us there. The Jacksonville people made quite a to-do over the three of us, and we stayed through two lively and happy weeks. On the way back to New York, Grace and I stopped in Washington, where I had several conferences with members of the Department. I received assurance that I should soon be transferred to a pleasanter post; perhaps to a post in France. The intimations were that my transfer would be made in three or four months; and Grace and I decided that the best plan would be for her to remain for that short time with her parents in New York, while I went back and closed up affairs. So, when I sailed for Corinto, I sailed alone.

XXVI

I T was now 1912. I arrived back in Corinto near the end of March. The town was just as I had left it; my house was very different. But the expectation of an early transfer kept me in high spirits. A month passed; two months passed. In the latter part of June I received a cablegram. I held it in my hands for a moment, experimenting with the powers of second sight. Was it France? If not, where? I opened the message and found that it was from my brother, telling me that our father was dead. This was the closest that death had yet to strike me. The day's work was over; it was night; I stood leaning against the door-post with the thin slip of paper in my hand, weeping quietly. Nothing else could have served me so well at that moment as the opportunity to weep quietly and alone. I went to bed with memories of my days of childhood unreeling in my mind.

The third month passed, and the fourth month was passing; it was surely now but a matter of days before I should receive my transfer. On July 29 word reached me of a ministerial crisis in Managua. President Diaz had dismissed General Mena from the Ministry of War. Mena had refused to hand over his authority and had withdrawn the armed forces and taken up positions around the capital. I immediately cabled this news to the Department of State and telegraphed it to Commander Terhune of the U.S.S. *Annapolis*, who, a few days before, had sailed down to San Juan del Sur, the cable station. On the morning of August 1, the *Annapolis* was back at Corinto. General Mena, in the meantime, was fortifying the positions that

Consul and Sentry, Nicaragua

commanded Managua, and the situation was unquestionably serious.

President Diaz did not follow the example of his predecessor and flee; instead, he called upon the United States to maintain him in the position in which it had placed him. On August 3, Commander Terhune, under orders, landed with one hundred bluejackets and five officers from the *Annapolis*, and with arms and ammunition proceeded to Managua to act as a Legation guard. The *Annapolis* remained at her anchorage with twenty-odd bluejackets left aboard under the command of a young lieutenant named Lewis. One other American ship, the collier *Justin*, was in port. On the sixth, the *Justin* received orders from Washington to proceed to Panama for a force of marines. On the eleventh the American minister called me on the phone and informed me that General Mena had begun bombarding Managua.

The bombardment of the capital continued. Refugees began pouring into Corinto. The American members of the Mixed Claim Commission and other Americans from Managua made the Consulate their headquarters. Many refugees coming down reported that the rebel fire was centered on the Legation. One significant rumor was that the old Zelaya followers in the district of Leon would rise and array themselves under the Mena standard. On the fourteenth the *Justin* returned to Corinto bringing three hundred and fifty-six marines under the command of Major Smedley D. Butler. This entire force entrained for Managua to reinforce the Legation guard.

On the sixteenth, Dr. Toribio Tijerino, Delegate of the President in the Department of Leon, Chinandega, and the Segovias, arrived in Corinto. (The President had delegated his authority in the areas which he could not control from the capital.) Dr. Tijerino reported that the situation in Leon was critical; that General Mena had succeeded in supplying arms and ammunition to los Liberales in that stronghold of Zelayaism, and that an uprising in that city was imminent. After making this report, Dr. Tijerino returned to Chinandega, a fair-sized city fifteen miles up the railroad from Corinto. I at once called the Legation on the telephone to give the Minister this information, which was of particularly vital importance because of Leon's position, halfway between Managua and the

port of Corinto. The Minister inclined to pooh-pooh the report. The bombardment had subsided, and he felt the situation was well in hand. Quite naturally, with a Legation guard
of nearly five hundred American marines and sailors, he had a
sense of security. Nevertheless, I continued and told him that I
had heard that a large quantity of arms and ammunition had
been smuggled into Leon in wagons, under cover of being
farm produce. While I was talking with the Minister, the telephone wire snapped. A few minutes later I learned that the
telegraph wires had been cut. Corinto had no direct communication with Managua by telephone, telegraph, or rail for the
next two weeks.

Two days later, Dr. Tijerino came down again to Corinto,
bringing with him three hundred government troops as far as
Paso Caballos. (Paso Caballos was the narrow inlet and wide
salt marsh, three or four miles above the town, that separated
Corinto from the mainland and made it actually an island. The
railroad ran over a long bridge across the pass.) Dr. Tijerino reported that there had been an uprising in Leon and the insur-
rectionists had taken the city with great slaughter; that they
were on their victorious way to the port; and that they were
now approaching Chinandega and would soon get to Corinto.
It was a day or two before we got full news about the capture
of Leon. There had not been a battle but a massacre. The insurgents had fallen on the government garrison, numbering
five or six hundred, and killed them to a man. No quarter was
allowed. Two American soldiers of fortune, Dodd and Phillips,
were fighting with the government forces; wounded, they
were taken to the hospital; but the rebels attacked the hospital,
killing every wounded soldier in it, including the two Americans. Thus Managua was cut off from Corinto, and the American forces forming the Legation guard from their base.

Dr. Tijerino's report created great excitement. The Comandante addressed a communication to me stating that he did
not have a sufficient force at his command to maintain peace
and order and protect lives and property at the port, and requested that the American forces assume that responsibility. I
conferred with Lieutenant Lewis and a six-pounder was taken
off the ship, mounted on a flat car, manned, and placed at the
juncture of the railroad and the main street. A machine gun

was mounted at the corner of the custom house. A patrol consisting of fourteen bluejackets from the *Annapolis* was detailed for duty at night. Several times each night, for ten nights, I made the rounds of this patrol with the ensign in command. During that period, I did not take off my clothes for the purpose of going to bed. American and foreign women and children I had placed each night aboard the *Annapolis* and *Justin*. I kept the Consulate open all night as headquarters for the American landing force. All the Americans and most of the foreigners made it their headquarters. There were thirty to forty men there every night during the "siege." The stewards of the *Annapolis* kept a caldron of coffee for the patrol. I drank, I judge, a couple of quarts a night. Dr. Tijerino resented the establishment of the American patrol. His plan was to bring his troops in and himself take military control of the port. The Comandante stood by his request to the American Consul. Thereupon, the General (he was a general as well as a doctor) threatened to put the Comandante and all his staff in prison on Cardon Island. I advised Dr. Tijerino that the American force, small as it was, was better able to hold the port without bloodshed than any force he could bring in. The next day he took his soldiers and went back to Chinandega. I was glad to see him go. For the time, the responsibility for Corinto rested on me, and I was determined that there should be no bloodshed there if I could prevent it. The horror of what had happened in Leon made my determination stronger.

But I was not rid of Tijerino. The next day he was back in Corinto, and sent a note through me to the commanding officer of the *Annapolis* requesting that he be furnished with a hundred rifles and ammunition and provisions from the ship. He became very indignant when he was informed that it was not possible to grant his request. On the following morning, he sent me a note requesting that I call a conference of all the consuls in Corinto, to be held at the Comandancia at three o'clock, to consider the best means of maintaining peace and order at the port. I replied to him that I should be glad to request the consuls to meet at the American Consulate at the hour indicated. I did that, and informed the General. He sent back word that he would not attend the conference but would transmit a note in which he would state his intention of

sending the Comandante with all his force, including the police force, to the front, and installing himself as chief local authority at the port; leaving the maintenance of peace and order
and the protection of lives and foreign interests to the American forces. The hour for the meeting arrived and with it the
consular representatives at Corinto of England, France, and
Italy. Every American in Corinto was present. Dr. Tijerino had
not put in his appearance; so I requested Lieutenant Lewis to
go across the street, where the General had his headquarters,
and urge him to come over to the meeting, since there was
neither time nor necessity for diplomatic correspondence. A
half-dozen bluejackets were on guard in front of the Consulate. The Lieutenant took them with him and made his way
through the gathering crowd across to Dr. Tijerino's office.
The General refused to come over, whereupon Lieutenant
Lewis became out of patience, placed him under arrest,
marched him between the bluejackets across the street, and
delivered him to me in the Consulate. Of course, the Lieutenant had been far more urgent than I had intended or anticipated.

The news spread like wildfire. Instantly, it seemed, the street
in front of the Consulate was jammed with a surging crowd.
The six American bluejackets with an ensign stood lined across
the entrance of the Consulate with fixed bayonets. Every
American present realized that the moment was charged with
every possibility of danger; for the crowd continued to press
forward. General Tijerino approached me, and with a dramatic
gesture unbuckled his sword, took his revolver from his hol-
ster, laid both weapons on my desk and said, "Sir, I am your
prisoner." Then immediately he launched into an eloquent
and incendiary speech, in a voice loud enough to reach the already excited crowd outside. He began by charging me with
having placed under arrest the President of Nicaragua; the
which was virtually true. He declared that he would protest to
the Central American governments and to the world. (He did
send protests to the Presidents of Guatemala, Salvador, and
Honduras, but none of those rulers took any action, so far as I
ever learned.) He called on patriotic Nicaraguans to resent the
indignity to which he had been subjected. There were *vivas*
from the crowd. At the beginning of the General's speech, I

had hastily called Lieutenant Lewis and asked him to take personal charge of the bluejackets and to use every means to avoid anything like a clash. I then cut the General's speech off by attempting to make as a dramatic gesture as he had made on his entrance. I gave him back his revolver and with my own hands rebuckled his sword upon him; at the same time declaring that he was in no sense a prisoner; that no indignity was intended to him personally or in his capacity of Delegate of the President; that the American officer had only been over-zealous in the desire that the conference have the benefit of the General's wisdom and judgment in the vital matters to be discussed. The gesture ended the speech, but I am sure it did not fool the General; he was too intelligent a man for that. And the gesture also ended the conference. The consular representatives went away; Lieutenant Lewis personally conducted the General back to his headquarters, and the crowd dispersed.

General Tijerino spent all the next day in his office. He was busy getting his protests out to the world. On the following day, he sent me another request. This time it was that he be furnished with a train in order that he might go back with his troops for the defense of Chinandega. Now this was a serious request. When the uprising in Leon cut the railroad line in the middle, there was a train standing in Corinto that would make the trip the next morning to Managua and on to Granada. Of course, it did not start. That train was vital to Corinto; more vital than the American ships and guns; for every day it went up as far as Chinandega and brought back vegetables, chickens, eggs and milk, and a huge tank on a flat car filled with water. Nothing to eat was grown on the island that was Corinto; and every hole dug in the ground gave only brackish water. That train was Corinto's guaranty against a food and water famine.

I debated the matter, and talked with Lieutenant Lewis and Mr. Leonard about it. Two reasons inclined me to grant the General's request; I was anxious to make amends as far as I possibly could for the affront he had received, and I was equally anxious to embrace any plan by which I should never again lay eyes on Tijerino. I let him have the train on his solemn and many-times repeated oath that he would send it back immediately. I later called in the engineer in charge of the train and impressed on him the vital necessity of bringing it

back to Corinto. The engineer, I saw, understood the seriousness of the matter. He was a bright man, much too bright to
be running a train in Nicaragua; he should have had Tijerino's
job. The General loaded his troops on. They filled the four
coaches inside, outside and on top. They left Corinto with
many *vivas*. The General did not keep his word. When he
reached Chinandega, he refused to let the train come back.
The engineer was powerless; but, while he waited, a train
pulled in from the direction of Leon, and the locomotive
stood panting with the cowcatcher pointed toward Corinto.
Then my engineer and his fireman conceived and carried out a
plot in which they risked their lives. They watched and saw
that everybody, including the crew, got off the train that had
just arrived; then they hopped aboard the locomotive, opened
the throttle, and brought the train down to Corinto. Had it
been in my power, I should have awarded the engineer some
kind of a cross. As it was, we were better off; the kidnapped
train had five coaches and a newer and bigger locomotive.

The entire plan, after all, worked out; for I never again laid
eyes on Tijerino. Two days after he left Corinto, the rebel
forces came down from Leon and captured Chinandega. In
the fight, Tijerino's son, who was his adjutant, was killed; and
he himself lost an eye, was captured and made a prisoner. With
the fall of Chinandega, rumors came down to Corinto that
the rebels would next attack and capture the port. The port
and custom house constitute the grand prize in every Latin-
American revolution. On receipt of the news from Chinandega, we transferred the six-pounder to Paso Caballos, where
it would command the railroad, and placed Captain Meriwether of the collier *Justin* and a guard of five in charge. News
also leaked down to us that Captain Terhune had attempted
to come from Managua to Corinto with a force of his bluejackets, and had been met at Leon by the rebel army, forced to
detrain and march back to the capital. Following the outbreak
of the insurrection, the Department cabled that the U.S.S.
Denver had been ordered to Corinto; more than sufficient
time had passed for her to make the trip, and we were much
puzzled as to where the *Denver* could be.

Later in the afternoon, two days after the capture of
Chinandega, Captain Meriwether telephoned me from Paso

Caballos that a locomotive carrying a flag of truce had approached the other end of the bridge and was waiting for a signal to cross the pass. He asked what he should do. I asked him how much of a train the locomotive had. He answered that he could not tell, as only the engine could be seen from the Corinto side, but that he would find out. He did, and telephoned down that there was only one coach. I told him to let them cross. The train brought a commission of seven or eight civilians, representing the rebel forces in Chinandega, who stated to Captain Meriwether that they had come to confer with the Comandante of Corinto. Captain Meriwether telephoned to ask if he should allow them to come down into town. I answered, yes, but not without having hesitated. When the train came down, I met the commission and invited them to hold the conference in the Consulate. They thanked me politely, and politely informed me that, since their business was not with the American officials but with the local Nicaraguan authorities, and concerned only Nicaragua, they would prefer to meet in the Comandancia. These interchanges were taking place in the middle of the street; the commission would not enter the Consulate even for a preliminary conference. The Comandante, almost crouching behind me, begged piteously that I prevent the conference from being held in the Comandancia; with or without good reason, he was in fear for his life. I pressed my invitation, and the commission firmly declined. They pointed out to me that the matter in hand was purely internal, one in which the American government had no concern or authority. The commission was composed of educated men; the spokesman was a lawyer and a graduate of the University of Pennsylvania; they had come down armed with a great array of books on international law; however, without these books they knew, probably, ten times as much international law as I did; and aside from their overlooking the existing facts, they were in every respect right. I reminded them that it was upon my word that they had been allowed to come down into Corinto to confer. They bowed, and countered by saying that they could have made the entry by force had they so decided.

I realized that, in permitting the commission to come down into the town, I had committed a tactical blunder. I knew that the insurrection, begun by Mena, had in Leon and the districts to the west developed into an uprising of the old Zelaya element; that it required only a spark to convert Corinto into an exploded powder magazine. The crowd in the street had grown to a dense throng that kept pressing in. The firm stand taken by the commission brought forth loud cries of *"Viva la revolución! Viva la república! Viva Zelaya! Abajo los americanos!"* I had before me a problem of extrication.

I stood firmly against the commission, on such grounds as I had; and we finally reached the compromise that the conference would be held on neutral territory. We agreed upon the house of the Italian Vice-Consul. It was nearly dark. I said to the trembling Comandante that there would be no danger in going into the conference as arranged; that he should not, however, take any definite step before he had apprised me of the demands made by the commission.

We waited anxiously. The Consulate was crowded. Every American man and many of the foreign men in Corinto were there. It was nearly ten o'clock when a messenger came from the conference bringing a note for me from the Comandante. The note stated that the commission had served an ultimatum on him to the effect: If the port is not turned over within six hours, beginning from midnight, General Vaca, of the revolutionary army, will come down with a force of three thousand men and take it. From the Americans who crowded the Consulate came the many-times repeated expression, "Where in the hell is the *Denver*?"

I had to think fast, if my thinking was to serve my purpose. I was fundamentally aware that the whole mess was, strictly, Nicaragua's business; that it would be better if we were entirely out of it, or better still if we had never gotten into it. But I was also aware of the fact that we were in it. The plan I intended to stick to was to do my utmost to prevent bloodshed and looting, perhaps massacre, at Corinto and to hold the port open, at least, as long as the American forces were cut off in the interior. However, I was not fully aware of another element that had entered—the fascination of the game I had been called on to play. I formed a little inner council consisting of Lieutenant Lewis, Captain Meriwether, Mr. Leonard, and Judge Shoenrich and Judge Thompson, members of the

Mixed Claim Commission, who had fled from Managua and were among the refugees at the Consulate. We decided upon a reply that the Comandante should make to the commission, and we drafted it at once. The reply stated that the Comandante would, in order to avoid violence and bloodshed, be willing to turn the port over to the revolutionists; but having already, for the purpose of preserving peace and order, invoked the aid of the American forces present, he did not feel that he could comply with the demands of the commission, unless the American Consul was brought into the conference.

An hour later, we received a message that the commission desired to conger with the Comandante and the American Consul at the Consulate. At this point, Lieutenant Lewis, a very zealous young man, as we have seen, but not an exceptionally bright one, devised a bit of strategy that gave all of us a laugh for many a day thereafter. Indeed, it was a stroke that entirely redeemed him from mediocrity in our eyes. Requested to escort the commission to the Consulate, he suggested that he station the whole of his patrol of fourteen bluejackets at intervals between the Consulate and the place where the conference was meeting. The night was dark; there were no street lamps in Corinto, and the Lieutenant and an ensign took their lanterns and started out to station the patrol and fetch the commission. A few steps from the door of the Italian Vice-Consul, the commissioners discerned by the light of the lanterns the glimmer of a white uniform and the glint of a rifle, and heard a sharp challenge, "Halt! Who goes there?" Lieutenant Lewis approached the sentry, gave the satisfactory information, and received the order to "Pass on." Fourteen times within the distance of four blocks the party was thus challenged; and, it is probable that, by the time the commissioners reached the Consulate, Lieutenant Lewis's plan to give them a magnified idea of the American force in Corinto had worked.

I welcomed the commission and listened to its demands for the immediate surrender of the port. I told them that I felt they had forestalled any awkward complications by asking the American Consul into the conference; that, however, by their own declarations on arriving in Corinto, they had neither instructions nor authority to deal with the American officials;

that, therefore, I did not see how there could be any guarantee of the terms we might arrive at in the present conference;
that before I could take any steps it would be necessary for
them to secure from the military leader of the revolution instructions and authority for them to deal with the American
Consul. Earlier in the evening, I had ordered Dan to prepare a
bountiful roast beef supper, with no limits on the supply of
beverages. Our impasse was forgotten in the feast that followed. Party lines, political antagonisms, individual and national aspirations were all melted down into one strong
current of fellowship and brotherhood. Liberales and Conservadores actually shed tears on one another's shoulders at the
woes of their common country. The American consul was a
"prince," and *los americanos* were "all right." At about two
o'clock in the morning we succeeded, not without physical
difficulties, in loading the commissioners on their train and
starting them back to Chinandega.

But the commissioners were sober the next day; and in the
afternoon, Captain Meriwether telephoned that they were
again at the pass under a flag of truce. We had decided the
night before that all future conferences would be held at Paso
Caballos. I asked Captain Meriwether to inform the commission that I should be up at Paso Caballos as soon as I could
and confer with them. The Captain told me that they were
much disappointed at not being allowed to come down into
the town. I took my time about getting up to the pass; for I realized that time was the most important factor in the game I
was playing. I went up to Paso Caballos weighing in my mind
the statement I intended to make, and wondering what the result of it would be. I stood on a little knoll under a tree; the
commission was in front of me; at my side stood the ensign
whom Lieutenant Lewis has sent to accompany me to the conference; around me were grouped the men in charge of our
six-pounder. When I began to speak I realized suddenly that I
was very tired. Ten nights out of bed, running on black coffee,
was telling on me. The men who had been keeping the vigil
with the six-pounder were haggard. The commissioners appeared obnoxiously fresh and alert. The scene took on an air of
unreality, the air of opéra bouffe, and I was merely playing a
part, a rather ridiculous part. I did not state the points suc-

cinctly that I had come to lay down. I made an address to the commissioners, bringing the points in as I went along: Any transfer of the port to the revolutionists must be made in an orderly manner—No armed force, except the necessary police force, must be installed in Corinto—Whatever authority and government was set up would have to be purely civilian. When I had finished talking, the commissioners agreed to the terms. Their decision instantly brought back the realities. I was again face to face with the impending actualities of the situation. I ventured one more stroke to gain time: I required of the commissioners that they get from General Vaca a written communication addressed to me and over his own signature, stating that he held himself bound by the terms, before any of their conditions could be entered upon. The commissioners willingly promised to do this and to return with the required document the next day. They boarded their train and returned to Chinandega. The ensign who had accompanied me to Paso Caballos, a young Southerner, was the only officer on the *Annapolis* with whom my relations were not fully cordial—he himself had pointedly indicated that he did not wish them so. After the parley he came up to me and wrung my hand. He appeared to be proud that we were both Americans. But things around me had already slipped back into the realm of unrealities, and his gesture and words seemed merely parts in a play.

On the next morning Captain Terhune with a force of one hundred marines and bluejackets from the Legation guard was in Corinto, having made his way down from Managua. Before the morning passed the U.S.S. *Denver* arrived with five hundred marines. When the commissioners from the revolution came back in the afternoon, I had them brought down into the town, and the conference was held at the Consulate between them and Captain Terhune of the *Annapolis*, Captain Washington of the *Denver*, and myself. We refused to turn over the port. I went to bed that night and slept soundly; and, of course, without any thought that I was having a hand in establishing a precedent that Japan was to cite to us twenty years later.

On the following day, the U.S.S. *California* arrived with Rear Admiral W.H.H. Southerland. Four hundred marines were landed from the *California*, and the cruiser proceeded to

Panama for an additional force. The Admiral transferred his flag to the *Annapolis*. Marine Headquarters were established at the Consulate, and in an open space in the town a marine camp was set up under the name of Camp Dixie. During the day Captain Terhune said that he wanted to talk with me. He told me how, when he was making his way with his small force from Managua to Corinto, one of his men had shot and killed a young Nicaraguan. This was the first bloodshed by an American, and the Captain, who was a fine, generous-hearted man, was deeply disturbed by it. The Nicaraguan had been seen under a bridge where the railroad crossed a small river; the American shot him on the supposition that he was tampering with the bridge; Captain Terhune was of the opinion that the young fellow was only trying to catch some fish. I said to the Captain that he was right in feeling that it was a terrible thing to have killed a boy who was, probably, innocent even of mischief; but that, under the circumstances, I did not think that he should assume the guilt personally. For nearly an hour, midst the clatter and clutter of the landing forces, he and I paced back and forth on the waterfront, while he tried to work the matter off his mind and conscience. I know he did not succeed in doing it then; because he brought it up again and talked it over with Admiral Southerland and me. The Admiral assured him that what had happened was in the course of military action, and advised him to put the incident out of his mind. Whether Captain Terhune was ever able to do this, I cannot know.

While the marines were setting up camp, Mr. Palacio ran to me with the complaint that they were taking mahogany that he had on the waterfront ready for shipment, and using it for firewood. I at once reported his complaint to the Admiral. The marines themselves were astonished to learn that they were burning mahogany. This action, however, was something less than vandalism; for among the uses to which mahogany is put in Nicaragua is the making of cartwheels and railroad ties.

On September fourth, the *California* came back from Panama with seven hundred and fifty marines aboard. Within a few days, there was a fleet of eleven warships under command of Admiral Southerland. Captain Halstead, whom I had known since my first year at Corinto, was in command of

the *California*. The Admiral assigned to me a bluejacket
guard. Wherever I went, my "naval attaché" followed a few
paces behind. I am sure this measure was not taken for my protection—I needed no protection—but to impress the native
population. The population was likewise duly impressed when
I paid my official visit to Admiral Southerland. As I left the
flagship, every vessel in the fleet, one after another, boomed a
salute of seven guns, seventy-seven in all. The thunder startled
the country for miles around. It threw the dogs of Corinto
into a panic; the whole canine colony of the port started yelping and running as though they were mad. If any of them are
still alive, they are, I judge, running yet.

On September twenty-sixth, General Mena surrendered. On
the twenty-seventh he was brought to Corinto, and on the
next day deported to Panama aboard the U.S.S. *Cleveland*. On
October third, the American forces began bombarding Barranca. On the following day Barranca and Coytepe were taken
by assault, with four Americans killed and eight wounded;
forty Nicaraguans killed and seventy-five wounded. On October sixth, American forces entered Leon, the last stronghold of
the Mena revolution. The first step of the American intervention was finished. Admiral Southerland was ready to transfer
his flag back to the *California* and return to the United States.
He had been a frequent visitor at the Consulate, and so much
admired a gray parrot which I owned that I made him a present of the bird. Before the *California* sailed, Captain Halstead
gave a breakfast for me aboard, that was attended by the other
captains in the fleet. The marines remained and had their base
at Corinto.* But excitement and tension subsided, and affairs
fell into the course of daily routine.

On the surface, the reasons for armed intervention of the
United States in Nicaragua appear to be based solely on considerations of concessions and loans. Those who have opposed
the imperialism of the United States in the Caribbean region
have, for the most part, opposed it on those grounds. I am
sure that the reasons go deeper; that they are based upon a

---

*Just before writing these lines I read that three months hence seven hun-
dred American marines will be withdrawn from Nicaragua, ending the occupation begun in 1909.

policy of government that has been running and growing stronger since 1826, a policy of government that is a part of the tradition of the State and Navy Departments (and, as to foreign affairs, Administrations may come and Administrations may go, but the State and Navy Departments go on forever). This policy held that the security of the United States depended upon controlling an inter-oceanic canal across Central America. For more than fifty years, the United States made tentative efforts for a Nicaragua Canal. Down to the purchase of the unfinished Panama Canal, it was agreed that the Nicaragua route was the most practicable and feasible of all. This policy of government now holds that, even with the American ownership of the Panama Canal, the security of the United States still depends upon domination of the very possible route across Nicaragua. Only a year or so before the 1909 revolution, Zelaya was endeavoring to open secret negotiations with Japan for the acquisition of the Nicaragua route, and a copy of his letter broaching the matter was in the hands of the State Department. This policy embraces also the control of certain potential naval bases guarding the sea paths on the Atlantic side to any canal across Central America. The State and Navy Departments may feel that they can rest easier, since now a treaty with Nicaragua has been negotiated and proclaimed by both countries granting the United States rights in perpetuity to construct, operate, and maintain a canal across Nicaragua. These are, I believe, fundamental facts in the Caribbean policy of the United States; and, I think, those who oppose that policy should take these facts into consideration and not lay all their stress upon the profits made by holders of concessions and clippers of loan coupons. I leave it to a financial accountant to compute how long it will take before the expenditures for intervention will begin to show a strictly business profit. Concessions, loans, and revolutions are important factors, but, for the government, their chief importance lies in their connection with its fundamental policy. It is my opinion that the relations of the United States to all the islands of the Caribbean and to Panama, Nicaragua, and the other Central American countries, as well, depend almost entirely upon how far we can go toward abolishing the possibility and fear of war between the United States and any other great

power; and that, of course, comprehends the complete abolishment of war.

XXVII

*T*he Autobiography of an Ex-Colored Man was brought out
in Boston while the revolution was in progress. Copies
were sent to me, and the book was read by many of the naval
and marine officers. But I had written scarcely a line of new
work in my more than three years in Nicaragua. For some time
I had been carrying in my mind the plan to write a poem in
commemoration of the fiftieth anniversary of the signing of
the Emancipation Proclamation. By some mental twist I had
kept thinking that the anniversary would fall in 1915. In early
October, I read in my copy of *The New York Age* that colored
people in various parts of the United States had been celebrating the anniversary of the preliminary proclamation, which
Lincoln signed September 22, 1862; and I suddenly found that
I had three months, instead of three years, in which to write
my poem. I went to work feverishly, but under some disadvantages; one room in the Consulate was still used as marine headquarters; there were two machine guns on the front porch
with marine guards; at night, thirty or forty marines slept on
the porch at the rear of the house; of quiet, privacy, or peace, I
had little. Nevertheless, I did manage to work. I found the
hours after midnight best. But throughout the day, my mind
was so absorbed with making the poem that the affairs of
Nicaragua and of the United States, too, took a secondary
place. I finished the poem in about six weeks and mailed it to
Brander Matthews. He, feeling that it ought to appear on the
exact date of the anniversary, submitted it to the *New York
Times*, where it was printed January 1, 1913. On the following
day *The Times* printed a fairly long and quite laudatory editorial comment on the poem. The writer of the editorial went so
far as to say, "While there would be hesitation in pronouncing
this poem a work of genius, there would be difficulty in ex-
plaining why it did not deserve to be so described."

The poem as originally written consisted of forty-one stanzas. After a struggle in which my artistic taste and best judgment won, I cut off the last fifteen stanzas—something which

I did not find easy to do. The main theme of the poem, as I had carried it in my mind, was fifty years of struggle and achievement. As the poem took form, it made a rapid sweep back over the two hundred and ninety-four years between 1619 and 1913, and, beginning with the eleventh stanza—

> This land is ours by right of birth,
> This land is ours by right of toil;
> We helped to turn its virgin earth,
> Our sweat is in its fruitful soil

it affirmed our well-earned claims to a share in the commonwealth; reaching in the twenty-sixth stanza a note of faith in the future. At that point, it took a turn and brought into view the other side of the shield, ending on a note of utter despair. I saw that I had written two poems in one. I saw that the last third of the composition, though it voiced the verities, was artistically out of place, and, moreover, that it nullified the theme, purpose, and effect of the poem as a whole. I recognized that the last fifteen stanzas required another and different setting.

I decided to make a separate poem out of the deleted fifteen stanzas, but I never attempted to have them printed. I grew, more and more, to fear that they contained an element of empty rhetoric that was absent in the major portion of the original poem. However, if I were today writing that "major portion" of the poem, I should question the superiority in the absolute of so-called white civilization over so-called primitive civilization.

President Taft was defeated in the November elections. After his defeat, he sent a long list of nominations to the Senate; in the list I was named as Consul to the Azores. I was disappointed that I had not been named for a post in France, but I was too glad to get away from Corinto to feel the disappointment very keenly. I knew nothing about the Azores, but, looking the islands up in the catalogue of consular posts, I found that the climate was pleasant, and the standards of living far above those of Nicaragua. I knew that my duties would not be of the kind required at Corinto, and I anticipated the opportunity to go on with my writing. I also calculated that I would be within rather easy distance to Europe. I saw that I should be faced with a new language, Portuguese; but I felt sure that I should have little trouble with it, since it was allied so closely to Spanish. But the Democratic majority in the Senate, having in mind the fifteen hungry years endured by their constituents and the fat years just ahead, refused to confirm the nominations made by an outgoing Republican president. And that was the status of my case when I reached the United States.

When I got to New York, I found Rosamond on the eve of sailing for Europe. He had been serving as the executor of our father's estate, and had waited only to talk with me about certain matters in connection with it. I went first to Washington and talked with the officials at the State Department with respect to my appointment to the Azores. They seemed to feel optimistic about the list of nominations being sent back to the Senate and being confirmed. Grace and I went to Jacksonville. I found my mother cheerful but looking much older.

My father had left, in addition to several parcels of real estate, fifteen thousand dollars in mortgages, negotiated through a local house of which a Judge W. B. Owen, a man in whom he had entire confidence, was the head. I was in Jacksonville only a week or two before I heard that the Florida Realty Trust Company was on the rocks. I attended a meeting called by the investors in the concern, but I felt safe because my father's investments were secured not by bond or stock issues of the company, but by individual first mortgages locked up in his safe at home. As I was leaving the meeting, a lawyer whom I knew well called me aside and whispered in my ear that I had better look into my "first mortgages." The company went smash. Judge Owen, it appeared, lost his mind. I talked with the business manager, who declared to me over and over that the only way he saw out for himself was to commit suicide. I engaged a lawyer and he uncovered the divers methods these financial second-story men had employed to fleece their clients. They had, in my father's case, in two instances, recorded a mortgage on a piece of property twenty-four hours before they delivered to him a document purporting to be a first mortgage deed. After three or four years of litigation, we recovered only a fraction of my father's investments with this company; hundreds of others lost all they had. I don't think

Judge Owen went to an asylum, and the business manager did not have the decency to commit suicide. Not a step was ever taken to punish a single one of the respectable scoundrels connected with this concern.

I remained in Jacksonville six or seven months on leave of absence; then I went back to Washington. The heads at the Department of State with whom I talked were not so optimistic now. Wilbur J. Carr, who examined me for my entrance into the Service, and who became First Assistant Secretary of State, suggested that I go and have a talk with the Secretary of State. As the reader knows, the then Secretary of State was William Jennings Bryan, a man who superficially was a statesman, but fundamentally was a political spoilsman. He was the Secretary of State who wrote to the newly appointed Receiver General of Customs for the Dominican Republic:

My dear Mr. Vick:

Now that you have arrived and are acquainting yourself with the situation, can you let me know what positions you have at your disposal with which to reward deserving Democrats? Whenever you desire a suggestion from me in regard to a man for any place there call on me.

The same who had written to President Wilson:

We have so many deserving Democrats and so few places to give that I would like if all of them would be willing to serve for a short time so that we could pass the offices around. . . . If you do not approve of the suggestions in regard to George Fred Williams, would you like to have me look for a good Democrat who would like a winter's stay in Greece?

Nevertheless, I went to see him to press my case and to ask if my name would again be sent to the Senate for the post at the Azores. I had not seen Mr. Bryan since the days of the Spanish-American War. Then I saw him a number of times, a handsome young colonel, still in his thirties, marching at the head of his Nebraska regiment, which was in camp in Jacksonville. There, because he had already been the national standard bearer of the Democratic Party, he attracted more attention than did even General Fitzhugh Lee; now, I saw him still young in years, but old in looks. His antique aspect was emphasized by his wearing clothes that literally flapped about him. Mr. Bryan received me cordially and I stated my errand. With much arching of the eyebrows, drawing down of the corners of the mouth, and many gesticulations, he informed me without words directly to the effect that I, as a Republican appointee, ought to feel grateful if I was left in the Service at all. Mr. Bryan seemed to have no idea that the plan he had in mind would be blocked by the merit system, so far as the Consular Service was concerned. I left the Secretary of State with this clearly in mind: I was up against politics plus race prejudice; I might be allowed to remain at my present post; if so, I should be there for another four years at least, perhaps for another eight. I came to the definite conclusion that life was too short for me to spend eight years more of it in Corinto. I wrote out my resignation. The problem was more serious than my resignation from Stanton School; notwithstanding, it caused me only little more hesitation. I dropped my letter in the mail box, and marked another turn on the way along which I have come.

PART FOUR

XXVIII

I RETURNED to Jacksonville discouraged and disturbed. I had
burned my bridges, but I could not entirely keep down the
question as to the wisdom of my action. I had given up a secure position carrying retirement and a pension, and placed
myself where I had to make a new start, without knowing what
direction I should take. Nevertheless, deep down I felt sure
that, if the question was still open, I should close it as I had
already done. Several colored citizens approached me with
respect to the principalship of the New Stanton. The idea did
not appeal to me. It struck me that to become principal of
Stanton again would be to make a complete circle of my life
path, ending where I had begun. I thought seriously about re-
suming the practice of law. Jacksonville had become a bustling,
go-getter, money-mad city; it was, at the time, a boom town;
and I figured that it would offer me a good field as a lawyer.
Most of the colored men I talked with had caught the get-
rich-quick fever; they told me many marvelous tales of fortunes suddenly made, of how such and such a person had
bought a piece of property for a few hundred dollars and,
within a short time, sold it for many thousands. This sort of
talk was substantiated by considerable material evidence; a
number of these colored men lived in finer houses than were
occupied by anybody, except the quite rich white citizens, in
the Jacksonville I had formerly known. Among them, the
ownership of automobiles had passed the stage of being a novelty. And they were as loud in their praises and as firm in their
faith in the future of Jacksonville as was the local board of
trade or club of Rotarians. I could not help but be infected by
their enthusiasm and, from the advice they gave me, I gathered that among the very few things that Jacksonville lacked
was just such a lawyer as I should be. The Negro Masons of
the state were building a five- or six-story Masonic Temple,
and I went so far as to speak tentatively for office space.

Jacksonville was also making a bid for the moving picture industry; there were three or four studios already located there. While I was floundering, I thought to make a try at this new art field. I wrote a half-dozen short scenarios, Grace working with me on them, and promptly sold three of them, at prices ranging from twenty-five to fifty dollars each. We saw the exhibition of the first picture, and were so disappointed in it that we were actually ashamed to see the others.

Grace was having her first experience of really living in the South. The colored people we knew were very nice to her; they gave dinners and receptions and parties; they took us on long automobile rides; all of which she enjoyed. But those affairs, naturally, subsided; and, even had they not, it was not possible to live wholly within that circumscribed world. Many things on the outside, notwithstanding her hearsay knowledge of conditions, she resented so strongly that it was plain that she would have the greatest difficulty in adjusting herself to them. Some of these things seemed, in themselves, trivial; so trivial as to be ridiculous; but the truth is, these trivialities, taken with what they signify, are often vital and far-reaching. Grace and I were walking along the street one day, and, passing a man whom I knew, I raised my hat. He, in turn, smiled pleasantly but sheepishly, and nodded his head. Grace asked me, "Who is that man?" "He is Mr. Bours," I replied. "He was a member of the school board when I was principal of Stanton." A little farther along, I saw two men approaching. One of the men I did not know, the other I had known for twenty years. The man I knew was "Colonel" Carter, the editor of one of Jacksonville's newspapers. The "Colonel" was a fine man, and, speaking from a racial point, an *exceptional* Southern white man. One day, during the time I was running *The Daily American*, I was in his office when his wife came in. He said at once, "Mr. Johnson, do you know Mrs. Carter?" She interrupted by saying, "Why, I've known him nearly all my life." And this was true and, furthermore, meant that she had known me before the "Colonel" had come to Jacksonville. During the time I was writing for the theater in New York, a very beautiful and socially prominent Jacksonville young lady decided to go on the stage. "Colonel" Carter gave her a letter to me in which he asked me to use my best efforts in her behalf. The young lady presented the letter, and I introduced her at the offices of Klaw and Erlanger. She did not go on the stage, but before the end of a full season she married one of the outstanding light opera stars. At that happy event, she did not forget my efforts; she sent me an invitation to the wedding. None but an exceptional Southern white man would or could have done either of these two things. As the distance between the two approaching men and Grace and me lessened, I began to speculate upon what the "Colonel," in the presence of another white man and on the public highway, would do. He had seen us, and, I judge, his brain was working faster than mine. When he was within say, fifty feet of us he did an amazingly quick-witted thing; he took his hat entirely off and began scratching his head violently. As he passed, he smiled, bowed, and said, "How do you do?" I had felt like kicking myself for having "seen" Mr. Bours at all. I felt a bit sorry for "Colonel" Carter.

Certainly, the refusal to tip one's hat to a colored woman and to address a Negro as Mister or Missis are trivialities, but they connote the whole system of race prejudice, hatred, and injustice; their roots go to the very core of the whole matter. I have heard many Negroes brush aside these trivial things. The position they take is: What does it matter?—It doesn't hurt us—We should be foolish to endanger our economic and financial good or, it may be, our security of life and limb, by taking umbrage at these trifles. All of which is true enough, if nothing can be done to alter the situation. But there are instances in which it can be altered, if only by taking one's self out of it. These are trivialities, but for myself, I wish as little dealings or relations as possible with a man who will expect me to tip my hat when he is with his wife and will refuse to do the same thing when I am with mine. This mere trifle declares that, actually, there is no common ground on which we can stand; and I shall, whenever it is possible for me to do so, avoid standing on any ground with him.

On another day I was standing in the bank with which my father had done business when Dr. John C. L'Engle, the white-haired, aristocratic president, beckoned me to his desk. He talked to me for some minutes about my father, in the characteristically terse manner for which he was well known in

Jacksonville. He told me, too, that he had attended my father's funeral, and how much he had been affected by the singing of *We'll Understand It Better By and By*. Then quite abruptly he asked, "Do you intend to stay in Jacksonville?" I replied that I was not sure. He then said, "You can't do it. If you had never gone away, it would be a different matter. But Jacksonville is not the Jacksonville you used to know. Don't try it." These words from a wise man added to the doubts which for weeks had been gathering and growing thicker and darker.

D—— made a flying visit to Jacksonville. He brought with him his little daughter, a cute child three or four years old. She made a remark that circulated in town for days afterwards. D——'s step-mother had taken her to church; it was, probably, the first time the child had ever been in a church, and of course she had not seen *The Green Pastures*. On the front seat sat William De Lyon; he it was who had been a partner in the brickmason firm that gave me my first job. He was now a very old man with beautiful, silvery hair that he wore reaching down to his shoulders. The child nudged her guardian and asked in an awestruck whisper, "Is that God?" I saw little of D——; he was in town only a few days. When I talked with him he exhibited much interest in my situation, mixed, it seemed to me, with a degree of sympathetic condescension. But I may have been sensitive on the point.

Rosamond was in London. When, on the death of our father, he had gone to Jacksonville, he had become engaged to Nora Floyd, who as a small girl had been one of his piano pupils. The date set for their wedding was approaching, but Rosamond was supervisor of music at Hammerstein's Opera House in London and could not afford to leave to come to Jacksonville. It was finally arranged that the marriage would take place in London. Nora went over with her mother. The news that Rosamond's fiancée was going to Europe to be married grew into a sensation in Jacksonville when clippings that my brother sent over showed that news and pictures of the wedding had been given front page space in three or four of the London dailies.

Secretary Bryan had small success in his efforts to oust men from the Consular Service in order to make places for "deserving Democrats"; but Secretary Burleson had wholesale success with domestic patronage. This whole patronage business, as it developed under the new administration had, it seemed to me, a significance beyond the substitution of one set of partisan officeholders for another set. The South, it appeared, had taken the election of a Southern-born president, the first (to be elected) in sixty-four years, together with a Cabinet in which the proportion of Southern-born portfolio holders was one-half, as a signal that the country had been turned over not only to the Democratic Party in general, but to the South in particular. One of the effects of this impression held, I should say, by a majority of Southern white people, was a determination to nullify what remained of the Negro's national citizenship. Going back to the days of Reconstruction, the Negro in the South had always felt, no matter what his local status might be, that he was a citizen of the United States. This feeling was manifest especially when such a Negro entered a federal building. There he felt that he was on some portion, at least, of the ground of common citizenship; that he left most of the galling limitations on the outside. This, in reality, was only little more than a feeling; but, at that, it was worth something. The only place in the South where a Negro could pretend to a share in the common rights of citizenship was under the roof of a federal building. In parts of Florida, at any rate, efforts were made to take even that away from him. In several communities near Jacksonville, newly appointed postmasters cut "Jim Crow" windows at the side, through which Negroes were to get their mail, *without coming into the post office.* There they had to stand in sun or rain until the last white person on the inside had been served. The steps begun during President Wilson's first term to sweep away the remaining vestiges of the Negro's federal citizenship would have gone far had they not been halted by the World War.

Rosamond's absence in London added to my dilemma about my future. Property affairs needed the attention of one of us; and I saw more plainly each day that it was my mother's desire for me to remain in Jacksonville; she wanted one of us near her. My mother's desire tugged unremittingly at my heartstrings. I struggled through many indecisions, lying awake, at times, for hours in the night. I was at the fork, at the crossroads; no, I was standing lost in the woods. I did not know which direction to take, but I knew whichever I took would be fateful. I finally arrived at a fixed purpose. Just how I reached it I cannot tell. Was I governed by prescience or led by the wish? Was it blind luck or just a good guess? Someone has said that a large part of the whole business of life is good guessing. That someone was, I think, pretty close to the truth. I had a tearful parting from my mother when I carried out my purpose of returning to New York. I reassured her with the promise that I should come back to Jacksonville as often as I possibly could. Toward the end of the summer of 1914 Grace and I started north.

New York was more changed for me than ever. Grace's parents had followed the tide uptown and moved to Harlem. And in Harlem we made our home. It was now that I came to know well my wife's parents. My mother-in-law, a lovely, intelligent, and cultured woman, took, for me, all the point out of the ancient joke. In time, through mutual affection, she grew to take, very largely, the place of a mother in my life. I found in my father-in-law a good friend and, moreover, an exceedingly interesting character: a man without a day of formal schooling, but full of wisdom and a knowledge of the world. He had a collection of books that made one of the best small libraries I ever saw, every book an important one. He is still an insatiable reader and still maintains a disdain for "trash." His reading makes conversation and discussion with him, sometimes, an exciting experience. He has a philosophy of life, to which he attributes the fact that he has reached the age of eighty, hale and hearty; and its main elements are moderation and regularity. He gets up every morning at the same hour, a very early one, drinks a cup of coffee and, no matter what the weather, goes out. It is jokingly said that he opens up Harlem. He comes back and by breakfast time has read the morning paper. He takes a nap at a certain hour; must have his dinner precisely on the minute; has certain evenings for the movies, certain nights for reading, and a certain hour for going to bed. For years he has gone every Sunday morning to the Ethical

Society. Nothing less than some *force majeure* can change his schedule. Notwithstanding this seeming inflexibility, he is a man of tender sympathies. For many years he has been a generous contributor to causes, especially to Negro causes and institutions. I have never ceased to find him interesting and stimulating.

My sole justification to myself in making the decision to return to New York was that I should have opportunity to make my way by writing. I had done it once; why couldn't I do it again? At all events, I should be exerting my efforts in a field where the goal was great enough to call up my energies and enthusiasm. My first opportunity came from a quarter which I had not given consideration. I had been in New York only a few weeks when Fred R. Moore, the owner and publisher of *The New York Age*, the oldest of the New York Negro newspapers, offered me the position of editor of the paper. I agreed to write the editorials, but made the arrangement to have what I wrote in the main appear under my name as contributing editor, a title I copied from Theodore Roosevelt. I wrote *The Age* editorials for ten years; those that I signed being printed in double columns under the caption, "Views and Reviews." I got great gratification out of the fact that the articles in those double columns quickly began to attract the attention of readers and also of other Negro editors.

But writing the editorials for *The New York Age* neither took all my time nor paid me as much as I needed to earn. I tried again for Broadway. I wrote the words for a half-dozen or so popular songs, collaborating with various composers, and I did some work with Jerome Kern on a new play for Marie Cahill; but I found that I had lost the touch for Broadway. I simply couldn't turn the trick again; I don't think that anybody else has ever been able to do it. A vogue of that kind is a vogue, and is about as exempt from recapture as past time. My failure to effect a "comeback" on Broadway led to some extremely blue days for me. For the first time in my life I was confronted with the actual want of money. I turned to writing "art songs," and did a number of them with Harry T. Burleigh, with Will Marion Cook, and with my brother. *Sence You Went Away*, which I wrote with

Rosamond, was sung by John McCormack and made some money. At this point, I took a part in the organization of the American Society of Composers, Authors, and Publishers. We gave an organization dinner at Luchow's in Fourteenth Street. I sat at the speakers' table next to Victor Herbert, whose music I had so long admired but whom I had not known personally. The Society has grown to be the richest and most powerful organization of its kind in the world. Its membership fee is ten dollars a year, and it distributes something like a million and a half dollars to its members annually. This it can do because through a law it succeeded in having passed by Congress it is enabled to collect a royalty on all mechanical, electrical, and radio reproductions and also upon the professional use of the music written by its members. Then the chance came for me to put into English the libretto of *Goyescas*, the Spanish grand opera produced at the Metropolitan Opera House in 1915. In doing this piece of work I kept two objects (not always attained in the translations of grand opera librettos) in mind: to make it singable and sensible. Seeing my name and work in the program of the Metropolitan gave me a new sensation.

Señor Periquet, the librettist of the opera, and I got to be very good friends. He was sufficiently impressed with my work on *Goyescas* to enter into a contract with me to be the English translator of his plays for the United States. I did translate one of them, but was not able to find anyone willing to produce it, so I never did another. Periquet was ruddy, with light hair and gray eyes and of a gay temperament. Enrique Granados, the composer of the opera, was a directly opposite type. He was olive in complexion, with black hair and dark, sad, dreamy eyes. His manner was quiet, almost apologetic. He had a high reputation as a composer in Spain, but he had always been poor and struggling. He had come to New York to witness the American première of his work, bringing his wife with him and leaving their six children at home. The opera was not a startling success, but Granados was quietly happy; it had made his fortune. He had never thought, perhaps, of there being so much money in the world; at any rate, of so much of it coming to him. Prospects of simple but secure life in Spain for himself and family were rosy.

The night before Granados sailed for home, I took dinner with him and his wife and Periquet at the Hotel Claridge. After dinner, he played for us—he possessed remarkable virtuosity. His wife sat demurely listening; Periquet, between numbers and after Granados had finished playing, continued his importunities for the composer and his wife to give up their plan of returning to Spain by way of England, and to wait for the Spanish steamer on which he, Periquet, was going to sail. But Granados in his quiet way clung to his plan. He then had something like ten thousand dollars in gold and banknotes in a belt strapped around his waist, and he was eager to get back home to his children. It may have been that he needed to count his fortune over in his own country before he could feel that it was real money and really his. He pressed Periquet to change and sail with him, but the latter was explosive in the expression of his determination to sail on none other than a Spanish steamer. He did not consider it safe, he said, to return over the more northern route. Granados and his wife sailed. They were crossing the channel in the *Sussex* when she was torpedoed by a German submarine, and both of them were lost. The treasure that he was carrying home helped to carry him down. It took me a long while after the news to get that evening at the Claridge out of my mind. If Periquet could have been only a little more persuasive; or if Granados had been only a little less eager to get home.

Naturally, I turned my hand also to literary writing. This was nearly a decade before the big magazines threw their pages open to Negro writers and principal publishers had begun to feel that they would like to have at least one Negro author added to their lists. I greatly missed Richard Watson Gilder and Dr. Ward, both of whom had always been ready to talk with me and to consider my work for publication. However, I did establish cordial relations with Robert Underwood Johnson, who had succeeded Mr. Gilder as editor of *The Century*, and went often to see Brander Matthews.

The first new contact I made was with H. L. Mencken, then one of the editors of *Smart Set*. Mr. Mencken had made a sharper impression on my mind than any other American then writing, and I wanted to know him. As a reason for going to

see him, I took along a one-act play, *Mañana de Sol*, which I
had translated from the Spanish of Serafín and Joaquín Álvarez
Quintero. I sent my name in, feeling not entirely confident
that I should see Mr. Mencken, but he came out almost
promptly. We sat and talked for thirty, forty, perhaps, forty-five
minutes; and I kept wondering how a man as busy as he could
give so much time to a mere stranger. I had never been so fascinated at hearing anyone talk. He talked about literature,
about Negro literature, the Negro problem, and Negro music.
He declared that Negro writers in writing about their own race
made a mistake when they indulged in pleas for justice and
mercy, when they prayed indulgence for shortcomings, when
they based their protests against unjust treatment on the
Christian or moral or ethical code, when they argued to prove
that they were as good as anybody else. "What they should
do," he said, "is to single out the strong points of the race and
emphasize them over and over and over; asserting, at least on
these points, that they are *better* than anybody else." I called to
his attention that I had attempted something of that sort in
The Autobiography of an Ex-Colored Man. He was particularly
interested in Negro music, and I afterwards sent him copies of
songs by Burleigh and Cook and Johnson. Through some correspondence which we had about the songs, I discerned that
his chief interest in them was not that of an editor but of a musician. Mr. Mencken did not accept the play, but my visit was
the beginning of a very pleasant relation. His parting advice
was that I center my efforts on prose rather than poetry; I
gathered that his opinion of poetry and poets was not exceedingly high. When I left him I felt buoyed up, exhilarated. It
was as though I had taken a mental cocktail.

In the meantime, I contributed some poems to *The Crisis*.
One of these, "The White Witch," a poem that puzzles many
people who read it—I consider its meaning quite plain—
figured rather sensationally in a court scene in Boston, where
colored citizens were attempting by legal steps to prohibit
the exhibition of the moving picture, *The Birth of a Nation*.
One of the attorneys for the picture people rose in court,
waving a copy of *The Crisis* in his hand, and tried to make
the poem evidence that such a picture as *The Birth of a Nation* was an absolute necessity in the United States.

With the coming of the presidential campaign of 1916, I found myself again taking a hand in politics; but this time I had a deeper interest and a stronger influence. I felt convinced that the maintenance of such national citizenship rights as the Negroes still held depended upon throwing the Southern oligarchy at Washington out of power; and I bent all my energies, especially through my editorials in *The Age*, toward that end. My distrust and dislike of the attitude of the Administration centered upon Woodrow Wilson, and came nearer to constituting keen hatred for an individual than anything I have ever felt. In addition to writing as strongly as I could, I volunteered as a speaker and campaigner for Hughes through New York and Massachusetts. In the midst of the campaign, the *Philadelphia Ledger* offered two thousand dollars in prizes for editorials on the candidates of the two major parties; one thousand dollars in three prizes for editorials on "Why Hughes Should Be Elected," and similar amounts for editorials on "Why Wilson Should Be Elected." By the terms of the contest, only bona fide editors of newspapers could enter; about eight hundred editors took part. The time limit had nearly expired before it struck me that I was a bona fide editor, and might take a chance. I wrote my article, and was compelled to send it by special delivery in order to get it to Philadelphia in time. I was awarded the third prize for a Hughes editorial. The Negro press gave me unanimous congratulations and hailed my success as a feather in the cap of Negro journalism.

On the day before election, I was at Republican headquarters in New York when Mr. Hughes came in to pay a visit. I was introduced to him as the man who had written one of the prize-winning editorials on "Why Hughes Should Be Elected." He graciously expressed his appreciation; though, in all probability, he had not read the article. That night he made the closing speech of his campaign at Madison Square Garden. I was among those seated on the platform. Mr. Hughes did not make a back-stage entrance; he strode down the long center aisle, Mrs. Hughes swinging on his arm, and tripping along at his side as gayly as a girl, while the thousands stood up and cheered. It must have been a tremendous moment for them both. On election night I was with those invited to listen to the returns at headquarters—no broadcasting in those far-off days. A committee of gentlemen received returns as telegraphed in, and chalked them up on a blackboard. At about ten or ten-thirty o'clock the great states east of Mississippi had been heard from, and enthusiasm reached the point of jubilation. The word went out "Hughes elected!" Newsboys were shrilly crying up and down the streets, "Extra! Hughes elected!" The crowds shouted "Hughes elected!" The committee telephoned the news to Mr. Hughes at his hotel, and he went to bed, President of the United States.

I felt jubilant, too. Had I not had a hand in overthrowing the Southern oligarchy? Toward midnight a lull came over Republican headquarters. It appeared that returns from the far western states were coming in rather slowly. A little after midnight, I went upstairs, where I found a vacant room and sat down to write an editorial on the election, which would go to press within twenty-four hours. I put down the heading, "Thank God for Hughes," and under that caption wrote my article. When I had finished, I came down and peeped into the large room. A good part of the brilliant assemblage had left, and the lull that I had noted before seemed to have deepened. However, I did not stop to ask any questions; I slipped out and started for Harlem. When I got out of the Subway at 135th Street and Lenox Avenue, I felt hungry and I stopped in a restaurant to get something to eat. Before I came out, I heard newsboys crying, "Extra! Wilson elected!" I thought it was a hoax, but I bought a newspaper and read it avidly. After the first shock of amazement, the thought that struck me most forcibly was that I should have to get to work and write another leading article to fill the column.

XXIX

EARLY in the summer of 1916 I was in Jacksonville on a third visit to my mother since I had moved to New York. While there I received a letter from J. E. Spingarn, inviting me to be a member of a conference on questions relating to the Negro, which would be attended by both white and colored people, and would be held at his country place, Troutbeck, at Amenia, New York. At the bottom of the letter, W. E. B. Du Bois had scribbled, "Do come." I wrote back that I gladly accepted membership in the conference and that I should certainly attend. The meeting was held in August and lasted three days. Mr. Spingarn, then Chairman of the Board of Directors of the National Association for the Advancement of Colored People, was host to the conference. A half hundred of the most influential and progressive Negroes in the country, and of white people interested in the cause of Negro rights, participated in the sessions. At one of these, the group was dazzled by the beauty and fired by the crusading zeal of Inez Milholland. Another session was attended and addressed by the Governor of the state, Charles S. Whitman. I was chosen, through the suggestion of Mr. Spingarn, I am sure, to make the remarks introducing Governor Whitman. During the conference I had a talk with Oswald Garrison Villard, in which he said that one of the most effective steps the Negro in New York could take would be to march down Fifth Avenue in a parade of silent protest.

The conference was held at a time when the fundamental rights of the Negro were in a state of flux. At no time since the days following the Civil War had the Negro been in a position where he stood to make a greater gain or sustain a greater loss in status. The great war in Europe, its recoil on America, the ferment in the United States, all conspired to break up the stereotyped conception of the Negro's place that had been increasing in fixity for forty years, and to allow of new formations. What new forms these conceptions would assume depended largely upon what attitude and action the Negro himself and the white people willing to stand with him would take. Those gathered at the conference determined to help shape them more in accordance with real democracy and the heart's desire of the Negro. The Amenia Conference came at an hour of exigency and opportunity, and took its place in the list of important events in the history of the Negro in the United States.

Late in the fall, I received another letter from Mr. Spingarn. In this letter he asked me if I would not take a place in the National Association for the Advancement of Colored People. The offer was a genuine surprise. I had not received the slightest intimation of its likelihood; nevertheless, under my surprise I was aware that what had come to me was in line with destiny. Out of such tenuous stuff had it come—the unspoken reactions between me and two other men, J. E. Spingarn and W. E. B. Du Bois—that it could not have been other than the resultant of these mysterious forces that are constantly at work for good or evil in the life of every man. A short while before, a tentative offer, and a flattering one, had been made to me, which, I am confident, I could have taken up; but I hesitated and doubted and did not make an attempt to do so. When I received Mr. Spingarn's letter, it at once seemed to me that every bit of experience I had had, from the principalship of Stanton School to editorship on *The New York Age*, was preparation for the work I was being asked to undertake. The Board of Directors created the position of Field Secretary, and in that capacity I began work with the Association in December 1916.

Our offices were situated in two small rooms at 70 Fifth Avenue. The office staff consisted of four persons, Roy Nash, secretary; myself; Frank M. Turner, bookkeeper; and Richetta G. Randolph, stenographer. Both Mr. Turner and Miss Randolph, the best confidential secretary I have known or known of, are still with the Association. Across the hall, Dr. Du Bois, the editor of *The Crisis*, had quarters occupying considerably more space. *The Crisis* was the organ of the Association, but was maintained as a distinct business entity, with a separate staff, then numbering eight or ten persons. The magazine had been established five years before, and in that time had grown to have a circulation of thirty thousand. It was, I believe, the only radical publication in the country that was self-supporting. And here the word "radical" is used in a relative sense. *The Crisis* voiced the protests of the Association, but in the English-speaking world, most of those protests had passed out of the radical program with the signing of the Magna Carta at Runnymede seven hundred years before. The central purpose of the National Association for the Advancement of Colored People was nothing more or less than to claim for the Negro common equality under the fundamental law of the United States; to insist upon the impartial application of that law; to proclaim that democracy stultified itself when it barred men from its benefits solely on the grounds of race and color. And yet, things relative are as real as things absolute. In parts of the country—say, for example, darkest Mississippi—it was, and still is, actually radical to hark back to the demands made by the barons on King John, and insist upon the right of Negroes to enjoy common security of life and property; upon their right, when charged with crime, to a fair trial by a jury of their peers before a duly constituted court of justice; upon the application for them of the principle, "No taxation without representation"; upon the right of qualified Negro citizens to cast a vote. "Negro radicalism" that went no farther than this has times without number been met with violence and even death. Communists, who advocate and work for the overthrow of the entire governmental system, run no such risks as the Negro "radical" who insists upon the impartial interpretation and administration of existing law.

In 1916, the Association was a small organization. It had its inception in a call issued February 12, 1909, the one-hundredth anniversary of the birth of Abraham Lincoln, for a conference to consider the civil state of the Negro. In the following year a temporary organization, composed of both white and colored people, was formed; and in 1911 the Association was incorporated under the laws of New York, with a board of thirty directors, constituted of about equal numbers of white and colored members. From its beginning, the organization took an unequivocal stand against disfranchisement, against inequitable public schooling for Negro children, against segregation and all forms of public discrimination based on race or color, and against mob violence and lynching. For thirty years past the accepted status of the Negro as a citizen had been steadily declining. In some respects it was lower than it had been at the close of the Civil War. In the whole South, the home of the overwhelming masses of the race, he had been completely disfranchised, segregated, and "Jim Crowed" in nearly every phase of life, and mobbed and lynched and burned at the stake by the thousands. There had been the isolated declarations of the Afro-American Council in 1890 and 1898; and the pronouncements of the Niagara Movement in 1905 and the several years following, pronouncements on which the program of the National Association for the Advancement of Colored People was based; but the race as a whole had adopted soft-speaking, conformity, and sheer opportunism as the methods for survival. Concerted effort inspired by high courage and idealism seemed to be wholly lacking. It looked as though the Negro would let his rights and his claim to rights go by default. In that quarter, whence came the champions of justice to the Negro from the whites, there had been a shifting of front, and there was a more or less general admission that the noble crusade had been undertaken in vain. Most of what had been gained as a result of the war had been yielded in the struggle on the field where public sentiment is won or lost.

And so, when the National Association for the Advancement of Colored People announced its platform of Equality for the Negro, a great many people were startled. Such a platform, as was to be expected, aroused fierce antagonisms to the organization. It was denounced as radical, revolutionary, subversive; and those at its head were branded as dangerous busybodies or idealistic fanatics. But the most telling attack on the Association was made by those who called it a "social equality" society; for that had the effect of making a good many white friends of the Negro's cause uneasy, and of placing Negroes themselves on the defensive. This term, "social equality," is, at the same time, a most concrete and a most elusive obstacle in the Negro's way. It is never defined; it is shifted to block any path that may be open; it is stretched over whole areas of contacts and activities; it is used to cover and justify every form of restriction, injustice, and brutality practiced against the Negro. The mere term makes cowards of white people and puts Negroes in a dilemma.

Very few, even among the most intelligent Negroes, could find a tenable position on which to base a stand for social among the other equalities demanded. When confronted by the question, they were forced by what they felt to be self-respect, to refrain from taking such a stand. As a matter of truth, self-respect demands that no man admit, even tacitly, that he is unfit to associate with any of his fellow men (and that is aside from whether he wishes to associate with them or not). In the South, policy exacts that any pleas made by a Negro—or by a white man, for that matter—for fair treatment to the race, shall be predicated upon a disavowal of "social equality." Booker T. Washington, in his great Atlanta speech, felt the necessity of declaring, "In all things purely social we can be as separate as the five fingers, and yet one as the hand in all things essential to material progress." It was this figure of speech, this stroke of consummate diplomacy, that made the whole of his eloquent plea swallowable for Southern throats, and straightway brought him recognition as a statesman. And a fine figure of speech it is, but it does not stand logical analysis. Beyond the ineptitude of its implication that separated fingers (though separated only socially) can constitute an efficient hand, is the fact that it raises an illimitable question: of what do "all things essential to material progress" consist? An elimination of the things deemed "purely social" by Dr. Washington's white hearers, would have left a very narrow margin, perhaps only a mudsill level of things on which to co-operate like one as the hand.

There ought not be any intellectual dilemma in this question for a self-respecting Negro. He can, without apology to himself or to anyone else, stand for social equality on any definition of the term not laid down by a madman or an idiot. Certainly, he does not mean that he is watching to sneak or break into somebody's parlor, or to present himself uninvited for a dinner or a party, or that he has intentions of seizing some Nordic maiden by the hair and dragging her off to be his woman. Certainly, he knows that nothing can compel social intercourse. He sees many Negroes that no force within the race can compel him to invite to his house; and he sees many white people that he would not, under any circumstances, have in his house. But he holds: There should be nothing in law or public opinion to prohibit persons who find that they have congenial tastes and kindred interests in life from associating with each other, if they mutually desire to do so.

But I am fully aware that in writing as I have in the last page or two I have been arguing about "social equality" only from the surfaces of the question. And these surfaces give the whole matter the aspect of a preposterous and absurd farce; especially in the region where "social equality" is talked about most. For, in that region, a white gentleman may not eat with a colored person without the danger of serious loss of social prestige; yet he may sleep with a colored person without incurring the risk of any appreciable damage to his reputation. But behind and under the paradoxes lies a definite significance, a significance so seldom allowed to come into the open that most Negroes have not even thought about it; that white women, even those in the South, are, probably, not entirely aware of it; but which every thinking Southern white man understands clearly: *"Social equality" signifies a series of far-flung barriers against amalgamation of the two races; except so far as it may come about by white men with colored women.*

The platform of the Association startled a great many Negroes. Many there were who, while longing for the objectives set forth, felt timid about the methods proposed for attaining them. They feared that a full statement of the Negro's case, and an open avowal of the determination to prosecute it, would retard rather than hasten the results aimed at; that a frontal attack would do the Negro's cause more harm than good. And many there were who definitely opposed the association, who fought it covertly and openly. This particular opposition to the organization was, in a large degree, an inheritance from the Niagara Movement. It was the Niagara Movement, inaugurated by Dr. Du Bois in 1905, that marked, with respect to the question of the Negro's civil rights, a split of the race into two well-defined parties—one, made up from the preponderating number of conservatives, under the leadership of Booker T. Washington and the other, made up from the militant elements, under the leadership of W. E. B. Du Bois. Between these two groups there were incessant attacks and counter-attacks; the former declaring that the latter were visionaries, doctrinaires, and incendiaries; the latter charging the former with minifying political and civil rights, with encouraging opposition to higher training and higher opportunities for Negro youth, with giving sanction to certain prejudiced practices and attitudes toward the Negro, thus yielding up in fundamental principles more than could be balanced by any immediate gains. One not familiar with this phase of Negro life in the twelve- or fourteen-year period following 1903 (the year of publication of *The Souls of Black Folk*) cannot imagine the bitterness of the antagonism between these two wings. When the National Association for the Advancement of Colored People was organized, the Du Bois wing merged to help form the new organization, and the old antagonism, in a considerable measure, was transferred. In 1916, the situation, in brief, was as follows: Booker T. Washington had died the year before, but the conservative mass of Negroes, together with a large part of the white South and the greater proportion of the Northern whites at all interested in the Negro, stood firm under the banner of the Tuskegee Idea; Negro militants and white champions of equal rights for the Negro were grouped together in the National Association; in addition, there was a third group, under the leadership of Monroe Trotter, editor of the *Boston Guardian*. Mr. Trotter, in many respects an able man, zealous almost to the point of fanaticism, an implacable foe of every form and degree of race discrimination, waged, during this period referred to, a relentless and often savage fight through his newspaper against Dr. Washington and the Tuskegee Idea. Mr. Trotter, however, could not work, except alone; and, although there were numbers of people who subscribed to his opinions, he lacked capacity to weld his followers into a form that would give them any considerable group effectiveness.

During the first seven years, the growth of the Association was slow and the result only of continual effort. The organization was lacking funds and the strength that comes from numbers, but it made a valiant use of the only effective weapon available—agitation. It agitated through mass meetings, through leaflets and pamphlets, *The Crisis*, and any other publication that would open its pages. It had sent Elizabeth Freeman, a young white woman, exceptionally fitted for the job, to investigate the burning alive of a Negro in Waco, Texas, and had published to the world the gruesome details of her findings. Later, Roy Nash went to Abbeyville, South Carolina, and investigated the lynching of Anthony Crawford, a prosperous Negro, who was lynched mainly because of the fact that he was well-to-do and independent. I threw myself wholeheartedly into this work. In 1916 there were sixty-eight branches in Northern and Western cities. There were three branches in three Southern cities, New Orleans, Shreveport, Louisiana, and Key West, Florida, with a total of three hundred and forty-eight members. My first step as Field Secretary was an effort to organize in the South. It was my idea that the South could furnish numbers and resources to make the Association a power. This idea did not meet with the unqualified approval of all the members of the Board of Directors. There were some who feared that a large membership in the South might cause the organization to modify its position; they felt that it could be freer to speak and act if not hampered by responsibility for Southern branches. It was, however, my deep conviction that the aims of the Association could never be realized by only hammering at white America; I felt convinced that it would be necessary to awaken black America, awaken it to a sense of its rights and to a determination to hold fast to such as it possessed and to seek in every orderly way possible to secure all others to which it was entitled. I realized that, regardless of what might be done *for* black America, the ultimate and vital part of the work would have to be done by black America itself; and that to do that work black America needed an intelligent program. A large majority of the Board agreed with me in my plan for organizing the South. I took the preparatory step of drafting a manual for branches, setting forth the aims of the Association, the plan for organizing branches, and the laws by which branches would be governed; then I wrote a letter stating my purpose to key persons in some twenty cities, and asking them to call a conference of twenty-five representative people to meet with me on a date specified. I started on the actual work early in January 1917; beginning at Richmond, Virginia, and going as far south as Tampa, Florida. At each conference, with the exception of one city, a branch organization was set up and arrangements planned for a mass meeting at which a drive for members would be made. On my way back, I retraced the ground I had covered and addressed these mass meetings.

The results of the trip were not overwhelmingly successful, but, at least to me, they were encouraging. They did, in fact, lay the groundwork for what, two years later, the Association called its "Southern Empire." By that time, through supplementary work done by Mary E. Talbert in the Southwest, there were alert, aggressive, intelligently directed branches in almost every Southern state, and the South was contributing an amount for the national work greater than what had been the total general fund of the organization in 1916. At the close of 1919, there were three hundred and ten branches in the Association, one hundred and thirty-one of them being in the South.

Nor were the results of the trip uniform; in some cities the idea of making a united stand and a concerted effort for citizenship rights was seized upon more enthusiastically than in others. But I was impressed with the fact that everywhere there was a rise in the level of the Negro's morale. The exodus of Negroes to the North, pulled there to fill the labor vacuum in the great industries, was in full motion; the tremors of the war in Europe were shaking America with increasing intensity; circumstances were combining to put a higher premium on Negro muscle, Negro hands, and Negro brains than ever before; all these forces had a quickening effect that was running through the entire mass of the race. This effect was especially noticeable in Atlanta. The mass meeting I addressed in that city was held in the splendid Negro theater. The meeting had been well advertised, and the crowd took up every available bit of space in the auditorium. As I sat on the platform, I noticed that a number of policemen were stationed in the theater. In other days, this would have placed a hand of chilling restraint on the proceedings, but now it had no such effect. Each person who took part spoke out frankly and courageously about the business that had brought the people together; and the more frank and courageous the utterance, the louder and longer was it cheered and applauded. I don't know what those Atlanta policemen thought about the meeting, but, so far as I could see, they did nothing more than look and listen. Atlanta grew to be one of the strongest branches in the Association; reaching a membership of more than a thousand.

The organization conference which was held at Atlanta was unique; it was the only one in which no woman was invited to take part. There were present fifty or so of the leading colored men of the city; lawyers, doctors, college professors, public school teachers, editors, bankers, insurance officials, and businessmen. Some of these men I had known before, but most of them were strangers. From the whole group, a very young man who acted as secretary of the conference became singled out in my mind. I saw him several times and was impressed with the degree of mental and physical energy he seemed to be able to bring into play and center on the job in hand. I did not need to guess that the representative conference and the extraordinary mass meeting were largely results of his efforts. I left Atlanta having made a strong mental note about him.

Within a few weeks after I got to New York, the United States entered the World War. Shortly thereafter, Mr. Nash resigned the secretaryship and entered the army, and I took the place of acting secretary. In the fall, I put before the Board what I believed to be the qualifications of the young man I had met in Atlanta and urged that he be offered a place in the national office. Many of the members of the Board were somewhat doubtful about a very young man from the deep South, and utterly unknown; and, furthermore, they were thinking in terms of a new secretary. Nevertheless, I pressed the case of my candidate, and was finally authorized to write to him. I did so. He hesitated for a while, and I could not blame him, for he had a position and a promising outlook with an insurance company; and the salary that we offered him was very small. However, in the end he wrote that he would accept the offer. So, at the beginning of 1918, Walter White came to New York to be assistant secretary of the Association, and to carry through, later, the series of lynching investigations that were to make his name nationally known. A few days later, John R. Shillady, the newly elected secretary, took up his work.

The months between the resignation of Mr. Nash and the coming of Mr. White and Mr. Shillady were strenuous. The organization was beginning to show signs of greater growth, and there were only three of us at the office to do the necessary work. I spent part of my time in the office and part of it on the road. But Mary White Ovington, who was one of the founders of the Association, and who had been its volunteer secretary at the beginning, when there were no salaried officers, came in almost daily and helped.

It was in this period that I rushed to Memphis to make an investigation of the burning alive of Ell Persons, a Negro, charged with being an "axe murderer." I was in Memphis ten days; I talked with the sheriff, with newspaper men, with a few white citizens, and many colored ones; I read through the Memphis papers covering the period; and nowhere could I find any positive evidence that Ell Persons was the man guilty of the crimes that had been committed. And, yet, without a trial, he was burned alive on the charge. I wrote out my findings, and they were published in a pamphlet that was widely circulated.

On the day I arrived in Memphis, Robert R. Church drove me out to the place where the burning had taken place. A pile of ashes and pieces of charred wood still marked the spot. While the ashes were yet hot, the bones had been scrambled for as souvenirs by the mobs. I reassembled the picture in my mind: a lone Negro in the hands of his accusers, who for the time are no longer human; he is chained to a stake, wood is piled under and around him, and five thousand men and women, women with babies in their arms and women with babies in their wombs, look on with pitiless anticipation, with sadistic satisfaction while he is baptized with gasoline and set afire. The mob disperses, many of them complaining, "They burned him too fast." I tried to balance the sufferings of the miserable victim against the moral degradation of Memphis, and the truth flashed over me that in large measure the race question involves the saving of black America's body and white America's soul.

It was in this period that the Association won the first of its victories in reaffirming the Negro's constitutional rights. From the United States Supreme Court it gained, in the Louisville Segregation Case, a unanimous decision declaring that laws which established residential segregation by race were unconstitutional. It is true that the Association, through its president, Moorfield Storey, had had a hand in winning the decision handed down by the Supreme Court in 1915 declaring "grandfather clauses" unconstitutional;* but the Segregation Case was the Association's case from the beginning; with its Louisville branch it fought that case through all the courts of Kentucky, up to and through the Supreme Court. In the

---

*Speaking generally, these grandfather clauses in the amended constitutions of the Southern states enumerated as necessary to the rights of suffrage a list of property, literacy, and character qualifications of high standard; and then provided that none of these qualifications need be met by any persons who had the right to vote or who had an ancestor who had a right to vote before the time of the close of the Civil War. There were, of course, numbers of colored people who could have qualified under the ancestor proviso, but the right was not worth the risk of attempting to establish it.

Supreme Court, the case was argued by Mr. Story; I had the privilege of hearing him.

It was also in this period that the Association, under the lead of J. E. Spingarn, undertook to see that provision was made for the training of colored men to be officers in the army.* Mr. Spingarn made efforts to have them admitted to the regular training camps; on one occasion I went with him as one of a committee to see Secretary of War Newton D. Baker about their admission to the regular camps; but such an arrangement "simply *could not be made.*" This decision could not be charged to any personal attitude of Mr. Baker; for not even Secretaries of War can override a fixed policy of the army bureaucracy at Washington. The arrangement finally made was for a special training camp at Des Moines.

This arrangement brought down on Mr. Spingarn some sharp criticism, criticism from within and without the Association. He was denounced by some as going back on a basic principle of the organization of which he was a high officer. At any rate, his critics could not charge him with being a doctrinaire; he had faced a situation—several hundred thousand Negroes in the armies of the United States, and not a chance for one of them to be an officer, unless he had already received the required training—and he met it practically. Mr. Spingarn is one of the most finely sensitive souls that I know, and, probably, he was wounded by some of the criticisms hurled at him, but he never showed it. From the Des Moines Camp, 678 colored men received commissions as officers in the army. The common sense of the matter and the pride the race took in the results snuffed criticism out.

When I went with the committee to see Secretary Baker, it was my first visit to Washington after our declaration of war. As I passed the White House and entered the State, Army, and Navy Building, I saw a sight which gave me food for thought.

---

*There were four Negro regiments in the regular army, but, practically, no commissioned officers. 2,290,527 Negroes were registered, 458,838 were examined, and 342,277 were accepted and drafted for service. Of the total number of registrants in the United States, 26.84 per cent of the whites were accepted for full military service, and 31.74 per cent of the Negroes. Including the regular army regiments and National Guard units, 380,000 Negro soldiers were mobilized for the World War.

Those were the days when the nation was in a panic over the rumors of pro-Germans and spies in their midst, and troops were thrown around these two buildings for their protection. And every man of the troops guarding the home of the President and the offices of the three principal departments of the government was a black man.

In the middle of this same summer, on July 2, the colored people of the whole country were appalled by the news of the East St. Louis massacres, a riot in which four hundred thousand dollars' worth of property was destroyed, nearly six thousand Negroes driven from their homes, hundreds of them killed, some burned in the houses set afire over their heads. This occurrence was the more bitterly ironical because it came when Negro citizens, as others, were being urged to do their bit to "make the world safe for democracy."

But the reaction to the East St. Louis Massacre was widespread. Congress passed a resolution calling for an investigation. At a hearing before the Committee on Rules of the House of Representatives, Congressman Dyer, of Missouri, among other things, said:

I have visited out there and have interviewed a number of people and talked with a number who saw the murders that were committed. One man in particular who spoke to me is now an officer in the United States Army Reserve Corps, Lieut. Arbuckle, who is here in Washington somewhere, he having come here to report to the Adjutant General.

At the time of these happenings he was in the employ of the Government, but he was there on some business in East St. Louis. He said that he saw a part of this killing, and he saw them burning railway cars in yards, which were waiting for transport, filled with interstate commerce. He saw members of the militia of Illinois shoot Negroes. He saw policemen of the city of East St. Louis shoot Negroes. He saw this mob go to the homes of these Negroes and nail boards up over the doors and windows and then set fire and burn them up. He saw them take little children out of the arms of their mothers and throw them into the fires and burn them up. He saw the most dastardly and most criminal outrages ever perpetrated in this country, and this is undisputed. And I have talked with others; and my opinion is that over five hundred people were killed on this occasion.

Congressman Rodenberg, of Illinois—East St. Louis is in Illinois—in his remarks before the Committee said:

Now, the plain, unvarnished truth of the matter, as Mr. Joyce told Secretary Baker, is that civil government in East St. Louis completely collapsed at the time of the riot. The conditions there at the time beggar description. It is impossible for any human being to describe the ferocity and brutality of that mob. In one case, for instance, a little ten-year-old boy, whose mother had been shot down, was running around sobbing and looking for his mother, and some members of the mob shot the boy, and before life had passed from his body they picked the little fellow up and threw him in the flames.

Another colored woman with a little two-year-old baby in her arms was trying to protect the child, and they shot her and also shot the child, and threw them in the flames. The horror of that tragedy in East St. Louis can never be described. It weighted me down with a feeling of depression that I did not recover from for weeks. The most sickening things I ever heard of were described in the letters that I received from home giving details of that attack.

As is usual in such occurrences, Negroes were singled out and held legally responsible. The Association secured a staff of lawyers headed by Charles Nagel, Secretary of Commerce under Taft, for their defense, and it also raised a fund for the relief of those who had been made destitute by the riot.

I attended a meeting of the executive committee of our Harlem branch. They were discussing plans to register a protest against the East St. Louis massacre; the plan most favored was a mass meeting at Carnegie Hall. Recalling Mr. Villard's remarks at the Amenia Conference, I suggested a silent protest parade. The suggestion met with immediate acceptance. It was agreed that the parade should not be made merely an affair of the Association and the Harlem branch, but of the colored citizens of all Greater New York. A large committee, including the pastors of the leading churches and other men and women of influence, was formed, and preparations were gone about with feverish enthusiasm. On Saturday, July 28, nine or ten thousand Negroes marched silently down Fifth Avenue to the sound of muffled drums. The procession was headed by children, some of them not older than six, dressed in white. These were followed by the women dressed in white, and bringing up the rear came the men in dark clothes. They carried banners; some of which read:

MOTHER, DO LYNCHERS GO TO HEAVEN?
GIVE ME A CHANCE TO LIVE.
TREAT US SO THAT WE MAY LOVE OUR COUNTRY.
MR. PRESIDENT, WHY NOT MAKE AMERICA SAFE
FOR DEMOCRACY?

Just ahead of the man who carried the American flag went a streamer that stretched half across the street and bore this inscription:

YOUR HANDS ARE FULL OF BLOOD

The streets of New York have witnessed many strange sights, but, I judge, never one stranger than this; never one more impressive. The parade moved in silence and was watched in silence. Among the watchers were those with tears in their eyes. Negro Boy Scouts distributed to those lined along the sidewalks printed circulars which stated some of the reasons for the demonstration:

We march because by the Grace of God and the force of truth, the dangerous, hampering walls of prejudice and inhuman injustices must fall.

We march because we want to make impossible a repetition of Waco, Memphis, and East St. Louis, by rousing the conscience of the country and bringing the murderers of our bothers, sisters, and inno-cent children to justice.

We march because we deem it a crime to be silent in the face of such barbaric acts.

We march because we are thoroughly opposed to Jim-Crow Cars, Segregation, Discrimination, Disfranchisement, LYNCHING, and the host of evils that are forced on us. It is time that the Spirit of Christ should be manifested in the making and execution of laws.

We march because we want our children to live in a better land and enjoy fairer conditions than have fallen to our lot.

Within less than a month after the silent protest, news flashed up from Texas about the "Houston affair." A battalion of the Twenty-Fourth Infantry, one of the Negro regiments of the regular army, was stationed at Fort Sam Houston. Late in

Negro Silent Protest Parade, July 28, 1917

the night of August 23 the city of Houston was "shot up"; two Negroes and seventeen white people, five of the latter being Houston policemen, were killed. The Negro soldiers were charged by the local authorities with being responsible for the killings, but the whole incident seemed somewhat wrapped in mystery. Great pressure was brought to have the soldiers tried in the courts of Texas on charges of murder, and, at one time, it looked as though the government might yield to it, but the men were tried by court martial.

The Association promptly sent Martha Gruening to Houston to get at the facts. Miss Gruening found that there had been cumulating bad feeling between the soldiers and the Houston police; that the friction was due chiefly to the fact that the local authorities had objected to the policing of the men while in the city by the usual methods of establishing a provost guard, and had insisted on that duty being placed in the hands of the local police; that the police had been insulting and brutal in enforcing their powers; that, without need, the police had cruelly clubbed a number of soldiers; that on the day preceding the shooting, Corporal Baltimore, the most popular non-commissioned officer and one of the most experienced soldiers in the regiment, had been seriously beaten; that the news reached the camp that he had been killed.

The Association attempted to assist in the defense of the men through the services of a white Texas attorney, A. J. Houston, son of Sam Houston. Sixty-three members of the regiment were court-martialed, and on December 11, early in the morning before it was quite daylight, almost surreptitiously, thirteen of them were hanged. The Negroes of the country were agony-stricken. Not that they questioned the findings of the court, but they felt that the fiendish baitings by which the men had been goaded should have been taken as extenuating circumstances, and, too, that the men should have been afforded their right of appeal to their Commander-in-Chief, the President. They thought back over the fifty years of the Negro regiments in the regular army; how in that time those regiments had been stationed in every section of the country without ever a serious blot on their record for discipline and soldierly conduct, except in two incidents, and both of those incidents had happened in Texas; and they felt that the primary cause of the trouble lay not in the Negro soldiers but in Texas.

In a second court martial, five more of the men were sentenced to be hanged, fifty-one to life imprisonment, and five to long terms. Before the court was finally discontinued, eleven more of the men received the death sentence, bringing the number condemned to die up to sixteen.

A committee of four, consisting of the Rev. George Frazier Miller, Frank M. Hyder, F. A. Cullen, representing the Harlem branch of the Association, and myself, hastened to Washington to see President Wilson, taking a petition of twelve thousand signers, asking executive clemency for the condemned men.

A short while before, I had gone to Washington with a delegation to see the President, but his secretary, Mr. Tumulty, acted as a buffer. This time the Presdient received us graciously. He asked us to be seated. Mr. Wilson did not sit behind his desk, he sat out from it in a comfortable chair, and we sat grouped in a sort of semi-circle in front of him. But almost immediately I rose, as spokesman for the committee, and presented the petition. In presenting it I said:

We come as a delegation from the New York Branch of the National Association for the Advancement of Colored People, representing the twelve thousand signers to this petition which we have the honor to lay before you. And we come not only as the representatives of those who have signed this petition, but we come representing the sentiments and aspirations and sorrows, too, of the great mass of the Negro population of the United States.

We respectfully and earnestly request and urge that you extend executive clemency to the five Negro soldiers of the Twenty-Fourth Infantry now under sentence of death by court martial. And understanding that the cases of the men of the same regiment who were sentenced to life imprisonment by the first court martial are to be reviewed, we also request and urge that you cause this review to be laid before you and that executive clemency be shown also to them.

We feel that the history of this particular regiment and the splendid record for bravery and loyalty of our Negro soldiery in every crisis of the nations give us the right to make this request. And we make it not only in the name of their loyalty, but also in the name of the unquestioned loyalty to the nation of twelve million Negroes—a loyalty which today places them side by side with the original American stocks that landed at Plymouth and Jamestown.

The hanging of thirteen men without the opportunity of appeal to the Secretary of War or to their Commander-in-Chief, the President of the United States, was a punishment so drastic and unusual in the history of the nation that the execution of additional members of the Twenty-Fourth Infantry would to the colored people of the country savor of vengeance rather than justice.

It is neither our purpose nor is this the occasion to argue whether this attitude of mind on the part of colored people is justified or not. As representatives of the race we desire only to testify that it does exist. This state of mind had been intensified by the significant fact that, although white persons were involved in the Houston affair, and the regiment to which the colored men belonged was officered entirely by white men, none but colored men, so far as we have been able to learn, have been prosecuted or condemned.

We desire also respectfully to call to your attention the fact that there were mitigating circumstances for the action of these men of the Twenty-Fourth Infantry. Not by any premeditated design and without cause did these men do what they did at Houston; but by a long series of humiliating and harassing incidents, culminating in the brutal assault on Corporal Baltimore, they were goaded to sudden and frenzied action. This is borne out by the long record for orderly and soldierly conduct on the part of the regiment throughout its whole history up to that time.

And to the end that you extend the clemency which we ask, we lay before you this petition signed by white as well as colored citizens of New York; one of the signers being a white man, a president of a New York bank, seventy-two years of age, and a native of Lexington, Kentucky.

And now, Mr. President, we would not let this opportunity pass without mentioning the terrible outrages against our people that have taken place in the last three-quarters of a year; outrages that are not only unspeakable wrongs against them, but blots upon the fair name of our common country. We mention the riots at East St. Louis, in which the colored people bore the brunt of both the cruelty of the mob and the processes of law. And we especially mention the savage burnings that have taken place in the single state of Tennessee within nine months; the burnings at Memphis, Tennessee; at Dyersburg, Tennessee; and only last week at Estill Springs, Tennessee, where a Negro charged with the killing of two men was tortured with red-hot irons, then saturated with oil and burned to death before a crowd of American men, women, and children. And we ask that you, who have spoken so nobly to the whole world for the cause of humanity, speak against these specific wrongs. We realize that your high position and the tremendous moral influence which you wield in the world will give a word from you greater force than could come from any other source. Our people are intently listening and praying that you may find it in your heart to speak that word.

The presentation of the petition was finished; the President did not rise, and I retook my seat. He talked with us about the mission that had brought us to the White House. We were surprised when he admitted that he had not heard of the burning at Estill Springs. He asked us to give him the facts about it; and declared that it was hard for him to think that such a thing could have taken place in the United States. We pressed him for a promise to make a specific utterance against mob violence and lynching. He demurred, saying that he did not think any word from him would have special effect. We expressed our conviction that his word would have greater effect than the word of any other man in the world. Finally, he promised that he would "seek an opportunity" to say something.

Mr. Wilson talked on with us in a sociable manner. He sat with his knees straight, his elbows resting on the arms of his choir, his hands joined at the tips of his fingers and thumbs, and pointing in front of him in the shape of a wedge. I had seen him only once before, and then at a distance, when he had marched in a preparedness parade in New York; now I was sitting within six feet of him and regarding him intently. I had thought of him as an extremely austere man; as he talked, I realized that the official air had been dropped, and that he was, as we say, very human. His head, no longer inclined forward, rested back easily, and the sternness of his face relaxed and, occasionally in a smile, became completely lost. He asked us questions about the colored people, and we answered them as wisely as we could. He chatted a short while longer, even recounting one or two slight reminiscences of his youthful days in the South. We had been with the President a few minutes longer than a half-hour when he rose, signifying that the interview was at an end. We left with a last plea in behalf of the condemned men of the Twenty-Fourth Infantry. When I came out, it was with my hostility toward Mr. Wilson greatly shaken; however, I could not rid myself of the conviction that at bottom there was something hypocritical about him.

The President did take some action. He prohibited the execution of any more American soldiers—except in the forces at the front—before the sentences of the courts martial had been reviewed by the War Department; and of the sixteen men of the Twenty-Fourth condemned to die, he, after a review of their cases, commuted the sentences of ten to life imprisonment and affirmed the death sentences of six. He also did "find an opportunity" to make a strong utterance against mob violence and lynching. (So it may be that my estimate of Mr. Wilson was actually colored and twisted by prejudice.) The Association continued its efforts for the men in prison; it secured the commutation of sentences of some and, finally, the release on parole of the entire number.

All that happened in Houston just before and on that night in August will probably never be known. The nineteen executed men went to death and the fifty-odd others to prison without "talking." Barlett James was one of the white officers of the regiment, the Captain of Company L, a West Pointer and an experienced soldier. The military investigation showed that on the night of August 23 he was in the company street with the men of his company gathered round him. It showed that a detail from the men who had left camp came back to induce the main portion of the battalion to join them; that an appeal was made to Company L, and that Captain James said, "The men of Company L are going to stay with their captain." Captain James was in the list of witnesses for the court martial; but seven days before the date set for the opening of the trial, he went to his quarters and blew out his brains. And so, a witness who might have shed light on the mystery as to why sixty-odd men of the regiment were not prevented from leaving camp with arms and ammunition did not testify.

XXX

NINETEEN seventeen was a busy year for me. Yet I made the time to collect my published and unpublished poems and issue them in a little volume entitled *Fifty Years and Other Poems*. Brander Matthews wrote a word of introduction for the book. In the middle of the summer, I attended a three-day conference of the Intercollegiate Socialist Society that was held at Belleport, Long Island. I was on the program, but I did not make a talk on economic or social conditions; instead, I read a paper on the contribution of the Negro to American culture.

Some of the contributions that the Negro has made to America are quite obvious—for example, his contribution of labor—and their importance, more or less, has long been recognized. But the idea of his being a generous contributor to the common cultural store and a vital force in the formation of American civilization was a new approach to the race question.

The common-denominator opinion in the United States about American Negroes is, I think, something like this: These people are here; they are here to be shaped and molded and made into something different and, of course, better; they are here to be helped; here to be given something; in a word, they are beggars under the nation's table waiting to be thrown the crumbs of civilization. However true this may be, it is also true that the Negro has helped to shape and mold and make America; that he has been a creator as well as a creature; that he has been a giver as well as a receiver. It is, no doubt, startling to contemplate that America would not and could not be precisely the America it is, except for the influence, often silent, but nevertheless potent, that the Negro has exercised in its making. That influence has been both active and passive. Any contemplation of the Negro's passive influence ought to make America uneasy. Estimate, if you can, the effect upon the making of the character of the American people caused by the opportunity which the Negro has involuntarily given the dominant majority to practice injustice, wrong, and brutality for three hundred years with impunity upon a practically defenseless minority. There can be no estimate of the moral damage done to every American community that has indulged in the bestial orgy of torturing and mutilating a human being and burning him alive. The active influences of the Negro have come out of his strength; his passive influences out of his weaknesses. And it would be well for the nation to remember that for the good of one's own soul, what he needs most to guard against, most to fear, in dealing with another, is that one's weakness, not his strength.

My paper, despite the fact that it was removed from the main topic of the conference, was received well, and gave rise to some interesting discussion. A young man, Herbert J. Seligmann, who was reporting the conference for the *New York Evening Post* was enthusiastic about it. He asked for my manuscript and made a summary of it for his newspaper. Paragraphs of his summary actually went round the world; they were copied in American and European periodicals, and I got clippings from as far away as South Africa and Australia. The statement that evoked the greatest interest—and some controversy—was that the only things artistic in America that have sprung from American soil, permeated American life, and been universally acknowledged as distinctively American, had been the creations of the American Negro.

I was, of course, speaking of the principal folk-art creations of the Negro—his folklore, collected by Joel Chandler Harris under the title of *Uncle Remus*, his dances, and his music, sacred and secular. Some years later, I modified that statement by excepting American skyscraper architecture. In making the original statement I certainly had no intention of disparaging the accomplishments of the other groups, the aboriginal Indians and the white groups. The Indians have wrought finely, and what they have done sprang from the soil of America; but it must be admitted that their art-creations have in no appreciable degree permeated American life. In all that the white groups have wrought, there is no artistic creation—with the exception noted above—born of the physical and spiritual forces at work peculiarly in America, none that has made a universal appeal as something distinctly American.

One other statement in Mr. Seligmann's summary of my paper which was widely copied was that the finest artistic contribution that this country could offer as its own to the world was the American Negro spirituals.

It is, however, in his lighter music that the Negro has given America its best-known distinctive form of art. I would make no extravagant claims for this music, but I say "form of art," without apology. This lighter music has been fused and then developed, chiefly by Jewish musicians, until it has become our national medium for expressing ourselves musically in popular form, and it bids fair to become a basic element in the future great American music. The part it plays in American life and its acceptance by the world at large cannot be ignored. It is to this music that America in general gives itself over in its leisure hours, when it is not engaged in the struggles imposed upon it by the exigencies of present-day American life. At these times, the Negro drags his captors captive. On occasions, I have been amazed and amused watching white people dancing to a Negro band in a Harlem cabaret; attempting to throw off the crusts and layers of inhibitions laid on by sophisticated civilization; striving to yield to the feel and experience of abandon; seeking to recapture a taste of primitive joy in life and living; trying to work their way back into that jungle which was the original Garden of Eden; in a word, doing their best to pass for colored.

It was early in 1917 that a number of liberals organized the Civic Club. In the discussions of the plans, the question of Negro membership was brought up. Finally, after considerable debate, it was settled upon that there would be no bar to membership on account of race or color. Dr. Du Bois and I were invited to become charter members, and we did. The Club had quarters, at first, in the Hotel Marquis; later, it moved into leased quarters on 12th Street, just off Fifth Avenue. The organization quickly became an influence in civic matters. One of the first of the special committees formed was one on The Negro in New York, under the chairmanship of Marie Jenney Howe. Other members on that committee that I remember were Fola LaFollette, Paula Jacobi, and Mary White Ovington. The first case undertaken was that of admittance to interneship at Bellevue Hospital of a young colored woman doctor. Mrs. Howe worked earnestly on the case and it was won, but the young lady did not take the interneship; she got married.

The Civic Club grew to be a strong influence in the life of Negro New Yorkers. The Negro membership increased to twenty-five or thirty. I served for a number of years on the executive committee and, finally, served as president.

XXXI

WITH the opening of 1918, Mr. White, as assistant secretary, and Mr. Shillady, as the new secretary, came to the

Association; and my individual responsibility and work lessened. Mr. Shillady had great ability as a systematizer and organizer. He laid out the work of the increasing staff according to the most modern and approved methods. He planned a national drive for membership that was eminently successful. And he conducted the first adequate statistical study of lynching ever made. He sent two research workers to the Congressional Library at Washington, who read the newspapers back over a period of thirty years and extracted the data regarding every lynching that had been published. They set down the names, sex, and age of the victim; the place, date, and manner of each lynching; and the charge upon which each victim was lynched. These data were compiled and tabulated by Mr. Shillady, and published in a book of over a hundred pages, under the title of *Thirty Years of Lynching in the United States.* The most startling fact revealed was that the common opinion that Negroes were lynched only for rape was without foundation. The figures showed that of the more than three thousand Negroes lynched in the thirty-year period, less than seventeen per cent had even been charged with rape. They showed that Negroes had been lynched for "talking back" to white persons, for "not driving out of the road" to let white persons pass. They also showed that more than fifty Negro women had been lynched; against whom, of course, the "usual crime" could not be charged. This publication was of a value beyond estimation in the Association's fight against lynching. The Association began to take on magnitude. The office staff was added to. H. J. Seligmann was taken on as Director of Publicity, and William Pickens, already widely known as an orator, was taken on as Associate Field Secretary. The clerical staff in the office was increased to a dozen or more persons.

Very early in the year I went on the road speaking and organizing. The field was ready to be harvested. The war and the exodus had shaken the Negroes of the entire country loose from their traditional moorings of standpatism and timidity. They were awake and eager. My speaking was not confined to the colored people; in the North, I addressed many white audiences.

The experiences that came to me through these meetings were varied; some of them thrilling, some pathetic, and some humorous. I remember how the pathos of one situation gripped me. I was addressing a white forum in a Mid-Western industrial city, which, at that time, had only a very small Negro population. As is generally the case under such conditions, these people were disoriented. But a delegation of them waited on me when I had finished my address, and asked if I would not come and speak to a meeting of colored people and organize them into a branch of the Association. It was late, but, when I learned that an audience was waiting for me in the little colored church, I went. When I reached the church, I found it jammed to suffocation. As I went up the aisle to the pulpit, there was no applause—a demonstration I had become accustomed to—the people seemed to regard me with a worshipful silence, as though I were some sort of messiah. When I spoke to them, they hung on my words with such confidence and childlike faith that I could have wept, wept because of my own lack of power to deliver them.

In my trip through the Middle West, I reached a large colored church one Sunday morning and found that the whole service had been turned over to me. I was sitting with the pastor in his study waiting for the time to begin, when he asked me what my text was to be. I stammered that I really had no text, and that I was going to make a talk, not deliver a sermon. "But," he demanded, "aren't you a preacher?" I had to admit that I was not. He grew angry at my admission, and spoke to me as though he had been taken in. He declared that he could not allow any secular topic to take the place of the regular morning service. I told him there were phases of my subject that had a decidedly spiritual bearing, and that I did not think his congregation would consider them out of place. He reluctantly yielded, and did so, I felt, really because he had counted on a Sunday morning off and had not prepared a sermon.

The error this pastor had made in considering me a clergyman was based on a double confusion. I was frequently referred to in the newspapers, and introduced to audiences (incorrectly) as "ex-Minister to Venezuela and Nicaragua," and to many people, "preacher" comes up spontaneously as the synonym for "minister." In fact, after my engagement to Grace became known, one of her admirers called her up to josh her about the absurd rumor he had heard that she was going to marry a preacher.

I found that the matter of professional titles was not a minor one in many a place where I spoke. At a meeting in a Southern city, the preacher who was down on the program to make the remarks that would introduce me to the audience, leaned over, as we sat on the platform, and whispered. "What might be your entitlements?" "No entitlements," I whispered back, "just Mister. Introduce me as Mr. Johnson." With deep sincerity he whispered back again, "I can't do it. I can't introduce you to these people as just Mister." And he didn't; he introduced me as "Professor Johnson."

My meetings quite commonly served a double purpose; an occasion for me to make a speech on the work of the Association and to organize a branch or add to membership; and an opportunity for local talent, especially musical talent, to display itself. Good music helped a meeting, if it was not too good, and if there was not too much of it. For the main purpose of the meeting I preferred spirited singing by the audience to solos by individual artists. One soloist, however, I shall never forget. He was a powerful, ebony-hued baritone who unwittingly metamorphosed *Danny Deever* into a stirring race song by dramatically declaiming:

> "'What makes that rear-rank breathe so 'ard?'
>   Said Files-on-Parade.
>   'It's bitter cold, it's bitter cold,'
>   The *colored* sergeant said."

I received once a laboriously written and marvelously spelled letter. The writer assured me that he had heard a great deal about me and the wonderful society for the advancement of colored people of which I was "the head." He informed me that he was colored and that the state of his affairs had reached a point so low as to be critical; and concluded with the request that I *advance him* about ten dollars.

My work on the road carried me into the far South, and I had opportunity to observe closely the operation of two powerful forces that were at work on the Negro's status—the exodus and the war. Negroes were migrating to the North in great numbers, and I observed the anomaly of a premium

being put on this element of the population that had generally been regarded as a burden and a handicap to the South.
Here, it seemed, was a splendid chance to get rid of a lot of
"lazy, worthless people," but some communities were so
loath to lose them that they obliged railroad ticket agents to
adopt a policy of not selling tickets to Negroes to go North.
In many instances Negroes were forcibly restrained from
leaving.

The demands of the war were also working great changes. A
train that I was on stopped at Waycross, Georgia. I saw a great
crowd around the station and on the tracks, and got out of my
coach to see what it was all about. I found a long train loaded
with Negro troops who were on their way "over there," and
witnessed the incredible sight of white women, together with
colored women, all dressed alike in a Red Cross looking uniform, busy distributing to the men neatly wrapped packages of
whatever things such committees gave to soldiers leaving for
the front.

I reached Jacksonville a day or two before the date of a mass
meeting that was being held in the National Guard armory.
Let me here go back to a time when I was in Jacksonville three
or four years prior to this meeting. The armory, built, of
course, out of the tax funds of Duval County, was then brand-
new. The drill room was the finest and largest auditorium in
Jacksonville; its use as a municipal auditorium was among the
advantages set forth in the project for building the armory. Its
first use under this head was for a musical affair that had been
promoted by a committee of white women. These ladies had
arranged to have Coleridge-Taylor's *Hiawatha* sung, and for
the principal rôle had engaged a tenor from Atlanta. A small
group of colored people wanted very much to hear the can-
tata, and they asked me if I would not see if it could be
arranged for them to do so. I telephoned Mrs. Lund, who was
on the committee, and stated the case. She seemed very much
pleased that there were colored people who wanted to hear the
class of music that was to be sung. She asked how many there
would be. I told her, probably twenty-five. She assured me
that seats would be arranged for them and they would be welcome. The group was delighted. They asked me if I was going
with them. I answered that I had been lucky enough to hear

Hiawatha under better circumstances, and would not go. The next day, Mrs. Lund rang me up. She was very much perturbed. She gave me to know that the militia officer in charge of the armory had countermanded the arrangements that had been made; he had declared that Negroes could not be allowed in the armory. I asked Mrs. Lund if she thought the militia officer knew that the music to be sung was the work of a Negro composer. She did not answer that. Indeed, it is doubtful whether Mrs. Lund, as competent a musician as she was, or any other lady of the committee, knew that Coleridge-Taylor was a Negro.

The mass meeting that was to be held at the armory was for the purpose of stimulating the sale of Liberty Bonds. Fully a half of the auditorium was filled with colored people, and they subscribed liberally. On the platform was a large committee composed of white and colored citizens. Both white and colored speakers addressed the audience. By the white speakers, especially, great emphasis was laid on "*our* country" and "what *we* must do" to win the war for democracy. I don't know whether the same militia officer was still in charge of the armory or not.

But all of the forces were not favorable. These changes that I have alluded to were, after all, slight in proportion to the underlying mass of prejudice and bigotry. The Ku Klux Klan was beginning to gain the tremendous power it possessed a year or so later; and clouds were gathering that, within twelve months, would blot the light from the skies for the Negro. It was while I was in Jacksonville on this trip that I received a letter from Mr. Shillady asking me to go to Quitman, Georgia, and talk with a young colored man who knew a great deal about the "Mary Turner lynching," and to try and have him come on to New York. Walter White had, a short while before, investigated this lynching and reported that this young colored man had driven the wagon of the white undertaker who took charge of the bodies of the victims; and that he, probably, could divulge the names of some of the members of the mob. Mr. White's investigation of this lynching, one of the most monstrous in all the records, made a national sensation. It was his first important job in this work for which he was so well fitted; not the least of his advantages being that his race could not be detected from his appearance.

I proceeded to Quitman, arriving late in the afternoon. I went to the house of a colored doctor. He was fearful; so much so that he communicated his fears to me. He said that the town was still alive over the lynching, and much incensed over Mr. White's disclosures; and that it would not be safe for me to go out that night, because my appearance in a town the size of Quitman would be sure to arouse suspicion. He put out all the lights in the house at about nine o'clock and we went to bed. I did not sleep. The slightest sound gave me a start, for I could not but judge that the doctor's precautions were necessary. The very fact that he had taken me in was proof that he was no coward.

The next day I started out to find my young man. I found him in one of those dingy restaurants for Negroes, common in the South. He told me that his mother ran the place. It was located in the Negro quarter. There were ill-kept tables in the front, and a battered pool table in the back. I talked with him a long while, using all persuasion I could bring to bear to have him consent to come North and state all he knew about the lynching, or give me the names of such members of the mob as he knew. He refused to do either. He said that if he went North, he would leave his mother at the mercies of the lynchers; and if he gave me the names, suspicion would point directly to him. The common sense of the position he took was unassailable.

While I was talking with him, an automobile drove up at the front. It was a small roadster or coupé, but it was loaded down with six men, all white. They were a pretty tough-looking lot. They called for the young fellow to come out. He said to me, "There they are now. What'll I tell 'em if they ask about you?" I did not see how they could know that I was in town, but I told him to say what I had told the doctor to say, in case of any questions—that I was taking subscriptions for a colored newspaper. He went out, and remained talking with the men longer than was pleasant for me. When he came in, he summed up what the men had said to him into—"They asked me what you were doing here, and I told them you were taking subscriptions. They told me to keep my damned mouth shut."

I got out of Quitman that afternoon and I did not feel safe or comfortable until the train had crossed the Florida line.

At a meeting that I addressed in one of the Western cities, I received the impulse to make a definite start on a piece of literary work I had long been nursing in my mind. I had long been planning that at some time I should take the primitive stuff of the old-time Negro sermon and, through art-governed expression, make it into poetry. I felt that this primitive stuff could be used in a way similar to that in which a composer makes use of a folk theme in writing a major composition. I believed that the characteristic qualities: imagery, color, abandon, sonorous diction, syncopated rhythms, and native idioms, could be preserved and, at the same time, the composition as a whole be enlarged beyond the circumference of mere race, and given universality. These ideas I had revolved, but I had not yet set myself to the task of working them out. For several years, I had been excusing myself on the ground of not having time.

It was Sunday, and I had been addressing meetings in various colored churches. I had finished my fourth talk, and it was after nine o'clock at night. However, to my surprise and irritation, the local committee informed me that I was scheduled for still another address. I protested the lateness of the hour, but was told that for the meeting at this church we were just in good time.

When we reached the church an "exhorter" was concluding a dull sermon. I was ushered to the platform, where I sat and listened to two more short, uninteresting efforts. These were but preliminaries, curtain-raisers, for the main event, a sermon by a famed evangelist.

At last he rose. He was a dark brown man, handsome in his gigantic proportions. I think the presence of a "distinguished visitor" on the platform disconcerted him a bit, for he started in to preach a formal sermon from a formal text. He was flat. The congregation sat apathetic and dosing. He must have realized that he was neither impressing the "distinguished visitor" nor giving the congregation what it expected; for, suddenly and without any warning for the transition, he slammed the Bible shut, stepped out from behind the pulpit,

and began intoning the rambling Negro sermon that begins
with the creation of the world, touches various high spots in
the trials and tribulations of the Hebrew children, and ends
with the Judgment Day. There was an instantaneous change in
the preacher and in the congregation. He was free, at ease, and
the complete master of himself and his hearers. The congregation responded to him as a willow to the winds. He strode
the pulpit up and down, and brought into play the full gamut
of a voice that excited my envy. He intoned, he moaned, he
pleaded—he blared, he crashed, he thundered. A woman
sprang to her feet, uttered a piercing scream, threw her handbag to the pulpit, striking the preacher full in the chest, whirled
round several times, and fainted. The congregation reached a
state of ecstasy. I was fascinated by this exhibition; moreover,
something primordial in me was stirred. Before the preacher
finished, I took a slip of paper from my pocket and somewhat
surreptitiously jotted down some ideas for my first poem.

It had been thirty years since I had heard such a sermon. I
still had my somewhat vague, youthful memories; but this
fresh exhibition of the potentialities of the material I planned
to use was just what I needed to start me on the work. In the
course of several weeks, I finished "The Creation" to my satisfaction. It was published in *The Freeman*.

In writing "The Creation," I had to consider a question
that had to be settled then and there for the whole group of
poems—the question of form and medium. I at once discarded the use of conventionalized Negro dialect, for reasons
which I set forth fully in the Preface to the poems when they
were published in book form.* Furthermore, it was not my intention to paint the picturesque or comic aspects of the old-
time Negro preacher—I considered them extraneous—my aim
was to interpret what was in his mind, to express, if possible,
the dream to which, despite limitations, he strove to give utterance. I chose a loose rhythmic instead of a strict metric
form, because it was the first only that could accommodate itself to the movement, the abandon, the changes in tempo, and
the characteristic syncopations of the primitive material.

* *God's Trombones—Seven Negro Sermons in Verse*. New York, The Viking
Press, 1927.

In "The Creation" I was happy over the results of my experiments. Following its publication in *The Freeman*, it received numerous commendations. It has since been included in a dozen or more anthologies. One of the first to pronounce the poem an excellent one was William Stanley Braithwaite, with whom in these years I had formed a close and helpful friendship. I was happy, too, over the fact that I had at last made an opening on this piece of work; but seven years elapsed before I formulated the subject matter and chose the title of the second poem of the group that I wrote—"Go Down, Death."

I addressed a mass meeting in Carnegie Hall and made the most effective speech of my whole career as a platform speaker. It was a great meeting; and the famous auditorium was packed to capacity. As I sat on the platform I felt depressed, almost listless. When I rose, every nerve in my brain and body quickened by the intensity of feeling that came across the footlights from the audience to me. As I talked, I was lifted up and swept along by the sense of demi-omnipotence which comes to a speaker at those moments when he realizes that by an inflection of the voice or a gesture of the hand, he is able to sway a mass of people. It is a sensation that intoxicates; and it carries within itself all the perils of intoxication. Words surged to be uttered; and uttered, they were effective beyond their weight and meaning. One passage of my speech had an electrical effect:

I can never forget what I felt on the day I saw "The Buffaloes," New York's own black regiment swing out of Madison Square into the most magnificent street in the world. They were on their way to receive a stand of colors to be presented by the Union League Club. I followed them up Fifth Avenue as they marched, with a vision in their eyes and a song on their lips, going to fight, perhaps to die, to secure for others what they themselves were yet denied. They halted in front of the club, and in a mighty chorus sang *The Star Spangled Banner*. Then from the balcony the Governor of the state came down and presented the colors. As he gave the flag into their keeping, he raised his voice, trembling with emotion, and cried out, "Bring it back! Bring it back, boys! Bring it back!" And the answer welled up in my heart: Never you fear, Mr. Governor, they will bring it back; perhaps tattered and torn, but they will bring it back. And they will bring it back as they have always done whenever it has been committed to their hands, without once letting it trail in the dust, without putting a single stain of dishonor upon it. Then it is for you, Mr. Governor, for you, gentlemen of the Union League Club, for you, the people of America, to remove those stains that are upon it, upon it as these men carry it into battle, the stains of Disfranchisement, of Jim-Crowism, of Mob Violence, and of Lynching. . . .

The emotional tension of the audience snapped with an explosion of cheers and applause. I continued, finishing the passage:

The record of the black men on the fields of France gives us the greater right to point to that flag and say to the nation: Those stains are still upon it; they dim its stars and soil its stripes; wash them out! Wash them out!

But I do not think my voice reached farther than the length of my outstretched arms. I stood silent and waited for the tumult in the audience and tumult within me to subside.

I read these words over now. They are cold. They strike me as a rather flamboyant piece of oratory. If it were not for my own memory, I should doubt that they ever possessed the power to do what they did do. So I come back to my theory that the inner secret of sheer oratory is not so much in the *what* is said as in the combination of the *how*, *when*, and *where*. The *how* is the most important of these factors, and its chief virtue lies in "timing"; that is, in the ability of the speaker to set up a series of rhythmic emotional vibrations between himself and his hearers. I have witnessed the accomplishment of this feat by oldtime Negro preachers using pure incoherencies.

At the beginning of the fall of 1918, Rosamond and I received a telegram from Jacksonville stating that our mother had been taken sick. We at once put into execution what we had been planning, to have her and our sister come to New York to live. Rosamond was at this time director of the New York Music School Settlement for Colored People. The school was located in two imposing adjoining houses in 130th Street, between Lenox and Seventh Avenues. My mother arrived very ill, but in a few weeks she rallied, and we had hopes of her recovery. Then she had a relapse and began to sink, and day by day our hopes grew fainter. I spent every hour with her that I possibly could;

often sitting by her bed through the night. She had heard talk about the meeting that was to be held at Carnegie Hall; and she kept repeating how sorry she was that she could not go to hear me speak. I told her that I might not go to speak. She insisted that I should; and she urged my sister to go also. Christmas came drearily for us, and New Year's still more drearily; for we now knew that death was distant only in days. On the night of January 6, I went to Carnegie Hall to speak; my sister remained at home. After my speech, I went back to my mother's bedside. She died early the next morning. Of this, the most poignant sorrow in my life, I am unable to write.

After my mother's death, Rosamond and I had our father's body brought to New York and buried in the same plot with hers. We both gained a deep sentimental satisfaction in knowing that, after the many and varied intervening years, they rested together in a piece of the soil of the city where they first met.

XXXII

IN the late spring of 1919, I spoke at another mass meeting in Carnegie Hall. It was a meeting in protest against lynching, and Charles Evans Hughes was the chief speaker. Immediately after this meeting, I started on a speaking tour of the branches of the Association on the Pacific Coast and to organize new branches there. I talked from San Diego to Seattle. Many of the meetings were large and enthusiastic, but, on the whole, the trip was uneventful. It was, however, interesting to meet large numbers of worthwhile colored people; something I did not have the opportunity of doing on my visit to California fourteen years before. And now there were so many more of them.

On the trip I had to bear with a certain amount of lionizing. Toward the end it began to wear on me. In one of the large cities of the Northwest, I arrived at about eight o'clock in the morning after ten hours of effort to get some sleep on a train that was swaying and bumping over mountains. A committee met my train, and I was informed that a breakfast would be given for me at ten o'clock. There were twelve people at the breakfast. Immediately after breakfast, we piled into three or

four automobiles and drove, it seemed to me, over the whole
county, a county larger, I judge, than some of the Eastern
states. When we drove back into the city I was taken to see a
number of prominent citizens, among them, the editors of the
daily newspapers. I protested gently. I was met by "just one
more," and "just one more," and "the dinner will not be until
six o'clock." I knew the meeting that night was to be an important one. I knew, too, that I should be up against what a
public speaker is always up against, his record of past performances. Certainly, I could not end a speech by saying, "I wasn't
as good tonight as you may have been led to expect, but the
committee kept me on the go all day, and wore me out."

I finally lost the restraint that I usually try to maintain, and
commanded the committee to take me to my stopping place at
once, and told them not to expect me at the dinner before the
meeting, to be given in my honor. They all seemed hurt; the
chairman acted as though I had struck him in the face. I was
sorry afterwards, for it is a terrible thing to wound friends who
are sincerely endeavoring to be kind. But my action was in
sheer self-defense. After that experience I could understand
what Elbert Hubbard meant by what he was said to have included in his printed terms: "One hundred dollars a lecture.
One hundred and fifty dollars if entertained."

I addressed a meeting in Spokane. Just before leaving the
next afternoon for Seattle, I was walking up and down the railroad station platform, talking with two gentlemen who had
come to see me off. My train came in and stood at the station
for a quarter of an hour or so. A porter from the train approached me and said, "This is James Weldon Johnson, isn't
it?" I was accustomed to having porters and waiters on trains
address me by my name; and always regarded it as a high mark
of distinction. The porter added: "Madame Schumann-Heink
is on the train, and she asks if you won't come to her drawing
room when you come aboard."

I judged that she had seen me from her window and, out of
curiosity, had asked the porter who I was. However, when I
went to her drawing room, she talked as though she knew
something about me. I stayed with her more than an hour. She
did most of the talking and talked most of the while about the
war. Her emotions, it appeared, were still torn by the fact that

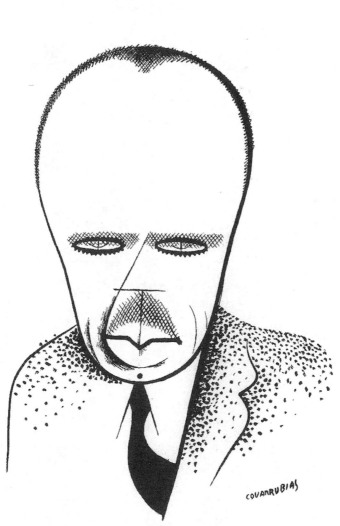

Caricature by Covarrubias

she had sons who found it necessary to fight each other. Her words manifested the heart of the infinite mother, and I was deeply moved. She talked a little about music and art, and mentioned the fact that she had given her old home on Michigan Avenue in Chicago for a conservatory of music for Negro students. I left Madame Schumann-Heink feeling that I had had the opportunity of being in the presence of not only a great artist but a grand woman.

I returned east by way of Vancouver and the Canadian Rockies, reaching Cleveland, the latter part of June, to attend the first of the larger annual conferences of the Association. At the Cleveland conference, the Southern branches made themselves felt. Their delegates were among the most aggressive and outspoken. They proved their sincerity by demanding that the next conference be held in the South. They declared that the Association should demonstrate its own sincerity and courage by stating the case for equality of all the rights of citizenship in the South as well as in the North. They argued, and soundly, that the branches in the South should not be expected to do this if the national body refrained. Such a challenge could not be brushed aside. Atlanta made the bid for the conference, and the bid was backed up by an official invitation from the city. The national body voted that it would meet there the following May (1920).

The Red Summer of 1919 broke in fury. The colored people throughout the country were disheartened and dismayed. The great majority had trustingly felt that, because they had cheerfully done their bit in the war, conditions for them would be better. The reverse seemed to be true. There was one case, at least, in which a returned Negro soldier was lynched *because of the fact* that he wore the uniform of a United States soldier. The Ku Klux Klan had reached ascendancy. Reports from overseas had come back giving warning that the returned Negro soldiers would be a dangerous element and a menace; that these black men had been engaged in killing white men, and, so, had lost the sense of the inviolability of a white man's life; that they had frequently been given the treatment accorded only to white men in America, and, above all, that many of them had been favorably regarded by white women. One of the chief recruiting slogans of the Klan was the necessity of united action to keep these men in their place.

During the summer, bloody riots occurred in Chicago, Omaha, in Longview, Texas, in Phillips County, Arkansas, in Washington, and other communities. The riot in the national capital lasted three days, during which Negroes were hunted through the streets, dragged from street cars, beaten, and even killed. These pogroms brought from Claude McKay this cry of defiant despair sounded from the last ditch:

> If we must die—let it not be like hogs
> Hunted and penned in an inglorious spot,
> While round us bark the mad and hungry dogs,
> Making their mock at our accursed lot. . . .
>
> Oh, Kinsmen! We must meet the common foe
> Though far outnumbered let us show us brave,
> And for their thousand blows deal one death-blow!
> What though before us lies the open grave?
> Like men we'll face the murderous, cowardly pack,
> Pressed to the wall, dying, but fighting back!*

The riots in Phillips County, Arkansas, were the most brutal of all these outbursts of violence, and the most memorable, because out of them came a law case in which the Association won its second important constitutional victory. Early in 1919, when the price of cotton had soared to undreamed-of heights, Negro farmers in and about Elaine, Arkansas, who were realizing no greater profit than when the price of cotton was at its nadir, organized to see if they could not by legal steps force a statement of accounts and a fair settlement from their landlords. They were holding a meeting one night in a little church at Hoop Spur in an effort to raise the fee of a Little Rock firm of white lawyers—father and son—which they had engaged to take their case. Without warning the church was fired upon by a deputy sheriff and his posse. In the mêlée, the deputy sheriff was killed. The church was burned to the ground.

A reign of terror followed. Between two hundred and three hundred Negroes were hunted down in the fields and swamps

*Quoted from *Harlem Shadows*, by Claude McKay, New York, 1922, Harcourt, Brace and Company.

to which they fled, and shot down like animals. Many of them had no idea of what the trouble was about. The two white lawyers barely escaped violence. They fled the state and settled in Detroit. Then, in accordance with common policy, the onus of what had taken place was put on the Negroes. A large number of them were indicted on the charge of conspiracy to massacre the whites and seize the land. A farcical trial lasting three-quarters of an hour was held in a courthouse that was filled with and surrounded by a mob. The jury, after being out five minutes, brought in a verdict that condemned twelve of the Negro farmers to death. Sixty-seven others received sentences of life imprisonment and long terms. What they were all actually guilty of was attempted assault on the peonage system—the system by which the Negro in the agricultural South is as effectively robbed of his labor as ever he was under slavery.

The Association took up the defense of these men and, after fighting their cases for five years through the courts of Arkansas and twice up to the United States Supreme Court, won the decision from the latter court in which it virtually reversed itself. The decision declared that the Negroes, though tried in a duly constituted court, had not had a trial according to due process of law, because the court had been dominated by a mob. This was the reverse of the position taken by the Supreme Court in the famous Leo Frank case. Ultimately, the twelve farmers condemned to die were freed, and the sixty-odd others released from prison.

Early in August of the Red Summer, our national office received a letter from the president of our branch in Austin, Texas, a branch of more than three hundred members, stating that he had been cited to appear in court and to bring all books and papers and correspondence belonging or pertaining to the National Association for the Advancement of Colored People; and that he had complied. Mr. Shillady telegraphed the Attorney General of Texas offering any information concerning the Association that might be desired. He then left immediately for Austin. On arriving there, he first met with a committee of the local branch, then called at the Governor's office, but that office was closed. At the Attorney General's office he had an interview with the acting Attorney General and gave him full information as to the purpose and methods of the Association, together with copies of its principal publications. The object of Mr. Shillady's visit to Austin was to ascertain why the books and papers of the local branch had been subpœnaed and to give the state official a fuller record than could be obtained from an examination of those documents. On the morning of his arrival he was haled before a local judge and examined in camera, being subjected to many questions, pertinent and impertinent, by a group of inquisitors. When he left this secret court of inquiry, he started for his hotel, and just across the street from it he was overtaken by a group of men who had been present at the inquiry. They quickly surrounded him and beat him severely. Mr. Shillady was a nonresistant and during the assault did not raise a hand. Of course, it is possible that he would have been killed had he defended himself. Among Mr. Shillady's assailants were a constable and a county judge. The Governor of Texas publicly expressed his satisfaction at the treatment Mr. Shillady had been given.

When this attack on Mr. Shillady took place, I was at Hampton Institute, where I had gone for a brief vacation. I had been there but two or three days before I received the telegram informing me of what had happened. I left immediately for New York. I met Mr. Shillady when he arrived at the Pennsylvania Station. His face and body were badly bruised; moreover, he was broken in spirit. I don't think he was ever able to realize how such a thing could happen in the United States to an American, free, white, and twenty-one. He never fully recovered spiritually from the experience.

We, the Association's officers, found ourselves faced by two disturbing conditions: We realized that there was a campaign of considerable proportions on to intimidate our members in Southern communities and stamp out the organization; in a number of instances this campaign was successful. We also found that there had arisen a division throughout the whole membership as to the wisdom of holding the next annual conference in Atlanta. Many felt that the meeting should be canceled, postponed, or transferred to a Northern city. The officers and the majority of the Board of Directors, together with the greater part of the membership, stood for the decision made at Cleveland. The Atlanta branch stood firm; so the national officers could not have done less, even had they wished to. As the Atlanta conference drew nigh, in the same degree it became a test of courage.

XXXIII

THE United States had seized Haiti in 1915. For the seizure of an independent nation, we offered the stock justifications: protection of American lives and American interests, and the establishment and maintenance of internal order. Had all these reasons been well founded, they would not have constituted justification for the complete seizure of a sovereign state at peace with us.

But they were not all well founded. American lives were not and never had been jeopardized in Haiti; and, if American business ventures were not as profitable as had been expected, that could not be wholly charged to the Haitian government. Nor could it be said that the United States or any other country had sustained loss through any default of Haiti on its foreign obligations. It is true, there was internal disorder; but that disorder was not so great or so menacing to us as the disorder then prevalent in our next-door neighbor across the Rio Grande. Perhaps the distinction lay in the difference in size between Haiti and Mexico. The underlying reasons were not given. They were, however, those involved in long-standing policies of the State and Navy Departments at Washington.

An army of marines had been landed in Haiti, as had been the case in Nicaragua. In Nicaragua, however, the American forces were there in accordance with the wishes of the government; they were there to sustain that government in power. In Haiti, the American forces seized the power and made themselves the government. Haiti was quickly developed into a very nice job-holding colony for "deserving Democrats." Harsh conditions resulted from this situation because a number of Haitians were deluded by the idea that they had the patriotic right to arm themselves and defend their native land against the invaders. Probably, they thought that the majority of the people in the United States who were at all familiar with American history would recognize them as patriots. The term that the majority of the American people learned to apply to them was, "bandits."

In spite of the fact that the lid was kept down tight, reports of the harsh conditions due to the American occupation kept leaking through to us. The Association considered having me go to Haiti and make an investigation. I went to see Theodore Roosevelt and talked the matter over with him. He was enthusiastic about such a mission, and thought I ought to be able to do a good job. He talked in his naturally energetic manner, snapping out the words and biting them off. He talked for quite a while about the weaknesses of the Administration at Washington. He was especially strong in expressing his opinion about its refusal to accept his offer to raise a division of volunteers for the war. He made no effort to conceal the deep disappointment he felt. He told me that it was in his plans to have one brigade made up of Negro troops and to place it under the command of Charles Young as a brigadier general.* I expressed myself bitterly about the retirement of Colonel Young and the shunting of him off from a generalship. Mr. Roosevelt dictated and signed a letter for my use; and, as I left him, he slapped me on the shoulder and wished me good luck. I did not go to Haiti, however, until February 1920. Herbert Seligmann sailed with me, but after several weeks there he was taken seriously ill and returned home.

I had been reading up on Haiti on the trip down, but I was not quite prepared for my first sight of the country. I had, of course, seen enough of the tropics to know that every island there is not a palm-covered coral bed jutting only from a few feet to a few hundred feet above the ocean's level; but I was surprised at the high ranges of purple-colored mountains that we saw as we ran down the Haitian coast. The city of Port-au-Prince surprised me still more, for it is not only situated on one of the most beautiful bays in the world, but I found it the finest city of all the Latin-American seaports that I had seen. I

---

*Charles Young was the third Negro to graduate from West Point (1889) and was a splendid soldier and officer. At the outbreak of the World War he held the rank of major. Over his protest and despite his desire for service, he was retired in 1917 with the rank of colonel; but was detailed to organize a constabulary in Liberia. He died there, but his body was brought home and buried with military honors in the Arlington National Cemetery.

had also been familiarizing myself with Haitian history, and in doing that I met with other surprises. I learned that Haiti was the second independent republic in the Western Hemisphere; the United States being the first. I learned that its aid had made possible the independence of the third republic, Venezuela, as early as it was achieved. I learned that the war in Haiti by which black slaves liberated themselves worked a more complete social revolution than the war by which the slaves were freed in the United States. Our Civil War freed the slaves in name only. It left them illiterate, homeless, and penniless, and at the economic mercy of their former masters. Masses of them merely entered a new slavery in which there was neither legal nor moral obligation on the masters; there was not even so much as a financial interest in the "new slaves." In Haiti, the large plantations were cut up into small parcels, and the former slaves settled on plots of ground, which they cultivated, perhaps poorly, but as independent farmers. Some families had cultivated the same plot of ground for a hundred years or more; and so there was no such thing in Haiti as a peon class, a class, the creation of which is one of the curses of Mexico.

For a while, I was something of a "man of mystery" in Port-au-Prince. I was stopping at the best hotel; I entertained important people there and at the Café Dereix; I cashed drafts at the bank; and I appeared to have important business. What that business was remained, on the whole, a question; for nobody knew just what it was, except the people to whom I discussed it, and they were, if anything, more anxious than I to have the matter considered confidential.

My aim was to gather information and shades of opinion from as many sources as I possibly could; and in trying to carry it out, I talked with a large number of persons. I talked with almost every important Haitian, many of them men of wide political knowledge and experience, who realized the difficulty of the situation, but were determined to take every feasible step for the restoration of Haitian independence. I talked also with members of the radical group, the group whose slogan was, "Down with the Americans!" and which stood for taking steps, feasible or not.

I called to see ex-President Légitime, a grand old gentle-man; indeed, a jet-black Frenchman of the courtly school. He returned the call, taking lunch with me at my hotel. He spoke frankly of the wrongs and evils that had resulted from American rule. I saw President Sudre Dartiguenave twice. I believed that he was a patriot at heart, but he was in a delicate position and was extremely guarded in what he said to me. It seemed to me to be his intention to have me form my opinions from what he did not say. I spent an evening with Louis Borno, who succeeded M. Dartiguenave in the presidency. M. Borno, a lawyer, was a former Secretary of State for Foreign Affairs. He was one of the most accomplished men I have met; tall, slender, bronze-colored, with the face and hands of an artist; a linguist, a fine poet, and a very astute statesman. Our conversation lasted a couple of hours and was genuinely pleasant, but on every vital topic M. Borno was guarded. I saw a great deal of M. Sanon, who had resigned as Secretary of Foreign Affairs rather than sign the Haitian-American Convention by which Haiti was forced to abdicate its sovereignty. A huge man, pure black, and with exceptional intellectual powers. I saw as much of M. Price-Mars, formerly Secretary of the Haitian Legation at Washington, a gentle scholar, as slight in bulk as Sanon was huge, and also pure black. I frequently saw most of the men who are today reassuming the control of their country.

But the man with whom my visit to Haiti had the most far-reaching relations was the least pretentious of all that I met. He was Georges Sylvain, small and shy, but quite distin-guished. He was a well-known lawyer, a former Haitian minis-ter to France, and a man of letters. Some of his literary work had been crowned by the French Academy; he had addressed the Sorbonne and had been made a member of the Légion d'Honneur. With him, the cause of Haiti seemed to dominate every other interest. He gave me a good deal of information about Haiti, and about American misrule, which he knew I was going to make use of in the United States in the interest of the Haitians. In return, he asked me what I thought the Haitians themselves ought to do. All the Haitians I talked with complained bitterly of conditions; they had learned that I had been named as a member of the Republican National Advisory

Committee for the approaching presidential campaign, and they piled these complaints up for me, seeming to feel that, if the Democratic administration, under which the oppressive conditions had been put upon them, was replaced by a Republican administration, I, by laying their complaints before the new régime, could have those conditions removed. They reckoned not at all how infinitesimal was the influence that my position carried. M. Sylvain was the first to ask me what I thought were some of the things the Haitians themselves could do.

The plan I suggested to M. Sylvain was one for organizing sentiment among the Haitians and for setting up machinery by which they could take united action. I told him that external help could not be effective unless the Haitian people were active. I gave him a full explanation of the central idea and the working methods of the National Association for the Advancement of Colored People, and urged upon him that a similar organization be established in Haiti, with headquarters in Port-au-Prince, and branches in the other important cities and towns. He followed the suggestion, and at a mass meeting held in the theater at Port-au-Prince the Union Patriotique was organized. This organization exerted a vital force in advancing the restoration of Haitian independence to the point it has reached. It is sad that M. Sylvain did not live to see the fuller realization of his hopes and efforts.

I talked with foreigners as well as Haitians. I made a point of seeing the several Americans who were conducting mercantile businesses in Port-au-Prince; without exception, they expressed sentiments that leaned toward the Haitians. I also talked with a number of our marine officers. I now knew their language; and in my talks with them I spent a tidy sum on *goutte d'or* (a famous brand of Haitian rum). I found that the rum had the effect of lessening restraint and inducing frankness. The effect was so potent in several instances that my marine friends appeared to become oblivious to the fact that they were talking with a Negro—an American Negro. One of them summed up the situation for me by declaring, "The trouble with Haiti is that these niggers down here with a little money and education think they are as good as *we* are." Another one related to me an incident that occurred at a fire. He told me that the fire was gaining headway, and they were calling on everybody to give a hand; that standing on the sidewalk was a Haitian dressed in a silk hat, Prince Albert coat, and patent leather shoes; that when his command to this Haitian to take hold of the hose was ignored, he "gave him a kick that landed him one way in the gutter and his silk hat another." A gentleman, black or white, dressed in a silk hat, Prince Albert coat, and patent leather shoes, under a tropic sun, has always struck me as ludicrous, but this incident did not strike me as humorous.

Some of the marines related to me details of their fights in the hills and back country with the "bandits." One of them told me about a "bandit hunt"; how they finally came upon a crowd of natives engaged in the popular pastime of cock-fighting, and how they "let them have it" with machine gun and rifle fire. It was evident that for many of the American boys who had enlisted in the marines and been sent to Haiti, "hunting bandits" was a great adventure and a very thrilling sport. I used these accounts given me by the marine officers, together with other reports that I gathered, as the basis for an estimate of the number of Haitians that had been killed by the American forces of the occupation.

I had the opportunity to take a peep into social life in the Haitian capital. I visited a number of the beautiful villas on the heights above Port-au-Prince. I had the privilege of going to the Cercle Bellevue, the leading club, where the men talked understandingly about world affairs. I attended the closing exercises of the Normal School, where the girls acted out one of Molière's plays with a verve and finish that was surprising to me. And I was present at a charity ball given at the French Legation, the grandest affair of the kind I had ever witnessed. I was forced to conclude that Haitian society in Port-au-Prince moved on a level that for wealth and culture could not be matched by the colored people in any city in the United States.

In my last two weeks in Haiti I made a ten-day trip in a Ford through the country, as far north as Cap Haïtien. I satisfied my curiosity to see the inside of some of the native huts. These huts were ingeniously built of thin strips of wood plaited about the heavier uprights and plastered outside and inside with clay, the whole covered with a thatched roof. There were generally two rooms or more. The floor was usually of hard clay. In almost every instance the outer walls were white-washed or tinted blue, or pink, or yellow. On the inside, the cabins were kept very clean and the yards about them were swept daily. An æsthetic touch, flowers or a gorgeous shrub or vine, was common. Nowhere did I see the filth and squalor that is hardly ever missing in and around the log cabins of the South. And yet, some Americans, who were, doubtless, sincerely anxious to see the Haitians make progress, felt that they would be essentially advanced if, instead of living in these native huts—so well adapted to their needs and their environment—they lived in American-built cottages with glass windows and a front porch, and covered by a tin roof and a mortgage. The Haitian peasants were kindhearted, hospitable, and polite. They were, naturally, ignorant of a great many things, but far from being stupid; indeed, they were rather quick-witted and imaginative. The countrywomen were magnificent as they filed along the roads by scores and by hundreds, taking farm and garden products to the town markets. Their baskets balanced on their colored-turbaned heads, the large, gold loops in their ears pendulating to their steps, they strode along lithe and straight, almost haughtily, carrying themselves like so many Queens of Sheba. The weather was fine, and I enjoyed the trip as though it were only a pleasure jaunt. I stopped in a village where they were celebrating a feast day, and saw a native dance. The men and women danced in a thatched-roof pavilion without walls. They danced in a ring, to the music of drums of various sizes and pitch. There was the same ring going round and round on shuffling feet, one heel stamping out the rhythm of a monotonous chant, in the same manner that I had seen as a child in the African village in Nassau, and observed later in the "ring shouts" in Negro churches in the South. When I crossed the mountains, I saw scenery as wonderful as any my eyes had beheld.

The sensation of my trip to Haiti came in my visit to Cap Haïtien. I telegraphed to Lemuel W. Livingston that I was coming. Up to a short time before, he had been the American Consul at Cap Haïtien, having served about twenty years at the same post. He had also during nearly all that time been the correspondent of the Associated Press. Livingston and two or three of his friends met me on the road ten or fifteen miles out of Cap Haïtien, and I drove into the city with them. I took dinner with my old friend. I had not seen him for many years. I was glad to talk with him about past things; but, more important, there were things I wanted to ask him about Haiti that I did not feel I could ask anyone else. He had married a charming Haitian woman, whose father, I learned, was a man of some wealth. Livingston's marriage furnished his main reason for never wishing to be transferred from Cap Haïtien. After dinner we went to the club, a spacious and well-appointed building. There, he introduced me to a number of men, some of them white. White men having residence or business in the Cape were glad to have the privileges of the club. While Livingston and I were playing billiards, I told him what the chief desire was that had brought me to Cap Haïtien—to make the trip up to Christophe's citadel. He told me it was a strenuous trip, and would require some preparation, but that there was no reason why I could not make it.

I drove, starting at daylight, in my Ford to the little village of Milot. There at the inn I met the man with whom I had arranged to furnish me with three horses and six men. Two of the horses turned out to be mules, but a mule is much superior to a horse for mountain climbing. We started out supplied with food and coffee. Just beyond the village, at the foot of the mountain, are the ruins of Sans Souci, Christophe's palace. The palace of the great black king of Northern Haiti was a copy, more or less and on a smaller scale, of Versailles. It was the work of French architects and builders; and when it was finished it was, beyond question, the most palatial residence in the Americas.

Christophe built this citadel in the first decade of the nineteenth century on the top of a mountain more than three thousand feet high, which dominates the fertile plains of Northern Haiti. He built it as a last stronghold against the French if they attempted to retake Haiti. The trip up took a little more than two hours and was over a narrow, precipitous, at times dangerous path. After I had ridden an hour and a half, I reached a sudden turn in the path and caught the first view of the great fortress. The sight was amazing, it was dumbfounding, I could scarcely believe my own eyes. There, from the pinnacle of the mountain, rose the massive walls of brick and stone to a height of more than one hundred feet. On three sides the walls are sheer with the sides of the mountain; the other side is approached by the path.

The first sight to attract my attention after I entered the citadel was fifty long, solid brass cannons, with which Christophe had commanded the path. How he ever got those cannon up there, nobody seemed to know. I was told that the Haitian government had had offers for them as metal, but that nobody seemed to know how to get them down. I explored the vast structure for several hours, its storerooms, its dungeons, its subterranean passages, its chapel. There was a fountain from which the water still bubbled up—a sort of physical mystery to me, as I saw no greater height from which it could come—and there was a dark opening into which one dropped a stone without ever hearing it strike bottom. In places the walls were from eight to twelve feet thick. Some idea of the size of the citadel may be gained from the statement that Christophe built it to quarter thirty thousand soldiers. The more I saw of it, the more the wonder grew on me not only as to the execution but as to the mere conception of such a work. I should say that it is the most wonderful ruin in the Western Hemisphere, and, for the amount of human energy and labor sacrificed in its construction, can be compared to the pyramids of Egypt. As I stood on the highest point, where the sheer drop from the walls was more than two thousand feet, and looked out over the rich plains of Northern Haiti, I was impressed with the thought that, if ever a man had the right to feel himself a king, that man was Christophe when he walked around the parapets of his citadel.

I did my best to get some pictures with my small kodak, but without much success. Since that time many photographs have been made of it from airplanes. Christophe's citadel had been written about, but forgotten. I think I may claim that I rediscovered it for the United States. When I returned home, I lectured about it and wrote about it, publishing with some of my articles the snapshots I had taken. What I said and wrote was in some degree responsible for a new literary interest in Haiti. John W. Vandercook talked with me about Christophe and his citadel before he went down and wrote his book, *Black Majesty**; and William B. Seabrook talked with me about Haiti before he went down and wrote *The Magic Island.*[†] Among my friends and acquaintances, my trip started a sort of pilgrimage to the black republic.

When I got back to Port-au-Prince, I went directly to the steamship office to arrange for my passage to New York. I was told that there was nothing I could get on the next ship nor on the next. There was only one line of steamships touching Haiti, the United States–owned Panama Line; the Dutch and German lines had been suspended. It was May, and the Panama Canal employees were going home as fast as they could on the vacations allowed them by the government. The ships reached Port-au-Prince loaded beyond capacity. I waited, but without any assurances that I could get passage.

While I was waiting, a farewell luncheon was given me at Pétionville, a village up on the mountainside above Port-au-Prince. About a dozen prominent Haitians were present, including M. Sanon and M. Price-Mars. The luncheon gave me an opportunity of emphasizing to this group the necessity for organization of the Haitians. I also made it an opportunity to offer a gratuitous suggestion. My suggestion was that Creole be made a written language. I said that in my opinion one of the greatest handicaps of Haiti was the fact that her masses, though possessing native intelligence, were absolutely illiterate. They had no means of receiving or communicating thoughts through the written word. For a reason that I cannot explain, the French language in the French-Colonial settlements in America containing a Negro population divided itself into two branches, French and Creole. This is true of Louisiana, Martinique, Guadeloupe, and Haiti. I think it is strange, because nothing like it happened with the Spanish language. Creole is an Africanized French, but it must not be thought of as a mere dialect. The French-speaking person cannot understand Creole, excepting a few words, until he learns it. It is a distinct, grammatically constructed, graphic, and very expressive language. A merchant woman, following the native

*Harper & Brothers, New York, 1928.
[†]Harcourt, Brace & Co., New York, 1929.

Christophe's Citadel

idiom, will say, "You do not wish anything beautiful if you do not buy this."

I elicited from the group, that, possibly, less than a half-million Haitians knew and used the French in addition to Creole, while more than two million knew and used only Creole; that the children of the masses studied French for a few years in school, but it never became their everyday language. I expressed as strongly as I could my belief that, while French should be retained as the language of literature and culture, Creole should be made the common written and printed tongue; that it be used in much the same way that Papaimento is used in Curaçao. I emphatically declared to my listeners that books and newspapers made available to the masses through Creole would be a greater power for liberating and raising up the Haitian people than any other I could think of. My suggestion was politely received, but aroused no enthusiasm. For the educated Haitians are exceedingly proud of their French traditions and of the fact that French is their tongue. They consider the French language a precious heritage and their strong link with world culture. On this latter point, they are, of course, right.

The middle of May was approaching, and I was growing desperate. I simply had to get back to the United States; and not because I could not have spent the time pleasantly waiting for a ship, but because the Atlanta conference of the Association was set for the latter part of the month, and I *had* to be there. I had been one of those at the national office who had most loudly proclaimed that the conference should not be postponed or transferred to some other city; that it should be held in Atlanta, despite any risks. I now plainly saw that if I were absent it would be a thing that I could not explain away in a lifetime; that the most polite response the explanation of not being able to secure passage on a ship would receive would be a smile, which in words would take the form of that very expressive vulgarism, "Oh yeah?"

In my extremity, I made arrangements with a native fisherman to take me in his boat from Port-au-Prince to Santiago, Cuba, a distance of about two hundred miles. I planned to take a train from Santiago to Havana, and to go from there to Key West or New York.

My next-room neighbor at the Hotel Bellevue was a Mr. Cochran. He was the owner of a large tobacco shop in Washington. He had been the owner of a hotel here, but had sold it at a high profit during the war, when hotel space in the capital was worth anything a proprietor had the lack of conscience to charge for it. With the money from the sale he had come to Haiti and made investments. He showed a decided liking for me. One day he apologetically confessed that I was the "first educated colored man" he had ever known. He backed up his sentiments by making me a very good offer to remain with him in Haiti as a kind of manager for his ventures—an offer I, of course, had to decline.

Mr. Cochran and two of his American friends and I were playing bridge on the upper piazza of the Hotel, when I disclosed to him my plan for getting back to the United States. He became greatly concerned. He declared that I shouldn't think of carrying out any such plan; that the trip from Port-au-Prince across the Mona Passage in a small boat would be not only very uncomfortable but hazardous. There was a Panama Line steamer bound for New York in port that morning. Mr. Cochran stopped the bridge game, went to his room and got two boxes of cigars, and asked me to come along with him. We went aboard the ship and into the captain's cabin. The captain seemed glad to see Mr. Cochran and gladder to get a supply of cigars double the quantity he had usually received. My friend quickly came to the point—wouldn't the captain take me to New York—business of the most urgent sort. The captain came back just as promptly—it was impossible—the ship was loaded to the gunwales—not an inch of space left—there were already more passengers aboard than she was chartered to carry—if anything happened to her on the trip, he would be in danger of losing his master's license. But Mr. Cochran was a determined man; he would not accept a refusal. Finally, the captain said that I might come aboard and go up as a deck passenger, for there were no accommodations. I was overjoyed and thanked him. Mr. Cochran, I hardly knew how to thank.

I hurriedly packed and got aboard, and began the most uncomfortable four or five days that I can remember. I, of course, had no stateroom; not a bunk; not even a steamer chair. The voyage was rough, and I was in that state of constant semi-nausea which is many times more disagreeable than outright seasickness. The ship was far from being a vessel de luxe, and often I had no place where I could sit down. I paid the steward to place a makeshift bed for me on one of the wooden benches in the smoking room, and there I slept. But I could never get to bed before twelve or one o'clock, for until that hour the room was filled with men gambling. They used all the tables for gambling, and shot dice on the floor. These men who crowded the smoking room were Canal employees of the artisan class—engineers, machinists, plumbers, electrical workers, and helpers. They were rough; their language was coarse and profane. But I gave the best attention I could to what they said, because it presented an interesting and important view of life, a view that I was unfamiliar with, a view that disclosed one of the most discouraging aspects of the racial situation. One expression that they constantly used brought to me more vividly than anything else ever had a realization of the Negro's economic and industrial plight, of how lean a chance was his with his white brothers of the proletariat. The expression which I heard at a hundred times was, "Never let a nigger pick up a tool." "Never let a nigger pick up a tool." "Never let a nigger pick up a tool."

This expression echoed in my mind for a long time, and the answer to it was, I knew, that in the practical processes of dealing with the race question there is nothing more fundamental and vital than the lowering and sweeping away of economic and industrial barriers against the Negro. For no condition under which he struggles oppresses the Negro more than the refusal of a fair and equal chance to earn a living—to say nothing of earning it in ways in which he is able to prove himself well fitted. It is at once unfair, unreasonable, and cruel to declare to the Negro that, when he has grown to the stature of a full American citizen, he will be acknowledged as such, and at the same time to deny him the basic means of accomplishing the very thing demanded. And of this unfairness, this unreasonableness, this cruelty, the American people as a whole are guilty.

When economic and industrial avenues are open to the Negro, many of the most perplexing phases of the race question
will automatically disappear.

XXXIV

I GOT back to New York just in time to go to Atlanta. I was
disturbed at hearing of the number of persons who had
decided not to go. Mr. Shillady himself had decided not to
attend the conference. He confessed to me, "I think I have the
moral courage, but I find that I have no physical courage."
Mr. Seligmann was not yet fully recovered from his Haitian illness and so could not go; Edward Bernays took his place and
handled the publicity for us. Miss Ovington, Mr. White, and
Mr. Pickens of the national office had already gone. Arthur B.
Spingarn, chairman of our legal committee, and I made the
trip down together.

When Mr. Spingarn and I reached Atlanta, the Pullman
porter put our bags out, and, when we alighted, both his and
mine were in the hands of one and the same red-cap. As we
followed the red-cap along the platform and up the stairs, I
could see through the back of his head how his brain was
working on a serious problem which increased in imminence
with each step that he took. And the problem was whether to
break the laws of Georgia by taking the white man through the
Jim-Crow exit with me, or by taking me through the white
folks' exit with him. I was so curious about his mental
processes and their probable result, that I lost sight of the fact
that the poor fellow and ourselves were between the upper and
nether millstones of all the power of the sovereign State of
Georgia. I could not help but muse over the paradoxicalness of
the situation; for Atlanta, like every other Southern community, was a city in which there was not a white household
worth going into in which Negroes did not go and even live
and sleep. The finer and wealthier the household, the more
certain was this to be true. Negroes kept such houses clean,
they took care of the children, they nursed the sick, they were
entrusted with the family treasures and family secrets, and with
their own black hands they prepared the food; yet, the entrance to the Union Station, as wide as a city street, was too

narrow for the two races to pass in and out of together. The superficial observer will, quite naturally, conclude that the so-called race problem in the South is based upon an innate racial antipathy; indeed, the opposite is more nearly true. The red-cap showed real courage and successfully risked the chance of taking us both through the main entrance.

The Northern members of the Association who went down to Atlanta did so feeling that they were performing a rather heroic action, but it developed that the feeling was not warranted. Of course, it is true that they went without knowing what might happen. There was considerable tenseness at the first sessions, a mass meeting held on Sunday afternoon at the largest colored church in the city. The mayor of Atlanta was present and made the address of welcome; and, after making allowance for the strong implications that we would not have any trouble so long as we remembered that we were in Atlanta and not in New York or Boston, it was a very good address of welcome. In lieu of Mr. Shillady, I was on the program for the keynote speech, the speech in which the aims of the Association would be set forth and its achievements rehearsed. I was in a position where I did not dare to pussyfoot, even if I wanted to do so. The conference ran along easily and quite pleasantly. I believe that the authorities of Atlanta felt that the city was on trial, and I think that some special instructions must have been given to policemen, street car conductors, and such others as might come in direct contact with the delegates, for there was more than the wonted public courtesy and a noticeable elasticity in the traditional racial bounds.

Back in New York, I began at once to get my Haitian material into shape. But I interrupted this work long enough to go to Chicago and, armed with a badge and a pass as a member of the national Advisory Committee—insignia of quite an empty honor—attended the Republican Convention which nominated Warren G. Harding for president and broke General Leonard Wood's heart. In fairness, I should modify the "empty honor" stricture; for Herbert Parsons did write me a letter asking that I prepare some material on the Negro for inclusion in the campaign book. The letter followed me to Haiti and back to New York.

Shortly after my return to our office, Mr. Shillady resigned, and I was appointed, for a second time, Acting Secretary. At the meeting of the Board of Directors in October I was elected Secretary, and became the first Negro to hold that position. Early during my secretaryship Mrs. Addie W. Hunton and Robert W. Bagnall were added to our staff.

Immediately upon getting back from Chicago, I again took up work on the data I had gathered in Haiti. I wrote a series of four articles for *The Nation*, single articles for several other publications, and prepared a lecture on Self-Determining Haiti. In the meantime, I made a trip to Marion, Ohio, and talked with Senator Harding. I calculated that the most advantageous break possible to be gained for Haiti could be secured through him as the Republican presidential candidate. I found Mr. Harding an exceedingly busy man; Republican politicians from all over the country were flocking to Marion to see him; but, when he learned the nature of my visit, he became instantly interested and gave me plenty of time. I went over the whole Haitian situation, going back to the efforts of the Washington Administration at the close of 1914 to force American control on Haiti; I rehearsed the steps taken later through the Ford Mission and those taken still later through the Fuller Mission; I pointed out that the overthrow and assassination of President Guillaume and the attending consequences did not constitute the cause of the American occupation of Haiti in July 1915, but merely furnished the long-awaited opportunity; I spoke of the influence upon the actions taken by the United States in Haiti that Roger L. Farnham, Vice-President of the National City Bank of New York had exercised. I stressed that, in establishing the occupation, American marines had killed three thousand Haitians, many of them unarmed persons; I emphasized the contradiction in the preachments of President Wilson about the self-determination of small nations and the military seizure under his administration of a weak but friendly republic.

Mr. Harding was quick to see the importance of this data as campaign material, but he was cautious. He wanted me to give him the fullest verification possible of all the facts, in order that he might be on solid ground in using them. I said to him that in addition to the statement I was presenting, I could furnish him with copies of documents that would substantiate all the charges except one; and this I did do on a second visit to Marion. Regarding the charge that American marines had killed three thousand Haitians, I told him that I had arrived at the number after the widest inquiry I could make and upon what I believed was a conservative estimate.*

Mr. Harding's handsome face was a study while I talked with him. Despite his occasional grave and cautious protestations, I could see that he looked upon the Haitian matter as a gift right off the Christmas tree. He could not conceal his delight. I sat directly opposite him at a flat-top desk. In my anxiety to impress him, I leaned forward with my arms on the desk. He sat in a swivel chair, smoking cigarette after cigarette, and listening intently. From time to time he leaned back in his chair and blew clouds of smoke upward. Once, toward the latter part of the interview, when he came back down into position, he reached into his hip pocket, brought out a big plug of tobacco and, cutting off a generous mouthful, began to chew. After he became president, the W.C.T.U. sent him a petition requesting that he discontinue smoking cigarettes as an example to the youth of the country. I wonder what the dear ladies would have done had they known he was a tobacco chewer. I left the Senator satisfied with the results of my mission.

Mr. Harding made of the Haitian matter a campaign issue that struck Washington like a bombshell. The Administration was thrown on the defensive and, through Secretary Daniels, a naval investigation was promptly instituted. The prime purpose of this investigation was to give a whitewash to the marines; nevertheless, the light had been turned on, and some of the more brutal abuses in Haiti were abolished. The bombshell hurled by Mr. Harding brought out return fire from those on the defensive:—the Haitian government was so rotten with graft that our government was compelled to take charge in order to straighten out and purify things—the people of Haiti had sunk to such depths of degradation that it was our moral duty to step in and lift them up—they had regressed

---

*This estimate was, a short while later, more than confirmed by General Barnett, of the marines, who in a published report put the number of "indiscriminate killings of Haitians" at 3250; the number of marines killed at 13; and the number of Haitians wounded "impossible to estimate."

to cannibalism—there was a case in which an American marine had been killed and his vital organs taken out and eaten raw. This tale of atrocity logically raised a question that the naval inquiry did not go into. The question as to which was more reprehensible, the alleged custom in Haiti of eating a human being without cooking him, or the authenticated custom in the United States of cooking a human being without eating him. The Haitian custom would have, at least, a utilitarian purpose in extenuation.

Under President Harding, a Senate investigation was held. This investigation also, on the whole, was a whitewash. The Senate Committee felt that there should be a liberal civil government in Haiti, but under the tutelage of the United States for a period of years; however, some further reforms were effected. The latest governmental step taken was the appointment of the Forbes Commission to Haiti by President Hoover. This Commission recommended a number of reforms and broader policies, and the final withdrawal of American military authority. President Hoover also sent down a commission headed by Dr. R. R. Moton, of Tuskegee, which made valuable recommendations for the betterment of educational and social conditions. And so, during these more than twelve years, through the efforts of the Haitians themselves, and their friends in the United States, the restoration of Haitian independence has been going forward by degrees. The work is not yet completed, but a great deal has been done. All this while the Association had kept up its fight for a free Haiti. We have held mass meetings, we have disseminated publicity, we have appeared at the hearings of Senate committees, and we have brought all pressure we possibly could to bear on both the Senate and the President. Haiti freed will owe a great debt to the National Association for the Advancement of Colored People.

My two interviews with Mr. Harding at Marion established a cordial relationship. I saw him a number of times in Washington after he became President. On my first visit, he shook hands with me as I was leaving and laughed as he said, "We certainly made a good shot with the Haitian material." I replied, "We certainly did."

XXXV

IN the latter part of 1919 I had taken the first steps for the Association toward securing the enactment of a federal law against lynching. In this period, the number of lynchings was not so high as it had been in former years, but the barbarous manner in which victims were put to death could not have been surpassed by the fiends in hell. The colored people of the whole country agonized over these recurring outbreaks of inhuman savagery. As an example, merely: Henry Lowery, a Negro, shot and killed a white man and his daughter at Nodena, Arkansas; the killings resulting from a dispute about money that the white man owed the Negro. Lowery escaped but was captured by officers of the law. These officers surrendered him to a mob. The mob chained him to a log and lynched him. A part of the account of the lynching given in the Memphis, Tennessee, *Press*, in its issue of January 27, 1921, by one of its special correspondents who was an eye witness, reads:

More than 500 persons stood by and looked on while the Negro was slowly burning to a crisp. A few women were scattered among the crowd of Arkansas planters, who directed the gruesome work. . . .

Not once did the slayer beg for mercy despite the fact that he suffered one of the most horrible deaths imaginable. With the Negro chained to a log, members of the mob placed a small pile of leaves around his feet. Gasoline was then poured on the leaves, and the carrying out of the death sentence was under way.

Inch by inch the Negro was fairly cooked to death. Every few minutes fresh leaves were tossed on the funeral pyre until the blaze had passed the Negro's waist. As the flames were eating away his abdomen, a member of the mob stepped forward and saturated the body with gasoline. It was then only a few minutes until the Negro had been reduced to ashes. . . .

Even after the flesh had dropped away from his legs and the flames were leaping toward his face, Lowery retained consciousness. Not once did he whimper or beg for mercy. Once or twice he attempted to pick up the hot ashes and thrust them in his mouth in order to hasten his death. Each time the ashes were kicked out of his reach by a member of the mob. . . .

Words fail to describe the sufferings of the Negro. Even after his legs had been reduced to the bones he continued to talk with his captors, answering all questions put to him. . . .

This incident was not unique; the national office of the Association had dealt with a number of cases equally atrocious, and had tried through publicity and protest to make them means of arousing the conscience of the nation against the Shame of America, the shame of being the only civilized country in the world, the only spot anywhere in the world where such things could be. These happenings caused in me reactions that ran the gamut from towering but impotent rage to utter dejection, and always set me wondering at the thoughtlessness of people who take it as a matter of course that American Negroes should love their country.

I had gone down to Washington to see if Senator Capper, at that time the President of our Topeka branch, would introduce a bill in the Senate for us. He expressed complete willingness to do so, but suggested that the measure would stand a better chance if we could get his colleague, Senator Curtis, to sponsor it. He took me over to Senator Curtis's office and gave me a very favorable introduction to him. Senator Curtis said that he would be glad to introduce a resolution in the Senate that would call for an investigation of lynching. An investigation was less than we wanted; we had in our office a record of the facts for thirty years back, but I felt that a Senate investigation would be a beginning, at least. When I left Curtis, I went over to the House Office Building and saw Representative L. C. Dyer, who had made efforts to bring before Congress a bill to make lynching a federal crime. Mr. Dyer said that he believed an anti-lynching bill could, eventually, be passed in the House if it could be gotten out on the floor; that the first great difficulty was to get such a bill reported out favorably from the committee. I told him that I believed the National Association for the Advancement of Colored People could stir the Judiciary Committee to favorable action on an anti-lynching bill. Mr. Dyer welcomed our co-operation.

Nothing definite was done, however, until the opening of the Sixty-seventh Congress in the spring of 1921. On April 11, Mr. Dyer introduced H.R. 13, a bill "to insure to persons within the jurisdiction of every state the equal protection of the laws, and to punish the crime of lynching." The bill was at once referred to the Committee on the Judiciary and ordered to be printed. We joked a bit about it, but neither Mr. Dyer nor I was dismayed at the number 13, which the bill had drawn. We dug up notable precedents in which 13 had proved lucky. Within a short time, the entire machinery of the Association, its full organized strength and all the collateral force it could marshal, were thrown behind the measure.

The length of anything like a detailed account of the fight for the passage of the Dyer Anti-Lynching Bill, would, for inclusion here, be too much out of proportion to the length of this story. For nearly two years, during the periods when Congress was in session, I spent the greater part of my time in Washington. I tramped the corridors of the Capitol and the two office buildings so constantly that toward the end, I could, I think, have been able to find my way about blindfolded. I could almost say as much for the trip up Pennsylvania Avenue to the White House. My experience as a lobbyist brought me into personal contact with almost every outstanding man in both branches of Congress, and with a great many who were not outstanding. In seeing some of them I was often given precedence over people who had been waiting long before I arrived. Martin B. Madden, Chairman of the Appropriations Committee, arranged with me for a signal on the door to his private office that gave me access while others were waiting in the reception rooms. Once when I went in to see Senator Medill McCormick, one of the clerks, after taking in my name, told me that the Senator wanted me to come around and into his private office. When I got in he said, "Come on, let's take a ride and talk things over." And, leaving a half-dozen or so people waiting, we got into his car and rode out into the country, then back to the Capitol. He was a thin, nervous, high-strung, and, I thought, somewhat erratic man, but he was often impulsively warm-hearted. Once, when the filibuster was on in the Senate, and the supporters of the Dyer bill had gained a point, he waved to me from his place on the floor to where I sat in the gallery as though we were alumni of the same college and our football team had just scored. Theodore Burton, of Ohio, gave me the privilege of his office as a place where I could write or read or just sit down and rest; Senator Calder, of New York, did likewise. I always felt fully at ease in the offices of Senators Capper, Curtis, Shortridge, Willis, and

Watson, and of Frank W. Mondell, majority leader in the House, and Congressman Dyer, and Hamilton Fish. Matters concerning the bill frequently made it necessary for me to see Andrew J. Volstead, who as chairman of the House Judiciary Committee exercised great influence in having the bill reported favorably; also Nicholas Longworth, then on the House Steering Committee, and Senators Lodge and Borah.

I saw and talked with every man in Congress who was interested in the bill or who, I thought, could be won over to it. Early I learned the trick of sitting in the Senate lobby and sending my card in to members I wanted to see. At times when the Senate was in session, this saved considerable energy; and I found it an easy method of catching men who were hard to see in their offices. I discovered, to my surprise, that a Senator who was not making a speech, or waiting to make one, welcomed any good excuse to come off the floor. But it was not all easy sailing. Many of the men I tried to reach were cold. Often my tower of hopes came crashing down and had to be built up all over again. Sometimes my heart was as sore and weary as my feet.

The Anti-Lynching Bill was reported out of the House Judiciary Committee on October 20. This meant that the bill would be placed on the calendar; but being placed on the calendar did not mean that it would be reached promptly; nor even that Congress might not adjourn without reaching it at all. Mr. Dyer informed me that the only method of securing prompt action was to have the Steering Committee place the bill among other measures to be considered, and then to have a special rule made on it by the Committee on Rules. He advised me to get to work on the influential Republican members of both Committees. I did. I saw them many times and brought to bear on each one all the suasion and pressure I could command. I kept in touch with our New York office by mail, telegraph, and telephone; and members of the Committee who needed greater suasion and pressure began to receive letters and telegrams from their constituents back home.

On December 19, Mr. Campbell, Chairman of the Rules Committee, rose on the floor and moved the adoption of a special rule. The Democrats, led by the Southern Representatives, immediately began filibustering tactics by walking off the floor

and leaving the House without a quorum. Finally, Speaker
Gillette ordered the doors locked and the arrest of members by
the Sergeant-at-Arms. By eight o'clock at night, after a three-
hour wait, enough members were found and brought in to
make a quorum. A vote on the special rule was then taken, and
the rule adopted. On the following day, Mr. Volstead attempted to have the House go into Committee of the Whole
for consideration of the bill. The opposition repeated its tactics
of the previous day. But the Speaker repeated his methods and a
quorum was obtained. The House went into Committee of the
Whole and the bill was read. The leaders hesitated to attempt to
push the measure any further before the holiday recess. Forty
Republicans had gone on a junketing trip to Panama, and
twenty others had been sent to convey the body of Representative Elston, of California, who had died, back to the State (I
don't know whether the latter trip came under the head of junketing or not). These absences reduced the Republican working majority to so narrow a margin that the leaders feared to try
a definite test of strength. However, the groundwork was now
fully laid for bringing the measure properly before the House of
Representatives when Congress reassembled in January. The
Association had been working at high pressure. It had roused
the colored people of the country; it had secured the co-operation of the Negro press, and enlisted the aid of many influential
agencies and individuals. A constant shower of communications
urging the passage of the bill was being poured on members of
Congress. The Dyer bill brought out the greatest concerted action I have yet seen the colored people take.

I was back in Washington on January 10. The Anti-
Lynching Bill was taken up on that day, but side-tracked for a
week for the Post Office Appropriation Bill. On the seven-
teenth, debate was resumed; then consideration was postponed another week for another appropriation bill. I began to
suffer qualms of anxiety. I wondered if the men with whom I
had been dealing were merely giving me and the Association
and the Negroes of the country a little "run-around." In the
morning on the twenty-fourth, I went to see Mr. Mondell. He
told me that the Dyer bill would not be taken up because there
was another appropriation bill to be disposed of. He said that

some of the leaders wanted more time, and that it might be best to leave it until the thirtieth, then keep it up until it was passed. He added that he had called a meeting of Republican leaders in the Speaker's room, to discuss the matter, and was on his way there. We came out of his office together; he went to the Speaker's room, and I went to my accustomed place in the gallery to sit and read the morning papers, while waiting for the opening hour. While the roll was being droned out, I saw Mr. Mondell beckoning me from the floor to meet him in the lobby. When I reached him, he told me rather excitedly that the Dyer bill would be taken up the next day, whether the appropriation bill was out of the way or not, and pushed through to a finish.

Debate opened on the next day and grew more bitter as it went along. Speeches of the most truculent character were made by Representatives Sisson, of Mississippi, and Blanton, of Texas, both of whom spoke not only in favor of the mob rule, but in utter defiance of anything the federal government might propose to do about it. Most of the Southern opponents of the bill argued that rape was the cause of lynching, and that, in such cases, the white community simply went mad and was not accountable for its acts which, after all, were in fulfillment of a "higher law." Mr. Sisson put it more crassly when he declared that lynching would never stop until black rascals kept their hands off white women. It had been part of my work to keep the sponsors of the bill supplied with facts and figures. They had the figures from me showing that less than seventeen per cent of the victims of lynching in thirty-three years had even been charged by the mob with rape. But the piece of data that completely swept away the "usual crime" argument, was a list of dates and places, and of the names of sixty-four Negro women who had been lynched. The supporters of the bill made some good speeches and used the statistics that had been furnished to them with telling effect. The most eloquent of these speeches was made by Burke Cochran, a Democrat.

The news that the Anti-Lynching Bill was being debated jammed the galleries on the following day; the majority of the crowd being Negroes. There was intense excitement. At a point in one of the speeches, the Negroes in the galleries broke the rules and rose and cheered. A voice from the floor shouted, "Sit down, you niggers!" And a voice from the galleries shouted back, "You're a liar! We're not niggers." The Speaker announced that he would have the galleries closed if there was any further applause. At three o'clock the bill went to a vote, and at three-thirty the Speaker declared it passed by a vote of 230 to 119.

A wave of thanksgiving and jubilation swept the colored people of the country. I was exceedingly happy. But I realized that the fight in the Senate would be harder; and without pausing I started on this second part of my task. The bill was promptly referred to the Senate Committee on the Judiciary; the formation of that committee at once presented the practical difficulty of most of the influential Republican members being men who were not sensitive to Negro votes. On the committee were Chairman Knute Nelson, from Minnesota; Senator Cummings, from Iowa; Senator Brandagee, from Connecticut; Senator Borah, from Idaho; Senator Dillingham, from Vermont; Senator Colt, from Rhode Island; Senator Shortridge, from California; and Senator Sterling, from South Dakota. But the greatest difficulty was the overwhelming number of constitutional lawyers in the Senate, very few of whom seemed willing to leave a decision in the constitutionality of the bill to the Supreme Court.

The question of constitutionality stood highest between Senator Borah and the support of the bill; and the bill had been placed in the hands of a sub-committee of five, three Republicans and two Democrats, of which he was chairman. I talked with the Senator. He said to me at the beginning that he did not require any further facts about lynching; that he was convinced of its infamy and the necessity for its abolishment. He went on to say that the problem before him was the constitutionality of the measure, and the more he studied it, the greater was his doubt. He asked to be provided with briefs on the bill by lawyers who considered it constitutional. Such briefs were prepared by Moorfield Storey, Herbert K. Stockton, W. H. Lewis, Butler R. Wilson, and James A. Cobb, and given to Senator Borah. In the meantime, the bill hung in his sub-committee. At another time when I saw him he said with warmth that he would do anything in his power, as a Senator, to save the life of a single Negro from a lynching mob, but he could not support a measure that he did not believe was constitutional. He stated that he would try to find a way to make the legislation constitutional as well as adequate, and that a refusal on his part to champion the bill would come only from a decision that it was totally unconstitutional. Once when I saw him he looked at me squarely from under his shaggy eyebrows, but with that expression characteristic of him, which makes you uncertain as to whether he is in earnest or laughing at you, and said, "Let me give you a suggestion. Lay this bill aside and try for an Amendment to the Constitution that would enable its enactment." He indicated that he would be willing to draft the resolution. I emphatically expressed my doubt that any such amendment could ever be ratified by a sufficient number of states for its adoption.

I kept pressing Senator Lodge, the Republican leader in the Senate, for a report of the bill out of committee. The Association doubled its efforts. A memorial to the Senate urging the enactment of the Dyer Anti-Lynching Bill was prepared. This petition was signed by twenty-four state Governors; thirty-nine mayors of cities; forty-seven jurists and lawyers; eighty-eight bishops and churchmen, including three archbishops; twenty-nine college presidents and professors; thirty editors, and thirty-seven other prominent and influential citizens. A committee of three, Archibald H. Grimké, president of our Washington branch; Butler R. Wilson, president of our Boston branch; and myself, waited on Senator Lodge and requested him to present the memorial. He consented to do so, and did on May 6. But the bill still hung in the sub-committee.

On May 18, Senator Borah telegraphed me that the report of his committee on the bill was being urged and asked that all briefs not yet filed be sent at once. I went immediately to see the Senator, and found him in no pleasant mood. He informed me that Senator Lodge had ordered a report on the bill, and that he intended to hold it no longer, but to report it to the full committee the following Monday. He complained that sufficient time for a thorough study of the constitutionality of the measure had not been allowed, and therefore he would report the bill in accordance with the only opinion he had up to the time been able to form. He added, as though talking to himself, that he would get out of the Senate before he would do anything to pull anybody's political chestnuts out of the fire. This remark, perhaps, referred to the coming election in which Senator Lodge would be up for return to the Senate. I was dismayed by this sudden turn in the prospects of the legislation. I recognized that Senator Borah was the most commanding figure in the Senate, and I had been nurturing the hope that he would, in the end, take upon himself the championing of the bill. I felt that that would mean the battle already half won. But the mischief had been done, and I realized that, if the bill went along, it would go without his help. He did report the bill back to the full committee when he said he would, and the report was adverse; the Senator voting with the two Democrats. On the first of June, I directed a letter to each member of the Senate, calling attention to the fact that in the single month of May, twelve Negroes had been lynched, five of them burned alive; that on May 6, the day on which Senator Lodge presented the memorial to the Senate, a mob at Kirbin, Texas, had burned three Negroes alive, one immediately after another.

On June 27, I received a letter from Senator Lodge, marked "Confidential," in which he advised me that the Judiciary Committee was preparing to report the bill out. The committee reported it out on the twenty-ninth, and set a date for hearings. I appeared before the committee at these hearings and, in addition to the other things that I had to say, took my one fling in setting myself up as a constitutional lawyer. The gist of the argument against the constitutionality of the measure was that lynching is murder, and, therefore, the federal government has no more constitutional right to step into a state and punish lynching than it has to do likewise and punish murder. In my statement to the Committee I said:

The analogy between murder and lynching is not a true one. Lynching is murder, but it is also more than murder. In murder, one or more individuals take life, generally, for some personal reason. In lynching, a mob sets itself up in place of the state and acts in place of due processes of law to mete out death as a punishment to a person accused of a crime. It is not only against the act of killing that the federal government seeks to exercise its power through the proposed law, but against the act of the mob in arrogating to itself the functions of the state and substituting its actions for the due processes of law guaranteed by the Constitution to every person accused of crime. In murder, the murderer merely violates the law of the state. In lynching, the mob arrogates to itself the powers of the state and the functions of government. The Dyer Anti-Lynching Bill is aimed against lynching not only as murder, but as anarchy—anarchy which the states have proven themselves powerless to cope with.

The bill was put into the hands of Senator Shortridge to be brought up on the floor. My heart sank as I thought of the gap between a Borah and a Shortridge. Mr. Shortridge, as a Senator, was rather pompous of style; he seemed to have schooled himself in the graces of the statesman of a former generation. I judged that Daniel Webster was his model, for in speaking he employed the Websterian tone, and even wore his right hand in the bosom of his long coat. Late in August, I was assured by Senator McCormick, and also by Senators Curtis and Watson, that the Senate Steering Committee would meet within a day or two, and that the Anti-Lynching Bill would be placed on the program of measures to be taken up for consideration before Congress adjourned. The committee did meet on the thirtieth and place the bill on the program.

I kept urging upon the Senate leaders personally that the bill be taken up for consideration, and our national office kept up organized pressure. On September 21, at the noon hour—the hour for the opening of regular sessions—I walked with Senator Curtis from his office over to the Capitol. At the entrance we met Senator Lodge and Senator Watson. A hurried conference was held, and Senator Lodge, addressing his colleagues as "Charlie" and "Jim," gave orders for the recognition of Senator Shortridge and the taking up of the bill for consideration by two o'clock. At two o'clock Senator Shortridge was recognized and given the floor. Before he proceeded, he was interrupted by Senator McNary, who asked to be allowed to place before the Senate, House amendments to a certain resolution. Senator Shortridge, with exceeding courtliness, yielded to "the gentleman from Oregon." Immediately thereafter, he was interrupted by Senator Warren, who asked to be allowed to report on a joint resolution for the Committee on Appropriations, and he likewise yielded to "the gentleman from Wyoming." The opposition had not anticipated the move for the bill, but they quickly sensed why Senator Shortridge was

THE SHAME OF AMERICA

Do you know that the <u>United States</u> is the <u>Only Land on Earth</u> where human beings are <u>BURNED AT THE STAKE?</u>

In Four Years 1918-1921, Twenty-Eight People were publicly BURNED BY AMERICAN MOBS

3436 People Lynched, 1889-1921

For What Crimes Have Mobs Nullified Government and Inflicted the Death Penalty?

The Alleged Crimes	The Victims	Why Some Mob Victims Died
Murder	1266	For turning out of road for white boy in auto
Rape	573	Being a relative of a person who was lynched
Crimes against the Person	493	Jumping a labor contract
Crimes against Property	380	Being a member of the Non-Partisan League
Miscellaneous Crimes	548	"Talking back" to a white man
Absence of Crime	176	"Insulting" white man
	3436	

Is Rape the "Cause" of Lynching?

Of 3,436 people murdered by mobs in our country, only 573, or less than 17 per cent, were even accused of the crime of rape.

83 WOMEN HAVE BEEN LYNCHED IN THE UNITED STATES

Do lynchers maintain that they were lynched for "the usual crime?"

AND THE LYNCHERS GO UNPUNISHED

THE REMEDY

The Dyer Anti-Lynching Bill Is Now Before the United States Senate

The Dyer Anti-Lynching Bill was passed on January 26, 1922, by a vote of 230 to 119 in the House of Representatives.

The Dyer Anti-Lynching Bill Provides:

That culpable State officers and assistants shall be tried in Federal Courts as failures of State courts to act, and that a county in which a lynching occurs shall be fined $10,000, recoverable in a Federal Court.

The Principal Question Raised Against the Bill Is upon the Ground of Constitutionality.

The Constitutionality of the Dyer Bill Has Been Affirmed by

The Judiciary Committee of the House of Representatives
The Judiciary Committee of the Senate
The United States Attorney-General, legal adviser of Congress
Judge Guy T. Goff, of the Department of Justice

The Senate has been petitioned to pass the Dyer Bill by

24 Lawyers and Jurists including late former Attorneys General of the United States
19 State Supreme Court Justices
24 State Governors
3 Archbishops, 25 Bishops and prominent churchmen
39 Mayors of large cities, north and south

The American Bar Association at its meeting in San Francisco, August 9, 1922, adopted a resolution asking for further legislation by Congress to punish and prevent lynching and mob violence.

Fifteen State Conventions of 1922 (3 of them Democratic) have inserted in their party platforms a demand for national action to stamp out lynching.

The Dyer Anti-Lynching Bill is not intended to protect the guilty, but to secure to every person accused of crime trial by due process of law.

THE DYER ANTI-LYNCHING BILL IS NOW BEFORE THE SENATE
TELEGRAPH YOUR SENATORS TODAY YOU WANT IT ENACTED

If you want to help the organization which has brought to light the facts about lynching, the organization which is fighting for 100 per cent Americanism, not for some of the people some of the time, but for all of the people, white or black, all of the time

Send your check to J. E. SPINGARN, Treasurer of the

NATIONAL ASSOCIATION FOR THE ADVANCEMENT OF COLORED PEOPLE

70 FIFTH AVENUE, NEW YORK CITY

on the floor. At this point, Senator Pat Harrison, the keenest parliamentarian in the upper house, I think, raised the point of order that the resolution reported by Senator Warren was debatable. A long and complicated parliamentary wrangle ended in the ruling by the Chair that Senator Harrison and *not* Senator Shortridge was entitled to the floor. Senator Harrison took the floor and proceeded to hold it for nearly two hours, and the Democratic filibuster was on.

When Senator Shortridge regained the floor, he did what he should have done in the first instance; without a preliminary word or gesture he said, "I move that the Senate proceed to the consideration of House Bill 13, being Calendar number 822—" Before he could give the title of the bill, Senator Harrison raised the point of no quorum. The roll call showed a quorum. Senator Heflin made a motion to adjourn, which was voted down. (Here it was that Senator McCormick waved to me in the gallery.) Senator Shortridge then went on with his speech in support of the bill It was an eloquent speech, a logical speech, a good speech; but on his call for a vote, the point of no quorum was sustained. I felt that a bit of stupid courtesy had cost us the opportunity of having the bill taken up for consideration.

The Senate adjourned until November 20. At the opening of Congress, the Association had had placed in the hands of each member of the Senate a copy of a full-page advertisement which had been inserted in *The New York Times* and seven other daily papers in various cities, including the *Washington Star* and the *Atlanta Constitution*, with a total circulation of 1,633,803. The advertisement, which was published at a cost of $5136.93, set forth the salient facts about lynching, and probably caused more intelligent people to think seriously on the shame of America than any other single effort ever made.

Senator Shortridge again made the motion to take up the bill for immediate consideration, but now the Democratic filibuster was organized, and under the leadership of Senators Underwood and Harrison, with Heflin butting in, was at once put into operation. The tactics embraced leaving the chamber without a quorum, raising points of order, and making extended speeches, the subject matter of which was limited only by the limits of the universe. The filibuster was not met by any determined aggression on the part of the Republicans. Except by Senators Shortridge, Edge, Willis, and New, no actual fight for the consideration of the bill was made on the Republican side. The majority leaders seemed to feel that they would have done their duty and cleared their own skirts when they allowed the Southern Democrats to "put themselves on record" and, in doing so, assume responsibility for the failure of the measure. Senator Underwood, the Democrat leader, laid down an ultimatum to the Republican leaders; namely, that the opposition would not allow any government business whatsoever to be transacted until the Anti-Lynching Bill was withdrawn, not only for the remainder of the extra session, but for the entire remaining term of the Sixty-Seventh Congress. Such a withdrawal would, of course, necessitate a repassage of the bill by the House. Once or twice during the fight, I caught a glance from Senator Borah. This time I felt sure he was laughing at me, and somewhat maliciously.

At the close of the week, Saturday, December 2, the Republican leaders felt that the "record" had been made and they were ready to abandon the Anti-Lynching Bill. On that morning, I conferred with Senator Lodge, with Senator Curtis, and with Senator Watson, and pleaded with each of them not to abandon the bill on the terms laid down by the filibusters. Each of them said to me that the bill would not be abandoned on any such terms. That night the Republican Senators held a caucus to discuss the question. The morning papers announced that the caucus, after a heated session of more than two hours, had voted to abandon the bill; that nine Senators, however, did vote to keep up the fight until the fourth of March if necessary.

It would be difficult for me to tell just what my feelings were. I think disgust was the dominant emotion. What I had for a week been sensing would happen—the betrayal of the bill by Republican leaders—had happened. I knew that they had been making no determined effort to have the bill taken up for consideration. My thoughts were made the more bitter by a fact which I knew and which every Senator admitted, the fact that the bill would have been passed had it been brought to a vote.

I immediately sent to Senator Lodge, to Senator Curtis, and to Senator Watson the following telegram:

IN MY TALK WITH YOU SATURDAY MORNING REGARDING DYER ANTI-
LYNCHING BILL I URGED THAT MEASURE BE NOT ABANDONED ON TERMS
OF DEMOCRATIC FILIBUSTERS EVEN THOUGH EXIGENCIES REQUIRED
THAT IT BE LAID ASIDE FOR PRESENT STOP YOU SAID TO ME BILL WOULD
NOT BE ABANDONED ON TERMS LAID DOWN BY FILIBUSTERS STOP MORN-
ING PAPERS STATE THAT AT CAUCUS YESTERDAY IT WAS DECIDED THAT
BILL BE PERMANENTLY WITHDRAWN AND NOT BROUGHT UP AGAIN BE-
TWEEN NOW AND MARCH FOURTH STOP WILL YOU PLEASE LET ME KNOW
IF NEWSPAPER REPORTS ARE CORRECT

JAMES WELDON JOHNSON

By Special Delivery I received from Senator Lodge the following reply:

Personal   United States Senate
                              Committee on Foreign Relations,
                                     December 4, 1922.

Dear Sir:

I received your telegram of last evening. I do not know what you
mean by saying that I said to you in our conversation that "the bill
would not be abandoned on terms laid down by filibusters." I never
said anything of the kind. I never mentioned terms to you in any way.
There was no question of terms. The bill was either to be laid aside or
kept before the Senate. There was no question of terms at all. I explained to you that the bill could not become law even if the effort to
take up the bill continued until March 4th, that it was equally impossible to change the rules, and that the only question that the conference would decide was whether they would give up all business of the
session—put aside the ship subsidy bill, the farmers' extension of
credits bill, and all the supply bills, and in addition a large number of
confirmations—or whether they would withdraw the Dyer bill and
not press it during the coming session, which begins today. The conference agreed not to press the bill further and instructed me to say
precisely what I said in the newspapers, so far as I have seen the newspaper report. I wish to repeat to you that I said nothing whatever
about terms because nothing of that sort arose, and the words you attribute to me were never uttered by me. Nothing of that sort was
said.

Very truly yours,

H. C. LODGE.

James Weldon Johnson, Sec'y
National Association for the Advancement of Colored People,
1333 R Street, N.W.
Washington, D.C.

It is, of course, possible that Senator Lodge forgot what he said to me. Almost as promptly I received from Senator Watson the following note:

> United States Senate
> Committee on Finance,
> December 4, 1922.

Hon. James Weldon Johnson
Nat'l Assn. for the Advancement
   of Colored People,
Washington, D.C.

Dear Johnson:
If you come to my office, I will tell you what happened. There is too much about it to place within the limits of an ordinary letter.
> Yours, etc.
> JAMES E. WATSON.

The Dyer Anti-Lynching Bill did not become a law, but it made of the floors of Congress a forum in which the facts were discussed and brought home to the American people as they had never been before. Agitation for the passage of the measure was, without doubt, one of the prime factors in reducing the number of lynchings in the decade that followed to less than one-third of what it had been in the preceding decade—to one-tenth of what it was in the first decade of the keeping of the record. It served to awaken the people of the Southern states to the necessity of taking steps themselves to wipe out the crime; and this, I think, was its most far-reaching result.

I went to Washington occasionally after my period of lobbying for the Dyer bill on various other matters. I went down to see young Theodore Roosevelt, then Assistant Secretary of the Navy, and talked with him about the barriers that were being raised against the Negroes enlisted in the Navy, a service in which they had a long and praiseworthy record. When I had about finished with the interview, I mentioned to Mr. Roosevelt that I was going over to see Mr. Slemp, secretary to President Coolidge, on a matter. Mr. Roosevelt asked, "Do you know Mr. Slemp?" I replied that I did not know him personally. He then said, "Wait a moment." He called Mr. Slemp on the telephone, and with some highly complimentary remarks about me, said that I was coming over to the Executive Offices. When I got over, Mr. Slemp was prepared to meet me and gave me a hearty welcome. We talked over the matter in hand; then he said to me, "I'd like to have you meet the President." This looked as though the procedure of official form was being turned round. I don't know how many American citizens have had an official say to them, "I'd like to have you meet the President." Mr. Slemp took me in and gave me a rather flattering introduction to President Coolidge, and withdrew. The President was, I think, more embarrassed than I. He, it appeared, did not want to say anything or did not know just what to say. I was expecting that he would make, at least, an inquiry or two about the state of mind and condition of the twelve million Negro citizens of the United States. I judged that curiosity, if not interest, would make for that much conversation. The pause was painful (for me at least) and I led off with some informational remarks; but it was clear that Mr. Coolidge knew absolutely nothing about the colored people. I gathered that the only living Negro he had heard anything about was Major Moton. I was relieved when the brief audience was over, and I suppose Mr. Coolidge was, too.

XXXVI

I GOT immense satisfaction out of the work which was the main purpose of the National Association for the Advancement of Colored People; at the same time, I struggled constantly not to permit that part of me which was artist to become entirely submerged. I had little time and less energy for creative writing, but in 1921 I began work on an anthology of poetry by American Negroes. My original idea was extremely modest; I planned to start with Paul Laurence Dunbar and sift the work of all the Negro poets from him down to Claude McKay and his contemporaries, with a view to publishing in a small volume thirty or forty of the poems that I judged to be up to a certain standard.

Before I had gone very far with the work, I realized that such a book, being the first of its kind, would be entirely devoid of a background. America as a whole knew something of Dunbar, but it was practically unaware that there were such things as Negro poets and Negro poetry. So I decided to write an introduction; and the introduction developed into a forty-two page essay on "The Creative Genius of the Negro." In that essay I called attention to the American Negro as a folk artist, and pointed out his vital contributions, as such, to our national culture. In it I also made a brief survey of Negro poetry. I began with Phillis Wheatley, who, brought in 1761 on a slave ship from Africa to Boston when she was nine years old, became the second woman in America to publish a volume of poetry, and touched on the most significant work from among the thirty-odd Negro poets between her and Dunbar. I also went a little afield and mentioned some of the Negro poets of the West Indies and South America, giving most space to Plácido, the popular poet of Cuba. My selections for the anthology proper increased to three or four times the number I had originally planned for, but I felt that in the case of this particular book, there was more to be gained by being comprehensive than would be lost by not being exclusive. The use of "Aframerican" in the introductory essay to designate Negroes of either North America, South America, or the West Indies gave some currency in this country to the term as a substitute for "Negro" or "colored" or "Afro-American." The word was coined, so far as I know, by Sir Harry H. Johnston. It is on all points a good word, but in its use in this country it quickly acquired a slightly derisive sense, a sense due mainly, perhaps, to the stamp put upon it by H. L. Mencken. Mr. Mencken and George S. Schuyler, the Negro satirist, are the only American writers who continue to make frequent use of it. Many white people, when they wish to be especially considerate, are in doubt about the term most acceptable to Negroes. There are indeed puzzlingly subtle distinctions, to which colored people are more or less sensitive. The adjective "colored" and the generic designations "Negroes," "the Negro," and "the Negro race" are always in order; but, "a Negro man," "a Negro woman," etc., are somewhat distasteful. "Negress" is considered unpardonable. *The Book of American Negro Poetry** was published early in 1922.

*Harcourt, Brace and Company, New York, 1922.

Later in the same year, Claude McKay published his *Harlem Shadows*. He did not follow up this book of poems, but turned to prose. That, together with his long absence from the United States, has caused him to be partially forgotten as a writer of verse, but *Harlem Shadows* proclaims him one of the finest of modern American poets. Jean Toomer followed with *Cane*, a series of realistic stories of Negro life, interspersed with original lyrics of great beauty. Strangely, he never worked further the rich vein he had struck; this single book, however, made a deep impression on the critics and is still referred to as one of the best pieces of latter-day American prose. The extraordinary poems of Anne Spencer attracted attention; there were beginnings by others, and the Negro "literary revival" was under way.

Shortly after the publication of *Harlem Shadows*, Claude McKay decided to go to Russia. He had for a time been associate editor with Max Eastman of the *Liberator*, and was familiar with and interested in the Soviet experiment. Grace and I gave a farewell party for him at our apartment in Harlem. There were present seven or eight white persons prominent in the literary world and a dozen or so colored guests. News about the party leaked out. Harlem was not yet accustomed to social gatherings of the sort, and the local Negro papers referred to it as the "black and white" party.

In 1924, Jessie Fauset published *There is Confusion*,* a novel of life among intelligent and fairly well-to-do Northern Negroes. Almost simultaneously, came Walter White's *The Fire in the Flint*,† a novel that gave a sectional view of life in the South, and aroused wide comment and sharp controversy. In this period literary prizes were awarded for several years through *The Crisis*, edited by W. E. B. Du Bois, and *Opportunity*, edited by Charles S. Johnson. The *Opportunity* awards were each time made at a dinner attended by two or three hundred people, many of them white writers and others interested in literature. In 1924 and 1925 came volumes of poetry by Countee Cullen and Langston Hughes, followed by novels by Nella Imes and Rudolph Fisher and by books of prose and

*Boni and Liveright, New York.
†Alfred A. Knopf, New York.

poetry by a dozen other writers. The leading publishers opened their doors and the important magazines opened their pages to these writers—and the Negro "literary revival" was in full swing.

In 1925, with my brother, who made the piano arrangements, I collected a group of sixty-one Negro spirituals. For the collection I wrote forty pages of preface in which I gave the history of the spirituals, the probable theories as to their origin, and an estimate of them as music and poetry. The collection was published under the title of *The Book of American Negro Spirituals.** It was an instantaneous success, and is still in demand. It is, I believe, probably the best collection of Negro spirituals in print, and would have made headway under any conditions; but we were fortunate in having it come out just at the propitious moment. We followed the next year with a second collection; and although it contained as many numbers as beautiful and interesting as those in the first collection, it has not approached the success of its forerunner.

The research which I did in collecting the spirituals and gathering the data for my introductory essay had an effect on me similar to what I received from hearing the Negro evangelist preach that Sunday night in Kansas City. This work tempered me to just the right mood to go on with what I had started when I wrote "The Creation." I was in touch with the deepest revelation of the Negro's soul that has yet been made, and I felt myself attuned to it. I made an outline of the second poem that I wrote of this series. It was to be a "funeral sermon." I decided to call it "Go Down, Death."

On Thanksgiving Day, 1926, I was at home. After breakfast I went to my desk and began to work in earnest on the poem. As I worked, my own spirit rose till it reached a degree almost of ecstasy. The poem shaped itself easily and before the hour for dinner I had written it as it stands published. Grace had dinner guests Lucille Miller and Crystal Bird. I read the poem to this little group. Between Thanksgiving and the Christmas holidays, I wrote the prayer, "Listen, Lord." My plan was to write seven "sermons," and I had finished only two. I decided to go to Great Barrington, Massachusetts, and write the other

*The Viking Press, New York.

five. I found the thermometer there around 18 below zero, but
I stayed two weeks and brought the finished poems back with
me to New York. The poem that gave me the hardest work was
"The Crucifixion." I realized that its effectiveness depended
upon a simplicity which I found more difficult to achieve than
the orotundity of "The Creation" and "The Prodigal Son" or
the imagery of "Go Down, Death" and "The Judgment Day."

When I finished the poems, I decided that they needed a
preface; and I wondered if I was condemned to do a preface
for every book that I should write. I did a preface, telling
something about the old plantation preacher and setting forth
at some length my reasons for not writing the poems in conventionalized Negro dialect. Next to writing "The Crucifixion," my greatest difficulty was in finding a title for the book.
I toyed and experimented with at least twenty tentative titles. I
narrowed them down to *Listen, Lord*; *Cloven Tongues*; *Tongues
of Fire*; and *Trumpets of the Lord*, or *Trumpeters of the Lord*. I
liked the last two titles, but saw that "Trumpets" or "Trumpeters" would be a poetic cliché. Suddenly, I lit upon "trombone." The trombone, according to the Standard Dictionary,
is: "A powerful brass instrument of the trumpet family, the
only wind instrument possessing a chromatic scale enharmonically true, like the human voice or the violin, and hence very
valuable in the orchestra." I had found it, the instrument and
the word, of just the tone and timbre to represent the old-time
Negro preacher's voice. Besides, there were the traditional jazz
connotations. So the title became *God's Trombones—Seven Negro Sermons in Verse.**

In 1925 I was awarded the Spingarn Medal. The Spingarn
Medal, established by J. E. Spingarn, has now for eighteen
years been awarded annually for "the highest or noblest
achievement by an American Negro during the preceding year
or years," and is the most distinguished badge of merit that an
American Negro may wear. The Medal was awarded to me as
"author, diplomat, and public servant." *God's Trombones* won
for me the Harmon Award, consisting of a gold medal and a
check for four hundred dollars. I was elected a member of the
Board of Trustees of Atlanta University, and became a member

*The Viking Press, New York, 1927.

of the committee that brought about the merger of Atlanta
with Morehouse College and Spelman College to form the
greater Atlanta University. Talledega College and Howard
University conferred on me the degree of Litt. D.

During this period, I went to a great many "literary" parties.
At such gatherings I met and came to know a large number of
American literary and artistic celebrities—great and near-
great—and some of the stars of the theater and of Hollywood.
I also made the acquaintance of a few European celebrities. At
the Van Vechtens' I met Theodore Dreiser. I had formed a
stern mental image of Mr. Dreiser, picturing him as a morose
and dour individual. But at dinner he impressed me as being
more jovial than somber; indeed, he contributed a full share to
the jollity of the occasion. In the home of Alma Wertheim, I
became acquainted with several of the foremast composers,
musicians, and conductors of the modern school. It was there
that I met Louis Gruenberg, who had already, while living in
Vienna, made a setting of "The Creation," scored for voice
and orchestra. It was partly through Mrs. Wertheim's interest
in modern music that the work was given a production at
Town Hall under the direction of Sergei Koussevitzky, with a
portion of the Boston Symphony Orchestra, and Jules Bledsoe
as soloist. At a dinner at the Lewis Gannetts', I met Count
Karolyi, former President of Hungary, and his wife. The
Count, much to my surprise, was deeply interested in the
American race question, and talked to me earnestly to learn
what I could tell him about the Negro in the United States.
He was particularly curious about race intermixture and amalgamation as a solution of the problem. The guest of honor and
his wife left earlier than the others of us. When our host, who
had seen them out, came back into the room, he laughingly
related that the Count, in saying good-by, had expressed satisfaction at the apparent confirmation of his idea of race intermixture and social intermingling as a way out; for he had
gained the impression that my wife was white and that another
of the guests, a beautiful brunette, was colored. Between me
and the people to whose homes I went and those I met in
them, there grew some friendships, several of them deep and
abiding. I went to two or three parties in Greenwich Village.

At one of these, I remember, costume of some kind was *de rigueur*. I was taken in hand by a Russian who had been connected with the theater in his own country. My regular clothes were discarded; then the Russian took a single narrow length of an oriental-looking fabric, and with amazing deftness wound it round my head as a turban, passed it under my arm, around my waist, draped my loins, and, presto, I was some sort of denizen of the desert. The transformation pleased me highly, despite some disturbing qualms about exhibitionism.

In turn, Grace and I entertained occasionally at our home in Harlem. And so did Walter White and his wife at their home. Some of the parties we gave were gay; more than once we closed the evening, or began the morning, by all going to one of the Harlem cabarets to dance. But the most lasting impression I have of any of the gatherings at my home is of Clarence Darrow, sitting under a lighted lamp, the only one in the room left lighted, reading in measured tones from his book, *Farmington*. I retain a memory of the Lincoln-like beauty of the man, the beauty of sheer simplicity of his prose, the rising and falling melody of his voice, and the group seated about him drinking in the three elements combined—Ruby Darrow, no doubt, musing, "This wonderful man is my husband"—Carl Van Vechten, the most sophisticated of American novelists, sitting back in the shadow, but not so far back that his face does not show emotions straining for tears—Fania Marinoff, seated on the floor, her head thrust slightly forward, her lips parted, her dark eyes glistening, herself unconsciously revealing an unblemished line of beauty of head and face and throat—the whole group silent, as the words falling, falling, slip through their minds and lodge in their hearts with strange stirrings. Then to change the mood, Mr. Darrow takes up Newman Levy's *Opera Guyed*,* and reads "Samson and Delilah," then "La Traviata," and then "Thaïs"; his sober voice and manner against the wit and ribald humor of the poems make us chuckle and roar. The author of the poems tries to maintain a becoming modesty, but we are ready to forgive him for chuckling as heartily as the rest of us. Mr. Darrow, for his own delight, repeats the concluding lines of "Thaïs" several times over.

*Alfred A. Knopf, New York, 1923.

Now, in partial repayment, Paul Robeson gives a reading of "The Creation," and "Listen, Lord," and Clarence Darrow quotes to him the words of Agrippa to Saint Paul, "Almost thou persuadest me to be a Christian."

This was the era in which was achieved the Harlem of story and song; the era in which Harlem's fame for exotic flavor and colorful sensuousness was spread to all parts of the world; when Harlem was made known as the scene of laughter, singing, dancing, and primitive passions, and as the center of the new Negro literature and art; the era in which it gained its place in the list of famous sections of great cities. This universal reputation was the work of writers. The picturesque Harlem was real, but it was the writers who discovered its artistic values and, in giving literary expression to them, actually created the Harlem that caught the world's imagination. Very early, Langston Hughes discovered these values and gave them their first expression in poetry. The prose about this Harlem is voluminous. The writers who came to parties and went sight-seeing in Harlem found stimulating material for their pens. Then other writers flocked there; many came from far, and depicted it in many ways and in many languages. They still come; the Harlem of story and song still fascinates them.

But there is the other real and overshadowing Harlem. The commonplace, work-a-day Harlem. The Harlem of doubly handicapped black masses engaged in the grim, daily struggle for existence in the midst of this whirlpool of white civilization. There are dramatic values in that Harlem, too; but they have hardly been touched. Writers of fiction, white and black, have limited their stories to Harlem as a playground, and have ignored or not recognized the fundamental, relentless forces at work and the efforts to cope with them. This is, of course, understandable; picturesque and exotic phases of life offer the easier and more alluring task for the fictionist. But the sterner aspects of life in Harlem offer a unique and teeming field for the writer capable of working it. Under these aspects lie real comedy and real tragedy, real triumphs and real defeats. The field is waiting, probably for some Negro writer.

The two books about Harlem that were most widely read
and discussed were Carl Van Vechten's *Nigger Heaven*,* and
Claude McKay's *Home to Harlem*.† Mr. Van Vechten's novel
ran through a score of editions, was published in most of the
important foreign languages, and aroused something of a national controversy. For directly opposite reasons, there were
objections to the book by white and colored people. White objectors declared that the story was a Van Vechten fantasy; that
they could not be expected to believe that there were intelligent, well-to-do Negroes in Harlem who lived their lives on
the cultural level he described, or a fast set that gave at least a
very good imitation of life in sophisticated white circles. Negro
objectors declared that the book was a libel on the race, that
the dissolute life and characters depicted by the author were
non-existent. Both classes of objectors were wrong, but their
points of view can be understood. Negro readers of the book
who knew anything knew that dissolute modes of life and dissolute characters existed in Harlem; their objections were
really based upon the chagrin and resentment at the disclosures to a white public. Yet, Mr. McKay's book dealt with low
levels of life, a lustier life, it is true, than the dissolute modes
depicted by Mr. Van Vechten, but entirely unrelieved by any
brighter lights; furthermore, Mr. McKay made no attempt to
hold in check or disguise his abiding contempt for the Negro
bourgeoisie and "upper class." Still, *Home to Harlem* met with
no such criticism from Negroes as did *Nigger Heaven*. The
lusty primitive life in *Home to Harlem* was based on truth, as
were the dissolute modes of life in *Nigger Heaven*; but Mr. Van
Vechten was the first well-known American novelist to include
in a story a cultured Negro class without making it burlesque
or without implying reservations and apologies.

Most of the Negroes who condemned *Nigger Heaven* did
not read it; they were estopped by the title. I don't think they
would now be so sensitive about it; as the race progresses it
will become less and less susceptible to hurts from such causes.
Whatever the colored people thought about *Nigger Heaven*,

*Alfred A. Knopf, New York, 1926.
†Harper & Brothers, New York, 1928.

speaking of the author as a man antagonistic to the race was entirely unwarranted. Carl Van Vechten had a warm interest in colored people before he ever saw Harlem. In the early days of the Negro literary and artistic movement, no one in the country did more to forward it than he accomplished in frequent magazine articles and by his many personal efforts in behalf of individual Negro writers and artists. Indeed, his regard for Negroes as a race is so close to being an affectionate one, that he is constantly joked about it by his most intimate friends. His most highly prized caricature of himself is one done by Covarrubias in black-face, and presented to him on his birthday. Mr. Van Vechten's birthday, that of young Alfred Knopf, and mine, fall on the same day of the same month. For four or five years we have been celebrating them jointly, together with a small group of friends. Last summer we celebrated at the country place of the Knopfs. In a conversation that Blanche Knopf, Lawrence Langner, and I were carrying on, something about the responsibility for children came up. Mr. Van Vechten interrupted Mrs. Knopf with an opinion of his own on the subject, to which she retorted, "Carl, you don't know anything about it, because you are not a parent." Mr. Van Vechten responded with, "You're mistaken; I am the father of four sons." And Alfred Knopf flashed out, "If you are, they must be the four Mills Brothers." Mr. Van Vechten joined in the outburst of laughter. From the first, my belief had held that *Nigger Heaven* is a fine novel.

My own literary efforts and what part I played in creating the new literary Harlem were, however, mere excursions; my main activity was all the while the work of the Association. But doubled activities began to tell on me, and my doctor began to give warning. I had been helped to keep the pace because Miss Ovington had generously given me and Grace the use of her place, Riverbank, in the Berkshire Hills, for several summers. In 1926 I bought a little place in the township of Great Barrington, Massachusetts. I rode one day by an overgrown place where a little red barn was all that stood out amongst the weeds; the house on the place had burned down. A bright little river ran under a bridge and circled round behind the barn. On inquiry, I learned that there were five acres in the tract, and I said, "This is just the place for me." Grace and I studied the possibilities and decided that we could remodel the barn, keeping the interior, with the old hand-hewn beams, just as it was. We did; and named the place Five Acres. There, we have made our home ever since for a part of the year.

To get outdoor exercise I took up golf. For four or five years I was a votary of the game—though remaining a dub. One day in September, 1925, I was on the links of a club over in New Jersey, when a messenger ran up and told me that I was wanted for a long-distance telephone call. I rushed to the clubhouse and found that the call was from Detroit. I talked for a half-hour with the officers of our branch there.

The Negro population in Detroit had in a little over a decade increased from some ten thousand to some seventy-five thousand or more. This had brought about an actual physical pressure in their housing conditions. Several Negroes, to escape this pressure, bought homes in new neighborhoods, but were evicted from them by organized violence; in several instances the houses being practically destroyed by bombs. Dr. Ossian Sweet, a Negro physician, had bought a house in a modest white neighborhood of mechanics, clerks, and small tradesmen, but he hesitated for several months about moving in because of the assaults that had been made on the homes bought by other Negroes in white neighborhoods. Finally, he asked for police protection and with his wife moved in. With his household goods, he took in guns and a supply of ammunition. There also went in with Dr. Sweet his two brothers and some of his men friends, making eleven in all in the house. The police guarded the house that night and the next day. Late in the afternoon a crowd began gathering, and the police guard was increased; but the police did not disperse the crowd. As darkness came on, the street became jammed with people and others were constantly arriving. Later, stones began to hit the house; there was no interference from the police; a rifle cracked, and Leon Breiner, a white man in the crowd, fell dead. All of the inmates of the house, with the exception of the doctor's wife, were taken to jail and held without bail. The situation in Detroit was inflammable. Our branch officer there was calling on the national office for counsel and assistance.

I hurried back to the city and consulted Arthur B. Spingarn. Walter White was dispatched immediately to Detroit and there he took the first steps to allay passions and arrange for legal defense. The Association engaged a staff of six lawyers, headed by Clarence Darrow and Arthur Garfield Hays. The eleven defendants were indicted for first-degree murder. During the trial, Mr. White spent most of his time in Detroit, and Mr. Spingarn made several trips there. I undertook to raise money for the defense of the case. The issue was segregation by mob violence and the simple question was: Does the common axiom of Anglo-Saxon law, that a man's house is his castle, apply to a Negro American citizen? We set our organization machinery in motion, and I issued an appeal to the country in which we called for the raising of a Defense Fund, a fund for the Detroit cases and any other cases that would involve the Negro's constitutional rights. The response was spontaneous; within four months a sum in excess of $75,000 was raised. (A third of this amount was contributed by the American Fund for Public Service.) The trial of the eleven defendants resulted in a disagreement.

The second trial began in the following spring. In this trial the defendants demanded to be tried separately, and the state elected to proceed against Henry Sweet, the doctor's youngest brother, who admitted that he had fired the shot from the house. I attended the second trial. We had three lawyers, Clarence Darrow and two local lawyers. The courtroom was filled each day; and on the last day, when Mr. Darrow addressed the jury, not another person could have been squeezed in. The doors were jammed and the corridors packed. I had the opportunity of hearing Clarence Darrow for the defense, at his best, in a famous case. He talked for nearly seven hours. I sat where I could catch every word and every expression of his face. It was a wonderful performance. Clarence Darrow, the veteran criminal lawyer, the psychologist, the philosopher, the humanist, the apostle of liberty, was bringing into play every bit of skill, drawing on all the knowledge, and using every power that he possessed upon the twelve men who sat in front of him. At times his voice was as low as though he was coaxing a child. At such times, the strain upon the listeners to catch his words made them appear rigid. At other times, his words came like flashes of lightning and crashes of thunder. He closed his argument with a plea that left no eyes dry. When he finished, I walked over to him to express my appreciation and thanks. His eyes were wet. He placed his hands on my shoulders. I tried to stammer out a few words, but broke down and wept. The jury brought in a verdict of "Not guilty," and the Association had won another victory in its fight to maintain the common rights of citizenship for the Negro.

Before the Detroit case was over, the Association undertook another case involving the Negro's constitutional rights. In a section of the Texas law regulating primary elections, was the following clause: "However, in no event shall a Negro be eligible to participate in a Democratic Party primary election held in the State of Texas, and should a Negro vote in a Democratic primary election, such ballot shall be void, and election officials are herein directed to throw out such ballot and not count the same." Similar provisions in most of the Southern states constitute the "white primary," which, due to the one-party political system, is the most effective method of disfranchising the Negro. In these states, there is no law that prohibits Negroes from voting in the general elections, but the functions of the general elections have been transferred to the primary election. The persons winning nominations in the primary election are already elected, and the general election becomes merely perfunctory. For example, in the Texas gubernatorial campaign of 1926, in the first Democratic primary, with six candidates in the field, 735,186 votes were cast; in the run-off, with the candidates narrowed down to Dan Moody and Governor "Ma" Ferguson, 793,766 votes were cast. But in the general election in the same campaign, only 89,263 votes were cast.

The Association undertook a test of the Texas law, taking up the case of Dr. A. L. Nixon, a Negro physician of El Paso, who, though qualified as a Democrat, was denied the right to vote in the Democratic primary. This case was fought for two years, through the courts of Texas to the Supreme Court. At the end, the Supreme Court handed down a unanimous decision declaring white primary laws unconstitutional.

The scope of my activities had widened; I had become a member of the national committee of the American Civil

Liberties Union and had taken an earnest part in the fight in behalf of minority groups in general and in the fight for the restoration and maintenance of free speech, which was still circumscribed by the wartime prohibitions that had been placed on it. When Charles Garland refused to accept an inheritance of a million or more dollars, the American Fund for Public Service was organized and chartered, mainly through the efforts of Roger N. Baldwin, who was a friend of Mr. Garland, for the express purpose of taking over and administering this money. I was made a member of the board of twelve directors charged with the duty of disbursing the fund; later, I was chosen president of the board. Once, when the Fund was being organized, Mr. Garland lunched with us. He was an uncommonly handsome young man and extremely reticent. He turned his inheritance over merely with the request that it be given away *as quickly as possible, and to "unpopular" causes, without regard to race, creed, or color.* In doing this, he made no gesture of any kind. He simply did not want the money, and refused to take it. He wished only to be left free to follow the life he had planned to live. It was a strange experience to look upon a man in the flesh and in his right mind who could act like that about a million dollars. For a while the fund, which was for the most part in First National Bank stock, increased faster than we could get rid of it, and I was surprised at learning that giving away money, if it is done at all judiciously, is a difficult job.

Shortly after my return from Detroit I found myself at the center of a sensational fight for free speech. Three organizations, the League of Neighbors, the Union of East and West, and the Fellowship of Faiths, had planned to celebrate Peace Week. For the close of the week a mass meeting was scheduled to be held at the Morris High School; the speakers to be Judge Jacob Panken, Rev. Albert Thomas, Arthur Garfield Hays, and myself. The permission for the use of the school was revoked because Mr. Hays and I were among the speakers. The American Civil Liberties Union immediately took up the matter, and in a letter to the Board of Education charged that Mr. Hays and I had been barred from speaking because our names were on a blacklist kept by the board. This the school board denied. The Union decided to bring a test case to determine the right of the Board of Education to maintain a blacklist against public speakers, and promptly filed an application for the use of the auditorium of the Stuyvesant High School for a discussion of "Old-Fashioned Free Speech," with John Haynes Holmes, John Nevin Sayre, Arthur Garfield Hays, and myself as the speakers. The application was denied. The case was taken before the Board of Education and into the courts, with Samuel Untermeyer and Morris Ernst representing the Union. After continual efforts extending over more than two years the case was won, and the Board of Education approved the application for the meeting in the auditorium of the Stuyvesant High School. By that time I had recovered from the shock of being classed as a dangerous and un-American character. I felt fully reinstated when I was invited to take part in the unveiling of the bust of Whittier at the Hall of Fame.

My work as secretary of the Association, together with the books I had published, caused an increasing demand for me on the lecture platform. Calls for me came from forums, women's clubs, and from colleges and universities. I filled as many of these as time and energy permitted. Some of the forums I addressed had always a goodly number of wild-tongued radicals in the audience. These, I discovered, loved nothing better than having a speaker to bait. During the period for questions they often "treated me rough" because I did not hold that all of the ills and disadvantages suffered by the Negro could be wholly accounted for by the theory of economic determinism. At times, I encountered churlishness. Once a man rose and said, "I want to ask you a frank question. Isn't the chief objection to the Negro due to the fact that he has a bad odor?" In reply, I agreed that there were lots of bad-smelling Negroes; but, in turn, I asked my questioner if he thought the expensive magazine advertisements about "B.O." were designed to attract an exclusive Negro patronage. I remarked that I did not think so, since they were generally illustrated with pictures of rather nice-looking white girls.

I learned that by keeping my temper I could deal with irrationality, even with cases of violent race prejudice, but I was completely nonplused by the gentle old lady who would come up after a talk before a woman's club and dilate to me on the qualities of her colored butler or cook, as evidence of the high opinion she held of the Negro. I did not question that her colored help possessed all the excellencies she ascribed to them, but I was, nevertheless, at a loss for just the proper comment to make about it. My embarrassment was the greater because I knew that the gentlewoman was being actuated by a sincere desire to say something nice to me. And yet, as I think of it, there perhaps is no good reason why I should not always express to the gentle old lady my appreciation of the fact that she is providing one or two Negroes with jobs. I enjoyed talking before women's clubs, because that gave me frequent opportunities to talk about literature and art, and to read my poems. At a number of colleges and universities I talked about the æsthetic as well as about the sterner factors in the race question. Through arrangements made by Helen R. Bryan of Philadelphia, I spoke before the high and normal schools of that city on Negro art and literature. I think that the students and teachers in general gained information from these talks; I am sure that at least one result was a marked psychological effect on the few colored students in the overwhelming mass of white students—the emergence of a new pride and self-respect, which I could not help but note in their words and in their faces as they grouped around me after each talk. In the spring of 1927, I was invited to the University of North Carolina to hold seminars for a week on the sociological and artistic phases of Negro life. I believe this invitation was unprecedented. This was one of the most interesting episodes in my whole career. As I faced those groups of Southern white young men, I felt a greater desire to win them over than I had felt with any other group I ever talked to; and to win them over by the honest truth. I was not sure that I could do it, but, I think, to a good extent, I did. My course increased in popularity; so much so that my last talk was adjourned from the classroom to one of the assembly halls because of the additional number of students in English who attended. At the end of the week, I addressed the student body and citizens of Chapel Hill in the University Chapel.

On this visit to the University of North Carolina I formed some friendly relations. I met Paul Green, the playwright, and Elizabeth Lay Green, his wife. It was very interesting to talk with them about Negro literature and drama. I talked, too, with Howard W. Odum and Guy B. Johnson, who were

Mr. and Mrs. Johnson at
Fisk University

Two Views of
"Five Acres"

directing the work at the University in digging up and making a record of Negro folk material, a work second only to that done by Fisk University in preserving and bringing to the attention of the world the Negro spirituals. After my address in the University Chapel, a young lady introduced herself to me as Mrs. Katherine Elmore. Her husband, Lee Elmore, was connected with the Department of Dramatics at the University. She asked me if I would come to her home and meet some friends. I was happy to go. A dozen or so people came in, and the evening was a delightful one. There was talk about a great many things, with the race problem left out. I read from *God's Trombones*—the book was just coming off the press. In a letter that Mrs. Elmore wrote to her mother, Mrs. Laura T. Huyck, in Albany, she spoke about me. I was in Albany to make an address the following winter and met Mr. and Mrs. Huyck. Since then, among the pleasantest days that Grace and I have passed have been the week-ends that we have spent each summer at their beautiful place at Rennselaerville, New York. On one of these visits I was talking with Mrs. Huyck, who is a constant reader, and suggested an idea I had by asking her why, instead of always taking in, she did not cultivate an art-means of giving out, of giving expression to herself. She put the question back to me somewhat quizzically: "Why, what shall I do? I believe I am too old to start to take up the piano again." I ventured, "Well—why not try painting?" She laughed the suggestion away as preposterous, saying that she had never had a pencil or brush in her hand. But her secretary gave her a set of pastel colors and boards as a present the following Christmas, and she did, without any instruction or direction, begin to work with them. Grace and I were at her home in Albany in the spring and both of us were surprised by the pictures she had made. I could hardly credit my eyes. Since then she has held two exhibitions at the Durand-Ruel Galleries in East Fifty-Seventh Street, New York City, and received the praise of the art critics. One of her pictures was bought by the Brooklyn Museum of Art.

I regard it as curious, almost as a matter of destiny, when I think of the number of times my life has touched the life of some other individual in an apparently cursory and transient way, and then consider how that contact marked the beginning of an important phase in my own life. I have no intention of depreciating my own intelligence and industry, but the farther back I am able to look, the more clearly I discern that such results as I have gained may be, in a fair degree, traced to "lucky breaks." If I were giving an exhortation on the subject to young people, I should say, "*Do not trust to luck,* but be, in every way, as fully prepared as possible to measure up to the 'lucky breaks' when they come."

I attended another important conference on the race question. It was held for three days at New Haven in one of the fraternity houses of Yale University. Twenty-five men, white and colored, made up the conference. Arthur B. Spingarn and I represented the National Association for the Advancement of Colored People. At this conference I met Edwin R. Embree, then Vice-President of the Rockefeller Foundation, and Dr. Thomas Elsa Jones, the new President of Fisk University. In the remarks that I made introducing the round-table discussion which I led, I said, "It is a common error to think of the race situation as static, as a problem that will remain fixed until it is solved. What we call the race problem is not what it was a hundred years ago, or fifty years ago, or twenty or even ten years ago. The situation is constantly shifting and changing. It has never remained the same in any two generations. And it has never shifted more rapidly than it is shifting at the present time. The situation is a shifting one, therefore the means and methods of meeting it must also change." Mr. Embree made a summary of the conference, and commented with emphasis on that statement. A while later, I saw Mr. Embree again at dinner at the house of Julius Rosenwald, in Chicago, but I had no idea then what this association would lead to.

I spoke one Sunday morning for the Ethical Culture Society in New York. As I sat on the platform, I noted D—— in the audience. He waited until the exercises were over to speak to me. I was glad of this because I had seen only little of him during these busy years. He introduced me to a very beautiful girl who was with him, as the young lady he was going to marry. I didn't fear that he was going to commit bigamy because I knew he had had matrimonial difficulties and that he and his wife were divorced. As soon as the young lady opened her mouth, I noted her Southern drawl. D——, always quick-eyed and mentally alert and, without a doubt, a mind reader with regard to me, promptly gave me the information that she was from Louisiana. The information surprised me in no manner. D——, in the confessions he used to make, had more than once confided to me the strange and strong attraction that Southern white women possessed for him. There was certainly nothing unnatural in his experience. A situation which combines the forbidden and the unknown close at hand could not do less than create a magnified lure. White men, where the races are thrown together, have never, for themselves, taken great pains to disguise that fact. There is no sound reason to think that this mysterious pull exerts itself only one direction across the color line, or that it confines itself to only one of the sexes; the pull is double and inter-crossed. It is possible that Dame Nature never kicks up her heels in such ecstatic abandon as when she has succeeded in bringing a fair woman and a dark man together; and vice versa. Nor are there any facts on which to base a belief that, under comparable conditions, it would be more difficult for a colored man to win the love of a white woman (I am not here considering marriage, which is governed by a number of things aside from love) than for a white man to win the love of a colored woman. This is a thought well nigh impossible for the average white man to think; at least, with any equanimity. The primitive spirit of possessive and egotistic maleness is broad enough to embrace the women of other men, but its egotistic quality brooks no encroachment on the women of the clan. This primitive maleness is not limited to the white man, it is a masculine trait that may be traced back through many ages and among many races. The Negro, the Negro in the South possesses it; the difference being his lack of power to give it authority. In this whole situation, further complicated by the primitive antagonisms of femaleness, the sensitive nerve of the race problem in the South is embedded.

I saw D—— and his fiancée occasionally after they were married, they seemed perfectly happy. I enjoyed hearing her talk. In that delicious drawl she informed me: "I never knew that colored people had any problem till D—— told me about it. I used to see lots of them where I lived; sometimes I used to go to the quarter of the town where most of them lived, and they always seemed so happy to me." The three of us were at dinner one night at the Civic Club, when she proudly told me that she was going to have a baby; that she hoped it was going to be a boy, and that he would be the first colored president of the United States. I gave her my best wishes, but added that, according to rumors that had been current, Warren Gamaliel Harding had beaten her prospective heir to that distinction. The baby was a boy; and a girl followed, both of them lovely children. I did not see D—— frequently, but our old intimacy was in some measure re-established. He had made considerable money. He told me that it cost him twenty thousand dollars a year to live. He had put nearly all he could get together in the then recent Florida real estate boom and the burst of the bubble had hit him hard. One day in the summer of 1930, Grace, who was reading the *New York Times*, startled me with the cry that D—— was dead. I snatched the paper, and read that he had risen early, gone into the bathroom, and shot himself through the heart. At the hospital, where he died a few hours afterwards, his last words were that he was just tired of life.

Death has grieved me more deeply, but never has it more terribly shocked me.

In the elections of 1928, an effort was made to draft me as a candidate for Congress from the district in which the majority of Negroes in Harlem lived. I spent a disagreeable couple of hours at the rooms of the County Committee. Samuel Koenig, Chairman, and members of the committee made a strong attempt to impress on me that it was my duty not only to the Republican Party but to my race to accept the nomination. I had no more ambition to be a Congressman than I had to be a prize fighter; and—in other words—I told them so. They would not take "No" for an answer then and there, and urged me to consider the matter for a few days. I consented to do that, but my mind was quite made up. I did not see that I owed the Republican Party any duty that called on me for such a disruption of my plans and violation of my tastes. But I realized how important a thing it would be to have a Negro in Congress, and at the end of a few days, I wrote Mr. Koenig a letter definitely declining the nomination and urging the naming of some other colored man. A colored man was nominated but failed by a narrow margin to be elected.

My fervor as a Republican partisan had for some time been cooling off until now it was quite cold. Indeed, five years before, in speaking at the annual conference of the Association that was held in Kansas City, I had said:

As soon as the Negro is able he should go into the Democratic primaries and vote for what he believes to be the best men for the local offices. For a long time, he should not bother himself about helping to elect Republican presidents—or Democratic ones either. By eschewing national Republican politics he will undermine all arguments about his being a mere tool and monkeypaw of alien Yankee domination. By such a course, he will be building from the ground up. In common sense, the chief concern of a Negro in the South is to have a voice in electing the judges of the local courts, the county prosecuting attorney, the sheriff, the members of the school board. Unless he holds a federal job, it is sheer nonsense for a Negro in Mississippi to boast that he voted for Harding. If he can't get equitable school facilities for his children, or is in danger of being railroaded in the courts, or mobbed, or lynched, President Harding can't help him—in Mississippi. Of course, if the same Negro were in China, the President could send the entire navy to his assistance.

This statement did not meet with enthusiastic applause. To a gathering of Negroes, at that time, it sounded like heresy. Today, it is precisely what a great proportion of the race is attempting to do.

XXXVII

IN the spring of 1929, Mr. Embree, who had become the President of the Julius Rosenwald Fund, offered me a Fund fellowship that would enable me to devote a year exclusively to writing. Nothing could have been more welcome, and I gratefully accepted the fellowship and planned to enter on it in the fall. I had just decided on this arrangement, when I received a telephone call from E. C. Carter, editor of *The Inquiry*, and secretary of the American Council of the Institute of Pacific Relations. I had had the opportunity of getting to know Mr. Carter through serving with him on a committee at the National Interracial Conference that was held in Washington the previous winter. Mr. Carter was calling to ask me if I wouldn't go as a member of the American group to the third biennial conference of the Institute. I don't think I quite caught the import of the invitation, so Mr. Carter said he would run down to my office and talk the matter over. He told me about the Institute—and I was ashamed of myself for knowing so little of so important a body—and that the coming conference would be held in Kyoto, Japan, and that my actual expenses would be allowed. I was tempted to question what motives the gods in the guise of Mr. Embree and Mr. Carter might have in bringing me two such boons simultaneously. The entrance on my fellowship was postponed (the time began when I was in the middle of the Pacific on the homeward voyage).

There was nothing exciting in the trip over. We sailed the latter part of September from Seattle. I made some cordial acquaintances aboard ship; my most constant companion being Mrs. Kuo-Wai Tsu, a Chinese lady, who was returning home after attending the tenth anniversary reunion of her class at Wellesley College. I learned that she was a relative of General Chiang Kai-Shek. She and I talked together a great deal—her English was flawless—we walked the deck together, and danced together. I began by thinking to explore as far as I could the mysteries of the oriental female mind in comparison with those of America, Europe, and South America; I ended by concluding that, essentially, they were all one. But perhaps my friend's years at Wellesley had left her not wholly oriental.

On the morning that we approached the harbor in Yokohama, the sun burst through the mists and struck the summit of Fujiyama with a shaft of light. The snow-capped cone, glittering above the dark sloping sides of the mountain, seemed suspended in air. It was an awful sight as well as one of transcending beauty. I judge there is no experience more fascinating for the American or European traveler than the first landing in Japan. Strange lands are many, but I surmise that in none, other than Japan, is found such perfection of strangeness—strangeness which at once excites the sense of wonder and satisfies the sense of beauty.

I was in a fever to get ashore but, before I could, I was surrounded by a half-dozen reporters. They were as enterprising
and insistent as their New York or Chicago brothers could be.
They interviewed and photographed me. They asked me many
questions about the Negroes in the United States and the
National Association for the Advancement of Colored People.
They were surprisingly familiar with the aims and work of the
organization. What would be the future of the Negroes?
Would they turn Communistic? Would they eventually merge
with the whites? Would I bring up the question of the Negro
in the Institute? Would I write a book on Japan? I had already
learned some lessons about giving out spoken interviews on
important questions, and my answers were guided by them. I
was glad when the reporters left, and I rushed to my stateroom
to finish packing and close up my hand luggage. Just as I
started at the job, Mrs. Kuo came to the door and said she had
decided to make the trip up to Tokyo; would I wait for her?
The night before, I had asked her if she had ever visited Tokyo
and she had told me "No" and with a definite intimation that
she had no desire to see the Japanese capital. And now, as I was
preparing to dash ashore, she asked me to wait for her. I did
wait until she was ready—fully forty minutes. No occidental
woman could have done it better.

Before I finished with my luggage, three reporters came into
my stateroom; three of the same who had been interviewing
and photographing me. One of them asked, "Mr. Johnson,
did you see Fujiyama this morning?" I answered that I had.
"Mr. Johnson," he continued, "the people of Japan would be
greatly honored to have from you a poem on Fujiyama." With
that, he planked a pad down in front of me and offered me a
pencil. I was never so taken unawares in my life. I lamely explained that with so inspiring a subject together with the
Japanese language, a fitting poem would come spontaneously,
but such a thing was impossible to a poet working in the barbarous English tongue. They went away quite disappointed.

The electric train, swift, clean, efficiently run, landed us in
Tokyo. I went at once to the Imperial Hotel, where I had
made a reservation before leaving the United States. It was
lucky that I had done so; the hotel was crowded; the engineers
of the world were holding their convention in Tokyo.

The Imperial, as is of course known, is one of the great cosmopolitan hotels of the world. Everyone who stops there either achieves or has thrust upon him one of two divergent opinions as to its architecture and its plan. Americans, in particular, debate the question, because of the nationality of the architect. I know very little about the æsthetics of architecture, but I could see that the Imperial was not truly oriental or occidental. Nevertheless, I thought it a very skillful combination of Japanese beauty and American convenience. I admired greatly the low roofs, flowering courts, the tiled lobby and corridors; and I was thankful for my private bath and shower with running hot and cold water, the box spring mattress on my bed, and the easy chairs in my room.

Before I went to Japan, a lady, a friend of mine who had just returned from there, advised me that I should by no means stop at the Imperial in Tokyo, but that I should go to a strictly native hotel if I wanted to gain a sense of Japanese life. She warned me, however, that I should have to sleep on a mat and would have no comfortable furniture, and that the Japanese have no ideas about the difference of sex in the use of toilets and baths. She told me of an experience she had had in a bath. She was in the very midst of her ablutions, when a Japanese gentleman who had used the bath just before her re-entered, and without the slightest sign of embarrassment said to her, "Excuse me, Madam, but I think I left my spectacles in here." He had left them, and he got them and went out.

The next morning when I passed through the lobby on my way to breakfast, I stopped at the news-stand and bought a copy of the newspaper published in English. I also bought copies of all the papers printed in Japanese, when the diminutive boy at the counter showed me that my picture was in each one of them. Articles accompanied these pictures, but I never made any attempt to find out what I was quoted as saying. I had long suffered a dread of reading anything in American newspapers that quoted me on any important question. As I was leaving the stand, the diminutive boy took a postcard out of his pocket and said to me, "Sign? Sign?" I divined that he wanted me to autograph the card for him. When I got my glasses adjusted and looked at it I saw that it was a picture card of Fujiyama. At the side of the mountain was my face which the boy had neatly cut out of one of the newspapers and pasted on the card. I felt highly complimented, and signed it.

I remained in Tokyo three days, then left for Kyoto, where the Conference was to be held. The arrangements for members of the Conference were all that thoughtfulness and courtesy could demand. We found ourselves quasi-guests of the Japanese government. We had been accorded the courtesy of the Port of Yokohama; and been furnished with passes on all railroad and street car lines in Japan, and with franks for telegraph services.

The trip to Kyoto takes about ten hours. On the train which I took I was glad to find Mr. and Mrs. E. C. Carter. Doctor Ignazo Nitobe, the distinguished Japanese statesman and chairman of the Japanese group in the Conference, was also on the same train. Each hour I spent in Japan increased my wonder for Japanese efficiency. There was something absolutely uncanny about all enterprises, all plans, all arrangements moving along without a discernible hitch. There was the railroad, smooth, rapid; the cars in such fine, simple taste; the dining car service excellent and cheap. Soon after leaving Tokyo we partly circled Fujiyama, and had a revolving and swiftly changing view of the mighty mountain. As we skimmed along, I sat on the observation platform, watching the landscape as it unrolled from the train. Nothing met the eye that was sprawling, nothing squalid, nothing ugly. Every patch of land where foothold was possible was cultivated. More and more that perfection of strangeness that is Japan took hold on me.

Kyoto pleased me more than Tokyo. It is a very ancient city and was the capital of Japan for a thousand years before Tokyo became the seat of government. Why the word "Tokyo" is a rearrangement of the letters in the word "Kyoto" some Japanese told me, but, foolishly, I neglected to make either a written or a mental note of it. Kyoto is a city of nearly a million, but it is much more serene than Tokyo, more purely Japanese. It is still the home of the Japanese ancient art handicrafts. During the week I had before the Conference convened I spent some time in the handicraft district watching the curious processes in the making of cloisonné and lacquer and the delicate inlays of gold, silver, and copper. I became interested in Japanese prints, and wanted to purchase some, but thought I had better get some idea about them before I made any purchases. I went into a bookshop and asked for the best book on prints; they sold me a volume by Arthur Davison Ficke, the American poet. I had been with Mr. Ficke in his home a few weeks before I left for Japan, and it vexed me a little to have to pay a double price for the book of a fellow author, which, by the rules of the game, I might have "boned."

The headquarters of the Conference were at the Myako Hotel, and an old and picturesque building located in the outskirts and on a hill that overlooked the whole city. Many wings and additions that had been put on from time to time gave a quaint, rambling effect to the exterior, and made of the interior a labyrinthian puzzle. Attempts at modernizing it had been carried out, but not always successfully. As I remember, to reach certain floors by the elevators, you rode to the floor above and walked down. With many of the other members of the Conference, I stopped at the Kyoto Hotel down in the city. The Kyoto is a ten- or twelve-story brick building, and as modern and up-to-date as any hotel of its size in San Francisco or New York. I felt that the Kyoto carried its ideal of Western efficiency farther than was necessary or even good business. For instance, the waiters were men, dressed in somber tuxedo jackets; while at the Myako, the meals were served by dainty, doll-like Japanese maids in gayly colored kimonos. It appeared that I was doomed to be limited in my observations and study of "native" life.

On the night before the opening of the Conference, the members of the American group, with the Philippine group included, and their relatives and friends, about a hundred in all, dined in a body at the Myako Hotel. I sat at the left of a charming young matron; I knew that she was married because I glanced quickly at her place card and read, "Mrs. Frederick Vanderbilt Field." As we were unfolding our napkins, she turned to me with a smile and asked, "Mr. Johnson, don't you commute in the summers from Hillsdale, New York, down to the city?" I answered, "Why, yes, on Sunday nights I often go to Hillsdale to catch the New York Central, but sometimes I take the New York, New Haven and Hartford out of Great Barrington." Mr. and Mrs. Field lived at Lenox in the summer, and we had more than once ridden down to New York in the same car; but it was in Japan that we came to know each other.

I was tremendously interested in the Conference and learned things about the Far Eastern question that had hitherto rested in that zone of hazy ideas which surrounds everyone's definite knowledge. I contributed as much as I was able to contribute to the round-table discussions. Out of it all, the truth that came home most directly to me was the universality of the race and color problem. Negroes in the United States are prone, and naturally, to believe that their problem is *the* problem. The fact is, there is a race and color problem wherever the white man deals with darker races. The thing unique about the Negro problem in the United States, a uniqueness that has its advantages and disadvantages, is that elsewhere the problem results from the presence of the white man in the midst of a darker civilization, and in the United States, from the presence of the Negro in the midst of a white civilization.

I was curious about the techniques of the Conference. I closely studied the technique of the Japanese and Chinese groups. The discussion of those questions that related specifically to the differences of interests between Japan and China was, generally, a battle of Chinese intellectual agility against Japanese power and might, with the occidental groups acting as interpreters, arbitrators, and pacifiers. The discussion of those questions relating to differences of interest between the oriental and occidental groups was based upon differences in cultures, in philosophies, in religions; at no point were racial differences allowed to come near the surface. It was also the technique of the Japanese and Chinese in the occidental-oriental questions, not only not to mention racial differences but, for the purposes of discussion, to ignore completely their existence. I knew, and I am sure every member of the Japanese and Chinese groups, as well as of the American, British, Canadian, Australian, and New Zealand groups, knew that back of all the economic arguments for the Oriental Exclusion Act passed by the United States were reasons based on differences of race and color. I, of course, realized that this question of race and color was loaded, and, if brought out, might explode and wreck the Conference. Yet, I never became fully satisfied that this ostrich-like behavior, this studied ignoring of a factor so basic to every question being considered, was the wisest policy. It seemed to me to give a slight tinge of insincerity to the atmosphere of a Conference which was earnestly striving to bring about a better understanding and a more cordial relationship between the East and the West.

In questions of differing interests between the Japanese and Chinese groups there was a frankness that was missing when the questions were of differing interests between the occidental and oriental groups. Once, on the part of the Japanese, the frankness was brutal, but, in my opinion, revealed the truth of the situation. Yosuke Matsuoka, of the Japanese group, and former vice-president of the South Manchurian Railway, enraged, like a bull at the hands of the picador, by the lances of international law thrust into him by one of the doctors of philosophy of the Chinese group, burst out, "If Japan in the war with Russia had known of the secret treaty signed by Li Hung Chang and Libanov, there would today be no Manchurian problem; Japan would have taken South Manchuria and held it against Russia. She made her mistake in not taking it when nobody could have stopped her." The words were equivalent to a prediction of what happened this year, 1933, when nobody *could* stop her.

I had difficulty, often embarrassing, but which I shared with a good many others, of not being able always to distinguish Japanese from Chinese by their physical traits. I let that pass, but I constantly strove to get at their distinguishing mental traits. I had boundless admiration for the energy, the enterprise, the genius for organization and execution, and that uncanny efficiency of the Japanese. But all that weighed hardly as much in my balances as the keen intelligence, the poise, the broad and deep philosophy of life of the Chinese. China is, I believe, the only great people that has managed to get along without anthropomorphic Gods as the essence and apex of a national religion. A philosophy of human conduct, more than anything else, seems to fill that place. This is reflected in Chinese character. Intelligent Japanese and Chinese are both stung to the quick by our Exclusion Act, and both resent it, but it appeared to me that, while the Japanese smart under it, the Chinese are able to rise above it. One reason for this, I thought, was the fact that the Chinese are more self-contained and not so solicitous of the approbation of the white world as are the Japanese. I myself reacted differently to these two peoples; the Japanese left me rather cold. Not during the time I was at the Conference did I form cordial relations with any Japanese. Among the Chinese at the Conference, I formed some warm friendships. A difference between the Japanese and Chinese women who were members of the Conference seemed, to me, notable. The Japanese women, for the most part, sat demure, with little or nothing to say; a number of the Chinese women joined freely in the discussions and even mounted the rostrum at the assemblies and pronounced addresses. This, though, may be partly accounted for by the fact that nearly every one of the Chinese women had an adequate mastery of the English language, an implement that the Japanese women, generally, lacked.

I, however, did enter into friendly relations with a Japanese who had been a student at the Union Theological Seminary; we discovered that we had a mutual friend in Dr. Harry Ward. He invited me to dinner and I went; knowing that for once, anyhow, I should get a glimpse of real Japanese life. The night was rainy and chilly, and I had momentary regrets, when just after we entered his gate, I found that I had to take off my shoes and walk in sandals over a wet stone pavement to the house. At the entrance to the house we were met by his wife and daughter, a girl of about fourteen. They met us on their knees and, bowing low a number of times until their foreheads touched the earth, they kept uttering what I supposed were words of welcome to the lord of the house and his honorable guest. I felt the awkwardness of my position. My Western ideas made me revolt at the sight of these women abasing themselves before me in such a manner. The house was neat, almost bare of furniture, and practically one room; but, by those ingenious translucent partitions, it could be divided into a number of apartments. This gentleman was Western enough to have a dining room table. On it, he himself cooked the national dish, Sukiaki, in a sort of chafing dish of stone. The wife served but did not eat with us. The meal was delicious; and since then I have eaten Sukiaki often in the Japanese restaurants in New York.

At about the middle of the Conference, I received a letter, which is given below. I have never been able to feel sure whether this letter, although it bore every mark of authenticity, was the heart cry of a Japanese schoolboy or whether Wallace Irwin was in Japan and composed it:

Oct. 23.

Mr. Johnson,
Nara City, Nara Hotel.
Venerable Mr. Johnson:

Please excuse my discourtesy that I have sent this letter to you.

I am a Japanese boy—fifteen years old. I am a boy who express agreement against your opinion—for the black race agitation. I have been deeply sympathetise with them in their situation, on hearing. I am glad you came Japan to attend the meeting. Because, venerable Mr., I hope put myself in your agitation. I think, to do so, is that I will extremely satisfied, reason why, I am a Japanese. I pray that you make me associate with you, and you lead me to your agitation. If you admit my entreaty, I will do my best for your agitation.

Mr. May you admit this my entreaty.

Sir, Please admit my entreaty.

Please excuse written very poor English.

Very truly yours,
MASAO KAJIMA,
Shimonoseki City, Nagaskicho, Sasayama.

The Institute had made a point of drawing in a number of young men, some of whom interested me more than did many of the older members of the Conference. One of these was Malcolm MacDonald, son of Ramsay MacDonald. He constantly took part in discussions of the most involved questions of world politics and economics. He looked like a boy—he was only twenty-eight—and that made the grasp he had of world affairs and the masterful manner in which he was able to evidence it seem the more amazing. Another, and considerably younger, was the Hon. W. W. Astor. We lunched together and he remarked to me, "I am half American, you know." I knew that he was a little more than half, but I said to him that the fact that his mother was one of the Langhorne sisters of Virginia was generally known to Americans; this seemed to please him a great deal. He then recounted to me how his mother had helped in forwarding the fortunes of Roland Hayes in

London. But, for the most part, he talked about books, and talked very brilliantly. I began to speculate upon whether there was something special in English education or social life that made for early mental maturity.

One day a tall, slender, typically American young man approached me. He started to introduce himself but I interrupted him, saying, "How do you do, Mr. Rockefeller?" He invited me to have lunch; and we were joined by James G. McDonald, of the Foreign Policy Association. We chatted pleasantly about the Conference and of one thing and another. A day or two later, I was talking with Edouard Lavergne, the French observer at the Conference, and he said to me that Mr. McDonald had asked him how was my French, and that he had assured him that it was very good. I thanked M. Lavergne for vouching for me, but we were both puzzled to understand why Mr. McDonald was interested in knowing whether I spoke French well or ill. The puzzle was solved when Mr. McDonald and Mr. Rockefeller (the third) told me of their plan to have a French table on the voyage back. There would be four at the table, themselves, Adolphe Pervy, a young Frenchman, and me. We should speak only French at table, and there would be a fine of ten cents for each lapse into English. I said how pleased I would be to join the table, but expressed a doubt that, after making some purchases I had my eyes on, I should have enough dimes to pay for my lapses.

The table was a success. We spoke French at meals for the fifteen days of the voyage, and no one paid a fine. Of course, the rule wasn't actually a hard one, because if you didn't know how to say it, you could remain silent. However, we did talk constantly and on a great many subjects. Several times we discussed the American race question. Mr. Rockefeller interested me much as a person. At first, it seemed not quite congruous that this modest, unassuming, almost shy young man represented such tremendous power. But under his quiet manner, earnestness and a sense of responsibility were steadily revealed.

On every ship there always happens to be one, at least, of those genial busybodies who are never completely happy unless they are carrying out some plan to make everybody else on board happy. There was a man on our ship who, when we were a couple of days out from Honolulu, circulated a petition in the dining salon that requested the captain to wireless the office in Honolulu for permission to put the ship under extra steam so that the passengers might have an additional period of daylight in the Hawaiian capital. He brought the petition to our table and handed it to Mr. Rockefeller, who read it and passed it along. The others of us glanced through it and, without any particular thought, signed our names. The petition man came back in a few minutes with this message, "The captain says that if Mr. Rockefeller will head the petition, he will wireless the Honolulu office." The answer he got was, "Tell the captain I'll speak to him about it." Mr. Rockefeller, following some statements I had made in our table discussions, had evinced more than casual interest in the race question. He confessed that he knew next to nothing about it, and that it was something he wanted to know a great deal about. So a number of times, he and I remained at table after everyone else had left the salon, talking, in English of course, about various phases of the American race problem. The night that the petition was circulated was one of the times that we remained. Before we went on deck, I, out of more than curiosity, asked him if he was going to sign the petition to speed up the ship. "No," he said, "I won't sign it; 'John D. Rockefeller' is more than merely my name."

At the close of the Conference, I realized that I had had a glimpse at only one level of Japanese life, the upper level; and I regretted it. I had stolen a little time off and walked some of the meaner streets of Tokyo and Kyoto, but that had afforded me only a very superficial glance at life on that plane. No opportunity was available to observe Japanese life as a whole; the time which was not taken up by the affairs of the Institute was almost wholly consumed by official entertainments in the grand style. Many luncheons, teas, and dances were given. I do not think I was wrong in feeling that the number and the lavishness of these entertainments went beyond the promptings of mere hospitality, even of that of the Japanese. We were entertained by the Mayor and Chamber of Commerce of Kyoto, and by the Governor of the Osaka Prefecture together with the Mayor and Chamber of Commerce of the city. After the luncheon in Osaka, we witnessed a puppet show. The Japanese

James Weldon Johnson

PHOTOGRAPH BY DORIS ULMANN

puppets are not miniature figures worked on strings; they are large-sized dolls and are carried through the play in the hands of human actors, who, however, do this so skillfully that they lose themselves to the spectators and seem to impart their human qualities to the dolls. The play was a tragedy that held the audience with mounting emotional interest to the end. In Kyoto, Baron and Baroness Fujimura gave a garden party, with geisha dances by three of Japan's most famous cinema stars. I thought that the beauty of the girls and their costumes exceeded that of their style of dancing. In Tokyo, Baron and Baroness Shidehara gave a garden party. Baron and Baroness Mitsui threw open their residence for a garden party and the performance of a "No" play. This example of Japanese ancient classic drama was to me impressive but rather tedious; not at all so absorbing and moving as the puppet show. I could not pretend, even to others, that I derived as much from the drama, interpreted mainly through spoken words that were incomprehensible, as from the puppet show, interpreted through the universal medium of pantomime. On our last night in Japan a ball was given for us at one of the Tokyo clubs; and on the day we sailed we were tendered a luncheon by Viscount Eiichi Shibusawa, the "Grand Old Man" of Japan, who, despite his ninety years, made a speech, and in English.

The culminating social event was a garden party given by the Emperor. The invitations, bearing the Imperial golden, sixteen-petaled chrysanthemum, caused a flutter of excitement. An official informed a group of us that in all the history of Japan less than two hundred foreigners had before this been included among those invited to such a fête. The etiquette of the occasion caused some anxiety and considerable inconvenience: No lady dressed in mourning or wearing a veil would be admitted. Gentlemen were expected to wear frock or cutaway coats and silk hats. The question of silk hats grew serious and developed into something of a panicky scramble; they were borrowed, rented, and reluctantly purchased. On the day of the garden party, the heads of the foreign male guests presented a historical pageant of the top-hat making industry.

I was among the number of those who had not included a silk hat in their wardrobe. I had left one at home that I had not had on my head in more than fifteen years, and I did not want

to spend money for another piece of useless headgear. I spoke
to one of the clerks at the Imperial about getting me a hat. He
assured me that he would do so. On the morning of the party,
he told me that the hat was there. I tried it on; it was a brand-
new, latest style hat of Japanese make and fitted me becom-
ingly. I asked how much the rental would be. "Five yen." I
objected that it was exorbitant; in truth, I fancied the hat, and
after some bargaining purchased it for ten yen. And now I own
two useless silk hats. The number of guests at the Emperor's
garden party was as many as two thousand, I judged. The gardens were as extensive as they were beautiful: after we entered
the gates, we walked, it seemed, a mile or more before we
reached the place where we were to stand as the Emperor
passed by. The crowd lined both sides of the gravel walk. The
group I was with stood directly opposite the members of the
Japanese Cabinet and the foreign diplomats. We chatted and
laughed as we waited, and the wait was long. There were several false signals. Finally, there was the blast of a trumpet. The
Japanese guests set the example and became silent. There was
no craning of necks, though the Emperor was approaching. I
had, I don't know why, expected to hear loud banzais. Instead,
there was a hush. As the Emperor and his retinue passed, not a
sound could be heard but the crunching of the gravel under
their feet. I noted that the Japanese did not look at him, but
stood with their eyes cast down. The foreigners did not follow
that example. What I saw was a young man, under medium
size, dressed in a khaki military uniform, walking by with easy
grace; and yet, he was an imperious figure. His retinue consisted of a dozen or so persons; all of the ladies were dressed in
native costumes, except the Princess Chichibu, who wore
Western dress, and of whom a sight was worth a trip to Japan.

In Honolulu I found that I was scheduled to speak at a
luncheon at the superlatively elegant hotel on Waikiki. The
luncheon was tendered to the American members of the Institute by the Hawaiian group. I spoke for twenty-odd minutes. I
began, according to the thing expected, by paying tribute to
the beauty of Honolulu and to its importance as the birthplace
of the Institute. Then I spoke of the significance of the Institute and the Kyoto Conference. So far, so good. What I was

saying met with unstinted appreciation. Then I brought in the race factor as a vital force that would have to be considered in the plans and purpose of the Institute. The air began to chill, but I had started down a path on which I could not halt and off which I could not turn. I saw what was ahead but I had no choice; I had to keep going. I went steadily on and finished to mild applause. Racial differences were also "ignored" in Hawaii; at least, at that time, and in making such a public speech, I had violated a Hawaiian taboo. Three people—I like to name them, Mrs. E. C. Carter, Miss Elizabeth Green, who lived in Honolulu, and M. Pervy, the young Frenchman—told me that I had made a "great speech and spoken the truth." But such a reception for a speech was a new experience for me, and for a couple of days I felt depressed about it. But I came out of the depression confident that I had never made a less popular or a better speech in my life.

On the day of our arrival in San Francisco Mr. Rockefeller and I were among the speakers (his maiden speech) at a luncheon of the Chamber of Commerce. I sat next to and talked with one of the most interesting men I have ever met, Captain Dollar, founder of the Dollar Steamship Line. On my way to New York I stopped over in Chicago to fill several lecture engagements that had been booked before I went to Japan.

XXXVIII

BACK in New York, I immediately got down to work. I remained in the city during the winter, and in the spring went to Five Acres, where I continued my writing. During the year I wrote and published *Black Manhattan** and *Saint Peter Relates an Incident of the Resurrection Day*.† In *Black Manhattan* I attempted to set down the story of the Negro in New York. As a background for present-day Harlem, I began with the "Harlem" of 1626, the year of the establishment of the settlement of New Amsterdam, when the Negro population was eleven, or a little above five per cent of the total non-Indian population. For the sake of the story, I kept down to a small

---

*Alfred A. Knopf, New York, 1930.
†The Viking Press, New York, 1930.

degree the discussion of sociological and economic factors, and eschewed all statistical data. One of the prime purposes in writing the story was to set down a continuous record of the Negro's progress on the New York theatrical stage, from the attempted classical performances of the African Company, at the corner of Bleecker and Mercer Streets in 1821, down to *The Green Pastures* in 1930. I considered that this record alone, done for the first time, was sufficient warrant for the book. In *Saint Peter Relates an Incident of the Resurrection Day*, I attempted an ironic poem about the unknown soldier. The poem was written "While meditating upon Heaven and Hell and Democracy and War and America and the Negro Gold Star Mothers." The book was printed for private distribution only.

Mr. Embree came to New York frequently, and I was in Chicago several times to fill lecture engagements. Once when I was there I found him in the throes of literary composition. He discussed with me the theme of his work: that Negroes in America were evolving into a new race; Brown America, he termed it. On this theme he wrote a truly remarkable book.* Before one of his trips to New York he wrote and asked me if it would be possible to arrange for a meeting with some of the principals of the cast of *The Green Pastures*; he was an enthusiastic admirer of the play. The arrangement was made and Mr. Embree gave a dinner at his hotel, with Richard B. Harrison, "The Lawd," as the chief guest. It was one of the happiest parties I ever attended. Mr. Embree had that afternoon been at the meeting of the Spingarn Medal Award Committee, of which he is a member, and he had the pleasure of announcing that Mr. Harrison had been awarded the medal. During the dinner an effort was made to draw from Mr. Harrison what had been the psychological effects upon him of playing the character of the Omnipotent for so long a time. At the direct question, he paused for a moment; we listened, watching him; his fine, beautiful countenance glowed and he said, "If it has had any effect, it has been to deepen my sense of humility." He need not have framed his answer in words; for a man cannot be this or that and hide it; God stamps it in his face.

* *Brown America*. New York, The Viking Press, 1931.

I saw Mr. Rosenwald again at the funeral of Louis Marshall. I had been asked to serve as an honorary pallbearer—Mr. Marshall had been one of the most valuable and active members of the Legal Committee of the Association. While the honorary pallbearers were waiting in the chapel, I chatted with Mr. Rosenwald and with Judge Benjamin N. Cardozo, the only ones I knew personally. Mr. Rosenwald took the trouble to introduce me to several. He gave me a flattering introduction to Alfred E. Smith. Mr. Smith regarded me for a moment with what appeared like cool curiosity; at least, there was no evidence of any kind of interest. Perhaps he found it difficult to reconcile Mr. Rosenwald's introduction with the incarnate exhibit confronting him.

Toward the end of my fellowship year, Dr. Thomas Elsa Jones, President of Fisk University, came to see me. He talked about the University—and no one can hear President Jones talk about Fisk without feeling the galvanic force of his tremendous energy and enthusiasm—and said that he wanted me on the faculty. The place he wanted me to fill was, in a general way, like that of Robert Frost at Amherst. I was to be guide and mentor of students who had the ambition and gave some evidence of talent to be writers. I was to have entire freedom to organize and carry on this work as I felt was best. The idea and plan were fascinating. The trustees of the University created the Adam K. Spence Chair of Creative Literature, and I was elected as the first occupant.

At the end of the year, I resigned as secretary of the Association, after fourteen years of service with the organization. I was elected to membership on the Board of Directors and made a vice-president. The Rosenwald Fund extended the period of my fellowship through to the time when I should begin my duties at Fisk University. In that period I revised *The Book of American Negro Poetry*, enlarging it to include the younger group of poets, and making the biographical notes critical as well. I also made a beginning on this present volume.

In the spring of 1931, a committee of my friends, headed by staff members of the Association, gave me a farewell dinner at the Hotel Pennsylvania. Three hundred persons attended the dinner, and I experienced the ordeal of hearing one's friends say extremely nice and generous things about one before a large company. In this respect, I was fortunate in the speakers; they were: Walter White, W. E. B. Du Bois, J. E. Spingarn, Miss Mary White Ovington, Robert W. Bagnall, Heywood Broun, M. Dantes Bellegarde, the Haitian Minister to the United States, Mrs. Mary McLeod Bethune, and Carl Van Doren. Arthur B. Spingarn was toastmaster; a letter of tribute from the Hon. Wilbur J. Carr, First Assistant Secretary of State, was read, and Countee Cullen contributed an original poem. Before the speaking began, my brother sat at the piano and played over and sang a number of our old Broadway songs. Many of the guests were old enough to join heartily in the choruses of *The Congo Love Song*, *The Maiden with the Dreamy Eyes*, *Under the Bamboo Tree*, and one or two others. Among those who sang most gleefully was Edward B. Marks, our first publisher, who was seated at the speakers' table. This reminiscent part of the program proved so popular that for a while I wondered if the dinner was being given in my honor or Rosamond's.

In the winter I began my work at Fisk University. It was a grateful relief from the stress and strain that had entered into so considerable a part of my life; and I wondered how I had been able, in such degree as I had, to make of myself a man of action, when I was always dreaming of the contemplative life. Not all of the stress and strain that I experienced while executive head of the Association resulted from efforts to deal with the outside forces antagonistic to the Negro race; much of it came from endeavors to rouse Negroes themselves from apathy, to win over hostile factions and bring about joint action within the race. It would be wrong to think that the Negroes marched as one united and zealous band under the banner of the Association; there were envies, bickerings, rancors, and pure maliciousness to contend with, as well as honest opposition. Negroes among themselves sometimes declare that we are the most disjoined and discordant group in the world, but I judge that we are, after all, merely human. If we could achieve the superhuman state of complete unity on an intelligent plan, not all the forces arrayed against us would be able to block our march forward.

There are moments when I miss the thrill of action. At times when there is a pitched battle between justice and wrong, I have a longing to be back in the thick of the fight. But there are thrills also in the contemplative life; and in it there are also fields on which causes may be won. I am almost amused at the eagerness with which I go to meet my classes. The pleasure of talking to them about the things that I have learned and the things that I have thought out for myself is supreme. And there is no less pleasure in drawing from them the things that they have learned and the things that they have thought out for themselves. I realize that, though I am nominally the teacher, there are many new things that I shall be taught. In touch with the youth of my race in a great university in the midst of the South; I shall be zealous to learn what they are thinking, how the world looks to them, and what goals they are pressing toward. I feel that on this favorable ground I shall be able to help effectively in developing additional racial strength and fitness and in shaping fresh forces against bigotry and racial wrong.

I find that looking backward over three-score years does not lessen my enthusiasm in looking forward. What I have done appears as very little when I consider all that the will to do set me as a task, and what I have written quite dwarfed alongside my aspirations; but life has been a stirring enterprise with me, and still is; for the willingness is not yet over and the dreams are not yet dead.

I am sometimes questioned concerning my glance forward. I am questioned by people who want to know my views about the future of the Negro in the United States:—Will the race continue to advance? Is the national attitude toward the Negro changing; and if so, is it for the better? Will the Negro turn to Communism? My answer always is that the race will continue to advance. In giving that answer, I assume no prophetic attributes; I base it on the fact that the race has given a three-hundred-year demonstration of its ability to survive and advance under conditions and in the face of obstacles that will not, by any discernible probabilities, ever again be so hard. That, I think, gives a definite earnest for the future. His "past performances" give the Negro increasing self-confidence to undertake what is before him. And, today, his self-confidence may be increased by only looking around him and noting what a mess the white race has made of civilization. By looking around, he can only conclude that, while no other race would probably have done any better, no other race could hardly have done worse. He can at any time negatively increase his own racial self-esteem by taking an objective observation of the brutality, meanness, lawlessness, graft, crowd hysteria, and stupidity of which the white race is capable.

Despite the many contrary appearances and all the numerous actual inequalities and wrongs that persist, I feel certain that in the continuous flux of the factors in the race problem the national attitude toward the Negro is steadily changing for the better. When it is borne in mind that the race problem in America is not the problem of twelve million moribund people intent upon sinking into a slough of ignorance, poverty, and decay in the midst of our civilization, in spite of all efforts to save them—*that would indeed be a problem*—but is, instead, the question of opening new doors of opportunity at which these millions are constantly knocking, the crux shifts to a more favorable position, and gives a view that makes it possible to observe that faster and faster the problem is becoming a question of mental attitudes toward the Negro rather than of his actual condition. The new doors of opportunity have been slowly but gradually opening and I believe that changing mental attitudes will cause them to be opened more and more rapidly. I see some signs of these changes in the South; and I think it among the probabilities that a gradual revolution will be worked out there by enlightened white youth, moved consciously by a sense of fair play and decency, and unconsciously by a compulsion to atone for the deeds of their fathers.

I believe that economic factors will work toward the abolishment of many of the inequalities and discriminations in the South. That section, the poorest of the country, must yield to pressure against the policy of maintaining a dual educational system, a dual railroad system, dual public park systems, and draining duplications in many another economic and civic enterprise. The absurdity of a man going into business and at the start barring the patronage of one-third to one-half of the community must eventually counterbalance all the prejudices that bolster up such an unsound practice. This process will be hastened by the growth of the economic strength of Negroes themselves. I here stress the South not under any misapprehension that it is the only section of prejudice and discrimination against Negroes, but because it is *in the South* that the race problem must be solved; because it will not be completely solved in any other section of the country until it is solved there; because essentially the status of the Negro in all other sections will depend upon what it is in the South.

Will the Negro turn to Communism? I do not think so. A restless fringe in the larger cities may go over, but the race shows practically no inclination to do so, either among the intellectuals or the masses. No group is more in need or more desirous of a social change than the Negro, but in his attitude toward Communism he is displaying common sense. There are no indications that the United States will ever adopt Communism, and it is more than probable that in this country it will, in its present form, continue to be an outlawed political and economic creed; then, for the Negro to take on the antagonisms that center against it, in addition to those he already carries, would from any point of view, except that of fanaticism, be sheer idiocy. I feel that the Negro should not hesitate at revolution that would bring in an era which fully included him in the general good, but, despite the enticing gestures being made, I see absolutely no guarantees that Communism, even if it could win, would usher in such an era. Indeed, I do not see that political and economic revolutions ever change the hearts of men; they simply change the bounds within which the same human traits and passions operate. If any such change should tomorrow take place in the United States, the Negro would not find himself miraculously lifted up, but still at the lower end of the social scale, and still called upon to work and fight persistently to rise in that scale. The only kind of revolution that would have an immediately significant effect on the American Negro's status would be a moral revolution—an upward push given to the level of ethical ideas and practices. And that, probably, is the sole revolution that the whole world stands in need of.

Often I am asked if I think the Negro will remain a racial entity or merge; and if I am in favor of amalgamation. I answer that, if I could have my wish, the Negro would retain his racial identity, with unhampered freedom to develop his own qualities—the best of those qualities American civilization is much in need of as a complement to its other qualities—and finally stand upon a plane with other American citizens. To convince America and the world that he was capable of doing this would be the greatest triumph he could wish and work for. But what I may wish and what others may not wish can have no effect on the elemental forces at work; and it appears to me that the result of those forces will, in time, be the blending of the Negro into the American race of the future. It seems probable that, instead of developing them independently to the utmost, the Negro will fuse his qualities with those of the other groups in the making of the ultimate American people; and that he will add a tint to America's complexion and put a perceptible permanent wave in America's hair. It may be that nature plans to work out on the North American continent a geographical color scheme similar to that of Europe, with the Gulf of Mexico as our Mediterranean. My hope is that in the process the Negro will be not merely sucked up but, through his own advancement and development, will go in on a basis of equal partnership.

If I am wrong in these opinions and conclusions, if the Negro is always to be given a heavy handicap back of the common scratch, or if the antagonistic forces are destined to dominate and bar all forward movement, there will be only one way of salvation for the race that I can see, and that will be through the making of its isolation into a religion and the cultivation of a hard, keen, relentless hatred for everything white. Such a hatred would burn up all that is best in the Negro, but it would also offer the sole means that could enable him to maintain a saving degree of self-respect in the midst of his abasement.

But the damage of such a course would not be limited to the Negro. If the Negro is made to fail, America fails with him. If America wishes to make democratic institutions secure, she must deal with this question right and righteously. For it is in the nature of a truism to say that this country can actually have no more democracy than it accords and guarantees to the humblest and weakest citizen.

It is both a necessity and to the advantage of America that she deal with this question right and righteously; for the well-being of the nation as well as that of the Negro depends upon taking that course. And she must bear in mind that it is a question which can be neither avoided nor postponed; it is not distant in position or time; it is immediately at hand and imminent; it must be squarely met and answered. And it cannot be so met and answered by the mere mouthings of the worn platitudes and humanitarianism, of formal religion, or of abstract democracy. For the Negroes directly concerned are not in far-off Africa; they are in and within our midst.

*   *   *

My glance forward reaches no farther than this world. I admit that through my adult life I have lacked religiosity. But I make no boast of it; understanding, as I do, how essential religion is to many, many people. For that reason, I have little patience with the zealot who is forever trying to prove to others that they do not need religion; that they would be better off without it. Such a one is no less a zealot than the religionist who contends that all who "do not believe" will be consigned to eternal hell fires. It is simply that I have not felt the need of religion in the commonplace sense of the term. I have derived spiritual values in life from other sources than worship and prayer. I think that the teachings of Jesus Christ embody the loftiest ethical and spiritual concepts the human mind has yet borne. I do not know if there is a personal God; I do not see how I can know; and I do not see how my knowing can matter. What does matter, I believe, is how I deal with myself and how I deal with my fellows. I feel that I can practice a conduct toward myself and toward my fellows that will constitute the basis for an adequate religion, a religion that may comprehend spirituality and beauty and serene happiness.

As far as I am able to peer into the inscrutable, I do not see that there is any evidence to refute those scientists and philosophers who hold that the universe is purposeless; that man, instead of being the special care of a Divine Providence, is a dependent upon fortuity and his own wits for survival in the midst of blind and insensate forces. But to stop there is to stop short of the vital truth. For mankind and for the individual this state, what though it be accidental and ephemeral, is charged with meaning. Man's sufferings, his joys, his aspirations, his defeats, are just as real and of as great moment to him as they would be if they were part of a mighty and definite cosmic plan.

The human mind racks itself over the never-to-be-known answer to the great riddle, and all that is clearly revealed is the fate that man must continue to hope and struggle on; that each day, if he would not be lost, he must with renewed courage take a fresh hold on life and face with fortitude the turns of circumstance. To do this, he needs to be able at times to touch God; let the idea of God mean to him whatever it may.

THE END

INDEX

EDITORIALS FROM
THE NEW YORK AGE

Do You Read Negro Papers?

IN THE last issue of The Age there was an interesting communication from Mr. T. L. McCoy, of Raleigh, North Carolina, regarding Negro newspapers and their readers. Mr. McCoy has been working in the journalistic field, and he states that the work is hard and the harvest far from bountiful.

In his effort to secure colored subscribers and readers he has met with a great deal of discouragement. We can well believe that he is not exaggerating the gloomy side of his experiences.

It appears that the chief objection to Negro papers which he encounters from some of the people he approaches is summed up in these words, "I cannot find any news in the Negro newspapers."

The Negro paper is not primarily a newspaper, any more than a religious weekly is a newspaper.

If a man wants news he should buy one of the great dailies with resources for gathering almost instantaneously the reports of happenings from every point on the globe. All the news that a sensible man would expect to find in a colored paper is that growing out of our church, fraternal and other organizations and out of our social life, or the record of an event that in some way touches the race.

Negro weeklies make no pretense at being newspapers in the strict sense of the term. They have a more important mission than the dissemination of mere news. It is not their work to herald that there has been a wreck off the Fiji Islands or that the Russians have captured Przemyls.

They are race papers. They are organs of propaganda. Their chief business is to stimulate thought among Negroes about the things that vitally concern them.

Some colored people make an open boast that they never read Negro papers. It is safe to bet that these same people never do anything toward the development and upbuilding of the race.

It is also safe to bet that they wouldn't buy groceries from a Negro even if his stock was as good, his prices as cheap, and his store as convenient as any other man's.

One more safe wager is that they are people who are getting along pretty well, and are not much bothered about how anybody else gets along; especially those of their own race.

In effect, they paraphrase the famous report of old Commodore Vanderbilt, and say, "Damn the race!"

Do you read Negro papers?

October 22, 1914

President Wilson's "New Freedom" and the Negro

WHEN a man gets mad or drunk, he blurts out the truth; that is, the truth which he would not utter under normal conditions. President Wilson got mad at the delegation from the Equal Rights League, that had an audience with him last week, and he blurted out the truth, the truth about how he really feels toward the Negro.

The country now knows what his innermost sentiments are. There may have been other Presidents who held the same sort of sentiments; but Mr. Wilson bears the discreditable distinction of being the first President of the United States, since Emancipation, who openly condoned and vindicated prejudice against the Negro.

In effect, the President dismissed the delegation summarily. It was given out from the White House that the audience terminated as it did because the spokesman of the delegation lost his temper and became insolent and offensive in his remarks. Anyone who will carefully read the reports of the incident can see that it was really the President who lost his temper and that it was only the President who made any remark that could be termed offensive. And he lost his temper because he did not like being told the truth about a disagreeable subject. If Mr. Wilson's heart and his brain had been on the right side on this question, he could have patiently listened to whatever was said.

The general charge of "insolence" savors too much of a false standard of dignity; or worse, it smacks just a bit of a despatch that might be received from any Southern community at any time, which reads, "Negro lynched: cause, insolence to white man."

The President is quoted as saying that he had not been addressed in such a manner since he entered the White House. We are prepared to believe that is true; but, what could he expect under the circumstances?

Could he expect men making a plea for fundamental justice for their own race to indulge in the polished, dispassionate and soulless phrases to which he himself is given? Could he expect them to talk as though they were discussing an appointment to some fourth-class post-office?

We do not know what Mr. Trotter said, but it is certain, if he had in any way overstepped the bounds of propriety, the facts would have been clearly set forth in the newspaper reports.

No man with any sense of fairness can justify the President's segregation policy. It is wrong in general, because it is contrary to law, because it is contrary to the spirit of democracy and Christianity, because it is contrary to enlightened humanitarian thought. It is wrong in particular, because it is contrary to what has been the common practice for fifty years, and because it is enforced against a class of colored people that furnish no reason for it. The colored clerks in the Departments are all men and women of education and no small degree of culture. In fact, it is not an overdrawn statement to say that, in educational equipment, the colored department clerks average above the white clerks in the same grade; for, whereas a colored college graduate must seek such a position, the white university man can go into unlimited higher vocations open to him.

As Negroes, we resent the President's attitude and action. As an integral part of the republic, we are mortified to see the head of the nation make himself an apologist for discrimination between citizens on the basis of color.

The President has preached "The New Freedom," he has raised his voice against religious prejudice, he has used the influence of the United States, backed up by the power of its army and navy, in the interest of the landless peons of Mexico; but not one word has he uttered for fair play to the ten million Negroes in this country; not one word of hope or encouragement has he thrown out to them; but whenever he has used his great influence, it has been against them and for their humiliation.

Mr. Wilson, the men who waited upon you did not go to ask any favors; neither did they go to have a Sunday School lecture read to them from a primary catechism; nor to be patted on the head and told to be "good little niggers and run home"; no, those men went as citizens of the United States to you as the Chief Magistrate of the nation to ask that you investigate and correct an unwarranted wrong that had been put upon their race, a wrong which if permitted to grow would eventually rob that race of self-respect and place upon it an official government badge of inferiority; that is what they went to ask, and it vexes you, it makes you angry, they shall not be allowed another audience. Great God! what can be this Democratic Administration's conception of Democracy?

In this whole matter, Mr. Wilson's attitude, while not in keeping with his position as President of this great nation, is, at least, explainable by what we know of him. But it is incomprehensible where those members of the delegation and other colored men who voted for Wilson two years ago ever got the idea that he would act differently from the way in which he has acted. What single deed or utterance in his whole life has there ever been that could be so construed or twisted as to give them the faintest hope that Mr. Wilson would prove a second Lincoln? or even a second-rate Lincoln?

It is, perhaps, after all, a good thing that the incident happened as it did. If Mr. Wilson had listened to the delegation, and made some cautious and perfunctory remarks about "looking into the matter, etc.," nobody would ever have known that the Equal Rights committee had waited upon him, and, most probably, nothing would ever have been done.

As it is, the attention of the country has been focused upon this wrong, and the judgment of the American people, which at bottom stands for fair play, will be brought to bear upon it. It is probable that public opinion will call a halt on this retrocession to ante-bellum tenets, and blot out this reproach on our national government.

To the Administration and all who stand against giving the Negro in this country a fair and equal chance—you had as well take notice now as later: The Negro question will never be settled until it is settled right. You may evade, you may postpone, you may circumvent, but it will ever spring up to confront and confound you.

Do not delude yourselves with the thought that we are so weak that life and spirit can be crushed out of us, that we can eventually be ground down and reduced to nothing. We are of a race that has never despaired or died: other races may wither before you, other races may come and pass away, but we are of a Race Eternal, we are of the Mother of Races.

We are ten million loyal citizens of this republic; we have helped to till its soil and we have helped to fight its battles; whatever share of national duty, however humble it may have been, that has fallen to our hands we have striven faithfully to perform; we are earnestly endeavoring to fit ourselves to perform a larger and nobler share of that duty—what more can you require?

We ask no more than an equal chance; but that much we demand.

November 19, 1914

22 Calibre Statesmen

Won't some member of the Senate or the House offer a resolution to gag the Negrophobes in Congress? One week, a bill is introduced to exclude absolutely from the country all immigrants of African descent, regardless of qualifications. The next week, a bill is introduced making the intermarriage of blacks and whites a crime. And, now, before we can recover from these two blows aimed at us, here comes the favorable return of a bill for the separation of the races on street cars and all other public conveyances in the District of Columbia.

What can be the conception of public duty of these men who are the instigators of this tireless attack upon us? What can be the size of their souls? As small as their minds must be, can't they find some other subject to occupy them? Can't they devote their meagre ability toward an effort to straighten out the mess into which the Democratic party has put the whole country? Or can't they, at least, sit still in Congress and listen to men who have something to offer for the general welfare of the nation, and then try to vote intelligently?

Some man with a .22 calibre brain and a heart the size and softness of a hickory nut gets into Congress. He gets there because there is such a thing as race prejudice. Were it not for race prejudice this same man would be, at best, a $700 a year country lawyer. In Congress he finds himself entirely outclassed by men of breadth and depth; and he realizes that there is only one way by which he can attract publicity and convince the people back home that he is doing something to save the country, and that is by introducing some bill against the unoffending and long-suffering Negro. Perhaps he does not expect the bill to pass, but he feels that he has discharged his moral duty, and made a record which again entitles him to the votes of his patriotic constituency.

The trouble with this breed of "statesmen" is that they were born more than fifty years too late; for it is more than fifty years since the occupation of slave driver and slave catcher went out of existence.

If the brains and hearts of these men were right, they could not help but see and feel that the best interests of their communities lie in the fair and humane consideration of the race question. They have a great opportunity. More than that, they have an awful responsibility; for largely upon what they now say and do depend the future peace, happiness and security of their own posterity.

If these men cannot rise to a comprehension of the great general problems before the country; if they have nothing to contribute toward the great general welfare of the nation; then, for the love of Mike (pardon the slang), let them keep still.

February 22, 1915

Uncle Tom's Cabin and The Clansman

TEN or twelve days ago the New York dailies printed a despatch from Atlanta, Ga., which stated that a theatrical company was forbidden to play the usual version of "Uncle Tom's

Cabin" in that city. This action was taken on account of a protest made by some local organization. However, the play was changed and given the Arcadian title of "Old Plantation Days," the offensive parts were expurgated, Simon Legree was transfigured into a sort of benevolent patriarch, Uncle Tom was made into a happy old darkey who greatly enjoyed being a slave and who ultimately died of too much good treatment, and so, a performance was given that was, no doubt, a great success, and offended nobody's sensibilities. All of which is very amusing.

A few days later the New York dailies printed a despatch from Washington which stated that "The Birth of a Nation," a moving picture play founded on Thomas Dixon's novel, "The Clansman," had been given its initial performance at The White House.

"The Clansman" did us much injury as a book, but most of its readers were those already prejudiced against us. It did us more injury as a play, but a great deal of what it attempted to tell could not represented on the stage. Made into a moving picture play it can do us incalculable harm. Every minute detail of the story is vividly portrayed before the eyes of the spectators. A big, degraded looking Negro is shown chasing a little golden-haired white girl for the purpose of outraging her; she, to escape him, goes to her death by hurling herself over a cliff. Can you imagine the effect of such a scene upon the millions who seldom read a book, who seldom witness a drama, but who constantly go to the "movies"?

This play was passed by the Board of Censors, and is scheduled to open in one of the New York theatres this week. Due to the efforts of Prof. Joel E. Spingarn, the Board of Censors was induced to demand a second exhibition, and, as a result, its former approval was withdrawn. But the Board has no legal authority, and the producers can proceed without its approval; if they do, it will be up to the police. Prof. Spingarn deserves great credit, even if the steps he has already taken do not result in stopping the play.

Some years ago the Irish in this section of the country broke up every performance of a farce comedy called "McFadden's Flats," because in it Irishmen were represented wearing green whiskers and raising pigs in the parlor. Not long ago they stopped the dramas being performed by the Irish players from Ireland, because some of the characters were objectionable. But here comes a stupendous moving picture play that seriously attempts to hold the American Negro up before the whole country as a degraded brute, and further, to make him the object of prejudice and hatred.

We, as law-abiding citizens, call upon the mayor and the police to see that the decision of the Board of Censors be sustained; that either the objectionable features be cut out or the production prohibited.

Let the 100,000 colored citizens of this city stand united and determined to see that this picture shall not be produced in such a manner as will misrepresent and vilify us as a race.

March 14, 1915

The Passing of Jack Johnson

IT IS the old, old story of one fight too many. It is a demonstration of the old truth that in a contest of age with skill and experience against youth with strength and endurance, Youth, in the end, will always triumph.

From a pugilistic point of view, it was a great fight. And, however much we may cultivate the finer sensibilities, however much we may decry the exercise of brute force, still there is something in a great fight and a clean and fearless fighter that stirs every man with red blood in his veins. Johnson fought a great fight. He showed no sign of the yellow streak, and it must be remembered, too, that it was the fight of one lone black man against the world. And he proved that he has not only been a great winner, but that he could also be a good loser. After the battle was over he was manly and sportsmanlike enough to say:

"It was a clean knockout and the best man won. It was not a matter of luck. I have no kick coming."

Johnson was the perfect athlete, the master boxer and always the square sportsman. Even those who hate him concede that no greater fighter ever put on a glove. Had it not been for

certain bad personal breaks, he would have been the most popular idol pugilism ever had; for he possesses all the elements
that make for popularity. Even so, it is hardly probable that
Willard will ever become the world known figure that Johnson
is. There is not, perhaps, a spot on the globe where Jack Johnson's name is not familiar; while it is doubtful that Willard's
name will ever go beyond English speaking countries.

Johnson's bad personal breaks deprived him of the sympathy and approval of most of his own race; yet it must be admitted that with these breaks left out of the question, his record as
a pugilist has been something of a racial asset. The white race,
in spite of its vaunted civilization, pays more respect to the argument of force than any other race in the world. As soon as
Japan showed that it could fight, it immediately gained the respect and admiration of the white race. Jack Johnson compelled some of this same sort of respect and admiration in an
individual way.

One of the delusions fostered by the Anglo-Saxon is that
white men are superior to those of "lesser breed" not only intellectually, but also in physical strength and stamina; that
physical stamina is a matter of mind, and the white man's
mind being superior he can stand the gruelling grind that
takes the heart out of other men. Before the Johnson-Jeffries
fight, the papers were full of statements to the effect that the
white man had the history of Hastings and Agincourt behind
him, while the black man had nothing but the history of the
jungle; that when the white man looked the black man in the
eye, the black man would wilt. But the black man did not
wilt. He not only looked the white man in the eye, but hit
him in the eye. Johnson effectually punctured this old and pet
delusion; and so we say his pugilistic record is something of a
racial asset.

Frederick Douglass had a portrait of Peter Jackson hung on
the wall of his library, and he used to say that Peter was doing
his part to solve the race question. Were it not for the unfortunate "breaks" referred to, Jack's niche would be greater than
Peter's.

When Johnson licked Jeffries, most of the states passed laws
prohibiting the exhibition of moving pictures of prize fights.
Of course it would be degrading to the morals of the people to

see a black man conquering a white one. (Some of this moral fervor expended against the "Birth of a Nation" would be very creditable.) Now that a white man has licked Johnson, the law looks funny, doesn't it?

We notice that Willard will draw the color line.

He labels himself, by this, not as the greatest fighter in the world, but merely as the greatest white fighter. So, after all, Jack Johnson goes down as the last real champion, a fighter who was ready to match his strength and skill against all comers.

April 8, 1915

A Trap

WORD comes to us indirectly that the producers of "The Birth of a Nation" are showing their kindly feelings toward the Negro by offering to introduce into the first part of the picture some views of Hampton Institute. If this is true, the Dixon-Griffith combination is laying a trap in which, we are quite sure, the Hampton people will be too wise to walk.

If there was ever a case for the application of the old saw, "Beware of the Greeks bearing gifts," this is one. No good will toward the Negro need be expected or hoped for from Tom Dixon and his associates. There is absolutely nothing in their hearts but blind hatred for the race; and any protestation to the contrary is based on some hidden motive.

This "The Birth of a Nation" gang is evidently feeling the attacks made on their hell-inspired production; but it is not for Hampton to save them. If the picture can be killed, let it die, from first scene to last; for there isn't enough good in it to merit saving any part. The whole representation was conceived only in hatred for the North and contempt for the Negro; so let it die! Kill it!

The final effect of introducing views of Hampton Institute into the first part of the "Birth of a Nation" would be to have spectators feel at the end of the play that education for Negroes is a failure. In doing this the producers would obtain the powerful endorsement of Hampton and thereby disarm criticism and repel attack, and still not change the main lessons taught by the play.

It is inconceivable that the Dixon-Griffith people after spending thousands of dollars to produce a picture whose sole purpose is to convince the North that it made a mistake in fighting to free the slaves, and to convince the nation that it must "keep the nigger down," it is inconceivable, we say, that these people would consider introducing into their picture views from a colored school in such a manner and to such an extent as to change the whole play into a propaganda of glorious uplift for the Negro. No such change of heart can be expected.

The offer to introduce these views, if it has been made, is nothing more than a trap. A trap, as we said, into which Dr. Frissell and the Hampton authorities will be too wise to walk.

May 6, 1915

"The Poor White Musician"

PERHAPS nothing should astonish us during these days of war, when the world seems to be up side down; but the following letter written to The Globe is in a tone so unusual and unexpected that we reproduce it in full:

Editor of The Globe, Sir—Why does society prefer the Negro musician? is a question which is not infrequently discussed by white musicians; yes, I dare say, by artists. The Negro musician is to-day engaged at most of the functions given by society, especially its dances. Why this preference should be given to the Negro "so-called" musician, who hasn't the slightest conception of music, rather than to the Caucasian musician, who has spent well nigh a fortune—aside from numerous years of painstaking study—is incomprehensible.

Surely it isn't because of the oft-refuted contention that ragtime music demands the Negro musician, for the white musician has proven time and again that he can render a ragtime selection better than the Negro. Why should a famous dancing couple prefer a Negro orchestra for their dancing exhibitions? Even the New York hotels are now beginning to discard the white musician for the Negro. It will not be long before the poor white musician will be obliged to blacken his face to make a livelihood or starve.

EUGENE DE BUERIS.

New York, September 8.

Was a more pitiful wail ever uttered? And is it not difficult to grasp that fact that it is a white man and not a Negro who is uttering the wail?

The writer is evidently a New York musician, and he cannot understand why the Negro musicians of this city are making competition so strong for their white professional brothers. Some persons not acquainted with the facts might jump to the conclusion that the colored men work cheaper than the whites, but it is certain that Mr. De Bueris would have been glad to make that charge in his letter, if such were the case.

On this point let us relate an amusing incident which happened a few days ago. A society lady called up on the telephone a man who makes a business of supplying musicians, and asked the price for a band of ten men. The man she called up is a colored man and supplies colored musicians, but as his office is on Broadway, such a thought seems not to have been anywhere near the lady's mind. He told her what ten men would cost for an evening. She was amazed and said to him, "Why I can get colored musicians for that price!"

The fact is, colored musicians charge more than white musicians; so we can see that after all there is some excuse for the bewilderment of Mr. De Bueris. Let us see if we can't enlighten him a bit.

When he refers to the colored players as "so-called musicians" he may think he is slurring them, but, instead, he is slurring the white society people, and hotel and cafe proprietors who prefer Negro musicians. But Mr. De Bueris is all wrong in belittling the musical ability of these men. They may not have spent "as many fortunes or as many years of painstaking study" as the white musicians, but what has that to do with natural musical ability? Nothing. It only goes to show that white men need to spend fortunes and years of study in order to play music as well, or almost as well, as Negroes do naturally. Let Mr. De Bueris think of what would happen to the white musicians if the colored men spent fortunes and years in study, and let him be thankful.

There are good and sufficient reasons why Negro musicians are preferred at social affairs. Modern music and modern dancing are both Negro creations.

Since ragtime music has swept the world and become universally known as American music, there have been attempts to rob the Negro of the credit of originating it; but this is in accord with an old habit of the white race; as soon as anything is recognized as great, they set about to claim credit for it. In this manner they have attempted to rob the Negro of the credit of originating the plantation stories and songs. We all remember how after the Russo-Japanese war attempts were made to classify the Japanese as white. In the same way, scholars have "doubted" that the Zulus are real Negroes. Had Jack Johnson continued as champion, somebody would have tried to prove that he was not a real Negro. By this method, the white race has gathered to itself credit for originating nearly all the great and good things in the world. It has taken credit for what has been accomplished by the ancient Egyptians, the East Indians and the Arabs, by the simple process of declaring those black people to be white.

The truth is, the pure white race has not originated a single one of the great, fundamental intellectual achievements which have raised man in the scale of civilization.

The alphabet, the art of letters, of poetry, of music, of sculpture, of painting, of the drama, of architecture; numbers, the science of mathematics, of astronomy, of philosophy, of logic, of physics, of chemistry; the use of metals and the principles of mechanics were all invented or discovered by darker and, what are, in many cases, considered inferior, races. The pure white race did not originate even the religion it uses.

But all of this is another story; let us get back to the "poor white musician."

Not only is modern American music a Negro creation, but the modern dances are also. The dance steps which society debutantes are now learning and those which are the latest thing on the stage have been known among Negroes for years. Then it is only natural that when it comes to making music for modern dancing, the Negro musician should be the real thing.

In a way, Mr. De Beuris is right when he says that white musicians can play ragtime as well as Negro musicians; that is, white musicians can play exactly what is put down on the paper. But Negro musicians are able to put into the music something that can't be put on the paper; a certain abandon which seems to enter in the blood of the dancers; and that is the answer to Mr. De Beuris' question, that is the secret, that is why Negro musicians are preferred.

And let us add a word to the Negro musician upon efficiency in his work. He cannot afford to run along merely upon his great natural gift.

This letter written to The Globe shows that the white musicians feel his competition, and that means that they will stop at nohing to put him out of business. Let the Negro musician improve and develop himself. He may not be able to spend a fortune, but he can, by some slight sacrifices, put in his spare time on painstaking study. It is only in this way that he can continue to hold his own.

September 23, 1915

Stranger Than Fiction

A COUPLE of years ago the writer of these columns wrote and published anonymously a novel entitled, "The Autobiography of an Ex-Colored Man." The book aroused considerable comment and produced a wide difference of critical opinion between reviewers on Northern and Southern publications. Northern reviewers generally accepted the book as a human document, while Southern reviewers pronounced the theme of the story utterly impossible. A few of the Northern reviewers were in doubt as to whether the book was fact or fiction.

Here are extracts from the reviews in three newspapers which illustrate the three sorts of opinion expressed by the critics:

"Naturally the name of the writer of "The Autobiography of an Ex-Colored Man" can never be divulged by the publishers of this most remarkable human document. That it is not fiction we are prepared to believe from the sincerity and directness of the work as well as from the fact that it would be impossible for any one to portray such a character without making a hero of the subject if he were a colored man, and it is unthinkable and impossible that a white man could ever gain such an interior view of the life of a person of colored blood. As a dispassionate selfanalysis it would rank with the confessions of St. Augustine, and, as a human document, is far superior to the famous "Diary" of Marie Bashkirtseff which electrified the word some years ago.—Portland (Me.) Express.

Here is an extract from the review of one of the undecided critics:

It is a remarkable human document, being the story of a colored man who was sufficiently light in color to pass as a white man * * *. If the story be a true one, it is more remarkable than any piece of fiction ever written of the colored race * * *. That is just the puzzling thing about the book. It reads more like fiction than fact, yet there is a semblance of truth in it * * *. It is an X-ray portraiture of the soul of a Negro * * *. The most wonderful story of self-revelation, either in fact or fiction, that has been published in many years.—Springfield (Mass.) Union.

Here is a representative opinion of the Southern reviews, which pronounced the idea around which the story was built to be absurd and impossible:

The publishers' note stating that the book gives "a glimpse behind the scenes of the race drama" is not borne out. The publishers' assertion that the mistreatment of the Negroes by white persons in America is "actually and constantly forcing an unascertainable number of fair complexioned people over into the white race" is based upon ignorance of the fact that it is not by complexion alone that race is ascertainable. Only ignorance can see any possibility of a mixture of Anglo-Saxons to distinguish between a North American mixed blood and a white person.—Louisville Courier-Journal.

We reproduced the opinion from the Maine and Massachusetts papers only to throw into stronger relief the opinion from the Courier-Journal. Here is a writer calmly asserting that the slightest tinge of African blood is discernible, if not in the complexion, then in some trait or characteristic betraying inferiority. This is, of course, laughable. Seven-tenths of those who read these lines know of one or more persons of colored blood who are "passing."

But the cause of our digging through our files of clippings about "The Autobiography of an Ex-Colored Man" was the recent news in the New York dailies concerning the sensational developments in the proceedings to break the will of Mrs. Frank Leslie, widow of Frank Leslie, the great magazine publisher, in which it was alleged that she was a daughter of Charles Follin, of Louisiana, and that her mother was a Negro slave.

Mrs. Leslie was one of the remarkable women of this city. On the death of her husband, the various Leslie publications were in a precarious condition. She took them in hand and, by energy and intelligence, placed them on a paying basis. When she died she left an estate of almost two million dollars.

If Mrs. Leslie was a colored woman, and there are reasons to believe the allegation to be true—a large sum was spent by those who make the allegation in an investigation of Mrs. Leslie's history and pedigree; and in "Who's Who" no mention is made of Mrs. Leslie's mother—we say, if she was a colored woman, her case is stranger than any fiction.

December 23, 1915

Saluting the Flag

WE recently received the following letter, written in a boyish hand:

615 Cherry St., Des Moines, Ia.
March 20, 1916.

Mr. James W. Johnson,
   Contributing Ed. New York Age, New York.
Dear Sir: Please find enclosed clipping from the Evening Tribune of this city, date of 18th instant. The incident is very peculiar, and I am anxious to have your comment upon same. Was the Juvenile Judge justified in his ruling? Should this boy be compelled to salute the flag? Are the boy's contentions justified by the facts in the case as cited by him?
                    Very truly,
                              G. H. EDMUNDS.

The case referred to in the above letter has attracted some attention. Hubert Eaves, a colored boy eleven years old, refused to salute the American flag in accordance with the rules of the public schools of Des Moines. He was taken before the judge of the Juvenile Court, who, after hearing the case, ordered the boy to go back to school and salute the flag.

The clipping sent by G. H. Edmunds gives an extended account of the hearing. It appears that both parents of the boy were present in court and upheld him in his position. It also appears that the parents and the boy belong to a "sanctified" sect known as the Sanctified Holy Church; and the mother is reported as saying that the Holy Ghost told Hubert not to salute the flag. However, we pass over everything except the statements made by Hubert himself. The following two reasons were the ones given by him:

"I won't salute the flag at school for I do not think it is right. It doesn't have God in it.

"In the second place I haven't any country. It all belongs to the white man. If it wasn't for God, I would not be here. The white man doesn't want us."

Now, we shall take Hubert seriously. We shall assume that he knows the full weight and significance of his words; that he is actuated by conscientious scruples, and not merely led away by religious vagaries.

Carefully read the reasons stated above and we cannot but see that either one would be stronger, single and alone, than are the two of them coupled together. In fact, coupled together, they are contradictory.

In the first place, Hubert declines to salute the flag because "it doesn't have God in it"; and in the second place, he inadvertently blames God for placing him in a country against which he (Hubert) has such bitter feelings. If it is God's fault that Hubert is in such a country as he feels this to be, we do not see how it would make saluting the flag any easier for him even if it did "have God in it" and the salutation were made a solemn religious ceremony. It would seem that his second reason would make him feel as bitter against God as he does against the country.

Many people make the mistake of supposing that every human act must be classified either as right or wrong. They do not realize that there is a class of acts which, in themselves, are neither right nor wrong. And, strange to say, it is over this neuter class that many of the fiercest human conflicts have been waged. In the whole human family there is no difference of opinion as to honest dealing and truth telling being right and thieving and lying being wrong. But people will differ seriously over the right or wrong involved in going to see a circus; and wars have been fought to settle questions equally as trivial. If it may be said that there is nothing of right in the mere act of saluting the flag of one's native land, it can be said with equal certainty that there is nothing wrong in it.

Hubert, in his second reason for not saluting the flag says, "I haven't any country. It all belongs to the white man." This statement would be more rational than the first, if it were true. But is it true? It is not. Three hundred years of labor and loyalty makes this country belong to the Negroes as much as it belongs to anybody else; and a good deal more than it belongs to many who are living under its flag. Of course, we have been wronged, we are still being wronged, many of our rights are still denied us, but the American Negro is not going to renounce his rights because some people in the country are opposed to his having them. No, he is going to work and fight until his every right is recognized and accorded. If he should lie down and say, "I haven't any country. It all belongs to the white man," he would not deserve a country.

Hubert seems to feel that the country is all wrong; that God is no where in it; Hubert is mistaken. Although many, sometimes a majority, of the people in this country are wrong, yet that abstract thing we call the Country is right, and is always making for the right. It was the spirit of righteousness that gave birth to this country, and that spirit, sooner or later, in spite of opposition, always makes its power felt. For two centuries there were enough people living under the American flag who were in favor of human bondage to make the country accept it, but at last the spirit of righteousness arose and swept the land like a flame, and slavery was destroyed. Finally, every other wrong against the Negro will righted.

We say to Hubert that if God is anywhere, he is in the flag.

We realize that in the beginning we assumed more for this eleven-year-old boy than his slight shoulders should be made to bear. It is hardly to be doubted that the attitude which he has assumed is due more to the teachings of the "Sanctified Holy Church" than to anything else.

To our correspondent we say that we think the judge of the Juvenile Court was right in ordering Hubert to go back to school and conduct himself in accordance with the rules.

April 4, 1916

Responsibilities and Opportunities of the Colored Ministry

No one who travels over the country, especially through the South, can fail to be impressed with this fact: The most complete and powerful organization in the race is the Negro church. No other medium that we have can compare with the church in strength of appeal, breadth of influence and finality of authority.

In this respect the colored churches relatively constitute a more powerful organization than do the white churches. For while white people are influenced religiously by their churches, they are influenced in matters social, industrial, financial and political through other well established mediums. On the other hand, the only medium through which many millions of colored people can be reached and influenced is the church. Then it goes without saying there rests upon colored ministers greater race responsibilities and opportunities than upon any other single set of men.

The writer has several times said in this column that if the white churches of this country should unite in taking a real Christian stand on the race question, a miraculous change would be brought about; a similar statement may be made about the colored churches. If the colored churches of this country would unite in taking an intelligent and unselfish stand on all questions of vital interest to the race, there would also be brought about a miraculous change. The taking of such a stand depends entirely upon the colored ministers. It is first necessary that they come to realize the responsibilities and opportunities that their position gives them.

Of course, there are many of our ministers who do realize these responsibilities and opportunities, but the great majority, those that reach the mass of millions, have not progressed beyond the standard of ante-bellum days. They are still consuming all of their time in the pulpit, and using up some mental and a great deal of muscular energy in efforts to expound what Paul said. The things that Paul said are, of course, important and it is the duty of a minister to preach and teach them, but there are things being said by men living to-day and in this very country important enough to the race to be worthy of some of the time usually devoted to Paul.

Here is a great work which must begin with the intelligent and progressive ministers. The work of making this powerful organization not only the instrument for promoting our spiritual welfare, but our welfare as men and citizens.

February 8, 1917

Under the Dome of the Capitol

THE WRITER was present last week when Mr. Moorfield Storey argued the Louisville Segregation Ordinance Case for the National Association for the Advancement of Colored People before the United States Supreme Court at Washington. There were fifteen or twenty representative colored men at the hearing. We should like to have been possessed of the power to sound the inmost thoughts of these colored men and of the white people present and of the Justices on the bench while the two lawyers who pled the case for the other side were talking. The writer for himself must confess that at times he experienced a strange sensation while listening to the Negro discussed before this highest tribunal in the land as something just outside of American citizenship; indeed, as something just below humanity.

Both the lawyers for the other side appeared to be able men and doubtless the reasons they gave were the best that could be given to bolster up and excuse so bad a law, so undemocratic, so unconstitutional a law. But one not familiar with the case might have thought that they were pleading to have the homes of the white people of the South protected from wild beasts or against the presence of lepers. And as we sat there we wondered how far the presence of so many respectable and intelligent colored men would go to offset such an argument.

At two o'clock Chief Justice White announced a recess of thirty minutes. The writer and two other American citizens, one colored and the other white, went down in the basement to the public lunch room to get something to eat. We were met by an employee who told us we could not be served. When asked why, he informed us that Senator Overman (of North Carolina), on becoming chairman of the committee that has charge of the Capitol and grounds, issued an order that no colored person should be served in either of the lunch rooms.

This, under the very dome of the Capitol of the greatest democracy in the world! It was a thing to arouse all the hates and furies and put murder in a man's heart.

We went across to the Congressional Library and were served just as any other American citizens. The man who is responsible for the rules that govern the Library building is from the civilized state of Massachusetts.

At two-thirty we returned to the Court and heard Mr. Storey's strong plea for right and justice and humanity, and the writer felt that the better and greater part of this nation does stand for right and justice, and will ultimately see that right and justice are done. The Overmans and the Vardamans and the others of their ilk who are now in high places will not and cannot dominate long. They are riding now just as their predecessors did in the fifties, and they are going to fall just the same.

The basic spirit of America is democracy, and though that spirit is often thwarted it is constantly struggling forward and will finally prevail. When the opposing forces were at the height of their strength, the better part of this nation arose and struck down slavery. The better part of this nation changed the organic law of the land and made us citizens. And the better part of this nation is going to see that we are given full and equal justice.

The Overmans and the Vardamans and all like them will pass away, the great spirit of democracy will live and press forward forever. It only remains for us to try to keep pace with it, and we shall surely come into our own. That is my faith.

May 3, 1917

The Silent Parade

THE colored citizens of New York are arranging to hold on Saturday a silent parade of protest on Fifth avenue. It is proposed to have ten thousand men, women and children march with banners bearing inscriptions that set forth the services of labor and loyalty which the race has given to the country and the wrongs and injustices which it has been made to suffer in return.

If this purpose is successfully carried out, it will be the most effective effort ever made by the American Negro to let the nation know that he resents these wrongs and will be satisfied with nothing less than the treatment which is the rightful due of every American citizen.

It ought to be a great success. Out of the colored population of Greater New York, there should be not ten thousand but twenty thousand marchers. Such a sight as that, twenty thousand colored school children, men and women marching in silent dignity as a protest against the treatment to which the race is submitted in the United States would be so impressive that New York City and the entire country would be compelled to take notice. In fact, the effect would be felt all over the world. No mass meeting, however great, and no speeches, however eloquent, could accomplish as much.

And this is just the time for such a demonstration; with Waco and Memphis and East St. Louis still fresh in our memory and with America waging a war in the name of humanity and democracy. Such a demonstration should be made not only by the Negroes of New York, but by the Negroes in each city in the country where it is possible to do so. These demonstrations should be made now and simultaneously.

July 26, 1917

An Army with Banners

LAST Saturday the silent protest parade came off, and it was a greater success than even the committee had dared to hope it would be. Some of the New York papers estimated the number of marchers in line as high as fifteen thousand. It was indeed a mighty host, an army with banners.

No written word can convey to those who did not see it the solemn impressiveness of the whole affair. The effect could be plainly seen on the faces of the thousands of spectators that crowded along the line of march. There were no jeers, no jests, not even were there indulgent smiles; the faces of the onlookers betrayed emotions from sympathetic interest to absolute pain. Many persons of the opposite race were seen to brush a tear from their eyes. It seemed that many of these people were having brought home to them for the first time the terrible truths about race prejudice and oppression.

The power of the parade consisted in its being not a mere argument in words, but a demonstration to the sight. Here were thousands of orderly, well-behaved, clean, sober, earnest people marching in a quiet, dignified manner, declaring to New York and to the country that their brothers and sisters, people just like them, had been massacred by scores in East St. Louis for no other offense than seeking to earn an honest living; that their brothers and sisters, people just like them, were "Jim Crowed" and segregated and disfranchised and oppressed and lynched and burned alive in this the greatest republic in the world, the great leader in the fight for democracy and humanity.

The impact of this demonstration upon New York city was tremendous. And it is not strange that it was so. More than twelve thousand of us marching along the greatest street in the world, marching solemnly to no other music than the beat of muffled drums, bearing aloft our banners on which were inscribed not only what we have suffered in this country, but what we have accomplished for this country, this was a sight as has never before been seen.

But, after all, the effect on the spectators was not wholly in what they saw, it was largely in the spirit that went out from the marchers and overpowered all who came within its radius. There was no holiday air about this parade. Every man, woman and child that took part seemed to feel what it meant to the race. Even the little six year old tots that led the line seemed to realize the full significance of what was being done. And so it was that these thousands and thousands moving quietly and steadily along created a feeling very close to religious awe.

When the head of the procession paused at 30th Street I looked back and saw the long line of women in white still mounting the crest of Murray Hill, the men's column not yet in sight; and a great sob came up in my throat and in my heart a great yearning for all these people, my people, from the helpless little children just at my hand back to the strong men bringing up the rear, whom I could not even see. I turned to Dr. DuBois at my side and said, "Look!" He looked, and neither of us could tell the other what he felt.

It was a great day. An unforgettable day in the history of the race and in the history of New York City.

August 3, 1917

Experienced Men Wanted

An Age reader at Jacksonville, Florida, sends us a circular which is being distributed in connection with the army recruiting stations at Jacksonville, Tampa, Miami, Pensacola and Tallahassee, and which reads as follows:

"NON-COMMISSIONED OFFICERS WANTED
WHITE MEN
Married or Single
EXPERIENCED IN THE HANDLING
OF COLORED MEN
For Enlistment as Non-Commissioned Officers in the Service,
Battalions, Engineer Corps
NATIONAL ARMY"

"Experienced in the handling of colored men." That is about the most conspicuous example of grouping the Negro with the mule that has ever been brought to my attention. But aside from that, what kind of white non-commissioned officers does the War Department think it will get by allowing recruiting stations to advertise in the South for white men "experienced in handling colored men?" Does the War Department have any idea of what it means in the South to have experience in handling Negroes? It generally means to have the qualifications of a slave driver, of a chain-gang guard, of an overseer of the roughest kind of labor. It means to be devoid of sympathetic understanding and human kindness. Of course, if it is absolutely necessary to have white non-commissioned officers over colored troops, the Department can find lots of white men in the South who make intelligent and sympathetic officers; but it will not find these men by advertising there for white men who are *"experienced in handling Negroes."*

The War Department has adopted a policy of training Southern troops in the North and Northern troops in the South. In line with this policy, I would suggest, since the Department seems to deem it necessary that colored troops be commanded by white officers, that all white officers for colored troops be Northern men. It is true that the sort of Southern white man the Department would get by the above advertisement would have more "experience," but it would be experience of the wrong kind, it would be experience that would render him incapable of looking upon the men of his command as comrades in arms.

It is true that some of the finest and truest officers that the colored regiments of the regular army have are white men of Southern birth; but these men are entirely devoid of any "ex-

perience in handling Negroes" in the Southern sense. They
went to West Point in their teens. Direct from West Point they
went into the army and there have come to know the glorious
traditions of the four crack colored regiments of the service,
and to respect them and the men who made them. There is no
plane of comparison between these officers and men taken out
of civil life in the South and given command because of their
"experience in handling Negroes."

Getting down to common sense and plain justice, since colored men must be in strictly colored regiments, *all non-commissioned officers of these regiments should be colored men: more,
all line officers of those regiments should be colored men; and
there is no good reason why, ultimately, all the field officers of
those regiments should not be colored.*

But if it is decreed that white men must officer colored regiments, then at least let them be Northern white men who
have had no "experience."

November 8, 1917

"Why Should a Negro Fight?"

THE above heading is the heading of an editorial in the Plainfield (N.J.) Courier-News of the 11th of this month. The
Courier-News editorial was called forth by a letter written by
some colored person to the editor asking reasons why the Negro should fight to protect the country. Two Age readers in
Plainfield sent us the article and asked us to reply to it.

The letter which was sent to the editor of the Courier-News
reads as follows:

Plainfield Courier:

Dear Sir: I am a buyer of your paper and I note in your column
there are questions asked and answered. This is a question I should
like you answer me. Why is it a Negro man should go to protect a
country and public places when in it he can not even go in and drink
a glass of ice cream soda nor even his female sex?

E.R.

In the first place, this a very lightweight letter. The person writing it picked out the weakest argument that could possibly be found. Of course, the denial of the privilege of drinking ice cream soda in certain places on account of race or color is a phase of the denial of full citizenship and common democracy; but it is trivial to single it out as a reason why the Negro should not do his part in this great war. If the duty of the Negro to fight was really a question in the mind of the writer of the letter, it seems that he should have backed up his inquiry with such arguments as the lynching and burning alive of Negroes, without any effort on the part of authorities to punish the perpetrators of these crimes; the disfranchisement and "Jim Crowing" of the race, even of those who are bearing arms and wearing the uniform; the shutting out of Negroes from many of the fields of occupation; the criminally unfair division of the public school funds in many states; the absence of even handed justice in the courts of many of the states, and other arguments that would carry weight.

In the second place, the letter contained a needless request for information. Any Negro outside of an insane asylum can by ten minutes of thought on the matter arrive at reasons why the race must do its full part in this war, which will outweigh any doubts there may have been in his mind.

America is the American Negro's country. He has been here three hundred years; that is, about two hundred years longer than most of the white people. He is a citizen of this country, declared so by the Constitution. Many of the rights and privileges of citizenship are still denied him, but the plain course before him is to continue to perform all of the duties of citizenship while he continually presses his demands for all of the rights and privileges. Both efforts must go together; to perform the duties and not demand the rights would be pusillanimous; and to demand the rights and not perform the duties would be futile.

It is a fact that the Negro is denied his full rights as a citizen, and that a good many people in the country are determined that he shall never have them; then the task before the Negro is to force the accordance of those rights, and that he cannot do by refusing to perform the duties. In fact, the moment he ceases to perform the duties of citizenship he abdicates the right to claim the full rights of citizenship.

As regards the present war, the central idea behind Germany is force; if that idea wins, it will be worse for the American Negro and all the other groups belonging to submerged and oppressed peoples; so the American Negro should do all in his power to help defeat it.

Then, too, a German victory would mean the almost absolute destruction of France. France, the fountain of liberal ideas, the nation which more than any other in the world has freed itself from all kinds of prejudices, the nation which endeavors to practice as well as preach the brotherhood of man. The destruction of France would be the greatest blow to liberty that could now be dealt.

These are a few of the plain, logical reasons, based largely upon self-interest; besides there are other and more altruistic reasons; we leave the purely sentimental reasons out of consideration.

So much for the letter written to the Courier-News; now for the editorial written in answer to the letter. Here is the first sentence from it:

A Negro should fight for this country because this nation freed him from the bonds of slavery.

Now if the editor of the Courier-News put up such an argument as that to a jackass he would get his brains kicked out. What was the slavery "from which this nation freed us?" It was the slavery into which this nation put us and held us for two hundred and fifty years. Can a man throw you into prison without cause in order to place you under a debt of gratitude to him for taking you out?

The editor of the Courier-News goes on to say:

The Negro who tries to put himself on the level with white men socially is an enemy of the Negro race. The greatest men of that race have condemned those who are always finding fault because they cannot obtain service in hotels, restaurants and ice cream parlors patronized by the whites. It is the duty of these dissatisfied Negroes to open restaurants and ice cream parlors of their own and endeavor to conduct them better than any white man conducts his place of business.

We do not know from what part of the country the editor of the Courier-News hails, but his definition of "social equality" sounds very much as though it was made in Alabama or Mississippi. There is no more social equality in drinking ice cream soda in a public place than there is in riding in the same subway car. And where does this editor get his information that the greatest men of the race have condemned those who found fault because hotel and other public accommodations were refused to colored people?

His suggestion that Negroes should have their own hotels, theatres and other public places is impracticable. It would be impossible for the Negro or any other group in this country to duplicate the machinery of civilization. If a colored man is passing through Denver or Salt Lake City, is he to go without food and lodging because there are not enough Negroes in either of those cities to maintain a hotel or a restaurant? But even if the Negro could duplicate all of the machinery of civilization in the country and live his life separate and apart, would it be wise to have him do it? We are now trying to cut the hyphen out of our body politic, would it be wise to deliberately create another?

It is curious to note the amount of ego that goes with the attitude of the editor of the Courier-News on this question. He sits writing his little article shaming Negroes for wanting to associate with white people, not imagining for a moment that there are colored people who not only would not seek him for a social equal, but who probably might refuse to accept him as one. If he should be stopping at the Van-Astor hotel, and a colored man came in to register, the first thought to crop up in his mind would be, "Here is a Negro who wants to get into a hotel where I, a white man, and other white men are stopping," not knowing that what the Negro wants is something to eat and a place to sleep and that he is willing to pay for the best he can afford.

This ego is characteristic off all white people who talk like the editor of the Courier-News. They feel, when a Negro protests against discrimination and "Jim Crowism" that he is trying to get away from his race and associate with white people. When a self-respecting Negro so protests, the thought of merely associating with white people is the farthest from his mind; he is contending for a common democratic right which all other citizens of the country have, that of being accommodated in public places when he is clean, orderly and is able and willing to pay the price; or he is protesting against being forced to accept inferior service for the price of the best service, and he is especially resenting the badge of inferiority which being "Jim Crowed" places upon him.

This article of the Courier-News runs on for the length of a column, nearly all of it being a diatribe against Negroes who are seeking "social equality," meaning those who object to being "Jim Crowed" and shut out of theatres and hotels and restaurants and other public places where orderly conduct and the price are the only requisites exacted from other citizens. So it is not worth the while to quote any more of it.

We wish to say that there are many sound and solid reasons why the Negro should fight for his country, aside from the reasons that are altruistic and sentimental; but the editor of the Courier-News in using up a column of his more or less valuable space in answering the letter of E. R. failed to strike upon a single one.

The letter written to the Courier-News was lightweight, but the editor's article in answer to it did not weigh as much as the letter. His article is entirely apart from the mark.

June 29, 1918

"Negro" With a Big "N"

ONE of our readers in Newark recently sent us some correspondence which he had had with Mr. Ochs, owner of the New York Times, relative to the policy of that great paper in always printing the word "Negro" with a small "n." Our correspondent wrote to Mr. Ochs complaining of this policy of The Times and received the following letter in reply:

Dear Sir:

Mr. Ochs has asked me to acknowledge your letter presenting arguments for spelling the word "Negro" with a capital letter.

The question has often been discussed. Generally the small letter is used in newspapers. From our point of view, the capitalization of the word would tend to accentuate a separateness of the colored portion of the population. That is just what we should avoid, is it not? Our view is that we should no more capitalize "negro" than "white." It would be calling special attention to the hue of a man's skin, accentuating a difference among Americans of different colors.

Yours very truly,

R. H. GRAVES,

RHG/B   Sunday Editor.

It is hard to believe that this letter is from the Sunday Editor of the New York Times. We would not expect a letter of such weak reasoning from a backward child. In the first place, it brings a smile that hurts our face to think of the editorial staff of The Times delicately considering not to do anything that would "tend to accentuate a separateness of the colored portion of the population." In the second place, any ten year old boy ought to be able to see the fallacy of the grammatical reason that is usually given in support of using the small "n" in "Negro." The argument it that the word "Negro" is an adjective, and adjectives are not written with capital letters.

This argument entirely ignores the fact that words in a living language have no fixed value or meaning. Many words are born and go through various changes in meaning; often they absolutely die; and sometimes they are reborn with still a different shade of meaning. For example, several centuries ago the word "wench" was a perfectly proper term to be applied to a woman, especially if she was a servant; but let any lady now apply the term to her cook, and she will have a fight on hand or the job of looking for another cook or both. There are also words that are born as outcasts, but finally acquire good standing in a language; the classic example in the American language is the word "blizzard."

This argument also ignores the fact that there are two kinds of grammar—grammatical grammar and logical grammar. Grammatical grammar rules that a singular subject must take a verb in the singular; but we may say, "The committee has decide thus and so." The use of a singular or plural verb depends upon whether we are thinking of the committee as a single body or as made up of several individuals.

Grammarians, who write the rules, are always trying to establish grammatical grammar, to give words a fixed and unchangeable status, but the people, who use the language, are constantly overriding the grammarians and establishing logical grammar; that is, giving to words the status and meaning which they have come to have through use.

We all know that philological research will show that the word "Negro" was originally an adjective meaning black. This is especially true of the Latin languages; for example in Spanish, *un hombre negro* means a black man, and *un caballo negro* means a black horse. But logical grammar and just a little plain, common sense tells us that when the word "Negro" is used not to qualify, but to denominate a race of people it is no longer an adjective, it is a proper name and should be written with a capital letter.

The Sunday Editor of The Times says: "Our view is that we should no more capitalize 'negro' than 'white.' It would be calling special attention to the hue of a man's skin, accentuating a difference among Americans of different colors." It seems here that he has the whole thing backwards. When he writes the word "negro" with a small letter it is an adjective and means black. When he writes the word "Negro" with a capital letter it is not an adjective, it is a proper name and does not necessarily mean black. So there is less danger of calling special attention to the hue of a man's skin in writing "Negro" than is writing "negro."

The history and growth of the use of the word "Negro" is somewhat curious. For a good many years the more advanced elements of the race objected to the term, and there are still many that object to it. We frankly admit that there are grounds for their objection. The growth of the use of the word is due mainly to two things; the fact that some years ago certain race leaders determined to redeem the word, and to the fact that it is a shorter word than "colored" and so fits better in the headlines. The headline writer can make a display in bigger type when he says, "NEGRO BURNED AT THE STAKE" than he could by saying, "COLORED MAN BURNED AT THE STAKE." The headline writer has, perhaps, done more to make the word general than anybody else.

Of course, there arises a question as to the wisdom of adopting a name that needed to be "redeemed." Why name a boy Benedict Arnold when he could be as easily named George Washington? Nor can it be helped but noticed that white people themselves, when they wish to speak softly to and about the race use the adjective "colored." The Sunday Editor of The Times does it in his letter. It must also be admitted that the term, "The Negro" sets us off absolutely. So far as names go, at least, it would be much easier to go from "colored American" to "American citizen" than from "The Negro" to "American citizen." In fact, it may be said that so long as the race is exclusively known as "The Negro" it will not be a full participator in American democracy.

But the race leaders who adopted "Negro" to redeem it had their good reasons. We are a separate people with needs different from the rest of the population; so the men who had to talk and write for the race felt the need of some concrete term; they could not be continually writing in adjectival phrases. Other race names were tried, "Afro-American," "Ethio-American," etc., but they were all found too clumsy. So "Negro" has come to be the race name used generally by the writers and newspaper men of the race; and whatever objections there may be to it, it is the best concrete term for the race that has yet been found.

But what's in a name? Our condition is the main thing to be changed; the name will take care of itself. However, we do insist that sticklers for grammatical grammar and others recognize that the word "Negro" when used to designate a race, is not an adjective, but a proper name, and should be written with a capital letter.

August 17, 1918

Protesting Women and the War

MISS Alice Paul has issued to the members of the National Woman's party an appeal to protest with all the strength and vigor they have in order to get the Suffrage Amendment through the Senate. She declared, "If enough women protest, and protest with sufficient vigor, the Federal Suffrage Amendment will be passed." She urged upon all who would not be able to take part in the protest demonstration in front of the White House on September 16, to contribute financially to the fall election campaign in the West, when voting women will be called upon to protest through their votes against the Democratic party's continued blocking of the amendment enfranchising women.

Miss Paul said further: "The Suffrage Amendment is still blocked in the Senate. The Administration and the Senate show no signs of acting on it."

Of course, Miss Paul must know the reason why the Suffrage Amendment is being blocked in the Senate. It is being blocked because the Southern senators, and they control the Senate, are opposed to it. And the Southern senators are opposed to it because they are opposed to the enfranchisement of colored women in the South.

This is the irony of the whole Negro problem; the white people of the South have to deny themselves many of the good things that they need and want because they are not willing for the Negro to have them too. They deny themselves compulsory education laws because these laws would also compel the colored child to go to school. The white women of the South evidently would like to have the vote, but their Senators must fight against the national enfranchisement of women because they do not want colored women in the South to be enfranchised.

The question might arise in the minds of some, why are these politicans so afraid of giving the vote to the colored women of the South, could they not disfranchise them as easily as they have disfranchised the men? There comes the rub; we believe the Southern politicians know just what we know, and that is that the colored women, if given the vote, could not be kept out of their rights so easily as the colored men have been kept out. Often as a matter of compliment men say that the women are the most worthy sex. That is no compliment when applied to colored women, it is simply a statement of fact.

Three-fourths of what the Negro has amounted to in America is due to the colored women. For the past fifty years they have struggled on patiently and bravely, never shirking. Negro fathers who are lazy, trifling and no good, who have deserted wife and children when the load grew a little heavy, can be counted by the thousands; but the Negro mothers have stuck, they have slaved and sacrificed to keep these same children fed and clothed and in school. The colored mother who deserts her post is such a *rara avis* that she may be said not to exist.

If these women who have struggled so heroically for fifty years and held the race together are given the vote, it may be depended upon that they will put up a better fight to hold it and exercise it than the men have put up. Perhaps the Southern politicians know this.

But this is the thought that struck us when we read Miss Paul's call upon the women of the country to protest; the white women of the United States have more privileges and power than any women in the world; it seems that they have about everything that the feminine heart could desire; the only thing they appear to lack is the symbol of political power, the ballot, and for this they are protesting. They are not only demanding it in spoken and written language and by all the pressure they are able to bring upon the national law making body, they are protesting by demonstrations in front of the President's house.

Now, if it is right for these women who have so much to go to such lengths while the country is at war because they have not yet been given the ballot, why is it wrong for the Negro to protest during the war because members of the race are burned alive at the stake?

This war is going to bring many changes, but it is not going to work any miracles for the Negro. It is simply giving him the chance to work out his own salvation, and if he doesn't start to working out that salvation now, he had just as well leave the job alone. If he thinks that by merely going along and doing his duty humbly and faithfully, somebody is coming along after the war and say, "Well done, thou good and faithful servant, come up higher," he is in for the biggest disappointment in his history. The Negro, just as the women of America and the laboring classes of England, have got to take intelligent thought and action now to insure any future benefits which they hope to gain.

September 21, 1918

The Japanese Question in California

SENATOR Phelan of California comes out in the press this week in a most gloomy prediction for this state. He foresees in the increase of the birth rate of Japanese there the complete overwhelming of the white race. He bases his gloomy predictions on the conditions which allow Japanese women to come into California as the wives of Japanese men already living there. One of the stipulations the gentleman's agreement between Japan and the United States was that Japan would allow no more of her laborers to come to this country. The wives of laborers were, however, excepted; as a result large numbers of Japanese women have been steadily coming in as wives of the laborers already here.

It is against these women that Senator Phelan raises his warning. He says they not only work as laborers, but are giving birth to large families and thereby increasing the Japanese population, in spite of immigration restrictions. He says:

> These women work in the fields as laborers and so circumvent the agreement, and then they give birth to children and thus defeat the purpose of the agreement by increasing the horde of non-assimilable aliens who are crowding the white men and women off the land. If this is not checked now it means the end of the white race in California, the subversion of American institutions and the end of our Western civilization. The fight is on. On which side do you stand?

The feeling against the Japanese on the Pacific Coast is almost entirely economic. But it is not, as some might suppose, because the Japanese work for less wages than the whites and so reduce the standards of living; it is because the Japanese work harder and longer than the whites, because they can make money where the whites fail, because they set too hard a pace in work for the whites to follow.

The Japanese have gotten on the land, and certain products of the land on the Pacific Coast are wholly in their control. They almost completely control the truck farm products and the berry products of that whole region. They work on the land longer hours, they cultivate it more painstakingly, and they get better results from it than the whites. The white man does not want to work that hard. He wants some time to ride around in his Ford and to socialize. As a result he can't stand the competition, and he is being driven off the land. From this arises the prejudice against the Japanese on the Coast. We could wish that that was the cause of prejudice against Negroes in the South.

The Japanese are fast coming into possession of the land in California and other Pacific States. In the public markets of Seattle the finest vegetable and fruit stalls are owned by Japanese; and they have white men and women working for them. These Japanese are getting possession of the land and they are making money, and their money they are investing in business. If they keep it up for a generation longer, they will be in a position to defy Senator Phelan and all others like him.

It is an eye-opener to any colored man to see what the Japanese have done on the Pacific Coast, in spite of prejudice and laws against them. One can ride for miles and miles and see nothing but Japanese at work on the land. One can arrive at a station and see car after car being loaded with berries; and all of the loading, all of the shipping, all of the clerking, all of the handling both of the berries and the money being done by Japanese.

Nevertheless, we think that Senator Phelan's forecast is too dark. We do not think that Japanese thrift will mean the "end of the white race in California and the subversion of American institutions and Western civilization." The Japanese are not trying to overthrow anything in California; they are only asking to be let alone to extract the best living they can out of the soil by their own labor.

If industry and thrift on the part of Japanese farmers mean the end of the white race in California—well, let it end; for the truth would be that it had already reached the point of decay and rot if it could not stand the fair competition of hard work, industry and energy expended on the soil

July 12, 1919

The "Jim Crow" Car in Congress

LAST WEEK Congressman Madden of Illinois went before the House Interstate and Foreign Commerce Committee and urged the abolition of the "Jim Crow" car in interstate railroad traffic. This he did in support of a bill which he has introduced requiring "equal and identical rights, accommodations and privileges" for both races on railway trains. Mr. Madden declared that the Government has no right to draft its citizens in defense of the flag and at the same time say to them that their rights are inferior to those of other citizens of the United States. He added that Chinese and Japanese are allowed to ride on trains on equal conditions with the whites.

Representative Rayburn of Texas and Sanders of Louisiana, members of the committee, answered Mr. Madden by stating that the Negroes of the South did not want to ride in the cars with the white people.

Mr. Rayburn said: "You want to force the Negroes to ride in the cars with the white people, when the Negroes themselves would rather ride in separate cars than be mixed up with white people."

Mr. Sanders said: "We of the South contend that the Negro prefers separate accommodations. Our Negroes down South, knowing they are not welcome in the white man's coach, don't go in."

Both Mr. Rayburn and Mr. Sanders hold the egotistic position of the Southern white man on this matter; that is, that with colored people who protest against the "Jim Crow" car it is a question of riding with white people. It is not a question of riding with white people, it is a question of paying equal fare for inferior accommodations, and of having to submit to the humiliation of being compelled to ride in this inferior place which is designated for them and no one else. To say that the white people are compelled to ride in the first class car is only to play with words.

Many people in the North make the same mistake regarding hotel accommodations. They think that a colored man in going to a white hotel is seeking to be with white people. The truth of the matter is he is looking for something to eat and a decent place to sleep. This whole idea is only a demonstration of the supreme egotism of the white man. He thinks to himself that the Negro looks up to him as a paragon, as the one thing to be desired and to be near. In truth, the Negro often looks down on him as the most damnable hypocrite, scoundrel and savage that the world ever saw.

The greatest illumination is shed on the mind of Mr. Sanders of Louisiana by his use of the phrase, "Our Negroes down South." Mr. Sanders is here using the phrase in just about the same sense as it was used by the slaveholders of Louisiana before the Civil War.

Sooner or later the Government must face this question of discrimination on the railroads which it is operating. And if the Government ceases to operate the railroads, the Supreme Court of the United States must face the question, at least, as it applies to interstate traffic.

We wish more power to Mr. Madden of Illinois.

September 13, 1919

A Real Poet

FOR YEARS the great poet has been regarded as the highest manifestation of the intellectual, esthetic, and in many cases spiritual, powers of a race. In the names that have come down through history it is those of the great poets that blaze out brightest. It is chiefly upon the achievements of such poets that races and peoples claim greatness for themselves.

There are, of course, four names which in their influence and appeal stand on a level with or even above the greatest poets. They are Buddha, Confucius, Christ and Mohammed. But these four great religious teachers were after all great ethical poets. Judged in every light they do represent the highest peaks of the genius of the races that produced them. But these names are limited to oriental races. No occidental race has yet produced a great religious teacher. Among the occidental peoples the great poet still stands almost unrivaled. There are other lists, of course, that contain names of wide influence and appeal. For example, the soldiers' list can show Alexander, Cæsar and Napoleon. But there is not an occidental people in which the final test would not put its greatest poet above its greatest soldier.

The times are slightly changed and the glamor about the poet may be somewhat dimmed. We are living in a very material age, and the man of science, the man who is able to bend the forces of nature to the well being of humanity is coming into ascendency. There may come a time when from achievements in science there will spring names that will shed a luster as bright and enduring as the names of Homer, Shakespeare, Dante, Moliere and Goethe.

However, to my mind, this is improbable. The materialism of the present age may be but a transitory state. Moreover, although the scientist may contribute what in the ultilitarian sense is far more important to humanity, he can never take hold of the imaginations of men and stir their souls like the poet. It therefore seems that as long as man loves the beautiful the great poet will hold his supreme place.

I have indulged in this rather weighty sounding introduction simply to induce a train of thought. I wish my readers to think of the production of poets by a race as a vital thing. It is vital not only as an indication of the development of the race but it is vital as to the place and recognition which that race is given by the world at large.

In accordance with the temper of the age, and more particularly, in accordance with false ideas with which the mind of the Negro in America has been impregnated, we Aframericans are prone to think of one of our number who conducts a successful corner grocery store as being far more vital and important as a factor in our progress than one who turns out a sheaf of poems, even though the poems are real poetry. We are prone to think of the grocer as one who is laying foundations stones in our racial greatness and of the poet as doing little more than wasting his time.

Without disparaging the successful grocer, I must say that this evaluation is all wrong. It would be interesting, if it were possible, to calculate how many successful Negro grocers it would take to equal the force of Paul Laurence Dunbar as a factor in the progress of the race and in having the progress recognized by the world. I am now driving at the truth contained in the words of Jesus Christ when He said, "Man shall not live by bread alone." If the race would develop its greatness and highest possibilities it needs not only to support its grocers but also to appreciate its poets.

All of this is merely introductory to a few words to call attention to a Negro poet who has risen like a new and flaming star on the horizon. The poet is Claude McKay.

Mr. McKay deserves a full and prompt appreciation. We should not do in his case what were guilty of in the case of Dunbar, that was, not to recognize or not even to know his greatness until it was acclaimed by the whites.

Mr. McKay is a real poet and a great poet. I mean by this that he has both the poetic endowment and the ability to make that endowment articulate, and he is yet far from his full growth. He is still a young man. He is a poet of beauty and a poet of power. No Negro poet has sung more beautifully of his own race than McKay and no Negro poet that equalled the power with which he expresses the bitterness that so often rises in the heart of the race. As an example of that power we quote his sonnet, "If We Must Die," written after the terrible riots in the summer of 1919:

> If we must die, let it not be like hogs
> Hunted and penned in an inglorious spot,
> While round us bark the mad and hungry dogs,
> Making their mock at our accursed lot.
> If we must die, O let us nobly die,
> So that our precious blood may not be shed
> In vain; then even the monsters we defy
> Shall be constrained to honor us though dead!
>
> O kinsmen! we must meet the common foe!
> Though far outnumbered let us show us brave,
> And for their thousand blows deal one deathblow!
> What though before us lies the open grave?
> Like men we'll face the murderous, cowardly pack,
> Pressed to the wall, dying, but fighting back!

The race ought to be proud of a poet capable of voicing it so fully. Such a voice is not found every day.

Mr. McKay's volume, "Harlem Shadows," published by Harcourt, Brace & Company, New York, is already attracting the attention of the critics of the country. What he has achieved in this little volume sheds honor upon the whole race.

May 20, 1922

Marcus Garvey's Inferiority Complex

IN REPLY to certain statements made by William Pickens regarding the Universal Negro Improvement Association, Marcus Garvey is quoted in the "Negro World" of August 19 as delivering himself as follows:

"You know some of us lose knowledge of ourselves sometimes. In the tropics, where I come from, you will find every well-to-do Negro losing knowledge of himself. That is, the moment a white man smiles with him, pats him on the shoulder and invites him to dinner for once, he loses knowledge of himself, and starts to believe that he is a white man. I wonder if anybody has patted Pickens on the shoulder; I wonder if anybody has taken Pickens by the hand; I wonder if anybody has invited Pickens to dinner, and I would not doubt that he has been invited to dinner, because I have seen him recently very much in the company of white folks, and any time a Negro gets into the company of white folks he becomes a dangerous Negro."

Has Mr. Garvey any realization of the revelation he is making of himself when he expresses such a sentiment as the above? Evidently, Mr. Garvey does not see that he is placing himself in a position far more contemptible and ignominious than the one in which he seeks to place Mr. Pickens. When Mr. Garvey expresses the belief that at any time a Negro associates with white people he feels so flattered that he becomes a boot-licking sycophant and a parasite, he is revealing what the Freudian psychologists would call an inferiority complex.

What becomes of Mr. Garvey's boasts about the equality and even the superiority of the Negro if within himself he feels that a Negro cannot sit down with a white man, look him in the face and talk with him, or eat with him—in a word, that a Negro and a white man cannot extend to each other the simple courtesies of life—without the Negro feeling himself greatly flattered and having his head turned? If this is true, any boasts about the Negro's equality is sheer humbug. If this is true, the future of the U.N.I.A. under Mr. Garvey's leadership hangs on a very slender thread.

Suppose some day a white man should invite Mr. Garvey to dinner and he did summon enough courage to go. According to his beliefs, the Negroes of the U.N.I.A. would from that hour henceforth be minus a Moses. It appears that Mr. Garvey's only security in maintaining his sense of equality and superiority is to steer clear of white folks.

Mr. Garvey pretends to speak for the colored people in the tropics where he came from. We feel more inclined to believe that he is speaking for his own subconscious self and that he is expressing the way he would feel if "patted on the shoulder" by a white man. However, Mr. Garvey knows more about the people of his home than we do. But, we can give him the information that in the United States, at least, there are hundreds and thousands of colored people who can and do associate with white people and without feeling themselves in any way flattered by the association. They take it simply as a matter of common human relations, as a matter of course. We can also inform Mr. Garvey that there are masses of white people with whom these same hundreds and thousands of colored people in the United States would refuse to associate.

We can also inform Mr. Garvey that there are a great many white people in the United States who can and do associate with colored people without being in any degree condescending or patronizing; they, too, take such association simply as a matter of common human relations, as a matter of course.

Any colored man who feels, like Mr. Garvey, that no Negro can associate with white people without feeling flattered and becoming a bootlicker may well question whether or not he actually does believe in his own equality.

If Mr. Garvey cannot understand the implications of his attack on Mr. Pickens he ought to go and have himself psychoanalyzed, and he will find that he has an inferiority complex. His over loud boastings about his own equality are obvious indications of that complex.

September 2, 1922

The New Exodus

THE EXODUS of Negroes from the South is assuming proportions that are causing great alarm among the white people of that section. The principal newspapers of Georgia are discussing the question pro and con. Some of them are endeavoring to belittle the whole movement. The Atlanta "Constitution" is inclined to attach small importance to it and to attribute the movement such as it is, more to economic than to other reasons.

On the other hand, the Macon "News" regards the present situation as a most serious one. It quotes Mr. Stanley, the Commissioner of Labor of Georgia, who makes an estimate the Negroes are leaving the state at the rate of two hundred and fifty and upwards a day.

A number of prominent leaders of the African Methodist Episcopal Church met in Atlanta and after discussing the situation issued a report upon it. The report set up that the colored people "are giving away the earnings of a lifetime; they are ruining our church membership; they are breaking up our churches to the extent that they often take the pastor with them." The report makes a plea for fair treatment. On this point the report as published in the Atlanta "Constitution" says, "The 'Constitution' has pleaded for years that, while we are separate here from a social standpoint, our interests are common and that the Negro should be given a fair chance to make the most of himself and family."

We can easily understand how the leaders of the colored churches in the South feel about this movement. It will very seriously affect their organizations. But the churches will not be the only ones to suffer. Colored business and professional men will suffer just the same. What the colored leaders, religious, professional and business, ought to avoid in this situation is exactly what some of them did when the movement was on several years ago. They should not appeal to the white people to help stop the exodus either by persuasion or prohibition. They should make it an opportunity to demand the removal as far as possible of the main causes for the exodus.

These leaders are in a position where they do not need to make an appeal. They can make a strong, unqualified demand and place the burden of responsibility upon the white people. For example, we have one of these religious leaders commending the following statement which occurred in an editorial in the "Constitution."

"The Negro belongs in the South. He has shown remarkable physical, mental, moral and material development in the South. He deserves fair treatment."

That sort of statement is too wishy-washy and sentimental. Why does the Negro belong in the South. Any man worth his salt belongs where he can do best. There is nothing sacred about the Negro having been born in the South. History is filled with examples of men who have left the lands in which their forefathers have lived for thousands of years when their conditions became oppressive and they felt that they could better themselves. If the Negro can come North and better his condition economically, educationally and politically, he would be nothing less than a fool to stay in the South simply because he was born there.

We hope that this movement will assume such proportions as will make the white South realize that it can no longer treat the Negro as he has been treated and still keep him in the South. We also hope that the colored leaders in the South will take advantage of the opportunity that this movement offers to demand fairer treatment, treatment that will at least include freedom from peonage, a fair share of the educational fund, the right to vote under the same qualifications required of other citizens, common justice in the courts and the abolishment of lynching. However, whether the South concedes fairer treatment to the Negro or not, we hope the movement will keep up. The longer it keeps up, still more will the South be inclined to give fairer and still fairer treatment.

But under all circumstances the Negro will be better off if a million or two of them can come out of the South. As we said before, there are too many of them packed up there. This condition makes Negroes cheap in every respect, not only as labor but as life. It will be far better for them to spread over the country. We only hope that they will not crowd into the cities in large numbers. As many as are able should try and get on the land in the Middle West and in the Northwest.

Let the exodus keep up and let Negroes North and South, leaders and masses, endeavor to take the fullest strategic advantage of the movement.

March 3, 1923

SELECTED ESSAYS

The Riots

I REACHED Washington early in the evening of July 22. As the train neared the capital I could feel the tenseness of the situation grow. It showed itself in the air of the passengers as they read the newspapers, with their glaring headlines telling of the awful night before and intimating that the worst was yet to come. As I passed through the cars on my way to the diner and back, men and women glanced up at me with what seemed to be a look of mild surprise; with a glance which seemed to say, "This man must indeed have very important business in Washington."

The porters and waiters plainly showed the strain under which they were doing their work—the strain of suppressed excitement with, perhaps, an added sense of dread of going into something, they knew not what. They moved about quietly, in fact, grimly and entirely without their customary good humor and gaiety. One of the porters who knew who I was questioned the wisdom of my going through with the trip. I may have felt that his question was not absolutely without reason, but I did not admit it. When I left the car he said to me, "Take good care of yourself." I assured him that I would spare no effort to do so.

I had made many trips to Washington—some as a mere visitor, some as a member of the Government's Foreign Service, some for the purpose of placing for the National Association matters affecting the race before men high in authority and position; and so I had experienced varied emotions on making the trip to the Nation's Capital, but none like the emotions experienced on this trip. I knew it to be true, but it was almost an impossibility for me to realize as a truth that men and women of my race were being mobbed, chased, dragged from street cars, beaten and killed within the shadow of the dome of the Capitol, at the very front door of the White House. It was almost an impossibility for me to realize that, perhaps, my own life would not be safe on the public streets.

When we reached the Northwest Section of the city, I found the whole atmosphere entirely different. I had expected to find the colored people excited and, perhaps, panicky; I found them calm and determined, unterrified and unafraid. Although on the night before shots had blazed all through the night at the corners of Seventh and T Streets and Fourteenth and U, I could detect no signs of nervousness on the part of the colored people living in the section. They had reached the determination that they would defend and protect themselves and their homes at the cost of their lives, if necessary, and that determination rendered them calm.

Still, under the outward calm there was a tautness that could be sensed. Wild rumors had been circulating all day foreboding terrible things; and these things, whatever they might be, the colored people had made up their minds to meet. But as darkness came on, the rain began to fall, and later it fell in torrents; so it may be that the rain had something to do with the things that did not happen.

That evening I met with a half-dozen of the influential colored men of the city. We talked over what had happened and discussed the steps already taken by the authorities and by the colored citizens and such steps as we thought it well to take on the following day.

The next morning Mr. Seligmann and I had a conference with Major Pullman, Chief of Police, regarding the protection of colored citizens. At this interview Mr. Seligmann secured for the information of the National Office and for purposes of publicity data regarding all the alleged cases of attacks on women which had been put forward as the cause of the riots. Our conference with Major Pullman lasted an hour; he expressed a desire to have us talk with Commissioner Brownlow and made an appointment with him for us at two o'clock in the afternoon. Before we left Major Pullman's office a committee consisting of Dr. A. M. Curtis, young Dr. Curtis and Mr. Emmett J. Scott, accompanied by Captain Doyle of the 8th Police Precinct, came to ask that the Police Department swear in a number of colored men as Special Officers to aid in preserving law and order. Mr. Seligmann and I remained and gave our support to the committee. However, it was plain that

Major Pullman was not favorable to the plan. He suggested that the committee take the matter up with his superior, Commissioner Brownlow. Mr. Seligmann and I then informed the committee of our appointment with the Commissioner at two o'clock, and invited them to go.

In the afternoon we had a long conference with Commissioner Brownlow. The whole situation was gone over, and the plan of commissioning colored men as Special Officers was brought up. The Commissioner was stronger in his opposition than the Chief of Police.

In the evening I attended a meeting of the Executive Committee of the Washington Branch to learn what the branch had done and was doing, and to offer such suggestions as I might. I found that the branch had been active as far back as July 9 when it sent a strong letter to all four of the Washington daily papers, calling their attention to the fact that they were sowing the seeds of a race riot by their inflammatory headlines and sensational news articles. After the outbreak of the riots a committee had been appointed which went before Commissioners Brownlow and Gardner and before Major Pullman to urge that effective action be taken to prevent assaults upon defenseless colored people who were the victims of the attacks. Members of the Legal Committee had spent considerable time in court in connection with the trials of the men who had been arrested for carrying weapons for their protection. A committee was set at work obtaining affidavits from victims of the riot who had been wounded or injured. And at this meeting the Legal Committee was authorized to interview all colored persons charged with rioting and offer them legal assistance.

On the following morning I went to the Capitol and talked at length with three influential Senators. I went over the whole situation, not only local, but national, with these Senators, and did my best to show them what I considered to be the principal causes of the trouble. I also spoke to each one of them regarding a Congressional investigation of the whole question of mob violence. I was able to secure from one of these Senators, who has been in Congress for twenty-five years and is a member with experience and prestige, and who is also a strong advocate of justice for the Negro, the promise that he would father a resolution calling for such an investigation and a printed report on the same.

In the afternoon I went to the office of the *Washington Post* and talked with the city editor. It was the *Post* which on Monday morning had published the "Mobilization for Tonight" call to the idle service men in Washington to meet near the Knights of Columbus hut, on Pennsylvania Avenue, and organize a "clean up." When I handed the city editor my card, he appeared glad to see me. He seemed to be under the impression that I had come down from New York for the express purpose of telling the colored people in Washington to be "good." He called a reporter and asked me to tell him what the Association was doing and proposed to do in the matter.

I lost no time in telling him that the organization which I represented stood for law and order; that all the fights it had made in behalf of the colored people had been made through and under the law; but that my reason for calling on him was not to discuss that phase of the situation. I then proceeded to tell him frankly and directly how responsible were the *Washington Post* and the other Washington dailies for what had taken place.

I talked with him for, perhaps, half an hour. During the whole time he stood as one struck dumb; at least, he answered not a word. I realized that the man was scared through and through. He asked me before I left if I thought the riots were over. I told him I thought they were, unless the whites again took the aggressive. I was surprised to see the next morning that the *Post* published some of the things I had said.

The next day, accompanied by Mr. R. C. Bruce, I made similar visits to the offices of the *Washington Times* and the *Washington Star*. In the afternoon I talked again with one of my Senators. At night I left for New York.

I returned disquieted, but not depressed over the Washington riot; it might have been worse. It might have been a riot in which the Negroes, unprotected by the law, would not have had the spirit to protect themselves.

The Negroes saved themselves and saved Washington by their determination not to run, but to fight—fight in defense of their lives and their homes. If the white mob had gone on unchecked—and it was only the determined effort of black men that checked it—Washington would have been another and worse East St. Louis.

As regrettable as are the Washington and the Chicago riots, I feel that they mark the turning point in the psychology of the whole nation regarding the Negro problem.

The Crisis, 1919

Self-Determining Haiti

I. THE AMERICAN OCCUPATION

To know the reasons for the present political situation in Haiti, to understand why the United States landed and has for five years maintained military forces in that country, why some three thousand Haitian men, women, and children have been shot down by American rifles and machine guns, it is necessary, among other things, to know that the National City Bank of New York is very much interested in Haiti. It is necessary to know that the National City Bank controls the National Bank of Haiti and is the depository for all of the Haitian national funds that are being collected by American officials, and that Mr. R. L. Farnham, vice-president of the National City Bank, is virtually the representative of the State Department in matters relating to the island republic. Most Americans have the opinion—if they have any opinion at all on the subject—that the United States was forced, on purely humane grounds, to intervene in the black republic because of the tragic coup d'etat which resulted in the overthrow and death of President Vilbrun Guillaume Sam and the execution of the political prisoners confined at Port-au-Prince, July 27–28, 1915; and that this government has been compelled to keep a military force in Haiti since that time to pacify the country and maintain order.

The fact is that for nearly a year before forcible intervention on the part of the United States this government was seeking to compel Haiti to submit to "peaceable" intervention. Toward the close of 1914 the United States notified the government of Haiti that it was disposed to recognize the newly-elected president, Theodore Davilmar, as soon as a Haitian commission would sign at Washington "satisfactory protocols" relative to a convention with the United States on the model of the Dominican-American Convention. On December 15, 1914, the Haitian government, through its Secretary of Foreign Affairs, replied: "The Government of the Republic of Haiti would consider itself lax in its duty to the United States and to itself if it allowed the least doubt to exist of its

irrevocable intention not to accept any control of the administration of Haitian affairs by a foreign Power." On December
19, the United States, through its legation at Port-au-Prince,
replied that in expressing its willingness to do in Haiti what
had been done in Santo Domingo it "was actuated entirely by
a disinterested desire to give assistance."

Two month later, the Theodore government was overthrown by a revolution and Vilbrun Guillaume was elected
president. Immediately afterwards there arrived at Port-au-
Prince an American commission from Washington—the Ford
mission. The commissioners were received at the National
Palace and attempted to take up the discussion of the convention that had been broken off in December, 1914. However,
they lacked full powers and no negotiations were entered into.
After several days, the Ford mission sailed for the United
States. But soon after, in May, the United States sent to Haiti
Mr. Paul Fuller, Jr., with the title Envoy Extraordinary, on a
special mission to apprise the Haitian government that the
Guillaume administration would not be recognized by the
American government unless Haiti accepted and signed the
project of a convention which he was authorized to present.
After examining the project the Haitian government submitted to the American commission a counter-project, formulat-
ing the conditions under which it would be possible to accept
the assistance of the United States. To this counter-project Mr.
Fuller proposed certain modifications, some of which were accepted by the Haitian government. On June 5, 1915, Mr. Fuller
acknowledged the receipt of the Haitian communication regarding these modifications, and sailed from Port-au-Prince.

Before any further discussion of the Fuller project between
the two governments, political incidents in Haiti led rapidly to
the events of July 27 and 28. On July 27 President Guillaume
fled to the French Legation, and on the same day took place a
massacre of the political prisoners in the prison at Port-au-
Prince. On the morning of July 28 President Guillaume was
forcibly taken from French Legation and killed. On the afternoon of July 28 an American man-of-war dropped anchor in
the harbor of Port-au-Prince and landed American forces. It
should be borne in mind that through all of this the life of not
a single American citizen had been taken or jeopardized.

The overthrow of Guillaume and its attending consequences did not constitute the cause of American intervention
in Haiti, but merely furnished the awaited opportunity. Since
July 28, 1915, American military forces have been in control of
Haiti. These forces have been increased until there are now
somewhere near three thousand Americans under arms in the
republic. From the very first, the attitude of the Occupation
has been that it was dealing with a conquered territory. Haitian forces were disarmed, military posts and barracks were
occupied, and the National Palace was taken as headquarters
for the Occupation. After selecting a new and acceptable president for the country, steps were at once taken to compel the
Haitian government to sign a convention in which it virtually
foreswore its independence. This was accomplished by
September 16, 1915; and although the terms of this convention
provided for the administration of the Haitian customs by
American civilian officials, all the principal custom houses of
the country had been seized by military force and placed in
charge of American Marine officers before the end of August.
The disposition of the funds collected in duties from the time
of the military seizure of the custom houses to the time of their
administration by civilian officials is still a question concerning
which the established censorship in Haiti allows no discussion.

It is interesting to note the wide difference between the
convention which Haiti was forced to sign and the convention
which was in course of diplomatic negotiation at the moment
of intervention. The Fuller convention asked little of Haiti and
gave something, the Occupation convention demands everything of Haiti and gives nothing. The Occupation convention
is really the same convention which the Haitian government
peremptorily refused to discuss in December, 1914, except that
in addition to American control of Haitian finances it also provides for American control of the Haitian military forces. The
Fuller convention contained neither of these provisions. When
the United States found itself in a position to take what it had
not even dared to asked, it used brute force and took it. But
even a convention which practically deprived Haiti of its independence was found not wholly adequate for the accomplishment of all that was contemplated. The Haitian constitution
still offered some embarrassments, so it was decided that Haiti

must have a new constitution. It was drafted and presented to the Haitian assembly for adoption. The assembly balked—chiefly at the article in the proposed document removing the constitutional disability which prevented aliens from owning land in Haiti. Haiti had long considered the denial of this right to aliens as her main bulwark against overwhelming economic exploitation; and it must be admitted that she had better reasons than the several states of the United States that have similar provisions.

The balking of the assembly resulted in its being dissolved by actual military force and the locking of doors of the Chamber. There has been no Haitian legislative body since. The desired constitution was submitted to a plebiscite by a decree of the President, although such a method of constitutional revision was clearly unconstitutional. Under the circumstances of the Occupation the plebiscite was, of course, almost unanimous for the desired change, and the new constitution was promulgated on June 18, 1918. Thus Haiti was given a new constitution by a flagrantly unconstitutional method. The new document contains several fundamental changes and includes a "Special Article" which declares:

All the acts of the Government of the United States during its military Occupation in Haiti are ratified and confirmed.

No Haitian shall be liable to civil or criminal prosecution for any act done by order of the Occupation or under its authority.

The acts of the courts martial of the Occupation, without, however, infringing on the right to pardon, shall not be subject to revision.

The acts of the Executive Power (the President) up to the promulgation of the present constitution are likewise ratified and confirmed.

The above is the chronological order of the principal steps by which the independence of a neighboring republic has been taken away, the people placed under foreign military domination from which they have no appeal, and exposed to foreign economic exploitation against which they are defenseless. All of this has been done in the name of the Government of the United States; however, without any act by Congress and without any knowledge of the American people.

The law by which Haiti is ruled today is martial law dispensed by Americans. There is a form of Haitian civil government, but it is entirely dominated by the military Occupation. President Dartiguenave, bitterly rebellious at heart as is every good Haitian, confessed to me the powerlessness of himself and his cabinet. He told me that the American authorities give no heed to recommendations made by him or his officers; that they would not even discuss matters about which the Haitian officials have superior knowledge. The provisions of both the old and the new constitutions are ignored in that there is no Haitian legislative body, and there has been none since the dissolution of the assembly in April, 1916. In its stead there is a Council of State composed of twenty-one members appointed by the president, which functions effectively only when carrying out the will of the Occupation. Indeed the Occupation often overrides the civil courts. A prisoner brought before the proper court, exonerated, and discharged, is, nevertheless, frequently held by the military. All government funds are collected by the Occupation and are dispensed at its will and pleasure. The greater part of these funds is expended for the maintenance of the military forces. There is the strictest censorship of the press. No Haitian newspaper is allowed to publish anything in criticism of the Occupation or the Haitian government. Each newspaper in Haiti received an order to that effect from the Occupation, *and the same order carried the injunction not print the order*. Nothing that might reflect upon the Occupation administration in Haiti is allowed to reach the newspapers of the United States.

The Haitian people justly complain that not only is the convention inimical to the best interests of their country, but that the convention, such as it is, is not being carried out in accordance with the letter, nor in accordance with the spirit in which they were led to believe it would be carried out. Except one, all of the obligations in the convention which the United States undertakes in favor of Haiti are contained in the first article of that document, the other fourteen articles being made up substantially of obligations to the United States assumed by Haiti. But nowhere in those fourteen articles is there anything to indicate that Haiti would be subjected to military domination. In Article I the United States promises to "aid the Haitian government in the proper and efficient development of its agricultural, mineral, and commercial resources and in the es-

tablishment of the finances of Haiti on a firm and solid basis."
And the whole convention and, especially, the protestations of
the United States before the signing of the instrument can be
construed only to mean that that aid would be extended
through the supervision of civilian officials.

The one promise of the United States to Haiti not contained in the first article of the convention is that clause of Article XIV which says, "and, should the necessity occur, the
United States will lend an efficient aid for the preservation of
Haitian independence and the maintenance of a government
adequate for the protection of life, property, and individual
liberty." It is the extreme of irony that this clause which the
Haitians had a right to interpret as a guarantee to them against
foreign invasion should first of all be invoked against the Haitian people themselves, and offer the only peg on which any
pretense to a right of military domination can be hung.

There are several distinct forces—financial, military, bu-
reaucratic—at work in Haiti which, tending to aggravate the
conditions they themselves have created, are largely self-
perpetuating. The most sinister of these, the financial en-
gulfment of Haiti by the National City Bank of New York,
already alluded to, will be discussed in detail in a subsequent
article. The military Occupation has made and continues to
make military Occupation necessary. The justification given is
that it is necessary for the pacification of the country. Pacification would never have been necessary had not American
policies been filled with so many stupid and brutal blunders;
and it will never be effective so long as "pacification" means
merely the hunting of ragged Haitians in the hills with machine guns.

Then there is the force which the several hundred American
civilian place-holders constitute. They have found in Haiti the
veritable promised land of "jobs for deserving democrats" and
naturally do not wish to see the present status discontinued.
Most of these deserving democrats are Southerners. The head
of the customs service of Haiti was a clerk of one of the
parishes of Louisiana. Second in charge of the customs service
of Haiti is a man who was Deputy Collector of Customs at
Pascagoula, Mississippi [population, 3,379, 1910 Census]. The
Superintendent of Public Instruction was a school teacher in

Louisiana—a State which has not good schools even for white children; the financial advisor, Mr. McIlhenny, is also from Louisiana.

Many of the Occupation officers are in the same category with the civilian place-holders. These men have taken their wives and families to Haiti. Those at Port-au-Prince live in beautiful villas. Families that could not keep a hired girl in the United States have a half-dozen servants. They ride in automobiles—not their own. Every American head of a department in Haiti has an automobile furnished at the expense of the Haitian Government, whereas members of the Haitian cabinet, who are theoretically above them, have no such convenience or luxury. While I was there, the President himself was obliged to borrow an automobile from the Occupation for a trip through the interior. The Louisiana school-teacher Superintendent of Instruction has an automobile furnished at government expense, whereas the Haitian Minister of Public Instruction, his supposed superior officer, has none. These automobiles seem to be chiefly employed in giving the women and children an airing each afternoon. It must be amusing, when it is not maddening to the Haitians, to see with what disdainful air these people look upon them as they ride by.

The platform adopted by the Democratic party at San Francisco said of the Wilson policy in Mexico:

The Administration, remembering always that Mexico is an independent nation and that permanent stability in her government and her institutions could come only from the consent of her own people to a government of her own making, has been unwilling either to profit by the misfortunes of the people of Mexico or to enfeeble their future by imposing from the outside a rule upon their temporarily distracted councils.

Haiti has never been so distracted in its councils as Mexico. And even in its moments of greatest distraction it never slaughtered an American citizen, it never molested an American woman, it never injured a dollar's worth of American property. And yet, the Administration whose lofty purpose was proclaimed as above—with less justification than Austria's invasion of Serbia, or Germany's rape of Belgium, without warrant other than the doctrine that "might makes right," has conquered Haiti. It has done this through the very period when, in the words of its chief spokesman, our sons were laying down their lives overseas "for democracy, for the rights of those who submit to authority to have a voice in their own government, for the rights and liberties of small nations." By command of the author of "pitiless publicity" and originator of "open covenants openly arrived at," it has enforced by the bayonet a covenant whose secret had been well guarded by a rigid censorship from the American nation, and kept a people enslaved by the military tyranny which it was his avowed purpose to destroy throughout the world.

II. WHAT THE UNITED STATES HAS ACCOMPLISHED

WHEN the truth about the conquest of Haiti—the slaughter of three thousand and practically unarmed Haitians, with the incidentally needless death of a score of American boys—begins to filter through the rigid Administration censorship to the American people, the apologists will become active. Their justification of what has been done will be grouped under two heads: one, the necessity, and two, the results. Under the first, much stress will be laid upon the "anarchy" which existed in Haiti, upon the backwardness of the Haitians and their absolute unfitness to govern themselves. The pretext which caused the intervention was taken up in the first article of this series. The characteristics, alleged and real, of the Haitian people will be taken up in a subsequent article. Now as to results: The apologists will attempt to show that material improvements in Haiti justify American intervention. Let us see what they are.

Diligent inquiry reveals just three: The building of the road from Port-au-Prince to Cape Haitien; the enforcement of certain sanitary regulations in the larger cities; and the improvement of the public hospital at Port-au-Prince. The enforcement of certain sanitary regulations is not so important as it may sound, for even under exclusive native rule, Haiti has been a remarkably healthy country and had never suffered from such epidemics as used to sweep Cuba and the Panama

Canal region. The regulations, moreover, were of a purely minor character—the sort that might be issued by a board of health in any American city or town—and were in no wise fundamental, because there was no need. The same applies to the improvement of the hospital, long before the American Occupation, an effectively conducted institution but which, it is only fair to say, benefited considerably by the regulations and more up-to-date methods of American army surgeons—the best in the world. Neither of these accomplishments, however, creditable as they are, can well be put forward as a justification for military domination. The building of the great highway from Port-au-Prince to Cape Haitien is a monumental piece of work, but it is doubtful whether the object in building it was to supply the Haitians with a great highway or to construct a military road which would facilitate the transportation of troops and supplies from one end of the island to the other. And this represents the sum total of the constructive accomplishment after five years of American Occupation.

Now, the highway, while doubtless the most important achievement of the three, involved the most brutal of all the blunders of the Occupation. The work was in charge of an officer of Marines who stands out even in that organization for his "treat 'em rough" methods. He discovered the obsolete Haitian *corvée* and decided to enforce it with the most modern Marine efficiency. The *corvée*, or road law, in Haiti provided that each citizen should work a certain number of days on the public roads to keep them in condition, or pay a certain sum of money. In the days when this law was in force the Haitian government never required the men to work the roads except in their respective communities, and the number of days was usually limited to three a year. But the Occupation seized men wherever it could find them, and no able-bodied Haitian was safe from such raids, which most closely resembled the African slave raids of past centuries. And slavery it was—though temporary. By day or by night, from the bosom of their families, from their little farms or while trudging peacefully on the country roads, Haitians were seized and forcibly taken to toil for months in far sections of the country. Those who protested or resisted were beaten into submission. At night, after long hours of unremitting labor under armed taskmasters, who swiftly discouraged any slackening of effort with boot or rifle butt, the victims were herded in compounds. Those attempting to escape were shot. Their terror-stricken families meanwhile were often in total ignorance of the fate of their husbands, fathers, brothers.

It is chiefly out of these methods that arose the need for "pacification." Many men of the rural districts became panic-stricken and fled to the hills and mountains. Others rebelled and did likewise, preferring death to slavery. These refugees largely make up the "caco" forces, to hunt down which has become the duty and the sport of American Marines, who were privileged to shoot a "caco" on sight. If anyone doubts that "caco" hunting is the sport of American Marines in Haiti, let him learn the facts about the death of Charlemagne. Charlemagne Peralite was a Haitian of education and culture and of great influence in his district. He was tried by an American courtmartial on the charge of aiding "cacos." He was sentenced, not to prison, however, but to five years of hard labor on the roads, and was forced to work in convict garb on the streets of Cape Haitien. He made his escape and put himself at the head of several hundred followers in a valiant though hopeless attempt to free Haiti. The America of the Revolution, indeed the America of the Civil War, would have regarded Charlemagne not as a criminal but a patriot. He met his death not in open fight, not in an attempt at his capture, but through a dastard deed. While standing over his camp fire, he was shot in cold blood by an American Marine officer who stood concealed by the darkness, and who had reached the camp through bribery and trickery. This deed, which was nothing short of assassination, has been heralded as an example of American heroism. Of this deed, Harry Franck, writing in the June *Century* of "The Death of Charlemagne," says: "Indeed it is fit to rank with any of the stirring warrior tales with which history is seasoned from the days of the Greeks down to the recent world war." America should read "The Death of Charlemagne" which attempts to glorify a black smirch on American arms and tradition.

There is a reason why the methods employed in road building affected the Haitian country folk in a way in which it might not have affected the people of any other Latin-American country. Not since the independence of the country has there been any such thing as a peon in Haiti. The revolution by which Haiti gained her independence was not merely a political revolution, it was also a social revolution. Among the many radical changes wrought was that of cutting up the large slave estates into small parcels and allotting them among former slaves. And so it was that every Haitian in the rural districts lived on his own plot of land, a plot on which his family had lived for perhaps more than a hundred years. No matter how small or how large that plot is and whether he raises much or little on it, it is his and he is an independent farmer.

The completed highway, moreover, continued to be a barb in the Haitian wound. Automobiles on this road, running without any speed limit, are a constant inconvenience or danger to the natives carrying their market produce to town on their heads or loaded on the backs of animals. I have seen these people scramble in terror often up the side or down the declivity of the mountain for places of safety for themselves and their animals as the machines snorted by. I have seen a market woman's horse take flight and scatter the produce loaded on his back all over the road for several hundred yards. I have heard an American commercial traveler laughingly tell how on the trip from Cape Haitien to Port-au-Prince the automobile he was in killed a donkey and two pigs. It had not occurred to him that the donkey might be the chief capital of the small Haitian farmer and that the loss of it might entirely bankrupt him. It is all very humorous, of course, unless you happen to be the Haitian pedestrian.

The majority of visitors on arriving at Port-au-Prince and noticing the well-paved, well-kept streets, will at once jump to the conclusion that this work was done by the American Occupation. The Occupation goes to no trouble to refute this conclusion, and in fact it will by implication corroborate it. If one should exclaim, "Why, I am surprised to see what a well-paved city Port-au-Prince is!" he would be almost certain to receive the answer, "Yes, but you should have seen it before the Occupation." The implication here is that Port-au-Prince was a mudhole and that the Occupation is responsible for its clean and well-paved streets. It is true that at the time of the intervention, five-years ago, there were only one or two paved streets in the Haitian capital, but the contracts for paving the entire city had been let by the Haitian Government, and the work had already been begun. This work was completed during the Occupation, *but the Occupation did not pave, and had nothing to do with the paving of a single street in Port-au-Prince.*

One accomplishment I did expect to find—that the American Occupation, in its five years of absolute rule, had developed and improved the Haitian system of public education. The United States has made some efforts in this direction in other countries where it has taken control. In Porto Rico, Cuba, and the Philippines, the attempt, at least, was made to establish modern school systems. Selected youths from these countries were taken and sent to the United States for training in order that they might return and be better teachers, and American teachers were sent to those islands in exchange. The American Occupation in Haiti has not advanced public education a single step. No new buildings have been erected. Not a single Haitian youth has been sent to the United States for training as a teacher, nor has a single American teacher, white or colored, been sent to Haiti. According to the general budget of Haiti, 1919–1920, there are teachers in the rural schools receiving as little as six dollars a month. Some of these teachers may not be worth more than six dollars a month. But after five years of American rule, there ought not to be a single teacher in the country who is not worth more than that paltry sum.

Another source of discontent is the Gendarmerie. When the Occupation took possession of the island, it disarmed all Haitians, including the various local police forces. To remedy this situation the Convention (Article X), provided that there should be created,—

without delay, an efficient constabulary, urban and rural, composed of native Haitians. This constabulary shall be organized and officered by Americans, appointed by the President of Haiti upon nomination by the President of the United States. . . . These officers shall be replaced by Haitians as they, by examination conducted under direction of a board to be selected by the Senior American Officer of this constabulary in the presence of a representative of the Haitian Government, are found to be qualified to assume such duties.

During the first months of the Occupation officers of the Haitian Gendarmerie were commissioned officers of the marines, but the war took all these officers to Europe. Five years have passed and the constabulary is still officered entirely by marines, but almost without exception they are ex-privates or non-commissioned officers of the United States Marine Corps commissioned in the gendarmerie. Many of these men are rough, uncouth, and uneducated, and a great number from the South, are violently steeped in color prejudice. They direct all policing of city and town. It falls to them, ignorant of Haitian ways and language, to enforce every minor police regulation. Needless to say, this is a grave source of continued irritation. Where the genial American "cop" could, with a wave of his hand or club, convey the full majesty of the law to the small boy transgressor or to some equally innocuous offender, the strong-arm tactics for which the marines are famous, are apt to be promptly evoked. The pledge in the Convention that "these officers be replaced by Haitians" who could qualify, has, like other pledges, become a mere scrap of paper. Graduates of the famous French military academy of St. Cyr, men who have actually qualified for commissions in the French army, are denied the opportunity to fill even a lesser commission in the Haitian Gendarmerie, although such men, in addition to their pre-eminent qualifications of training, would, because of their understanding of local conditions and their complete familiarity with the ways of their own country, make ideal guardians of the peace.

The American Occupation of Haiti is not only guilty of sins of omission, it is guilty of sins of commission in addition to those committed in the building of the great road across the island. Brutalities and atrocities on the part of American marines have occurred with sufficient frequency to be the cause of deep resentment and terror. Marines talk freely of what they "did" to some Haitians in the outlying districts. Familiar methods of torture to make captives reveal what they often do not know are nonchalantly discussed. Just before I left Port-au-Prince an American Marine had caught a Haitian boy stealing sugar off the wharf and instead of arresting him he battered his brains out with the butt of his rifle. I learned from the lips of American Marines themselves of a number of cases of rape of Haitian women by marines. I often sat at tables in the hotels and cafes in company with marine officers and they talked before me without restraint. I remember the description of a "caco" hunt by one of them; he told how they finally came upon a crowd of natives engaged in the popular pastime of cock-fighting and how they "let them have it" with machine guns and rifle fire. I heard another, a captain of marines, relate how he at a fire in Port-au-Prince ordered a "rather dressed up Haitian," standing on the sidewalk, to "get in there" and take a hand at the pumps. It appeared that the Haitian merely shrugged his shoulders. The captain of marines then laughingly said: "I had a pretty heavy pair of boots and I let him have a kick that landed him in the middle of the street. Some-one ran up and told me that the man was an ex-member of the Haitian Assembly." The fact that the man had been a member of the Haitian Assembly made the whole incident more laugh-able to the captain of marines.

Perhaps the most serious aspect of American brutality in Haiti is not to be found in individual cases of cruelty, numer-ous and inexcusable though they are, but rather in the Ameri-can attitude, well illustrated by the diagnosis of an American officer discussing the situation and its difficulty: "The trouble with this whole business is that some of these people with a little money and education think they are as good as we are," and this is the keynote of the attitude of every American to every Haitian. Americans have carried American hatred to Haiti. They have planted the feeling of caste and color preju-dice where it never before existed.

And such are the "accomplishments" of the United States in Haiti. The Occupation has not only failed to achieve any-thing worth while, but has made it impossible to do so be-cause of the distrust and bitterness that it has engendered in the Haitian people. Through the present instrumentalities no matter how earnestly the United States may desire to be fair to Haiti and make intervention a success, it will not succeed. An entirely new deal is necessary. This Government forced the Haitian leaders to accept the promise of American aid and American supervision. With that American aid the Hai-tian Government defaulted its external and internal debt, an obligation, which under self-government the Haitians had scrupulously observed. And American supervision turned out to be a military tyranny supporting a program of economic exploitation. The United States had an opportunity to gain the confidence of the Haitian people. That opportunity has been destroyed. When American troops first landed, although the Haitian people were outraged, there was a feeling nevertheless which might well have developed into cooperation. There were those who had hopes that the United States, guided by its traditional policy of nearly a century and a half, pursuing its fine stand in Cuba, under McKinley, Roosevelt, and Taft, would extend aid that would be mutually beneficial to both countries. Those Haitians who indulged this hope are disappointed and bitter. Those members of the Haitian Assembly who, while acting under coercion were nevertheless hopeful of American promises, incurred unpopularity by voting for the Convention, are today bitterly disappointed and utterly disillusioned.

If the United States should leave Haiti today, it would leave more than a thousand widows and orphans of its own making, more banditry than has existed for a century, resentment, hatred and despair in the heart of a whole people, to say nothing of the irreparable injury to its own tradition as the defender of the rights of man.

III. GOVERNMENT OF, BY, AND
FOR THE NATIONAL CITY BANK

FORMER articles of this series described the Military Occupation of Haiti and the crowd of civilian place holders, as among the forces at work in Haiti to maintain the present status in that country. But more powerful though less obvious, and more sinister, because of its deep and varied radications, is the force exercised by the National City Bank of New York. It seeks more than the mere maintenance of the present status in Haiti; it is constantly working to bring about a condition more suitable and profitable to itself. Behind the Occupation, working conjointly with the Department of State, stands this great banking institution of New York and elsewhere. The financial potentates allied with it are the ones who will profit by the control of Haiti. The United States Marine Corps and the various office-holding "deserving Democrats," who help maintain the status quo there, are in reality working for great financial interests in this country, although Uncle Sam and Haiti pay their salaries.

Mr. Roger L. Farnham, vice-president of the National City Bank, was effectively instrumental in bringing about American intervention in Haiti. With the administration at Washington, the word of Mr. Farnham supersedes that of anybody else on the island. While Mr. Bailley-Blanchard, with the title of minister, is its representative in name, Mr. Farnham is its representative in fact. His goings and comings are aboard vessels of the United States Navy. His bank, the National City, has been in charge of the Banque Nationale d'Haiti throughout the Occupation.* Only a few weeks ago he was appointed receiver of the National Railroad of Haiti, controlling practically the entire railway system in the island with valuable territorial concessions in all parts.† The $5,000,000 sugar plant at Port-au-Prince, it is commonly reported, is about to fall into his hands.

---

*The National City Bank originally (about 1911) purchased 2,000 shares of the stock of the Banque Nationale d'Haiti. After the Occupation it purchased 6,000 additional shares in the hands of three New York banking firms. Since then it has been negotiating for the complete control of the stock, the balance of which is held in France. The contract for this transfer of the Bank and the granting of a new charter under the laws of Haiti were agreed upon and signed at Washington last February. But the delay in completing these arrangements is caused by the impasse between the State Department and the National City Bank, on the one hand, and the Haitian Government on the other, due to the fact that the State Department and the National City Bank insisted upon including in the contract a clause prohibiting the importation and exportation of foreign money into Haiti subject only to the control of the financial adviser. To this new power the Haitian Government refuses to consent.

†Originally, Mr. James P. McDonald secured from the Haitian Government the concession to build the railroads under the charter of the National Railways of Haiti. He arranged with W. R. Grace & Company to finance the concession. Grace and Company formed a syndicate under the aegis of the National City Bank which issued $2,500,000 bonds sold in France. These bonds were guaranteed by the Haitian Government at an interest of 6 per cent on $32,500 for each mile. A short while after the floating of these bonds, Mr. Farnham became President to the company. The syndicate advanced another $2,000,000 for the completion of the railroad in accordance with the concession granted by the Haitian Government. This money was used, but the work was not completed in accordance with the contract made by the Haitian Government in the concession . The Haitian Government then refused any longer to pay the interest on the mileage. These happenings were prior to 1915.

Now, of all the various responsibilities, expressed, implied, or assumed by the United States in Haiti, it would naturally be supposed that the financial obligation would be foremost. Indeed, the sister republic of Santo Domingo was taken over by the United States Navy for no other reason than failure to pay its internal debt. But Haiti for over one hundred years scrupulously paid its external and internal debt—a fact worth remembering when one hears of "anarchy and disorder" in that land—until five years ago when under the financial guardianship of the United States interest on both the internal and, with one exception, external debt was defaulted; and this in spite of the fact that specified revenues were pledged for the payment of this interest. Apart from the distinct injury to the honor and reputation of the country, the hardship on individuals has been great. For while the foreign debt is held particularly in France which, being under great financial obligations to the United States since the beginning of the war, has not been able to protest effectively, the interior debt is held almost entirely by Haitian citizens. Haitian Government bonds have long been the recognized substantial investment for the well-to-do and middle class people, considered as are in this country, United States, state, and municipal bonds. Non-payment on these securities has placed many families in absolute want.

What has happened to these bonds? They are being sold for a song, for the little cash they will bring. Individuals closely connected with the National Bank of Haiti are ready purchasers. When the new Haitian loan is floated it will, of course, contain ample provisions for redeeming these old bonds at par. The profits will be more than handsome. Not that the National Bank has not already made hay in the sunshine of American Occupation. From the beginning it has been sole depositary of all revenues collected in the name of the Haitian Government by the American Occupation, receiving in addition to the interest rate a commission on all funds deposited. The bank is the sole agent in the transmission of these funds. It has also the exclusive note-issuing privilege in the republic. At the same time complaint is widespread among the Haitian business men that the Bank no longer as of old accommodates them with credit and that its interests are now entirely in developments of its own.

Now, one of the promises that was made to the Haitian Government, partly to allay its doubts and fears as to the purpose and character of the American intervention, was that the United States would put the country's finances on a solid and substantial basis. A loan for $30,000,000 or more was one of the features of this promised assistance. Pursuant, supposedly, to this plan, a Financial Adviser for Haiti was appointed in the person of Mr. John Avery McIlhenny. Who is Mr. McIlhenny? That he has the cordial backing and direction of so able a financier as Mr. Farnham is comforting when one reviews the past record and experience in finance of Haiti's Financial Adviser as given by him in "Who's Who in America," for 1918–1919. He was born in Avery Island, Iberia Parish, La.; went to Tulane University for one year; was a private in the Louisiana State militia for five years; trooper in the U.S. Cavalry in 1898; promoted to second lieutenancy for gallantry in action at San Juan; has been a member of the Louisiana House of Representatives and Senate; was a member of the U.S. Civil Service Commission in 1906 and president of the same in 1913; Democrat. It is under his Financial Advisership that the Haitian interest has been continued in default with the one exception above noted, when several months ago $3,000,000 was converted into francs to meet the accumulated interest payments on the foreign debt. Dissatisfaction on the part of the Haitians developed over the lack of financial perspicacity in this transaction of Mr. McIlhenny because the sum was converted into francs at the rate of nine to a dollar while shortly after the rate of exchange on French francs dropped to fourteen to a dollar. Indeed, Mr. McIlhenny's unfitness by training and experience for the delicate and important position which he is filling was one of the most generally admitted facts which I gathered in Haiti.

At the present writing, however, Mr. McIlhenny has become a conspicuous figure in the history of the Occupation of Haiti as the instrument by which the National City Bank is striving to complete the riveting, double-locking and bolting of its financial control of the island. For although it would appear that the absolute military domination under which Haiti is held would enable the financial powers to accomplish almost anything they desire, they are wise enough to realize that a day of reckoning, such as, for instance, a change in the Administration in the United States, may be coming. So they are eager and anxious to have everything they want signed, sealed, and delivered. Anything, of course, that the Haitians have fully "consented to" no one else can reasonable object to.

A little recent history: in February of the present year the ministers of the different departments, in order to conform to the letter of the law (Article 116 of the Constitution of Haiti, which was saddled upon her in 1918 by the Occupation* and Article 2 of the Haitian-American Convention†) began work on the preparation of the accounts for 1918–1919 and the budget for 1920–1921. On March 22 a draft of the budget was sent to Mr. A. J. Maumus, Acting Financial Adviser, in the absence of Mr. McIlhenny who had at the time been in the United States for seven months. Mr. Maumus replied on March 29, suggesting postponement of all discussion of the budget until Mr. McIlhenny's return. Nevertheless, the Legislative body, in pursuance of the law, opened on its constitutional date, Monday, April 5. Despite the great urgency of the matter in hand, the Haitian administration was obliged to mark time until June 1, when Mr. McIlhenny returned to Haiti. Several conferences with the various ministers were then undertaken. On June 12, at one of these conferences, there arrived in the place of the Financial Adviser a note stating that he would be obliged to stop all study of the budget "until the time when certain affairs of considerable importance to the well-being of the country shall be finally settled according to recommendations made by me to the Haitian Government." As he did not give in his note the slightest idea what these important affairs were, the Haitian Secretary wrote asking for information, at the same time calling attention to the already

---

*"The general accounts and the budgets prescribed by the preceding article must be submitted to the Legislative Body by the Secretary of Finance not later than eight days after the opening of the Legislative Session."

†"The President of Haiti shall appoint, on the nomination of the President of the United States, a Financial Adviser who shall be attached to the Ministry of Finance, to whom the Secretary (of Finance) shall lend effective aid in the prosecution of his work. The Financial Adviser shall work out a system of public accounting, shall aid in increasing the revenues and in their adjustment to expenditures. . . ."

great and embarrassing delay, and reminding Mr. McIlhenny that the preparation of the accounts and budget was one of his legal duties as an official attached to the Haitian Government, of which he could not divest himself.

On July 19 Mr. McIlhenny supplied his previous omission in a memorandum which he transmitted to the Haitian Department of Finance, in which he said: "I had instructions from the Department of State of the United States just before my departure for Haiti, in a part of a letter of May 20, to declare to the Haitian Government that it was necessary to give its immediate and formal approval to:

1. A modification of the Bank Contract agreed upon by the Department of State and the National City Bank of New York.
2. Transfer of the National Bank of the Republic of Haiti to a new bank registered under the laws of Haiti, to be known as the National Bank of the Republic of Haiti.
3. The execution of Article 15 of the Contract of Withdrawal prohibiting the importation and exportation of non-Haitian money except that which might be necessary for the needs of commerce in the opinion of the Financial Adviser."

Now, what is the meaning and significance of these proposals? The full details have not been given out, but it is known that they are part of a new monetary law for Haiti involving the complete transfer of the Banque Nationale d'Haiti to the National City Bank of New York. The document embodying the agreements, with the exception of the clause prohibiting the importation of foreign money, was signed at Washington, February 6, 1920, by Mr. McIlhenny, the Haitian Minister at Washington and the Haitian Secretary of Finance. *The Haitian Government has officially declared that the clause prohibiting the importation and exportation of foreign money, except as it may be deemed necessary in the opinion of the Financial Adviser, was added to the original agreement by some unknown party.* It is for the purpose of compelling the Haitian Government to approve the agreements, including the "prohibition clause," that pressure is now being applied. Efforts on the part of business interests in Haiti to learn the character and scope of what was done at Washington have been thwarted by close secrecy. However, sufficient of its import has become known to understand the reasons for the unqualified and definite refusal of President Dartiguenave and the Government to give their approval. Those reasons are that the agreements would give to the National Bank of Haiti, and thereby to the National City Bank of New York, exclusive monopoly upon the right of importing and exporting American and other foreign money to and from Haiti, a monopoly which would carry unprecedented and extraordinarily lucrative privileges.

The proposal involved in this agreement has called forth a vigorous protest on the part of every important banking and business concern in Haiti with the exception, of course, of the National Bank of Haiti. This protest was transmitted to the Haitian Minister of Finance on July 30 past. The protest is signed not only by Haitians and Europeans doing business in that country but also by the leading American business concerns, among which are The American Foreign Banking Corporation, The Haitian-American Sugar Company, The Panama Railroad Steamship Line, The Clyde Steamship Line, and The West Indies Trading Company. Among the foreign signers are the Royal Bank of Canada, Le Comptoir Français, Le Comptoir Commercial, and besides a number of business firms.

We have now in Haiti a triangular situation with the National City Bank and our Department of State in two corners and the Haitian government in the third. Pressure is being brought on the Haitian government to compel it to grant a monopoly which on its face appears designed to give the National City Bank a strangle hold on the financial life of that country. With the Haitian government refusing to yield, we have the Financial Adviser who is, according to the Haitian-American Convention, a Haitian official charged with certain duties (in this case the approval of the budget and accounts), refusing to carry out those duties until the government yields to the pressure which is being brought.

Haiti is now experiencing the "third degree." Ever since the Bank Contract was drawn and signed at Washington increasing pressure has been applied to make the Haitian government accept the clause prohibiting the importation of foreign money. Mr. McIlhenny is now holding up the salaries of the President, ministers of departments, members of the Council of State, and the official interpreter. [These salaries have not been paid since July 1.] And there the matter now stands.

Several things may happen. The Administration, finding present methods insufficient, may decide to act as in Santo Domingo, to abolish the President, cabinet, and all civil government—as they have already abolished the Haitian Assembly—and put into effect, by purely military force, what, in the face of the unflinching Haitian refusal to sign away their birthright, the combined military, civil, and financial pressure has been unable to accomplish. Or, with an election and a probable change of Administration in this country pending, with a Congressional investigation foreshadowed, it may be decided that matters are "too difficult" and the National City Bank may find that it can be more profitably engaged elsewhere. Indications of such a course are not lacking. From the point of view of the National City Bank, of course, the institution has not only done nothing which is not wholly legitimate, proper, and according to the cannons of big business throughout the world, but has actually performed constructive and generous service to a backward and uncivilized people in attempting to promote their railways, to develop their country, and to shape soundly their finance. That Mr. Farnham and those associated with him hold these views sincerely, there is no doubt. But that the Haitians, after over one hundred years of self-government and liberty, contemplating the slaughter of three thousands of their sons, the loss of their political and economic freedom, without compensating advantages which they can appreciate, feel very differently, is equally true.

IV. THE HAITIAN PEOPLE

THE first sight of Port-au-Prince is perhaps most startling to the experienced Latin-American traveler. Caribbean cities are of the Spanish-American type—buildings square and squat, built generally around a court, with residences and business houses scarcely interdistinguishable. Port-au-Prince is rather a city of the French or Italian Riviera. Across the bay of deepest blue the purple mountains of Gonave loom against

the Western sky, rivaling the bay's azure depths. Back of the
business section, spreading around the bay's great sweep and
well into the plain beyond, rise the green hills with their white
residences. The residential section spreads over the slopes and
into the mountain tiers. High up are the homes of the well-to-
do, beautiful villas set in green gardens relieved by the flaming
crimson of the poinsettia. Despite the imposing mountains a
man-made edifice dominates the scene. From the center of the
city the great Gothic cathedral lifts its spires above the tranquil
city. Well-paved and clean, the city prolongs the thrill of its
first unfolding. Cosmopolitan yet quaint, with an old-world
atmosphere yet a charm of its own, one gets throughout the
feeling of continental European life. In the hotels and cafes the
affairs of the world are heard discussed in several languages.
The cuisine and service are not only excellent but inexpensive.
At the Café Dereix, cool and scrupulously clean, dinner from
hors d'œuvres to *glaces*, with wine, of course, recalling the famous ante-bellum hostelries of New York and Paris, may be
had for six gourdes [$1.25].

A drive of two hours around Port-au-Prince, through the
newer section of brick and concrete buildings, past the cathedral erected from 1903 to 1912, along the Champ de Mars
where the new presidential palace stands, up into the Peu de
Choses section where the hundreds of beautiful villas and
grounds of the well-to-do are situated, permanently dispels
any lingering question that the Haitians have been retro-
grading during the 116 years of their independence.

In the lower city, along the water's edge, around the market
and in the Rue Républicaine, is the "local color." The long
rows of wooden shanties, the curious little booths around the
market, filled with jabbering venders and with scantily clad
children, magnificent in body, running in and out, are no less
picturesque and no more primitive, no humbler, yet cleaner,
than similar quarters in Naples, in Lisbon, in Marseilles, and
more justifiable than the great slums of civilization's centers—
London and New York, which are totally without aesthetic redemption. But it is only the modernists in history who are
willing to look at the masses as factors in the life and development of the country, and in its history. For Haitian history,
like history the world over, has for the last century been that

of cultured and educated groups. To know Haitian life one must have the privilege of being received as a guest in the houses of these latter, and they live in beautiful houses. The majority have been educated in France; they are cultured, brilliant conversationally, and thoroughly enjoy their social life. The women dress well. Many are beautiful and all vivacious and chic. Cultivated people from any part of the world would feel at home in the best Haitian society. If our guest were to enter to the Cercle Bellevue, the leading club of Port-au-Prince, he would find the courteous, friendly atmosphere of a men's club; he would hear varying shades of opinion on public questions, and could scarcely fail to be impressed by the thorough knowledge of world affairs possessed by the intelligent Haitian. Nor would his encounters be only with people who have culture and savoir vivre; he would meet the Haitian intellectuals—poets, essayists, novelists, historians, critics. Take for example such a writer as Fernand Hibbert. An English authority says of him, "His essays are worthy of the pen of Anatole France or Pierre Loti." And there is Georges Sylvaine, poet and essayist, and conférencier at the Sorbonne, where his address was received with acclaim, author of books crowned by the French Academy, and an Officer of the Légion d'Honneur. Hibbert and Sylvaine are only two among a dozen or more contemporary Haitian men of letters whose work may be measured by world standards. Two names that stand out preeminently in Haitian literature are Oswald Durand, the national poet, who died a few years ago, and Damocles Vieux. These people, educated, cultured, and intellectual, are not accidental and sporadic offshoots of the Haitian people; they *are* the Haitian people and they are a demonstration of its inherent potentialities.

However, Port-au-Prince is not all of Haiti. Other cities are smaller replicas, and fully as interesting are the people of the country districts. Perhaps the deepest impression on the observant visitor is made by the country women. Magnificent as they file along the country roads by scores and by hundreds on their way to the town markets, with white or colored turbaned heads, gold-looped-ringed ears, they stride along straight and lithe, almost haughtily, carrying themselves like so many Queens of Sheba. The Haitian country people are kind-hearted, hospitable, and polite, seldom stupid but rather, quick-witted and imaginative. Fond of music, with a profound sense of beauty and harmony, they live simply but wholesomely. Their cabins rarely consist of only one room, the humblest having two or three, with a little shed front and back, a front and rear entrance, and plenty of windows. An aesthetic touch is never lacking—a flowering hedge of an arbor with trained vines bearing gorgeous colored blossoms. There is no comparison between the neat plastered-wall, thatched-roof cabin of the Haitian peasant and the traditional log hut of the South or the shanty of the more wretched American suburbs. The most notable feature about the Haitian cabin is its invariable cleanliness. At daylight the country people are up and about, the women begin their sweeping till the earthen or pebble-paved floor of the cabin is clean as can be. Then the yards around the cabin are vigorously attacked. In fact, nowhere in the country districts of Haiti does one find the filth and squalor which may be seen in any backwoods town in our own South. Cleanliness is a habit and a dirty Haitian is a rare exception. The garments even of the men who work on the wharves, mended and patched until little of the original cloth is visible, give evidence of periodical washing. The writer recalls a remark made by Mr. E. P. Pawley, an American, who conducts one of the largest business enterprises in Haiti. He said that the Haitians were an exceptionally clean people, that statistics showed that Haiti imported more soap per capita than any country in the world, and added, "They use it, too." Three of the largest soap manufactories in the United States maintain headquarters at Port-au-Prince.

The masses of the Haitian people are splendid material for the building of a nation. They are not lazy; on the contrary, they are industrious and thrifty. Some observers mistakenly confound primitive methods with indolence. Anyone who travels Haitian roads is struck by the hundreds and even thousands of women, boys, and girls filing along mile after mile with their farm and garden produce on their heads or loaded on the backs of animals. With modern facilities, they could market their produce much more efficiently and with far less effort. But lacking them they are willing to walk and carry. For a woman to walk five to ten miles with a great load of produce on her head which may barely realize her a dollar is doubtless primitive, and a wasteful expenditure of energy, but it is not a sign of laziness. Haiti's great handicap has been not that her masses are degraded or lazy or immoral. It is that they are ignorant, due not so much to mental limitations as to enforced illiteracy. There is a specific reason for this. Somehow the French language, in the French-American colonial settlements containing a Negro population, divided itself into two branches, French and Creole. This is true of Louisiana, Martinique, Guadeloupe, and also of Haiti. Creole is an Africanized French and must not be thought of as a mere dialect. The French-speaking person cannot understand Creole, excepting a few words, unless he learns it. Creole is a distinct tongue, a graphic and very expressive language. Many of its constructions follow closely the African idiom. For example, in forming the superlative of greatness, one says in Creole, "He is great among great men," and a merchant woman, following the native idiom, will say, "You do not wish anything beautiful if you do not buy this." The upper Haitian class, approximately 500,000, speak and know French, while the masses, probably more than 2,000,000, speak only Creole. Haitian Creole is grammatically constructed but has not to any general extent been reduced to writing. Therefore, these masses have no means of receiving or communicating thoughts through the written word. They have no books to read. They cannot read the newspapers. The children of the masses study French for a few years in school, but it never becomes their every-day language. In order to abolish Haitian illiteracy, Creole must be made a printed as well as a spoken language. The failure to undertake this problem is the worst indictment against the Haitian Government.

This matter of language proves a handicap to Haiti in another manner. It isolates her sister republics. All of the Latin-American republics except Brazil speak Spanish and enjoy an intercourse with the outside world denied Haiti. Dramatic and musical companies from Spain, from Mexico and from the Argentine annually tour all of the Spanish-speaking republics. Haiti is deprived of all such instruction and entertainment from the outside world because it is not profitable for French companies to visit the three or four French-speaking islands in the Western Hemisphere.

Much stress has been laid on the bloody history of Haiti and its numerous revolutions. Haitian history has been all too bloody, but so has that of every other country, and the bloodiness of the Haitian revolutions has of late been unduly magnified. A writer might visit our own country and clip from our daily press accounts of murders, robberies on the principal streets of our larger cities, strike violence, race riots, lynchings, and burnings at the stake of human beings, and write a book to prove that life is absolutely unsafe in the United States. The seriousness of the frequent Latin-American revolutions has been greatly overemphasized. The writer has been in the midst of three of these revolutions and must confess that the treatment given them on our comic opera stage is very little farther removed from the truth than the treatment which is given in the daily newspapers. Not nearly so bloody as reported, their interference with people not in politics is almost negligible. Nor should it be forgotten that in almost every instance the revolution is due to the plotting of foreigners backed up by their Governments. No less an authority than Mr. John H. Allen, vice-president of the National City Bank of New York, writing on Haiti in the May number of *The Americas*, the National City Bank organ, who says, "It is no secret that the revolutions were financed by foreigners and were profitable speculations."

In this matter of change of government by revolution, Haiti must not be compared with the United States or with England; it must be compared with other Latin American republics. When it is compared with our next door neighbor, Mexico, it will be found that the Government of Haiti has been more stable and that the country has experienced less bloodshed and anarchy. And it must never be forgotten that throughout not an American or other foreigner has been killed, injured or, as far as can be ascertained, even molested. In Haiti's 116 years of independence, there have been twenty-five presidents and twenty-five different administrations. In Mexico, during its 99 years of independence, there have been forty-seven rulers and eighty-seven administrations. "Graft" has been plentiful, shocking at times, but who in America, where the Tammany machines and the municipal rings are notorious, will dare to point the finger of scorn at Haiti in this connection.

And this is the people whose "inferiority," whose "retrogression," whose "savagery," is advanced as a justification for intervention—for the ruthless slaughter of three thousand of its practically defenseless sons, with the death of a score of our own boys for the utterly selfish exploitation of the country by American big finance, for the destruction of America's most precious heritage—her traditional fair play, her sense of justice, her aid to the oppressed. "Inferiority" always was the excuse of ruthless imperialism until the Germans invaded Belgium, when it became "military necessity." In the case of Haiti there is not the slightest vestige of any of the traditional justifications, unwarranted as these generally are, and no amount of misrepresentation in an era when propaganda and censorship have had their heyday, no amount of slander, even in a country deeply prejudiced where color is involved, will longer serve to obscure to the conscience of America the eternal shame of its last five years in Haiti. *Fiat justitia, ruat coelum!*

The Nation, 1920

The Book of American Negro Poetry

THERE IS, perhaps, a better excuse for giving an Anthology of American Negro Poetry to the public than can be offered for many of the anthologies that have recently been issued. The public, generally speaking, does not know that there are American Negro poets—to supply this lack of information is, alone, a work worthy of somebody's effort.

Moreover, the matter of Negro poets and the production of literature by the colored people in this country involves more than supplying information that is lacking. It is a matter which has a direct bearing on the most vital of American problems.

A people may become great through many means, but there is only one measure by which its greatness is recognized and acknowledged. The final measure of the greatness of all peoples is the amount and standard of the literature and art they have produced. The world does not know that a people is great until that people produces great literature and art. No people that has produced great literature and art has ever been looked upon by the world as distinctly inferior.

The status of the Negro in the United States is more a question of national mental attitude toward the race than of actual conditions. And nothing will do more to change that mental attitude and raise his status than a demonstration of intellectual parity by the Negro through the production of literature and art.

Is there likelihood that the American Negro will be able to do this? There is, for the good reason that he possesses the innate powers. He has the emotional endowment, the originality and the artistic conception, and, what is more important, the power of creating that which has universal appeal and influence.

I make here what may appear to be a more startling statement by saying that the Negro has already proved the possession of these powers by being the creator of the only things artistic that have yet sprung from American soil and been universally acknowledged as distinctive American products.

These creations by the American Negro may be summed up under four heads. The first two are the Uncle Remus stories, which were collected by Joel Chandler Harris, and the "spirituals" or slave songs, to which the Fisk Jubilee Singers made the public and the musicians of both the United States and Europe listen. The Uncle Remus stories constitute the greatest body of folklore that America has produced, and the "spirituals" the greatest body of folk-song. I shall speak of the "spirituals" later because they are more than folk-songs, for in them the Negro sounded the depths, if he did not scale the heights, of music.

The other two creations are the cakewalk and ragtime. We do not need to go very far back to remember when cakewalking was the rage in the United States, Europe and South America. Society in this country and royalty abroad spent time in practicing the intricate steps. Paris pronounced it the "poetry of motion." The popularity of the cakewalk passed away but its influence remained. The influence can be seen to-day on any American stage where there is dancing.

The influence which the Negro has exercised on the art of dancing in this country has been almost absolute. For generations the "buck and wing" and the "stop-time" dances, which are strictly Negro, have been familiar to American theatre audiences. A few years ago the public discovered the "turkey trot," the "eagle rock," "ballin' the jack," and several other varieties that started the modern dance craze. These dances were quickly followed by the "tango," a dance originated by the Negroes of Cuba and later transplanted to South America. (This fact is attested by no less authority than Vincente Blasco Ibañez in his "Four Horsemen of the Apocalypse.") Half the floor space in the country was then turned over to dancing, and highly paid exponents sprang up everywhere. The most noted, Mr. Vernon Castle, and, by the way, an Englishman, never danced except to the music of a colored band, and he never failed to state to his audiences that most of his dances had long been done by "your colored people," as he put it.

Any one who witnesses a musical production in which there is dancing cannot fail to notice the Negro stamp on all the movements; a stamp which even the great vogue of Russian dances that swept the country about the time of the popular dance craze could not affect. That peculiar swaying of the shoulders which you see done everywhere by the blond girls of the chorus is nothing more than a movement from the Negro dance referred to above, the "eagle rock." Occasionally the movement takes on a suggestion of the, now outlawed, "shimmy."

As for Ragtime, I go straight to the statement that it is the one artistic production by which America is known the world over. It has been all-conquering. Everywhere it is hailed as "American music."

For a dozen years or so there has been a steady tendency to divorce Ragtime from the Negro; in fact, to take from him the credit of having originated it. Probably the younger people of the present generation do not know that Ragtime is of Negro origin. The change wrought in Ragtime and the way in which it is accepted by the country have been brought about chiefly through the change which has gradually been made in the words and stories accompanying the music. Once the text of all Ragtime songs was written in Negro dialect, and was about Negroes in the cabin or in the cotton field or on the levee or at a jubilee or on Sixth Avenue or at a ball, and about their love affairs. To-day, only a small proportion of Ragtime songs relate at all to the Negro. The truth is, Ragtime is now national rather than racial. But that does not abolish in any way the claim of the American Negro as its originator.

Ragtime music was originated by colored piano players in the questionable resorts of St. Louis, Memphis, and other Mississippi River towns. These men did not know any more about the theory of music than they did about the theory of the universe. They were guided by their natural musical instinct and talent, but above all by the Negro's extraordinary sense of rhythm. Any one who is familiar with Ragtime may note that its chief charm is not in melody, but in rhythms. These players often improvised crude and, at times, vulgar words to fit the music. This was the beginning of the Ragtime song.

Ragtime music got its first popular hearing at Chicago during the world's fair in that city. From Chicago it made its way to New York, and then started on its universal triumph.

The earliest Ragtime songs, like Topsy, "jes' grew." Some of these earliest songs were taken down by white men, the words slightly altered or changed, and published under the names of the arrangers. They sprang into immediate popularity and earned small fortunes. The first to become widely known was "The Bully," a levee song which had been long used by roustabouts along the Mississippi. It was introduced in New York by Miss May Irwin, and gained instant popularity. Another one of these "jes' grew" songs was one which for a while disputed for place with Yankee Doodle; perhaps, disputes it even to-day. That song was "A Hot Time in the Old Town To-night"; introduced and made popular by the colored regimental bands during the Spanish-American War.

Later there came along a number of colored men who were able to transcribe the old songs and write original ones. I was, about that time, writing words to music for the music show stage in New York. I was collaborating with my brother, J. Rosamond Johnson, and the late Bob Cole. I remember that we appropriated about the last one of the old "jes' grew" songs. It was a song which had been sung for years all through the South. The words were unprintable, but the tune was irresistible, and belongs to nobody. We took it, re-wrote the verses, telling an entirely different story from the original, left the chorus as it was, and published the song, at first under the name of "Will Handy." It became very popular with college boys, especially at football games, and perhaps still is. The song was, "Oh, Didn't He Ramble!"

In the beginning, and for quite a while, almost all of the Ragtime songs that were deliberately composed were the work of colored writers. Now, the colored composers, even in this particular field, are greatly outnumbered by the white.

The reader might be curious to know if the "jes' grew" songs have ceased to grow. No, they have not; they are growing all the time. The country has lately been flooded with several varieties of "The Blues." These "Blues," too, had their origin in Memphis, and the towns along the Mississippi. They are a sort of lament of a lover who is feeling "blue" over the loss of his sweetheart. The "Blues" of Memphis have been adulterated so much on Broadway that they have lost their pristine hue. But when ever you hear a piece of music which has a strain like this in it:

you will know you are listening to something which belonged originally to Beale Avenue, Memphis, Tennessee. The original "Memphis Blues," so far as it can be credited to a composer, must be credited to Mr. W. C. Handy, a colored musician of Memphis.

As illustrations of the genuine Ragtime song in the making, I quote the words of two that were popular with the Southern colored soldiers in France. Here is the first:

> "Mah mammy's lyin' in her grave,
>   Mah daddy done run away,
>   Mah sister's married a gamblin' man,
>   An' I've done gone astray.
>   Yes, I've done gone astray, po' boy,
>   An' I've done gone astray,
>   Mah sister's married a gamblin' man,
>   An' I've done gone astray, po' boy."

These lines are crude, but they contain something of real poetry, of that elusive thing which nobody can define and that you can only tell that it is there when you feel it. You cannot read these lines without becoming reflective and felling sorry for "Po' Boy."

Now, take in this word picture of utter dejection:

> "I'm jes' as misabul as I can be,
>   I'm unhappy even if I am free,
>   I'm feelin' down, I'm feelin' blue;

> I wander 'round, don't know what to do.
> I'm go'n lay mah haid on de railroad line,
> Let de B. & O. come and pacify mah min'."

These lines are, no doubt, one of the many versions of the famous "Blues." They are also crude, but they go straight to the mark. The last two lines move with the swiftness of all great tragedy.

In spite of the bans which musicians and music teachers have placed on it, the people still demand and enjoy Ragtime. In fact, there is not a corner of the civilized world in which it is not known and liked. And this proves its originality, for if it were an imitation, the people of Europe, at least, would not have found it a novelty. And it is proof of a more important thing, it is proof that Ragtime possesses the vital spark, the power to appeal universally, without which any artistic production, no matter how approved its form may be, is dead.

Of course, there are those who will deny that Ragtime is an artistic production. American musicians, especially, instead of investigating Ragtime, dismiss it with a contemptuous word. But this has been the course of scholasticism in every branch of art. Whatever new thing the people like is pooh-poohed; whatever is popular is regarded as not worth while. The fact is, nothing great or enduring in music has ever sprung full-fledged from the brain of any master; the best he gives the world he gathers from the hearts of the people, and runs it through the alembic of his genius.

Ragtime deserves serious attention. There is a lot of colorless and vicious imitation, but there is enough that is genuine. In one composition alone, "The Memphis Blues," the musician will find not only great melodic beauty, but a polyphonic structure that is amazing.

It is obvious that Ragtime has influenced, and in a large measure, become our popular music; but not many would know that it has influenced even our religious music. Those who are familiar with gospel hymns can at once see this influence if they will compare the songs of thirty years ago, such as "In the Sweet Bye and Bye," "The Ninety and Nine," etc., with the up-to-date, syncopated tunes that are sung in Sunday

Schools, Christian Endeavor Societies, Y.M.C.A.'s and like gatherings to-day.

Ragtime has not only influenced American music, it has influenced American life; indeed, it has saturated American life. It has become the popular medium for our national expression musically. And who can say that it does not express the blare and jangle and the surge, too, of our national spirit?

Any one who doubts that there is a peculiar heel-tickling, smile-provoking, joy-awakening, response-compelling charm in Ragtime needs only to hear a skillful performer play the genuine article, needs only to listen to its bizarre harmonies, its audacious resolutions often consisting of an abrupt jump from one key to another, its intricate rhythms in which the accents fall in the most unexpected places but in which the fundamental beat is never lost in order to be convinced. I believe it has its place as well as the music which draws from us sighs and tears.

Now, these dances which I have referred to and Ragtime music may be lower forms of art, but they are evidence of a power that will some day be applied to the higher forms. And even now we need not stop at the Negro's accomplishment through these lower forms. In the "spirituals," or slave songs, the Negro has given America not only its only folksongs, but a mass of noble music. I never think of this music but that I am struck by the wonder, the miracle of its production. How did the men who originated these songs manage to do it? The sentiments are easily accounted for; they are, for the most part, taken from the Bible. But the melodies, where did they come from? Some of them so weirdly sweet, and others so wonderfully strong. Take, for instance, "Go Down, Moses"; I doubt that there is a stronger theme in the whole musical literature of the world.

Oppressed so hard they could not stand, Let my people go.   Go down, Mo-ses,

way down in E-gypt land,   Tell ole Pha-raoh, Let my people go.

It is to be noted that whereas the chief characteristic of Ragtime is rhythm, the chief characteristic of the "spirituals" is melody. The melodies of "Steal Away to Jesus," "Sing Low Sweet Chariot," "Nobody Knows de Trouble I See," "I Couldn't Hear Nobody Pray," "Deep River," "O, Freedom Over Me," and many others of these songs possess a beauty that is—what shall I say? poignant. In the riotous rhythms of Ragtime the Negro expressed his irrepressible buoyancy, his keen response to the sheer joy of living; in the "spirituals" he voiced his sense of beauty and his deep religious feeling.

Naturally, not as much can be said for the words of these songs as for the music. Most of the songs are religious. Some of them are songs expressing faith and endurance and a longing for freedom. In the religious songs, the sentiments and often the entire lines are taken bodily from the Bible. However, there is no doubt that some of these religious songs have a meaning apart from the Biblical text. It is evident that the opening lines of "Go Down, Moses,"

> "Go down, Moses,
>   'Way down in Egypt land;
> Tell old Pharaoh,
> Let my people go."

have significance beyond the bondage of Israel in Egypt.

The bulk of the lines to these songs, as is the case in all communal music, is made up of choral iteration and incremental repetition of the leader's lines. If the words are read, this constant iteration and repetition are found to be tiresome; and it must be admitted that the lines themselves are often very trite. And, yet, there is frequently revealed a flash of real, primitive poetry. I give the following examples:

"Sometimes I feel like an eagle in de air."

"You may bury me in de East,
You may bury me in de West,
But I'll hear de trumpet sound
In-a dat mornin'."

"I know de moonlight, I know de starlight;
I lay dis body down.
I walk in de moonlight, I walk in de starlight;
I lay dis body down.
I know de graveyard, I know de graveyard,
When I lay dis body down.
I walk in de graveyard, I walk troo de graveyard
To lay dis body down.

"I lay in de grave an' stretch out my arms;
I lay dis body down.
I go to de judgment in de evenin' of de day
When I lay dis body down.
An' my soul an' yo' soul will meet in de day
When I lay dis body down."

Regarding the line, "I lay in de grave an' stretch out my arms," Col. Thomas Wentworth Higginson of Boston, one of the first to give these slave songs serious study, said: "Never it seems to me, since man first lived and suffered, was his infinite longing for peace uttered more plaintively than in that line."

These Negro folksongs constitute a vast mine of material that has been neglected almost absolutely. The only white writers who have in recent years given adequate attention and study to this music, that I know of, are Mr. H. E. Krehbiel and Mrs. Natalie Curtis Burlin. We have our native composers denying the worth and importance of this music, and trying to manufacture grand opera out of so-called Indian themes.

But there is a great hope for the development of this music, and that hope is the Negro himself. A worthy beginning has already been made by Burleigh, Cook, Johnson, and Dett. And there will yet come great Negro composers who will take this music and voice through it not only the soul of their race, but the soul of America.

And does it not seem odd that this greatest gift of the Negro has been the most neglected of all he possesses? Money and effort have been expended upon his development in every direction except this. This gift has been regarded as a kind of side show, something for occasional exhibition; wherein it is the touchstone, it is the magic thing, it is that by which the Negro can bridge all chasms. No persons, however hostile, can listen to Negroes singing this wonderful music without having their hostility melted down.

This power of the Negro to suck up the national spirit from the soil and create something artistic and original, which, at the same time, possesses the note of universal appeal, is due to a remarkable racial gift of adaptability; it is more than adaptability, it is a transfusive quality. And the Negro has exercised this transfusive quality not only here in America, where the race lives in large numbers, but in European countries, where the number has been almost infinitesimal.

Is it not curious to know that the greatest poet of Russia is Alexander Pushkin, a man of African descent; that the greatest romancer of France is Alexander Dumas, a man of African descent; and that one of the greatest musicians of England is Coleridge-Taylor, a man of African descent?

The fact is fairly well known that the father of Dumas was a Negro of the French West Indies, and that the father of Coleridge-Taylor was a native-born African; but the facts concerning Pushkin's African ancestry are not so familiar.

When Peter the Great was Czar of Russia, some potentate presented him with a full-blooded Negro of gigantic size. Peter, the most eccentric ruler of modern times, dressed this Negro up in soldier clothes, christened him Hannibal, and made him a special body-guard.

But Hannibal had more than size, he had brain and ability. He not only looked picturesque and imposing in soldier clothes, he showed that he had in him the making of a real soldier. Peter recognized this, and eventually made him a general. He afterwards ennobled him, and Hannibal, later, married one of the ladies of the Russian court. This same Hannibal was great-grandfather of Pushkin, the national poet of Russia, the man who bears the same relation to Russian literature that Shakespeare bears to English literature.

I know the question naturally arises: If out of the few Negroes who have lived in France there came a Dumas; and out of the few Negroes who have lived in England there came a Coleridge-Taylor; and if from the man who was at the time, probably, the only Negro in Russia there sprang that country's national poet, why have not the millions of Negroes in the United States with all the emotional and artistic endowment claimed for them produced a Dumas, or a Coleridge-Taylor, or a Pushkin?

The question seems difficult, but there is an answer. The Negro in the United States is consuming all of his intellectual energy in this grueling race-struggle. And the same statement may be made in a general way about the white South. Why does not the white South produce literature and art? The white South, too, is consuming all of its intellectual energy in this lamentable conflict. Nearly all of the mental efforts of the white South run through one narrow channel. The life of every Southern white man and all of his activities are impassably limited by the ever present Negro problem. And that is why, as Mr. H. L. Mencken puts it, in all that vast region, with its thirty or forty million people and its territory as large as a half a dozen Frances and Germanys, there is not a single poet, not a serious historian, not a creditable composer, not a critic good or bad, not a dramatist dead or alive.

But, even so, the American Negro has accomplished something in pure literature. The list of those who have done so would be surprising both by its length and the excellence of the achievements. One of the great books written in this country since the Civil War is the work of a colored man, "The Souls of Black Folk," by W. E. B. Du Bois.

Such a list begins with Phillis Wheatley. In 1761 a slave ship landed a cargo of slaves in Boston. Among them was a little girl seven or eight years of age. She attracted the attention of John Wheatley, a wealthy gentleman of Boston, who purchased her as a servant for his wife. Mrs. Wheatley was a benevolent woman. She noticed the girl's quick mind and determined to give her opportunity for its development. Twelve years later Phillis published a volume of poems. The book was brought out in London, where Phillis was for several months an object of great curiosity and attention.

Phillis Wheatley has never been given her rightful place in American literature. By some sort of conspiracy she is kept out of most of the books, especially the text-books on literature used in the schools. Of course, she is not a *great* American poet—and in her day there were no great American poets— but she is an important American poet. Her importance, if for no other reason, rests on the fact that, save one, she is the first in order of time of all the women poets of America. And she is among the first of all American poets to issue a volume.

It seems strange that the books generally give space to a mention of Urian Oakes, President of Harvard College, and to quotations from the crude and lengthy elegy which he published in 1667; and print examples from the execrable versified version of the Psalms made by the New England divines, and yet deny a place to Phillis Wheatley.

Here are the opening lines from the elegy by Oakes, which is quoted from in most of the books on American literature:

> "Reader, I am no poet, but I grieve.
> Behold here what that passion can do,
> That forced a verse without Apollo's leave,
> And whether the learned sisters would or no."

There was no need for Urian to admit what his handiwork declared. But this from the versified Psalms still worse, yet it is found in the books:

> "The Lord's song sing can we? being
> in stranger's land, then let
> lose her skill my right hand if I
> Jerusalem forget."

Anne Bradstreet preceded Phillis Wheatley by a little over twenty years. She published her volume of poems, "The Tenth Muse," in 1750. Let us strike a comparison between the two. Anne Bradstreet was a wealthy, cultivated Puritan girl, the daughter of Thomas Dudley, Governor of Bay Colony. Phillis, as we know, was a Negro slave girl born in Africa. Let us take them both at their best and in the same vein. The following stanza is from Anne's poem entitles "Contemplation":

> "While musing thus with contemplation fed,
>   And thousand fancies buzzing in my brain,
>   The sweet tongued Philomel percht o'er my head,
>   And chanted forth a most melodious strain,
>   Which rapt me so with wonder and delight,
>   I judged my hearing better than my sight,
>   And wisht me wings with her awhile to take my flight."

And the following is from Phillis' poem entitled "Imagination":

> "Imagination! who can sing thy force?
>   Or who describe the swiftness of they course?
>   Soaring through air to find the bright abode,
>   The empyreal palace of the thundering God,
>   We on thy pinions can surpass the wind,
>   And leave the rolling universe behind,
>   From star to star the mental optics rove,
>   Measure the skies, and range the realms above,
>   There in one view we grasp the mighty whole,
>   Or with new worlds amaze the unbounded soul."

We do not think the black woman suffers much by comparison with the white. Thomas Jefferson said of Phillis: "Religion has produced a Phillis Wheatley, but it could not produce a poet; her poems are beneath contempt." It is quite likely that Jefferson's criticism was directed more against religion than against Phillis' poetry. On the other hand, General George Washington wrote her with his own hand a letter in which he thanked her for a poem which she had dedicated to him. He, later, received her with marked courtesy at his camp at Cambridge.

It appears certain that Phillis was the first person to apply to George Washington the phrase, "First in peace." The phrase occurs in her poem addressed to "His Excellency, General George Washington," written in 1775. The encomium, "First in war, first in peace, first in the hearts of his countrymen" was originally used in the resolutions presented to Congress on the death of Washington, December, 1799.

Phillis Wheatley's poetry is the poetry of the Eighteenth Century. She wrote when Pope and Gray were supreme; it is easy to see that Pope was her model. Had she come under the influence of Wordsworth, Byron, or Keats or Shelley, she would have done greater work. As it is, her work must not be judged by the work and standards of a later day, but by the work and standards of her own day and her own contemporaries. By this method of criticism she stands out as one of the important characters in the making of American literature, without any allowances for her sex or her antecedents.

According to "A Bibliographical Checklist of American Negro Poetry," compiled by Mr. Arthur A. Schomburg, more than one hundred Negroes in the United States have published volumes of poetry ranging in size from pamphlets to books of from one hundred to three hundred pages. About thirty of these writers fill in the gap between Phillis Wheatley and Paul Laurence Dunbar. Just here it is of interest to note that a Negro wrote and published a poem before Phillis Wheatley arrived in this country from Africa. He was Jupiter Hammon, a slave belonging to a Mr. Lloyd of Queens-Village, Long Island. In 1760 Hammon published a poem, eighty-eight lines in length, entitled "An Evening Thought, Salvation by Christ, with Penettential Cries." In 1788 he published "An Address to Miss Phillis Wheatley, Ethiopian Poetess in Boston, who came from Africa at eight years of age, and soon became acquainted with the Gospel of Jesus Christ." These two poems do not include all that Hammon wrote.

The poets between Phillis Wheatley and Dunbar must be considered more in the light of what they attempted than of what they accomplished. Many of them showed marked talent, but barely a half dozen of them demonstrated even mediocre mastery of technique in the use of poetic material and forms. And yet there are several names that deserve mention. George M. Horton, Frances E. Harper, James M. Bell and Alberry A. Whitman, all merit consideration when due allowances are made for their limitations in education, training and general culture. The limitations of Horton were greater than those of either of the others; he was born a slave in

North Carolina in 1797, and as a young man began to compose poetry without being able to write it down. Later he received some instruction from professors of the University of North Carolina, at which institution he was employed as a janitor. He published a volume of poems, "The Hope of Liberty," in 1829.

Mrs. Harper, Bell and Whitman would stand out if only for the reason that each of them attempted sustained work. Mrs. Harper published her first volume of poems in 1854, but later she published "Moses, a Story of the Nile," a poem which ran to 52 closely printed pages. Bell in 1864 published a poem of 28 pages in celebration of President Lincoln's Emancipation Proclamation. In 1870 he published a poem of 32 pages in celebration of the ratification of the Fifteenth Amendment to the Constitution. Whitman published his first volume of poems, a book of 253 pages, in 1877; but in 1884 he published "The Rape of Florida," an epic poem written in four cantos and done in the Spenserian stanza, and which ran to 97 closely printed pages. The poetry of both Mrs. Harper and of Whitman had a large degree of popularity; one of Mrs. Harper's books went through more than twenty editions.

Of these four poets, it is Whitman who reveals not only the greatest imagination but also the more skillful workmanship. His lyric power at its best may be judged from the following stanza from the "Rape of Florida":

> " 'Come now, my love, the moon is on the lake;
> Upon the waters is my light canoe;
> Come with me, love, and gladsome oars shall make
> A music on the parting wave for you.
> Come o'er the waters deep and dark and blue;
> Come where the lilies in the marge have sprung,
> Come with me, love, for Oh, my love is true!'
> This is the song that on the lake was sung,
> The boatman sang it when his heart was young."

Some idea of Whitman's capacity for dramatic narration may be gained from the following lines taken from "Not a Man, and Yet a Man," a poem of even greater length than "The Rape of Florida":

"A flash of steely lightning from his hand,
Strikes down the groaning leader of the band;
Divides his startled comrades, and again
Descending, leaves fair Dora's captors slain.
Her, seizing then within a strong embrace,
Out in the dark he wheels his flying pace;

  .   .   .   .   .

He speaks not, but with stalwart tenderness
Her swelling bosom firm to his doth press;
Springs like a stag that flees the eager hound,
And like a whirlwind rustles o'er the ground.
Her locks swim in dishevelled wildness o'er
His shoulders, streaming to his waist and more;
While on and on, strong as a rolling flood,
His sweeping footsteps part the silent wood."

It is curious and interesting to trace the growth of individuality and race consciousness in this group of poets. Jupiter Hammon's verses were almost entirely religious exhortations. Only very seldom does Phillis Wheatley sound a native note. Four times in single lines she refers to herself as "Afric's muse." In a poem of admonition addressed to the students at the "University of Cambridge in New England" she refers to herself as follows:

"Ye blooming plants of human race divine,
An Ethiop tells you 'tis your greatest foe."

But one looks in vain for some outburst or even complaint against the bondage of her people, for some agonizing cry about her native land. In two poems she refers definitely to Africa as her home, but in each instance there seems to be under the sentiment of the lines a feeling of almost smug contentment at her own escape therefrom. In the poem, "On Being Brought from Africa to America," she says:

"'Twas mercy brought me from my pagan land,
Taught my benighted soul to understand
That there's a God and there's a Saviour too;
Once I redemption neither sought or knew.
Some view our sable race with scornful eye,

'Their color is a diabolic dye.'
Remember, Christians, Negroes black as Cain,
May be refined, and join th' angelic train."

In the poem addressed to the Earl of Dartmouth, she speaks of
freedom and makes a reference to the parents from whom she
was taken as a child, a reference which cannot but strike the
reader as rather impassioned:

"Should you, my lord, while you peruse my song,
Wonder from whence my love of Freedom sprung,
Whence flow these wishes for the common good,
By feeling hearts alone best understood;
I, young in life, by seeming cruel fate
Was snatch'd from Afric's fancy'd happy seat;
What pangs excruciating must molest,
What sorrows labor in my parents' breast?
Steel'd was that soul and by no misery mov'd
That from a father seiz'd his babe belov'd;
Such, such my case. And can I then but pray
Others may never feel tyrannic sway?"

The bulk of Phillis Wheatley's work consists of poems addressed to people of prominence. Her book was dedicated to
the Countess of Huntington, at whose house she spent the
greater part of her time while in England. On his repeal of the
Stamp Act, she wrote a poem to King George III, whom she
saw later; another poem she wrote to the Earl of Dartmouth,
whom she knew. A number of her verses were addressed to
other persons of distinction. Indeed, it is apparent that Phillis
was far from being a democrat. She was far from being a democrat not only in her social ideas but also in her political ideas;
unless a religious meaning is given to the closing lines of her
ode to General Washington, she was a decided royalist:

"A crown, a mansion, and a throne that shine
With gold unfading, Washington! be thine."

Nevertheless, she was an ardent patriot. Her ode to General
Washington (1775), her spirited poem, "On Major General
Lee" (1776) and her poem, "Liberty and Peace," written in
celebration of the close of the war, reveal not only strong patri-

otic feeling but an understanding of the issues at stake. In her poem, "On Major General Lee," she makes her hero reply thus to the taunts of the British commander into whose hands he has been delivered through treachery:

"O arrogance of tongue!
And wild ambition, ever prone to wrong!
Believ'st thou, chief, that armies such as thine
Can stretch in dust that heaven-defended line?
In vain allies may swarm from distant lands,
And demons aid in formidable bands,
Great as thou art, thou shun'st the field of fame,
Disgrace to Britain and the British name!
When offer'd combat by the noble foe,
(Foe to misrule) why did the sword forego
The easy conquest of the rebel-land?
Perhaps TOO easy for thy martial hand.

What various causes to the field invite!
For plunder YOU, and we for freedom fight,
Her cause divine with generous ardor fires,
And every bosom glows as she inspires!
Already thousands of your troops have fled
To the drear mansions of the silent dead:
Columbia, too, beholds with streaming eyes
Her heroes fall—'tis freedom's sacrifice!
So wills the power who with convulsive storms
Shakes impious realms, and nature's face deforms;
Yet those brave troops, innum'rous as the sands,
One soul inspires, one General Chief commands;
Find in your train of boasted heroes, one
To match the praise of Godlike Washington.
Thrice happy Chief in whom the virtues join,
And heaven taught prudence speaks the man divine."

What Phillis Wheatley failed to achieve is due in no small degree to her education and environment. Her mind was steeped in the classics; her verses are filled with classical and mythological allusions. She knew Ovid thoroughly and was familiar with other Latin authors. She must have known Alexander Pope by heart. And, too, she was reared and sheltered in a wealthy and cultured family,—a wealthy and cultured Boston family; she never had the opportunity to learn life; she never found out her own true relation to life and to her surroundings. And it should not be forgotten that she was only about thirty years old when she died. The impulsion or the compulsion that might have driven her genius off the worn paths, out on a journey of exploration, Phillis Wheatley never received. But, whatever her limitations, she merits more than America has accorded her.

Horton, who was born three years after Phillis Wheatley's death, expressed in all of this poetry strong complaint at his condition of slavery and a deep longing for freedom. The following verses are typical of his style and his ability:

> "Alas! and am I born for this,
>   To wear this slavish chain?
> Deprived of all created bliss,
>   Through hardship, toil, and pain?
>
>   .   .   .
>
> Come, Liberty! thou cheerful sound,
>   Roll through my ravished ears;
> Come, let my grief in joys be drowned,
>   And drive away my fears."

In Mrs. Harper we find something more than the complaint and the longing of Horton. We find an expression of a sense of wrong and injustice. The following stanzas are from a poem addressed to the white women of America:

> "You can sigh o'er the sad-eyed Armenian
>   Who weeps in her desolate home.
> You can mourn o'er the exile of Russia
>   From kindred and friends doomed to roam.
>
>   .   .   .   .
>
> But hark! from our Southland are floating
>   Sobs of anguish, murmurs of pain,
> And women heart-stricken are weeping
>   O'er their tortured and slain.
>
>   .   .   .
>
> Have ye not, oh, my favored sisters,
>   Just a plea, a prayer or a fear

> For mothers who dwell 'neath the shadows
>   Of agony, hatred and fear?
>
>   .   .   .   .   .
>
> Weep not, oh my well sheltered sisters,
>   Weep not for the Negro alone,
> But weep for your sons who must gather
>   The crops which their fathers have sown."

Whitman, in the midst of "The Rape of Florida," a poem in which he related the taking of the State of Florida from the Seminoles, stops and discusses the race question. He discusses it in many other poems; and he discusses it from many different angles. In Whitman we find not only an expression of a sense of wrong and injustice, but we hear a note of faith and a note also of defiance. For example, in the opening to Canto II of "The Rape of Florida":

> "Greatness by nature cannot be entailed,
>   It is an office ending with the man,—
>   Sage, hero, Saviour, tho' the Sire be hailed,
>   The son may reach obscurity in the van:
>   Sublime achievements know no patent plan,
>   Man's immortality's a book with seals,
>   And none but God shall open—none else can—
>   But opened, it the mystery reveals,—
>   Manhood's conquest of man to heaven's respect appeals.
>
> "Is manhood less because man's face is black?
>   Let thunders of the loosened seals reply!
>   Who shall the rider's restive steed turn back,
>   Or who withstand the arrows he lets fly
>   Between the mountains of eternity?
>   Genius ride forth! Thou gift and torch of heav'n!
>   The mastery is kindled in thine eye;
>   To conquest ride! thy bow of strength is giv'n—
>   The trampled hordes of caste before thee shall be driv'n!
>
>   .   .   .   .   .
>
> " 'Tis hard to judge if hatred of one's race,
>   By those who deem themselves superior-born,
>   Be worse than that quiescence in disgrace,
>   Which only merits—and should only—scorn.

Oh, let me see the Negro night and morn,
Pressing and fighting in, for place and power!
All earth is place—all time th' auspicious hour,
While heaven leans forth to look, oh, will he quail or cower?

"Ah! I abhor his protest and complaint!
His pious looks and patience I despise!
He can't evade the test, disguised as saint;
The manly voice of freedom bids him rise,
And shake himself before Philistine eyes!
And, like a lion roused, no sooner than
A foe dare come, play all his energies,
And court the fray with fury if he can;
For hell itself respects a fearless, manly man."

It may be said that none of these poets strike a deep native
strain or sound a distinctively original note, either in matter or
form. That is true; but the same thing may be said of all the
American poets down to the writers of the present generation,
with the exception of Poe and Walt Whitman. The thing in
which these black poets are mostly excelled by their contemporaries is mere technique.

Paul Laurence Dunbar stands out as the first poet from the
Negro race in the United States to show a combined mastery
over poetic material and poetic technique, to reveal innate literary distinction in what he wrote, and to maintain a high level
of performance. He was the first to rise to a height from which
he could take a perspective view of his own race. He was the
first to see objectively its humor, its superstitions, its shortcomings; the first to feel sympathetically its heart-wounds, its
yearnings, its aspirations, and to voice them all in a purely
literary form.

Dunbar's fame rests chiefly on his poems in Negro dialect.
This appraisal of him is, no doubt, fair; for in these dialect
poems he not only carried his art to the highest point of perfection, but he made a contribution to American literature unlike
what any one else had made, a contribution which, perhaps, no
one else could have made. Of course, Negro dialect poetry was
written before Dunbar wrote, most of it by white writers; but

the fact stands out that Dunbar was the first to use it as a medium for the true interpretation of Negro character and psychology. And, yet, poetry does not constitute the whole or even the bulk of Dunbar's work. In addition to a large number of poems of a very high order done in literary English, he was the author of four novels and several volumes of short stories.

Indeed, Dunbar did not begin his career as a writer of dialect. I may be pardoned for introducing here a bit of reminiscence. My personal friendship with Paul Dunbar began before he had achieved recognition, and continued to be close until his death. When I first met him he had published a thin volume, "Oak and Ivy," which was being sold chiefly through his own efforts. "Oak and Ivy" showed no distinctive Negro influence, but rather the influence of James Whitcomb Riley. At this time Paul and I were together every day for several months. He talked to me a great deal about his hopes and ambitions. In these talks he revealed that he had reached a realization of the possibilities of poetry in the dialect, together with a recognition of the fact that it offered the surest way by which he could get a hearing. Often he said to me: "I've got to write dialect poetry; it's the only way I can get them to listen to me." I was with Dunbar at the beginning of what proved to be his last illness. He said to me then: "I have not grown. I am writing the same things I wrote ten years ago, and am writing them no better." His self-accusation was not fully true; he had grown, and he had gained a surer control of his art, but he had not accomplished the greater things of which he was constantly dreaming; the public had held him to the things for which it had accorded him recognition. If Dunbar had lived he would have achieved some of those dreams, but even while he talked so dejectedly to me he seemed to feel that he was not to live. He died when he was only thirty-three.

It has a bearing on this entire subject to note that Dunbar was of unmixed Negro blood; so, as the greatest figure in literature which the colored race in the United States has produced, he stands as an example at once refuting and confounding those who wish to believe that whatever extraordinary ability an Aframerican shows is due to an admixture of white blood.

As a man, Dunbar was kind and tender. In conversation he

was brilliant and polished. His voice was his chief charm, and was a great element in his success as a reader of his own works. In his actions he was impulsive as a child, sometimes even erratic; indeed, his intimate friends almost looked upon him as a spoiled boy. He was always delicate in health. Temperamentally, he belonged to that class of poets who Taine says are vessels too weak to contain the spirit of poetry, the poets whom poetry kills, the Byrons, the Burns's, the De Mussets, the Poes.

To whom may he be compared, this boy who scribbled his early verses while he ran an elevator, whose youth was a battle against poverty, and who, in spite of almost insurmountable obstacles, rose to success? A comparison between him and Burns is not unfitting. The similarity between many phases of their lives is remarkable, and their works are not incommensurable. Burns took the strong dialect of his people and made it classic; Dunbar took the humble speech of his people and in it wrought music.

Mention of Dunbar brings up for consideration the fact that, although he is the most outstanding figure in literature among the Aframericans of the United States, he does not stand alone among the Aframericans of the whole Western world. There are Plácido and Manzano in Cuba; Vieux and Durand in Haiti, Machado de Assis in Brazil; Leon Laviaux in Martinique, and others still that might be mentioned, who stand on a plane with or even above Dunbar. Plácido and Machado de Assis rank as great in the literatures of their respective countries without any qualifications whatever. They are world figures in the literature of the Latin languages. Machado de Assis is somewhat handicapped in this respect by having as his tongue and medium the lesser known Portuguese, but Plácido, writing in the language of Spain, Mexico, Cuba, and of almost the whole of South America, is universally known. His works have been republished in the original in Spain, Mexico and in most of the Latin-American countries; several editions have been published in the United States; translations of his works have been made into French and German.

Plácido is in some respects the greatest of all the Cuban poets. In sheer genius and the fire of inspiration he surpasses even the more finished Heredia. Then, too, his birth, his life and his death ideally contained the tragic elements that go into the making of a halo about a poet's head. Plácido was born in Habana in 1809. The first months of his life were passed in a foundling asylum; indeed, his real name, Gabriel de la Concepcion Valdés, was in honor of its founder. His father took him out of the asylum, but shortly afterwards went to Mexico and died there. His early life was a struggle against poverty; his youth and manhood was a struggle for Cuban independence. His death placed him in the list of Cuban martyrs. On the 27th of June, 1844, he was lined up against a wall with ten others and shot by order of the Spanish authorities on a charge of conspiracy. In his short but eventful life he turned out work which bulks more than six hundred pages. During the few hours preceding his execution he wrote three of his best known poems, among them his famous sonnet, "Mother, Farewell!"

Plácido's sonnet to his mother has been translated into every important language; William Cullen Bryant did it in English; but in spite of its wide popularity, it is, perhaps outside of Cuba the least understood of all Plácido's poems. It is curious to note how Bryant's translation totally misses the intimate sense of the delicate subtility of the poem. The American poet makes it a tender and loving farewell of a son who is about to die to a heart-broken mother; but that is not the kind of a farewell that Plácido intended to write or did write.

The key to the poem is in the first word, and the first word is the Spanish conjunction *Si* (if). The central idea, then, of the sonnet is, "If the sad fate which now overwhelms me should bring a pang to your heart, do not weep, for I die a glorious death and sound the last note of my lyre to you." Bryant either failed to understand or ignored the opening word, "If," because he was not familiar with the poet's history.

While Plácido's father was a Negro, his mother was a Spanish white woman, a dancer in one of the Habana theatres. At his birth she abandoned him to a foundling asylum, and perhaps never saw him again, although it is known that she outlived her son. When the poet came down to his last hours he remembered that somewhere there lived a woman who was his mother; that although she had heartlessly abandoned him; that although he owed her no filial duty, still she might, perhaps, on hearing of his sad end feel some pang of grief or sadness; so he tells her in his last words that he died happy and bids her not to weep. This he does with nobility and dignity, but absolutely without affection. Taking into account these facts, and especially their humiliating and embittering effect upon a soul so sensitive as Plácido's, this sonnet, in spite of the obvious weakness of the sestet as compared with the octave, is a remarkable piece of work.

In considering the Aframerican poets of the Latin languages I am impelled to think that, as up to this time the colored poets of greater universality have come out of the Latin-American countries rather than out of the United States, they will continue to do so for a good many years. The reason for this I hinted at in the first part of this preface. The colored poet in the United States labors within limitations which he cannot easily pass over. He is always on the defensive or the offensive. The pressure upon him to be propagandic is well nigh irresistible. These conditions are suffocating to breadth and to real art in poetry. In addition he labors under the handicap of finding culture not entirely colorless in the United States. On the other hand, the colored poet of Latin-American can voice the national spirit without any reservations. And he will be rewarded without any reservations, whether it be to place him among the great or declare him the greatest.

So I think it probable that the first world-acknowledged Aframerican poet will come out of Latin-America. Over against this probability, of course, is the great advantage possessed by the colored poet in the United States of writing in the world-conquering English language.

This preface has gone far beyond what I had in mind when I started. It was my intention to gather together the best verses. I could find by Negro poets and present them with a bare word of introduction. It was not my plan to make this collection inclusive nor to make the book in any sense a book of criticism. I planned to present only verses by contemporary writers; but, perhaps, because this is the first collection of its kind, I realized the absence of a starting-point and was led to provide one and to fill in with historical data what I felt to be a gap.

It may be surprising to many to see how little of the poetry

PREFACE: AMERICAN NEGRO POETRY   713

being written by Negro poets to-day is being written in Negro dialect. The newer Negro poets show a tendency to discard dialect; much of the subject-matter which went into the making of traditional dialect poetry, 'possums, watermelons, etc., they have discarded altogether, at least, as poetic material. This tendency will, no doubt, be regretted by the majority of white readers; and, indeed, it would be a distinct loss if the American Negro poets threw away this quaint and musical folk-speech as a medium of expression. And yet, after all, these poets are working through a problem not realized by the reader, and, perhaps, by many of these poets themselves not realized consciously. They are trying to break away from, not Negro dialect itself, but the limitations on Negro dialect imposed by the fixing effects of long convention.

The Negro in the United States has achieved or been placed in a certain artistic niche. When he is thought of artistically, it is as a happy-go-lucky, singing, shuffling, banjo-picking being or as a more or less pathetic figure. The picture of him is in a log cabin amid fields of cotton or along the levees. Negro dialect is naturally and by long association the exact instrument for voicing this phase of Negro life; and by that very exactness it is an instrument with but two full stops, humor and pathos. So even when he confines himself to purely racial themes, the Aframerican poet realizes that there are phases of Negro life in the United States which cannot be treated in the dialect either adequately or artistically. Take, for example, the phases rising out of life in Harlem, that most wonderful Negro city in the world. I do not deny that a Negro in a log cabin is more picturesque than a Negro in a Harlem flat, but the Negro in the Harlem flat is here, and he is but part of a group growing everywhere in the country, a group whose ideals are becoming increasingly more vital than those of the traditionally artistic group, even if its members are less picturesque.

What the colored poet in the United States needs to do is something like what Synge did for the Irish; he needs to find a form that will express the racial spirit by symbols from within rather than by symbols from without, such as the mere mutilation of English spelling and pronunciation. He needs a form that is freer and larger than dialect, but which will still hold the racial flavor; a form expressing the imagery, the idioms, the peculiar turns of thought, and the distinctive humor and pathos, too, of the Negro, but which will also be capable of voicing the deepest and highest emotions and aspirations, and allow of the widest range of subjects and the widest scope of treatment,

Negro dialect is at present a medium that is not capable of giving expression to the varied conditions of Negro life in America, and much less is it capable of giving the fullest interpretation of Negro character and psychology. This is no indictment against the dialect as dialect, but against the mould of convention in which Negro dialect in the United States has been set. In time these conventions may become lost, and the colored poet in the United States may sit down to write in dialect without feeling that his first line will put the general reader in a frame of mind which demands that the poem be humorous or pathetic. In the meantime, there is no reason why these poets should not continue to do the beautiful things that can be done, and done best, in the dialect.

In stating the need for Aframerican poets in the United Sates to work out a new and distinctive form of expression I do not wish to be understood to hold any theory that they should limit themselves to Negro poetry, to racial themes; the sooner they are able to write *American* poetry spontaneously, the better. Nevertheless, I believe that the richest contribution the Negro poet can make to the American literature of the future will be the fusion into it of his own individual artistic gifts.

Not many of the writers here included, except Dunbar, are known at all to the general reading public; and there is only one of these who has a widely recognized position in the American literary world, he is William Stanley Braithwaite. Mr. Braithwaite is not only unique in this respect, but he stands unique among all the Aframerican writers the United States has yet produced. He has gained his place, taking as the standard and measure for his work the identical standard and measure applied to American writers and American literature. He has asked for no allowances or rewards, either directly or indirectly, on account of his race.

Mr. Braithwaite is the author of two volumes of verses, lyrics of delicate and tenuous beauty. In his more recent and uncollected poems he shows himself more and more decidedly the mystic. But his place in American literature is due more to his work as a critic and anthologist than to his work as a poet. There is still another rôle he has played, that of friend of poetry and poets. It is a recognized fact that in the work which preceded the present revival of poetry in the United States, no one rendered more unremitting and valuable service than Mr. Braithwaite. And it can be said that no future study of American poetry of this age can be made without reference to Braithwaite.

Two authors included in the book are better known for their work in prose than in poetry: W. E. B. Du Bois whose well-known prose at its best is, however, impassioned and rhythmical; and Benjamin Brawley who is the author, among other works, of one of the best handbooks on the English drama that has yet appeared in America.

But the group of the new Negro poets, whose work makes up the bulk of this anthology, contains names destined to be known. Claude McKay, although still quite a young man, has already demonstrated his power, breadth and skill as a poet. Mr. McKay's breadth is as essential a part of his equipment as his power and skill. He demonstrates mastery of the three when as a Negro poet he pours out the bitterness and rebellion in his heart in those two sonnet-tragedies, "If We Must Die" and "To the White Fiends," in a manner that strikes terror; and when as a cosmic poet he creates the atmosphere and mood of poetic beauty in the absolute, as he does in "Spring in New Hampshire" and "The Harlem Dance." Mr. McKay gives evidence that he has passed beyond the danger which threatens many of the new Negro poets—the danger of allowing the purely polemical phases of the race problem to choke their sense of artistry.

Mr. McKay's earliest work is unknown in this country. It consists of poems written and published in his native Jamaica. I was fortunate enough to run across this first volume, and I could not refrain from reproducing here one of the poems written in the West Indian Negro dialect. I have done this not only to illustrate the widest range of the poet's talent and to offer a comparison between the American and the West Indian dialects, but on account of the intrinsic worth of the poem itself. I was much tempted to introduce several more, in spite of the fact that they might require a glossary, because however greater work Mr. McKay may do he can never do anything more touching and charming than these poems in the Jamaica dialect.

Fenton Johnson is a young poet of the ultra-modern school who gives promise of greater work than he has yet done. Jessie Fauset shows that she possesses the lyric gift, and she works with care and finish. Miss Fauset is especially adept in her translations from the French. Georgia Douglas Johnson is a poet neither afraid nor ashamed of her emotions. She limits herself to the purely conventional forms, rhythms and rhymes, but through them she achieves striking effects. The principal theme of Mrs. Johnson's poems is the secret dread down in every woman's heart, the dread of the passing of youth and beauty, and with them love. An old theme, one which poets themselves have often wearied of, but which, like death, remains one of the imperishable themes on which is made the poetry that has moved men's hearts through all ages. In her ingenuously wrought verses, through sheer simplicity and spontaneousness, Mrs. Johnson often sounds a note of pathos or passion that will not fail to waken a response, except in those too sophisticated or cynical to respond to natural impulses. Of the half dozen or so of colored women writing creditable verse, Anne Spencer is the most modern and least obvious in her methods. Her lines are at times involved and turgid and almost cryptic, but she shows and originality which does not depend upon eccentricities. In her "Before the Feast of Shushan" she displays an opulence, the love of which has long been charged against the Negro as one of his naïve and childish traits, but which in art may infuse a much needed color, warmth and spirit of abandon into American poetry.

John W. Holloway, more than any Negro poet writing in the dialect to-day, summons to his work the lilt, the spontaneity and charm of which Dunbar was the supreme master whenever he employed that medium. It is well to say a word here about the dialect poems of James Edwin Campbell. In dialect, Campbell was a precursor of Dunbar. A comparison of his idioms and phonetics with those of Dunbar reveals great differences. Dunbar is a shade or two more sophisticated and his phonetics approach nearer to a mean standard of the dialects spoken in the different sections. Campbell is more primitive and his phonetics are those of the dialect as spoken by the Negroes of the sea islands off the coasts of South Carolina and Georgia, which to this day remains comparatively close to its African roots, and is strikingly similar to the speech of the uneducated Negroes of the West Indies. An error that confuses many persons in reading or understanding Negro dialect is the idea that it is uniform. An ignorant Negro of the uplands of Georgia would have almost as much difficulty in understanding an ignorant sea island Negro as an Englishman would have. Not even in the dialect of any particular section is a given word always pronounced in precisely the same way. Its pronunciation depends upon the preceding and following sounds. Sometimes the combination permits of a liaison so close that to the uninitiated the sound of the work is almost completely lost.

The constant effort in Negro dialect is to elide all troublesome consonants and sounds. This negative effort may be after all only positive laziness of the vocal organs, but the result is a softening and smoothing which makes Negro dialect so delightfully easy for singers.

Daniel Webster Davis wrote dialect poetry at the time when Dunbar was writing. He gained great popularity, but it did not spread beyond his own race. Davis had unctuous humor, but he was crude. For illustration, note the vast stretch between his "Hog Meat" and Dunbar's "When de Co'n Pone's Hot," both of them poems on the traditional ecstasy of the Negro in contemplation of "good things" to eat.

It is regrettable that two of the most gifted writers included were cut off so early in life. R. C. Jamison and Joseph S. Cotter, Jr., died several years ago, both of them in their youth. Jamison was barely thirty at the time of his death, but among his poems there is one, at least, which stamps him as a poet of superior talent and lofty inspiration. "The Negro Soldiers" is a poem with the race problem as its theme, yet it transcends the limits of race and rises to a spiritual height that makes it one of the noblest poems of the Great War. Cotter died a mere boy of twenty, and the latter part of that brief period he passed in an invalid state. Some months before his death he published a thin volume of verses which were for the most part written on a sick bed. In this little volume Cotter showed fine poetic sense and a free and bold mastery over his material. A reading of Cotter's poems is certain to induce that mood in which one will regretfully speculate on what the young poet might have accomplished had he not been cut off so soon.

As intimated above, my original idea for this book underwent a change in the writing of the introduction. I first planned to select twenty-five to thirty poems which I judged to be up to a certain standard, and offer them with a few words of introduction and without comment. In the collection, as it grew to be, that "certain standard" has been broadened if not lowered; but I believe that this is offset by the advantage of the wider range given the reader and the student of the subject.

I offer this collection without making apology or asking allowance. I feel confident that the reader will find not only an earnest for the future, but actual achievement. The reader cannot but be impressed by the distance already covered. It is a long way from the plaints of George Horton to the invectives of Claude McKay, from the obviousness of Frances Harper to the complexness of Anne Spencer. Much ground has been covered, but more will yet be covered. It is this side of prophecy to declare that the undeniable creative genius of the Negro is destined to make a distinctive and valuable contribution to American poetry.

I wish to extend my thanks to Mr. Arthur A. Schomburg, who placed his valuable collection of books by Negro authors at my disposal. I wish also to acknowledge with thanks the kindness of Dodd, Mead & Co. for permitting the reprint of poems by Paul Laurence Dunbar; of the Cornhill Publishing Company for permission to reprint poems of Georgia Douglas Johnson, Joseph S. Cotter, Jr., Bertram Johnson and Waverley Carmichael; and of Neale & Co. for permission to reprint poems of John W. Holloway. I wish to thank Mr. Braithwaite for permission to use the included poems from his forthcoming volume, "Sandy Star and Willie Gee." And to acknowledge the courtesy of the following magazines: *The Crisis*, *The Century Magazine*, *The Liberator*, *The Freeman*, *The Independent*, *Others*, and *Poetry: A Magazine of Verse*.

JAMES WELDON JOHNSON.

NEW YORK CITY, 1921.

Lynching—America's National Disgrace

THE standard book on lynching, J. E. Cutler's "Lynch-Law," speaks of it as "a criminal practice which is peculiar to the United States." This definition was true when Cutler's book was published, not quite twenty years ago, and it still is true. The origin of the term is doubtful. To various Colonels and civilians named Lynch is ascribed the doubtful honor of establishing this form of crime in our country, in Revolutionary times, when the absence of courts of justice in country districts and the turmoil of American political upheaval caused men to band together for the maintenance of order, or for purposes of vengeance. Something not far from lynching occurred during the early wars with the Indians on the American Continent, and it may be said that this form of mob action is truly characteristic of uncivilized communities. Where society is still in the frontier stage, the settlement of disputes is left to individuals or groups of individuals. Thus in early days the bands of "regulators" notified undesirable characters to leave the community, prosecuted horse thieves and, in Revolutionary days especially, flogged Tories and tarred and feathered "informers," viz., persons accused of reporting American smuggling to the British authorities.

The term lynching, as used in those days, did not apply, as it does now, exclusively to the infliction of the death penalty. The usual penalty inflicted by the self-constituted courts was a severe flogging and a warning to leave the community, followed by severer punishment in case the warnings were not heeded. With the agitation for the abolition of slavery, lynching began to be an element in what has since crystallized into the race problem. Slave insurrections, notably the Nat Turner rebellion, were punished with the utmost severity and those suspected of having a share in them were often executed, shot, hanged, or even burned, without any form of trial. The abolitionists themselves met with mob action, as is well known, and in 1836, for denouncing the burning alive of a colored man who had been taken by a mob from jail in St. Louis, the Rev. E. P. Lovejoy had his printing office destroyed by a mob

and met death at the hands of a mob in 1837. Cutler quotes
Abraham Lincoln on "The Perpetuation of Our Political Institutions," an address containing a passage which well applies to
our day. Speaking of the spread of mob atrocities throughout
the country, Lincoln said:

> It would be tedious as well as useless to recount the horrors of all
> of them. Those happening in the State of Mississippi and at St. Louis
> are perhaps the most dangerous in example and revolting to human-
> ity. In the Mississippi case they first commenced by hanging the regu-
> lar gamblers—a set of men certainly not following for a livelihood a
> very useful or very honest occupation, but one which, so far from be-
> ing forbidden by the laws, was actually licensed by an act of the Leg-
> islature passed but a single year before. Next, negroes suspected of
> conspiring to raise an insurrection were caught up and hanged in all
> parts of the State; then, white men supposed to be leagued with the
> negroes; and finally, strangers from neighboring States, going thither
> on business, were in many cases subjected to the same fate. Thus
> went on this process of hanging, from gamblers to negroes, from ne-
> groes to white citizens, and from these to strangers, till dead men
> were literally dangling from the boughs of trees on every roadside,
> and in numbers almost sufficient to rival the native Spanish moss of
> the country as a drapery of the forest.

Lynching accompanied the border troubles that preceded
the Civil War, especially on the dark and bloody soil of Kansas,
but the recrudescence of lynching, in its present form, dates
from the period of Reconstruction, following the Civil War.
Much of the violence and terrorism of those days was due to
the then first organized Ku Klux Klan. This body was dissolved
in March, 1869, by proclamation of its Grand Wizard, and actually exterminated by the Federal Force bill of 1871, which
placed under the jurisdiction of Federal Courts the Ku Klux
outrages against freedmen and Northerners and Southerners
accused of favoring Reconstruction.

Lynching was an instrument in driving the negro out of
politics in the South, after the Reconstruction period. More
lynchings took place in the five-year period falling between
1889–1893 than in any subsequent period covering the same
amount of time. Lynching was not only—as it still continues
to be—an instrument for terrorizing negroes, keeping them
from voting and in the position of "inferior"; it has become

as well an instrument of economic exploitation, reinforcing peonage in the cotton-raising sections of the country, making it almost hopeless in many sections for colored men even to ask for simple justice, as many prominent white Southerners have publicly admitted. Governor Hugh M. Dorsey of Georgia on April 22, 1921, made a statement to a conference of citizens of that State dealing with the following phases of the problem: (a) The negro lynched; (b) the negro held in peonage; (c) the negro driven out by organized lawlessness; (d) the negro subject to individual acts of cruelty. The Governor's statement, which cited 135 cases of mistreatment of negroes in Georgia in the two preceding years, contained the following striking paragraphs:

> In some counties the negro is being driven out as though he were a wild beast. In others he is being held as a slave. In others, no negroes remain. In only two of the 135 cases cited is the "usual crime" against white women involved.
>
> As Governor of Georgia, I have asked you, as citizens having the best interests of the State at heart, to meet here today to confer with me as to the best course to be taken. To me it seems that we stand indicted as a people before the world. If the conditions indicated by these charges should continue, both God and man would justly condemn Georgia more severely than man and God have condemned Belgium and Leopold for the Congo atrocities. But worst than that condemnation would be the destruction of our civilization by the continued toleration of such cruelties in Georgia.

The first issue to be met in any discussion of contemporary American lynching is the question of "the usual crime," for the justification of lynching in the last thirty years has been based upon the contention that only by the summary and brutal method of mob murder could white women be protected from attacks of colored men. "To punish rape" has been the justification in face of persistent investigation and publication of the facts.

Those facts collected in "Thirty Years of Lynching," a statistical study based upon The Chicago Tribune's figures and other sources, and published by the National Association for the Advancement of Colored people, are as follows: During the thirty-year period, 1889–1918, less than one-fifth of the colored men done to death by lynching mobs were accused of "the usual crime," and in that period fifty colored and eleven white women were lynched. It should be borne in mind that a mob's accusation is not by any means equivalent to conviction, or even to an indictment for crime by a regularly constituted jury. In fact, in a number of cases in which investigators were sent to the scene of lynchings by the National Association for the Advancement of Colored People, their reports showed that the victim's guilt had not only not been proved, but that he was actually innocent of the crime charged. To take a recent five-year period, that of 1914–18, the number of negroes lynched in the United States, exclusive of those killed at East St. Louis in the riot, was 264. In only twenty-eight cases, or slightly more than one-tenth of the lynchings, was rape assigned as the cause.

If we compare these figures with the record for New York County, which is only a part of New York City, we find that in this county, in the single year 1917, there were 230 persons indicted for rape, of whom thirty-seven were indicted for rape in the first degree. That is, in just a part of New York City, nine more persons were indicted for rape in the first degree than there were negroes lynched on the charge of rape throughout the entire United States in a five-year period. Not one of the thirty-seven persons indicted in New York County was a negro.

To draw the comparison still closer it must be remembered that the evidence required by the Grand Jury of New York County to indict a person on the charge of rape must be more conclusive than the evidence required by or submitted to a lynching mob. The New York Grand Jury requires corroboration, direct or circumstantial; the unsupported word of a woman is not sufficient. The mob does not even require, in most cases, that the woman be certain as to the identity of the accused man.

I might add further that in 1911, when the Congressional Commission on Immigration made its study of crime in the United States, and investigated 2,262 cases in the New York Court of General Sessions, it found that the percentage of rape was lower for the negro than for either the foreign or native born whites. The actual figures were, for foreign-born whites, 1.8; for native-born whites, .8, and for negroes, .5. If to the fig-

ures of New York City were added the figures of other large
cities in the country, the rape record of the American negro
would dwindle into insignificance.

So much, then, for the lie that the negro is by nature a
rapist, or that he is more disposed to commit this crime than
any other race, and that lynching is punishment for that crime.
Fifteen years of investigation, made often at the risk of the in-
vestigator's life, and publication of the facts by the National
Association for the Advancement of Colored People have
done much to clear away this myth.

Meanwhile the task has been to acquaint the American
public with the facts, emphasizing not only the barbarities
that have accompanied the doing to death of people often
innocent, but also the menace that lynching and mob violence hold for all organized government and civilized society.
It is perhaps no longer necessary to dwell on the horrible
brutalities in which lynching mobs indulge, the mutilation of
victims, tortures applied such as shame the devices of savage
and uncivilized peoples, the public burning at the stake, before audiences of men, women, and even children, of human
beings. Eight colored men were publicly burned in the
United States in the year 1922, and of the fifty-three other
victims of American lynching mobs in that year the bodies of
three were publicly burned after the victims had been done
to death. So late as 1921 the country was treated to the horrible spectacle of newspapers announcing that a man was to
be burned in public, giving the time and place where the
event was to take place, and, after the burning, regaling their
readers with every horrible detail of the affair. I refer to the
burning alive of Henry Lowry, which took place at Nodena,
Ark., on the night of Jan. 26, 1921, and was fully reported,
before and after, in The Memphis Press and The News
Scimitar.

Of the menace of this sort of thing to the souls of the people who take part in it and witness it, no warning can be too
strong. The psychiatrist, Dr. A. A. Brill, lecturer at New York
University, has declared that no one can take part in a lynching
or witness it and remain thereafter a psychically normal human
being. Of the effect upon the children witnessing such brutal
scenes it is hardly necessary to speak. Two Presidents in recent

years have spoken of the danger of lynching to society and the nation. President Wilson, in a pronouncement on lynching and mob violence, published July 26, 1918, spoke of the situation as one which "vitally affects the honor of the nation and the very character and integrity of our institutions." In the course of that pronouncement President Wilson said: "There have been lynchings and every one of them has been a blow at the heart of ordered law and human justice. No man who loves America, no man who really cares for her fame and honor and character, or who is truly loyal to her institutions, can justify mob action while the courts of justice are open and the Governments of the States and the nation are ready and able to do their duty."

More recently, in a message to Congress, the late President Harding said: "Congress ought to wipe the stain of barbaric lynching from the banners of a free and orderly representative democracy."

Reinforcing the appeals of both these Presidents and their denunciation of the horror of lynching and its danger not only to the people of African descent but to our Government itself and to the people of all races, we had the spectacle a few years ago of Leo Frank, a white man, lynched in the State of Georgia after a trial dominated by a mob, with the Governor of the State threatened with physical violence. Only recently newspapers have reported a documentary confession by another man establishing Frank's innocence of the crime for which he was murdered by a mob. Instances of this sort could be multiplied indefinitely.

Great as has been the change in public opinion regarding this menace, a vast amount of work remains to be done. As was stated above, sixty-one persons were lynched in the United States during the year 1922; eight of these victims were burned alive. We have at least made this much progress that whereas lynching was condoned so little as fifteen years ago by newspaper editors, and even by clergymen in the pulpit, no reputable man in public life would now dare to utter such sentiments. The organized and persistent campaign against lynching first undertaken in this country by the National Association for the Advancement of Colored People has not been without avail so far as public sentiment is concerned, but the machinery for stopping lynching has been lamentably defective. Although again and again victims of lynching mobs have been proved innocent, it is only in the rarest instances that any effective action is taken for punishing the lynchers. I think that it is perfectly safe to say that for the more than 4,000 lynchings that have taken place in the United States during the past thirty-six years, not fifty people have been convicted for any offense whatever, and not twenty-five have been indicted for murder in the first degree. In the case of the respectable and peaceable colored janitor who was lynched last year (1923) at Columbia, Mo., and upon whose guilt the greatest doubt was subsequently cast, only one man was brought to trial, and when he was acquitted the case against the other men was dismissed.

State and local authorities throughout the United States have failed to deal with this issue of lynching. Now and again a determined Sheriff or a determined Governor, like the late Governor Bickett of North Carolina, cows and disperses a cowardly mob, but these cases of personal bravery on the part of officers of the law are so rare as to be almost negligible. We have, therefore, been confronted with a situation where from sixty to one hundred lynchings go unpunished every year in the United States and where the State and local machinery fail to function in stamping out this evil which disgraces the United States before the civilized world. We are, indeed, confronted with a complete breakdown and paralysis of the State before the mob. The States as a whole, have shown their absolute inability to cope with mob violence.

The conclusion to which the National Association for the Advancement of Colored People has finally been forced, after years of appeal to the State authorities and after its successful campaign to arouse public sentiment, is this: that the only effective machinery for stamping out lynching in the United States must be provided by fearless and strict enforcement of an adequate anti-lynching law. Such a bill, introduced in the last Congress by Representative Leonidas C. Dyer of Missouri and bearing his name—the Dyer Anti-Lynching bill—was passed by a vote of 230 to 119 in the House of Representatives and met a decisive check when a group of Southern Senators, under the leadership of Senator Underwood of Alabama, announced that they would filibuster and hold up the country's business, especially the budget, which was to come before the Senate at that time, threatening to deprive departments of the Government of funds necessary for their work. As the rules of the Senate permit unlimited debate, this group of Southern Senators was able to prevent even discussion of the Dyer bill in the Senate, although the facts concerning lynching had been made public at great length and in the most circumstantial detail during the debates in the House of Representatives and in the pages of the Congressional Record.

The main objection to the Dyer Anti-Lynching bill is that it infringes on State rights. It provides for a fine of $10,000 upon a county in which a lynching takes place, recoverable by the family or dependents of the victim; it also provides for the prosecution in Federal courts of lynchers and delinquent and negligent officers of the law. The objection is on constitutional grounds, the objectors maintaining that although the Constitution provides for equal protection of the laws, it contains no mandatory provision requiring Congress to accord that protection by legislation.

The bill is constitutional in the opinion of Moorfield Storey, former President of the American Bar Association, Attorney General Daugherty, Judge Guy D. Goff of the Department of Justice, and a number of lawyers who filed briefs during the Congressional fight. The supporters of the bill maintain that lynching is not simple murder, but a conspiracy by the mob which effectually substitutes the anarchy of mob action and mob justice for court trial and due process of law. It is a temporary overthrow of the State. The States are able to deal more or less adequately with simple murder, but are powerless against mob murder. The proponents also cite the failure of the States during thirty-five years to take any effective action whatever to stop lynching, and they point to the provision of the Dyer bill by which, with the enlargement of jurisdiction afforded by a federal court, lynchers and Sheriffs will not be tried by their own neighbors and constituents.

In the last Congress, however, it was not constitutional

questions that determined the fate of the Dyer Anti-Lynching bill. It was the unwillingness of Southern Senators even to allow this legislation to be discussed. Most of the lynchings in the United States take place in the Southern States. Of 3,224 lynchings recorded for the thirty-year period, 1889–1918, 2,834 took place in the South.

There is another phase of lynching, and that is its effect upon the relations of the races in this country. It has been estimated that 500,000 colored persons have come North in the period of one year. The migration has various causes. Not least among them is lynching. Lynching and mob violence are the reasons given as second, when not first, by nearly all migrants among whom systematic inquiry has been made. Such an inquiry was undertaken by the United States Department of Labor in 1917 and set forth in a report on negro migration at that time.

Some years ago I was talking with the Mayor of a Southern city who told me of driving through the country surrounding Gainesville, Fla., and seeing numbers of small farms deserted by colored farmers and tenants. There were even chickens running about the deserted farmsteads and apparently the places had been left as they were by the colored migrants. He could not account for the exodus until I reminded him that a short while before six colored people, one of them a woman, had been lynched in that vicinity because one colored man had shot a deputy sheriff who had come to arrest him without a warrant. Such a condition is true of many communities throughout the South. Every lynching, almost without exception, is followed by a departure of numbers of colored people.

The economic and social effects of lynching are clear. It is having a political effect also. The colored population of the United States are aroused over the question of lynching and the enactment of Federal and anti-lynching legislation as it has not been over any other situation or measure of recent times. They have been stimulated to organize political action, and in the last Congressional election colored votes retired Dr. Caleb R. Layton, Delaware's only representative in Congress, solely on the ground that Dr. Layton voted against the Dyer Anti-Lynching bill. Similar results took place in New Jersey, in

Michigan and in Wisconsin. The fate of the bill in Congress is being eagerly watched by the colored population of the United States, as well as by the thousands of white people to whom the stamping out of lynching has become a question involving not racial lines merely but the maintenance of order, good government and civilized society in their country.

Current History, 1924

PREFACE TO

The Second Book of Negro Spirituals

I N THIS the second book of American Negro Spirituals we are
continuing the work of putting these songs, characteristically arranged, in permanent form.

The present volume contains most of those old favorites
that largely for reasons of space were left out of the first. In it
will be found the familiar version of *Nobody Knows De Trouble
I See*. (The first volume contained the rare version of this
song.) There will also be found the stirring and triumphant
Walk Together Children, the apocalyptic *'Zekiel Saw De Wheel*,
and the poignantly sad *Sometimes I Feel Like a Motherless
Child*. Other old favorites are: *Sinner Please Don't Let Dis
Harves' Pass*, *Gwineter Ride Up In De Chariot*, *Lord I Want To
Be A Christian In-a My Heart*, *Gimme Yo' Han'*, *I Know De
Lord's Laid His Hands On Me*, *Walk In Jerusalem Jus' Like
John*, *De Ol' Ark's A-Moverin'*, and *Humble Yo'self De Bell
Done Ring*. Moreover, we are confident that even those who
are familiar with the Spirituals will be astonished at the number
of songs, lesser known but of remarkable beauty and quality,
here included. These are some of the songs in this volume
which need only to be heard to be loved: *My Soul's Been An-
chored In De Lord*, *God's A-Gwineter Trouble De Water*, *Dere's
A Han'writin' On De Wall*, *Walk, Mary, Down De Lane*, *Mary
Had A Baby*, *Chilly Water*, *I Want God's Heab'n To Be Mine*,
Death's Gwineter Lay His Cold Icy Hands On Me, *I Want to
Die Easy When I Die*, *My Lord Says He's Gwineter Rain Down
Fire*, *Same Train*, *In Dat Great Gittin' Up Mornin'*.

It would almost seem that the number of beautiful Spirituals is inexhaustible. In these two volumes of The Book of
American Negro Spirituals there have been collected and
arranged six score songs, and, despite the number of lost Spirituals, there are many score more. And the Spirituals, in a limited degree, are still in the making; as is evidenced by the
recent splendid collection made at the Penn Normal, Industrial and Agricultural School, St. Helena Island, South Car-

olina, by N. G. J. Ballanta, an accomplished African musician.
Considering the common source of the Spirituals, the absence
of monotony is more than surprising. Those who have heard J.
Rosamond Johnson and Taylor Gordon or Paul Robeson and
Lawrence Brown in recital must have remarked the unexpected variety displayed in a program made up exclusively of
Spirituals. These artists generally sing at a concert twenty to
twenty-five numbers, and yet they avoid approaching anything
like sameness. They often conclude programs even of such
length with the audience clamoring for more.

What is the secret of the wide variety and perennially fresh
appeal of the Spirituals? How is it that an audience can listen
to them for two hours without interlude and without bore-
dom or satiety? The Negro took as his basic material just his
native African rhythms and the King James version of the
Bible and out of them created the Spirituals;* how then was
he able to produce a body of five or six hundred religious
songs with so little monotony of treatment and effect? One
explanation is the fact that although the Spirituals in a general
classification fall under the heading "religious songs," all of
them are by no means religious in a narrow or special sense.
All of them are by no means songs of worship, though having
a religious origin and usage. In the Spirituals the Negro did
express his religious hopes and fears, his faith and his doubts.
In them he also expressed his theological and ethical views,
and sounded his exhortations and warnings. Songs of this
character constitute the bulk of the Spirituals. But in a large
proportion of the songs the Negro passed over the strict limits
of religion and covered nearly the whole range of group experiences—the notable omission being sex. In many of the Spirituals the Negro gave wide play to his imagination; in them he
told his stories and drew his morals therefrom; he dreamed his
dreams and declared his visions; he uttered his despair and
prophesied his victories; he also spoke the group wisdom and
expressed the group philosophy of life. Indeed, the Spirituals
taken as a whole contain a record and a revelation of the
deeper thoughts and experiences of the Negro in this country

---

*For an account of the origin and development of the Spirituals see preface
to first Book of American Negro Spirituals (New York, 1925), pp. 19–23.

for a period beginning three hundred years ago and covering
two and a half centuries. If you wish to know what they are
you will find them written more plainly in these songs than in
any pages of history. The Spirituals together with the secular
songs—the work songs and the sex songs—furnish a full expression of the life and thought of the otherwise inarticulate
masses of the Negro race in the United States.

A further explanation of the variety of the Spirituals lies in
the Negro's many-mooded nature; his sensitiveness and quick
response to the whole gamut of human emotions. And what
a range he has! I do not believe there is any other people in
the world that can be so lugubriously sad as the Negro, or so
genuinely gay. An added explanation is found in his lively
imagination, not yet wholly dulled by stereotyped ideas. For
illustration: the age-old symbol of death's convoy is a boat
crossing a stream or a ship leaving one port and entering another. The Negro has made frequent use in the Spirituals of
this classic symbol; but turn to the song, *Same Train*, and
you will see that he does not hesitate to scrap the stereotype
and create a new symbol out of his own everyday experiences. He dares to do this, and, what is more important, he
does it to the point of perfection. The imagery is not lessened; and see how the inevitability of death is insistently suggested in the inevitably recurring "Same train. Same train."

Above all, the Negro was using as his medium the infinitely
varied rhythmic patterns of his native African music, to which
he had added a new-found harmonic strength and melodic
beauty.* For these reasons he was able to fashion many kinds
of songs from what was practically the same materials. Songs
that are the cry of a lost soul and songs that are the voice of an
army with banners. Songs that are crooning lullabies and
songs like the thunders about Sinai. Pass from the pathos of
Sometimes I Feel Like A Motherless Child to the thrill of *Walk
Together Children*, from the intenseness of *Stan' Still Jordan* to
the exultancy of *Joshua Fit De Battle Ob Jericho*, from the lull
of *Swing Low Sweet Chariot* to the trumpeted-tongued procla-

---

*For a discussion of African rhythms and the "swing" of the Spirituals see
ibid., pp. 17–18 and 28–30. See also foreword to St. Helena Spirituals, N. G. J.
Ballanta, New York, 1925.

mation of *Go Down Moses*, and you will get an idea of the wide musical and poetical range spanned by the Spirituals that I have been trying to indicate.

The present volume contains sixty-one numbers. Every kind of Spiritual, as in the first Book, is here represented. There is, indeed, one kind that is extremely rare, the Spiritual based on the birth or infancy of Jesus. The crucifixion and the resurrection have been treated over and over by the creators of the Spirituals, but apparently the birth of Christ made very little appeal to them, and there are practically no "Christmas Spirituals." This is to me a quite curious fact. It would seem that the lowly birth of Jesus, from which more than one analogy could have been drawn, would have furnished the makers of the Spirituals with an inspiring theme, but, for reasons I am not able to give, it did not. It may be that the old-time plantation preacher, nonplussed by the Immaculate Conception, touched upon the birth of Christ only lightly or not at all, and, therefore, that part of the story of his life was not deeply impressed upon the bards.* Or it may be that the Negro preferred to think of Jesus as God, as almighty, all-powerful to help; and this idea of him could not easily be reconciled with his being born of a woman. Jesus, in the older Spirituals, is generally given a title of power. Sometimes he is referred to as "Massa Jesus"; most often he is called "King Jesus." One of the noblest and most inspiriting of all the Spirituals runs:[†]

> Ride on Jesus, Ride on Jesus.
> Ride on Conquering King;
> I wanter go to heab'n in de mornin'.

The reason may be due in part to the fact that the anniversary of the birth of Christ was not, in the South, in any sense a sacred or religious holiday. Up to within recent years, at least, it has been celebrated chiefly with gunpowder and whiskey. It has there been the most secular, even the most profane of all holidays. In slavery times it was the one day on which the slaves were given a sort of freedom. The liberty of coming and

*For reference to the work and offices of these bards see preface to first Book of Spirituals, pp. 21–23.

[†]For discussion of the poetry of the Spirituals see *ibid.*, pp. 38–42.

going was greatly enlarged. On many plantations whiskey was distributed. The day was one given over to a good time; to singing, dancing and visiting; to guzzling, gluttony, and debauchery. It is possible that it was a conscious part of the scheme of slavery to make Christmas a day on which the slaves through sheer excess of sensuous pleasure would forget their bonds. One sure result was that there was destroyed in the minds of the slaves any idea of connection between the birth of Christ and his life and death. At any rate, there are at most only two or three "Christmas Spirituals," and occasional lines referring to the birth of Jesus Christ here and there in other songs. In 1919 Miss Natalie Curtis published two songs, one she had found in Virginia entitled *Dar's A Star In De East*, and the other a song she got from St. Helena Island, South Carolina, entitled *Mary Had A Baby*. There are several versions of this latter song in the Ballanta collection. There was included in the Hampton collection (1909) a song entitled, *Rise Up Shepherd An' Foller*. Both *Mary Had A Baby* and *Rise Up Shepherd An' Foller*, characteristically harmonized and arranged, are in this volume.

In my opinion, the above observations are fairly good evidence that the "Christmas Spirituals" and the other songs containing lines referring to Christ's birth are of recent date. It is more than probable that they belong to a period quite some time after Emancipation; to a period in which there had come the development of a new idea not only of Christmas, but of Christ. This conclusion is further borne out by my inability through racking my early memories to recall anything like a "Christmas Spiritual," and by the fact that no Spiritual of that sort is found in the early standard collections.

There is no way of telling how much of this music has been lost beyond hope of retrieval. For more than a century the Negro had been singing his Spirituals before their beauty and significance were in the slightest degree recognized. It is only within the past fifty or sixty years that any worth-while effort has been made to collect and record these songs; and it is not probable that the original collections were anything near exhaustive. But the Negro and the world are lucky in that so great a mass of them has been saved. I say lucky because it was largely a matter of chance that practically all of this music was not completely lost. The Negro has been doubly lucky, because his music was preserved by others when he himself was unable to do the work, and because the amanuenses, in addition to their other qualifications, were men and women of honesty. The Spirituals were first collected and set down by white people from the North who came in contact with the Negroes of the South during or immediately after the Civil War.* These collectors might have omitted to make the exclusive Negro origin of the songs a part of the record; and so the task might have devolved some day upon the Negro to establish his title as their sole creator. The Negro was likewise lucky with regard to his folk tales. The plantation stories were collected and set down by a Southern white man,† who, had he failed to tell specifically where he got the tales and about their creators, might in time have been passed as an original and imaginative writer *influenced* by Negro life.

The Negro has not had such good fortune with the other folk contributions he has made to the common store of American art. Dancing, so far as it is a native art in America, has been dominated almost absolutely by Negro influence; and yet the Negro has received only the scantiest credit for his contribution. Of course, professional exponents who draw upon or exploit Negro dances do not pause to explain the fact, nor could they reasonably be expected to do so. I know of but one exception, Mr. Vernon Castle, perhaps the most noted, and, by the way, an Englishman, who always danced to the music of a colored band, and never failed to state that most of his dances had long been done "by your colored people," as he put it. Moreover, in great measure, the credit has been deliberately taken away; as witnessed by the number of white vaudeville performers and dancing instructors who promptly advertised themselves as "originators" of the world-encircling "Charleston." Something of the same sort has happened with regard to Negro secular music. The early black-face minstrels simply took such Negro songs as they wished and used them.

*For a history of the collection and preservation of the Spirituals see *ibid.*, pp. 46–49.

†The plantation stories were collected and published by Joel Chandler Harris under the title of *Uncle Remus.*

The first of the so-called Ragtime songs to be published were actually Negro secular folk songs that were set down by white men, who affixed their own names as the composers. In fact, before the Negro succeeded fully in establishing his title as creator of his secular music the form was taken away from him and made national instead of racial. It has been developed into the distinct musical idiom by which America expresses itself popularly, and by which it is known universally. For a long while the vocal form was almost absolutely divorced from the Negro; the separation being brought about largely through the elimination of dialect from the texts of songs. The vogue of the Blues, and the record of the origin and development of this latest vocal form written down by W. C. Handy and Abbe Niles, have gone far to recover the ground lost in this field. There was at one time much publicity discussion as to which of the white Jazz band leaders was entitled to the credit of originating the instrumental form. Now, however, there is a widening acknowledgement of the fact that this form, which has reached a point of development where it is commanding the attention of scholarly musicians, is based upon Negro rhythms and polyphonic structure, and was used by colored bands as far back as twenty years ago. By way of further digression, it is interesting to speculate upon how far one of the most distinctive qualities of Jazz, the orchestral tone-color, is to be credited to the Negro in a negative sense, indeed, to a lack. The charm of this tone-color results from the unorthodox composition of the Jazz orchestra. The composition of the Jazz orchestra is based upon instruments that do not demand long and arduous and expensive training under a master, but which, for anybody with a natural musical ear, are easily self-taught. The violin, which is the mainstay of the orthodox orchestra, is in the Jazz orchestra entirely eliminated or reduced to a place of least importance. The instrumental combination which gives to good Jazz music its peculiar power of excitation to motor response was not consciously designed; it, like Topsy, just happened and grew. At the same time, it cannot be overlooked that the two instruments which play the greater part in producing this effect are the African drum and the Aframerican banjo.

◆

There are no indications that the high regard attained by the Spirituals will be followed by any marked decline in interest. The vogue of these songs is by no means a suddenly popular fad; it has been reached through long and steady development in the recognition of their worth. Three generations ago their beauty struck a few collectors who were attuned to perceive it. A little while later the Fisk Jubilee Singers made them known to the world and gave them their first popularity, but it was a popularity founded mainly on sentiment. The chief effect of this slave music upon its white hearers then was that they were touched and moved with deepest sympathy for the "poor Negro." The Spirituals passed next through a period of investigation and study and of artistic appreciation. Composers began afterwards to arrange them so that their use was extended to singers and music-lovers. And then they made their appearance on concert programs and their appeal was greatly broadened. Today, the Spirituals have a new vogue, but they produce a reaction far different from the sort produced by their first popularity; the effect now produced upon white hearers is not sympathy for the "poor Negro" but admiration for the creative genius of the race. The Spirituals have passed through and withstood many untoward conditions on the long march to the present appreciation of their value; they have come from benighted disregard through scorn, apathy, misappraisal, even the ashamedness and neglect of the race that created them, to where they are recognized as the finest distinctive artistic contribution America can offer the world. The history of the Spirituals is sufficient evidence that they possess the germ of immortality. It is far this side of prophecy to say that they will last as long as anything artistic that has thus far been produced on this continent.

Has this music in any way been a vital force? Has its power brought about any change? What modification has it worked upon the nation and within the Negro? The Spirituals have exerted a gentle and little-considered influence for a good many years. For more than a half century they have touched and stirred the hearts of people and effected a softening down of some of the hard edges of prejudice against the Negro. Measured by length of years, they have wrought more in sociology than in art. Indeed, within the past decade and especially within the past two or three years they have been, perhaps, the main force in breaking down the immemorial stereotype that the Negro in America is nothing more than a beggar at the gate of the nation, waiting to be thrown the crumbs of civilization; that he is here only to receive; to be shaped into something new and unquestionably better. The common idea has been that the Negro, intellectually and morally empty, is here to be filled, filled with education, filled with religion, filled with morality, filled with culture, in a word, to be made into what is considered a civilized human being. All of this is, in a measure, true; but in a larger measure it is true that the Negro is the possessor of a wealth of natural endowments; that he has long been a generous giver to America; that he has helped to shape and mold it; that he has put an indelible imprint upon it; that America is the exact America it is today because of his influence. A startling truth it is that America would not be precisely the America it is except for the silent power the Negro has exerted upon it, both positive and negative. I say the truth is startling because I believe the conscience of the nation would be shocked by contemplation of the effects of the negative power the Negro has involuntarily and unwittingly wielded. This awakening to the truth that the Negro is an active and important force in American life; that he is a creator as well as a creature; that he has given as well as received; that he is the potential giver of larger and richer contributions, is, I think, due more to the present realization of the beauty and value of the Spirituals than to any other one cause.

The Spirituals have only just begun to exert an appreciable influence in art; and, strange to say, not at all or very little have they affected the field of music. The recent emergence of a younger group of Negro artists, preponderantly literary, zealous to be racial, or to put it better, determined to be true to themselves, to look for their art material within rather than without, got its first impulse, I believe, from the new evaluation of the Spirituals reached by the Negro himself. Almost suddenly the realization broke upon the Negro that in the Spirituals the race had produced one of the finest examples of folk-art in the world. The result was a leaping pride, coupled

with a consciousness of innate racial talents and powers, that
gave rise to a new school of Negro artists. In fact, it gave rise
to what can be termed The Negro Youth Movement, a movement which embodies self-sufficiency, self-confidence and self-
expression, and which is lacking in the old group sensitiveness
to the approbation or opinion of its white environment. Of
course, there have before been individual Negro writers actuated in the same way as this younger school, who have drawn
deeply on racial resources and material, but this group motiva-
tion, operating upon a larger group which is aware and responsive, is a new and significant thing.

The Negro was a long time in coming to a realization of
the true worth of the Spirituals*—and there are still some
faultily educated colored people who are ashamed of them—
but when he did, his eyes were opened to all of his own cultural resources.

Before going into how much farther the Spirituals may advance as a force in art, let us, in passing, give a moment's consideration to the distance the younger school of Negro artists
may cover. It is a fact beyond question that the Negro in the
United States has produced fine and distinctive folk-art.
Aframerican folk-art, an art by Africa out of America, Negro
creative genius working under the spur and backlash of American conditions, is unlike anything else in America and not the
same as anything else in the world; nor could it have been
possible in any other place or in any other times. With the
close of the creative period of the Blues, which appears to be
at hand, it is probable that the whole folk creative effort of the
Negro in the United States will have come to an end. The
Blues, in their primitive form, are pure folk songs. They are
the philosophical expression of the individual contemplating
his situation in relation to the conditions surrounding him. In
this respect they are the opposite of the Spirituals, which are
an expression of the group. And, as follows naturally, the Spirituals are essentially group songs, while the Blues are essentially solos. The date of the origin of the Blues cannot be
exactly fixed, but the internal evidence of the songs indicates

*For an account of the attitude of the colored people toward the Spirituals
see preface to first book of Spirituals, pp. 49–50.

that it is comparatively recent. The philosophical comment in
them is upon conditions which Negroes in the South have had
to face only since the Civil War: the courts, the law, the savagery of officers of the law, the chain gang, the life of work on
the railroads, and life in the cities; in a word, the Blues contain
the judgments of the ignorant and lower Negro masses upon
all the hard conditions of modern life they have been called on
to meet. Another evidence of this more or less recent origin is
a new note in them that is foreign to the traditional traits;
there is a note of pessimism, even of cynicism. Mr. Abbe Niles
in his foreword to "Blues" declares this philosophy is that of
choosing as the reaction to disaster laughter instead of tears,
and says it is summed up in the line:

> Got de blues, and too dam' mean to cry.

But this philosophizing, no matter upon what subject, generally centers around the separation of the man from the
woman or the woman from the man by the intervening conditions; and so for the most part, these songs resolve themselves
into the lament of a lover who is feeling "blue." Many of the
lines contain flashes of real primitive poetry. For these reasons,
the Blues are even more interesting and valuable as poetry
than they are as music.* For example, the lines:

> My man's got teeth like a lighthouse by de sea,
> An' when he smiles he th'ows a light on me.

The production of folk-art requires a certain naïveté, a certain insouciance, a sort of intellectual and spiritual isolation on
the part of the producing group that makes it indifferent to
preconceived standards. All of these, the Negro in the United
States is fast losing, and inevitably. The bulk of this Aframerican folk production has been music, music of many kinds,
songs of many kinds; but the urge and necessity upon the
Negro to make his own music, his own songs, are being de-

---

*For a more detailed discussion see foreword to *Blues*, A. & C. Boni, New
York, 1926, and the valuable treatise on Negro work songs and the Blues, *Negro Workaday Songs*, Odum and Johnson, University of North Carolina Press,
1926.

stroyed not only by the changing psychology but by such modern mechanisms as the phonograph and the radio. In fact, there are phonograph companies that make a business of furnishing colored people with close imitations of Negro folk songs. The production of genuine Aframerican folk-art must, sooner or later, cease. In time, even Negro dialect will be only a philological curiosity. Now, can the individual Negro artist produce a conscious art that will be as distinctively Aframerican as is the folk-art?

I doubt the possibility for the individual artists, especially the preponderating literary group, to produce anything comparable to the folk-art in distinctive values. Common education, common interests, a common language—all the environmental forces are against it. Through sheer conscious effort and determination something "different" might be produced, but most likely it would be something artificial and stillborn. I do not believe such effort is worth the while. But I do believe these artists can and will bring something new and vital *into American art*. They will bring to it something from the store of their racial genius:—warmth, color, movement, rhythm, abandon, freshness of unfettered imagination, the beauty of sensuousness, the depth and swiftness of emotion. This they can do by drawing fully on their racial resources and material, and through not being afraid of the truth. The writers, especially, have large opportunity to do their share by portraying Negro life as they alone can see and understand and interpret it, by painting it in true colors from the depths to the heights. And what a range they have! From the drollest comedy, through romance to the most overwhelming tragedy. No other group encompasses in its actual history and experiences in this country so wide and varied an emotional sweep as the Negro; and none but Negro artists can ever give it fullest artistic play. I am not even suggesting racial limits for Negro artists; any such bounds imposed would be strangling. I am rather restating what is axiomatic; that the artist produces his best when working at his best with the materials he knows best.

The environmental forces operating upon the individual Negro artists will not, I think, apply so inflexibly to those who may come in the fields of painting and the plastic arts. And less inflexibly still will they apply to the musicians. And this brings us back to a brief consideration of the spirituals as a force in music. What is to be the future of this music? Will it continue only as folk songs, to become some day merely an exhibit in our museum of artistic antiquities, or is it to be a force in the musical art of America? It is safe to say that for many generations the Spirituals will be kept alive as folk songs. I think it equally safe to say they will some day be a strong element in American music. They possess the qualities and powers; the trouble, so far, has been their almost absolute neglect and rejection by our serious composers. Our lesser musicians have been wiser and more diligent; they have taken the music the Negro created in lighter moods—Ragtime, Jazz, Blues—and developed it into American popular music. Indeed all the major folk creations of the Negro have been taken up and developed, except the Spirituals. The secular music has been developed and has become national and international; the dances have been developed with an almost equal result; we see even the development or degeneration of "Uncle Remus" into the popular bed-time stories. Why cannot this nobler music of the Negro in the hands of our serious composers be wrought into the greater American music that has so long been looked for?

I do not think the composers of any country have at their hands an unexplored mine of richer materials than American composers have in the Spirituals. Do our composers want themes for development into the greater forms, themes rooted in our artistic subsoil and having the vital spark of life? Let us suggest a few from the Spirituals; a choice can be made almost at random, sweet, plaintive, rhythmic, majestic:

Swing Low Sweet Chariot

Sinner Please Don't Let Dis Harves' Pass

My Lord Says He's Gwineter Rain Down Fire

Go Down Moses

I do not believe American composers will always overlook and pass over this fund of source material.

In the arrangements in this volume Mr. J. Rosamond Johnson has observed the same fidelity to the true characteristics of this music as he did in the First Book. However, he has here striven for greater simplicity. These arrangements will, we believe, prove interesting to the musician, but they will not be found too difficult for the average pianist.

JAMES WELDON JOHNSON

Great Barrington, Massachusetts.
1926.

The Dilemma of the Negro Author

T HE Negro author—the creative author—has arrived. He is here. He appears in the lists of the best publishers. He even breaks into the lists of the best-sellers. To the general American public he is a novelty, a strange phenomenon, a miracle straight out of the skies. Well, he *is* a novelty, but he is by no means a new thing.

The line of American Negro authors runs back for a hundred and fifty years, back to Phillis Wheatley, the poet. Since Phillis Wheatley there have been several hundred Negro authors who have written books of many kinds. But in all these generations down to within the past six years only seven or eight of the hundreds have ever been heard of by the general American public or even by the specialists in American literature. As many Negro writers have gained recognition by both in the past six years as in all the generations gone before. What has happened is that efforts which have been going on for more than a century are being noticed and appreciated at last, and that this appreciation has served as a stimulus to greater effort and output. America is aware today that there are such things as Negro authors. Several converging forces have been at work to produce this state of mind. Had these forces been at work three decades ago, it is possible that we then should have had a condition similar to the one which now exists.

Now that the Negro author has come into the range of vision of the American public eye, it seems to me only fair to point out some of the difficulties he finds in his way. But I wish to state emphatically that I have no intention of making an apology or asking any special allowances for him; such a plea would at once disqualify him and void the very recognition he has gained. But the Negro writer does face peculiar difficulties that ought to be taken into account when passing judgment upon him.

It is unnecessary to say that he faces every one of the difficulties common to all that crowd of demon-driven individuals who feel that they must write. But the Aframerican author faces a special problem which the plain American author knows nothing about—the problem of the double audience. It is more than a double audience; it is a divided audience, an audience made up of two elements with differing and often opposite and antagonistic points of view. His audience is always both white America and black America. The moment a Negro writer takes up his pen or sits down to his typewriter he is immediately called upon to solve, consciously or unconsciously, this problem of the double audience. To whom shall he address himself, to his own black group or to white America? Many a Negro writer has fallen down, as it were, between these two stools.

It may be asked why he doesn't just go ahead and write and not bother himself about audiences. That is easier said than done. It is doubtful if anything with meaning can be written unless the writer has some definite audience in mind. His audience may be as far away as the angelic host or the rulers of darkness, but an audience he must have in mind. As soon as he selects his audience he immediately falls, whether he wills it or not, under the laws which govern the influence of the audience upon the artist, laws that operate in every branch of art.

Now, it is axiomatic that the artist achieves his best when working at his best with the materials he knows best. And it goes without saying that the material which the Negro as a creative or general writer knows best comes out of the life and experience of the colored people in America. The overwhelming bulk of the best work done by Aframerican writers has some bearing on the Negro and his relations to civilization and society in the United States. Leaving authors, white or black, writing for coteries on special and technical subjects out of the discussion, it is safe to say that the white American author, when he sits down to write, has in mind a white audience— and naturally. The influence of the Negro as a group on his work is infinitesimal if not zero. Even when he talks about the Negro he talks to white people. But with the Aframerican author the case is different. When he attempts to handle his best known material he is thrown upon two, indeed, if it is permissible to say so, upon three horns of a dilemma. He must intentionally or unintentionally choose a black audience or a white audience or a combination of the two; and each of them presents peculiar difficulties.

If the Negro author selects white America as his audience he is bound to run up against many long-standing artistic conceptions about the Negro; against numerous conventions and traditions which through age have become binding; in a word, against a whole row of hard-set stereotypes which are not easily broken up. White America has some firm opinions as to what the Negro is, and consequently some pretty well fixed ideas as to what should be written about him, and how.

What is the Negro in the artistic conception of white America? In the brighter light, he is a simple, indolent, docile, improvident peasant; a singing, dancing, laughing, weeping child; picturesque beside his log cabin and in the snowy fields of cotton; naïvely charming with his banjo and his songs in the moonlight along the lazy Southern rivers; a faithful, ever-smiling and genuflecting old servitor to the white folks of quality; a pathetic and pitiable figure. In a darker light, he is an impulsive, irrational, passionate savage, reluctantly wearing a thin coat of culture, sullenly hating the white man, but holding an innate and unescapable belief in the white man's superiority; an everlastingly alien and irredeemable element in the nation; a menace to Southern civilization; a threat to Nordic race purity; a figure casting a sinister shadow across the future of the country.

Ninety-nine one-hundredths of all that has been written about the Negro in the United States in three centuries and read with any degree of interest or pleasure by white America has been written in conformity to one or more of these ideas. I am not saying that they do not provide good material for literature; in fact, they make material for poetry and romance and comedy and tragedy of a high order. But I do say they have become stencils, and that the Negro author finds these stencils inadequate for the portrayal and interpretation of Negro life today. Moreover, when he does attempt to make use of them he finds himself impaled upon the second horn of his dilemma.

II

It is known that art—literature in particular, unless it be sheer fantasy—must be based on more or less well established conventions, upon ideas that have some room in the general consciousness, that are at least somewhat familiar to the public mind. It is this that gives it verisimilitude and finality. Even revolutionary literature, if it is to have any convincing power, must start from a basis of conventions, regarding of how unconventional its objective may be. These conventions are changed by slow and gradual processes—except they be changed in a flash. The conventions held by white America regarding the Negro will be changed. Actually they are being changed, but they have not yet sufficiently changed to lessen to any great extent the dilemma of the Negro author.

It would be straining the credulity of white America beyond the breaking point for a Negro writer to put out a novel dealing with the wealthy class of colored people. The idea of Negroes of wealth living in a luxurious manner is still too unfamiliar. Such a story would have to be written in a burlesque vein to make it at all plausible and acceptable. Before Florence Mills and Josephine Baker implanted a new general idea in the public mind it would have been worse than a waste of time for a Negro author to write for white America the story of a Negro girl who rose in spite of all obstacles, racial and others, to a place of world success and acclaim on the musical revue stage. It would be proof of little less than supreme genius in a Negro poet for him to take one of the tragic characters in American Negro history—say Crispus Attucks or Nat Turner or Denmark Vesey—, put heroic language in his mouth and have white America accept the work as authentic. American Negroes as heroes form no part of white America's concept of the race. Indeed, I question if three out of ten of the white Americans who will read these lines know anything of either Attucks, Turner or Vesey; although each of the three played a rôle in the history of the nation. The Aframerican poet might take an African chief or warrior, set him forth in heroic couplets or blank verse and present him to white America with infinitely greater chance of having his work accepted.

But these limiting conventions held by white America do not constitute the whole difficulty of the Negro author in dealing with a white audience. In addition to these conventions regarding the Negro as a race, white America has certain definite opinions regarding the Negro as an artist, regarding the scope of his efforts. White America has a strong feeling that Negro artists should refrain from making use of white subject matter. I mean by that, subject matter which it feels belongs to the white world. In plain words, white America does not welcome seeing the Negro competing with the white man on what it considers the white man's own ground.

In many white people this feeling is dormant, but brought to the test it flares up, if only faintly. During his first season in this country after his European success a most common criticism of Roland Hayes was provoked by the fact that his programme consisted of groups of English, French, German, and Italian songs, closing always with a group of Negro Spirituals. A remark frequently made was, "Why doesn't he confine himself to the Spirituals?" This in face of the fact that no tenor on the American concert stage could surpass Hayes in singing French and German songs. The truth is that white America was not quite prepared to relish the sight of a black man in a dress suit singing French and German love songs, and singing them exquisitely. The first reaction was that there was something incongruous about it. It gave a jar to the old conventions and something of a shock to the Nordic superiority complex. The years have not been many since Negro players have dared to interpolate a love duet in a musical show to be witnessed by white people. The representation of romantic love-making by Negroes struck the white audience as somewhat ridiculous; Negroes were supposed to mate in a more primeval manner.

White America has for a long time been annexing and appropriating Negro territory, and is prone to think of every part of the domain it now controls as originally—and aboriginally—its own. One sometimes hears the critics in reviewing a Negro musical show lament the fact that it is so much like white musical shows. But a great deal of this similarity it would be hard to avoid because of the plain fact that two out of the four chief ingredients in the present day white musical show, the music and the dancing, are directly derived from the Negro. These ideas and opinions regarding the scope of artistic effort affect the Negro author, the poet in particular. So whenever an Aframerican writer addresses himself to white America and attempts to break away from or break through these conventions and limitations he makes more than an ordinary demand upon his literary skill and power.

At this point it would appear that a most natural thing for the Negro author to do would be to say, "Damn the white audience!" and devote himself to addressing his own race exclusively. But when he turns from the conventions of white America he runs afoul of the taboos of black America. He has no more absolute freedom to speak as he pleases addressing black America than he has in addressing white America. There are certain phases of life that he dare not touch, certain subjects that he dare not critically discuss, certain manners of treatment that he dare not use—except at the risk of rousing bitter resentment. It is quite possible for a Negro author to do a piece of work, good from every literary point of view, and at the same time bring down on his head the wrath of the entire colored pulpit and press, and gain among the literate element of his own people the reputation of being the prostitutor of his talent and a betrayer of his race—not by any means a pleasant position to get into.

This state of mind on the part of the colored people may strike white America as stupid and intolerant, but it is not without some justification and not entirely without precedent; the white South on occasion discloses a similar sensitiveness. The colored people of the United States are anomalously situated. They are a segregated and antagonized minority in a very large nation, a minority unremittingly on the defensive. Their faults and failings are exploited to produce exaggerated effects. Consequently, they have a strong feeling against exhibiting to the world anything but their best points. They feel that other groups may afford to do otherwise but, as yet, the Negro cannot. This is not to say that they refuse to listen to criticism of themselves, for they often listen to Negro speakers excoriating the race for its faults and foibles and vices. But these criticisms are not for the printed page. They are not for the ears and eyes of white America.

A curious illustration of this defensive state of mind is found in the Negro theatres. In those wherein Negro players give Negro performances for Negro audiences all of the Negro weaknesses, real and reputed, are burlesqued and ridiculed in the most hilarious manner, and are laughed at and heartily enjoyed. But the presence of a couple of dozen white people would completely change the psychology of the audience, and the players. If some of the performances so much enjoyed by strictly Negro audiences in Negro theatres were put on, say, in a Broadway theatre, a wave of indignation would sweep Aframerica from the avenues of Harlem to the canebrakes of Louisiana. These taboos of black America are as real and binding as the conventions of white America. Conditions may excuse if not warrant them; nevertheless, it is unfortunate that they exist, for their effect is blighting. In past years they have discouraged in Negro authors the production of everything but *nice* literature; they have operated to hold their work down to literature of the defensive, exculpatory sort. They have a restraining effect at the present time which Negro writers are compelled to reckon with.

This division of audience takes the solid ground from under the feet of the Negro writer and leaves him suspended. Either choice carries hampering and discouraging conditions. The Negro author may please one audience and at the same time rouse the resentment of the other; or he may please the other and totally fail to rouse the interest of the one. The situation, moreover, constantly subjects him to the temptation of posing and posturing for the one audience or the other; and the sincerity and soundness of his work are vitiated whether he poses for white or black.

The dilemma is not made less puzzling by the fact that practically it is an extremely difficult thing for the Negro author in the United States to address himself solely to either of these two audiences. If he analyzes what he writes he will find that on one page black America is his whole or main audience, and on the very next page white America. In fact, psychoanalysis of the Negro authors of the defensive and exculpatory literature, written in strict conformity to the taboos of black America, would reveal that they were unconsciously addressing themselves mainly to white America.

III

I have sometimes thought it would be a way out, that the Negro author would be on surer ground and truer to himself, if he could disregard white America; if he could say to white America, "What I have written, I have written. I hope you'll be interested and like it. If not, I can't help it." But it is impossible for a sane American Negro to write with total disregard for nine-tenths of the people of the United States. Situated as his own race is amidst and amongst them, their influence is irresistible.

I judge there is not a single Negro writer who is not, at least secondarily, impelled by the desire to make his work have some effect on the white world for the good of his race. It may be thought that the work of the Negro writer, on account of this last named condition, gains in pointedness what it loses in breadth. Be that as it may, the situation is for the time one in which he is inextricably placed. Of course, the Negro author can try the experiment of putting black America in the orchestra chairs, so to speak, and keeping white America in the gallery, but he is likely at any moment to find his audience shifting places on him, and sometimes without notice.

And now, instead of black America and white America as separate or alternating audiences, what about the combination of the two into one? That, I believe, is the only way out. However, there needs to be more than a combination, there needs to be a fusion. In time, I cannot say how much time, there will come a gradual and natural rapprochement of these two sections of the Negro author's audience. There will come a breaking up and remodeling of most of white America's traditional stereotypes, forced by the advancement of the Negro in the various phases of our national life. Black America will abolish many of its taboos. A sufficiently large class of colored people will progress enough and become strong enough to render a constantly sensitive and defensive attitude on the part of the race unnecessary and distasteful. In the end, the Negro author will have something close to a common audience, and will be about as free from outside limitations as other writers.

Meanwhile, the making of a common audience out of white and black America presents the Negro author with enough difficulties to constitute a third horn of his dilemma. It is a task that is a very high test for all his skill and abilities, but it can be and has been accomplished. The equipped Negro author working at his best in his best known material can achieve this end; but, standing on his racial foundation, he must fashion something that rises above race, and reaches out to the universal in truth and beauty. And so, when a Negro author does write so as to fuse white and black America into one interested and approving audience he has performed no slight feat, and has most likely done a sound piece of literary work.

The American Mercury, 1928

Race Prejudice and the Negro Artist

WHAT Americans call the Negro problem is almost as old as America itself. For three centuries the Negro in this country has been tagged with an interrogation point; the question propounded, however, has not always been the same. Indeed, the question has run all the way from whether or not the Negro was a human being, down—or up—to whether or not the Negro shall be accorded full and unlimited American citizenship. Therefore, the Negro problem is not a problem in the sense of being a fixed proposition involving certain invariable factors and waiting to be worked out according to certain defined rules. It is not a static condition; rather, it is and always has been a series of shifting interracial situations, never precisely the same in any two generations. As these situations have shifted, the methods and manners of dealing with them have constantly changed. And never has there been such a swift and vital shift as the one which is taking place at the present moment; and never was there a more revolutionary change in attitudes than the one which is now going on.

The question of the races—white and black—has occupied much of America's time and thought. Many methods for a solution of the problem have been tried—most of them tried *on* the Negro, for one of the mistakes commonly made in dealing with this matter has been the failure of white America to take into account the Negro himself and the forces he was generating and sending out. The question repeated generation after generation has been what shall we do with the Negro?—ignoring completely the power of the Negro to do something for himself, and even something to America. It is a new thought that the Negro has helped to shape and mold and make America. It is, perhaps, a startling thought that America would not be precisely the America it is to-day except for the powerful, if silent, influence the Negro has exerted upon it—both positively and negatively. It is a certainty that the nation would be shocked by a contemplation of the effects which have been wrought upon its inherent character by the negative power which the Negro has involuntarily and unwittingly wielded.

A number of approaches to the heart of the race problem have been tried: religious, educational, political, industrial, ethical, economic, sociological. Along several of these approaches considerable progress has been made. To-day a newer approach is being tried, an approach which discards most of the older methods. It requires a minimum of pleas, or propaganda, or philanthropy. It depends more upon what the Negro himself does than upon what someone does for him. It is the approach along the line of intellectual and artistic achievement by Negroes, and may be called the art approach to the Negro problem. This method of approaching a solution of the race question has the advantage of affording great and rapid progress with least friction and of providing a common platform upon which most people are willing to stand. The results of this method seem to carry a high degree of finality, to be the thing itself that was to be demonstrated.

I have said that this is a newer approach to the race problem; that is only in a sense true. The Negro has been using this method for a very long time; for a longer time than he has used any other method, and, perhaps, with farther-reaching effectiveness. For more than a century his great folk-art contributions have been exerting an ameliorating effect, slight and perhaps, in any one period, imperceptible, nevertheless, cumulative. In countless and diverse situations song and dance have been both a sword and a shield for the Negro. Take the Spirituals: for sixty years beginning with their introduction to the world by the Fisk Jubilee Singers, these songs have touched and stirred the hearts of people and brought about a smoothing down of the rougher edges of prejudice against the Negro. Indeed, nobody can hear Negroes sing this wonderful music in its primitive beauty without a softening of feeling toward them.

What is there, then, that is new? What is new consists largely in the changing attitude of the American people. There is a coming to light and notice of efforts that have been going on for a long while, and a public appreciation of their results. Note, for example, the change in the reaction to the Spirituals. Fifty years ago white people who heard the Spirituals were touched and moved with sympathy and pity for the "poor

Negro." To-day the effect is not one of pity for the Negro's condition, but admiration for the creative genius of the race.

All of the Negro's folk-art creations have undergone a new evaluation. His sacred music—the Spirituals; his secular music —Ragtime, Blues, Jazz, and the work songs; his folk lore—the Uncle Remus plantation tales; and his dances have received a new and higher appreciation. Indeed, I dare to say it is now more or less generally acknowledged that the only things artistic that have sprung from American soil and out of American life, and been universally recognized as distinctively American products, are the folk creations of the Negro. The one thing that may be termed artistic, by which the United States is known the world over, is its Negro-derived popular music. The folk creations of the Negro have not only received a new appreciation; they have—the Spirituals excepted—been taken over and assimilated. They are no longer racial, they are national; they have become a part of our common cultural fund. Negro secular music has been developed into American popular music: Negro dances have been made into our national art of dancing; even the plantation tales have been transformed and have come out as popular bedtime stories. The Spirituals are still distinct Negro folk songs, but sooner or later our serious composers will take them as material to go into the making of the "great American music" that has so long been looked for.

But the story does not halt at this point. The Negro has done a great deal through his folk-art creations to change the national attitudes toward him; and now the efforts of the race have been reinforced and magnified by the individual Negro artist, the conscious artist. It is fortunate that the individual Negro artist has emerged; for it is more than probable that with the ending of the creative period of Blues, which seems to be at hand, the whole folk creative effort of the Negro in the United States will come to a close. All the psychological and environmental forces are working to that end. At any rate, it is the individual Negro artist that is now doing most to effect a crumbling of the inner walls of race prejudice; there are outer and inner walls. The emergence of the individual artist is the result of the same phenomenon that brought about the new evaluation and appreciation of the folk-art creations. But it should be borne in mind that the conscious Aframerican artist is not an entirely new thing. What is new about him is chiefly the evaluation and public recognition of his work.

II

When and how did this happen? The entire change, which is marked by the shedding of a new light on the artistic and intellectual achievements of the Negro, the whole period which has become ineptly known as "the Negro renaissance," is the matter of a decade; it has all taken place within the last ten years. More forces than anyone can name have been at work to create the existing state; however, several of them may be pointed out. What took place had no appearance of a development; it seemed more like a sudden awakening, an almost instantaneous change. There was nothing that immediately preceded it which foreshadowed what was to follow. Those who were in the midst of the movement were as much astonished as anyone else to see the transformation. Overnight, as it were, America became aware that there were Negro artists and that they had something worth while to offer. This awareness first manifested itself in black America, for, strange as it may seem, Negroes themselves, as a mass, had had little or no consciousness of their own individual artists. Black America awoke first to the fact that it possessed poets. This awakening followed the entry of the United States into the Great War. Before this country had been in the war very long there was bitter disillusionment on the part of American Negroes—on the part both of those working at home and those fighting in France to make the world safe for democracy. The disappointment and bitterness were taken up and voiced by a group of seven or eight Negro poets. They expressed what the race felt, what the race wanted to hear. They made the group at large articulate. Some of this poetry was the poetry of despair, but most of it was the poetry of protest and rebellion. Fenton Johnson wrote of civilization:

I am tired of work; I am tired of building up somebody else's
    civilization.
Let us take a rest, M'lissy Jane.

You will let the old shanty go to rot, the white people's
     clothes turn to dust, and the Calvary Baptist Church sink
     to the bottomless pit.

Throw the children into the river; civilization has given us too
     many. It is better to die than it is to grow up and find
     out that you are colored.
Pluck the stars out of the heavens. The stars mark our destiny.
     The stars marked my destiny.
I am tired of civilization.

Joseph Cotter, a youth of twenty, inquired plaintively from
the invalid's bed to which he was confined:

> Brother; come!
> And let us go unto our God.
> And when we stand before Him
> I shall say,
> "Lord, I do not hate,
> I am hated.
> I scourge no one,
> I am scourged.
> I covet no lands,
> My lands are coveted.
> I mock no peoples,
> My people are mocked."
> And, brother, what shall you say?

But among this whole group the voice that was most powerful was that of Claude McKay. Here was a true poet of great
skill and wide range, who turned from creating the mood of
poetic beauty in the absolute, as he had so fully done in such
poems as "Spring in New Hampshire," "The Harlem Dancer,"
and "Flame Heart," for example, and began pouring out cynicism, bitterness, and invective. For this purpose, incongruous
as it may seem, he took the sonnet form as his medium. There
is nothing in American literature that strikes a more porten-
tous note than these sonnet-tragedies of McKay. Here is the
sestet of his sonnet, "The Lynching":

> Day dawned, and soon the mixed crowds came to view
> The ghastly body swaying in the sun:

> The women thronged to look, but never a one
> Showed sorrow in her eyes of steely blue;
> And little lads, lynchers that were to be,
> Danced round the dreadful thing in fiendish glee.

The summer of 1919 was a terrifying period for the American Negro. There were race riots in Chicago and in Washington and in Omaha and in Phillips County, Arkansas; and in Longview, Texas; and in Knoxville, Tennessee; and in Norfolk, Virginia; and in other communities. Colored men and women, by dozens and by scores, were chased and beaten and killed in the streets. And from Claude McKay came this cry of defiant despair sounded from the last ditch:

> If we must die—let it not be like hogs
> Hunted and penned in an inglorious spot.

> Oh, Kinsmen! We must meet the common foe:
> Though far outnumbered, let us still be brave,
> And for their thousand blows deal one death blow!
> What though before us lies the open grave?
> Like men we'll face the murderous, cowardly pack,
> Pressed to the wall, dying, but—fighting back!

But not all the terror of the time could smother the poet of beauty and universality in McKay. In "America," which opens with these lines:

> Although she feeds me bread of bitterness,
> And sinks into my throat her tiger's tooth,
> Stealing my breath of life, I will confess
> I love this cultured hell that tests my youth.

he fused these elements of fear and bitterness and hate into verse which by every test is true poetry and a fine sonnet.

The poems of the Negro poets of the immediate post-war period were widely printed in Negro periodicals; they were committed to memory; they were recited at school exercises and public meetings; and were discussed at private gatherings. Now, Negro poets were not new; their line goes back a long way in Aframerican history. Between Phillis Wheatley, who as a girl of eight or nine was landed in Boston from an African slave ship in 1761, and who published a volume of poems in 1773, and Paul Laurence Dunbar, who died in 1906, there were more than thirty Negroes who published volumes of verse—some of it good, most of it mediocre, and much of it bad. The new thing was the effect produced by these poets who sprang up out of the war period. Negro poets had sounded similar notes before, but now for the first time they succeeded in setting up a reverberating response, even in their own group. But the effect was not limited to black America; several of these later poets in some subtle way affected white America. In any event, at just this time white America began to become aware and to awaken. In the correlation of forces that brought about this result it might be pointed out that the culminating effect of the folk-art creations had gone far toward inducing a favorable state of mind. Doubtless it is also true that the new knowledge and opinions about the Negro in Africa—that he was not just a howling savage, that he had a culture, that he had produced a vital art—had directly affected opinion about the Negro in America. However it may have been, the Negro poets growing out of the war period were the forerunners of the individuals whose work is now being assayed and is receiving recognition in accordance with its worth.

III

And yet, contemporaneously with the work of these poets a significant effort was made in another field of art—an effort which might have gone much farther at the time had it not been cut off by our entry into the War, but which, nevertheless, had its effect. Early in 1917, in fact on the very day we entered the War, Mrs. Emily Hapgood produced at the Madison Square Garden Theater three plays of Negro life by Ridgley Torrence, staged by Robert Edmond Jones, and played by an all-Negro cast. This was the first time that Negro actors in drama commanded the serious attention of the critics and the general public. Two of the players, Opal Cooper and Inez Clough, were listed by George Jean Nathan among the ten actors giving the most distinguished performances of the year. No one who heard Opal Cooper chant the dream in the "Rider of Dreams" can ever forget the thrill of it. A sensational feature of the production was the singing orchestra of Negro

performers under the direction of J. Rosamond Johnson—
singing orchestras in theaters have since become common.
The plays moved from the Garden Theater to the Garrick, but
the stress of war crushed them out. In 1920, Charles Gilpin was
enthusiastically and universally acclaimed for his acting in
"The Emperor Jones." The American stage has seldom seen
such an outburst of acclamation. Mr. Gilpin was one of the ten
persons voted by the Drama League as having done most for
the American theater during the year. Most of the readers of
these pages will remember the almost national crisis caused by
his invitation to the Drama League Dinner. And along came
"Shuffle Along"; and all of New York flocked to an out of the
way theater in West Sixty-third Street to hear the most joyous
singing and see the most exhilarating dancing to be found on
any stage in the city. The dancing steps originally used by the
"policeman" in "Shuffle Along" furnished new material for
hundreds of dancing men. "Shuffle Along" was actually an
epoch-making musical comedy. Out of "Shuffle Along" came
Florence Mills, who, unfortunately, died so young but lived
long enough to be acknowledged here and in Europe as one of
the finest singing comediennes the stage had ever seen and an
artist of positive genius. In 1923 Roland Hayes stepped out on
the American stage in a blaze of glory, making his first appearances as soloist with the Boston Symphony Orchestra and later
with the Philharmonic. Few single artists have packed such
crowds into Carnegie Hall and the finest concert halls
throughout the country as has Roland Hayes; and, notwithstanding the éclat with which America first received him, his
reputation has continued to increase and, besides, he is rated
as one of the best box-office attractions in the whole concert
field. Miss Marian Anderson appeared as soloist with the
Philadelphia Symphony Orchestra and in concert at the
Lewisohn Stadium at New York City College. Paul Robeson
and J. Rosamond Johnson and Taylor Gordon sang Spirituals
to large and appreciative audiences in New York and over the
country, giving to those songs a fresh interpretation and a new
vogue.

Paul Robeson—that most versatile of men, who has made a
national reputation as athlete, singer, and actor—played in
Eugene O'Neill's "All God's Chillun" and added to his repu-

tation on the stage, and, moreover, put to the test an ancient taboo; he played the principal role opposite a white woman. This feature of the play gave rise to a more acute crisis than did Gilpin's invitation to the Drama League Dinner. Some sensational newspaper predicted race riots and other dire disasters, but nothing of the sort happened; the play went over without a boo. Robeson played the title role in a revival of "The Emperor Jones" and almost duplicated the sensation produced by Gilpin in the original presentation. There followed on the stage Julius Bledsoe, Rose McClendon, Frank Wilson, and Abbie Mitchell, all of whom gained recognition. At the time of this writing each of these four is playing in a Broadway production. Paradoxical it may seem, but no Negro comedian gained recognition in this decade. Negro comedians have long been a recognized American institution and there are several now before the public who are well known, but their reputations were made before this period. The only new reputations made on the comedy stage were made by women, Florence Mills and Ethel Waters. In addition there are the two famous Smiths, Bessie and Clara, singers of Blues and favorites of vaudeville, phonograph, and radio audiences. Of course there is Josephine Baker, but her reputation was made entirely in Europe. Nevertheless, these magical ten years have worked a change upon Negro comedy. Before Miller and Lyles brought "Shuffle Along" to New York, managers here could hardly conceive of a Negro musical comedy playing a Broadway house. When Williams and Walker, Cole and Johnson, and Ernest Hogan were in their heyday, people who wanted to see them had to go to theaters outside the great white-light zone. George Walker died before the "new day," and up to his retirement from the stage he kept up a constant fight for a chance for his company to play a strictly Broadway theater. Since "Shuffle Along," hardly a season has passed without seeing one or more Negro musical comedies playing in the finest theaters in New York. In fact, Negro plays and Negro performers in white plays on Broadway have become usual occurrences.

Odd has been the fate of the younger poets who were instrumental in bringing about the present state of affairs. It is a fact that none of them, with the exception of Claude McKay, quite succeeded in bridging over into it. Three of them, Roscoe Jamison, Lucian Watkins, and Joseph Cotter, are dead, all dying in their youth. Fenton Johnson is almost silent. And Claude McKay has for the past four or five years lived practically in exile. However, several of the older writers are busily at work, and there has sprung up in the last three or four years a group of newer creative writers. Countee Cullen and Langston Hughes have achieved recognition as poets. Jean Toomer, Walter White, Eric Walrond, and Rudolph Fisher have made a place among writers of fiction. And Claude McKay, after a period of silence as a poet, has published his *Home to Harlem*, a generally acclaimed novel. These are names that carry literary significance, and they take their places according to individual merit in the list of the makers of contemporary American literature. In addition, there are more than a score of younger writers who are not yet quite in the public eye, but will soon be more widely known. Writers such as these are bound to be known and in larger numbers, because their work now has the chance to gain whatever appreciation it merits. To-day the reagents that will discover what of it is good are at work, the arbiters of our national letters are disposed to regard their good work as a part of American literature, and the public is prepared to accept it as such. This has not always been the case. Until this recent period, the several achievements in writing that have come to light have been regarded as more or less sporadic and isolated efforts, and not in any sense as having a direct relation to the national literature. Had the existing forces been at work at the time, the remarkable decade from 1895 to 1905, which brought forth Booker T. Washington's *Up from Slavery*, W. E. Burghardt Du Bois's *The Souls of Black Folk*, Charles Chesnutt's stories of Negro life, and Paul Laurence Dunbar's poetry, might have signaled the beginning of the "Negro literary renaissance."

During the present decade the individual Negro artist has definitely emerged in three fields, in literature, in the theater, and on the concert stage; in other fields he has not won marked distinction. To point to any achievement of distinction in painting the Negro must go back of this decade, back to H. O. Tanner, who has lived in Europe for the past thirty-five years; or farther back to E. M. Bannister, who gained considerable recognition a half century ago. Nevertheless, there is the work of W. E. Scott, a mural painter, who lives in Chicago and has done a number of public buildings in the Middle West, and of Archibald J. Motley, who recently held a one-man exhibit in New York which attracted very favorable attention. The drawings of Aaron Douglas have won for him a place among American illustrators. To point to any work of acknowledged excellence in sculpture the Negro must go back of this decade to the work of two women, Edmonia Lewis and Meta Warrick Fuller, both of whom received chiefly in Europe such recognition as they gained. There are several young painters and sculptors who are winning recognition. But the strangest lack is that with all the great native musical endowment he is conceded to possess, the Negro has not in this most propitious time produced a single outstanding composer. There are competent musicians and talented composers of songs and detached bits of music, but no original composer who, in amount and standard of work and in recognition achieved, is at all comparable with S. Coleridge-Taylor, the English Negro composer. Nor can the Negro in the United States point back of this decade to even one such artist. It is a curious fact that the American Negro through his whole history has done more highly sustained and more fully recognized work in the composition of letters than in the composition of music. It is the more curious when we consider that music is so innately a characteristic method of expression for the Negro.

IV

What, now, is the significance of this artistic activity on the part of the Negro and of its reactions on the American people? I think it is twofold. In the first place, the Negro is making some distinctive contributions to our common cultural store. I do not claim it is possible for these individual artists to produce anything comparable to the folk-art in distinctive values, but I do believe they are bringing something fresh and vital into American art, something from the store of their own racial genius: warmth, color, movement, rhythm, and abandon; depth and swiftness of emotion and the beauty of sensuousness. I believe American art will be richer because of these elements in fuller quantity.

But what is of deeper significance to the Negro himself is the effect that this artistic activity is producing upon his condition and status as a man and citizen. I do not believe it an overstatement to say that the "race problem" is fast reaching the stage of being more a question of national mental attitudes toward the Negro than a question of his actual condition. That is to say, it is not at all the problem of a moribund people sinking into a slough of ignorance, poverty, and decay in the very midst of our civilization and despite all our efforts to save them; that would indeed be a problem. Rather is the problem coming to consist in the hesitation and refusal to open new doors of opportunity at which these peoples are constantly knocking. In other words, the problem for the Negro is reaching the plane where it is becoming less a matter of dealing with what he is and more a matter of dealing with what America thinks he is.

Now, the truth is that the great majority of Americans have not thought about the Negro at all, except in a vague sort of way and in the form of traditional and erroneous stereotypes. Some of these stereotyped forms of thought are quite absurd, yet they have had their opinions and attitudes regarding their fellow colored citizens determined by such a phrase as, "A nigger will steal," or "Niggers are lazy," or "Niggers are dirty." But there is a common, widespread, and persistent stereotyped idea regarding the Negro, and it is that he is here only to receive; to be shaped into something new and unquestionably better. The common idea is that the Negro reached America intellectually, culturally, and morally empty, and that he is here to be filled—filled with education, filled with religion, filled with morality, filled with culture. In a word, the stereotype is that the Negro is nothing more than a beggar at the gate of the nation, waiting to be thrown the crumbs of civilization. Through his artistic efforts the Negro is smashing this immemorial stereotype faster than he has ever done through any other method he has been able to use. He is making it realized that he is the possessor of a wealth of natural endowments and that he has long been a generous giver to America. He is impressing upon the national mind the conviction that he is an active and important force in American life; that he is a creator as well as a creature; that he has given as well as received; that he is the potential giver of larger and richer contributions.

In this way the Negro is bringing about an entirely new national conception of himself; he has placed himself in an entirely new light before the American people. I do not think it too much to say that through artistic achievement the Negro has found a means of getting at the very core of the prejudice against him, by challenging the Nordic superiority complex. A great deal has been accomplished in this decade of "renaissance." Enough has been accomplished to make it seem almost amazing when we realize that there are less than twenty-five Negro artists who have more or less of national recognition; and that it is they who have chiefly done the work. A great part of what they have accomplished has been done through the sort of publicity they have secured for the race. A generation ago the Negro was receiving lots of publicity, but nearly all of it was bad. There were front page stories with such headings as, "Negro Criminal," "Negro Brute." To-day one may see undesirable stories, but one may also read stories about Negro singers, Negro actors, Negro authors, Negro poets. The connotations of the very word "Negro" have been changed. A generation ago many Negroes were half or wholly ashamed of the term. To-day they have every reason to be proud of it.

For many years and by many methods the Negro has been overcoming the coarser prejudices against him; and when we consider how many of the subtler prejudices have crumbled, and crumbled rapidly under the process of art creation by the Negro, we are justified in taking a hopeful outlook toward the effect that the increase of recognized individual artists fivefold, tenfold, twentyfold, will have on this most perplexing and vital question before the American people.

Harper's, 1928

BLACK MANHATTAN

XV

DURING the term of exile of the Negro from the downtown theatres of New York, which began in 1910 and lasted for seven lean years, there grew up in Harlem a real Negro theatre, something New York had never had before; that is a theatre in which Negro performers played to audiences made up almost wholly of people of their own race. In several Southern cities there had been for a decade or more theatres where the audiences, on account of the laws separating the races in places of amusement, were strictly coloured. And in Chicago there was the Pekin Theatre, a Negro theatre patronized principally by coloured people. But the professional experience of Negro performers in New York had always been to play before audiences predominantly white. The rise of a Negro theatre in Harlem was, therefore, a new thing; and, because it was within the radius of the circle in which the theatrical forces of the country are centred, it proved to be a very important thing. It is not an exaggeration to say that it worked some vital changes. The Negro performer in New York, who had always been playing to white or predominantly white audiences, found himself in an entirely different psychological atmosphere. He found himself freed from a great many restraints and taboos that had cramped him for forty years. In all those years he had been constrained to do a good many things that were distasteful because managers felt they were things that would please white folks. Likewise he was forbidden to do some other things because managers feared they would displease white folks. One of the well-known taboos was that there should never be any romantic love-making in a Negro play. If anything approaching a love duet was introduced in a musical comedy, it had to be broadly burlesqued. The reason behind this taboo lay in the belief that a love scene between two Negroes could not strike a white audience except as ridiculous. The taboo existed in deference to the superiority stereotype that Negroes cannot be supposed to mate romantically, but do so in some sort of minstrel fashion or in some more primeval manner than white people. This taboo had been one of the most strictly observed.

In the middle theatrical period Cole and Johnson had come nearest to breaking it in their *Shoofly Regiment* and *Red Moon*. Williams and Walker never seriously attempted to do so. So, with the establishment of the Negro theatre in Harlem, coloured performers in New York experienced for the first time release from the restraining fears of what a white audience would stand for; for the first time they felt free to do on the stage whatever they were able to do.

This sense of freedom manifested itself in efforts covering a wide rage; efforts that ran all the way from crude Negro burlesque to Broadway drama. This intermediate and experimental theatrical period developed mainly in two Harlem theatres, the Lafayette and the Lincoln. Within several years both these houses had good stock-companies, and for quite a while their repertories consisted chiefly of downtown successes. The Lafayette Players developed into a very proficient organization that gave adequate presentations of *Madame X, The Servant in the House, On Trial, The Love of Choo Chin, Within the Law*, and other such plays. These melodramatic plays made a great appeal to Harlem audiences. To most of the people that crowded the Lafayette and the Lincoln the thrill received from these pieces was an entirely new experience; and it was all the closer and more moving because it was expressed in terms of their own race. For a time Negro sketches and musical shows were swept off the stage, but they are now back again.

The two stock-companies had as members some performers who came down from the days of the Isham, Williams and Walker, Cole and Johnson shows; and they also developed a number of young dramatic actors who became great Harlem favourites. There were Anita Bush, Inez Clough, Abbie Mitchell, Ida Anderson, Evelyn Ellis, Lottie Grady, Laura Bowman, Susie Sutton, Cleo Desmond, Edna Thomas, Charles Gilpin, Frank Wilson, Tom Brown, Charles Moore, Sidney Kirkpatrick, Lionel Monagas, A. B. Comathiere, Walter Thompson, "Babe" Townsend, Charles Olden, Andrew Bishop, Clarence Muse, Jack Carter. All of these names were as well known to Harlem as those of Broadway favourites to the rest of the city. Readers who are at all familiar with the present period of the Negro in the theatre will see that in this list there are those who did not remain limited to Harlem or to the circuit played by the Harlem stock-companies, but helped to place the Negro fairly and squarely on Broadway. The Negro theatre in Harlem, in which the coloured performed gained a new freedom and new incentives, proved to be the exact medium he needed through which to fit himself for the fresh start he was to make.

All through this intermediate period there were times when polite comedy and high-tension melodrama gave way to black-face farce, hilarious musical comedy, and bills of specialties. The black Harlem audiences enjoyed being thrilled, but they also wanted to laugh. And a Negro audience seems never to laugh heartier than when laughing at itself—provided it is a *strictly* Negro audience. There were several Negro producers who kept the older tradition alive: the Tutt brothers—Whitney and J. Homer—Irving C. Miller, and S. H. Dudley. Their productions always drew good houses. But in this field there stands out above them all a musical show produced at the Lafayette Theatre in 1913, which not only played to great local crowds, but brought Broadway up to Harlem. The piece was *Darktown Follies*, written and staged by Leubrie Hill, formerly a member of the Williams and Walker company. *Darktown Follies* drew space, headlines, and cartoons in the New York papers; and consequently it became the vogue to go to Harlem to see it. This was the beginning of the nightly migration to Harlem in search of entertainment. One visitor to the *Darktown Follies* was Florenz Ziegfeld, and a very much interested visitor he was. He bought the rights to produce the finale to the first act and several song numbers in his own *Follies*. The finale to the first act of *Darktown Follies* was one of those miracles of originality which occasionally come to pass in the world of musical comedy. Its title was "At the Ball," the tune was the sort of melody that, once heard, is unforgettable, and words and music were combined into a very clever piece of syncopation. But it was the staging that made it so striking. The whole company formed an endless chain that passed before the footlights and behind the scenes, round and round, singing and executing a movement from a dance called "ballin' the jack," one of those Negro dances which periodically come along and sweep the country. This finale was one of the greatest hits the *Ziegfeld Follies* ever had. One of the song numbers Mr. Ziegfeld took was "Rock Me in the Cradle of Love," which in the *Darktown Follies* had been sung by the Negro tenor to the bronze soubrette in a most impassioned manner, demonstrating that the love-making taboo had been absolutely kicked out of the Negro theatre. In 1915 Edward Sterling Wright came to the Lafayette Theatre with a very creditable presentation of *Othello*.

This period in Harlem filled in the gap between the second and third periods of the Negro in the theatre. The third period is now in full swing, and the Negro theatre in Harlem is also very much alive. At present, aside from the picture houses, there are three large Negro theatres in Harlem. The third was added when several years ago the Alhambra Theatre on Seventh Avenue near One Hundred and Twenty-fifth Street, long a Keith vaudeville house, was converted into a theatre for performances given by and for Negroes.

April 5, 1917, is the date of the most important single event in the entire history of the Negro in the American theatre; for it marks the beginning of a new era. On that date a performance of three dramatic plays was given by the Coloured Players at Garden Theatre in Madison Square Garden, New York, and the stereotyped traditions regarding the Negro's histrionic limitations were smashed. It was the first time anywhere in the United States for Negro actors in the dramatic theatre to command the serious attention of the critics and of the general press and public.

The plays were three one-act plays written by Ridgely Torrence; they were produced by Mrs. Emily Hapgood; the settings and costumes were designed by Robert Edmond Jones, and the staging was under his direction. The acting was fine; in several of the roles it was superb. In fact, nothing that has been done since has afforded Negro performers such a wide gamut for their powers. The praise of the critics was enthusiastic and practically unanimous.

The performance opened with *The Rider of Dreams*, a play of rustic Negro life, and a true comedy. The second play was *Granny Maumee*, a tragedy of the colour-line, which contained a vivid scene of voodoo enchantment. The play that closed the performance was *Simon the Cyrenian*, which was billed as "A Passion Interlude." It was the story of Simon, the black man who was Jesus' cross-bearer.

The casts of the three plays were:

The Rider of Dreams

A Comedy

Cast of Characters

Lucy Sparrow . . . . Blanche Deas
Booker Sparrow . . . . Joseph Burt
Madison Sparrow . . . . Opal Cooper
Dr. Williams . . . . Alexander Rogers

Granny Maumee

A Tragedy

Cast of Characters

Granny Maumee . . . . Marie Jackson Stuart
Pearl . . . . Fannie Tarkington
Sapphie . . . . Blanche Deas

Simon the Cyrenian

A Passion Interlude

"And as they led Him away, they laid hold upon one Simon, a Cyrenian . . . and on him they laid the cross, that he might bear it after Jesus." Luke xxiii, 26.

Cast of Characters

Procula . . . . Inez Clough
Drusus . . . . Andrew Bishop
Acté, Princess of Egypt . . . . Lottie Grady
Battus . . . . Theodore Roosevelt Bolin
Simon . . . . John T. Butler
Pilate . . . . Alexander Rogers
Barabbas . . . . Jesse Shipp
The Mocker with the Crown of Thorns . . . . Robert Atkin
The Mocker with the Scarlet Robe . . . . Thomas William
Egyptian Herald . . . . Frederick Slade
Centurion . . . . Jerome Osborne, Jr.
Longinus . . . . Ralph Hernandez
Soldiers . . . . $\begin{cases} \text{Jervis Wilson} \\ \text{Earl Taylor} \\ \text{Lisle Berridge} \end{cases}$
Attendants to Procula · · · · · · · · · · · · · · · · · · $\begin{cases} \text{Thomas William} \\ \text{Muriel Smith} \end{cases}$

Scene: The Garden of Pilate's House at Jerusalem.
Time: The day of Jesus' Crucifixion.

These plays, a rustic comedy, a voodoo tragedy, and the passion interlude, made a high demand on the versatility of the company: the first called for humorous characterization, the second for dramatic power, and the third for finished acting. The demand was fully measured up to. George Jean Nathan, in making his estimate of the ten most distinguished performers of the year, gave Opal Cooper for his work in *The Rider of Dreams* seventh place in the list of male actors, and Inez Clough for her portrayal of Procula, the wife of Pilate, in *Simon the Cyrenian*, ninth place among the women.

A glance at the casts of these plays will show some names that have by now become a bit familiar to the reader, and will also buttress the statement made earlier in this book that the accumulation of theatrical training and stage technique has made possible the higher development of each period of the Negro in the theatre over the period preceding. This knocks something of a hole in the popular idea that Negroes, because of their marked aptitude for the theatre, simply walk out on the stage and act. In certain exceptional cases they do, but generally they do not. We see the name Jesse Shipp. Mr. Shipp's professional experience goes back to the minstrel period, with Primrose and West's "Forty Whites and Thirty Blacks," and comes down through the Isham, the Cole and Johnson, and the Williams and Walker shows. At the present time Mr. Shipp is playing a part in *The Green Pastures*. Alex Rogers came down through the Williams and Walker shows. Miss Clough came down through the Isham and the Cole and Johnson shows and the Lafayette Players. Miss Deas came through the Cole and Johnson shows. In addition to Miss Clough, the Lafayette Players were represented by Andrew Bishop and Lottie Grady. One of those special exceptions was Opal Cooper. Mr. Cooper had never been on the professional stage before; his sole previous preparation was what he had gained as an entertainer in a night-club. John T. Butler, who played the role of Simon, was a post-office employee and had acquired his experience in amateur and semi-professional theatricals. Marie Jackson Stuart had long been a dramatic reader.

A notable feature of the production was the singing orchestra under the direction of J. Rosamond Johnson. A singing orchestra as part of a play was at the time a distinct innovation in the theatre in New York. The Coloured Players remained ten days at the Garden Theatre, then moved up to the Garrick with every promise of success; but the fates planned otherwise. The Coloured Players opened on April 5, 1917; and on the following day, April 6, the United States declared war against the Imperial German Government. They played at the Garrick for several weeks, but the increasing stress of the war was too great, even for stronger enterprises in the theatre, and it crushed them out. Nevertheless, this effort marked the beginning of the third, and present, period of the Negro in the American theatre. And it was Emily Hapgood, who has recently died, who first demonstrated the faith that the Negro could make a place on the legitimate stage. After the close of the war the effort was carried forward.

In addition to the theatre in Harlem, there has been another medium through which significant effect has been wrought in the Negro in the theatre; that medium is the night-clubs. To many, especially among coloured people, a Harlem night-club is a den of iniquity, where the Devil holds high revel. The fact is that the average night-club is as orderly as many a Sunday-school picnic has been. These clubs are patronized by many quite respectable citizens. Anyone who visits them expecting to be shocked is likely to be disappointed. Generally night-clubbers go simply to have a good time. They laugh and talk and they dance to the most exhilarating music. And they watch a first-rate revue. Certainly, there are infractions of the Volstead Act; but they also take place in the best-regulated homes. The larger clubs maintain permanent companies of performers; and such clubs as Connie's Inn, the Cotton Club, and Small's Paradise put on revues that are often better than what may be seen in the theatres downtown. The night-clubs have been the training ground for a good part of the talent that has been drawn upon by musical comedy and revues in the professional theatre; and not only for strictly Negro productions, but also for productions in which there have been mixed casts, as, for example, in *Show Boat* and *Golden Dawn*.

The night-clubs also constitute the stage for a number of crack Negro bands. Duke Ellington's is one of the most famous jazz bands in the country. Fletcher Henderson's is another, which, however, generally plays in a downtown club.

There are hundreds of musicians and hundreds of performers
connected with the night-clubs of Harlem. The waiters, cooks,
coat-room girls, doormen and others make up several more
hundreds. It has been estimated that there are something like
two thousand Negroes employed in these clubs.

The little-theatre movement has also been started and
restarted in Harlem, as the various efforts for establishment
flourished and died. There have been three or four definite and
partially successful efforts. The most successful was made by
the Krigwa Players, organized by W. E. Burghardt Du Bois in
connexion with the literary and artistic program of the *Crisis*
magazine. The Krigwa Players had the distinction of winning a
place in the Little Theatre Tournament, 1927, to compete for
the David Belasco trophy. The company did not win the trophy, but its play, *The Fool's Errand*, written by Eulalie Spence,
a New York coloured girl, was awarded one of the Samuel
French prizes for the best unpublished manuscript plays in the
contest.

XVI

O N December 15, 1919, John Drinkwater's *Abraham Lincoln* had its American *première* at the Cort Theatre in
New York, and Charles Gilpin, formerly with both the Lincoln
and the Lafayette companies, was drafted to create the role of
the Rev. William Custis, a Negro preacher who goes to the
White House for a conference between the President and the
black man constituting one of the strongest and most touching scenes in the play. The character of Custis was intended by
the playwright to be a representation of Frederick Douglass.
Drinkwater in writing the play had largely followed Lord
Charnwood's life of Abraham Lincoln, in which Douglass is
erroneously set down as "a well-known Negro preacher." The
playwright also made the error of putting Custis's lines into
dialect. He may, as a dramatist, have done this intentionally to
heighten the character effect; or he may, as an Englishman,
have done it through unfamiliarity with all the facts. In either
case, the dialect was such as no American Negro would ever
use. It was a slightly darkened pidgin-English or the form of
speech a big Indian chief would be supposed to employ in

talking with the Great White Father at Washington. However, Gilpin was a success in the role.

Meanwhile Eugene O'Neill was experimenting with the dramatic possibilities of the Negro both as material and as exponent. He had written a one-act play, *The Moon of the Caribbees*, in which the scene was laid aboard a ship lying in a West Indian harbour, and the characters were members of the ship's crew and Negro natives of the island. The play was produced at the Provincetown Playhouse, New York, in 1918, with a white cast. He had also written a one-act tragedy, *The Dreamy Kid*, in which all of the four characters were Negroes. *The Dreamy Kid* was produced at the Provincetown Playhouse, October 31, 1919, with a Negro cast and with Harold Simmelkjaer—who, despite the Danish name, is a Negro—in the title-role. This play was later revived with Frank Wilson as the Dreamy Kid. In the season of 1919–20 Butler Davenport's Bramhall Players produced at their playhouse in East Twenty-seventh Street a play called *Justice* with a mixed cast. Frank Wilson and Rose McClendon played important parts.

None of these efforts, so far as the Negro is concerned, evoked more than mildly favourable comment. But on November 3, 1920, O'Neill's *The Emperor Jones* was produced at the Provincetown Playhouse, with Charles Gilpin in the title-role, and another important page in the history of the Negro theatre was written. The next morning Gilpin was famous. The power of his acting was enthusiastically and universally acclaimed. Indeed, the sheer physical feat of sustaining the part—the whole play is scarcely more than a continuous monologue spoken by the principal character—demanded admiration. The Drama League voted him to be one of the ten persons who had done most for the American theatre during the year; and some of the readers of these pages will recall the almost national crisis that was brought on as a consequence of this action. As was the custom, the Drama League gave a dinner in honour of the ten persons chosen; and, as seemed quite natural to do, invited Mr. Gilpin. Thereupon there broke out a controversy that divided the Drama League, the theatrical profession, the press, and the public. Pressure was brought to have the invitation withdrawn, but those responsible for it stood firm. Then the pressure was centred upon Mr. Gilpin to induce him not to attend the dinner. The amount of noise and heat made, and of serious effort expended, was worthy of a weightier matter than the question of a dinner with a coloured man present as a guest. This incident occurred only ten years ago, but already it has an archaic character. It is doubtful if a similar incident today could provoke such a degree of asininity. Mr. Gilpin attended the dinner.

By his work in *The Emperor Jones* Gilpin reached the highest point of achievement on the legitimate stage that had yet been attained by a Negro in America. But it was by no sudden flight; it was by a long, hard struggle. Before being dined by the Drama League as one of those who had done most for the American theatre, he had travelled with small road shows playing one-night stands, been stranded more than once, been compelled to go back to work at his trade as a printer, been a member of a minstrel show, worked in a barber-shop, joined a street fair company, gone out with a concert company, tried being a trainer of prize-fighters, sung with a company of jubilee singers, worked as an elevator-boy and switchboard operator in an apartment house on Riverside Drive, been a railroad porter, played vaudeville, held a job as a janitor, and hesitated greatly about giving it up. His real theatrical career can be traced from Williams and Walker's company to Gus Hill's *Smart Set*, to the Pekin stock-company, to the Anita Bush Players at the Lincoln in Harlem, to the Lafayette Players, to John Drinkwater's *Abraham Lincoln*, and to *The Emperor Jones*. Mr. Gilpin was awarded the Spingarn Medal* in 1920. He died May 6, 1930.

Torrence and O'Neill were not the only playwrights of these latter days to experiment with the Negro as a theme for the theatre, but they were the first to use the Negro and Negro life as pure dramatic material. In 1905 there was produced at the Amsterdam Theatre (New York) *The Clansman* by the Rev. Thomas Dixon. This play was a rehash of the animosities of Reconstruction days, following the Civil War, and an attempt to intensify sentiment against the Negro. In 1909 *The Nigger*

*The Spingarn Medal was instituted in 1914 by J. E. Spingarn, treasurer of the National Association for the Advancement of Colored People, and is awarded annually for "the highest or noblest achievement by an American Negro during the preceding year or years."

by Edward Sheldon was produced at the New Theatre (New York). This play, too, was set in the Reconstruction period, but the situation was viewed from an almost opposite angle. In 1916 Robert Hilliard produced *Pride of Race* at the Maxine Elliot Theatre (New York) and played the leading role. This play was built on that bit of pseudo-science which holds that to a white person and a coloured person whose Negro blood cannot even be discerned there may be born a tar-black baby. These were plays of propaganda; they were played by wholly white casts; for them the Negro was merely thematic material. They did not contemplate him as an exponent.

The following year the Negro came back to the New York theatre in his more familiar role. In the summer of 1921 along came *Shuffle Along*, and all New York flocked to the Sixty-third Street Theatre to hear the most joyous singing and see the most exhilarating dancing to be found on any stage in the city. *Shuffle Along* was a record-breaking, epoch-making musical comedy. Some of its tunes—"I'm Just Wild about Harry," "Gipsy Blues," "Love Will Find a Way," "I'm Cravin' for That Kind of Love," "In Honeysuckle Time," "Bandana Days," and "Shuffle Along"—went round the world. It would be difficult to name another musical comedy with so many song hits as *Shuffle Along* had. Its dances furnished new material for hundreds of dancing performers. *Shuffle Along* was cast in the form of the best Williams and Walker, Cole and Johnson tradition; but the music did not hark back at all; it was up to the minute. There was, however, one other respect in which it did hark back; it was written and produced, as well as performed, by Negroes. Four men—F. E. Miller, Aubrey Lyles, Eubie Blake, and Noble Sissle—combined their talents and their means to bring it about. Their talents were many, but their means were limited, and they had no easy time.

They organized the show in New York and took it on a short out-of-town try-out, with Broadway as their goal. It was booked for an opening at the Howard Theatre, a coloured theatre in Washington. When the company assembled at the Pennsylvania Station, it was found that they did not have quite enough money for transportation, and there had to be quick scurrying round to raise the necessary funds. Such an ominous situation could not well be concealed, and there were misgivings and mutterings among the company. After all the tickets were secured, it took considerable persuasion to induce some of its members to go so far away from New York on such slim expectations.

They played two successful weeks at the Howard Theatre and so had enough money to move to Philadelphia, where they were booked to play the Dunbar Theatre, another coloured house. Broadway, their goal, looked quite distant even from Philadelphia. The managers, seeking to make sure of getting the company to New York, suggested to the owner of the Dunbar Theatre that it would be a good investment for him to take a half-interest in the show for one thousand dollars, but he couldn't see it that way. They played two smashing weeks at the Dunbar and brought the company intact into New York, but, as they expressed it, on a shoe-string. They went into the Sixty-third Street Theatre, which had been dark for some time; it was pretty far uptown for Broadway audiences. Within a few weeks *Shuffle Along* made the Sixty-third Street Theatre one of the best-known houses in town and made it necessary for the Traffic Department to declare Sixty-third Street a one-way thoroughfare. *Shuffle Along* played New York for over a year and played on the road for two years longer. It was a remarkable aggregation. There was a chorus of pretty girls that danced marvellously. The comedians were Miller and Lyles, and a funny black-face pair they were. Their burlesque of two ignorant Negroes going into "big business" and opening a grocery-store was a never-failing producer of side-shaking laughter. There was a quartet, the Four Harmony Kings, that gave a fresh demonstration of the close harmony and barber-shop chords that are the chief characteristics of Negro quartets. There was Lottie Gee, jauntiest of *ingénues*, and Gertrude Saunders, most bubbling of comediennes. There was Nobel Sissle with his take-it-from-me style of singing, and there was Eubie Blake with his amazing jazz piano-playing. And it was in *Shuffle Along* that Florence Mills, that incomparable little star, first twinkled on Broadway.

Shuffle Along pre-empted and held New York's interest in Negro theatricals for a year. In the fall of 1921 another venture was made, when Irving C. Miller, a brother of the Miller of

Shuffle Along, produced *Put and Take*, a musical comedy, at Town Hall (New York). *Put and Take*, by all ordinary standards, was a good show, but it was overshadowed by the great vogue of *Shuffle Along*. In the spring of 1923 Irving C. Miller had better success with *Liza*, a tuneful and very fast dancing show that he produced at a downtown theatre.

In the fall Miller and Lyles came out with a new play, *Runnin' Wild*, and opened at the Colonial Theatre, on upper Broadway, on October 29. The old combination had been broken. Miller and Lyles had remained together; Sissle and Blake had formed a separate partnership, and Florence Mills was lost to both sides; she was heading a revue at the Plantation, a downtown night-club. Notwithstanding, *Runnin' Wild*, even in the inevitable comparison with its predecessor, was a splendid show. It had a successful run of eight months at the Colonial. *Runnin' Wild* would have been notable if for no other reason than that it made use of the "Charleston," a Negro dance creation which up to that time had been known only to Negroes; thereby introducing it to New York, America, and the world. The music for the dance was written by Jimmie Johnson, the composer of the musical score of the piece. The Charleston achieved a popularity second only to the tango, also a Negro dance creation, originating in Cuba, transplanted to the Argentine, thence to the world via Paris. There is a claim that Irving C. Miller first introduced the Charleston on the stage in his *Liza*; even so, it was *Runnin' Wild* that started the dance on its world-encircling course. When Miller and Lyles introduced the dance in their show, they did not depend wholly upon their extraordinarily good jazz band for the accompaniment; they went straight back to primitive Negro music and had the major part of the chorus supplement the band by beating out the time with hand-clapping and foot-patting. The effect was electrical. Such a demonstration of beating out complex rhythms had never before been seen on a stage in New York. However, Irving C. Miller may indisputably claim that in his show *Dinah*, produced the next year at the Lafayette Theatre, he was the first to put another Negro dance, the "Black Bottom," on the stage. The "Black Bottom" gained a popularity which was only little less than that of the Charleston.

The Sissle and Blake show of this same year was *Chocolate Dandies*. In comparison with *Runnin' Wild*, its greatest lack lay in the fact that it had no comedians who approached the class of Miller and Lyles. But *Chocolate Dandies* did have Johnny Hudgins, and in the chorus a girl who showed herself to be a comedienne of the first order. Her name was Josephine Baker.

On May 7, 1923, there was witnessed at the Frazee Theatre what was the most ambitious attempt Negroes had yet made in the legitimate theatre in New York. The Ethiopian Art Players, organized by Raymond O'Neil and Mrs. Sherwood Anderson, presented Oscar Wilde's *Salome*; an original interpretation of Shakspere's *The Comedy of Errors*; and *The Chip Woman's Fortune*, a one-act Negro play by Willis Richardson. The acting of Evelyn Preer in the role of Salome, and her beauty, received high and well-deserved praise from the critics; and the work of Sidney Kirkpatrick, Laura Bowman, Charles Olden, and Lionel Monagas, all formerly of the Lafayette Players, won commendation. But the only play on the bill that was fully approved was *The Chip Woman's Fortune*. Some of the critics said frankly that however well Negroes might play "white" classics like *Salome* and *The Comedy of Errors*, it was doubtful if they could be so interesting as they would be in Negro plays, if they could be interesting at all. The Ethiopian Art Players had run up against one of the curious factors in the problem of race, against the paradox which makes it quite seemly for a white person to represent a Negro on the stage, but a violation of some inner code for a Negro to represent a white person. This, it seems, is certain: if they had put into a well-written play of Negro life the same degree of talent and skill they did put into *Salome* and *The Comedy of Errors*, they would have achieved an overwhelming success. But it appears that at the time no such play was available for them. Beginning June 4, the company played for a week at the Lafayette in Harlem.

In the same year *Taboo*, a play that had for its theme African voodooism, written by Mary Hoyt Wiborg, a white playwright, was produced at the Sam Harris Theatre (New York). The most important thing about this play was that in it Paul Robeson made his first appearance on the professional stage, playing the role of the voodoo king opposite Margaret Wycherly's voodoo queen. The outstanding feature of the play, however, was an African dance done by C. Kamba Simango, a native, and at the time a student at Columbia University. *Taboo*, after a brief run, was taken to London, where it was better received than in New York. Robeson went to London and acted his same role, playing opposite to Mrs. Patrick Campbell. 1923 also saw the production of *Roseanne*, a play of Negro life in the South, having to do with a transgressing preacher and his, finally, avenging congregation. The play, like *Taboo*, was the work of a white woman, Nan Bagby Stevens; it was produced at the Greenwich Village Theatre with a white cast, but failed. In the early part of 1924 it was produced with an all-Negro cast, Charles Gilpin and Rose McClendon in the principal roles. Later Robeson replaced Gilpin in the role of the preacher. With these plays may be grouped *Goat Alley*, a play of Negro life in the back alleys of Washington, written by Ernest H. Culbertson, a white playwright, and produced with a Negro cast at the Bijou Theatre (New York), June 20, 1921. The play was well written and capably acted, but failed. In 1927 it was revived at the Princess Theatre without greater success.

But on May 15, 1924, Eugene O'Neill produced at the Provincetown Playhouse a Negro play that made New York and the rest of the country sit up and take notice. The play was *All God's Chillun Got Wings*. The cast was a mixed one, with Paul Robeson in the principal role, playing opposite Mary Blair, a white actress. Public excitement about this play did not wait for the opening in the theatre, but started fully three months before; that is, as soon as it was seen through the publication of the play in the *American Mercury* that the two chief characters were a coloured boy and a white girl, and that the boy falls in love with the girl and marries her. When it was learned that the play was to be produced in a New York theatre with a coloured and a white performer in these two roles, a controversy began in the newspapers of the city that quickly spread; and articles, editorials, and interviews filed columns upon columns in periodicals throughout the country. The discussion in the press was, as might be expected, more bitter than it had been in the incident of the Drama League dinner to Charles Gilpin. The New York *American* and the *Morning*

Telegraph went further than other New York publications. For
weeks they carried glaring headlines and inciting articles. They
appeared to be seeking to provoke violence in order to stop
the play.

The New York *American* on March 18, eight weeks before
the opening, carried an article headed: "Riots Feared From
Drama—'All God's Chillun' Direct Bid for Disorders, the
View of George G. Battle—Thinks City Should Act." In the
article George Gordon Battle was quoted as saying: "The production of such a play will be most unfortunate. If the
Provincetown Players and Mr. O'Neill refuse to bow before
public opinion, the city officials should take action to ban it
from the stage." In the same article Mrs. W. J. Arnold, "a
founder of the Daughters of the Confederacy," was quoted as
saying: "The scene where Miss Blair is called upon to kiss and
fondle a Negro's hand is going too far, even for the stage. The
play may be produced above the Mason and Dixie [*sic*] line,
but Mr. O'Neill will not get the friendly reception he had
when he sent 'Emperor Jones' his other coloured play into the
South. The play should be banned by the authorities, because
it will be impossible for it to do otherwise than stir up ill feeling between the races."

An issue of the Hearst publication said editorially:

> Gentlemen who are engaged in producing plays should not make it
> any harder for their friends to protect them from censorship. They
> should not put on plays which are, or threaten to become, enemies of
> the public peace; they should not dramatize dynamite, because, while
> helping the box office, it may blow up the business.
>
> We refer to the play in which a white woman marries a black man
> and at the end of the play, after going crazy, stoops and kisses the
> Negro's hand.
>
> It is hard to imagine a more nauseating and inflammable situation,
> and in many communities the failure of the audience to scrap the
> play and mutilate the players would be regarded as a token of public
> anemia.

It would be still harder to imagine yellower journalism than
this, or why a thing that has happened more than once in actual life should be regarded as so utterly beyond conception as
a theatrical situation.

The opening night came, the theatre was crowded—the attacks had served as publicity—there was some feeling of tenseness on the part of the audience and a great deal on the part of the performers, but the play proceeded without any sign of antagonistic demonstration, without even a hiss or a boo. None of the appeals to prejudice, hate, and fear had had the intended effect. The pressure brought on Mayor Hylan and the Police Department got no further result than the refusal of permission to allow a group of children to appear in the opening scene. The public at large failed to be moved to any sense of impending danger to either the white or the black race because of this play. The outcome of the whole business proved that the rabid newspapers were not expressing public sentiment, but were striving to stir up a public sentiment.

All God's Chillun Got Wings did not prove to be another *Emperor Jones*. One sound reason why it did not was because it was not so good a play. It was dramatic enough, but the incidents did not link up along the inevitable line that the spectator was made to feel he must follow. It may be that as the play began to grow, Mr. O'Neill became afraid of it. At any rate, he side-stepped the logical question and let his heroine go crazy; thus shifting the question from that of a coloured man living with a white wife to that of a man living with a crazy woman; from which shift, so far as this particular play was concerned, nothing at all could be demonstrated. The play, as a play, did not please white people, and, on the other hand, it failed to please coloured people. Mr. O'Neill, perhaps in concession to public sentiment, made the white girl who is willing to marry the black student, and whom he is glad to get, about as lost as he could well make her. Coloured people not only did not consider this as any compliment to the race, but regarded it as absolutely contrary to the essential truth. However, the play ran for several weeks, and Paul Robeson increased his reputation by the restraint, sincerity, and dignity with which he acted a difficult role.

Mr. Robeson's reputation is now international. He played the leading Negro character in the London production of *Show Boat*. He played the title role in a successful revival of *The Emperor Jones* in Berlin early in 1930. And it has been an-

nounced that he will play Othello in a production to be made
of Shakspere's immortal tragedy at the Savoy Theatre, London, in May 1930.

Perhaps it was now time for New York again to sing and
dance and laugh with the Negro on the stage; and it soon had
the opportunity. On October 29, 1924, exactly one year after
the opening of *Runnin' Wild*, Florence Mills came to the
Broadhurst Theatre in *Dixie to Broadway*, and New York had
its first Negro revue. For the Florence Mills show broke away
entirely from the established traditions of Negro musical comedy. Indeed, it had to, because she was the star; and the traditions called for a show built around two male comedians,
usually of the black-face type. The revue was actually an enlarged edition of the one in which Miss Mills had been appearing at the Plantation. It was also the same revue that had been
played in London the season before under the title of *Dover to
Dixie* with her as the star. On the night of the production of
Dixie to Broadway New York not only found itself with a novelty in the form of a Negro revue, but also discovered that it
had a new artist of positive genius in the person of Florence
Mills. She had made a name in *Shuffle Along*, but in *Dixie to
Broadway* she was recognized for her full worth.

Florence Mills was born in Washington, D.C., January 25,
1895, and was on the stage practically all her life. She was a
child prodigy and began her career before she was six years old
as "Baby Florence Mills." As "Baby Florence" she appeared a
number of times as a singing and dancing entertainer in the
drawing-rooms of the diplomatic set at the capital. On one occasion Lady Pauncefote, wife of the British Ambassador, presented her with a gold bracelet. A very early photograph of
Florence shows her in a pose calculated chiefly to display this
piece of jewellery. The same photograph shows her wearing
two medals, won through her skill in cake-walking and buck-
dancing. She acquired these decorations as an amateur. Her
first professional appearance on the stage was noted as follows
in the Washington *Star*:

"The peerless child artist who has appeared before the most exclusive set in Washington, delighting them with her songs and dances, is
appearing this week at the Empire Theatre with the 'Sons of Ham'

company No. 2. As an extra attraction is Baby Florence singing 'Hannah from Savannah.' Baby Florence made a big hit and was encored for dancing.'

After this début she travelled for a while with a company as one of the "picks." Then she played in vaudeville with her two sisters, Olivia and Maude, in an act known as the Mills Sisters. Until she was twenty-five years old, she played from coast to coast in vaudeville or in one small road company or another, struggling hard, through that particularly hard sort of life, from a start of nine dollars a week up to four or five times that amount, and gaining a sure grasp on her art. Then, in the summer of 1921, in *Shuffle Along*, she came to Broadway—came from a Harlem cabaret to take the place of Gertrude Saunders —and fame and fortune met her there. Many of the good things of life came following; perhaps the best for her, after so many itinerant years, was the house she bought in Harlem, which her mother made home for her.

She left *Shuffle Along* to become the star of Lew Leslie's *Plantation Revue.* This revue proved so popular that Mr. Leslie took it to London. Miss Mills captured London completely. St. John Ervine, writing of her, said: "The success acquired by Miss Florence Mills, the American coloured girl playing in 'From Dover to Dixie' is something unequalled by any American playing here in the last decade. She is by far the most artistic person London has had the good fortune to see." When she returned from London, New York had the joy of seeing *Dixie to Broadway.*

In the spring of 1926 Miss Mills came out of the Plantation with a new revue called *Blackbirds*, and played at the Alhambra Theatre in Harlem for six weeks to packed houses. Early in the summer Mr. Leslie took the show to Paris, where it played for five months, then to London, where it had a six months' run. Miss Mills's popularity was unbounded. Her photographs were displayed everywhere, and her portrait was painted. News dispatches reported that the Prince of Wales was sixteen times a spectator of the revue, and that he always enthusiastically applauded "Little Twinks," and pronounced her "ripping."

"Ripping" will do, perhaps, as well as any other omnibus adjective in an attempt to define Florence Mills, but she was indefinable. One might best string out a list of words such as: pixy, elf, radiant, exotic, Peter Pan, wood-nymph, wistful, piquant, magnetism, witchery, madness, flame; and then despairingly exclaim: "Oh, you know what I mean." She could be whimsical, she could be almost grotesque; but she had the good taste that never allowed her to be coarse. She could be *risquée*, she could be seductive; but it was impossible for her to be vulgar, for she possessed a naïveté that was alchemic. As a pantomimist and a singing and dancing comedienne she had no superior in any place or any race. And yet, after all, did she really sing? The upper range of her voice was full of bubbling, bell-like, bird-like tones. And there, perhaps, is the comprehensive word the Prince might have used: "bird-like." It was rather a magical thing Florence Mills used to do with that small voice in her favourite song, "I'm a Little Blackbird Looking for a Bluebird"; and she did it with such exquisite poignancy as always to raise a lump in your throat.

She got back to New York from the European tour of *Blackbirds* on October 12, 1927. She came back decided to have a delayed operation for appendicitis performed. She came back also with all the plans laid to follow the course taken with her former success, and present *Blackbirds* to Broadway. But *Blackbirds of 1928* was produced without her.

She died in the hospital, November 1, 1927. It it not an exaggeration to say that her death shocked the theatrical world. Harlem was stunned and at first refused to believe the news could be true. Then there followed vague rumours of foul play. The papers devoted columns to her, news and editorial. The *Evening Journal* and the *Evening Graphic* carried the story of her life in serial form. The Negroes of New York mourned her deeply, for she was more their idol than any other artist of the race. Her funeral was one such as Harlem, perhaps all New York, had never seen before. Five thousand people were packed to suffocation in Mother Zion Church. The air quivered with emotion. Hall Johnson's choir sang Spirituals, and the whole throng wept and sobbed. A fellow actress rose at the end of the service to sing a song dedicated to the dead star; she started, she faltered, she struggled on; her efforts ended in a frantic cry: "Florence!" and she swayed and collapsed in a heap on the floor. Women fainted and men were unnerved. Under all there could be sensed a bewilderment, a resentment, at this act of God—Why did He do it?—we have so few—she was so young—she might have done so much more for us in the eyes of the world.

Outside the church more than a hundred thousand people jammed the streets. A detail of one hundred and fifty police was necessary to handle the crowd. The procession moved slowly through this dense mass. Eleven automobiles conveyed the flowers. Thirty coloured girls from the stage, dressed alike in grey, walked as an escort. The *cortège* followed. As One Hundred and Forty-fifth Street was neared, an airplane circled low and released a flock of blackbirds. They fluttered overhead a few seconds and then flew away.

XVII

IN October 1925 there was produced at the Frolic Theatre (New York) a play that was a departure for the Negro in the theatre. It was a serious drama, written by a coloured playwright, played by a mixed cast of fourteen white and three coloured performers, and with a Negro as the principal character. The play was *Appearances*, and it was distinctively a play with a message; but, surprising as it may be, the message had nothing to do with race. The play was an exposition of the *Servant in the House* idea. It was, in fact, a sort of dramatization of the doctrines of Christian Science, of the doctrine that simply by willing our subconscious forces into action we can accomplish the seemingly impossible. The load of such a message is generally more than any play can carry; and *Appearances* was pretty heavily weighted. It was only because the preachments of cheerful uplift were rendered with such direct, almost childlike simplicity that a New York audience listened without impatience. But the second act of the play, a court scene in which the hero through a conspiracy is *almost* convicted of assaulting a white woman, did have dramatic power and was well acted. It was this act that carried the play along. *Appearances* received fairly good notices and drew audiences for several weeks, but it did not appeal strongly enough to the general public to last.

The story of the writer of the play was actually better drama than the play. He was Garland Anderson, the bellboy and switch-board operator in an apartment hotel in San Francisco. As such he came into intimate contact with the guests and did not hesitate to give them his cheerful philosophy of life. They thought it "beautiful" and "wonderful" and felt that he ought to reach more people with his message. For several years he pondered over how to do this. Then he saw a performance of Channing Pollock's *The Fool* and resolved to write a play. He wrote the play and showed it to a number of people in San Francisco, among them Richard Bennett, who gave him encouragement. Al Jolson heard of the play and wired the author to send him the manuscript. He did so and a few days later followed in person. When Mr. Anderson arrived in New York Mr. Jolson told him he was sorry he could not produce the play; he did, however, give him a splendid letter and paid the expenses of his trip from San Francisco and furnished him enough money for a stay of a couple of months in New York.

Mr. Anderson now set about to get a producer, but without success. Then he decided to give a public reading of the play. Despite discouragements, he secured the grand ball room of the Waldorf-Astoria Hotel and on a Sunday afternoon read the play to some six hundred people. He made a trip to Washington and presented a copy of the manuscript to President Coolidge. He returned to New York and gave another public reading at the Manhattan Opera House. On June 19, 1925, L. W. Sagar, manager of the Central Theatre, accepted the manuscript for production and gave Mr. Anderson an option to buy a half-interest in the play, good until September 15. With his contract in his pocket he returned immediately to San Francisco. His efforts in New York had consumed seven months. During that time he had secured the approval and help of David Belasco, Heywood Broun, Majorie Rambeau, Nance O'Neill, Bill Robinson, and some others.

On his return to San Francisco he quickly sold a half-interest in the play to Messrs. H. S. and Fergus Wilkinson, guests at the hotel where he had worked, for fifteen thousand dollars. In two automobiles Mr. Anderson and his backers motored across the continent; the cars carrying streamers: "*San Francisco to New York—For the Opening Pro-*

duction of Appearances—*By Garland Anderson, the San Francisco Bellhop Playwright.*" Before leaving San Francisco the party was photographed with Mr. Anderson receiving a letter from the Mayor of San Francisco to be delivered to the Mayor of New York. On arrival in New York the party was photographed in front of City Hall with Mr. Anderson delivering his letter to Mayor Hylan.

The run of the play was not long, but, through the efforts of Mr. Anderson, it gained a second production in New York. At the present time, through his still further efforts, it is being played in London at the Royalty Theatre and appears to be making a good impression. The play may not be an altogether convincing argument for the theories it advances, but the author himself is.

In February 1926 David Belasco produced at the Belasco Theatre the sensational melodrama *Lulu Belle*, with a cast of sixty or more persons, above three-fourths of whom were coloured. The title-role was played with great realism by Lenore Ulric, and Ruby Lee, a female role second in importance only to Miss Ulric's, was played by Evelyn Preer. Edna Thomas, who had played in the Ethiopian Art Company with Miss Preer, had a small part; later she replaced Miss Preer. The role of George Randall, the principal Negro male character, was finely played by Henry Hull, a white actor, whose make-up and dialect were beyond detection. The play was written by Edward Sheldon and Charles MacArthur. The scenes of the four acts were: I, A street scene in the San Juan Hill district; II, the top floor of a Harlem boarding-house; III, a Harlem cabaret; IV, five years later—a luxurious apartment in Paris. The story was that of the rise of a beautiful little coloured wanton from the sidewalks of Harlem to an apartment on the avenue Marigny, Paris, provided for her by the Vicomte de Villars. The story ended in tragedy. Because of the manner in which it set on the stage scenes from new York life that were wholly Negro, and because of the large number of coloured performers in a mixed cast playing important roles, *Lulu Belle* was extremely significant in the history of the Negro in the theatre in New York.

Later in the same season Paul Robeson appeared as the star in *Black Boy*, a play by Jim Tully and Frank Dazey, which dealt with the rise and fall of a Negro prize-fighter. It was produced at the Comedy Theatre. *Black Boy* was not a success and did not add much to Mr. Robeson's prestige. The cast was a mixed one. Freddie Washington, a coloured actress, gave a remarkable performance in the role of a coloured girl who, in the play, passes for white, but finally declares she is coloured and goes to live with Black Boy.

In October another play was produced in New York with a large mixed cast, in which Negro principals were integral parts. It was *Deep River*, an opera with book by Laurence Stallings and music by Frank Harling. It was produced by Arthur Hopkins at the Imperial Theatre. The scene of the opera was Creole New Orleans of 1835. The piece was beautifully mounted and well sung, but it did not remain long. Nevertheless, it was a step for the Negro. Three of the important parts were played by coloured performers. Charlotte Murray, a contralto, sang a principal role, as did Jules Bledsoe, then a student and now well known. This was Mr. Bledsoe's first appearance on the theatrical stage, and his singing in the voodoo scene was one of the highest spots of the opera.

In one of the scenes—the quadroon ball—there was a beautiful winding staircase, down which Rose McClendon had to come slowly—ever so slowly—and walk through a *patio*, then off stage. It was a high test for poise, grace, and aristocratic bearing. She accomplished this feat every night in a manner that won great applause. Quoting Alexander Woolcott in the New York *World*: "When 'Deep River' was having its trial flight in Philadelphia Ethel Barrymore slipped in to snatch what moments she could of it. 'Stay till the last act if you can,' Arthur Hopkins whispered to her, 'and watch Rose McClendon come down those stairs. She can teach some of our most hoity-toity actresses distinction.' It was Miss Barrymore who hunted *him* up after the performance to say, 'She can teach them *all* distinction.'"

Several white Southern playwrights had essayed a portrayal of some phase of Negro life in the South, but the first to succeed in the New York theatre was Paul Green, of the University of North Carolina. He had written a number of one-act plays of Southern Negro life, some of which had been produced by amateurs. On December 28, 1926, his *In Abraham's*

Bosom was produced at the Provincetown Playhouse. *In Abraham's Bosom* was a beautiful though terrible play. It was closer and truer to actual Negro life and probed deeper into it than any drama of the kind that had yet been produced. There were twelve characters in the cast, ten coloured and two white. The Negro actors playing important parts were Rose McClendon, Abbie Mitchell, Frank Wilson, and Jules Bledsoe in the leading character. Later Frank Wilson replaced Mr. Bledsoe. Mrs. McClendon had acted and Mr. Bledsoe had sung two months before in *Deep River*. Before going on the stage, Mr. Bledsoe had been a student in medicine at Columbia University; and he had also for a long time been a student of music, especially of singing. He was divided within himself as to which line to follow, medicine or art. Whenever he was good enough to sing or play the piano or dance the Charleston (he is an expert), friends and acquaintances were unanimous in declaring that he ought to go on the stage. That, perhaps, may have helped him to decide. Like Robeson, who has made a national reputation as an athlete, as an actor, and as a singer, Bledsoe is a very versatile man. In *Deep River* he sang a heroic baritone role; in *In Abraham's Bosom* he played a dramatic and tragic part; and he was yet to play an entirely different character from either in *Show Boat*.

In Abraham's Bosom was a decided success. It enjoyed a long run and had several revivals. In 1927 it was awarded the Pulitzer Prize for the original American play best representing the educational value and power of the stage.

The New Playwrights produced *Earth*, by Em Jo Basshe, at the Fifty-second Street Theatre, March 9, 1927. *Earth* was a Negro play of considerable power, with religion and superstition as the main themes. The acting was creditable and there was also some effective singing. The entire cast was composed of coloured performers. The two leading roles were played by Inez Clough and Daniel Haynes. Miss Clough had long been known for her finished work; Mr. Haynes was a new-comer, but he made a splendid impression and demonstrated the potentialities he possessed.

In the summer of 1927, on June 11 and 12, two Negro musical plays were produced in New York: *Africana*, a revue, at the Sixty-third Street Theatre, with Ethel Waters as the star; and

Rang Tang, a new Miller and Lyles musical comedy, at the Majestic Theatre. In *Rang Tang* Miller and Lyles were as funny as ever in a very good show. They had a droll scene in an airplane which had come down at sea before they had finished the flight they were making to Africa. The company was good. Among the members were Evelyn Preer, Zaidie Jackson, and Daniel Haynes in a picturesque role as King of Madagascar, a part that gave his voice and physique great opportunities. But *Rang Tang* did not draw so well as its two predecessors. As one watched it, the thought arose that perhaps the traditional pattern of Negro musical comedy was a bit worn.

Africana opened the night before *Rang Tang*. It was a swift modern revue. There were several quite clever people in it, but Ethel Waters dominated the show. She did this nearly to the same degree that Florence Mills dominated her show, but with a technique almost in contrast. Miss Waters is tall, almost statuesque, with a head so beautiful that Antonio Salemme asked the privilege of doing it in bronze—the piece was purchased by Carl Van Vechten. She is not so versatile as was Florence Mills; she has not the vivacious energy or the elusive charm; nor can she dance like the sprite Miss Mills was. Miss Waters gets her audiences, and she does get them completely, through an innate poise that she possesses; through the quiet and subtlety of her personality. She never "works hard" on the stage. Her bodily movements, when she makes them, are almost languorous. Indeed, she is at her best when she is standing perfectly still, singing quietly. Her singing corresponds to her bodily movements; she never over-exerts her voice; she always creates a sense of reserved power that compels the listener. Her singing has made a great many songs widely poplar. "Dinah," and "I'm Coming, Virginia," are a part of her personality and fame. Miss Waters also has a disarming quality which enables her to sing some songs that many singers would not be able to get away with on the stage. Those who have heard her sing "Shake That Thing" will understand. Miss Waters began her career in a Harlem cabaret. She was engaged to take the lead in the Plantation revue in the absence of Florence Mills; at the same time Josephine Baker was in the chorus there. When Mrs. Reagan, a producer, was looking for a star to head the revue she was planning to put on in Paris, she went on a scouting trip to the Plantation. She tried to get Ethel Waters and, failing, took Josephine Baker; but that is really another story.

The reader has by now come to see that in this period of the Negro in the theatre the pendulum has swung or been made to swing from drama to music and from music to drama in something like regular intervals; and the pendulum now swung over to drama. On October 10 of this same year the Theatre Guild produced at the Guild Theatre *Porgy* by Dorothy and Du Bose Heyward. The play was a dramatization of Mr. Heyward's novel *Porgy*, one of the notable books of the year. Here was the second white Southerner—if in literary collaboration man and wife can be counted as one—to take Negro life in the South and work it into a successful play. *Porgy* was a folk-play and portrayed life among the Negroes of Catfish row in Charleston, South Carolina—simple fisher-folk. The play carried conviction through its sincere simplicity. But it did not run long on a monotonous level; at times it rose to heights of ecstasy and tragedy; and always it was suffused with Negro humour. Not only was the play well written, but it was remarkably mounted and staged. In the closing scene of the first act—in which the company gathered in Serena's room holding the wake over her murdered husband; singing and singing until they rise and break into religious frenzy, their swaying bodies and uplifted hands suddenly thrown in black shadows against the background of the whitewashed walls of the room; singing and singing—there have been few scenes in the New York theatre to equal it in emotional power. *Porgy* loomed high above every Negro drama that had ever been produced.

Equal to the writing and staging was the acting. The cast was a large one, sixty-six in all, with twenty-four principals, five of them white. Among the Negro principals the work of Frank Wilson as Porgy; Georgette Harvey as Maria, keeper of the cook-shop; Wesley Hill as Jake, captain of the fishing-fleet; Rose McClendon as Serena; and Evelyn Ellis as Crown's Bess, was outstanding. And far above medium was the work of Jack Carter as Crown, Leigh Whipper in the two roles of the undertaker and the crab-man, A. B. Comathiere as Simon Frazier, a lawyer, and Percy Verwayne as Sporting Life. In *Porgy* the Negro performer removed all doubts as to his ability to do acting that requires thoughtful interpretation and intelligent skill. Here was more than the achievement of one or two individuals who might be set down as exceptions. Here was a large company giving a first-rate, even performance, with eight or ten reaching a high mark. The evidence was massive and indisputable. *Porgy* was one of the great theatrical successes of the decade. It ran altogether in New York, in London, and on the road for more than two years.

Back swung the pendulum to music, singing, and dancing; and early in 1928 Lew Leslie produced *Blackbirds of 1928* at the Liberty Theatre (New York). *Blackbirds* set a pace for all revues, white as well as black. The show became a sort of New York institution; and out-of-town visitors came to the city with the conviction that it was something that had to be seen. Like *Shuffle Along*, it started several songs on a trip round the world. Those songs were: "I Can't Give You Anything but Love," "Magnolia's Wedding Day," "Diga Diga Do," and "I Must Have That Man." But above and beyond the singing of these songs was the singing in the burlesque of the wake scene from *Porgy*. This burlesque scene was staged similarly to the original, even to the shadows on the wall. But instead of Spirituals the blues—the "St. Louis Blues"—were sung, and with an effect equally electrical and almost as moving. This effect must have suggested even to the unthinking the close analogy, which does not exist, between the Negro folk-songs known as Spirituals and those known as blues. William Bolitho, writing about *Blackbirds* in the *World*, said of this scene:

They sang for the dead, in a shadowy chapel, in long prison-coloured overalls, shaking themselves, the shadows behind them, then the whole auditorium, and then at last I even thought of that most stable, buried thing in the whole universe, the biodynamic instincts of the human personality, with their great ancestral rhythms.

The great success of *Blackbirds* was mainly an ensemble success, a success of the whole company and the very excellent band. For while there were in the cast two very clever girls, Adelaide Hall and Ada Ward, and a fairly funny comedian, there was only one individual performer who stood out pre-eminently, and that was Bill Robinson. The same Bill Robinson had been a vaudeville head-liner for a good many years, but he was new to audiences in the legitimate theatres and utterly unknown to most of the dramatic critics. He was immediately pronounced the greatest tap-dancer in the world, and in a few weeks he was one of the most widely known men in the city. His stunt of dancing up and down a set of stair steps—a stunt that has since been much imitated—was acknowledged as a demonstration of the utmost perfection in tapping out intricate rhythms. The nicety with which each group of rhythms was executed was marvellous and never failed to give the listening spectator pleasurable surprise at the accomplishment of the feat.

A great deal was written about the dancing of Bill Robinson; probably as much as was ever written about any visiting Spanish or Russian dancer. Much of what was written was a serious consideration of his art. Mary Austin, writing in the *Nation* and making an analysis of the æsthetics underlying Mr. Robinson's work, said in part:

". . . He is proud of being able with the tappings of his feet to produce and coordinate more distinct simultaneous rhythms than any other American dancer. And by the postures of his lithe dark body and the motions of his slender cane so punctuate this rhythmic patter as to restore, for his audience, the primal freshness of their own lost rhythmic powers. It is only by the sincere unconsciousness of his genius that he is able to attain that perfection of stage performance, in which his audience is made happily to participate. For Bill Robinson does not know intellectually that the capacity for rhythmic coordination is the fundament, not only of art but all human achievement.

"Robinson is intelligent about his audience to the extent of having his own pleasure and competence in his dancing enhanced by this, and by that delicate concealment of effort—the *noblesse* of the aristocracy of art—by which the audience is left intact in its privilege of enjoyment. Those swift-vanishings from the stage to wipe away the sweat of muscles constrained to their uttermost, and bright-returns, having all the intriguing quality of bird flight, are as carefully studied as the lifting and placing of the cane are faithfully rehearsed. But they are all done after the fashion of true genius, which senses its effects rather than rationalizes them.

". . . One has to be slightly tone deaf or a superior mathematician to realize how much the appreciation of spatial relations has to do with our enjoyment of musical harmony. It is safe to say that Bill

Robinson's audience knows more than Bill of what, without any diminution of frank pleasure, is going on before its eyes. It probably does not realize any formal way that he is offering them the great desideratum of modern art, a clean short cut to areas of enjoyment long closed to us by the accumulated rubbish of the culture route. For Bill Robinson not only restores to us our primal rhythmic appreciations; he himself reaches the sources of his rhythmic inspiration by paths that the modern American artist would give one of his eyes— the eye filmed and colored by five thousand years of absorbed culture—to feel beneath his feet. . . .

"One suspects, too, a dawning appreciation on the part of such (American) audiences that in such release and return lies the chief gift of the Negro to contemporary art. . . ."

Blackbirds of 1928 ran at the one theatre in New York for more than a year; a second company toured other cities of the country.

A little before the opening of *Blackbirds* a unique venture was made at the Princess Theatre (New York). It was the presentation of a serious play written and produced as well as acted by Negroes. The play was *Meek Mose*, written by Frank Wilson and produced by Lester A. Walton. In the cast were a number of well-known and capable performers. Charles H. Moore played the principal role; among those supporting him were Sidney Kirkpatrick, Laura Bowman, and Susie Sutton. In addition to playing on the stage, Mr. Wilson had written several sketches and plays that had been produced in Harlem. It was the writing of plays while he was still a post-office employee that led him to the stage. But *Meek Mose* failed to interest Broadway.

Three weeks later, on February 27, Miller and Lyles appeared again on Broadway; this time at the theatre of their first good fortune, the Sixty-third Street. The show was called *Keep Shufflin'*, and, while far from being another *Shuffle Along*, it was also far from being a poor show. One thing, however, it seemed to demonstrate pretty clearly—that the traditional Negro musical-comedy pattern was about worn out or, at least, needed to be left unused for a time. In the mean while two great musical plays with mixed casts were playing in New York, *Golden Dawn* at Hammerstein's Theatre and *Show Boat* at the

Ziegfeld Theatre. In each of these companies there were some forty to fifty coloured performers. In *Show Boat* Jules Bledsoe played one of the featured parts, a character that ran straight through the play, and sang the most popular number of the whole show, "Old Man River."

On February 2, 1929, a play was put on at the Apollo Theatre that was in more ways than one sensational. It was a melodramatic play of Negro life in New York. It was far removed from *In Abraham's Bosom* and *Porgy*. It had no touch even with *All God's Chillun Got Wings*. The play was called *Harlem* and it was a portrayal of life in a Harlem railroad flat, of rent parties, of the "sweetback," of the "hot stuff man," of the "number king" and the number racket. And it also portrayed a distracted migrant mother from the South caught in this whirlpool and struggling to save herself, her husband, and her children from being submerged. The play depicted a low level of life, but it had vitality and power. The cast was large, sixty in number, all Negroes, except one. The acting was extremely realistic. The work of Inez Clough as the mother; Isabell Washington, a sister of Freddie Washington, as the wayward daughter; Ernest Whitman as the number king; and Billy Andrews as one of his runners, was especially good. Furthermore, the play was the work of a Negro writer, Wallace Thurman, in collaboration with William Jourdan, a white writer. It was a success.

In the summer of 1929, *Hot Chocolates*, the revue from Connie's Inn, a Harlem night-club, opened downtown at the Hudson Theatre. The piece was very fast, and it was funny and tuneful. The company disclosed no Florence Mills or Ethel Waters or Bill Robinson, but it did contain some very clever performers. A diminutive bit of femininity called Baby Cox made a hit. Her dancing was as fast as anything New York had ever seen. Nor did *Hot Chocolates* contain a list of song hits like *Shuffle Along* and *Blackbirds*, but one of its songs, "Ain't Misbehavin'," did have quite a vogue. It ran in New York about six months and on the road several months longer.

In *Porgy* the Negro removed any lingering doubts as to his ability to do intelligent acting. In *The Green Pastures* he es-

tablished conclusively his capacity to get the utmost subtleties
across the footlights, to convey the most delicate nuances of
emotion, to create the atmosphere in which the seemingly
unreal becomes for the audience the most real thing in life.
The Green Pastures is a play so simple and yet so profound, so
close to the earth and yet so spiritual, that it is as high a test
for those powers in the actor as any play the American stage
has seen—a higher test than many of the immortalized classics. It is a play in which the line between the sublime and
the ridiculous is so tenuous that the slightest strain upon it
would bring the whole play tumbling down. Take the place
that Heywood Broun pointed out where the coloured angels
are holding a fish fry in heaven, and the audience is chuckling
over the little black cherub with a bone in his throat, and
suddenly through the laughter rings out Gabriel's great line:
"Gangway for the Lord God Jehovah!" As Mr. Broun says, it
is the most stupendous entrance ever arranged for any actor.
And if the audience should laugh when the actor appears, the
play would be about done for. And no one laughs. The acting in *The Green Pastures* seems so spontaneous and natural
that one is tempted to believe the players are not really acting. In the light of the truth about the matter, this is a high
compliment.

The Green Pastures was produced at the Mansfield Theatre
on February 26, 1930. It is the work of Marc Connelly and
was suggested by Roark Bradford's Southern sketches *Ol'
Man Adam and His Chillun*. Mr. Connelly describes it as "an
attempt to present certain aspects of a living religion in the
terms of its believers. The religion is that of thousands of Negroes in the deep South." What Mr. Connelly actually did was
to work something very little short of a miracle. No one
seems able to remember any playwright, play, and company of
players that have together received such unanimous praise as
these three factors in the making of *The Green Pastures*. Almost as valuable as either of these factors is the work of the
Hall Johnson Choir in singing the Spirituals. It serves to
blend all the efforts into a magical whole. And there is something akin to poetic justice in the fact that Robert Edmond
Jones, who by his work in 1917 with the Hapgood Coloured

Players gave an earnest of his faith in the future, should have the satisfaction of bringing his larger experience and surer technique to *The Green Pastures*. The play was awarded the Pulitzer prize for 1929. In making their recommendation the jurors stated:

One play—*The Green Pastures* by Marc Connelly—towers so far above the other American plays of the season and comes so near to setting a new standard of excellence for the American drama of all time that the jurors desire with unusual enthusiasm to recommend it for the Pulitzer prize. . . . On this occasion, the jurors state emphatically that they have no second choice.

The cast is a large one and entirely coloured. It is headed by Richard B. Harrison, who plays God; and it is probable that no role more difficult or delicate was ever essayed on the stage; yet it does not seem possible that it could be more perfectly played. This is Mr. Harrison's first appearance on the professional stage, but for more than thirty years he has been a dramatic reader, giving readings for the most part in coloured churches and before coloured schools. For a long time he has carried an ambition to play a part that "fitted his personality," and a firm conviction that he would make good if he ever got the chance. The chance did not come until he was past sixty— but what a chance!

At least twenty parts in which the acting is of high merit could be singled out; but mention of the play cannot be made without mention also of the work of Wesley Hill, of *Porgy* fame, in the role of the Angel Gabriel, Daniel Haynes in the two roles of Adam and Hezdrel, Josephine Byrd and Florence Fields as the two charwomen who clean the Lord's private office, Tutt Whitney as Noah, and Charles H. Moore as Mr. Deshee. The complete program of the play is:

Laurence Rivers

presents

The Green Pastures

A Fable

by

Marc Connelly

Production Designed by Robert Edmond Jones
Music Under the Direction of Hall Johnson
Play Staged by the Author

Cast of Characters

(In the Order of Their Appearance)

Mr. Deshee .... Charles H. Moore
Myrtle .... Alicia Escamilla
First Boy .... Jazzlips Richardson, Jr.
Second Boy .... Howard Washington
Third Boy .... Reginald Blythwood
Randolph .... Joe Byrd
A Cook .... Frances Smith
Custard Maker .... Homer Tutt
First Mammy Angel .... Anna Mae Fritz
A Stout Angel .... Josephine Byrd
A Slender Angel .... Edna Thrower
Archangel .... J. A. Shipp
Gabriel .... Wesley Hill
The Lord .... Richard B. Harrison
Choir Leader .... McKinley Reeves
Adam .... Daniel L. Haynes
Eve .... Inez Richardson Wilson
Cain .... Lou Vernon
Cain's Girl .... Dorothy Randolph
Zeba .... Edna M. Harris
Cain the Sixth .... James Fuller
Boy Gambler .... Louis Kelsey
First Gambler .... Collington Hayes
Second Gambler .... Ivan Sharp
Voice in Shanty .... Josephine Byrd
Noah .... Tutt Whitney
Noah's Wife .... Susie Sutton
Shem .... Milton J. Williams

First Woman . . . . Dinks Thomas
Second Woman . . . . Anna Mae Fritz
Third Woman . . . . Geneva Blythwood
First Man . . . . Emory Richardson
Flatfoot . . . . Freddie Archibald
Ham . . . . J. Homer Tutt
Japheth . . . . Stanleigh Morrell
First Cleaner . . . . Josephine Byrd
Second Cleaner . . . . Florence Fields
Abraham . . . . J. A. Shipp
Isaac . . . . Charles H. Moore
Jacob . . . . Edgar Burks
Moses . . . . Alonzo Fenderson
Zipporah . . . . Mercedes Gilbert
Aaron . . . . McKinley Reeves
A Candidate Magician . . . . Reginald Fenderson
Pharaoh . . . . George Randol
The General . . . . Walt McClane
First Wizard . . . . Emory Richardson
Head Magician . . . . Arthur Porter
Joshua . . . . Stanleigh Morrell
First Scout . . . . Ivan Sharp
Master of Ceremonies . . . . Billy Cumby
King of Babylon . . . . Jay Mondaaye
Prophet . . . . Ivan Sharp
High Priest . . . . J. Homer Tutt

The King's Favorites . . . . {
Leona Winkler
Florence Lee
Constance Van Dyke
Mary Ella Hart
Inez Persand

Officer . . . . .Emory Richardson
Hezdrel . . . . Daniel L. Haynes
Another Officer . . . . Stanleigh Morrell

The Children

Philistine Bumgardner, Margery Bumgardner, Fredia Longshaw,
Wilbur Cohen, Jr., Verdon Perdue, Ruby Davis, Willmay Davis,
Margerette Thrower, Viola Lewis.

Angels and Townspeople

Amy Escamilla, Elsie Byrd, Benveneta Washington, Thula Oritz,
Ruth Carl, Geneva Blythwood.

Babylonian Band

Carl Shorter, Earl Bowie, Thomas Russell, Richard Henderson.

The Choir
Evelyn Burwell, Assistant Director

Sopranos—Bertha Wright, Geraldine Gooding, Marie Warren, Mattie
   Harris, Elsie Thompson, Massie Paterson, Marguerite Avery.
Altos—Ruthena Matson, Leona Avery, Mrs. Willie Mays, Viola Mick-
   ens, Charlotte Junius.
Tenors—John Warner, Joe Loomis, Walter Hilliard, Harold Foster,
   Adolph Henderson, William McFarland, McKinley Reeves,
   Arthur Porter.
Baritones—Marc D'Albert, Gerome Addison, Walter Whitfield, D. K.
   Williams.
Bassos—Lester Holland, Cecil McNair, Tom Lee, Walter Meadows,
   Frank Horace.

Synopsis of Scenes

Part I: Scene 1—The Sunday School. Scene 2—A Fish Fry. Scene
3—A Garden. Scene 4—Outside the Garden. Scene 5—A Roadside.
Scene 6—A Private Office. Scene 7—Another Roadside. Scene 8—A
House. Scene 9—A Hillside. Scene 10—A Mountain Top.

Part II: Scene 1—The Private Office. Scene 2—The Mouth of a
Cave. Scene 3—A Throne Room. Scene 4—The Foot of a Mountain.
Scene 5—A Cabaret. Scene 6—The Private Office. Scene 7—Outside
a Temple. Scene 8—Another Fish Fry.

The past seventy-five years have seen vast changes in the position of the Negro in the theatre. Beginning as a mere butt of
laughter, he has worked on up through minstrelsy and the
musical-comedy shows to become a creator of laughter; to become a maker of songs and dances for the people. This alone is
an achievement not to be despised. The past twenty years have
seen the Negro actor, after a set-back, emerge from the Negro
theatre of Harlem and finally make for himself a definite place
on the legitimate stage of New York, the theatrical capital of
the world. The last ten years have seen the growth of a list, surprisingly long considering all the conditions, of names that are
known in connexion with the theatre: Charles Gilpin, Paul
Robeson, Jules Bledsoe, Frank Wilson, Daniel Haynes, Wesley
Hill, Charles H. Moore, Richard B. Harrison, Florence Mills,
Rose McClendon, Evelyn Ellis, Ethel Waters, Inez Clough,

Abbie Mitchell, Evelyn Preer, F. E. Miller, Aubrey Lyles, Noble Sissle, Eubie Blake, Johnny Hudgins, and Bill Robinson. The list can be stretched to take in Josephine Baker, now of Europe and South America, and Turner Layton and Tandy Johnstone, now of London. Josephine Baker was not wholly unknown before her name became a household word in Europe; when she was with Sissle and Blake's *Chocolate Dandies* she was the real box-office attraction. She was only in the chorus, but was paid one hundred and twenty-five dollars a week and advertised as the highest paid chorus girl in the world. Billy Pierce, though he is not on the stage and though his influence has been exerted almost entirely through the white performer, cannot be omitted from this list. Mr. Pierce conducts a large and successful studio where he teaches dancers the art of tapping out intricate Negro rhythms with their feet. In the same categroy is Will Vodery, who for years has scored jazz orchestral arrangements for the Florenz Ziegfeld productions and for other Broadway musical shows. In this field Mr. Vodery stands among the foremost. He is at present on the staff of arrangers of the Fox Film Company.

As the progress of this period is traced, it can be seen that it is the Negro as an actor that has gained ground, gained in experience and in technique, and raised his position higher and higher in the world of the theatre. The Negro as a writer for the theatre has not kept pace; he has, in fact, lost ground, even in the special field where he was once prominent, the field of Negro musical shows. In the serious drama three attempts have been made in professional theatre, only one of which was successful. Coloured people often complain about the sort of light that is shed upon the race in most Negro plays. It may be—there is no certainty—that their remedy lies in the development of Negro playwrights. Some good reasons can be assigned for this discrepancy between the status of the actor and of the playwright, but they do not alter the fact.

The relation of Harlem to the latest phase of the development of the Negro in the theatre cannot be overlooked. New York is the centre from which all the main forces and activities of the American theatre radiate. And Harlem, with its cosmopolitan Negro population, its literary and artistic groups, its theatres, its cabarets and night-clubs, its theatrical clubs, and its little-theatre movement, with all of its elements that fire ambition, its opportunities for the nurture and development of talent, is within the radius of that centre. Here, then, was the field, and here were those best fitted to occupy it. There is no other city in the country where the same thing could have happened; and it could not have happened in New York had there been no Harlem at hand.

There are three other lines along which the Negro in New York has moved forward; three lines leading to the phonograph, radio, and screen audiences. For a long while Negroes have been making phonograph records. There have been jubilee singers, singers of Spirituals and of Negro comic songs. Bert Williams's royalties from the sale of his records was a very considerable sum. Roland Hayes, Paul Robeson, J. Rosamond Johnson, Taylor Gordon, and other artists have made records. But probably the Negro artists most popular with the phonograph audiences are the great singers of blues. The three Smiths, Mamie, Bessie, and Clara—not sisters—are known by all listeners to blues through the phonograph. It was Carl Van Vechten who first pointed out that the blues-singers were artists. When Mr. Van Vechten, by his articles in *Vanity Fair* and other publications, and by his personal efforts, was doing much so much to focus public attention upon the recent literary and artistic emergence of the Negro and upon the individual artists, he did not neglect the singers of this important and not fully evaluated genre of Negro folk-songs. In a *Vanity Fair* article (March 1926) he wrote of the singing of Ethel Waters, Bessie Smith, and Clara Smith and gave the following impression of Clara singing not from a record, but from a theatre stage:

Clara is a crude purveyor of the pseudo-folk-songs of her race. She employs, however, more nuances of expression than Bessie. Her voice flutters agonizingly between tones. Music critics would say that she sings off key. What she really does, of course, is to sing quarter tones. Thus she is justifiably billed as the "World's greatest moaner." She appears to be more of an artist than Bessie, but I suspect that this apparent artistry is spontaneous and uncalculated.

As she comes upon the stage through folds of electric blue

hangings at the back, she is wrapped in a black evening cloak bordered with white fur. She does not advance, but hesitates, turning her face in profile. The pianist is playing the characteristic strain of the Blues. Clara begins to sing:

> "All day long I'm worried;
> All day long I'm blue;
> I'm so awfully lonesome,
> I doan know what to do;
>
> So I ask yo', doctor,
> See if you can fin'
> Somethin' in yo' satchel
> To pacify my min'.
>
> Doctor! Doctor!

(Her tones become poignantly pathetic; tears roll down her cheeks.)

> Write me a prescription
>   fo' duh Blues,
> De mean ole Blues."

(Her voice dies away in a mournful wail of pain and she buries her head in the curtains.)

Clara Smith's tones uncannily take on the colour of the saxophone; again of the clarinet. Her voice is powerful or melancholy, by turn. It tears the blood from one's heart. One learns from her that the Negro's cry to a cruel Cupid is as moving and elemental as is his cry to God, as expressed in the Spirituals.

Indeed, the blues are as essentially folk-songs as the Spirituals. In the one the Negro expresses his religious reactions to hopes of a blissful life hereafter; in the other he expresses his secular and profane reactions to the ills of the present existence. In the Spirituals it is the exultant shout or the sorrow-laden cry of the group; in the blues it is always the plaint of the individual. It is my opinion that the blues are of more value as the repository of folk-poetry than of folk-music. Very often there is the flash of lines that have great primitive beauty and power.

Negroes broadcast from most of the important radio stations in New York. Some of these stations have coloured broadcasters regularly employed. From time to time groups are engaged by the manufacturing concerns that advertise over the radio, to furnish the entertainment on their programs. Indeed, Negro programs are now so popular that there are quite a number of white broadcasters who are doing Negro "stuff." the great favourites among these at present are Amos and Andy, whose imitations are so good that they are extremely popular with coloured people. Their work and style are very close to what Miller and Lyles first employed. Their vocabulary, especially the misuse of the letter "r" in such coined words as "regusted," is almost identical with the vocabulary made classic by the two Negro comedians. But radio offers less gain to the Negro in mere racial prestige than either the phonograph or the screen. The radio, though it seems so direct, is, after all, quite impersonal. One does not visualize the person, nor does one have any permanent record of his work.

As New York is the centre of the theatre, Los Angeles is the centre of the movies; nevertheless, New York furnishes a large proportion of the artists who appear on the screen. *Hallelujah* is the most recent of the more stupendous Negro screen productions, and King Vidor recruited and organized the company for it in New York and later transported the whole outfit to Los Angeles. His reason for doing so must have been that he considered New York the greatest source upon which he could draw for the best Negro talent.

The Negro as a race has not fared so well on the screen as on the stage. New York would probably go to the theatre to see any first-class performance by Negroes. But moving pictures are not made for one theatre or one city or even one section of the country; they are made to suit everybody as nearly as possible; so they are built on the greatest common denominator of public opinion and public sentiment. In no moving picture, then, has any Negro screen actor been permitted to portray as high a type as has been portrayed on the stage.

SELECTED POEMS

Under the Bamboo Tree

Down in the jungles lived a maid,
Of royal blood though dusky shade,
A marked impression once she made
Upon a Zulu from Matabooloo;
And ev'ry morning he would be
Down underneath a bamboo tree,
A waiting there his love to see,
And then to her he'd sing:

CHORUS

If you lak-a-me, lak I lak-a-you
And we lak-a-both the same
I lak-a say, this very day,
I lak-a change your name;
'Cause I love-a-you and love-a-you true
And if you love-a-me.
One live as two, two live as one
Under the bamboo tree.

And in this simple jungle way,
He wooed the maiden ev'ry day,
By singing what he had to say;
Once day he seized her and gently squeezed her,
And then beneath the bamboo green,
He begged her to become his queen;
The dusky maiden blushed unseen
And joined him in his song.

CHORUS

This little story strange but true,
Is often told in Mataboo
Of how this Zulu tried to woo
His jungle lady in tropics shady;
Although the scene was miles away,
Right here at home I dare to say,
You'll hear some Zulu ev'ry day,
Gush out this soft refrain:

CHORUS

FIFTY YEARS & OTHER POEMS

Fifty Years

1863–1913

O brothers mine, to-day we stand
   Where half a century sweeps our ken,
Since God, through Lincoln's ready hand,
   Struck off our bonds and made us men.

Just fifty years—a winter's day—
   As runs the history of a race;
Yet, as we look back o'er the way,
   How distant seems our starting place!

Look farther back! Three centuries!
   To where a naked, shivering score,
Snatched from their haunts across the seas,
   Stood, wild-eyed, on Virginia's shore.

Far, far the way that we have trod,
   From heathen kraals and jungle dens,
To freedmen, freemen, sons of God,
   Americans and Citizens.

A part of His unknown design,
   We've lived within a mighty age;
And we have helped to write a line
   On history's most wondrous page.

A few black bondmen strewn along
   The borders of our eastern coast,
Now grown a race, ten million strong,
   An upward, onward marching host.

Then let us here erect a stone,
    To mark the place, to mark the time;
A witness to God's mercies shown,
    A pledge to hold this day sublime.

And let that stone an altar be,
    Whereon thanksgivings we may lay,
Where we, in deep humility,
    For faith and strength renewed may pray.

With open hearts ask from above
    New zeal, new courage and new pow'rs,
That we may grow more worthy of
    This country and this land of ours.

For never let the thought arise
    That we are here on sufferance bare;
Outcasts, asylumed 'neath these skies,
    And aliens without part or share.

This land is ours by right of birth,
    This land is ours by right of toil;
We helped to turn its virgin earth,
    Our sweat is in its fruitful soil.

Where once the tangled forest stood,—
    Where flourished once rank weed and thorn,—
Behold the path-traced, peaceful wood,
    The cotton white, the yellow corn.

To gain these fruits that have been earned,
    To hold these fields that have been won,
Our arms have strained, our backs have burned,
    Bent bare beneath a ruthless sun.

That Banner which is now the type
    Of victory on field and flood—
Remember, its first crimson stripe
    Was dyed by Attucks' willing blood.

And never yet has come the cry—
  When that fair flag has been assailed—
For men to do, for men to die,
  That have we faltered or have failed.

We've helped to bear it, rent and torn,
  Through many a hot-breath'd battle breeze;
Held in our hands, it has been borne
  And planted far across the seas.

And never yet—O haughty Land,
  Let us, at least, for this be praised—
Has one black, treason-guided hand
  Ever against that flag been raised.

Then should we speak but servile words,
  Or shall we hang our heads in shame?
Stand back of new-come foreign hordes,
  And fear our heritage to claim?

No! stand erect and without fear,
  And for our foes let this suffice—
We've bought a rightful sonship here,
  And we have more than paid the price.

And yet, my brothers, well I know
  The tethered feet, the pinioned wings,
The spirit bowed beneath the blow,
  The heart grown faint from wounds and stings;

The staggering force of brutish might,
  That strikes and leaves us stunned and dazed;
The long, vain waiting through the night
  To hear some voice for justice raised.

Full well I know the hour when hope
  Sinks dead, and 'round us everywhere
Hangs stifling darkness, and we grope
  With hands uplifted in despair.

Courage! Look out, beyond, and see
   The far horizon's beckoning span!
Faith in your God-known destiny!
   We are a part of some great plan.

Because the tongues of Garrison
   And Phillips now are cold in death,
Think you their work can be undone?
   Or quenched the fires lit by their breath?

Think you that John Brown's spirit stops?
   That Lovejoy was but idly slain?
Or do you think those precious drops
   From Lincoln's heart were shed in vain?

That for which millions prayed and sighed,
   That for which tens of thousands fought,
For which so many freely died,
   God cannot let it come to naught.

To America

How would you have us, as we are?
Or sinking 'neath the load we bear?
Our eyes fixed forward on a star?
Or gazing empty at despair?

Rising or falling? Men or things?
With dragging pace or footsteps fleet?
Strong, willing sinews in your wings?
Or tightening chains about your feet?

O Black and Unknown Bards

O black and unknown bards of long ago,
How came your lips to touch the sacred fire?
How, in your darkness, did you come to know
The power and beauty of the minstrel's lyre?
Who first from midst his bonds lifted his eyes?
Who first from out the still watch, lone and long,
Feeling the ancient faith of prophets rise
Within his dark-kept soul, bursts into song?

Heart of what slave poured out such melody
As "Steal away to Jesus"? On its strains
His spirit must have nightly floated free,
Though still about his hands he felt his chains.
Who heard great "Jordan roll"? Whose starward eye
Saw chariot "swing low"? And who was he
That breathed that comforting, melodic sigh,
"Nobody knows de trouble I see"?

What merely living clod, what captive thing,
Could up toward God through all its darkness grope,
And find within its deadened heart to sing
These songs of sorrow, love, and faith, and hope?
How did it catch that subtle undertone,
That note in music heard not with the ears?
How sound the elusive reed so seldom blown,
Which stirs the soul or melts the heart to tears.

Not that great German master in his dream
Of harmonies that thundered amongst the stars
At the creation, ever heard a theme
Nobler than "Go down, Moses." Mark its bars,
How like a mighty trumpet-call they stir
The blood. Such are the notes that men have sung
Going to valorous deeds; such tones there were
That helped make history when Time was young.

There is a wide, wide wonder in it all,
That from degraded rest and servile toil
The fiery spirit of the seer should call
These simple children of the sun and soil.
O black slave singers, gone, forgot, unfamed,
You—you alone, of all the long, long line
Of those who've sung untaught, unknown, unnamed,
Have stretched out upward, seeking the divine.

You sang not deeds of heroes or of kings;
No chant of bloody war, no exulting pean
Of arms-won triumphs; but your humble strings
You touched in chord with music empyrean.
You sang far better than you knew; the songs
That for your listeners' hungry hearts sufficed
Still live,—but more than this to you belongs:
You sang a race from wood and stone to Christ.

Brothers

See! There he stands; not brave, but with an air
Of sullen stupor. Mark him well! Is he
Not more like brute than man? Look in his eye!
No light is there; none, save the glint that shines
In the now glaring, and now shifting orbs
Of some wild animal caught in the hunter's trap.

How came this beast in human shape and form?
Speak, man!—We call you man because you wear
His shape—How are you thus? Are you not from
That docile, child-like, tender-hearted race
Which we have known three centuries? Not from
That more than faithful race which through three wars
Fed our dear wives and nursed our helpless babes
Without a single breach of trust? Speak out!

I am, and am not.

                    Then who, why are you?

    I am a thing not new, I am as old
As human nature. I am that which lurks,
Ready to spring whenever a bar is loosed;
The ancient trait which fights incessantly
Against restraint, balks at the upward climb;
The weight forever seeking to obey
The law of downward pull;—and I am more:
The bitter fruit am I of planted seed;
The resultant, the inevitable end
Of evil forces and the powers of wrong.

    Lessons in degradation, taught and learned,
The memories of cruel sights and deeds,
The pent-up bitterness, the unspent hate
Filtered through fifteen generations have
Sprung up and found in me sporadic life.
In me the muttered curse of dying men,
On me the stain of conquered women, and
Consuming me the fearful fires of lust,
Lit long ago, by other hands than mine.
In me the down-crushed spirit, the hurled-back prayers
Of wretches now long dead,—their dire bequests.—
In me the echo of the stifled cry
Of children for their bartered mothers' breasts.
    I claim no race, no race claims me; I am
No more than human dregs; degenerate;
The monstrous offspring of the monster, Sin;
I am—just what I am. . . . The race that fed
Your wives and nursed your babes would do the same
To-day, but I—

                    Enough, the brute must die!
Quick! Chain him to that oak! It will resist
The fire much longer than this slender pine.
Now bring the fuel! Pile it 'round him! Wait!
Pile not so fast or high! or we shall lose

The agony and terror in his face.
And now the torch! Good fuel that! the flames
Already leap head-high. Ha! hear that shriek!
And there's another! wilder than the first.
Fetch water! Water! Pour a little on
The fire, lest it should burn too fast. Hold so!
Now let it slowly blaze again. See there!
He squirms! He groans! His eyes bulge wildly out,
Searching around in vain appeal for help!
Another shriek, the last! Watch how the flesh
Grows crisp and hangs till, turned to ash, it sifts
Down through the coils of chain that hold erect
The ghastly frame against the bark-scorched tree.

    Stop! to each man no more than one man's share.
You take that bone, and you this tooth; the chain—
Let us divide its links; this skull, of course,
In fair division, to the leader comes.

    And now his fiendish crime has been avenged;
Let us back to our wives and children.—Say,
What did he mean by those last muttered words,
"Brothers in spirit, brothers in deed are we"?

Fragment

    The hand of Fate cannot be stayed,
    The course of Fate cannot be steered,
    By all the gods that man has made,
    Nor all the devils he has feared,
    Not by the prayers that night be prayed
    In all the temples he has reared.

    See! In your very midst there dwell
    Ten thousand thousand blacks, a wedge
    Forged in the furnaces of hell,

And sharpened to a cruel edge
By wrong and by injustice fell,
And driven by hatred as a sledge.

A wedge so slender at the start—
Just twenty slaves in shackles bound—
And yet, which split the land apart
With shrieks of war and battle sound,
Which pierced the nation's very heart,
And still lies cankering in the wound.

Not all the glory of your pride,
Preserved in story and in song,
Can from the judging future hide,
Through all the coming ages long,
That though you bravely fought and died,
You fought and died for what was wrong.

'Tis fixed—for them that violate
The eternal laws, naught shall avail
Till they their error expiate;
Nor shall their unborn children fail
To pay the full required weight
Into God's great, unerring scale.

Think not repentance can redeem,
That sin his wages can withdraw;
No, think as well to change the scheme
Of worlds that move in reverent awe;
Forgiveness is an idle dream,
God is not love, no, God is law.

The White Witch

O, brothers mine, take care! Take care!
The great white witch rides out to-night,
Trust not your prowess nor your strength;
Your only safety lies in flight;
For in her glance there is a snare,
And in her smile there is a blight.

The great white witch you have not seen?
Then, younger brothers mine, forsooth,
Like nursery children you have looked
For ancient hag and snaggled tooth;
But no, not so; the witch appears
In all the glowing charms of youth.

Her lips are like carnations red,
Her face like new-born lilies fair,
Her eyes like ocean waters blue,
She moves with subtle grace and air,
And all about her head there floats
The golden glory of her hair.

But though she always thus appears
In form of youth and mood of mirth,
Unnumbered centuries are hers,
The infant planets saw her birth;
The child of throbbing Life is she,
Twin sister to the greedy earth.

And back behind those smiling lips,
And down within those laughing eyes,
And underneath the soft caress
Of hand and voice and purring sighs,
The shadow of the panther lurks,
The spirit of the vampire lies.

For I have seen the great white witch,
And she has led me to her lair,
And I have kissed her red, red lips

And cruel face so white and fair;
Around me she has twined her arms,
And bound me with her yellow hair.

I felt those red lips burn and sear
My body like a living coal;
Obeyed the power of those eyes
As the needle trembles to the pole;
And did not care although I felt
The strength go ebbing from my soul.

Oh! she has seen your strong young limbs,
And heard your laughter loud and gay,
And in your voices she has caught
The echo of a far-off day,
When man was closer to the earth;
And she has marked you for her prey.

She feels the old Antæan strength
In you, the great dynamic beat
Of primal passions, and she sees
In you the last besieged retreat
Of love relentless, lusty, fierce,
Love pain-ecstatic, cruel-sweet.

O, brothers mine, take care! Take care!
The great white witch rides out to-night.
O, younger brothers mine, beware!
Look not upon her beauty bright;
For in her glance there is a snare,
And in her smile there is a blight.

Mother Night

Eternities before the first-born day,
    Or ere the first sun fledged his wings of flame,
    Calm Night, the everlasting and the same,
A brooding mother over chaos lay.
And whirling suns shall blaze and then decay,
    Shall run their fiery courses and then claim
    The haven of the darkness whence they came;
Back to Nirvanic peace shall grope their way.

So when my feeble sun of life burns out,
    And sounded is the hour for my long sleep,
    I shall, full weary of the feverish light,
Welcome the darkness without fear or doubt,
    And heavy-lidded, I shall softly creep
      Into the quiet bosom of the Night.

Girl of Fifteen

Girl of fifteen,
I see you each morning from my window
As you pass on your way to school.
I do more than see, I watch you.
I furtively draw the curtain aside.
And my heart leaps through my eyes
And follows you down the street;
Leaving me behind, half-hid
And wholly ashamed.

What holds me back,
Half-hid behind the curtains and wholly ashamed,
But my forty years beyond your fifteen?

Girl of fifteen, as you pass
There passes, too, a lightning flash of time
In which you lift those forty summers off my head,
And take those forty winters out of my heart.

Down by the Carib Sea

I

Sunrise in the Tropics

Sol, Sol, mighty lord of the tropic zone,
Here I wait with the trembling stars
To see thee once more take thy throne.

There the patient palm tree watching
Waits to say, "Good morn" to thee,
And a throb of expectation
Pulses through the earth and me.

Now, o'er nature falls a hush,
Look! the East is all a-blush;
And a growing crimson crest
Dims the late stars in the west;
Now, a flood of golden light
Sweeps across the silver night,
Swift the pale moon fades away
Before the light-girt King of Day,
See! the miracle is done!
Once more behold! The Sun!

II

Los Cigarillos

This is the land of the dark-eyed *gente*,
Of the *dolce far niente*,
Where we dream away
Both the night and day,
At night-time in sleep our dreams we invoke,
Our dreams come by day through the redolent smoke,
As it lazily curls,
And slowly unfurls
From our lips,
And the tips
Of our fragrant *cigarillos*.

For life in the tropics is only a joke,
So we pass it in dreams, and we pass it in smoke,
Smoke—smoke—smoke.

Tropical constitutions
Call for occasional revolutions;
But after that's through,
Why there's nothing to do
But smoke—smoke;

For life in the tropics is only a joke,
So we pass it in dreams, and we pass it in smoke,
Smoke—smoke—smoke.

III

Teestay

Of tropic sensations, the worst
Is, *sin duda*, the tropical thirst.

When it starts in your throat and constantly grows,
Till you feel that it reaches down to your toes,
When your mouth tastes like fur
And your tongue turns to dust,
There's but one thing to do,
And do it you must,
Drink *teestay*.

Teestay, a drink with a history,
A delicious, delectable mystery,
"Cinco centavos el vaso, señor,"
If you take one, you will surely want more.

Teestay, teestay,
The national drink on a feast day;
How it coolingly tickles,
As downward it trickles,
Teestay, teestay.

And you wish, as you take it down at a quaff,
That your neck was constructed à la giraffe.
Teestay, teestay.

IV

The Lottery Girl

"Lottery, lottery,
Take a chance at the lottery?
Take a ticket,
Or, better, take two;
Who knows what the future
May hold for you?
Lottery, lottery.
Take a chance at the lottery?"

Oh, limpid-eyed girl,
I would take every chance,
If only the prize
Were a love-flashing glance
From your fathomless eyes.

"Lottery, lottery,
Try your luck at the lottery?
Consider the size
Of the capital prize,
And take tickets
For the lottery.
Tickets, *señor*? Tickets, *señor*?
Take a chance at the lottery?"

Oh, crimson-lipped girl,
With the magical smile,
I would count that the gamble
Were well worth the while,
Not a chance would I miss,
If only the prize
Were a honey-bee kiss
Gathered in sips
From those full-ripened lips,
And a love-flashing glance
From your eyes.

V

The Dancing Girl

Do you know what it is to dance?
Perhaps, you do know, in a fashion;
But by dancing I mean,
Not what's generally seen,
But dancing of fire and passion,
Of fire and delirious passion.

With a dusky-haired *señorita*,
Her dark, misty eyes near your own,
And her scarlet-red mouth,
Like a rose of the south,
The reddest that ever was grown,
So close that you catch
Her quick-panting breath
As across your own face it is blown,
With a sigh, and a moan.

Ah! that is dancing.
As here by the Carib it's known.

Now, whirling and twirling
Like furies we go;
Now, soft and caressing
And sinuously slow;
With an undulating motion,
Like waves on a breeze-kissed ocean:—
And the scarlet-red mouth
Is nearer your own,
And the dark, misty eyes
Still softer have grown.

Ah! that is dancing, that is loving,
As here by the Carib they're known.

VI

Sunset in the Tropics

A silver flash from the sinking sun,
Then a shot of crimson across the sky
That, bursting, lets a thousand colors fly
And riot among the clouds; they run,
Deepening in purple, flaming in gold,
Changing, and opening fold after fold,
Then fading through all of the tints of the rose into gray,
Till, taking quick fright at the coming night,
They rush out down the west,
In hurried quest
Of the fleeing day.

Now above where the tardiest color flares a moment yet,
One point of light, now two, now three are set
To form the starry stairs,—
And, in her fire-fly crown,
Queen Night, on velvet slippered feet, comes softly down.

Sence You Went Away

Seems lak to me de stars don't shine so bright,
Seems lak to me de sun done loss his light,
Seems lak to me der's nothin' goin' right,
    Sence you went away.

Seems lak to me de sky ain't half so blue,
Seems lak to me dat ev'ything wants you,
Seems lak to me I don't know what to do,
    Sence you went away.

Seems lak to me dat ev'ything is wrong,
Seems lak to me de day's jes twice as long,
Seems lak to me de bird's forgot his song,
    Sence you went away.

Seems lak to me I jes can't he'p but sigh,
Seems lak to me ma th'oat keeps gittin' dry,
Seems lak to me a tear stays in ma eye,
    Sence you went away.

Nobody's Lookin' but de Owl and de Moon

(A Negro Serenade)

De river is a-glistenin' in de moonlight,
De owl is set'n high up in de tree;
De little stars am twinklin' wid a sof' light,
De night seems only jes fu' you an' me.
Thoo de trees de breezes am a-sighin',
Breathin' out a sort o' lover's croon,
Der's nobody lookin' or a-spyin',
Nobody but de owl an' de moon.

Nobody's lookin' but de owl an' de moon,
An' de night is balmy; fu' de month is June;
Come den, Honey, won't you? Come to meet me soon,
W'ile nobody's lookin' but de owl an' de moon.

I feel so kinder lonely all de daytime,
It seems I raly don't know what to do;
I jes keep sort a-longin' fu' de night-time,
'Cause den I know dat I can be wid you.
An' de thought jes sets my brain a-swayin',
An' my heart a-beatin' to a tune;
Come, de owl won't tell w'at we's a-sayin',
An' cose you know we kin trus' de moon

'Possum Song

(A Warning)

'Simmons ripenin' in de fall,
You better run,
Brudder 'Possum, run!
Mockin' bird commence to call,
You better run, Brudder 'Possum, git out de way!
You better run, Brudder 'Possum, git out de way!
Run some whar an' hide!
Ole moon am sinkin'
Down behin' de tree.
Ole Eph am thinkin'
An' chuckelin' wid glee.
Ole Tige am blinkin'
An' frisky as kin be,
Yo' chances, Brudder 'Possum,
Look mighty slim to me.

Run, run, run, I tell you,
Run, Brudder 'Possum, run!
Run, run, run, I tell you,
Ole Eph's got a gun.
Pickaninnies grinnin'
Waitin' fu' to see de fun.
You better run, Brudder 'Possum, git out de way!
Run, Brudder 'Possum, run!

Brudder 'Possum take a tip;
You better run,
Brudder 'Possum, run!
'Tain't no use in actin' flip,
You better run, Brudder 'Possum, git out de way!
You better run, Brudder 'Possum, git out de way!
Run some whar an' hide.
Dey's gwine to houn' you
All along de line,
W'en dey done foun' you,
Den what's de use in sighin'?

Wid taters roun' you.
You sholy would tase fine—
So listen, Brudder 'Possum,
You better be a-flyin'.

Run, run, run, I tell you,
Run, Brudder 'Possum, run!
Run, run, run, I tell you,
Ole Eph's got a gun.
Pickaninnies grinnin'
Waitin' fu' to see de fun.
You better run, Brudder 'Possum, git out de way!
Run, Brudder 'Possum, run!

Brer Rabbit, You's de Cutes' of 'Em All

Once der was a meetin' in de wilderness,
All de critters of creation dey was dar;
Brer Rabbit, Brer 'Possum, Brer Wolf, Brer Fox,
King Lion, Mister Terrapin, Mister B'ar.
De question fu' discussion was, "Who is de bigges' man?"
Dey 'pinted ole Jedge Owl to decide;
He polished up his spectacles an' put 'em on his nose,
An' to the question slowly he replied:

"Brer Wolf am mighty cunnin',
Brer Fox am mighty sly,
Brer Terrapin an' 'Possum—kinder small;
Brer Lion's mighty vicious,
Brer B'ar he's sorter 'spicious,
Brer Rabbit, you's de cutes' of 'em all."

Dis caused a great confusion 'mongst de animals,
Ev'y critter claimed dat he had won de prize;
Dey 'sputed an' dey arg'ed, dey growled an' dey roared,
Den putty soon de dus' begin to rise.
Brer Rabbit he jes' stood aside an' urged 'em on to fight.
Brer Lion he mos' tore Brer B'ar in two;
W'en dey was all so tiahed dat dey couldn't catch der bref
Brer Rabbit he jes' grabbed de prize an' flew.

Brer Wolf am mighty cunnin',
Brer Fox am mighty sly,
Brer Terrapin an' 'Possum—kinder small;
Brer Lion's mighty vicious,
Brer B'ar he's sorter 'spicious,
Brer Rabbit, you's de cutes' of 'em all.

GOD'S TROMBONES

Seven Negro Sermons in Verse

Preface

A good deal has been written on the folk creations of the American Negro: his music, sacred and secular; his plantation tales, and his dances; but that there are folk sermons, as well, is a fact that has passed unnoticed. I remember hearing in my boyhood sermons that were current, sermons that passed with only slight modifications from preacher to preacher and from locality to locality. Such sermons were, "The Valley of Dry Bones," which was based on the vision of the prophet in the 37th chapter of Ezekiel; the "Train Sermon," in which both God and the devil were pictured as running trains, one loaded with saints, that pulled up in heaven, and the other with sinners, that dumped its load in hell; the "Heavenly March," which gave in detail the journey of the faithful from earth, on up through the pearly gates to the great white throne. Then there was a stereotyped sermon which had no definite subject, and which was quite generally preached; it began with the Creation, went on to the fall of man, rambled through the trials and tribulations of the Hebrew Children, came down to the redemption by Christ, and ended with the Judgment Day and a warning and an exhortation to sinners. This was the framework of a sermon that allowed the individual preacher the widest latitude that could be desired for all his arts and powers. There was one Negro sermon that in its day was a classic, and widely known to the public. Thousands of people, white and black, flocked to the church of John Jasper in Richmond, Virginia, to hear him preach his famous sermon proving that the earth is flat and the sun does move. John Jasper's sermon was imitated and adapted by many lesser preachers.

I heard only a few months ago in Harlem an up-to-date version of the "Train Sermon." The preacher styled himself "Son of Thunder"—a sobriquet adopted by many of the old-time preachers—and phrased his subject, "The Black Diamond Express, running between here and hell, making thirteen stops and arriving in hell ahead of time."

The old-time Negro preacher has not yet been given the niche in which he properly belongs. He has been portrayed only as a semi-comic figure. He had, it is true, his comics aspects, but on the whole he was an important figure, and at bottom a vital factor. It was through him that the people of diverse languages and customs who were brought here from diverse parts of Africa and thrown into slavery were given their first sense of unity and solidarity. He was the first shepherd of this bewildered flock. His power for good or ill was very great. It was the old-time preacher who for generations was the mainspring of hope and inspiration for the Negro in America. It was also he who instilled into the Negro the narcotic doctrine epitomized in the spiritual, "You May Have All Dis World, But Give Me Jesus." This power of the old-time preacher, somewhat lessened and changed in his successors, is still a vital force; in fact, it is still the greatest single influence among the colored people of the United States. The Negro today is, perhaps, the most priest-governed group in the country.

The history of the Negro preacher reaches back to Colonial days. Before the Revolutionary War, when slavery had not yet taken on its more grim and heartless economic aspects, there were famed black preachers who preached to both whites and blacks. George Liele was preaching to whites and blacks at Augusta, Ga., as far back as 1773, and Andrew Bryan at Savannah a few years later.* The most famous of these earliest preachers was Black Harry, who during the Revolutionary period accompanied Bishop Asbury as a drawing card and preached from the same platform with other founders of the Methodist Church. Of him, John Ledman in his *History of the Rise of Methodism in America* says, "The truth was that Harry was a more popular speaker than Mr. Asbury or almost anyone else in his day." In the two or three decades before the Civil War Negro preachers in the North, many of them well-educated and cultured, were courageous spokesmen against slavery and all its evils.

*See *The History of the Negro Church*, Carter G. Woodson.

The effect on the Negro of the establishment of separate and independent places of worship can hardly be estimated. Some idea of how far this effect reached may be gained by a comparison between the social and religious trends of the Negroes of the Old South and of the Negroes of French Louisiana and the West Indies, where they were within and directly under the Roman Catholic Church and the Church of England. The old-time preacher brought about the establishment of these independent places of worship and thereby provided the first sphere in which race leadership might develop and function. These scattered and often clandestine groups have grown into the strongest and richest organization among colored Americans. Another thought—except for these separate places of worship there never would have been any Spirituals.

The old-time preacher was generally a man far above the average in intelligence; he was, not infrequently, a man of positive genius. The earliest of these preachers must have virtually committed many parts of the Bible to memory through hearing the scriptures read or preached from in the white churches which the slaves attended. They were the first of the slaves to learn to read, and their reading was confined to the Bible, and specifically to the more dramatic passages of the Old Testament. A text served mainly as a starting point and often had no relation to the development of the sermon. Nor would the old-time preacher balk at any text within the lids of the Bible. There is the story of one who after reading a rather cryptic passage took off his spectacles, closed the Bible with a bang and by way of preface said, "Brothers and sisters, this morning—I intend to explain the unexplainable—find out the undefinable—ponder over the imponderable—and unscrew the inscrutable."

The old-time Negro preacher of parts was above all an orator, and in good measure an actor. He knew the secret of oratory, that at bottom it is a progression of rhythmic words more than it is anything else. Indeed, I have witnessed congregations moved to ecstasy by the rhythmic intoning of sheer incoherencies. He was a master of all the modes of eloquence. He often possessed a voice that was a marvelous instrument, a voice he could modulate from a sepulchral whisper to a crashing thunder clap. His discourse was generally kept at a high pitch of fervency, but occasionally he dropped into colloquialisms and, less often, into humor. He preached a personal and anthropomorphic God, a sure-enough heaven and a red-hot hell. His imagination was bold and unfettered. He had the power to sweep his hearers before him; and so himself was often swept away. At such times his language was not prose but poetry. It was from memories of such preachers there grew the idea of this book of poems.

In a general way, these poems were suggested by the rather vague memories of sermons I heard preached in my childhood; but the immediate stimulus for setting them down came quite definitely at a comparatively recent date. I was speaking on a Sunday in Kansas City, addressing meetings in various colored churches. When I had finished my fourth talk it was after nine o'clock at night, but the committee told me there was still another meeting to address. I demurred, making the quotation about the willingness of the spirit and the weakness of the flesh, for I was dead tired. I also protested the lateness of the hour, but I was informed that for the meeting at this church we were in good time. When we reached the church an "exhorter" was just concluding a dull sermon. After his there were two other short sermons. These sermons proved to be preliminaries, mere curtain-raisers for a famed visiting preacher. At last he arose. He was a dark-brown man, handsome in his gigantic proportions. He appeared to be a bit self-conscious, perhaps impressed by the presence of the "distinguished visitor" on the platform, and started in to preach a formal sermon from a formal text. The congregation sat apathetic and dozing. He sensed that he was losing his audience and his opportunity. Suddenly he closed the Bible, stepped out from behind the pulpit and began to preach. He started intoning the old folk-sermon that begins with the creation of the world and ends with Judgment Day. He was at once a changed man, free, at ease and masterful. The change in the congregation was instantaneous. An electric current ran through the crowd. It was in a moment alive and quivering; and all the while the preacher held it in the palm of his hand. He was

wonderful in the way he employed his conscious and unconscious art. He strode the pulpit up and down in what was actually a very rhythmic dance, and he brought into play the full
gamut of his wonderful voice, a voice—what shall I say?—not
of an organ or a trumpet, but rather of a trombone,* the instrument possessing above all others the power to express the
wide and varied range of emotions encompassed by the human
voice—and with greater amplitude. He intoned, he moaned,
he pleaded,—he blared, he crashed, he thundered. I sat fascinated; and more, I was, perhaps against my will, deeply
moved; the emotional effect upon me was irresistible. Before
he had finished I took a slip of paper and somewhat surreptitiously jotted down some ideas for the first poem, "The
Creation."

    At first thought, Negro dialect would appear to be the pre-
cise medium for these old-time sermons; however, as the
reader will see, the poems are not written in dialect. My reason
for not using the dialect is double. First, although the dialect is
the exact instrument for voicing certain traditional phases of
Negro life, it is, and perhaps by that very exactness, a quite
limited instrument. Indeed, it is an instrument with but two
complete stops, pathos and humor. This limitation is not due
to any defect of the dialect as dialect, but to the mould of convention in which Negro dialect in the United States has been
set, to the fixing effects of its long association with the Negro
only as a happy-go-lucky or a forlorn figure. The Aframerican
poet might in time be able to break this mould of convention
and write poetry in dialect without feeling that his first line will
put the reader in a frame of mind which demands that the
poem be either funny or sad, but I doubt that he will make the
effort to do it; he does not consider it worth the while. In fact,
practically no poetry is being written in dialect by the colored
poets of today. These poets have thrown aside dialect and discarded most of the material and subject matter that went into
dialect poetry. The passing of dialect as a medium for Negro

    *Trombones: A powerful brass instrument of the trumpet family, the only
wind instrument possessing a complete chromatic scale enharmonically true,
like the human voice or the violin, and hence very valuable in the orchestra.
—Standard Dictionary.

poetry will be an actual loss, for in it many beautiful things can be done, and done best; however, in my opinion, *traditional* Negro dialect as a form for Aframerican poets is absolutely dead. The Negro poet in the United States, for poetry which he wishes to give a distinctively racial tone and color, needs now an instrument of greater range than dialect; that is, if he is to do more than sound the small notes of sentimentality. I said something on this point in *The Book of American Negro Poetry*, and because I cannot say it better, I quote: "What the colored poet in the United States needs to do is something like what Synge did for the Irish; he needs to find a form that will express the racial spirit by symbols from within rather than by symbols from without—such as the mere mutilation of English spelling and pronunciation. He needs a form that is freer and larger than dialect, but which will still hold the racial flavor; a form expressing the imagery, the idioms, the peculiar turns of thought and the distinctive humor and pathos, too, of the Negro, but which will also be capable of voicing the deepest and highest emotions and aspirations and allow of the widest range of subjects and the widest scope of treatment." The form of "The Creation," the first poem of this group, was a first experiment by me in this direction.

The second part of my reason for not writing these poems in dialect is the weightier. The old-time Negro preachers, though they actually used dialect in their ordinary intercourse, stepped out from its narrow confines when they preached. They were all saturated with the sublime phraseology of the Hebrew prophets and steeped in the idioms of King James English, so when they preached and warmed to their work they spoke another language, a language far removed from traditional Negro dialect. It was really a fusion of Negro idioms with Bible English; and in this there may have been, after all, some kinship with the innate grandiloquence of their old African tongues. To place in the mouths of the talented old-time Negro preachers a language that is a literary imitation of Mississippi cotton-field dialect is sheer burlesque.

Gross exaggeration of the use of big words by these preachers, in fact by Negroes in general, has been commonly made; the laugh being at the exhibition of ignorance involved. What is the basis of this fondness for big words? Is the predilection due, as is supposed, to ignorance desiring to parade itself as knowledge? Not at all. The old-time Negro preacher loved the sonorous, mouth-filling, ear-filling phrase because it gratified a highly developed sense of sound and rhythm in himself and his hearers.

I claim no more for these poems than that I have written them after the manner of the primitive sermons. In the writing of them I have, naturally, felt the influence of the Spirituals. There is, of course, no way of recreating the atmosphere—the fervor of the congregation, the amens and hallelujahs, the undertone of singing which was often a soft accompaniment to parts of the sermon; nor the personality of the preacher— his physical magnetism, his gestures and gesticulations, his changes of tempo, his pauses for effect, and, more than all, his tones of voice. These poems would better be intoned than read; especially does this apply to "Listen, Lord," "The Crucifixion," and "The Judgment Day." But the intoning practiced by the old-time preacher is a thing next to impossible to describe; it must be heard, and it is extremely difficult to imitate even when heard. The finest, and perhaps the only demonstration ever given to a New York public, was the intoning of the dream in Ridgely Torrence's *Rider of Dreams* by Opal Cooper of the Negro Players at the Madison Square Theatre in 1917. Those who were fortunate enough to hear him can never, I know, forget the thrill of it. This intoning is always a matter of crescendo and diminuendo in the intensity—a rising and falling between plain speaking and wild chanting. And often a startling effect is gained by breaking off suddenly at the highest point of intensity and dropping into the monotone of ordinary speech.

The tempos of the preacher I have endeavored to indicate by the line arrangement of the poems, and a certain sort of pause that is marked by a quick intaking and an audible expulsion of the breath I have indicated by dashes. There is a decided syncopation of speech—the crowding in of many syllables or the lengthening out of which must be left to the reader's ear. The rhythmical stress of this syncopation is partly obtained by a marked silent fraction of a beat; frequently this silent fraction is filled in by a hand clap.

One factor in the creation of atmosphere I have included—
the preliminary prayer. The prayer leader was sometimes a
woman. It was the prayer leader who directly prepared the way
for the sermon, set the scene, as it were. However, a most impressive concomitant of the prayer, the chorus of responses
which gave it an antiphonal quality, I have not attempted to
set down. These preliminary prayers were often products
hardly less remarkable than the sermons.

The old-time Negro preacher is rapidly passing. I have here
tried sincerely to fix something of him.

New York City, 1927.

Listen, Lord—A Prayer

O Lord, we come this morning
Knee-bowed and body-bent
Before thy throne of grace.
O Lord—this morning—
Bow our hearts beneath our knees,
And our knees in some lonesome valley.
We come this morning—
Like empty pitchers to a full fountain,
With no merits of our own.
O Lord—open up a window of heaven,
And lean out far over the battlements of glory,
And listen this morning.

Lord, have mercy on proud and dying sinners—
Sinners hanging over the mouth of hell,
Who seem to love their distance well.
Lord—ride by this morning—
Mount your milk-white horse,
And ride-a this morning—
And in your ride, ride by old hell,
Ride by the dingy gates of hell,
And stop poor sinners in their headlong plunge.

And now, O Lord, this man of God,
Who breaks the bread of life this morning—
Shadow him in the hollow of thy hand,
And keep him out of the gunshot of the devil.
Take him, Lord—this morning—
Wash him with hyssop inside and out,
Hang him up and drain him dry of sin.
Pin his ear to the wisdom-post,
And make his words sledge hammers of truth—
Beating on the iron heart of sin.
Lord God, this morning—
Put his eye to the telescope of eternity,
And let him look upon the paper walls of time.
Lord, turpentine his imagination,
Put perpetual motion in his arms,
Fill him full of the dynamite of thy power,
Anoint him all over with the oil of thy salvation,
And set his tongue on fire.

And now, O Lord—
When I've done drunk my last cup of sorrow—
When I've been called everything but a child of God—
When I'm done travelling up the rough side of the
        mountain—
O—Mary's Baby—
When I start down the steep and slippery steps of death—
When this old world begins to rock beneath my feet—
Lower me to my dusty grave in peace
To wait for that great gittin' up morning—Amen.

The Creation

And God stepped out on space,
And he looked around and said:
I'm lonely—
I'll make me a world.

And far as the eye of God could see
Darkness covered everything,
Blacker than a hundred midnights
Down in a cypress swamp.

Then God smiled,
And the light broke,
And the darkness rolled up on one side,
And the light stood shining on the other,
And God said: That's good!

Then God reached out and took the light in his hands,
And God rolled the light around in his hands
Until he made the sun;
And he set that sun a-blazing in the heavens.
And the light that was left from making the sun
God gathered it up in a shining ball
And flung it against the darkness,
Spangling the night with the moon and stars.
Then down between
The darkness and the light
He hurled the world;
And God said: That's good!

Then God himself stepped down—
And the sun was on his right hand,
And the moon was on his left;
The stars were clustered about his head,
And the earth was under his feet.
And God walked, and where he trod
His footsteps hollowed the valleys out
And bulged the mountains up.

Then he stopped and looked and saw
That the earth was hot and barren.
So God stepped over to the edge of the world
And he spat out the seven seas—
He batted his eyes, and the lightnings flashed—
He clapped his hands, and the thunders rolled—

And the waters above the earth came down,
The cooling waters came down.

Then the green grass sprouted,
And the little red flowers blossomed,
The pine tree pointed his finger to the sky,
And the oak spread out his arms,
The lakes cuddled down in the hollows of the ground,
And the rivers ran down to the sea;
And God smiled again,
And the rainbow appeared,
And curled itself around his shoulder.

Then God raised his arm and he waved his hand
Over the sea and over the land,
And he said: Bring forth! Bring forth!
And quicker than God could drop his hand,
Fishes and fowls
And beasts and birds
Swam the rivers and the seas,
Roamed the forests and the woods,
And split the air with their wings.
And God said: That's good!

Then God walked around,
And God looked around
On all that he had made.
He looked at his sun,
And he looked at his moon,
And he looked at his little stars;
He looked on his world
With all its living things,
And God said: I'm lonely still.

Then God sat down—
On the side of a hill where he could think;
By a deep, wide river he sat down;
With his head in his hands,
God thought and thought,
Till he thought: I'll make me a man!

Up from the bed of the river
God scooped the clay;
And by the bank of the river
He kneeled him down;
And there the great God Almighty
Who lit the sun and fixed it in the sky,
Who flung the stars to the most far corner of the night,
Who rounded the earth in the middle of his hand;
This Great God,
Like a mammy bending over her baby,
Kneeled down in the dust
Toiling over a lump of clay
Till he shaped it in his own image;

Then into it he blew the breath of life,
And man became a living soul.
Amen. Amen.

The Prodigal Son

Young man—
Young man—
Your arm's too short to box with God.

But Jesus spake in a parable, and he said:
A certain man had two sons.
Jesus didn't give this man a name,
But his name is God Almighty.
And Jesus didn't call these sons by name,
But ev'ry young man,
Ev'rywhere,
Is one of these two sons.

And the younger son said to his father,
He said: Father, divide up the property,
And give me my portion now.

And the father with tears in his eyes said: Son,
Don't leave your father's house.
But the boy was stubborn in his head,
And haughty in his heart,
And he took his share of his father's goods,
And went into a far-off country.

There comes a time,
There comes a time
When ev'ry young man looks out from his father's house,
Longing for that far-off country.

And the young man journeyed on his way,
And he said to himself as he travelled along:
This sure is an easy road,
Nothing like the rough furrows behind my father's plow.

Young man—
Young man—
Smooth and easy is the road
That leads to hell and destruction.
Down grade all the way,
The further you travel, the faster you go.
No need to trudge and sweat and toil,
Just slip and slide and slip and slide
Till you bang up against hell's iron gate.

And the younger son kept travelling along,
Till at night-time he came to a city.
And the city was bright in the night-time like day,
The streets all crowded with people,
Brass bands and string bands a-playing,
And ev'rywhere the young man turned
There was singing and laughing and dancing.
And he stopped a passer-by and he said:
Tell me what city is this?
And the passer-by laughed and said: Don't you know?
This is Babylon, Babylon,
That great city of Babylon.
Come on, my friend, and go along with me.
And the young man joined the crowd.

Young man—
Young man—
You're never lonesome in Babylon.
You can always join a crowd in Babylon.
Young man—
Young man—
You can never be alone in Babylon,
Alone with your Jesus in Babylon.
You can never find a place, a lonesome place,
A lonesome place to go down on your knees,
And talk with your God, in Babylon.
You're always in a crowd in Babylon.

And the young man went with his new-found friend,
And bought himself some brand new clothes,
And he spent his days in the drinking dens,
Swallowing the fires of hell.
And he spent his nights in the gambling dens,
Throwing dice with the devil for his soul.
And he met up with the women of Babylon.
Oh, the women of Babylon!
Dressed in yellow and purple and scarlet,
Loaded with rings and earrings and bracelets,
Their lips like a honeycomb dripping with honey,
Perfumed and sweet-smelling like a jasmine flower;
And the jasmine smell of the Babylon women
Got in his nostrils and went to his head,
And he wasted his substance in riotous living,
In the evening, in the black and dark of night,
With the sweet-sinning women of Babylon.
And they stripped him of his money,
And they stripped him of his clothes,
And they left him broke and ragged
In the streets of Babylon.

Then the young man joined another crowd—
The beggars and lepers of Babylon.
And he went to feeding swine,
And he was hungrier than the hogs;
He got down on his belly in the mire and mud

And ate the husks with the hogs.
And not a hog was too low to turn up his nose
At the man in the mire of Babylon.

Then the young man came to himself—
He came to himself and said:
In my father's house are many mansions,
Ev'ry servant in his house has bread to eat,
Ev'ry servant in his house has a place to sleep;
I will arise and go to my father.
And his father saw him afar off,
And he ran up the road to meet him.
He put clean clothes upon his back,
And a golden chain around his neck,
He made a feast and killed the fatted calf,
And invited the neighbors in.

Oh-o-oh, sinner,
When you're mingling with the crowd in Babylon—
Drinking the wine of Babylon—
Running with the women of Babylon—
You forget about God, and you laugh at Death.
Today you've got the strength of a bull in your neck
And the strength of a bear in your arms,
But some o' these days, some o' these days,
You'll have a hand-to-hand struggle with bony Death,
And Death is bound to win.

Young man, come away from Babylon,
That hell-border city of Babylon.
Leave the dancing and gambling of Babylon,
The wine and whiskey of Babylon,
The hot-mouthed women of Babylon;
Fall down on your knees,
And say in your heart:
I will arise and go to my Father.

Go Down Death—A Funeral Sermon

Weep not, weep not,
She is not dead;
She's resting in the bosom of Jesus.
Heart-broken husband—weep no more;
Grief-stricken son—weep no more;
Left-lonesome daughter—weep no more;
She's only just gone home.

Day before yesterday morning,
God was looking down from his great, high heaven,
Looking down on all his children,
And his eye fell on Sister Caroline,
Tossing on her bed of pain.
And God's big heart was touched with pity,
With the everlasting pity.

And God sat back on his throne,
And he commanded that tall, bright angel standing at his
    right hand:
Call me Death!
And that tall, bright angel cried in a voice
That broke like a clap of thunder:
Call Death!—Call Death!
And the echo sounded down the streets of heaven
Till it reached away back to that shadowy place,
Where Death waits with his pale, white horses.

And Death heard the summons,
And he leaped on his fastest horse,
Pale as a sheet in the moonlight.
Up the golden street Death galloped,
And the hoofs of his horse struck fire from the gold,
But they didn't make no sound.
Up Death rode to the Great White Throne,
And waited for God's command.

And God said: Go down, Death, go down,
Go down to Savannah, Georgia,

Down in Yamacraw,
And find Sister Caroline.
She's borne the burden and heat of the day,
She's labored long in my vineyard,
And she's tired—
She's weary—
Go down, Death, and bring her to me.

And Death didn't say a word,
But he loosed the reins on his pale, white horse,
And he clamped the spurs to his bloodless sides,
And out and down he rode,
Through heaven's pearly gates,
Past suns and moons and stars;
On Death rode,
And the foam from his horse was like a comet in the sky;
On Death rode,
Leaving the lightning's flash behind;
Straight on down he came.

While we were watching round her bed,
She turned her eyes and looked away,
She saw what we couldn't see;
She saw Old Death. She saw Old Death
Coming like a falling star.
But Death didn't frighten Sister Caroline;
He looked to her like a welcome friend.
And she whispered to us: I'm going home,
And she smiled and closed her eyes.

And Death took her up like a baby,
And she lay in his icy arms,
But she didn't feel no chill.
And Death began to ride again—
Up beyond the evening star,
Out beyond the morning star,
Onto the glittering light of glory,
On to the Great White Throne.
And there he laid Sister Caroline
On the loving breast of Jesus.

And Jesus took his own hand and wiped away her tears,
And he smoothed the furrows from her face,
And the angels sang a little song,
And Jesus rocked her in his arms,
And kept a-saying: Take your rest,
Take your rest, take your rest.

Weep not—weep not,
She is not dead;
She's resting in the bosom of Jesus.

Noah Built the Ark

In the cool of the day—
God was walking—
Around in the Garden of Eden.
And except for the beasts, eating in the fields,
And except for the birds, flying through the trees,
The garden looked like it was deserted.
And God called out and said: Adam,
Adam, where art thou?
And Adam, with Eve behind his back,
Came out from where he was hiding.

And God said: Adam,
What hast thou done?
Thou hast eaten of the tree!
And Adam,
With his head hung down,
Blamed it on the woman.

For after God made the first man Adam,
He breathed a sleep upon him;
Then he took out of Adam one of his ribs,
And out of that rib made woman.
And God put the man and woman together
In the beautiful Garden of Eden,
With nothing to do the whole day long

But play all around in the garden.
And God called Adam before him,
And he said to him:
Listen now, Adam,
Of all the fruit in the garden you can eat,
Except of the tree of knowledge;
For the day thou eatest of that tree,
Thou shalt surely die.

Then pretty soon along came Satan.
Old Satan came like a snake in the grass
To try out his tricks on the woman.
I imagine I can see Old Satan now
A-sidling up to the woman.
I imagine the first word Satan said was:
Eve, you're surely good looking.
I imagine he brought her a present, too,—
And, if there was such a thing in those ancient days,
He brought her a looking-glass.

And Eve and Satan got friendly—
Then Eve got to walking on shaky ground;
Don't ever get friendly with Satan.—
And they started to talk about the garden,
And Satan said: Tell me, how do you like
The fruit on the nice, tall, blooming tree
Standing in the middle of the garden?
And Eve said:
That's the forbidden fruit,
Which if we eat we die.

And Satan laughed a devilish little laugh,
And he said to the woman: God's fooling you, Eve;
That's the sweetest fruit in the garden.
I know you can eat that forbidden fruit,
And I know that you will not die.

And Eve looked at the forbidden fruit,
And it was red and ripe and juicy.
And Eve took a taste, and she offered it to Adam,

To the mighty Roman Governor.
Great Pilate seated in his hall,—
Great Pilate on his judgment seat,
Said: In this man I find no fault.
I find no fault in him.
And Pilate washed his hands.
But they cried out, saying:
Crucify him!—
Crucify him!—
Crucify him!—
His blood be on our heads.
And they beat my loving Jesus,
They spit on my precious Jesus;
They dressed him up in a purple robe,
They put a crown of thorns upon his head,
And they pressed it down—
Oh, they pressed it down—
And they mocked my sweet King Jesus.

Up Golgotha's rugged road
I see my Jesus go.
I see him sink beneath the load,
I see my drooping Jesus sink.
And then they laid hold on Simon,
Black Simon, yes, black Simon;
They put the cross on Simon,
And Simon bore the cross.

On Calvary, on Calvary,
They crucified my Jesus.
They nailed him to the cruel tree,
And the hammer!
The hammer!
The hammer!
Rang through Jerusalem's streets.
The hammer!
The hammer!
The hammer!
Rang through Jerusalem's streets.

Jesus, my lamb-like Jesus,
Shivering as the nails go through his hands;
Jesus, my lamb-like Jesus,
Shivering as the nails go through his feet.
Jesus, my darling Jesus,
Groaning as the Roman spear plunged in his side;
Jesus, my darling Jesus,
Groaning as the blood came spurting from his wound.
Oh, look how they done my Jesus.

Mary,
Weeping Mary,
Sees her poor little Jesus on the cross.
Mary,
Weeping Mary,
Sees her sweet, baby Jesus on the cruel cross,
Hanging between two thieves.

And Jesus, my lonesome Jesus,
Called out once more to his Father,
Saying:
My God,
My God,
Why hast thou forsaken me?
And he drooped his head and died.

And the veil of the temple was split in two,
The midday sun refused to shine,
The thunder rumbled and the lightning wrote
An unknown language in the sky.
What a day! Lord, what a day!
When my blessed Jesus died.

Oh, I tremble, yes, I tremble,
It causes me to tremble, tremble,
When I think how Jesus died;
Died on the steeps of Calvary,
How Jesus died for sinners,
Sinners like you and me.

Let My People Go

And God called Moses from the burning bush,
He called in a still, small voice,
And he said: Moses—Moses—
And Moses listened,
And he answered and said:
Lord, here I am.

And the voice in the bush said: Moses,
Draw not nigh, take off your shoes,
For you're standing on holy ground.
And Moses stopped where he stood,
And Moses took off his shoes,
And Moses looked at the burning bush,
And he heard the voice,
But he saw no man.

Then God again spoke to Moses,
And he spoke in a voice of thunder:
I am the Lord God Almighty,
I am the God of thy fathers,
I am the God of Abraham,
Of Isaac and of Jacob.
And Moses hid his face.

And God said to Moses:
I've seen the awful suffering
Of my people down in Egypt.
I've watched their hard oppressors,
Their overseers and drivers;
The groans of my people have filled my ears
And I can't stand it no longer;
So I'm come down to deliver them
Out of the land of Egypt,
And I will bring them out of that land
Into the land of Canaan;
Therefore, Moses, go down,
Go down into Egypt,

And tell Old Pharaoh
To let my people go.

And Moses said: Lord, who am I
To make a speech before Pharaoh?
For, Lord, you know I'm slow of tongue.
But God said: I will be thy mouth and I will be thy tongue;
Therefore, Moses, go down,
Go down yonder into Egypt land,
And tell Old Pharaoh
To let my people go.

And Moses with his rod in hand
Went down and said to Pharaoh:
Thus saith the Lord God of Israel,
Let my people go.

And Pharaoh looked at Moses,
He stopped still and looked at Moses;
And he said to Moses: Who is this Lord?
I know all the gods of Egypt,
But I know no God of Israel;
So go back, Moses, and tell your God,
I will not let this people go.

Poor Old Pharaoh,
He knows all the knowledge of Egypt,
Yet never knew—
He never knew
The one and the living God.
Poor Old Pharaoh,
He's got all the power of Egypt,
And he's going to try
To test his strength
With the might of the great Jehovah,
With the might of the Lord God of Hosts,
The Lord mighty in battle.
And God, sitting high up in his heavens,
Laughed at poor Old Pharaoh.

And Pharaoh called the overseers,
And Pharaoh called the drivers,
And he said: Put heavier burdens still
On the backs of the Hebrew Children.
Then the people chode with Moses,
And they cried out: Look here, Moses,
You've been to Pharaoh, but look and see
What Pharaoh's done to us now.
And Moses was troubled in mind.

But God said: Go again, Moses,
You and your brother, Aaron,
And say once more to Pharaoh,
Thus saith the Lord God of the Hebrews,
Let my people go.
And Moses and Aaron with their rods in hand
Worked many signs and wonders.
But Pharaoh called for his magic men,
And they worked wonders, too.
So Pharaohs' heart was hardened,
And he would not,
No, he would not
Let God's people go.

And God rained down plagues on Egypt,
Plagues of frogs and lice and locusts,
Plagues of blood and boils and darkness,
And other plagues besides.
But ev'ry time God moved the plague
Old Pharaoh's heart was hardened,
And he would not,
No, he would not
Let God's people go.
And Moses was troubled in mind.

Then the Lord said: Listen, Moses,
The God of Israel will not be mocked,
Just one more witness of my power
I'll give hard-hearted Pharaoh.
This very night about midnight,

I'll pass over Egypt land,
In my righteous wrath will I pass over,
And smite their first-born dead.

And God that night passed over.
And a cry went up out of Egypt.
And Pharaoh rose in the middle of the night
And sent in a hurry for Moses;
And he said: Go forth from among my people,
You and all the Hebrew Children;
Take your goods and take your flocks,
And get away from the land of Egypt.

And, right then, Moses led them out,
With all their goods and all their flocks;
And God went on before,
A guiding pillar of cloud by day,
And a pillar of fire by night.
And they journeyed on in the wilderness,
And came down to the Red Sea.

In the morning,
Oh, in the morning,
They missed the Hebrew Children.
Four hundred years,
Four hundred years
They'd held them down in Egypt land.
Held them under the driver's lash,
Working without money and without price.
And it might have been Pharaoh's wife that said:
Pharaoh—look what you've done.
You let those Hebrew Children go,
And who's going to serve us now?
Who's going to make our bricks and mortar?
Who's going to plant and plow our corn?
Who's going to get up in the chill of the morning?
And who's going to work in the blazing sun?
Pharaoh, tell me that!

And Pharaoh called his generals,
And generals called the captains,
And the captains called the soldiers.
And they hitched up all the chariots,
Six hundred chosen chariots of war,
And twenty-four hundred horses.
And the chariots all were full of men,
With swords and shields
And shiny spears
And battle bows and arrows.
And Pharaoh and his army
Pursued the Hebrew Children
To the edge of the Red Sea.

Now, the Children of Israel, looking back,
Saw Pharaoh's army coming.
And the rumble of the chariots was like a thunder storm,
And the whirring of the wheels was like a rushing wind,
And the dust from the horses made a cloud that darked the
    day,
And the glittering of the spears was like lightnings in the
    night.

And the Children of Israel all lost faith,
The children of Israel all lost hope;
Deep Red Sea in front of them
And Pharaoh's host behind.
And they mumbled and grumbled among themselves:
Were there no graves in Egypt?
And they wailed aloud to Moses and said:
Slavery in Egypt was better than to come
To die here in this wilderness.

But Moses said:
Stand still! Stand still!
And see the Lord's salvation.
For the Lord God of Israel
Will not forsake his people.
The Lord will break the chariots,
The Lord will break the horsemen,

He'll break great Egypt's sword and shield,
The battle bows and arrows;
This day he'll make proud Pharaoh know
Who is the God of Israel.

And Moses lifted up his rod
Over the Red Sea;
And God with a blast of his nostrils
Blew the waters apart,
And the waves rolled back and stood up in a pile,
And left a path through the middle of the sea
Dry as the sands of the desert.
And the Children of Israel all crossed over
On to the other side.

When Pharaoh saw them crossing dry,
He dashed on in behind them—
Old Pharaoh got about half way cross,
And God unlashed the a waters,
And the waves rushed back together,
And Pharaoh and all his army got lost,
And all his host got drownded.
And Moses sang and Miriam danced,
And the people shouted for joy,
And God led the Hebrew Children on
Till they reached the promised land.

Listen!—Listen!
All you sons of Pharaoh.
Who do you think can hold God's people
When the Lord God himself has said,
Let my people go?

The Judgment Day

In that great day,
People, in that great day,
God's a-going to rain down fire.
God's a-going to sit in the middle of the air
To judge the quick and the dead.

Early one of these mornings,
God's a-going to call for Gabriel,
That tall, bright angel, Gabriel;
And God's a-going to say to him: Gabriel,
Blow your silver trumpet,
And wake the living nations.

And Gabriel's going to ask him: Lord,
How loud must I blow it?

And God's a-going to tell him: Gabriel,
Blow it calm and easy.
Then putting one foot on the mountain top,
And the other in the middle of the sea,
Gabriel's going to stand and blow his horn,
To wake the living nations.

Then God's a-going to say to him: Gabriel,
Once more blow your silver trumpet,
And wake the nations underground.

And Gabriel's going to ask him: Lord
How loud must I blow it?
And God's a-going to tell him: Gabriel,
Like seven peals of thunder.
Then the tall, bright angel, Gabriel,
Will put one foot on the battlements of heaven
And the other on the steps of hell,
And blow that silver trumpet
Till he shakes old hell's foundations.

And I feel Old Earth a-shuddering—
And I see the graves a-bursting—
And I hear a sound,
A blood-chilling sound.
What sound is that I hear?
It's the clicking together of the dry bones,
Bone to bone—the dry bones.
And I see coming out of the bursting graves,
And marching up from the valley of death,
The army of the dead.
And the living and the dead in the twinkling of an eye
Are caught up in the middle of the air,
Before God's judgment bar.

Oh-o-oh, sinner,
Where will you stand,
In that great day when God's a-going to rain down fire?
Oh, you gambling man—where will you stand?
You whore-mongering man—where will you stand?
Liars and backsliders—where will you stand,
In that great day when God's a-going to rain down fire?

And God will divide the sheep from the goats,
The one on the right, the other on the left.
And to them on the right God's a-going to say:
Enter into my kingdom.
And those who've come through great tribulations,
And washed their robes in the blood of the Lamb,
They will enter in—
Clothed in spotless white,
With starry crowns upon their heads,
And silver slippers on their feet,
And harps within their hands;—

And two by two they'll walk
Up and down the golden street,
Feasting on the milk and honey
Singing new songs of Zion,
Chattering with the angels
All around the Great White Throne.

And to them on the left God's a-going to say:
Depart from me into everlasting darkness,
Down into the bottomless pit.
And the wicked like lumps of lead will start to fall,
Headlong for seven days and nights they'll fall,
Plumb into the big, black, red-hot mouth of hell,
Belching out fire and brimstone.
And their cries like howling, yelping dogs,
Will go up with the fire and smoke from hell,
But God will stop his ears.

Too late, sinner! Too late!
Good-bye, sinner! Good-bye!
In hell, sinner! In hell!
Beyond the reach of the love of God.

And I hear a voice, crying, crying:
Time shall be no more!
Time shall be no more!
Time shall be no more!
And the sun will go out like a candle in the wind,
The moon will turn to dripping blood,
The stars will fall like cinders,
And the sea will burn like tar;
And the earth shall melt away and be dissolved,
And the sky will roll up like a scroll.
With a wave of his hand God will blot out time,
And start the wheel of eternity.

Sinner, oh, sinner,
Where will you stand
In that great day when God's a-going to rain down fire?

SAINT PETER RELATES AN INCIDENT

Saint Peter Relates an Incident of the Resurrection Day

Eternities—now numbering six or seven—
Hung heavy on the hands of all in heaven.
Archangels tall and fair had reached the stage
Where they began to show some signs of age.

The faces of the flaming seraphim
Were slightly drawn, their eyes were slightly dim.
The cherubs, too, for now—oh, an infinite while
Had worn but a wistful shade of their dimpling smile.

The serried singers of the celestial choir
Disclosed a woeful want of pristine fire;
When they essayed to strike the glad refrain,
Their attack was weak, their tone revealed voice strain.

Their expression seemed to say, "We must! We must!"
    though
'Twas more than evident they lacked the gusto;
It could not be elsewise—that fact all can agree on—
Chanting the selfsame choral æon after æon.

Thus was it that Saint Peter at the gate
Began a brand new thing in heaven: to relate
Some reminiscences from heavenly history,
Which had till then been more or less a mystery.

So now and then, by turning back the pages,
Were whiled away some moments from the ages,
Was gained a respite from the monotony
That can't help settling on eternity.

II

Now, there had been a lapse of ages hoary,
And the angels clamored for another story.
"Tell us a tale, Saint Peter," they entreated;
And gathered close around where he was seated.

Saint Peter stroked his beard,
And "Yes," he said
By the twinkle in his eye
And the nodding of his head.

A moment brief he fumbled with his keys—
It seemed to help him call up memories—
Straightway there flashed across his mind the one
About the unknown soldier
Who came from Washington.

The hosts stood listening,
Breathlessly awake;
And thus Saint Peter spake:

III

'Twas Resurrection morn,
And Gabriel blew a blast upon his horn
That echoed through the arches high and vast
Of Time and Space—a long resounding blast

To wake the dead, dead for a million years;
A blast to reach and pierce their dust-stopped ears;
To waken them, wherever they might be,
Deep in the earth or deeper in the sea.

A shudder shook the world, and gaping graves
Gave up their dead. Out from the parted waves
Came the prisoners of old ocean. The dead belonging
To every land and clime came thronging.

From the four corners of all the earth they drew,
Their faces radiant and their bodies new.

Creation pulsed and swayed beneath the tread
Of all the living, and all the risen dead.

Swift-winged heralds of heaven flew back and forth,
Out of the east, to the south, the west, the north,
Giving out quick commands, and yet benign,
Marshaling the swarming milliards into line.

The recording angel in words of thundering might,
At which the timid, doubting souls took fright,
Bade all to await the grand roll-call; to wit,
To see if in the Book their names were writ.

The multitudinous business of the day
Progressed, but naturally, not without delay.
Meanwhile, within the great American border
There was the issuance of a special order.

IV

The word went forth, spoke by some grand panjandrum,
Perhaps, by some high potentate of Klandom,
That all the trusty patriotic mentors,
And duly qualified Hundred-Percenters

Should forthwith gather together upon the banks
Of the Potomac, there to form their ranks,
March to the tomb, by orders to be given,
And escort the unknown soldier up to heaven.

Compliantly they gathered from each region,
The G.A.R., the D.A.R., the Legion,
Veterans of wars—Mexican, Spanish, Haitian—
Trustees of the patriotism of the nation;

Key Men, Watchmen, shunning circumlocution,
The sons of the This and That and of the Revolution;
Not to forget, there gathered every man
Of the Confederate Veterans and the Ku-Klux Klan.

The Grand Imperial Marshal gave the sign;
Column on column, the marchers fell in line;
Majestic as an army in review,
They swept up Washington's wide avenue.

Then, through the long line ran a sudden flurry,
The marchers in the rear began to hurry;
They feared unless the procession hastened on,
The unknown soldier might be risen and gone.

The fear was groundless; when they arrived, in fact,
They found the grave entirely intact.
(Resurrection plans were long, long past completing
Ere there was thought of re-enforced concreting.)

They heard a faint commotion in the tomb,
Like the stirring of a child within the womb;
At once they saw the plight, and set about
The job to dig the unknown soldier out.

They worked away, they labored with a will,
They toiled with pick, with crowbar, and with drill
To cleave a breach; nor did the soldier shirk;
Within his limits, he helped to push the work.

He, underneath the debris, heaved and hove
Up toward the opening which they cleaved and clove;
Through it, at last, his towering form loomed big and
        bigger—
"Great God Almighty! Look!" they cried, "he is a nigger!"

Surprise and consternation and dismay
Swept over the crowd; none knew just what to say
Or what to do. And all fell back aghast.
Silence—but only an instant did it last.

Bedlam: They clamored, they railed, some roared, some
        bleated;
All of them felt that somehow they'd been cheated.

The question rose: What to do with him, then?
The Klan was all for burying him again.

The scheme involved within the Klan's suggestion
Gave rise to a rather nice metaphysical question:
Could he be forced again through death's dark portal,
Since now his body and soul were immortal?

Would he, forsooth, the curious-minded queried,
Even in concrete, re-entombed, stay buried?
In a moment more, midst the pile of broken stone,
The unknown soldier stood, and stood alone.

v

The day came to a close.
And heaven—hell too—was filled with them that rose.
I shut the pearly gate and turned the key;
For Time was now merged into Eternity.

I gave one last look over the jasper wall,
And afar descried a figure dark and tall:
The unknown soldier, dust-stained and begrimed,
Climbing his way to heaven, and singing as he climbed:
Deep river, my home is over Jordan,
Deep river, I want to cross over into camp-ground.

Climbing and singing—
Deep river, my home is over Jordan,
Deep river, I want to cross over into camp-ground.

Nearer and louder—
Deep river, my home is over Jordan,
Deep river, I want to cross over into camp-ground.

At the jasper wall—
Deep river, my home is over Jordan,
Deep river,
Lord,
I want to cross over into camp-ground.

I rushed to the gate and flung it wide,
Singing, he entered with a loose, long stride;
Singing and swinging up the golden street,
The music married to the tramping of his feet.

Tall, black soldier-angel marching alone,
Swinging up the golden street, saluting at the great white
    throne.
Singing, singing, singing, singing clear and strong.
Singing, singing, singing, till heaven took up the song:
    Deep river, my home is over Jordan,
    Deep river, I want to cross over into camp-ground.

VI

The tale was done,
The angelic hosts dispersed,
    but not till after
There ran through heaven
Something that quivered
    'twixt tears and laughter.

My City

When I come down to sleep death's endless night,
The threshold of the unknown dark to cross,
What to me then will be the keenest loss,
When this bright world blurs on my fading sight?
Will it be that no more I shall see the trees
Or smell the flowers or hear the singing birds
Or watch the flashing streams or patient herds?
No. I am sure it will be none of these.

But, ah! Manhattan's sights and sounds, her smells,
Her crowds, her throbbing force, the thrill that comes
From being of her a part, her subtle spells,
Her shining towers, her avenues, her slums—
O God! the stark, unutterable pity,
To be dead, and never again behold my city.

If I Were Paris

Not for me the budding girl
Or the maiden in full bloom,
Sure of beauty and of charm,
Careless of the distant doom,
Laughing in the face of years
That stretch out so long and far,
Mindful of the things to be,
Heedless of the things that are;

But the woman sweetly ripe,
Under the autumn of her skies;
Thin lines of care about her mouth,
And utterless longing in her eyes.

Lift Every Voice and Sing

A group of young men in Jacksonville, Florida, arranged to celebrate Lincoln's birthday in 1900. My brother, J. Rosamond Johnson,
and I decided to write a song to be sung at the exercises. I wrote the
words and he wrote the music. Our New York publisher, Edward B.
Marks, made mimeographed copies for us, and the song was taught
to and sung by a chorus of five hundred colored school children.

Shortly afterwards my brother and I moved away from Jacksonville
to New York, and the song passed out of our minds. But the school
children of Jacksonville kept singing it; they went off to other schools
and sang it; they became teachers and taught it to other children.
Within twenty years it was being sung over the South and in some
other parts of the country. Today the song, popularly known as the
Negro National Hymn, is quite generally used.

The lines of this song repay me in an elation, almost of exquisite
anguish, whenever I hear them sung by Negro children.

Left every voice and sing
Till earth and heaven ring,
Ring with the harmonies of Liberty;
Let our rejoicing rise
High as the listening skies,

Let it resound loud as the rolling sea.
Sing a song full of the faith that the dark past has taught us,
Sing a song full of the hope that the present has brought us.
Facing the rising sun of our new day begun,
Let us march on till victory is won.

Stony the road we trod,
Bitter the chastening rod,
Felt in the days when hope unborn had died;
Yet with a steady beat,
Have not our weary feet
Come to the place for which our fathers sighed?
We have come over a way that with tears has been watered,
We have come, treading our path through the blood of the
    slaughtered,
Out from the gloomy past,
Till now we stand at last
Where the white gleam of our bright star is cast.

God of our weary years,
God of our silent tears,
Thou who hast brought us thus far on the way;
Thou who hast by Thy might
Led us into the light,
Keep us forever in the path, we pray.
Lest our feet stray from the places, our God, where we met
    Thee,
Lest, our hearts drunk with the wine of the world, we forget
    Thee;
Shadowed beneath Thy hand,
May we forever stand.
True to our God,
True to our native land.

Chronology

1871   Born James William Johnson June 17 in Jacksonville,
            Florida, second child of Helen Louise Dillet and James
            Johnson. (Helen Louise Dillet was born free in Nassau,
            the Bahamas, in 1842. James Johnson was born free in
            Richmond, Virginia, in 1830. They met in New York City
            and married in Nassau in April 1864. Their first child,
            Marie Louise, was born in 1868, and in 1869 they moved
            to Jacksonville, where Marie Louise died in 1870.) Mother
            teaches at the Stanton School, a school for African-Amer-
            icans established by the Freedmen's Bureau. Father works
            as headwaiter at the St. James, a luxury hotel. Family lives
            in a house in the LaVilla neighborhood.

1873–76   Brother John Rosamond (known as Rosamond) born
            August 11, 1873. At mother's initiative, parents adopt a
            teenage girl, Agnes Marion Edwards, who later teaches at
            the Stanton School. Family visits Nassau in 1876. Johnson
            enters first grade at the Stanton School, whose eight-
            month academic schedule is almost twice as long as the
            average public school year in Florida.

1878   Begins attending Ebenezer Methodist Episcopal Church,
            the largest African-American church in Jacksonville, largely
            at the prompting of his grandmother, Mary Dillet Barton,
            who hopes he will become a minister. Learns to play the
            piano.

1884   Travels to New York City with his grandmother Mary
            Barton and stays in Brooklyn for the summer. Works as a
            delivery boy for the Jacksonville *Times-Union* and then
            as an office boy for the editor of the paper, Charles H.
            Jones.

1885–87   Meets prominent African-American leaders Daniel A.
            Payne, bishop of the African Methodist Episcopal Church;
            Joseph C. Price, orator and educator; and Frederick Doug-
            lass, whose autobiography, *Life and Times of Frederick
            Douglass*, he had received as a prize at school. Speaks
            Spanish with Cuban friend Ricardo Rodriguez Ponce, who
            has come to live with the Johnson family, and becomes

fluent in the language. Develops friendship with Judson Douglass Wetmore, a light-skinned boy who can pass for white. (Johnson will later claim him as a model for the protagonist of *The Autobiography of an Ex-Colored Man*.)

1887   Graduates in May from the Stanton School. Moves to Atlanta in the fall to enter Atlanta University's Preparatory Division. Begins writing poetry. Studies a liberal arts curriculum with additional training in carpentry.

1888   Completes first year at the Preparatory Division and returns home in May. Yellow fever epidemic breaks out in Jacksonville in the summer, and the resulting quarantine prevents his return to Atlanta in the fall. Goes to work as a receptionist for a white physician, Thomas Osmond Summers, in Jacksonville.

1889   Tutored in classical languages and geometry in Jacksonville. Encouraged by Summers to read European literature and to continue writing verse. Goes with Summers to Washington, D.C., for several weeks in the spring. Returns to Atlanta for the fall semester.

1890   Graduates from the Preparatory Division. Enters Atlanta University's freshman class. Rosamond moves to Boston to study at the New England Conservatory of Music.

1891   Johnson meets Booker T. Washington while working in the university printing office. Declares his agnosticism. Teaches school in rural Henry County, Georgia, during the summer.

1892   First published poem, "To a Friend," published in the Atlanta University *Bulletin*. Wins the university's oratory contest for "The Best Methods of Removing the Disabilities of Caste from the Negro." Threatens to leave the university after he is required to publicly apologize for joining a group of students who refused to carve a Thanksgiving turkey as protest against school regulations, but is persuaded by his father and a dean to remain.

1893   Publishes three poems in the *Bulletin*. Leads a group of Atlanta University students to Chicago to work at the World's Columbian Exposition; en route, resists a conductor's attempts to force them to ride in the Jim Crow car instead of their previously chartered car. Finds work at the Exposition as a carpenter. Meets and begins friendship with Paul Laurence Dunbar, who discusses poetry with him. Returns to Atlanta in the fall. Writes first dialect poem, later published as "July in Georgy."

1894   Receives B.A. degree with honors from Atlanta University. Delivers graduation speech "The Destiny of the Human Race." Tours New England as a singer and fundraiser with the Atlanta University Quartet during the summer. Appointed principal of Stanton School at a salary of $75 a month.

1895   Visits the largest white grammar school in Jacksonville, which prompts complaints from local parents to the school board. Initiates the expansion of Stanton's curriculum when he offers a summer course for eighth-grade graduates; during his eight-year tenure as principal Stanton will begin to offer high school courses. Founds and edits the *Daily American*, an afternoon daily serving Jacksonville's African-American population, for which he writes editorials on a wide range of subjects.

1896   *Daily American* ceases publication for financial reasons. Johnson serves as secretary for the inaugural Atlanta University Conference on Negro Life. Makes second tour of New England with Atlanta University Quartet. Begins to study law at the office of attorney Thomas Ledwith. Writes drafts of poems "Sleep" and "Prayer at Sunrise."

1897   Rosamond returns to Jacksonville and urges Johnson to join him in composing songs, plays, and operas. The brothers write and produce a libretto for spring graduation exercises at Stanton. In December, Johnson publishes a letter in defense of education for African-Americans in the Florida *Times-Union*.

1898   Introduces Booker T. Washington as a speaker at an event celebrating the 25th anniversary of the Emancipation Proclamation. Becomes the first African-American from Duval Country to be admitted to the Florida bar. Writes poem "The Color Sergeant." Opens a law office in Jacksonville with Douglass Wetmore.

1899   Goes to New York City with Rosamond in the summer to seek a producer for their comic opera *Tolosa, or the Royal Document*, which satirizes American imperialism (it is never produced). Meets theatrical producer Oscar Hammerstein, actor and comedian Bert Williams, and composer Will Marion Cook. The brothers complete the dialect love song "Louisiana Lize," the first of many collaborative efforts with songwriter and performer Bob Cole; it is bought for $50 by May Irwin, a white singer. Johnson returns to Jacksonville in the fall.

1900   Writes lyrics to "Lift Ev'ry Voice and Sing," with music by Rosamond, for a ceremony celebrating Lincoln's birthday. Spends summer in New York City. May Irwin asks the brothers to write songs for the musical *The Belle of Bridgeport*. Johnson publishes a dialect poem, "Sence You Went Away," in *The Century Magazine*.

1901   Elected president of the Florida State Teachers Association, a black teachers' organization. Stanton School burns down in late May in a fire that destroys more than 150 blocks in the city. Jacksonville city council passes an ordinance requiring the segregation of streetcars. Johnson barely escapes lynching in Jacksonville when he is observed meeting a light-skinned woman, who is presumed white by his attackers, in a park. Returns to New York City with Rosamond. Writes, with music by Rosamond, "The Maiden with the Dreamy Eyes," sung in Anna Held's popular Broadway musical *The Little Duchess*. Works with Will Marion Cook on an opera, *The Cannibal King*, which is never completed. Contracts with Joseph W. Stern and Company as exclusive publishers of the Johnson brothers' songs.

1902   Returns to Jacksonville in February to teach in the relocated and much diminished Stanton School. In the summer, goes back to New York City to devote himself to songwriting career, living with Rosamond and Cole at the Hotel Marshall at 127 West 53rd Street. Becomes chief lyricist in the Broadway songwriting team, Cole and Johnson Brothers. "Under the Bamboo Tree" becomes the trio's first hit (400,000 copies sold within a year) when it is inserted into Marie Cahill's musical comedy *Sally in Our Alley*. Meets Grace Nail, daughter of Harlem entrepreneur John Bennett Nail, during a visit to Brooklyn in the summer. Resigns as principal of Stanton School in the fall. Publishes "Should the Negro Be Given an Education Different from That Given to the Whites?" in *Twentieth Century Negro Literature*, a collection of essays by prominent African-Americans edited by D. W. Culp.

1903   "Congo Love Song," sung by Marie Cahill, confirms na-
        tional success of Cole and Johnson Brothers songwriting
        team. Team begins writing *The Evolution of Ragtime*, a
        series of songs portraying the development of African-
        American music (songs are published in *Ladies' Home
        Journal* in 1905). Numerous Broadway musicals feature
        songs by Cole and Johnson Brothers. Begins taking
        courses at Columbia University, where he studies with
        Brander Matthews, professor of Dramatic Literature, who
        becomes a friend.

1904   Cole and Johnson Brothers writes two songs for
        Theodore Roosevelt's presidential campaign. Johnson
        joins Colored Republican Club of New York City, group
        associated with prominent black politician Charles Ander-
        son. Participates in the National Negro Business League,
        founded by Booker T. Washington; Johnson's paper "The
        Composition of Music as a Business" is read at the
        league's national meeting. Receives honorary master's de-
        gree from Atlanta University at spring commencement,
        where he meets W.E.B. Du Bois, whose *Souls of Black
        Folk* he admires.

1905   Submits group of poems to *Ladies' Home Journal* and re-
        ceives rejection letter praising his technical skill but criti-
        cizing the conventional nature of his subject matter.
        Travels in the spring to Denver and San Francisco with
        Cole and Rosamond, who are performing songs in
        vaudeville shows. Meets Jack Johnson, the prizefighter.
        Goes with Cole and Rosamond on a European tour in
        the summer, visiting Paris, Brussels, Antwerp, and Ams-
        terdam before arriving in London, where Cole and Rosa-
        mond have a six-week engagement at the Palace Theatre.
        Becomes president of the Colored Republican Club in
        New York City. Publishes magazine essay "The Negro of
        To-Day in Music" in October, praising the works of
        Samuel Coleridge-Taylor and Harry T. Burleigh, as well
        as those of Scott Joplin and other ragtime artists. Al-
        though sympathetic to its aims, he declines Du Bois's in-
        vitation to join the Niagara Movement, newly formed
        African-American group dedicated to pursuit of political
        and economic rights. Works on novel *The Autobiography
        of an Ex-Colored Man*. Collaborates with Cole and Rosa-
        mond on their last theatrical undertaking, *The Shoo-Fly
        Regiment*. Approached by Charles Anderson as a possible

candidate for the U.S. consular service, an offer he jokingly shrugs off.

1906   Johnson accepts renewed invitation from Anderson, and
        his application for the consular service is submitted to the
        Department of State via Booker T. Washington. Falls ill in
        Washington shortly after taking State Department exami-
        nations. Appointed U.S. consul in Puerto Cabello, the
        second largest port in Venezuela, by President Theodore
        Roosevelt. Receives enthusiastic letter of congratulations
        from Washington. Dissolves songwriting partnership and
        sails for South America, arriving in Puerto Cabello on
        May 28. During his three-year term in Venezuela, Johnson
        studies international law and diplomacy, writes poems (in-
        cluding "Brothers" and "O Black and Unknown Bards"),
        and works on *The Autobiography of an Ex-Colored Man*,
        while also serving as consul for Cuba, Panama, and
        France. Writes long letter to Washington describing racial
        situation in Venezuela, in which he notes the lack of dis-
        crimination while lamenting the loss of a distinct racial
        identity among Venezuelan people of color.

1907   Through Anderson, attempts unsuccessfully to be trans-
        ferred to a more favorable post. Travels on furlough to
        Jacksonville, Washington, D.C., and New York, where he
        spends time with Grace Nail. Returns to Venezuela late in
        the year.

1908   Publishes "O Black and Unknown Bards" in *The Century*.
        Receives word in June of his appointment as U.S. consul
        in Corinto, the chief Pacific port of Nicaragua. Revises
        draft of *The Autobiography of an Ex-Colored Man*.

1909   Travels to Washington in the spring for instruction on his
        new post before taking office in Corinto. Official work-
        load in Nicaragua occupies more of his time than his
        duties in Venezuela. Requests a leave of absence and in
        October travels to New York City, where he becomes en-
        gaged to Grace Nail.

1910   Marries Grace in New York City on February 10. They
        arrive in Nicaragua in the spring during an American-
        supported revolution against the Liberal government,
        though Corinto remains relatively peaceful. Revolution
        ends in August with the exile of President Zelaya. Con-
        tinues to seek a transfer out of Latin America, describing

his discontent in letters to Washington and to Anderson. Formally requests a transfer for health reasons from the State Department late in the year and suggests he be sent to one of several European consular posts.

1911   Bob Cole dies. Johnson requests leave and travels with Grace to the United States in November.

1912   Returns to Corinto without Grace in March. Father dies in Jacksonville. Uprising against the government of Adolfo Diaz begins in July, and American troops are sent to support government forces. When rebels demand to occupy Corinto in August, Johnson draws out negotiations to allow for the arrival of additional U.S. warships and Marines who succeed in keeping the port in government hands. *The Autobiography of an Ex-Colored Man* is published in Boston by Sherman, French and Company, appearing anonymously. (Johnson writes to his friend George Towns that "when the author is known, and known to be the one who could not be the main character of the story, the book will fall flat.") Initial sales are discouraging and the novel receives few reviews; praised by the *Springfield Republican* and by Jessie Fauset in *The Crisis*, the Nashville Tennessean calls it "an insult to Southern womanhood." Johnson learns that the State Department is planning to transfer him to a post in the Azores Islands, pending the approval of the newly elected Democratic administration of Woodrow Wilson. Granted leave to settle his father's estate and returns to New York in December. Sends poem "Father, Father Abraham" to *The Crisis*, which is published with a laudatory biographical note by Du Bois.

1913   "Fifty Years," a 41-stanza celebration in verse of the 50th anniversary of the Emancipation Proclamation, appears on the editorial page of the January 1 *New York Times*. The poem attracts considerable praise from both white and black readers, including Theodore Roosevelt, Booker T. Washington, and Charles Chesnutt, who writes Johnson that the poem is "the finest thing I ever read on the subject." Johnson changes his middle name from William to Weldon ("Jim Bill Johnson will not do for a man who pretends to write poetry or anything else," he writes George Towns). Travels to Jacksonville with Grace in March to manage affairs of his father's estate. Brander

Matthews reviews *The Autobiography of an Ex-Colored Man* favorably in *Munsey's Magazine* but sales remain slow, which Johnson blames on the "ultra-conservative" firm Sherman, French and Co. Johnson sends Matthews a manuscript of his collected poems. Meets in Washington with Wilbur Carr, director of the consular service, and Secretary of State William Jennings Bryan, and leaves convinced he will be sent back to Corinto. Resigns from the consular service in September. Visits New York City in the fall to see Grace's family and to look for employment. Writes screenplays, one of which is filmed as *Aunt Mandy's Chicken Dinner*, but is angered by the film and abandons screenwriting.

1914   Sends manuscript of poems to Boston poet William Stanley Braithwaite, who recommends that he submit it to Cornhill Publishers. Writes short protest poem "To America." Moves to Harlem with Grace in the fall, accepting position as editorial page editor at *The New York Age*, the oldest African-American newspaper in the city. Publishes daily editorials for the *Age* under the heading "Views and Reviews" for the next ten years. Writes lyrics for songs composed by Rosamond, and collaborates on unpublished songs with Lewis Muir and Jerome Kern. Publicly acknowledges his authorship of *The Autobiography of an Ex-Colored Man* to promote sales. Becomes a founding member of the American Society of Composers, Authors, and Publishers (ASCAP). Joins Sigma Pi Phi and Phi Beta Sigma fraternities. Publishes "The White Witch" in *The Crisis*.

1915   In March joins the National Association for the Advancement of Colored People (NAACP), founded in 1910 by Du Bois and others. Translates the libretto of *Goyescas*, an opera by Spanish composer Enrique Granados, which is produced at the Metropolitan Opera House. Supports the U.S. occupation of Haiti. Arranges for the printing of several thousand copies of Matthews' review of *The Autobiography of an Ex-Colored Man*; the publicity helps to sell the remaining copies of the first printing.

1916   Elected vice-president of the New York City chapter of the NAACP in May. Attends in August an NAACP-sponsored conference at the estate of Joel E. Spingarn in Amenia, New York, where he delivers a speech, "A

Working Program for the Future." Writes editorials in support of Republican presidential candidate Charles Evans Hughes in his campaign against Woodrow Wilson. Campaigns for Hughes in Cambridge, Massachusetts, upstate New York, and Harlem. Elected field secretary of the NAACP, at an annual salary of $2,000, by the board of directors in December. Goes to work at NAACP headquarters at 70 Fifth Avenue.

1917   Travels in January from Richmond, Virginia, to Tampa, Florida, on an organizing tour that results in the formation of 13 new NAACP branches. Meets Walter White, secretary of the Atlanta branch of the NAACP. Attends Supreme Court arguments in housing segregation case *Buchanan* v. *Worley* and is denied service in the public restaurant of the U.S. Capitol. Supports U.S. entry into World War I while protesting attempts to exclude black men from the armed forces. Goes to Memphis, Tennessee, to investigate the burning of Ell Persons by a lynch mob. Flanked by Du Bois, leads over 10,000 marchers down Fifth Avenue in New York on July 28 in a silent parade protesting lynchings and the recent rioting by white mobs in East Saint Louis, Illinois. Becomes acting secretary of the NAACP, serving until early 1918. Speaks at a conference of the Intercollegiate Socialist Society in Bellport, New York. With Du Bois, becomes charter member of the Civic Club, an interracial organization of progressive New Yorkers. Publishes *Fifty Years and Other Poems*, with an introduction by Brander Matthews, partly at his own expense in December.

1918   Meets with President Wilson as the leader of an NAACP delegation urging commutation of the death sentences of five black soldiers convicted of shooting policemen during racial disturbances in Houston, Texas. Hires Walter White as assistant secretary of the NAACP. Travels to New England, the Midwest, and the South on organizing tours (during 1918 the number of NAACP branches nearly doubles). Hears a minister give a sermon in a black church in Kansas City that begins with the creation of the world and ends in judgment day and makes notes that become the basis of "The Creation."

1919   Mother dies on January 7. Johnson speaks at an anti-lynching rally at Carnegie Hall. Travels more than 20,000

miles during the year promoting and organizing branches
of the NAACP, including a speaking tour of the Pacific
Coast states. Participates in the founding of the American
Civil Liberties Union. Lobbies U.S. Senate to investigate
recent violence against African-Americans in Washington,
Chicago, and other cities.

1920   Testifies in January before the House Judiciary Commit-
            tee in support of anti-lynching bill introduced by Con-
            gressman L. C. Dyer. Sails to Haiti in March and spends
            nearly two months investigating the American occupation
            since 1915. Advises lawyer Georges Sylvain to form an or-
            ganization similar to the NAACP to work for the restora-
            tion of Haitian sovereignty; his suggestion leads Sylvain
            and others to establish the Patriotic Union. Returns to
            New York in May. Appointed acting secretary of the
            NAACP in June after resignation of John R. Shillady.
            Publishes "Self-Determining Haiti," a four-part article
            condemning the American occupation, in *The Nation*.
            Poem "The Creation," a folk sermon in free verse drafted
            two years earlier, appears in *The Freeman*. Named secre-
            tary of the NAACP by the board of directors in Novem-
            ber, the first African-American to serve in that position.

1921   Opposes Marcus Garvey's "Back to Africa" program in
            New York Age editorials. Engages in extensive lobbying in
            support of the Dyer anti-lynching bill in the House and
            meets with President Warren Harding in an unsuccessful
            attempt to win his endorsement of the legislation.

1922   Dyer bill is passed by the House on January 26. Johnson
            compiles *The Book of American Negro Poetry*, the first
            anthology of African-American verse published by a ma-
            jor American trade press (Harcourt, Brace, and Com-
            pany). Campaigns for senators and representatives who
            support the Dyer bill. Advocates the formation of a new
            "Liberal Party" as a result of frustration with Republican
            inaction on civil rights issues. Lobbies for the Dyer bill
            in the Senate, but it is filibustered by Southern Demo-
            crats and then dropped from the legislative agenda by
            Senate Republicans.

1923–24   Leads successful NAACP effort to ensure black adminis-
            tration of a Tuskegee, Alabama, hospital for African-
            American veterans. Considers writing an expanded ver-
            sion of *The Autobiography of an Ex-Colored Man*; sends

the published book to Carl Van Vechten, who responds enthusiastically. Disappointed by the failure of the Progressive Party to address civil rights issues. Urges Northern black voters to move away from their traditional loyalty to the Republican Party and consider supporting sympathetic Democratic candidates in the 1924 national elections.

1925   Supports El Paso branch of the NAACP in legal challenge to Texas law excluding African-Americans from voting in the Democratic primary (law is declared unconstitutional by the U.S. Supreme Court in 1927). Awarded Spingarn Medal by the NAACP for his achievements as an "author, diplomat, and public servant." Edits, and writes lengthy preface for, *The Book of American Negro Spirituals*, which collects 61 spirituals arranged for piano by Rosamond. Awards Langston Hughes the poetry prize for "The Weary Blues" in a contest sponsored by Opportunity, the publication of the National Urban League. Contributes essay "Harlem: The Culture Capital" and poem "The Creation" to Alain Locke's landmark literary miscellany, *The New Negro*. Helps organize and raises funds for NAACP legal defense, headed by Clarence Darrow, of Dr. Ossian Sweet, his brother Henry, and nine other men charged with first-degree murder after the shooting death of a white man during a mob attack on Dr. Sweet's home in Detroit. Trial in December ends in a hung jury. (Henry Sweet is tried separately and acquitted in 1926; the charges against the other men are eventually dismissed.)

1926   Testifies before the Senate Judiciary Committee in support of a new anti-lynching bill (the committee refuses to report it to the floor). Edits and writes preface for *The Second Book of American Negro Spirituals*. Purchases a farm near Great Barrington, Massachusetts, and converts the barn into a summer cottage, Five Acres. Finishes poems "Go Down, Death" and "Listen, Lord" late in the year.

1927   Arranges with Alfred Knopf to reprint *The Autobiography of an Ex-Coloured Man* with an introduction by Carl Van Vechten (the spelling of "coloured" is Anglicized to appeal to British readers). Viking Press publishes *God's Trombones: Seven Negro Sermons in Verse*, with illustrations by Aaron Douglas. Johnson holds a week of seminars on social and artistic aspects of African-American life at the University of North Carolina in Chapel Hill. Begins writing satirical poem *Saint Peter Relates an Incident of the Judgment Day.*

1928   Receives Gold Award and $400 prize from the Harmon Foundation for *God's Trombones.* Receives honorary doctor of literature degrees from Howard University and Talledega College. Elected to the Board of Trustees of Atlanta University. Refuses offer from Republican county committee of nomination to run for Congress from the district containing Harlem.

1929   Receives Julius Rosenwald Fellowship in the summer. Takes a leave of absence from the NAACP for the remainder of 1929 and 1930 to devote himself to writing. Attends the third biennial conference of the Institute of Pacific Relations in Kyoto, Japan.

1930   Publishes *Black Manhattan*, a history of African-Americans in New York, with Alfred Knopf, and *Saint Peter Relates an Incident of the Judgment Day* in a small private edition. Resigns as secretary of the NAACP on December 17.

1931   Accepts appointment as the Adam K. Spence Chair of Creative Literature and Writing at Fisk University. Becomes vice-president and a member of the board of directors of the NAACP. Publishes a revised and enlarged edition of *The Book of American Negro Poetry.* NAACP honors him with a testimonial dinner in New York City attended by more than 300 guests.

1932   Begins teaching at Fisk in January with an annual base salary of $5,000; his courses include American literature after the Civil War and African-American writers. Shortly after Johnson arrives at Fisk, Vanderbilt professor Thomas Mabry invites him and Langston Hughes to a party that poet Allen Tate refuses to attend. ("There should be no social intercourse between the races," Tate writes Mabry, "unless we are willing for that to lead to marriage.") Johnson writes pamphlet *The Shining Life: An Appreciation of Julius Rosenwald.*

1933   Publishes autobiography *Along This Way* with Alfred Knopf. Critical response is enthusiastic. Profile "Dark Leader: James Weldon Johnson" is published in *The New Yorker.* Attends the Second NAACP Amenia Conference.

1934   Undergoes surgery in June for a tonsillar abcess. Appointed as visiting professor of literature for the fall semester at the New York University School of Education, becoming the first African-American to hold a position there (will return to NYU in the fall for the next three years to lecture). Publishes a defense of the NAACP program of integration, *Negro Americans, What Now?*, with Viking Press, in the fall. Lectures at other colleges and universities, including Oberlin, Swarthmore, Yale, the University of North Carolina, Northwestern, and the University of Chicago, over the next three years.

1935   Publishes *Saint Peter Relates an Incident: Selected Poems* in a trade edition.

1936   Declines to be considered to succeed John Hope as president of Atlanta University. Writes a pamphlet celebrating Hope's life and work.

1937   Publishes three essays in the collection *Our Racial and Cultural Minorities.*

1938   Celebrates birthday in Harlem on June 17, then goes to Maine with Grace to visit friends. On June 26 their car is struck during a thunderstorm by a train at an unguarded crossing near Wiscasset, Maine. Grace is severely injured and Johnson dies shortly after being freed from the car. After a funeral held on June 30 at the Salem Methodist Church in Harlem, his ashes are interred in the Nail family plot in Greenwood Cemetery, Brooklyn, New York.

Note on the Texts

This volume contains James Weldon Johnson's novel *The Autobiography of an Ex-Colored Man* (1912); his autobiography *Along This Way* (1933); 22 editorials written for *The New York Age* between 1914 and 1923; seven essays published between 1919 and 1928; three chapters from the history *Black Manhattan* (1930); and a selection of 25 poems.

Johnson began writing his only novel, *The Autobiography of an Ex-Colored Man*, while living in New York City just after 1900. By 1906, he had given a draft of two chapters to his friend Brander Matthews, a Columbia University professor with whom he had studied. Johnson continued to work on the novel during his two diplomatic appointments in Latin America, the first in Puerto Cabello, Venezuela (1906–1909), the second in Corinto, Nicaragua (1909–1912). *The Autobiography of an Ex-Colored Man* was published in Boston by Sherman, French and Company in the spring of 1912. It appeared anonymously because Johnson worried that it "would fall flat," as he wrote to his friend George Towns, if its author "was known to be the one who could not be the main character of the story." Johnson later acknowledged in an unpublished note to the manuscript of *Along This Way* that the protagonist was initially inspired by his boyhood friend and former legal partner J. Douglass Wetmore, although events in the final version of the book have little to do with Wetmore's life. Johnson declared his authorship of *The Autobiography of an Ex-Colored Man* two years after its publication.

In the early 1920s, Johnson considered revising the novel or writing a sequel, and he sent copies of the published book to Carl Van Vechten, Heywood Broun, and other writers. Although he ultimately decided not to expand or to heavily revise the novel, a new edition, entitled *The Autobiography of an Ex-Coloured Man*, was published by Alfred A. Knopf in 1927, with an introduction by Van Vechten. The changes made for the Knopf edition, although numerous, are largely alterations of spelling—Anglicized spellings such as "coloured," "grey," and "favourite," are used throughout—and punctuation, which for the most part is brought in line with predominant usage in 1927. (To cite one example, the comma followed by an em dash, which appears frequently in the 1912 text, is changed to an em dash throughout the Knopf edition.) Titles, which had appeared in quotation marks in the Sherman, French edition, are italicized; quotations are usually preceded by a colon in the Knopf edition, rather than the comma used in the earlier version. The word "around" was changed to read "round" throughout the Knopf edition. Word order in a sentence is occasionally rearranged. There were more substantive changes made for the Knopf edition as well, though such instances were few. At 90.2, "deeper feelings of sorrow" in the 1912 edition is changed to "deeper feelings." At 100.29–31, the sentence in the 1912 edition, "This spirit carries them so far at times as to make them sympathizers with members of their own race who are perpetrators of crime," is replaced in the Knopf edition by "This they generally do whenever white people are concerned." After "committed" at 112.7, the exclamations "murder! rape!" are omitted in the Knopf edition. At 121.20–22 the sentence, "There is nothing better in all the world that a man can do for his moral welfare than to love a good woman," does not appear in the Knopf edition. The present volume prints the text of the 1912 Sherman, French and Company edition of *The Autobiography of an Ex-Colored Man*.

Johnson's autobiography, *Along This Way*, was written in the early 1930s and published by the Viking Press in 1933. Johnson did not subsequently revise the book, and the Viking Press edition was the only one to appear in his lifetime. The text of the 1933 Viking Press edition of *Along This Way* is printed here. Copyright © 1933 by James Weldon Johnson; published by arrangement with Viking Penguin, a division of Penguin Putnam Inc.

In the fall of 1914, Johnson accepted a position managing the editorial page of *The New York Age*. Over the next ten years, he wrote editorials for the paper under the title "Views and Reviews." The present volume prints 22 of these editorials, which were not collected or revised by Johnson. The texts printed here are taken from the *Age*, and their publication dates are as follows.

Do You Read Negro Papers? October 22, 1914.
President Wilson's "New Freedom" and the Negro.
   November 19, 1914.
22 Calibre Statesmen. February 22, 1915.
Uncle Tom's Cabin and The Clansman. March 14, 1915.
The Passing of Jack Johnson. April 8, 1915.
A Trap. May 6, 1915.
"The Poor White Musician." September 23, 1915.
Stranger Than Fiction. December 23, 1915.
Saluting the Flag. April 4, 1916.
Responsibilities and Opportunities of the Colored Ministry.
   February 8, 1917.
Under the Dome of the Capitol. May 3, 1917.
The Silent Parade. July 26, 1917.

An Army with Banners. August 3, 1917
Experienced Men Wanted. November 8, 1917.
"Why Should a Negro Fight?" June 29, 1918.
"Negro" with a Big "N." August 17, 1918.
Protesting Women and the War. September 21, 1918.
The Japanese Question in California. July 12, 1919.
The "Jim Crow" Car in Congress. September 13, 1919.
A Real Poet. May 20, 1922.
Marcus Garvey's Inferiority Complex. September 2, 1922.
The New Exodus. March 3, 1923. Copyright © 1923 by James Wel-
    don Johnson. Reprinted by permission of the Literary Estate of
    James Weldon Johnson, Dr. Sondra Kathryn Wilson, Executor.

Of Johnson's many published articles and prefaces, seven essays
written between 1919 and 1928 are collected in this volume. He did
not revise these essays after they appeared in print, and for each the
text printed here is that of its first publication, as listed below:
The Riots. *The Crisis* 18 (1919).
Self-Determining Haiti. *The Nation* 111 (1920).
Preface to *The Book of American Negro Poetry*. *The Book of American
    Negro Poetry* (New York: Harcourt, Brace, and Company, 1922).
Lynching—America's National Disgrace. *Current History* 19 (1924).
    Copyright © 1924 by James Weldon Johnson. Reprinted by per-
    mission of the Literary Estate of James Weldon Johnson, Dr. Son-
    dra Kathryn Wilson, Executor.
Preface to *The Second Book of Negro Spirituals*. *The Second Book of
    Negro Spirituals* (New York: The Viking Press, 1926). Copyright ©
    1926 by James Weldon Johnson. Reprinted by permission of the
    Literary Estate of James Weldon Johnson, Dr. Sondra Kathryn
    Wilson, Executor.
The Dilemma of the Negro Author. *American Mercury* 15 (1928).
    Copyright © 1928 by James Weldon Johnson. Reprinted by per-
    mission of the Literary Estate of James Weldon Johnson, Dr. Son-
    dra Kathryn Wilson, Executor.
Race Prejudice and the Negro Artist. *Harper's Magazine* 157 (1928).
    Copyright © 1928 by James Weldon Johnson. Reprinted by per-
    mission of the Literary Estate of James Weldon Johnson, Dr. Son-
    dra Kathryn Wilson, Executor.

Shortly after receiving a Julius Rosenwald Fellowship in 1929,
which he used to dedicate himself to his writing while on a leave of
absence from the NAACP, Johnson wrote *Black Manhattan*, a history
of African-Americans in New York from 1626 to the twentieth century. In *Along This Way* Johnson wrote: "One of my prime purposes

in writing the story was to set down a continuous record of the Negro's progress on the New York theatrical stage, from the attempted classical performances of the African Company, at the corner of Bleecker and Mercer Streets in 1821, down to *The Green Pastures* in 1930. I considered that this record alone, done for the first time, was sufficient warrant for the book." *Black Manhattan* was published by Alfred A. Knopf in 1930 and was not subsequently revised by Johnson. The Knopf edition was the only one to appear during Johnson's lifetime, and it provides the text of the three chapters (15 through 17) from *Black Manhattan* printed here. These chapters are copyright © 1930 by James Weldon Johnson. Reprinted by permission of the Literary Estate of James Weldon Johnson, Dr. Sondra Kathryn Wilson, Executor.

Johnson published three collections of poetry: *Fifty Years and Other Poems* (1917), *God's Trombones* (1927), and *Saint Peter Relates an Incident* (1935). For all but one of the poems printed in this volume ("Under the Bamboo Tree"), the text of each poem is taken from its first book publication in one of Johnson's collections. The text of "Under the Bamboo Tree," a song whose lyrics were not collected by Johnson, has been transcribed from its first sheet-music publication, brought out by Joseph A. Stern in 1902. The poems from *Fifty Years and Other Poems* printed here are taken from the first edition, published by The Cornhill Company in Boston in 1917; except for "Nobody's Lookin' but de Owl an' de Moon" and "'Possum Song," these poems later appeared, sometimes in revised form, in *Saint Peter Relates an Incident*. *God's Trombones: Seven Negro Sermons in Verse*, a sequence of poems conceived as an integral work, was written in the mid-1920s and published by the Viking Press in 1927; the text of this edition is printed here. (Copyright © 1927 by James Weldon Johnson; published by arrangement with Viking Penguin, a division of Penguin Putnam Inc.) The four poems first collected in Johnson's selected-poems volume *Saint Peter Relates an Incident* are taken from the first edition of the book, published in 1935 by the Viking Press. The poems "My City," "Nobody's Lookin' but de Owl an' de Moon," "'Possum Song," "Under the Bamboo Tree," "Brer Rabbit, You's de Cutes' of 'Em All," "Saint Peter Relates an Incident of the Resurrection Day," and "If I Were Paris" are copyright © 1935 by James Weldon Johnson. Reprinted by permission of the Literary Estate of James Weldon Johnson, Dr. Sondra Kathryn Wilson, Executor.

This volume presents the texts of the original printings chosen for inclusion here, but it does not attempt to reproduce nontextual features of their typographic design. The texts are presented without change, except for the correction of typographical errors. Spelling, punctuation, and capitalization are often expressive features and are not altered, even when inconsistent or irregular. The following is a list of typographical errors corrected, cited by page and line number: 17.25, which is; 26.13, man; 26.15, to unpack; 27.35, waiting; 29.11, 17, Toussaint; 52.12, hale; 65.1, ambitions; 78.21, superogatory; 79.10, tailors; 97.25, all is; 108.26, Two; 246.10, in school; 500.17, committee; 517.10, them,; 519.31, sum in; 617.1–2, critism; 618.34, belittleing; 621.36, in; 622.19, an; 624.35, neough; 625.1, in beginning; 625.25, There; 631.9, *Experienced*; 638.14, "negro" . . . "white"; 644.24, in.; 646.18, lon gas; 647.21, terrrible; 648.27, belie fthat; 649.3, o fthe; 651.14, fo rthousands; 652.4, Northand; 677.17, been member; 695.22, Pharoah; 728.19, Gainsville; 772.16, 1917; 773.12, Sturat.

Notes

In the notes below, the reference numbers denote page and line of this volume (the line count includes headings). No note is made for material included in standard desk-reference books. Biblical references are keyed to the King James version. For further biographical background, references to other studies, and more detailed notes, see Eugene Levy, *James Weldon Johnson: Black Leader, Black Voice* (University of Chicago Press, 1973) and Sondra K. Wilson, editor, *The Selected Writings of James Weldon Johnson* (Oxford University Press, 1995, two volumes).

THE AUTOBIOGRAPHY OF AN EX-COLORED MAN

17.31   wars and rumors of wars]   Cf. Matthew 24:6.

18.4   "Peter Parley's History of the United States,]"   *The Tales of Peter Parley About America* (1827), first of a long series of children's educational books written pseudonymously by Samuel Griswold Goodrich.

18.5   "Tales of a Grandfather,"]   Walter Scott's *Tales of a Grandfather: Being Stories Taken from Scottish History* (1828).

25.10   "where the brook and river meet,"]   Cf. Henry Wadsworth Longfellow, "Maidenhood": "Standing with reluctant feet / Where the brook and river meet, / Womanhood and childhood fleet!"

45.12   Maceo and Bandera]   Antonio Maceo y Grajales (1845–96), military commander of revolutionary forces in Cuban wars of independence of 1868 and 1895; Quintín Bandera (1834–1906), general in Maceo's Mambi Army.

54.20–21   Jubilee songs . . . the Fisk singers]   The Jubilee Singers gained fame performing spirituals in concert tours in the United States and Europe. The group was organized in 1867 by George L. White, treasurer of Fisk University.

64.25   Peter Jackson]   West Indian–born boxer (1861–1901) known as the "Black Prince."

67.8   Du Maurier's conception]   In *Trilby* (1894), George Du Maurier's novel about an artist's model who becomes a great singer under the hypnotic sway of the musician Svengali.

95.22   "Jubilee Singers,"]   See note 54.20–21.

107.36 St. Paul's "It is hard to kick against the pricks."] Cf. Acts 26:14.

121.40 Eden Musée] Wax museum and variety theater formerly at 55 West 23rd St.

123.3 13th Nocturne] Chopin's Nocturne No. 13 in C minor (1837).

127.2 R. C. Ogden] Robert Curtis Ogden (1836–1913), merchant whose "Ogden movement" initiated education reform across the South; he served as president of the Hampton Institute board of trustees and as a trustee of the Tuskegee Institute.

127.2–3 Ex-Ambassador Choate] Joseph Hodges Choate (1832–1917), lawyer and diplomat who served as American ambassador to Great Britain from 1899 to 1905.

ALONG THIS WAY

144.15–16 *Tales of a Grandfather*] See note 18.5.

144.16–18 Samuel Lover . . . Handy Andy] *Handy Andy: A Tale of Irish Life* (1842), novel by Samuel Lover.

147.3 *Vashti—Or Until Death Do Us Part*] Novel (1869) by the popular Alabama author Augusta Evans Wilson (1835–1909).

184.7–8 Mr. Will Alexander of Atlanta] Will Winton Alexander (1884–1956), Methodist minister who helped found the Commission on Interracial Cooperation, which sought to improve race relations without directly attacking segregation.

188.5–6 T. Thomas Fortune] Journalist and civil rights leader (1856–1928), publisher of *The New York Age*.

191.11 Blind Tom] Thomas Greene Bethune (1849–1908), pianist and composer born in slavery in Columbus, Georgia. Bethune was a child prodigy and amazed audience with his musical and verbal recall and his ability to mimic natural and instrumental sounds; he could perform more than 700 pieces from memory. His white managers encouraged him to create an impression of idiocy in his public performances.

191.11 The Black Swan] Elizabeth Taylor Greenfield (1817?–76), popular African-American singer who performed in the United States and Britain in the 1850s; she was famous for her rich, resonant voice and her 27-note range.

236.1 Brander Matthews] American critic (1852–1929) and professor of English at Columbia.

236.34–35 *Roman Missal*] Liturgical book containing the prayers and readings for the Roman Catholic mass.

256.3–6 Hark! From the tomb . . . shortly lie.] Cf. Isaac Watts, Hymn 63 in *Hymns and Spiritual Songs* (1707).

276.16   Joseph Twitchell of Hartford] Congregational clergyman (1838–1918).

294.38   *The Geisha* and *The Runaway Girl*] *The Geisha* (1896), English operetta with music by Sidney Jones, libretto by Owen Hall, and lyrics by Harry Greenbank; *The Runaway Girl* (1898), operetta with music by Lionel Monckton and Ivan Caryll.

297.12   Harry B. Smith and Reginald DeKoven] Smith (1860–1936) wrote by his own account some 300 librettos, including *The Fortune Teller* (1898) and *The Girl from Utah* (1914); he collaborated on several works with De Koven (1859–1920), of which the most successful was *Robin Hood* (1891).

297.28   Oscar Hammerstein] Theatrical manager (1847–1919) whose productions included *Naughty Marietta* (1910).

298.1   *The Sultan of Zulu*] *The Sultan of Sulu* (1902), musical with book and lyrics by George Ade and music by Alfred G. Wathall.

298.9–11   Williams and Walker . . . Harry T. Burleigh] Bert Williams (1876?–1922) and George Walker (d. 1911), comedy team whose vehicles included *The Gold Bug* (1896), *In Dahomey* (1903), and *Abyssinia* (1906); Hogan (1860?–1909), stage performer and composer who starred in William Marion Cook and Paul Laurence Dunbar's musical *The Origin of the Cake; or, Clarindy* (1898); Cook (1869–1944), composer of shows including *In Dahomey*; Burleigh (1866–1949), singer and composer who became known for his arrangements of spirituals.

300.5   May Irwin] Popular actress (1862–1938) who achieved stardom in *The Widow Jones* (1895).

300.40   Amato] Pasquale Amato (1878–1942), Italian baritone who appeared in the original production of Puccini's *La Fanciulla del West* (1910).

322.1   Kurt Schindler] German-born composer, organist, and conductor (1882–1935).

327.4   *The Black Crook*] Musical melodrama (1866), the longest-running Broadway production up to that point.

334.21   Thais] Alexandrian courtesan who is the title character of Anatole France's 1890 novel.

336.32   *Still wie die Nacht*] Musical setting by Carl Bohm (1844–1920) of an anonymous German poem.

336.34–35 Dr. Johnson . . . hind legs.] Cf. Johnson's remark, quoted by Boswell in *The Life of Johnson*, volume 2, chapter 9: "Sir, a woman preaching is like a dog's walking on his hind legs. It is not done well; but you are surprised to find it done at all."

341.1   Weber and Fields] Joseph Weber (1867–1942) and Lew Fields (1867–1941) began performing as a comedy team in the 1870s and remained immensely popular until the team broke up in 1904; their shows include *Hurly Burly* (1898), *Hoity Toity* (1901), and *Twirly Whirly* (1902).

342.30   Harry Thurston Peck] Peck (1856–1914), a distinguished philologist and literary critic, edited *The Bookman* (1902–7) and taught at Columbia for 26 years. The revelation in 1910 of his involvement with a stenographer who sued him for breach of promise led to public ridicule, the collapse of his marriage, and his dismissal from Columbia.

343.33–34   "Train up a child . . . depart from it,"] Proverbs 22:6.

349.29–30   A silence . . . recorded in Rev. viii, 1,] "And when he had opened the seventh seal, there was silence in heaven about the space of half an hour."

352.7–8   *The Green Pastures*] Play (1930), by Marc Connelly, based on stories by Roark Bradford, in which Bible stories are retold in the style of a black southern preacher.

353.15   *Shuffle Along*] Musical comedy (1921) with lyrics by Noble Sissle and music by Eubie Blake; it featured the hit song "I'm Just Wild About Harry."

361.2   Peter Jackson] See note 64.25.

361.36   *Académie Julien*] The Académie Julian, institution founded in 1868 as a preparatory school for the Ecole des Beaux-Arts, and whose students included Bonnard, Vuillard, and Denis; many American artists studied there.

368.10   Marie Dressler] Comic actress (1869–1934) whose shows included *Higgledy Piggledy* (1904), *Twiddle Twaddle* (1906), and *Roly Poly* (1912).

373.38–39   Alton B. Parker's famous telegram] Upon receiving the Democratic presidential nomination in 1904, Parker sent a telegram to delegate William F. Sheehan declaring his view that the gold standard was "firmly and irrevocably established," and suggesting that his nomination be revoked if this position was unacceptable to the party.

380.14   Arthur A. Schomburg] Book collector (1874–1938) who served as curator of the Divison of Negro Literature, History, and Prints at the New York Public Library (1932–38). A portion of his personal collection is now housed in the Schomburg Center for Research in Black Culture.

426.38   Groce and Cannon] Leonard Groce of Texas and Lee Roy Cannon of Virginia, mercenaries fighting with Nicaraguan revolutionary forces, were executed on November 16, 1909.

432.22–23   "General" Lee Christmas] American railroad engineer (1863–1924) who had a long career as a mercenary in Central America; in Honduras he helped restore the ousted General Manuel Bonilla to power.

458.37 General Fitzhugh Lee] Former Confederate general (1886–90), a nephew of Robert E. Lee; he served as a general of U.S. volunteers during the Spanish-American War.

464.3 Secretary Burleson] Albert Sidney Burleson (1863–1937), postmaster general under Woodrow Wilson.

467.16 *Goyescas*] Opera by Enrique Granados y Campiña, first performed in New York in 1916.

472.9 Inez Milholland] Political activist (1886–1916) who campaigned for woman suffrage and civil rights and against American involvement in World War I.

472.14 Oswald Garrison Villard] Publisher (1872–1949) of the New York *Evening Post* and subsequently publisher and editor of *The Nation*.

499.22 *Danny Deever*] Poem by Rudyard Kipling, originally published in *Ballads and Barrack-Room Ballads* (1892).

508.21 Elbert Hubbard] American printer and prolific author (1859–1915) of inspirational essays such as "A Message to Garcia" (1899).

508.32 Madame Schumann-Heink] Ernestine Schumann-Heink (1861–1936), Czech-born contralto; she made her American debut in 1898, and had a repertory of 150 roles.

531.36 Herbert Parsons] New York congressman (1869–1925) and delegate to the Republican National Convention, 1908–20.

532.22–23 Ford mission . . . Fuller mission] See 661.7–29 in this volume.

533.26 Secretary Daniels] Josephus Daniels (1862–1948), Secretary of the Navy, 1913–21.

551.20 Major Moton] Robert R. Moton (1867–1940), educator who administered the Hampton Institute, then succeeded Booker T. Washington in 1915 as principal of the Tuskegee Institute. His title of "major" derived from his command of the student cadet corps at Hampton.

552.14 Plácido] Cuban poet (1809–44), born Gabriel de la Concepcíon Valdés, and known for poems of political protest; he was executed after being tried for involvement in a revolutionary plot.

552.24 Sir Harry H. Johnston] English colonial administrator, explorer, and artist (1858–1927) who served as commissioner and consul general for British Central Africa (now Malawi).

552.27 George S. Schuyler] Novelist and journalist (1895–1977); he was a columnist for *The Pittsburgh Courier* from 1924 to 1964, and his satirical novel *Black No More* was published in 1931.

553.12 Anne Spencer] Poet (1882–1975) whose work was published in *The Crisis* and in James Weldon Johnson's *Book of American Negro Poetry* (1922), but not collected in her lifetime; she established a Virginia branch of the NAACP in 1919 with Johnson's assistance.

553.36–37   Countee Cullen . . . Rudolph Fisher] Cullen's *Color* (1925) and Hughes' *The Weary Blues* (1926); Nella Larsen (who later married Dr. Elmer S. Imes) published *Quicksand* (1928) and *Passing* (1929); Rudolph Fisher's novels are *The Walls of Jericho* (1928) and *The Conjure Man Dies* (1932).

557.25   Fania Marinoff] Silent movie star, wife of Carl Van Vechten.

557.31–32   Newman Levy's *Opera Guyed*] A collection of light verse burlesquing the plots of well-known operas.

558.3–4   "Almost thou persuadest me to be a Christian."] Acts 26:28.

564.8   Roger N. Baldwin] Baldwin (1884–1981) was the founder and director of the American Civil Liberties Union.

564.32   Arthur Garfield Hays] Hays (1881–1954), counsel for the American Civil Liberties Union.

565.3–4   John Haynes Holmes, John Nevin Sayre] Holmes (1879–1964), Unitarian minister active in the founding of the NAACP; Sayre (1884–1977), a proponent of pacifism active in the ACLU.

576.5–6   nationality of the architect.] The Imperial was designed by Frank Lloyd Wright.

580.38   our Exclusion Act] The Immigration Act of 1924 entirely prohibited Japanese and Chinese immigrants from entering the U.S.

582.5   Wallace Irwin] Author of *Letters of a Japanese Schoolboy* (1909), which was followed by a sequel in 1923.

582.40   Roland Hayes] Hayes (1887–1977), a member of the Fisk Jubilee Singers, toured Europe in the early 1920s and became internationally known as a singer of spirituals and classical works.

587.22   Viscount Eiichi Shibusawa, the "Grand Old Man"] Banker and entrepreneur (1840–1931), instrumental in guiding Japan toward a modern economy.

590.25   Richard B. Harrison] Actor (1864–1935) and teacher of elocution; he gave nearly 2,000 performances as God ("De Lawd") in *The Green Pastures*.

EDITORIALS FROM *THE NEW YORK AGE*

608.4–5   famous report of old Commodore Vanderbilt] In October 1882, responding to a reporter's query about public opinion, Vanderbilt remarked: "The public be damned."

609.13   Mr. Trotter] William Monroe Trotter (1872–1934), editor and civil rights leader; he was the founder of *The Guardian* and active in the formation of the Niagara Movement (1905–7). He founded the National Equal Rights League in 1908.

609.35   "The New Freedom,"] Program of reforms promoted by Woodrow Wilson, emphasizing the lowering of tariffs, federal regulation of unfair business practices, and the creation of the Federal Reserve System.

613.30   Prof. Joel E. Spingarn] Spingarn (1875–1939), literary critic and publisher, was active in the NAACP and began awarding the Spingarn Medal in 1914.

614.22–25   a great fight] Jack Johnson, heavyweight champion of the world from 1908 to 1915, was defeated in Havana by Jess Willard on April 5, 1915.

621.8   "Diary" of Marie Bashkirtseff] Bashkirtseff (1858–84), a Ukrainian-born painter, kept a voluminous diary from the age of 13.

622.4–5   Mrs. Frank Leslie] Mrs. Leslie left the bulk of her estate to support the cause of woman suffrage. The will was challenged by a number of claimants including the grandchildren of Frank Leslie's disinherited sons from a previous marriage, who accused Mrs. Leslie of being the daughter of a black slave woman. Most of the money from the estate was lost to legal expenses and out-of-court settlements.

639.29   Miss Alice Paul] Social reformer (1885–1977), founder of the National Women's Party.

648.7–8   William Pickens . . . Universal Negro Improvement Association] Pickens, field secretary of the NAACP, was prominently involved in a public campaign urging the disbanding of the UNIA and the prosecution of Marcus Garvey for mail fraud.

SELECTED ESSAYS

669.10   "caco" forces] Peasants from the northern hills who fought for various political leaders and against the American occupation.

683.17   Fernand Hibbert] Novelist and dramatist (1873–1928) whose books included *Sena* (1905) and *Les Thazan* (1907).

683.19   Georges Sylvaine] Georges Sylvain (1866–1925) published *Cric? Crac!*, an adaptation of La Fontaine's fables into Creole, in 1901. He later founded the newspaper *La Patrie* and led intellectual resistance to the American occupation.

683.26   Oswald Durand] Poet (1840–1906) best known for *Choucoune* (1883), a pioneering long poem in Creole.

687.19   *Fiat justitia, ruat coelum!*] "Let justice be done, though heaven fall."

689.35   Mr. Vernon Castle]   Dancer (1887–1918) who performed widely
with his wife, Irene, and was known as the originator of the Castle walk,
turkey trot, and other popular dances.

691.1   like Topsy, "jes' grew."]   In chapter 20 of Harriet Beecher Stowe's
Uncle Tom's Cabin, the slave girl Topsy, when asked "Do you know who
made you?" replies: "I spect I grow'd. Don't think nobody never made me."

696.21   Col. Thomas Wentworth Higginson]   See Higginson's *Army
Life in a Black Regiment* (1870), chapter 9.

696.29–30   Mr. H. E. Krehbiel . . . Mrs. Natalie Curtis Burlin]   Henry
Edward Krehbiel (1854–1923), musicologist whose many books included
Afro-American Folksongs (1913); Burlin (1875–1921), ethnomusicologist who
followed up her early studies of American Indian music and culture with
Hampton Series Negro Folk-Songs, published in four volumes (1918–19).

696.35   Dett]   Robert Nathaniel Dett (1882–1943), composer, conductor,
and musical director the Hampton Institute.

710.22   Manzano]   Juan Francisco Manzano (1797–1854), whose poems
were published in English translation as *Poems by a Slave in the Island of
Cuba* (1840).

710.22   Machado de Assis]   Joaquim Maria Machado de Assis (1839–
1908), Brazilian novelist whose works include *Epitaph for a Small Winner*
(1880);

714.30   Willian Stanley Braithwaite]   Poet (1878–1962) best known for his
many anthologies of verse.

715.14   Benjamin Brawley]   English professor (1882–1939) at Harvard and
Morehouse College; author of the critical study *The Negro in Art and Literature in the United States* (1918).

716.6   Fenton Johnson]   Poet (1888–1958) whose first collection appeared
in 1913; he was also active as a magazine publisher and essayist.

716.8   Jessie Fauset]   Jessie Redmon Fauset (1885–1961), novelist whose
books include *Plum Bun and The Chinaberry Tree*.

716.10–11   Georgia Douglas Johnson]   Poet (1886–1966) whose first collection, *The Heart of a Woman*, appeared in 1918; her home was known as a
literary salon.

716.25   Anne Spencer]   See note 553.12.

716.34   John W. Holloway]   John Wesley Holloway (b. 1865) published
the poetry collection *From the Desert* in 1919.

716.38   James Edwin Campbell]   Poet (1867–96) whose collection in Gul-
lah dialect, *Echoes from the Cabin and Elsewhere*, appeared in 1895.

717.24   Daniel Webster Davis] Davis (1862–1913), teacher and Baptist minister whose collection *Weh Down Souf and Other Poems* appeared in 1897.

717.32–33   R. C. Jamison and Joseph S. Cotter, Jr.] Roscoe Conkling Jamison (1888–1918), poet whose work was collected in *Negro Soldiers and Other Poems* (1918); Cotter (1895–1919), poet whose work was collected in *The Band of Gideon and Other Lyrics* (1918).

720.30–31   Nat Turner rebellion] On August 22–24, 1831, insurgent slaves led by Nat Turner killed approximately 60 white men, women, and children in Southampton County, Virginia. More than 100 African-Americans were indiscriminately killed during the suppression of the revolt, and Turner and 20 others were hanged.

724.36   Dr. A. A. Brill] Psychoanalyst (1874–1948) and authorized translator of the writings of Freud.

725.22   Leo Frank] Frank (b. 1884), supervisor at the National Pencil Factory in Atlanta, Georgia, was tried and convicted in 1913 of the murder of Mary Phagan, a 13-year-old worker at the factory; after the governor of Georgia commuted his death sentence to life imprisonment, Frank was abducted from prison in August 1915 and lynched in Marietta, Georgia. Subsequent evidence indicated that the murder was committed by a factory worker who had testified against Frank at the trial; Frank was posthumously pardoned in 1986.

736.13–14   Abbe Niles] Wall Street lawyer who was an early jazz critic; he was closely associated with W. C. Handy, and wrote the foreword to Handy's *Blues: An Anthology* (1926).

736.36   like Topsy] See note 691.1.

756.35–757.9   I am tired of work . . . I am tired of civilization.] From Johnson's poem "Tired," which was published in the poetry annual *Others for 1919.*

757.12–24   Brother; come! . . . what shall you say?] Complete text of "And What Shall You Say?" from Joseph Seamon Cotter, Jr., *The Band of Gideon and Other Lyrics* (1918).

759.29–30   three plays . . . by Ridgley Torrence] *The Rider of Dreams, Granny Maumee,* and *Simon the Cyrenian*; see pp. 772–75 in this volume.

762.9   Eric Walrond] Writer and journalist (1898–1966), born in British Guyana, whose stories were collected in *Tropic Death* (1926).

FROM BLACK MANHATTAN

775.26–27   Volstead Act] Law passed in 1919 providing enforcement for the Eighteenth Amendment, which outlawed the production, distribution, and consumption of alcoholic beverages.

794.17   Antonio Salemme] Italian-born painter and sculptor (1892–1995)
who moved with his family to the U.S. in 1904.

SELECTED POEMS

816.10   Lovejoy] Elijah Lovejoy (1802–37), a newspaper editor of aboli-
tionist views, was killed while defending his printing press from an armed
mob in Alton, Illinois.

823.16   Antæan strength] In Greek mythology, the giant Antaeus, son of
Gaea (Earth), gained strength when thrown on the ground because of the renewed contact with his mother.

Library of Congress Cataloging-in-Publication Data

Johnson, James Weldon, 1871–1938.
  [Selections. 2004]
  Writings / James Weldon Johnson.
     p. cm. — (The Library of America; 145)
  Contents; The autobiography of an ex-colored man—Along
this way—New York Age editorials—Selected essays—
Black Manhattan—Selected poems.
ISBN 1–931082–52–9 (alk. paper)
  1. African Americans—Literary collections. 2. African
Americans. I. Library of America (Firm) II. Title: Autobiography
of an ex-colored man. III. Title: Along this way. IV. Title: New
York Age editorials. V. Title: Black Manhattan. VI. Title. VII.
Series

PS3519.O2625A6   2004
818'.52—dc21   2003044227

THE LIBRARY OF AMERICA SERIES

The Library of America fosters appreciation and pride in America's literary heritage by publishing, and keeping permanently in print, authoritative editions of America's best and most significant writing. An independent nonprofit organization, it was founded in 1979 with seed money from the National Endowment for the Humanities and the Ford Foundation.

This book is set in 10 point Linotron Galliard,
a face designed for photocomposition by Matthew Carter
and based on the sixteenth-century face Granjon. The paper
is acid-free Domtar Literary Opaque and meets the requirements
for permanence of the American National Standards Institute. The
binding material is Brillianta, a woven rayon cloth made by
Van Heek-Scholco Textielfabrieken, Holland. Composition
by Dedicated Business Services. Printing and binding
by R.R.Donnelley & Sons Company.
Designed by Bruce Campbell.